# Pokémon

## ADVENTURES

### GOLD & SILVER

**Pokémon ADVENTURES**
Volume 14
VIZ Kids Edition

Story by **HIDENORI KUSAKA**
Art by **SATOSHI YAMAMOTO**

© 2011 Pokémon.
© 1995-2011 Nintendo/Creatures Inc./GAME FREAK inc.
TM and ® and character names are trademarks of Nintendo.
© 1997 Hidenori KUSAKA and Satoshi YAMAMOTO/Shogakukan
All rights reserved.
Original Japanese edition "POCKET MONSTER SPECIAL"
published by SHOGAKUKAN Inc.

English Adaptation/Gerard Jones
Translation/HC Language Solutions
Touch-up & Lettering/Annaliese Christman
Design/Sam Elzway
Editor/Annette Roman

Printed in the U.S.A.

Published by VIZ Media, LLC
P.O. Box 77010
San Francisco, CA 94107

10 9 8 7 6 5 4 3 2 1
First printing, August 2011

www.vizkids.com

www.viz.com

PARENTAL ADVISORY
POKÉMON ADVENTURES
is rated A and is suitable
for readers of all ages.
ratings.viz.com

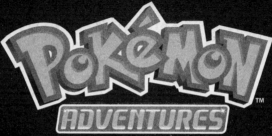

# POKÉMON™ ADVENTURES

GOLD & SILVER

14 VOLUME FOURTEEN

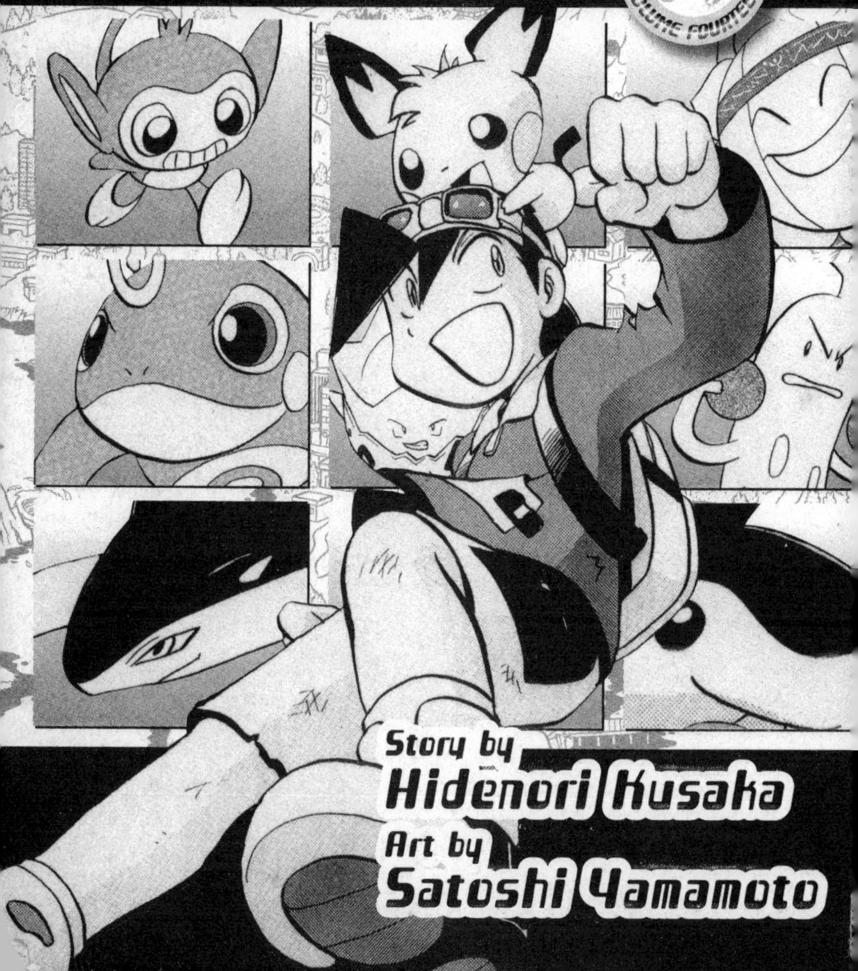

Story by
Hidenori Kusaka
Art by
Satoshi Yamamoto

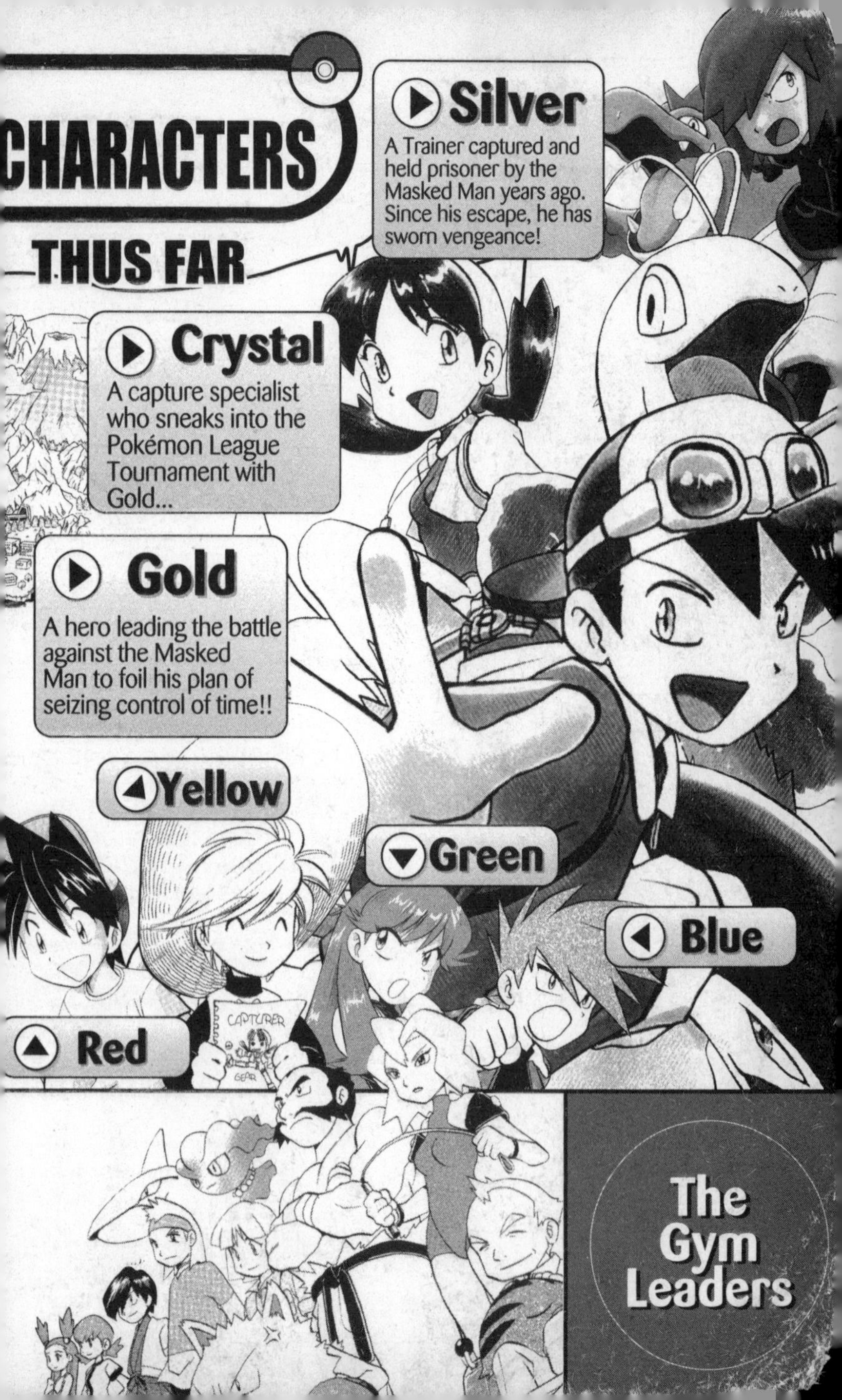

CHARACTERS THUS FAR
Silver
A Trainer captured and held prisoner by the Masked Man years ago. Since his escape, he has sworn vengeance!
Crystal
A capture specialist who sneaks into the Pokémon League Tournament with Gold...
Gold
A hero leading the battle against the Masked Man to foil his plan of seizing control of time!!
Yellow
Green
Blue
Red
CAPTURER
GEAR
The Gym Leaders

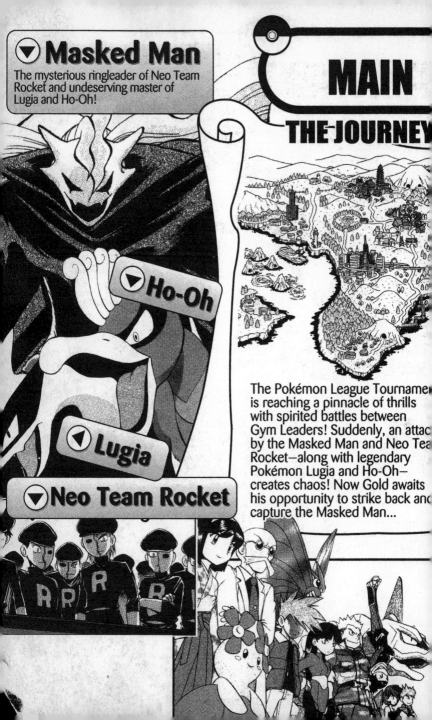

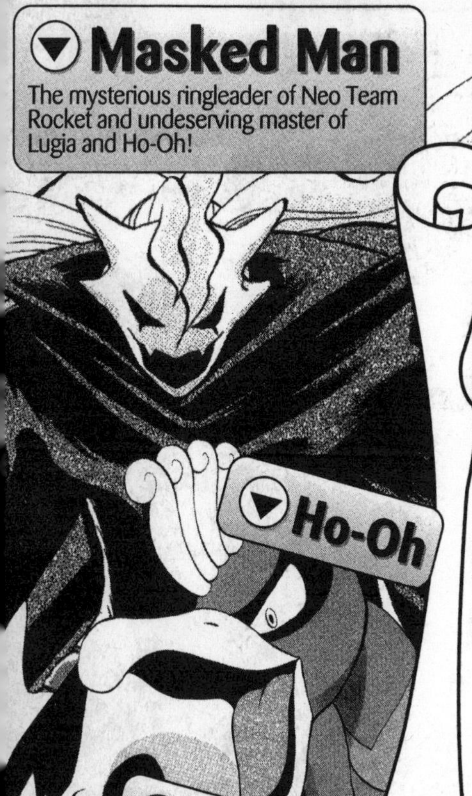
Masked Man
The mysterious ringleader of Neo Team Rocket and undeserving master of Lugia and Ho-Oh!
Ho-Oh
Lugia
Neo Team Rocket

# MAIN

## THE JOURNEY

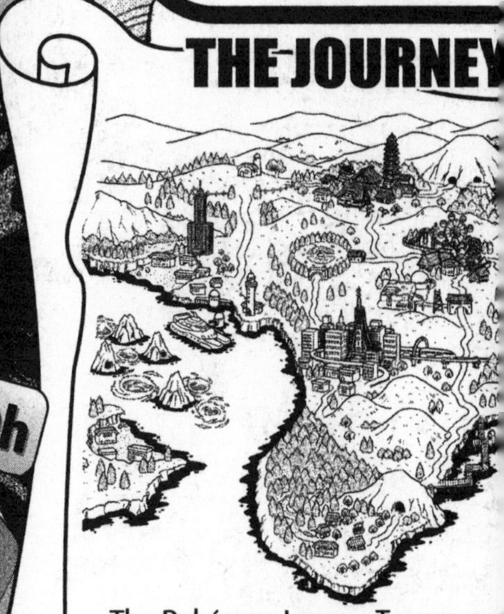

The Pokémon League Tourname
is reaching a pinnacle of thrills
with spirited battles between
Gym Leaders! Suddenly, an attac
by the Masked Man and Neo Tea
Rocket—along with legendary
Pokémon Lugia and Ho-Oh—
creates chaos! Now Gold awaits
his opportunity to strike back anc
capture the Masked Man...

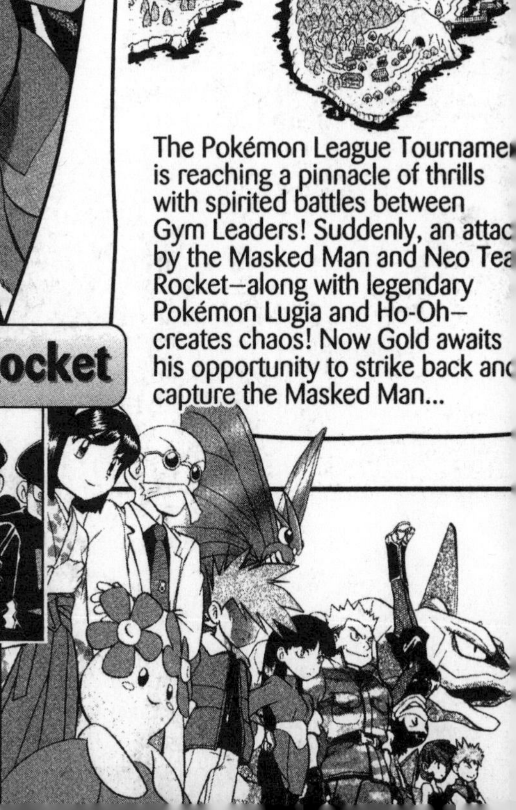

# CONTENTS

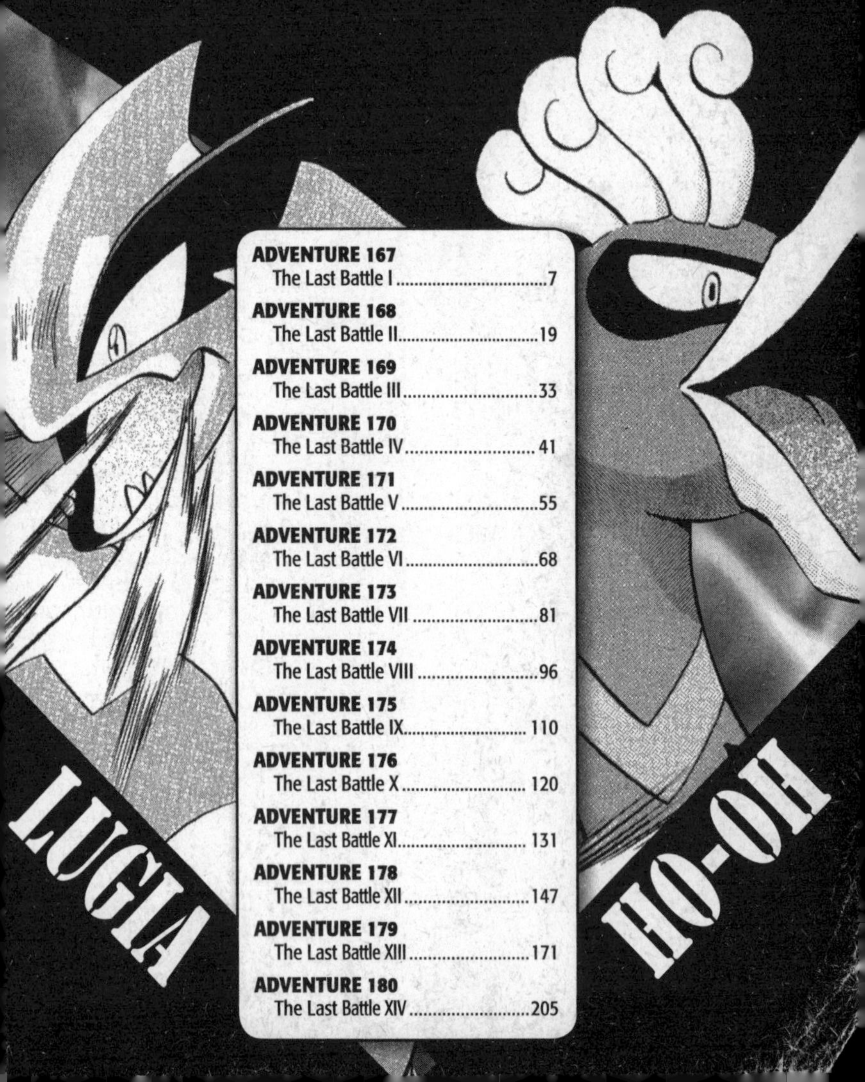
LUGIA
HO-OH

# The Last Battle I

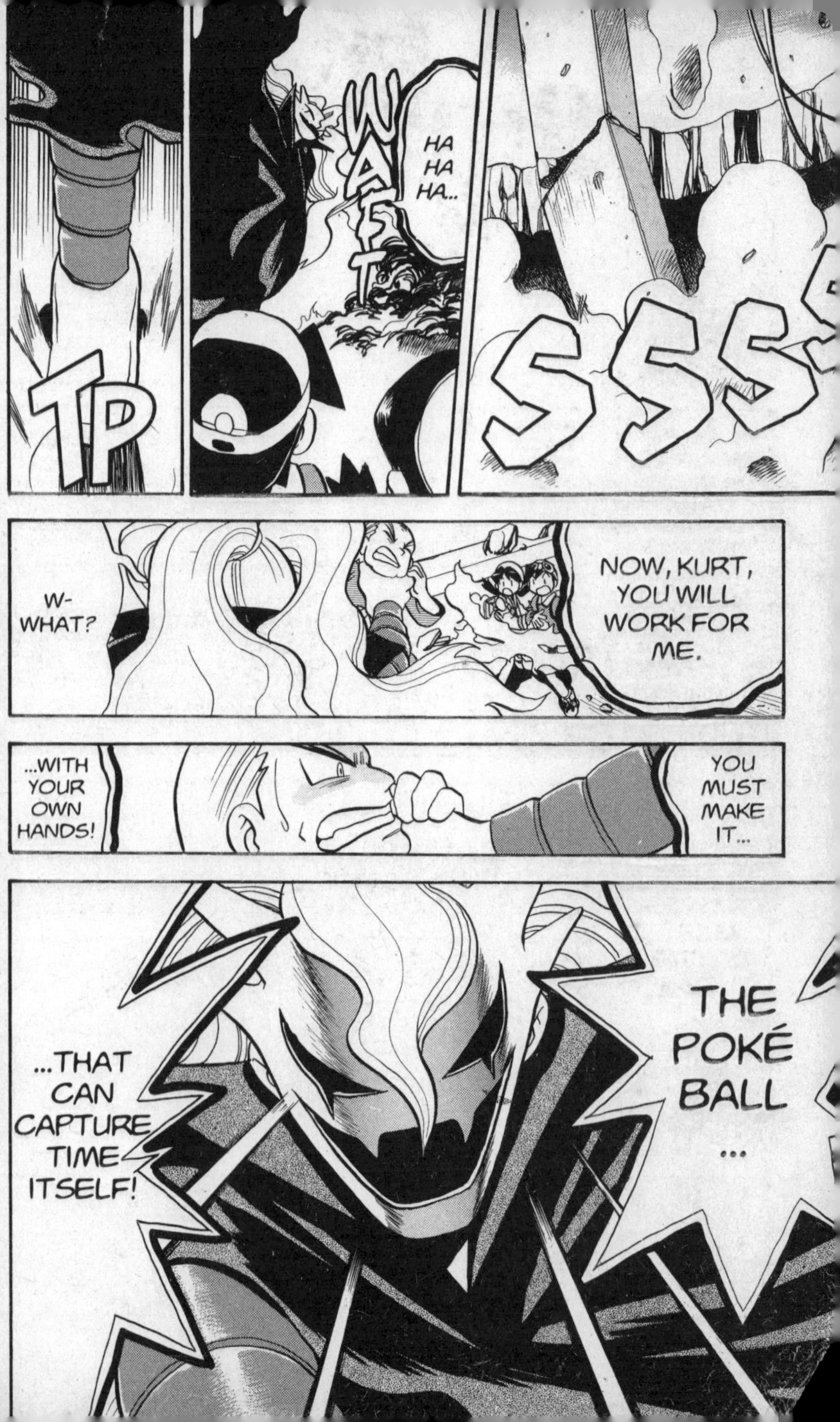
SSSS
HA HA HA...
WAFT
TP
NOW, KURT, YOU WILL WORK FOR ME.
W-WHAT?
YOU MUST MAKE IT...
...WITH YOUR OWN HANDS!
THE POKÉ BALL ...
...THAT CAN CAPTURE TIME ITSELF!

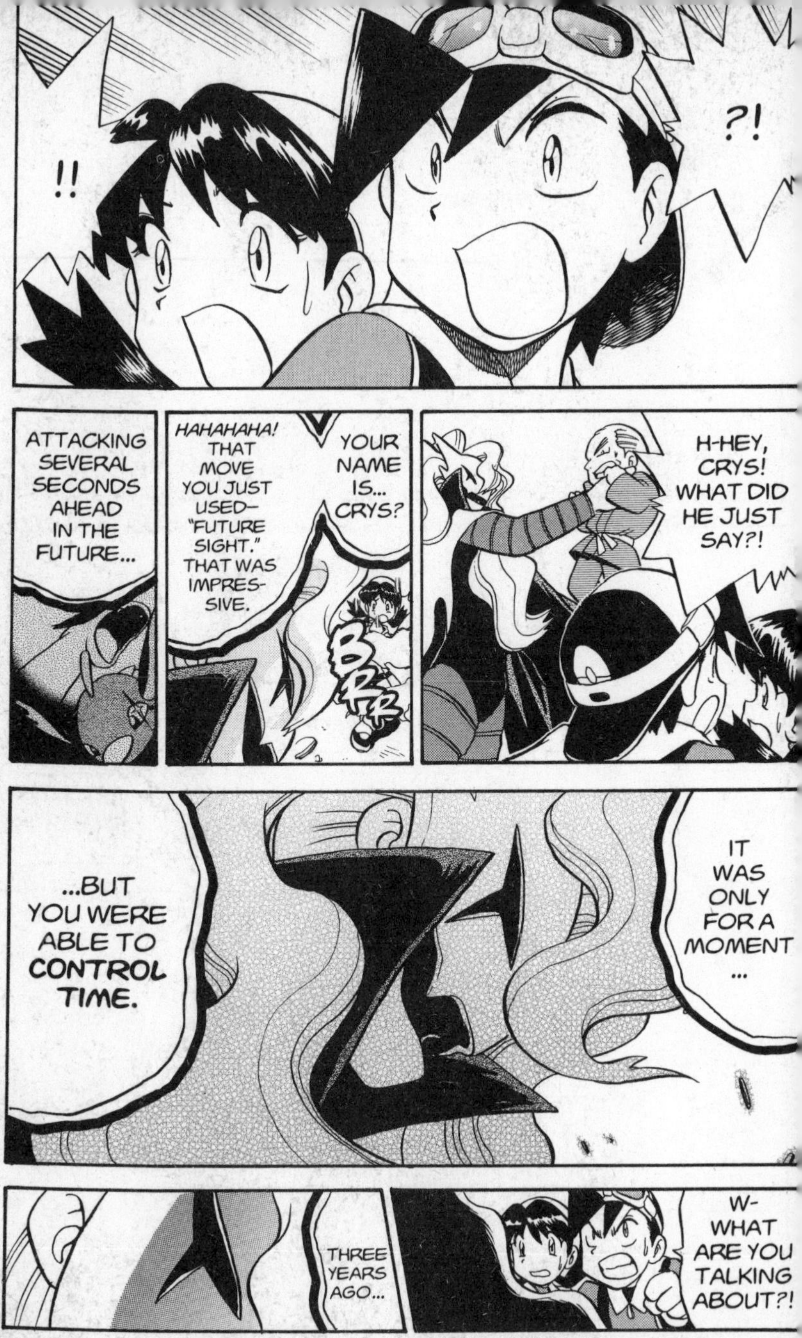
?!
!!
H-HEY, CRYS! WHAT DID HE JUST SAY?!
YOUR NAME IS... CRYS?
HAHAHAHA! THAT MOVE YOU JUST USED—"FUTURE SIGHT." THAT WAS IMPRES-SIVE.
BRR
ATTACKING SEVERAL SECONDS AHEAD IN THE FUTURE...
IT WAS ONLY FOR A MOMENT ...
...BUT YOU WERE ABLE TO **CONTROL TIME.**
W-WHAT ARE YOU TALKING ABOUT?!
THREE YEARS AGO...

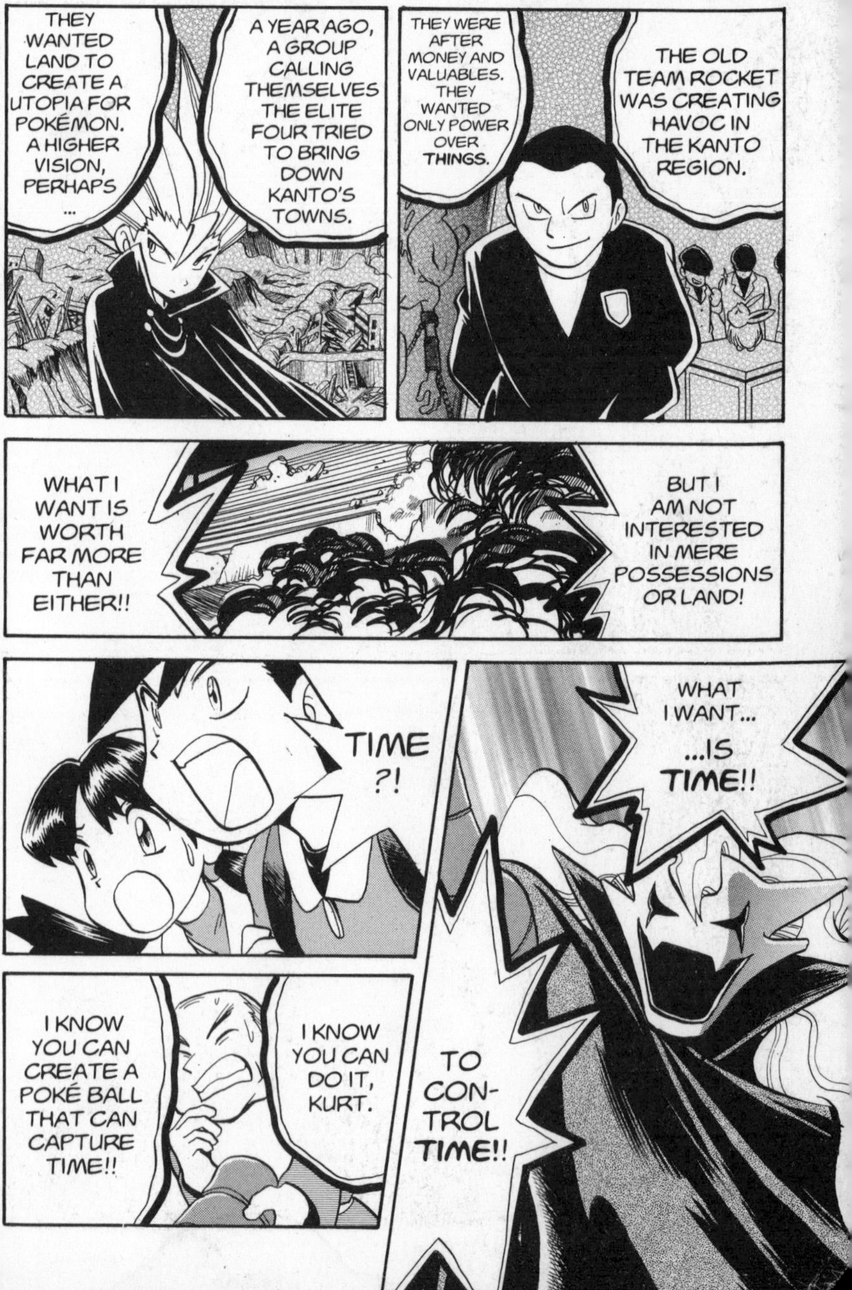
THE OLD TEAM ROCKET WAS CREATING HAVOC IN THE KANTO REGION.
THEY WERE AFTER MONEY AND VALUABLES. THEY WANTED ONLY POWER OVER THINGS.
A YEAR AGO, A GROUP CALLING THEMSELVES THE ELITE FOUR TRIED TO BRING DOWN KANTO'S TOWNS.
THEY WANTED LAND TO CREATE A UTOPIA FOR POKÉMON. A HIGHER VISION, PERHAPS...
BUT I AM NOT INTERESTED IN MERE POSSESSIONS OR LAND!
WHAT I WANT IS WORTH FAR MORE THAN EITHER!!
WHAT I WANT... ...IS TIME!!
TO CON-TROL TIME!!
TIME?!
I KNOW YOU CAN DO IT, KURT.
I KNOW YOU CAN CREATE A POKÉ BALL THAT CAN CAPTURE TIME!!

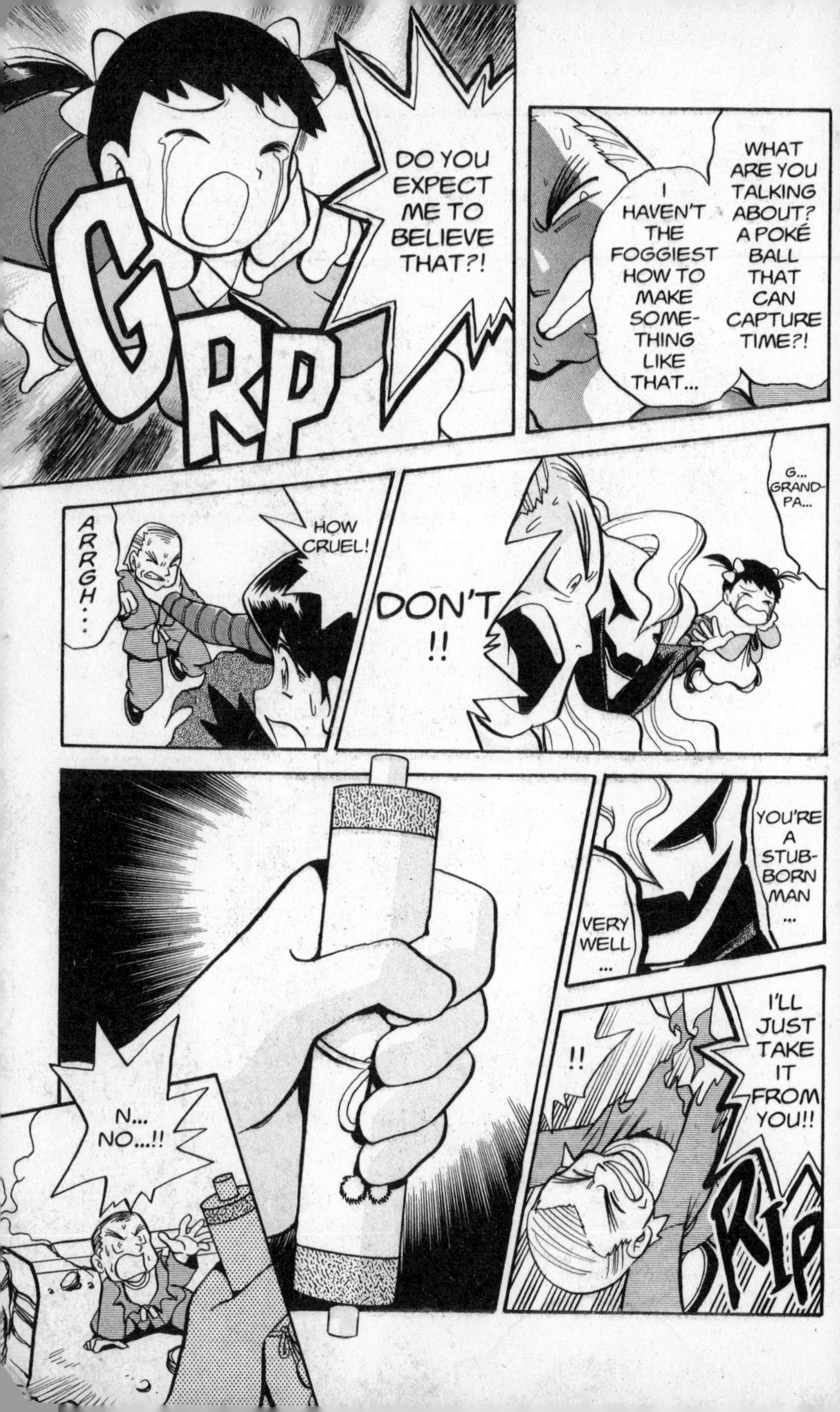
WHAT ARE YOU TALKING ABOUT? A POKÉ BALL THAT CAN CAPTURE TIME?!
I HAVEN'T THE FOGGIEST HOW TO MAKE SOME-THING LIKE THAT...
DO YOU EXPECT ME TO BELIEVE THAT?!
GRP
G... GRAND-PA...
DON'T !!
HOW CRUEL!
ARRGH...
YOU'RE A STUB-BORN MAN...
VERY WELL...
I'LL JUST TAKE IT FROM YOU!!
!!
RIP
N... NO...!!

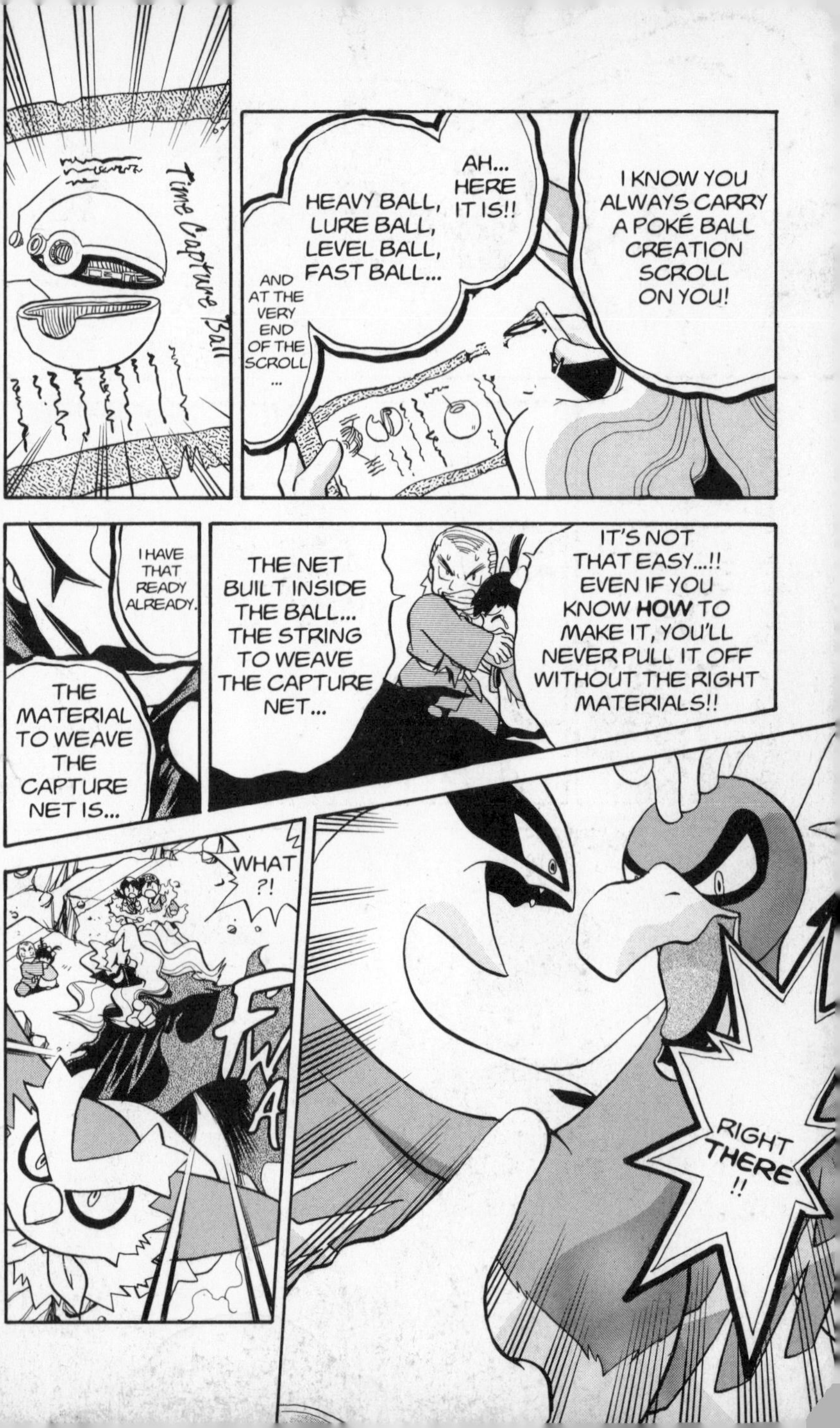
I KNOW YOU ALWAYS CARRY A POKÉ BALL CREATION SCROLL ON YOU!
AH... HERE IT IS!!
HEAVY BALL, LURE BALL, LEVEL BALL, FAST BALL...
AND AT THE VERY END OF THE SCROLL...
Time Capture Ball
IT'S NOT THAT EASY...!! EVEN IF YOU KNOW **HOW** TO MAKE IT, YOU'LL NEVER PULL IT OFF WITHOUT THE RIGHT MATERIALS!!
THE NET BUILT INSIDE THE BALL... THE STRING TO WEAVE THE CAPTURE NET...
I HAVE THAT READY ALREADY.
THE MATERIAL TO WEAVE THE CAPTURE NET IS...
RIGHT THERE!!
WHAT?!
FWA

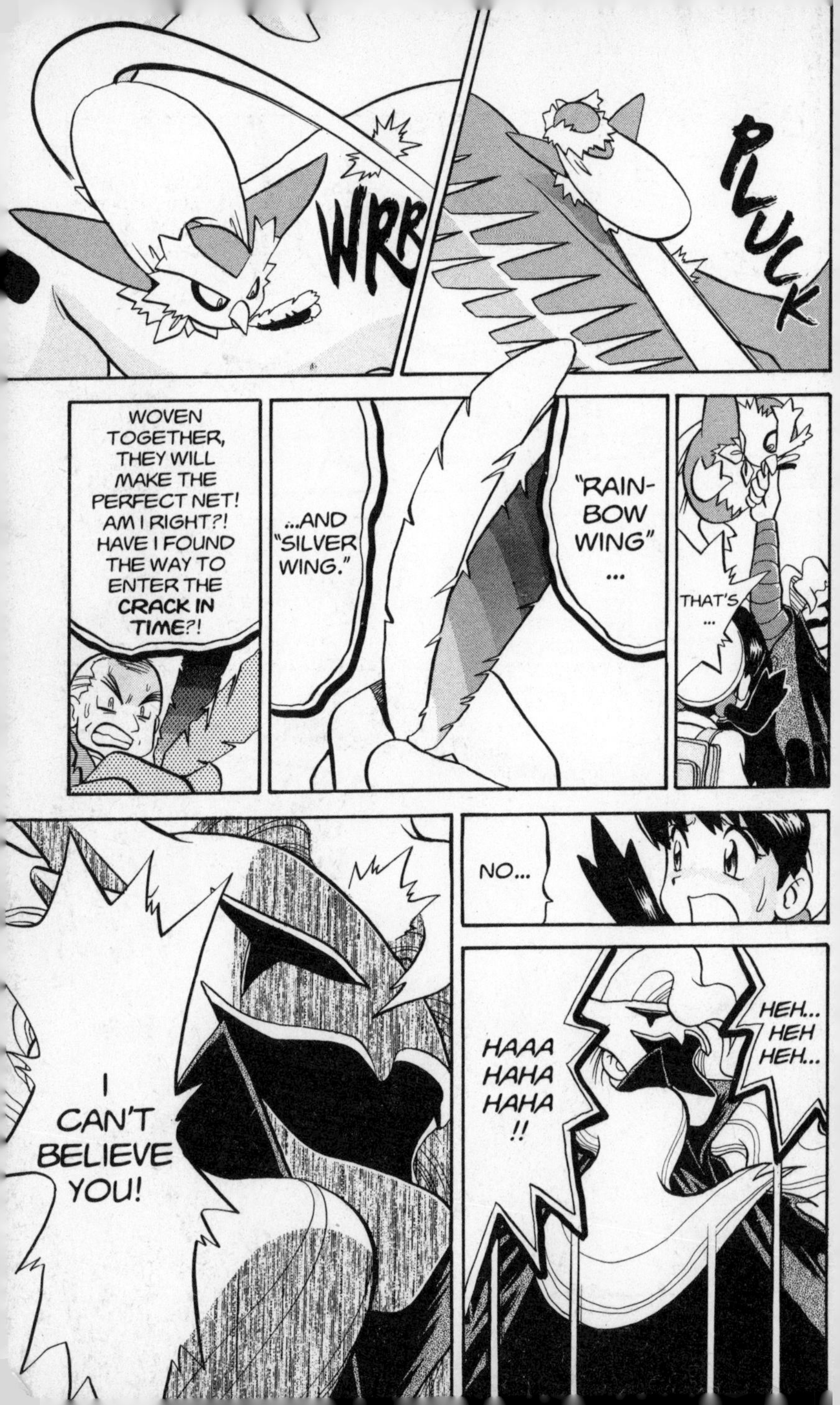
PLUCK
WRR
THAT'S...
"RAINBOW WING"...
...AND "SILVER WING."
WOVEN TOGETHER, THEY WILL MAKE THE PERFECT NET! AM I RIGHT?! HAVE I FOUND THE WAY TO ENTER THE **CRACK IN TIME**?!
NO...
HEH... HEH HEH...
HAAA HAHA HAHA !!
I CAN'T BELIEVE YOU!

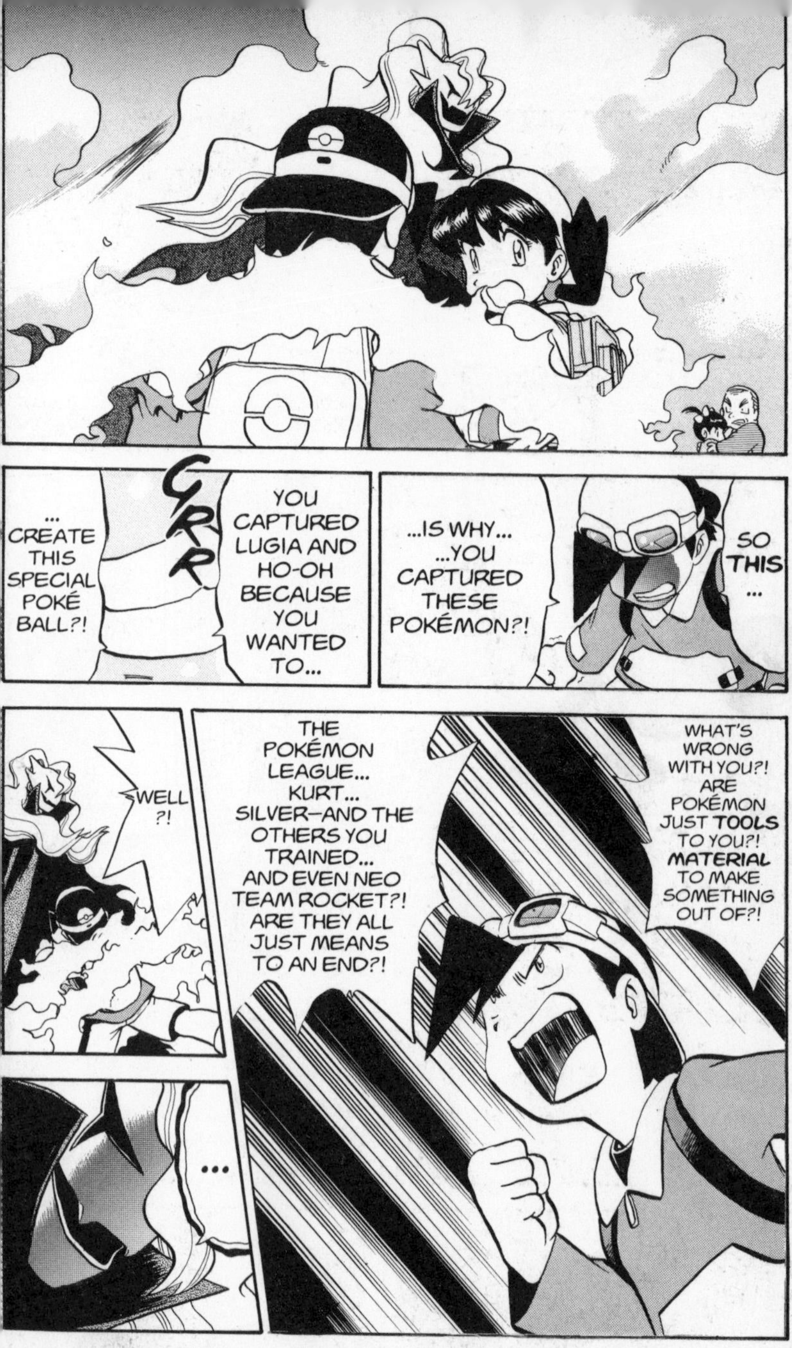
SO THIS...
...IS WHY... ...YOU CAPTURED THESE POKÉMON?!
YOU CAPTURED LUGIA AND HO-OH BECAUSE YOU WANTED TO...
GRR
... CREATE THIS SPECIAL POKÉ BALL?!
WHAT'S WRONG WITH YOU?! ARE POKÉMON JUST TOOLS TO YOU?! MATERIAL TO MAKE SOMETHING OUT OF?!
THE POKÉMON LEAGUE... KURT... SILVER—AND THE OTHERS YOU TRAINED... AND EVEN NEO TEAM ROCKET?! ARE THEY ALL JUST MEANS TO AN END?!
WELL?!
...

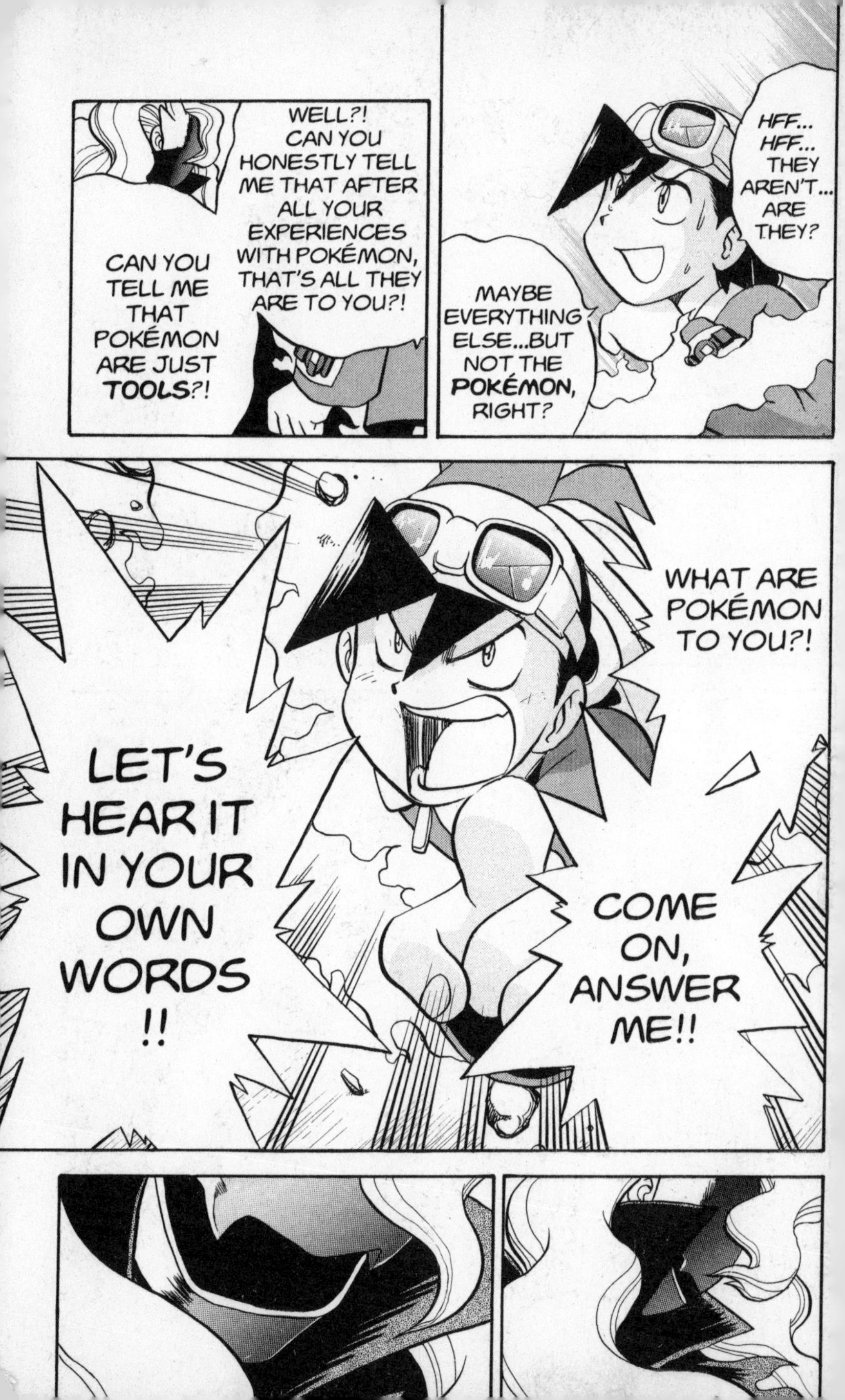
HFF... HFF... THEY AREN'T... ARE THEY?
MAYBE EVERYTHING ELSE...BUT NOT THE **POKÉMON**, RIGHT?
WELL?! CAN YOU HONESTLY TELL ME THAT AFTER ALL YOUR EXPERIENCES WITH POKÉMON, THAT'S ALL THEY ARE TO YOU?!
CAN YOU TELL ME THAT POKÉMON ARE JUST **TOOLS**?!
WHAT ARE POKÉMON TO YOU?!
COME ON, ANSWER ME!!
LET'S HEAR IT IN YOUR OWN WORDS!!

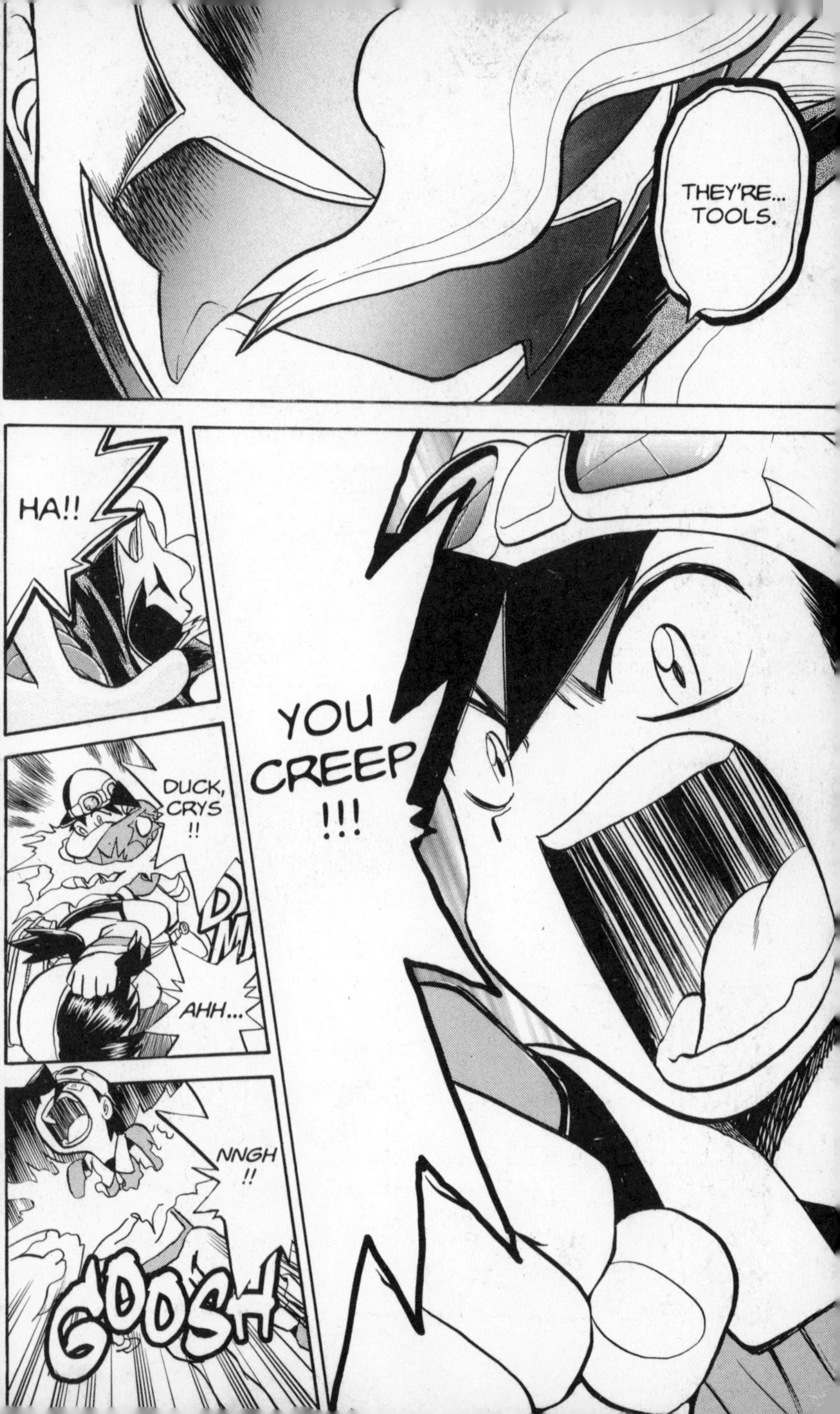
THEY'RE... TOOLS.
YOU CREEP !!!
HA!!
DUCK, CRYS !!
AHH...
NNGH !!
GOOSH

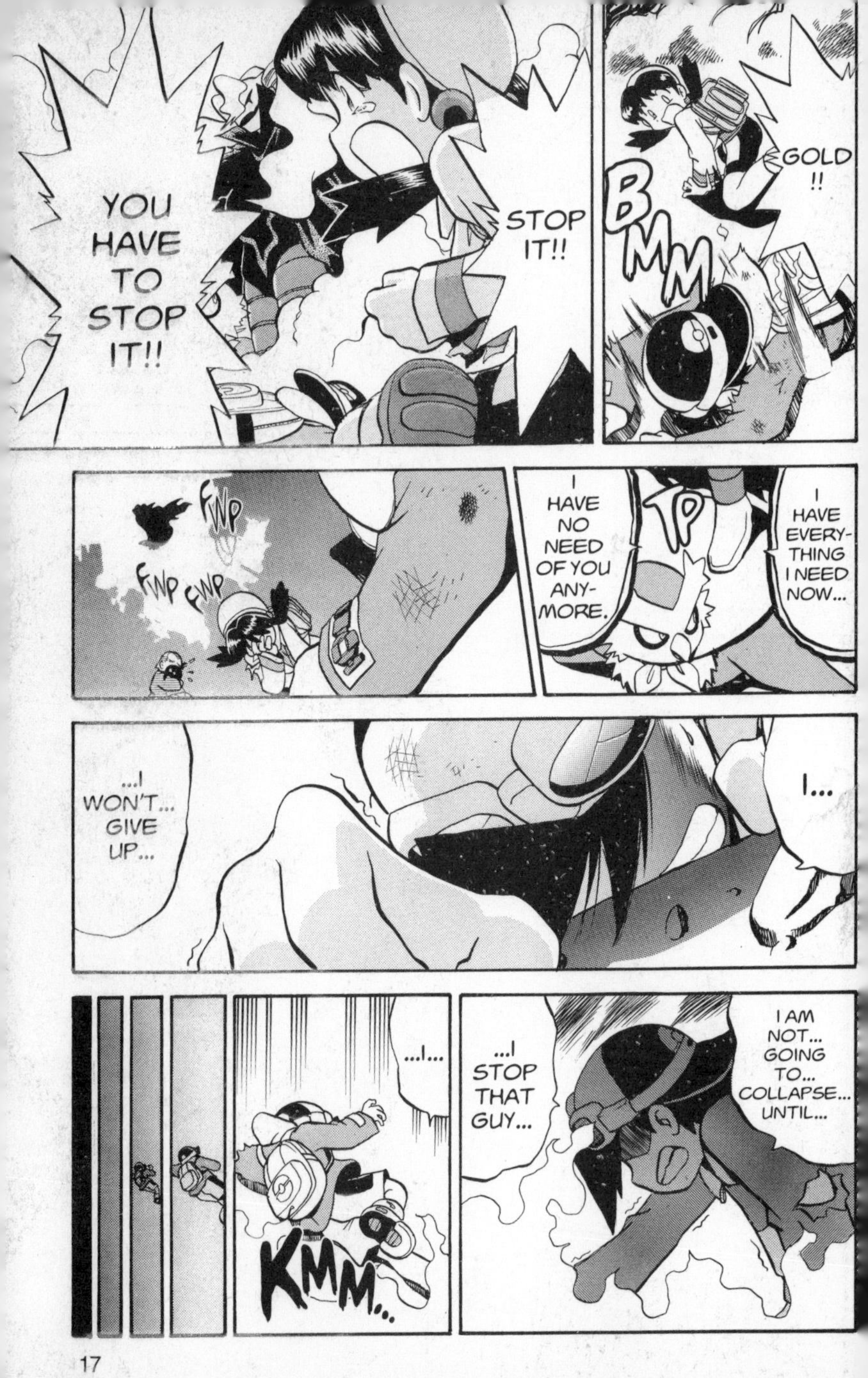
GOLD!!
BMM
STOP IT!!
YOU HAVE TO STOP IT!!
I HAVE EVERYTHING I NEED NOW...
TP
I HAVE NO NEED OF YOU ANYMORE.
FWP
FWP FWP
I...
...I WON'T... GIVE UP...
I AM NOT... GOING TO... COLLAPSE... UNTIL...
...I STOP THAT GUY...
...I...
KMM...

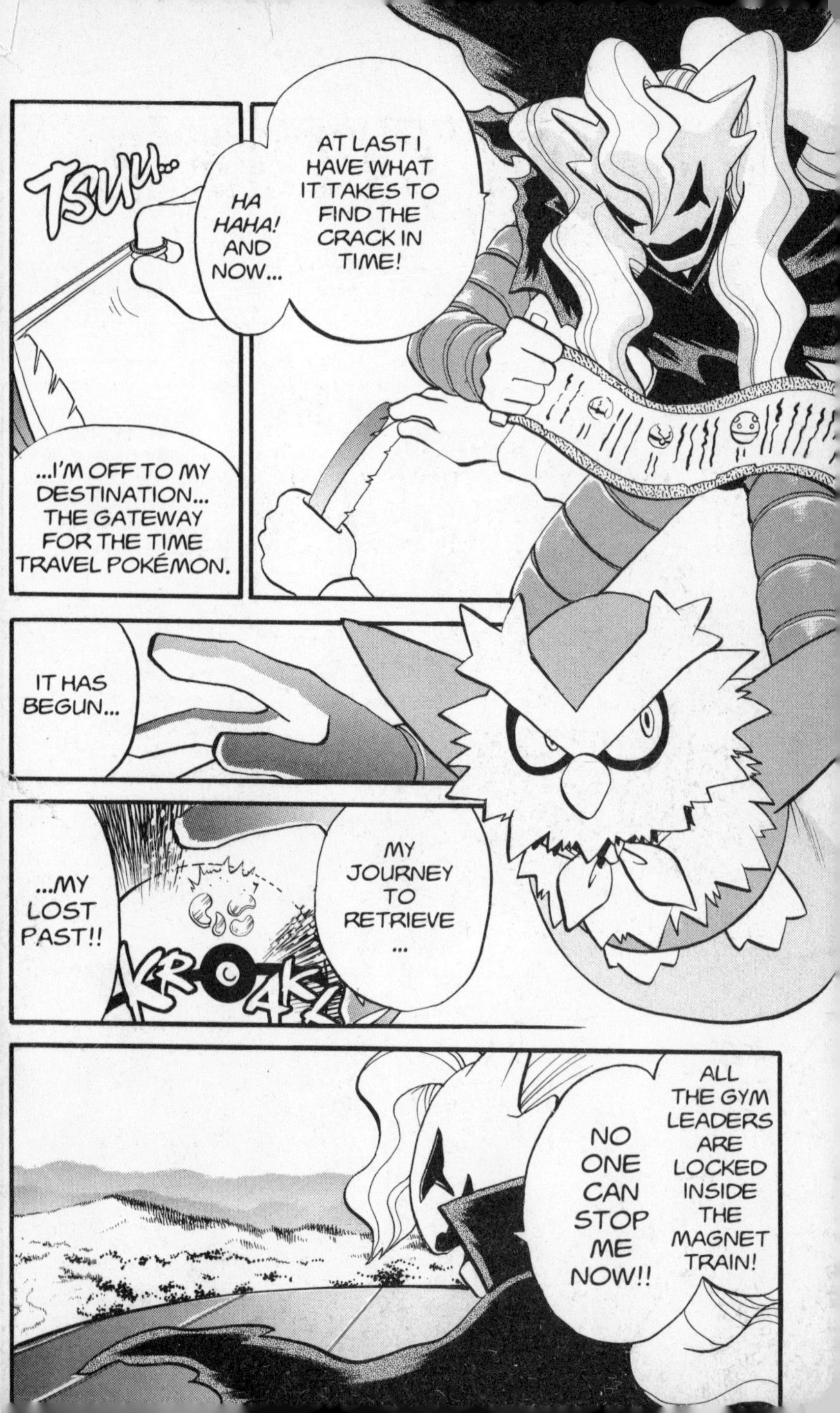
AT LAST I HAVE WHAT IT TAKES TO FIND THE CRACK IN TIME!
HA HAHA! AND NOW...
TSUU...
...I'M OFF TO MY DESTINATION... THE GATEWAY FOR THE TIME TRAVEL POKÉMON.
IT HAS BEGUN...
MY JOURNEY TO RETRIEVE ...
...MY LOST PAST!!
KROAK
ALL THE GYM LEADERS ARE LOCKED INSIDE THE MAGNET TRAIN!
NO ONE CAN STOP ME NOW!!

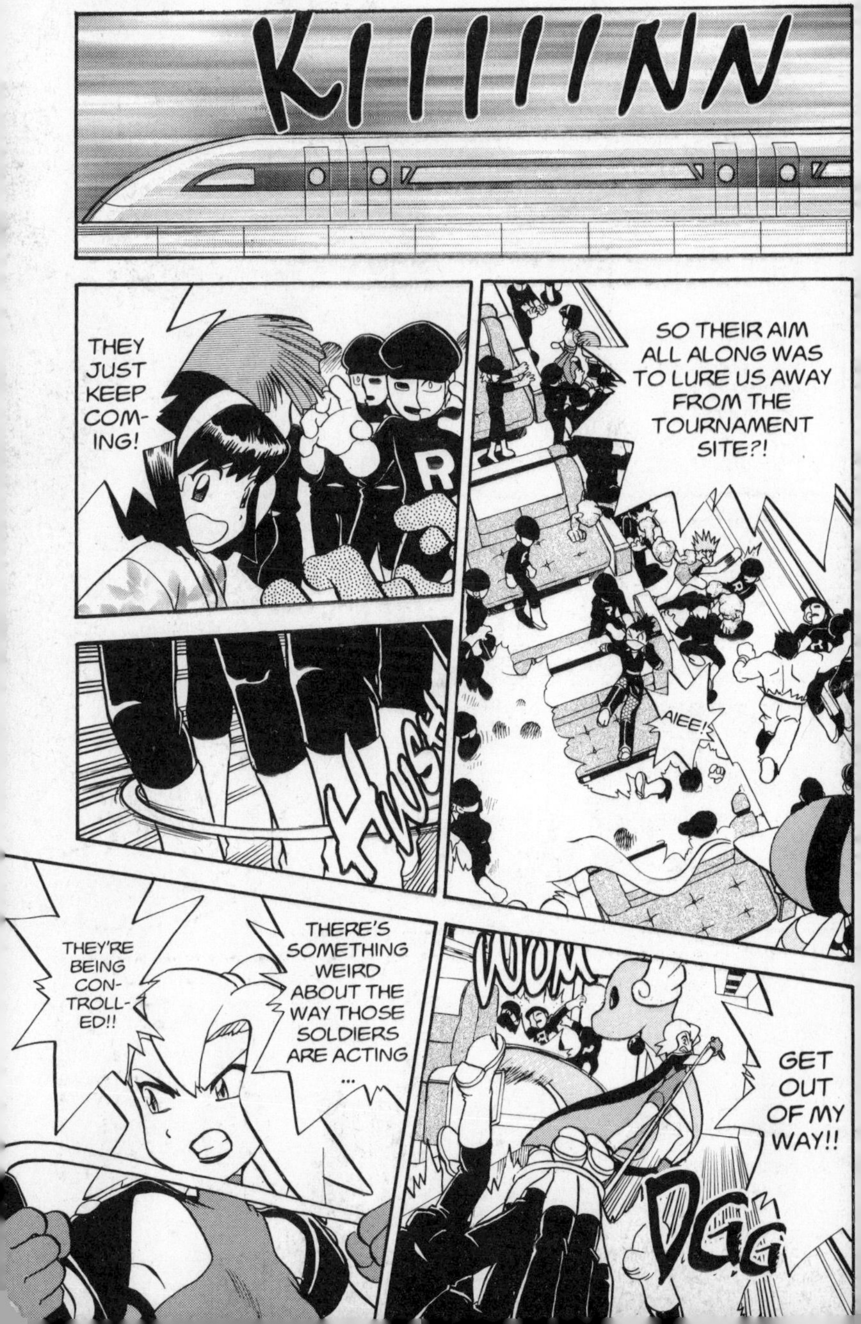
KIIIINN
SO THEIR AIM ALL ALONG WAS TO LURE US AWAY FROM THE TOURNAMENT SITE?!
AIEE!
THEY JUST KEEP COMING!
WUM
GET OUT OF MY WAY!!
DGG
THERE'S SOMETHING WEIRD ABOUT THE WAY THOSE SOLDIERS ARE ACTING ...
THEY'RE BEING CONTROLLED!!

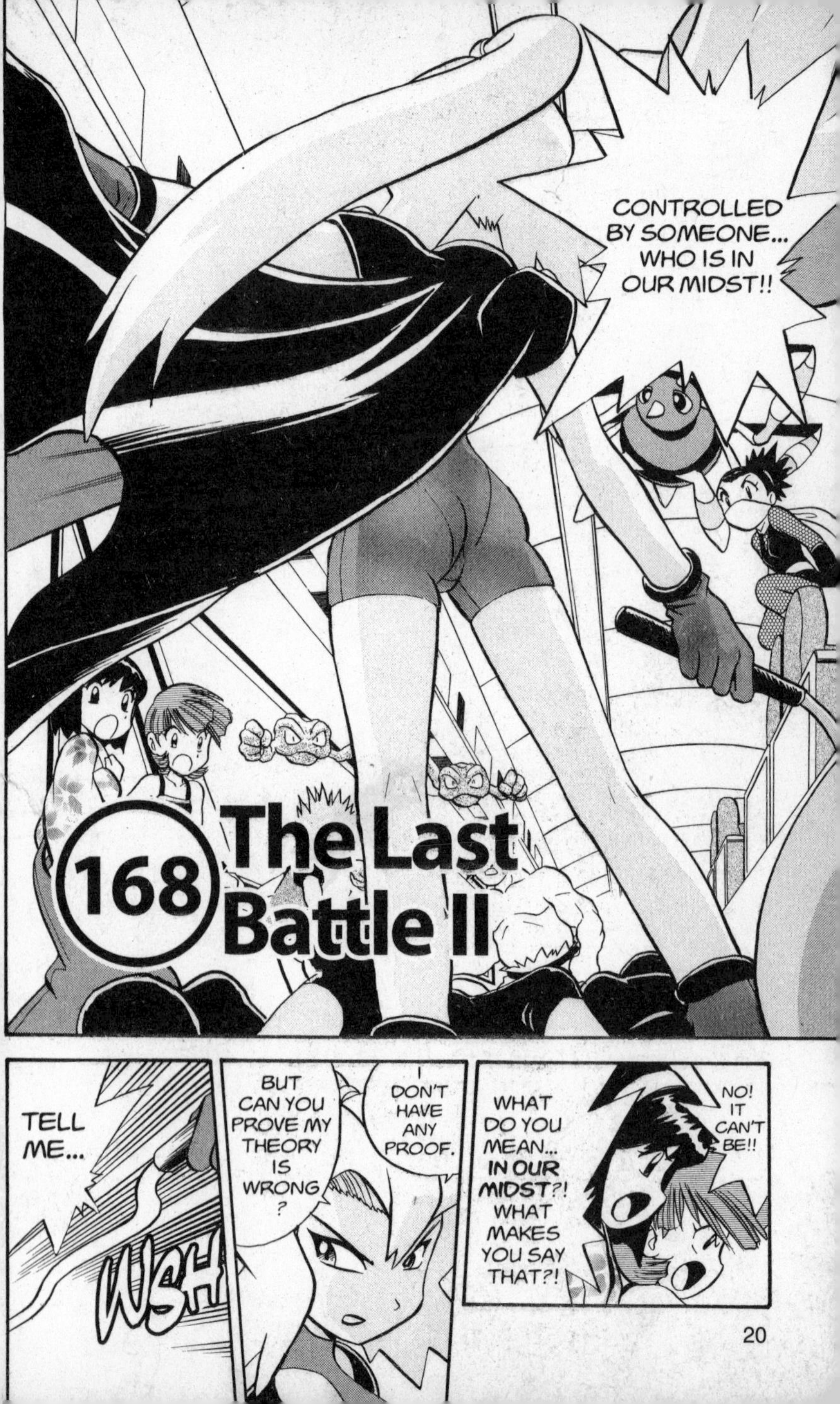
CONTROLLED BY SOMEONE... WHO IS IN OUR MIDST!!
168 The Last Battle II
NO! IT CAN'T BE!!
WHAT DO YOU MEAN... **IN OUR MIDST**?! WHAT MAKES YOU SAY THAT?!
I DON'T HAVE ANY PROOF.
BUT CAN YOU PROVE MY THEORY IS WRONG?
TELL ME...
WSH

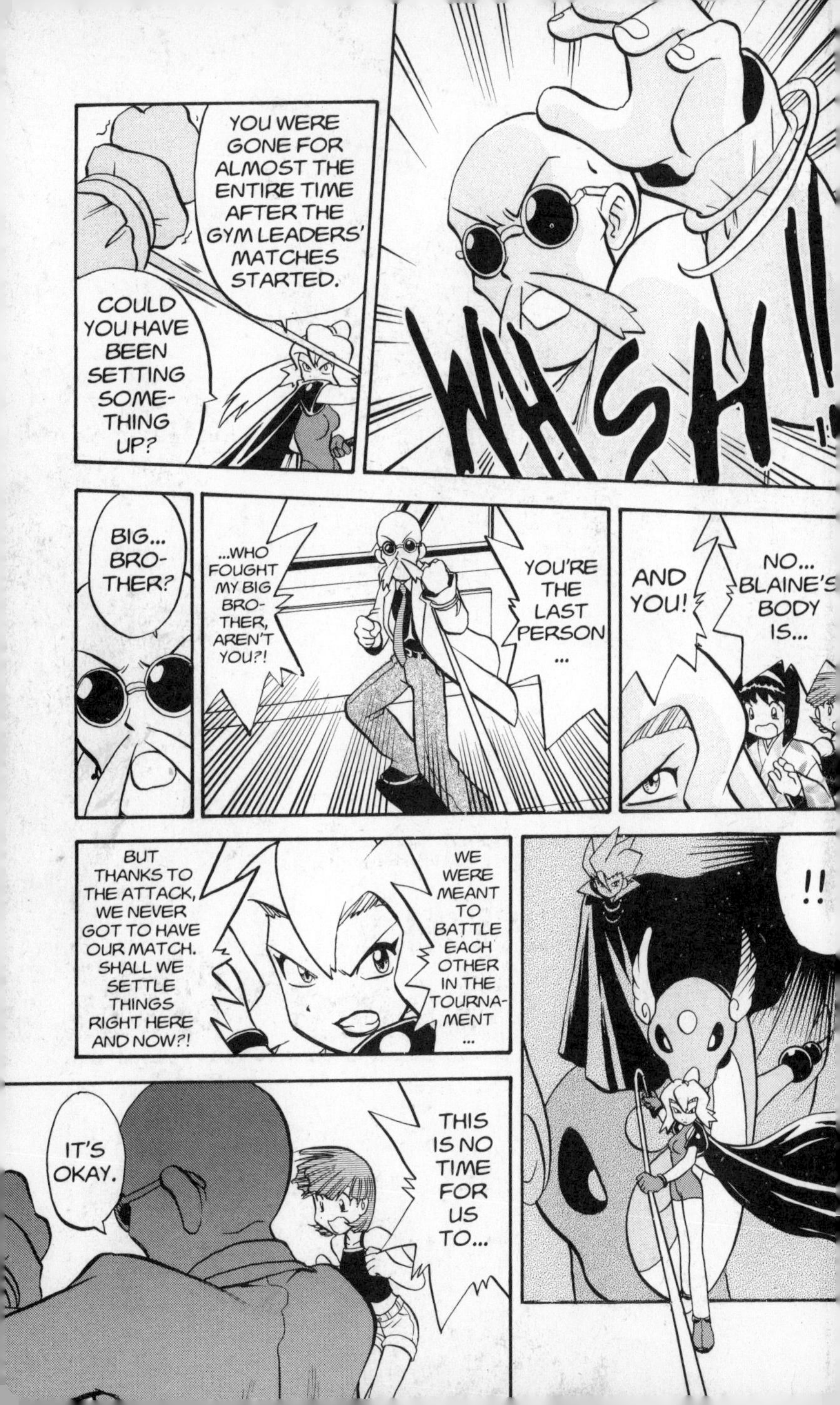
WHSH!!
YOU WERE GONE FOR ALMOST THE ENTIRE TIME AFTER THE GYM LEADERS' MATCHES STARTED.
COULD YOU HAVE BEEN SETTING SOME-THING UP?
NO... BLAINE'S BODY IS...
AND YOU!
YOU'RE THE LAST PERSON ...
...WHO FOUGHT MY BIG BRO-THER, AREN'T YOU?!
BIG... BRO-THER?
!!
WE WERE MEANT TO BATTLE EACH OTHER IN THE TOURNA-MENT ...
BUT THANKS TO THE ATTACK, WE NEVER GOT TO HAVE OUR MATCH. SHALL WE SETTLE THINGS RIGHT HERE AND NOW?!
THIS IS NO TIME FOR US TO...
IT'S OKAY.

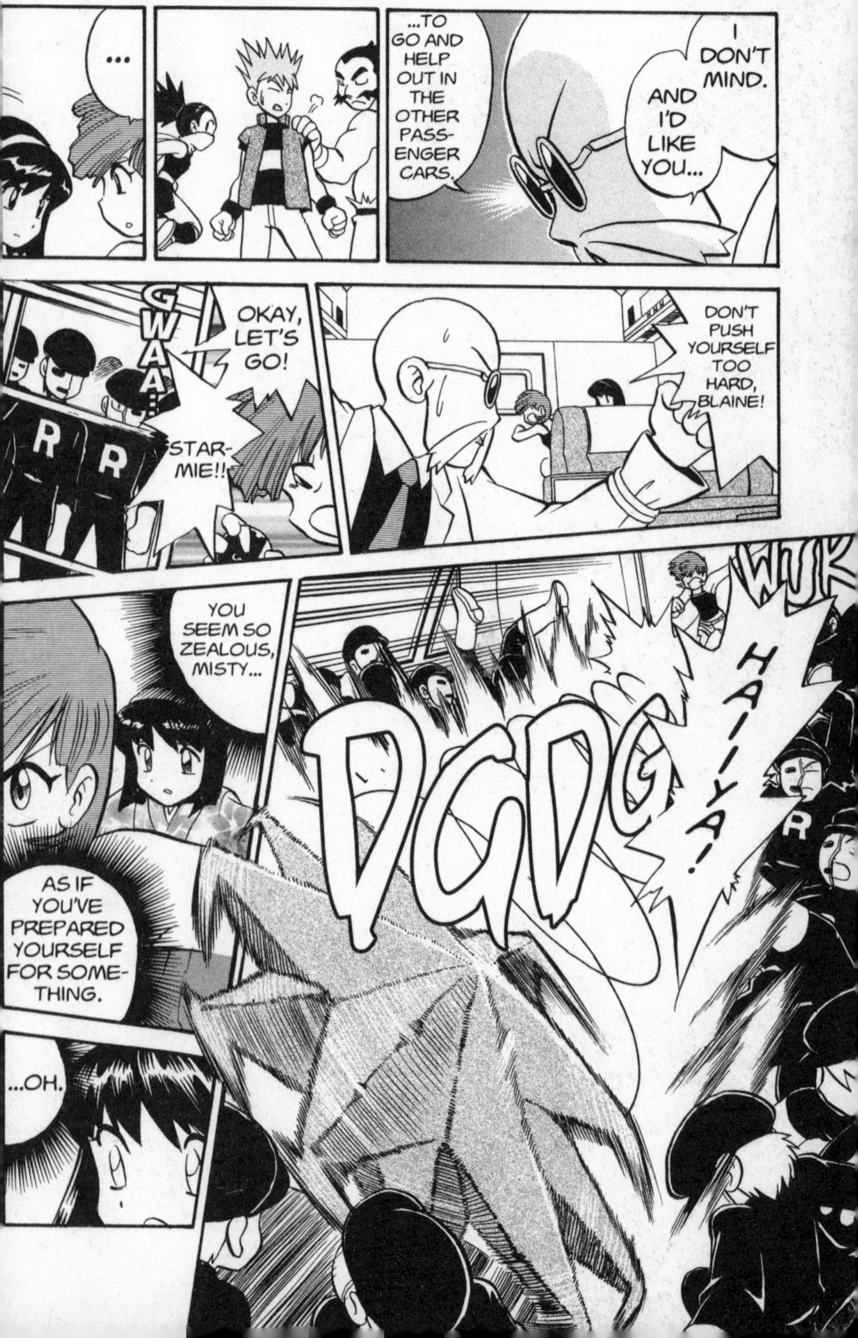
I DON'T MIND.
AND I'D LIKE YOU...
...TO GO AND HELP OUT IN THE OTHER PASSENGER CARS.
...
DON'T PUSH YOURSELF TOO HARD, BLAINE!
OKAY, LET'S GO!
GWAA!
STARMIE!!
WUK
HAIIYA!
DGDG
YOU SEEM SO ZEALOUS, MISTY...
AS IF YOU'VE PREPARED YOURSELF FOR SOMETHING.
...OH.

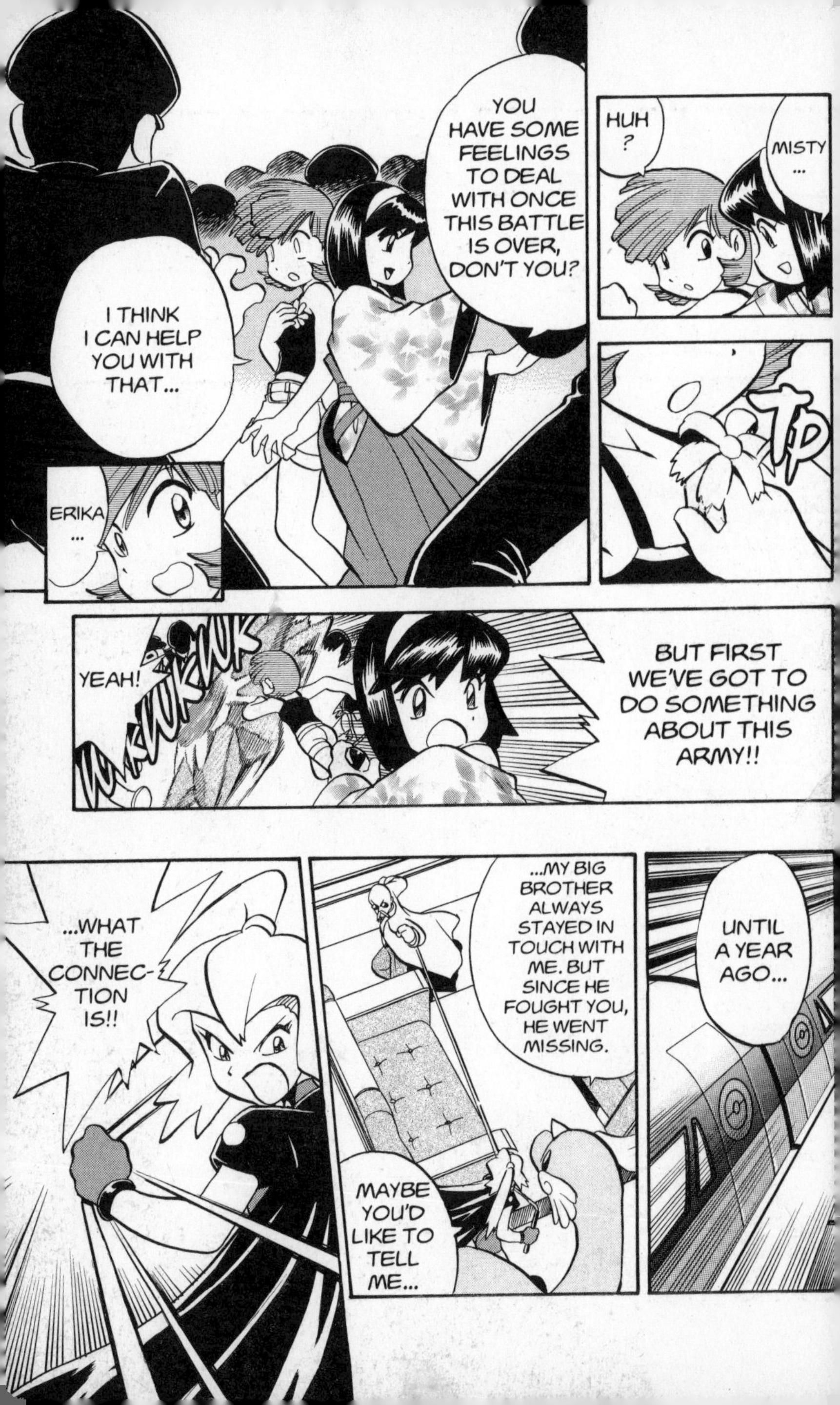
MISTY ...
HUH ?
TP
YOU HAVE SOME FEELINGS TO DEAL WITH ONCE THIS BATTLE IS OVER, DON'T YOU?
I THINK I CAN HELP YOU WITH THAT...
ERIKA ...
BUT FIRST WE'VE GOT TO DO SOMETHING ABOUT THIS ARMY!!
YEAH!
UNTIL A YEAR AGO...
...MY BIG BROTHER ALWAYS STAYED IN TOUCH WITH ME. BUT SINCE HE FOUGHT YOU, HE WENT MISSING.
MAYBE YOU'D LIKE TO TELL ME...
...WHAT THE CONNECTION IS!!

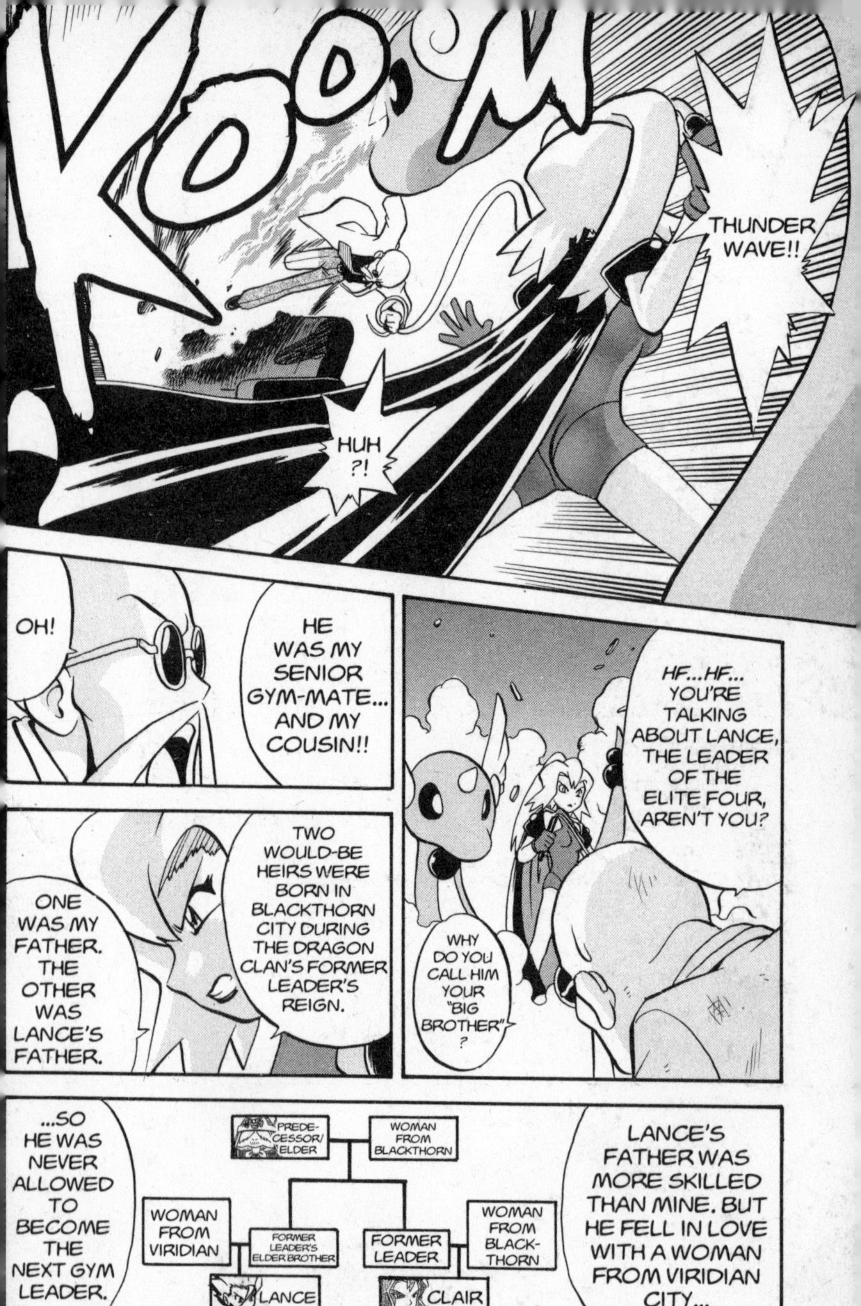
THUNDER WAVE!!
HUH ?!
HF...HF... YOU'RE TALKING ABOUT LANCE, THE LEADER OF THE ELITE FOUR, AREN'T YOU?
WHY DO YOU CALL HIM YOUR "BIG BROTHER"?
HE WAS MY SENIOR GYM-MATE... AND MY COUSIN!!
OH!
TWO WOULD-BE HEIRS WERE BORN IN BLACKTHORN CITY DURING THE DRAGON CLAN'S FORMER LEADER'S REIGN.
ONE WAS MY FATHER. THE OTHER WAS LANCE'S FATHER.
LANCE'S FATHER WAS MORE SKILLED THAN MINE. BUT HE FELL IN LOVE WITH A WOMAN FROM VIRIDIAN CITY...
PREDECESSOR/ ELDER
WOMAN FROM BLACKTHORN
WOMAN FROM BLACK-THORN
FORMER LEADER
FORMER LEADER'S ELDER BROTHER
WOMAN FROM VIRIDIAN
CLAIR
LANCE
...SO HE WAS NEVER ALLOWED TO BECOME THE NEXT GYM LEADER.

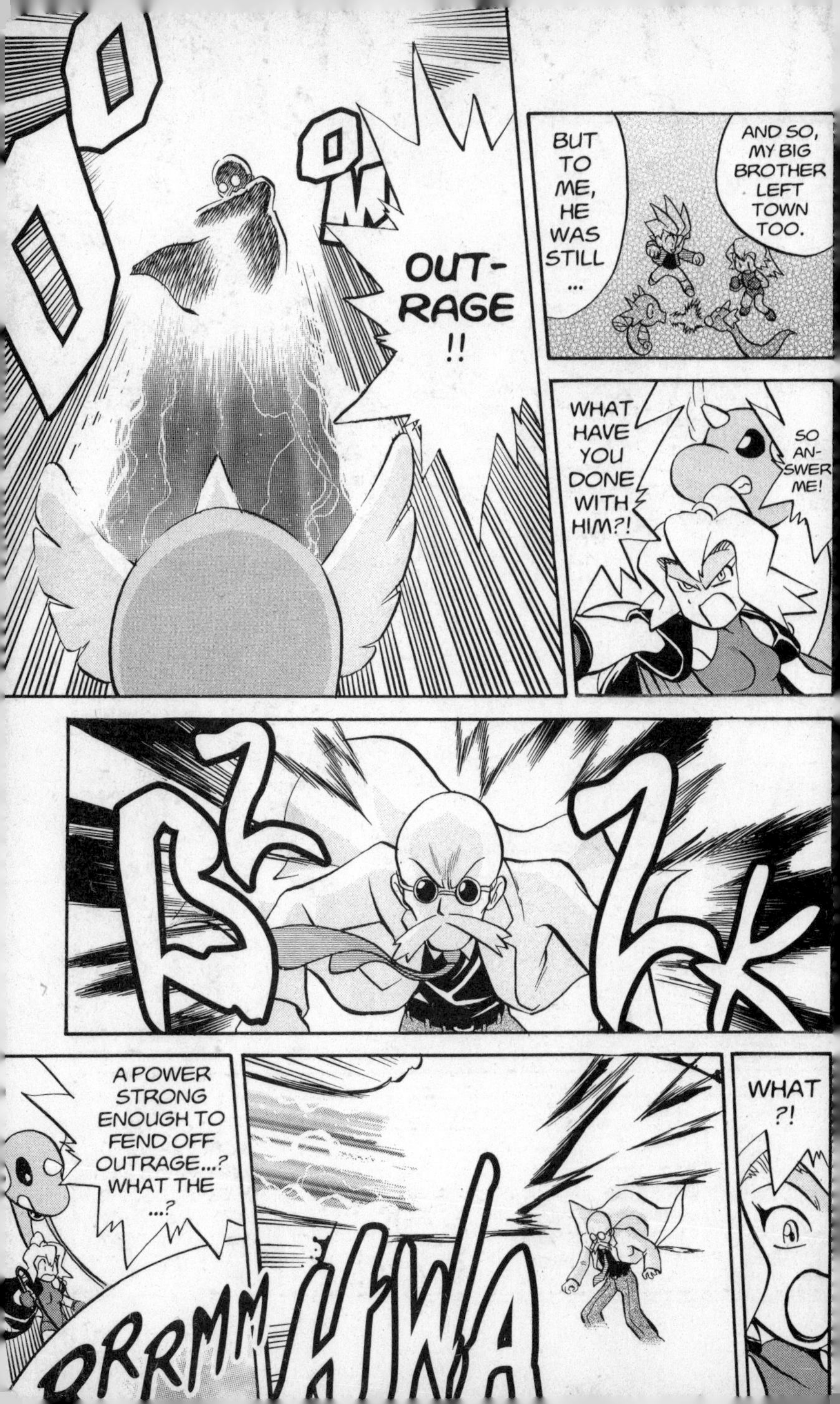
AND SO, MY BIG BROTHER LEFT TOWN TOO.
BUT TO ME, HE WAS STILL ...
WHAT HAVE YOU DONE WITH HIM?!
SO AN-SWER ME!
OUT-RAGE !!
WHAT ?!
A POWER STRONG ENOUGH TO FEND OFF OUTRAGE...? WHAT THE ...?

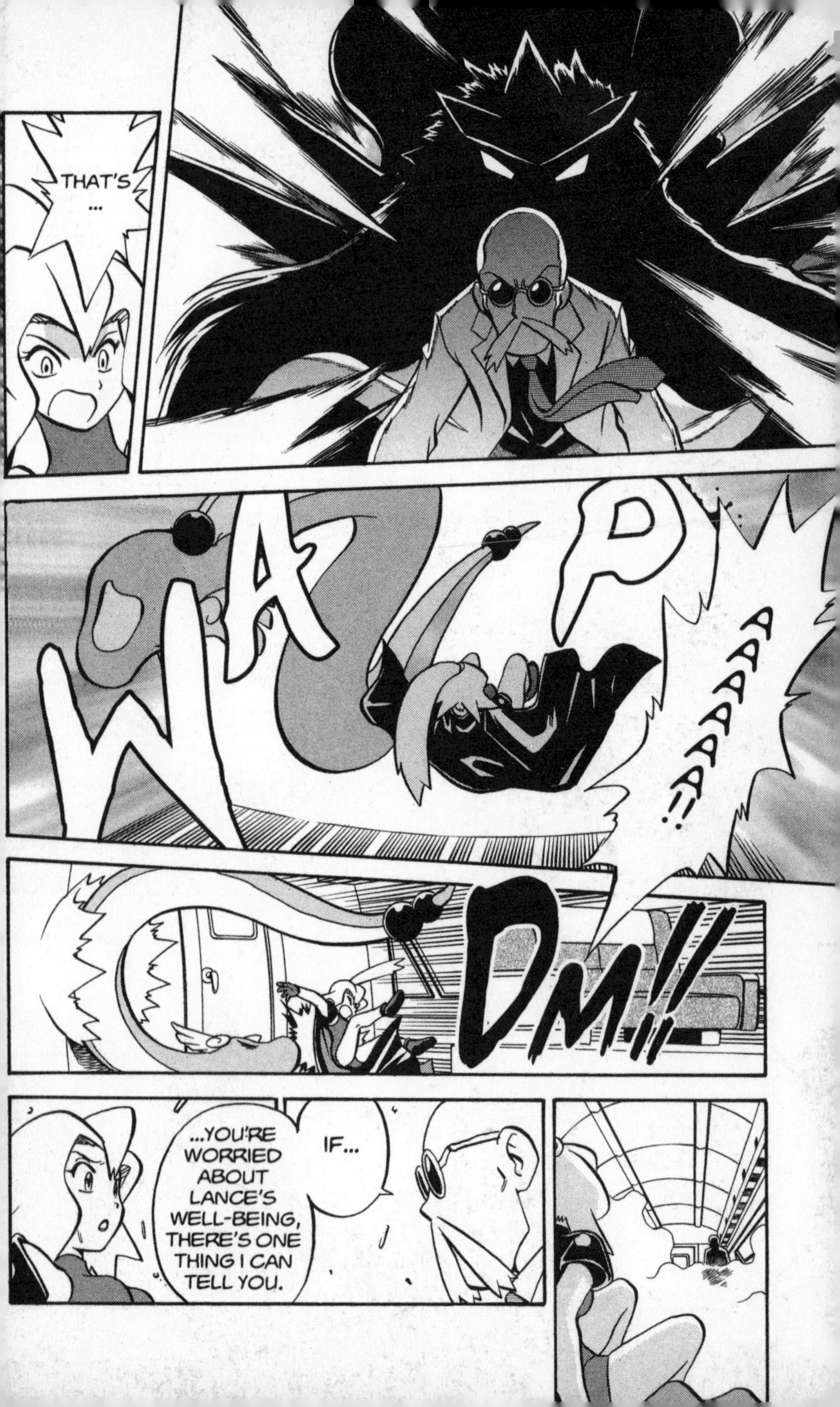
THAT'S ...
WAP
AAAAAAA!!
DM!!
IF...
...YOU'RE WORRIED ABOUT LANCE'S WELL-BEING, THERE'S ONE THING I CAN TELL YOU.

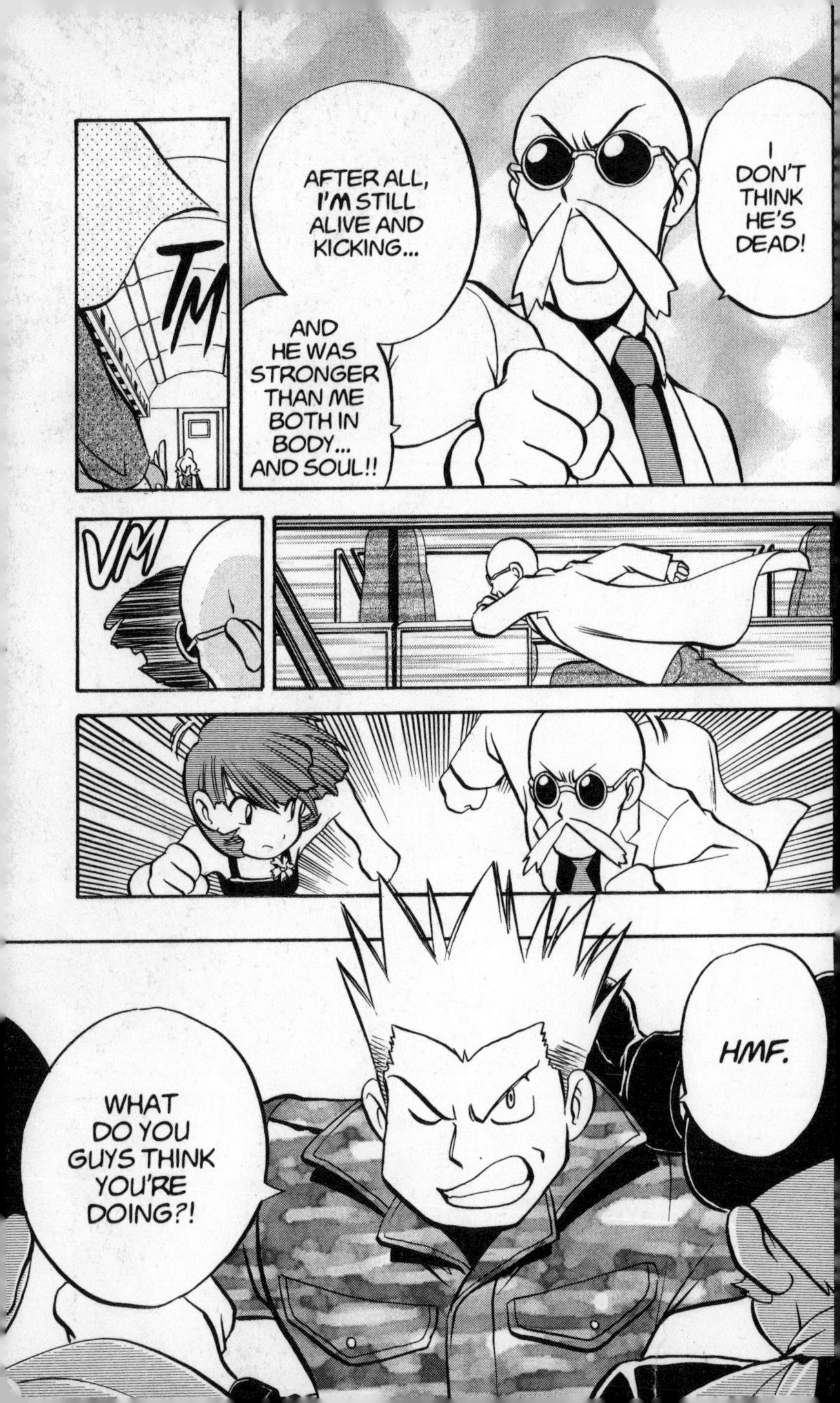
I DON'T THINK HE'S DEAD!
AFTER ALL, I'M STILL ALIVE AND KICKING...
AND HE WAS STRONGER THAN ME BOTH IN BODY... AND SOUL!!
TM
VM
HMF.
WHAT DO YOU GUYS THINK YOU'RE DOING?!

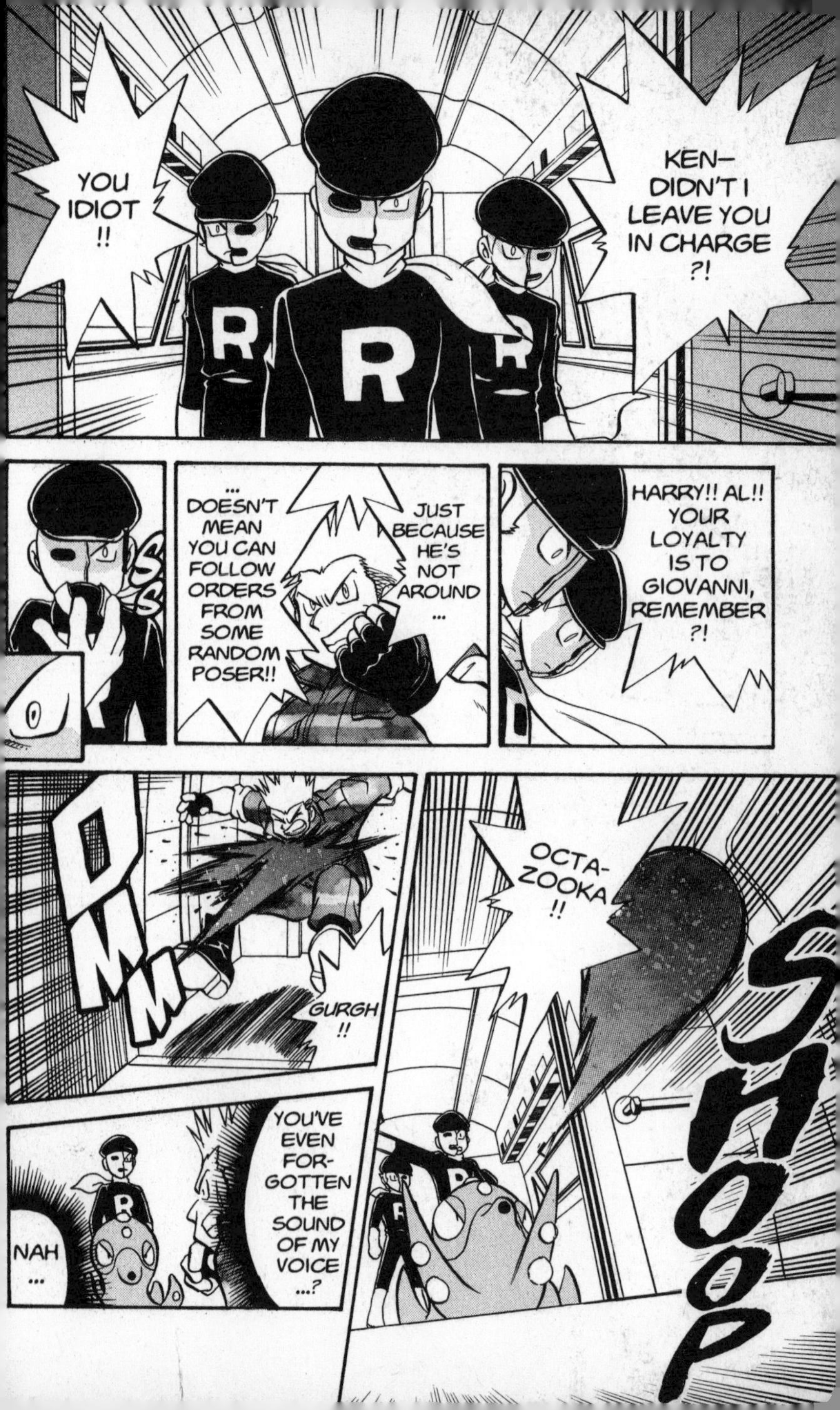

KEN— DIDN'T I LEAVE YOU IN CHARGE ?!
YOU IDIOT !!
HARRY!! AL!! YOUR LOYALTY IS TO GIOVANNI, REMEMBER ?!
JUST BECAUSE HE'S NOT AROUND ...
... DOESN'T MEAN YOU CAN FOLLOW ORDERS FROM SOME RANDOM POSER!!
SS
OCTA-ZOOKA !!
SHOOOP
DMMM
GURGH !!
YOU'VE EVEN FOR-GOTTEN THE SOUND OF MY VOICE ...?
NAH ...

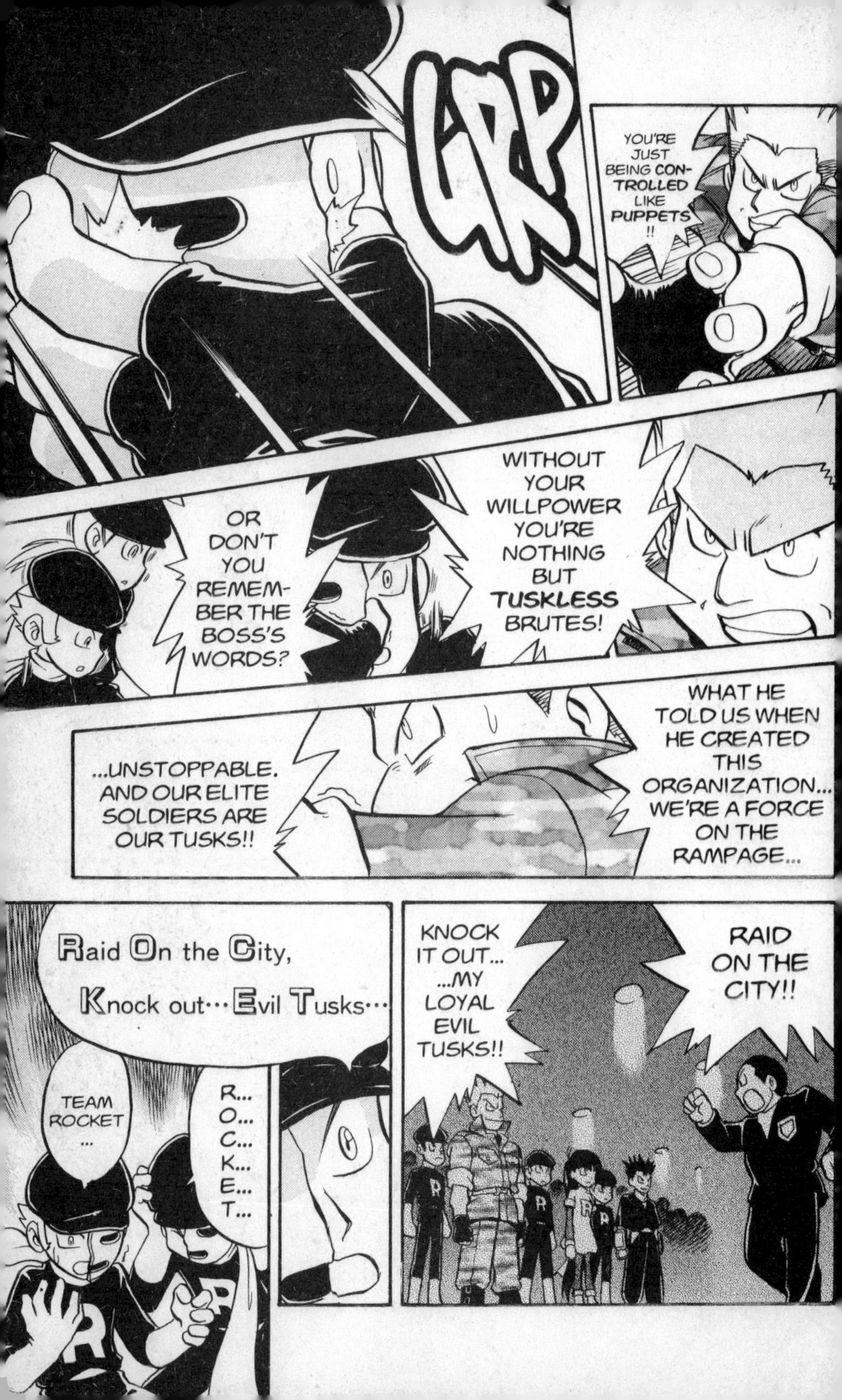
YOU'RE JUST BEING CONTROLLED LIKE PUPPETS!!
WITHOUT YOUR WILLPOWER YOU'RE NOTHING BUT TUSKLESS BRUTES!
OR DON'T YOU REMEMBER THE BOSS'S WORDS?
WHAT HE TOLD US WHEN HE CREATED THIS ORGANIZATION... WE'RE A FORCE ON THE RAMPAGE...
...UNSTOPPABLE. AND OUR ELITE SOLDIERS ARE OUR TUSKS!!
RAID ON THE CITY!!
KNOCK IT OUT... ...MY LOYAL EVIL TUSKS!!
Raid On the City,
Knock out··· Evil Tusks···
R... O... C... K... E... T...
TEAM ROCKET ...

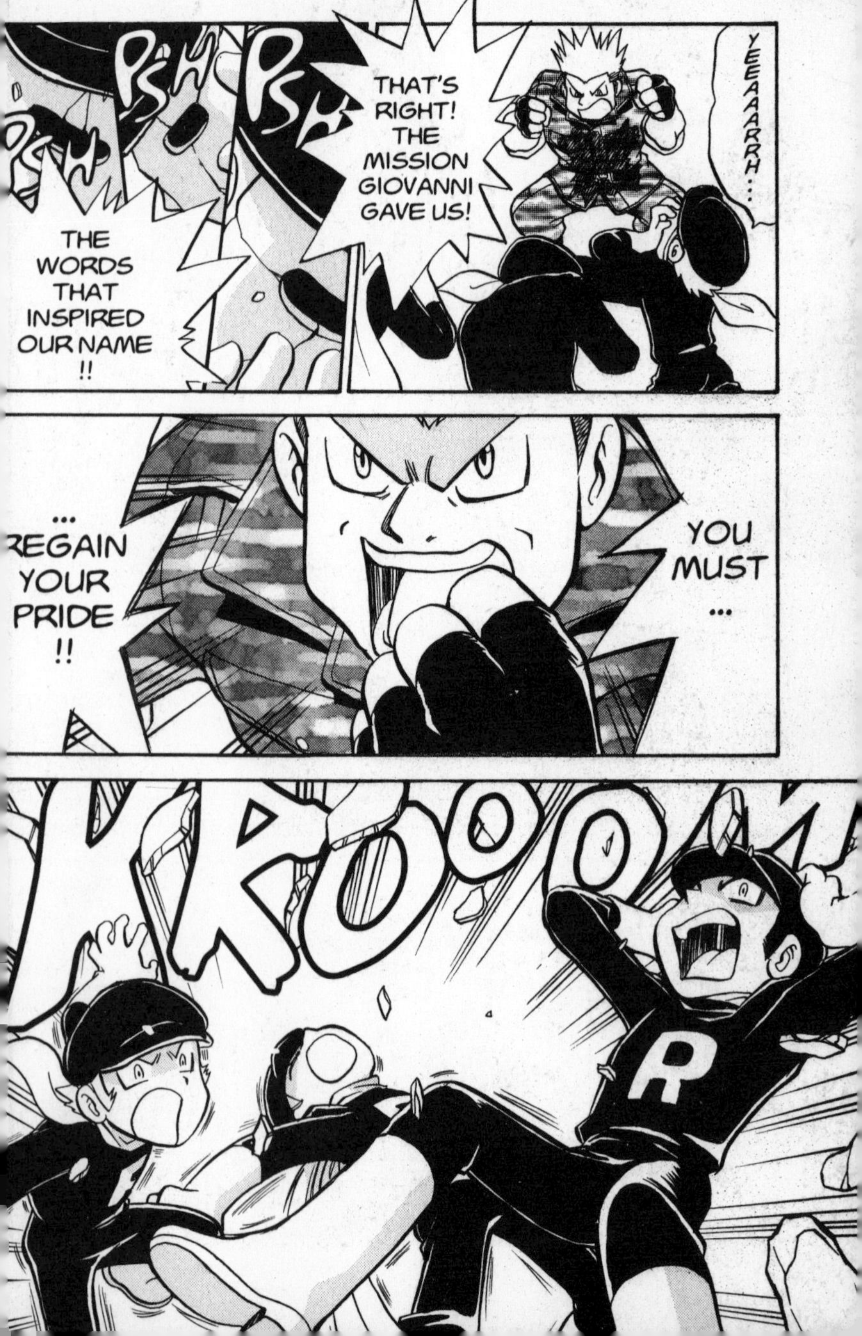
YEEAAARRH...
THAT'S RIGHT! THE MISSION GIOVANNI GAVE US!
PSH
PSH
THE WORDS THAT INSPIRED OUR NAME !!
YOU MUST ...
... REGAIN YOUR PRIDE !!

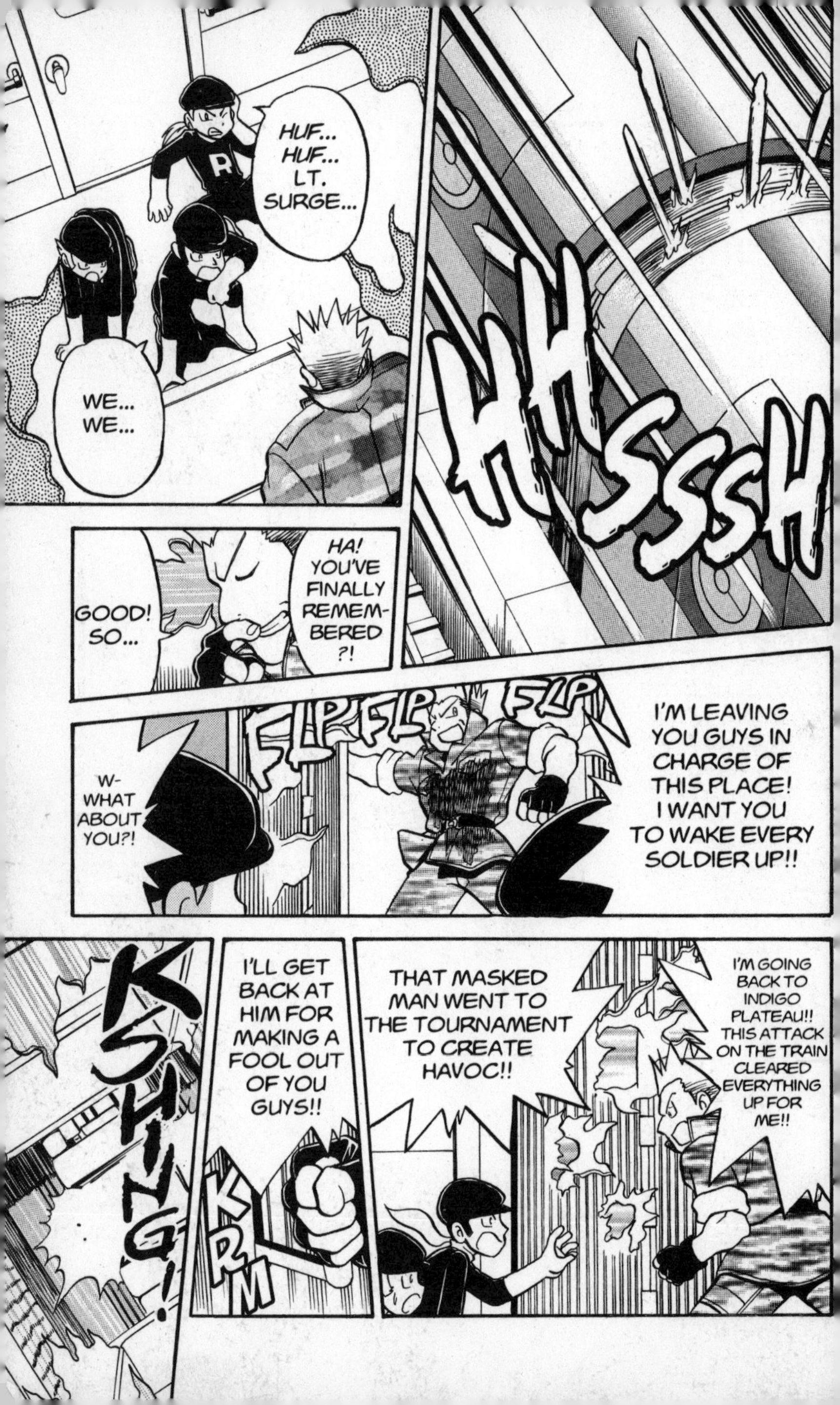
HHSSSH
HUF... HUF... LT. SURGE...
WE... WE...
HA! YOU'VE FINALLY REMEM-BERED ?!
GOOD! SO...
FLP FLP FLP
I'M LEAVING YOU GUYS IN CHARGE OF THIS PLACE! I WANT YOU TO WAKE EVERY SOLDIER UP!!
W-WHAT ABOUT YOU?!
I'M GOING BACK TO INDIGO PLATEAU!! THIS ATTACK ON THE TRAIN CLEARED EVERYTHING UP FOR ME!!
THAT MASKED MAN WENT TO THE TOURNAMENT TO CREATE HAVOC!!
I'LL GET BACK AT HIM FOR MAKING A FOOL OUT OF YOU GUYS!!
KRM
KSHING!

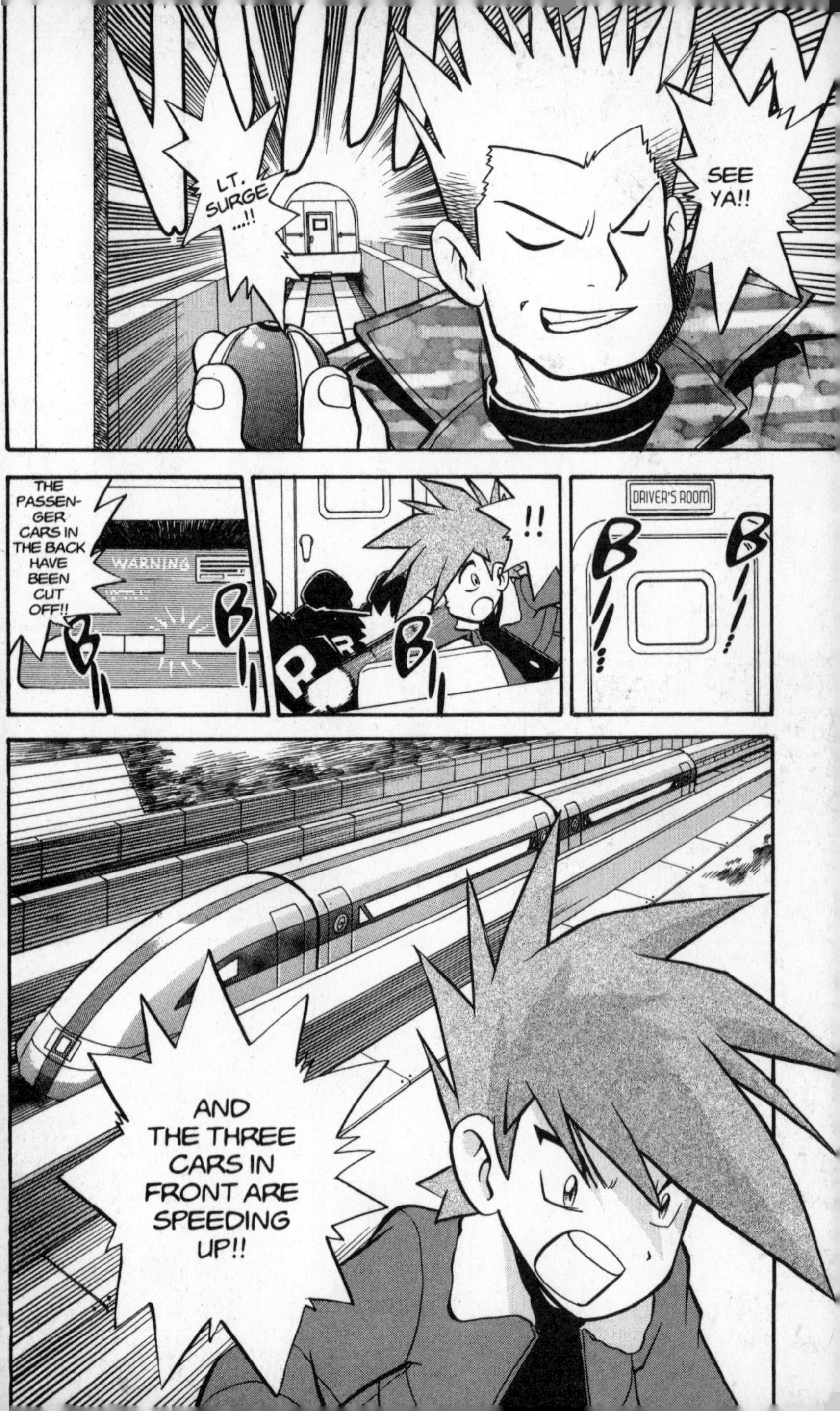

SEE YA!!
LT. SURGE ...!!
DRIVER'S ROOM
B B
!!
B
THE PASSENGER CARS IN THE BACK HAVE BEEN CUT OFF!!
WARNING
B B
AND THE THREE CARS IN FRONT ARE SPEEDING UP!!

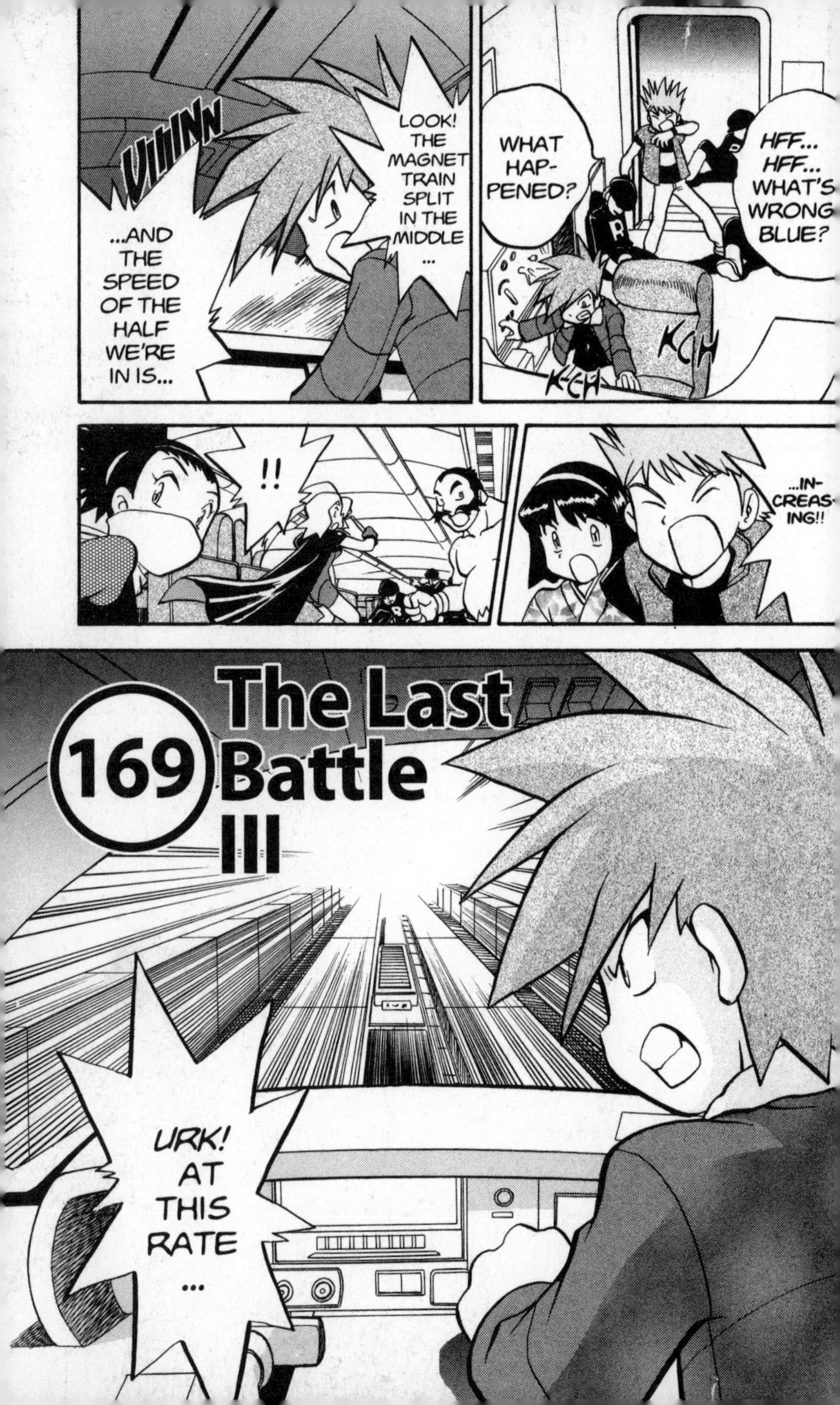
HFF... HFF... WHAT'S WRONG BLUE?
WHAT HAP-PENED?
K-CH
K-CH
LOOK! THE MAGNET TRAIN SPLIT IN THE MIDDLE ...
VIIIINN
...AND THE SPEED OF THE HALF WE'RE IN IS...
...IN-CREAS-ING!!
!!
169 The Last Battle III
URK! AT THIS RATE ...

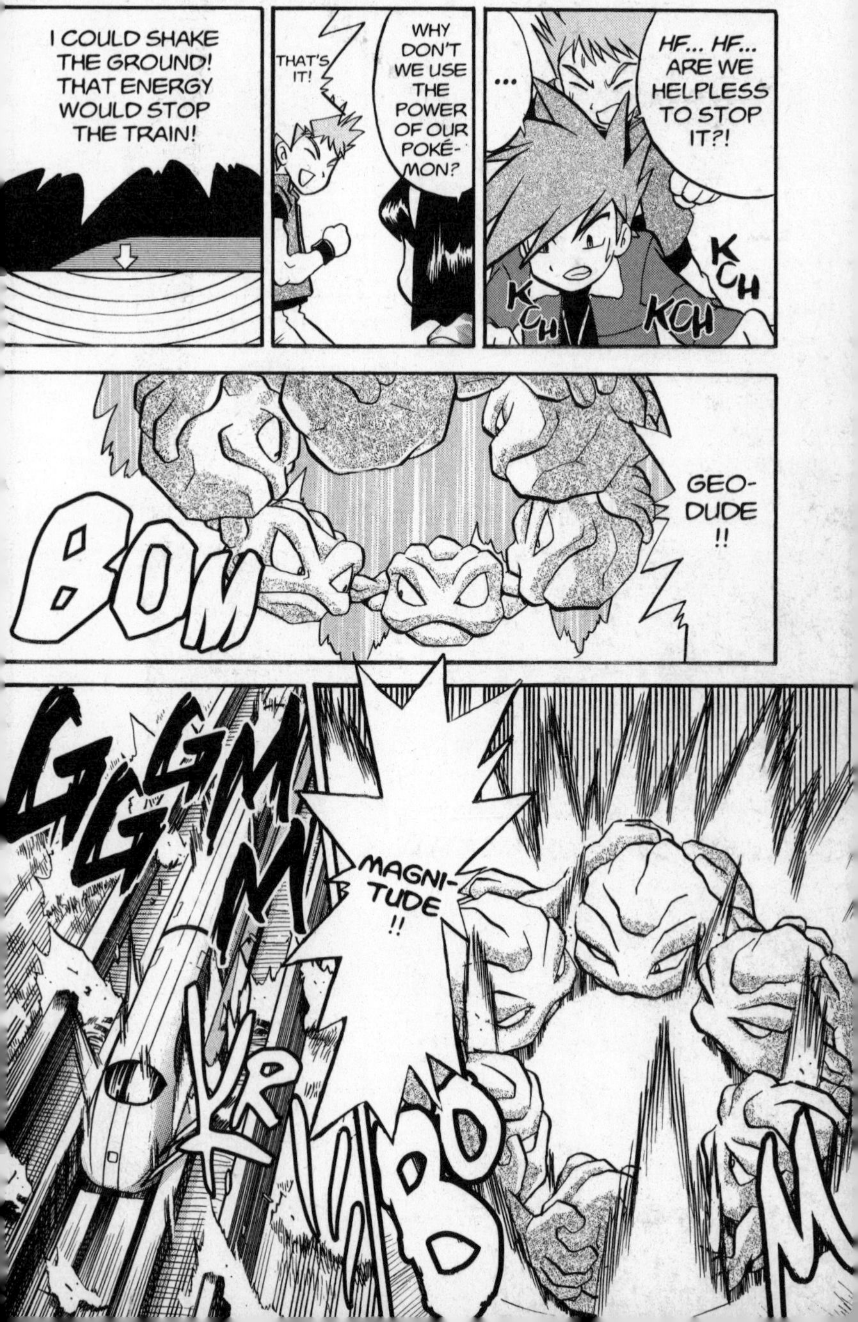
HF... HF... ARE WE HELPLESS TO STOP IT?!
...
KCH
KCH
KCH
WHY DON'T WE USE THE POWER OF OUR POKÉMON?
THAT'S IT!
I COULD SHAKE THE GROUND! THAT ENERGY WOULD STOP THE TRAIN!
GEODUDE!!
BOM
MAGNITUDE!!
GGGMM
KR
BOOM

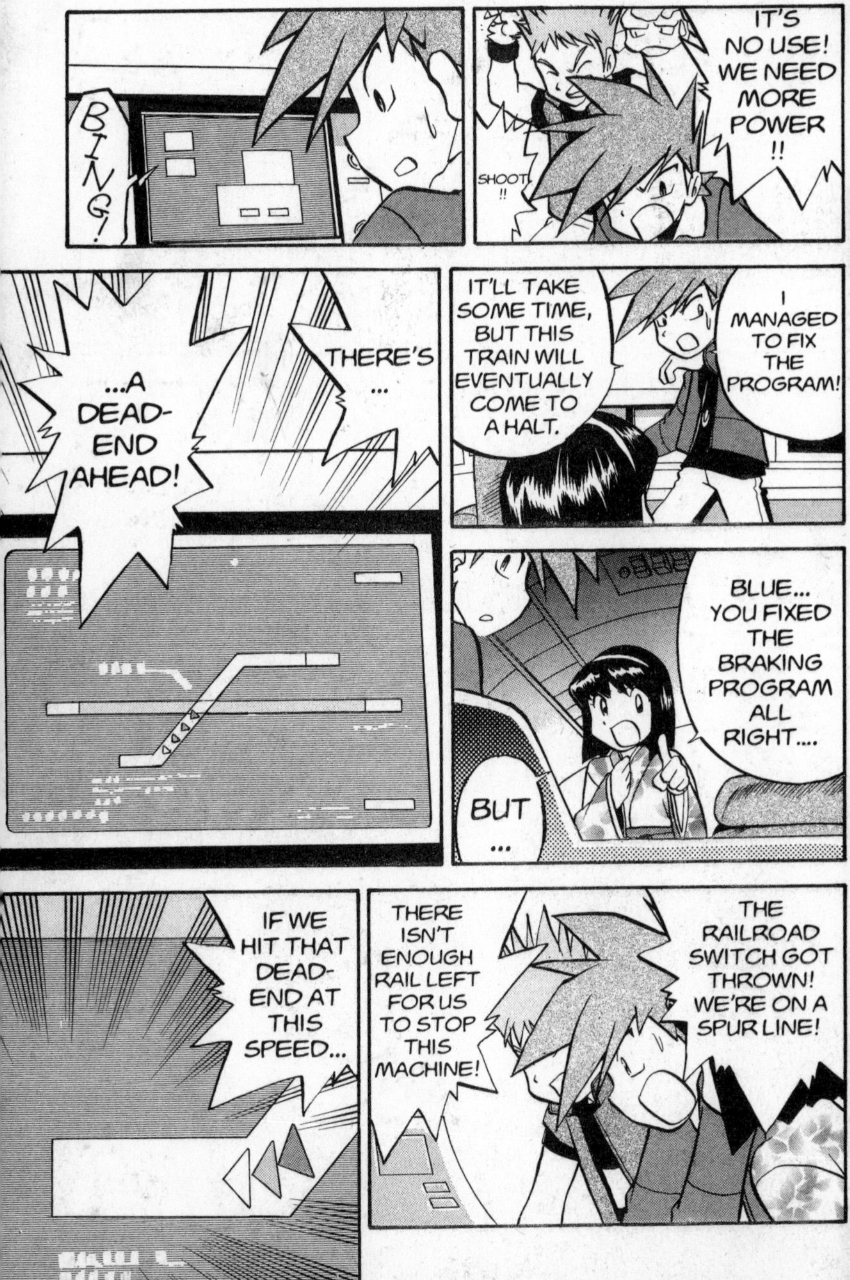
IT'S NO USE! WE NEED MORE POWER !!
SHOOT !!
BING!
I MANAGED TO FIX THE PROGRAM!
IT'LL TAKE SOME TIME, BUT THIS TRAIN WILL EVENTUALLY COME TO A HALT.
BLUE... YOU FIXED THE BRAKING PROGRAM ALL RIGHT....
BUT ...
THERE'S ...
...A DEAD-END AHEAD!
THE RAILROAD SWITCH GOT THROWN! WE'RE ON A SPUR LINE!
THERE ISN'T ENOUGH RAIL LEFT FOR US TO STOP THIS MACHINE!
IF WE HIT THAT DEAD-END AT THIS SPEED...

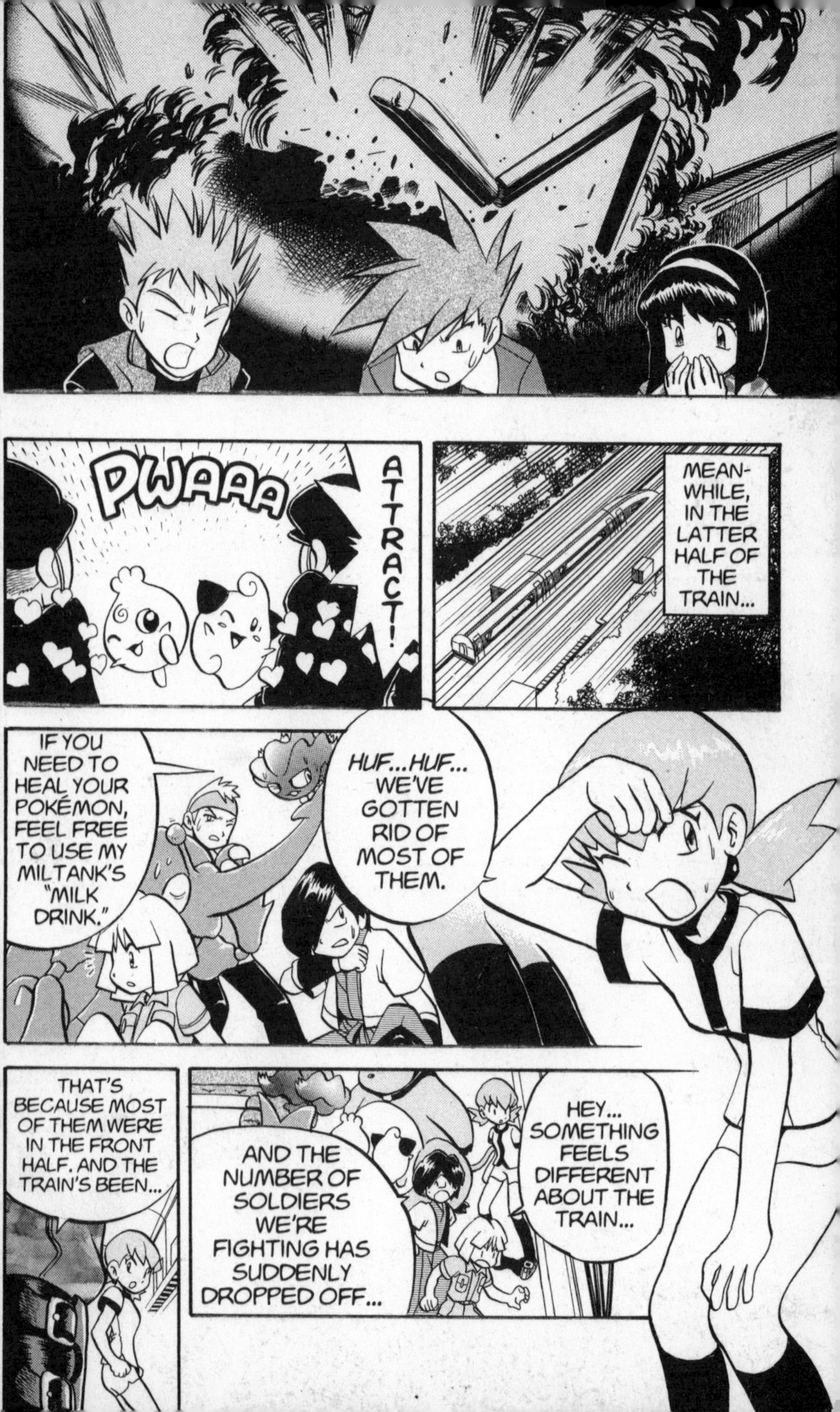
MEAN-WHILE, IN THE LATTER HALF OF THE TRAIN...
ATTRACT!
PWAAA
HUF... HUF... WE'VE GOTTEN RID OF MOST OF THEM.
IF YOU NEED TO HEAL YOUR POKÉMON, FEEL FREE TO USE MY MILTANK'S "MILK DRINK."
HEY... SOMETHING FEELS DIFFERENT ABOUT THE TRAIN...
AND THE NUMBER OF SOLDIERS WE'RE FIGHTING HAS SUDDENLY DROPPED OFF...
THAT'S BECAUSE MOST OF THEM WERE IN THE FRONT HALF. AND THE TRAIN'S BEEN...

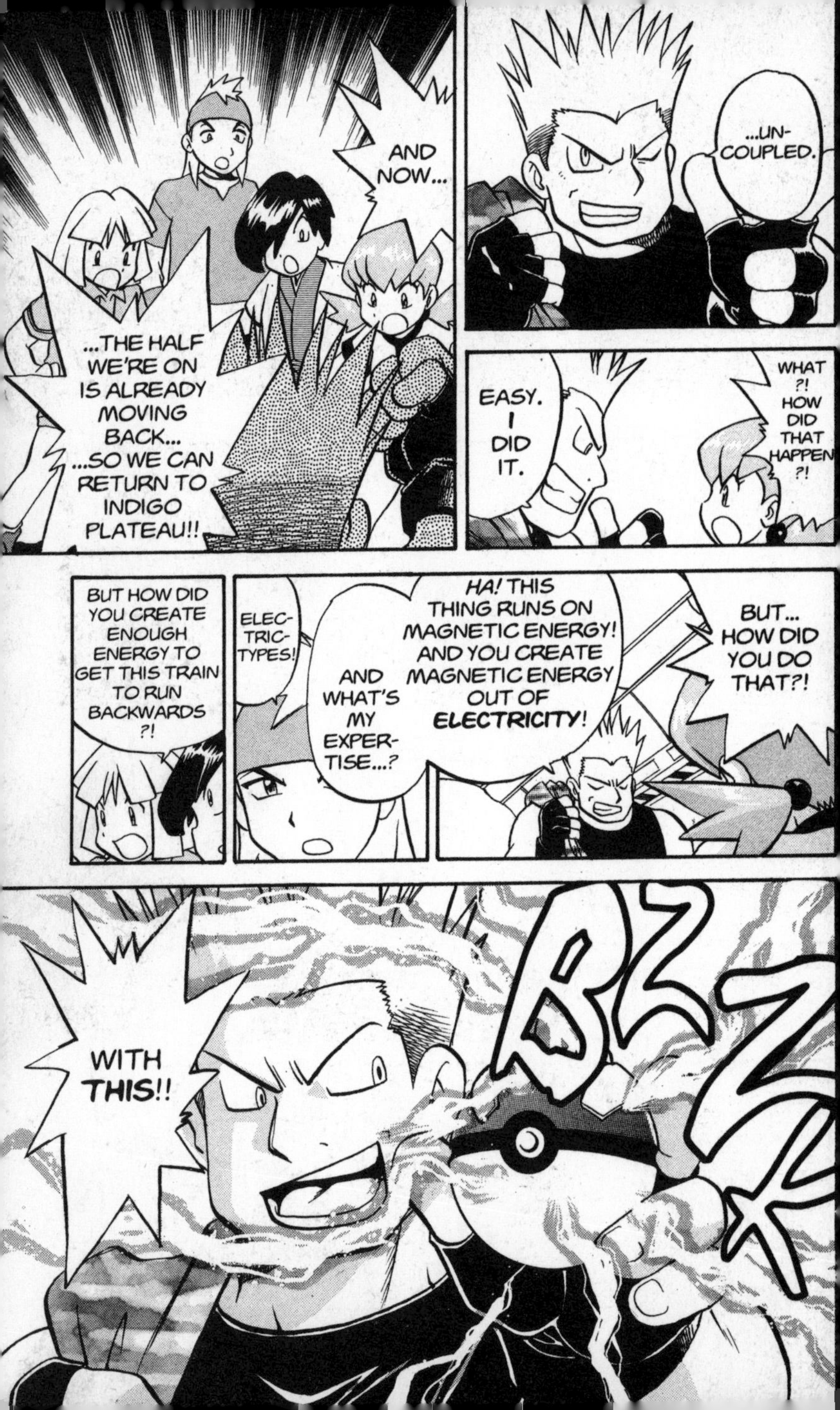
...UN-COUPLED.
WHAT?! HOW DID THAT HAPPEN?!
EASY. I DID IT.
AND NOW...
...THE HALF WE'RE ON IS ALREADY MOVING BACK... ...SO WE CAN RETURN TO INDIGO PLATEAU!!
BUT... HOW DID YOU DO THAT?!
HA! THIS THING RUNS ON MAGNETIC ENERGY! AND YOU CREATE MAGNETIC ENERGY OUT OF ELECTRICITY!
AND WHAT'S MY EXPERTISE...?
ELECTRIC-TYPES!
BUT HOW DID YOU CREATE ENOUGH ENERGY TO GET THIS TRAIN TO RUN BACKWARDS?!
BZZT
WITH THIS!!

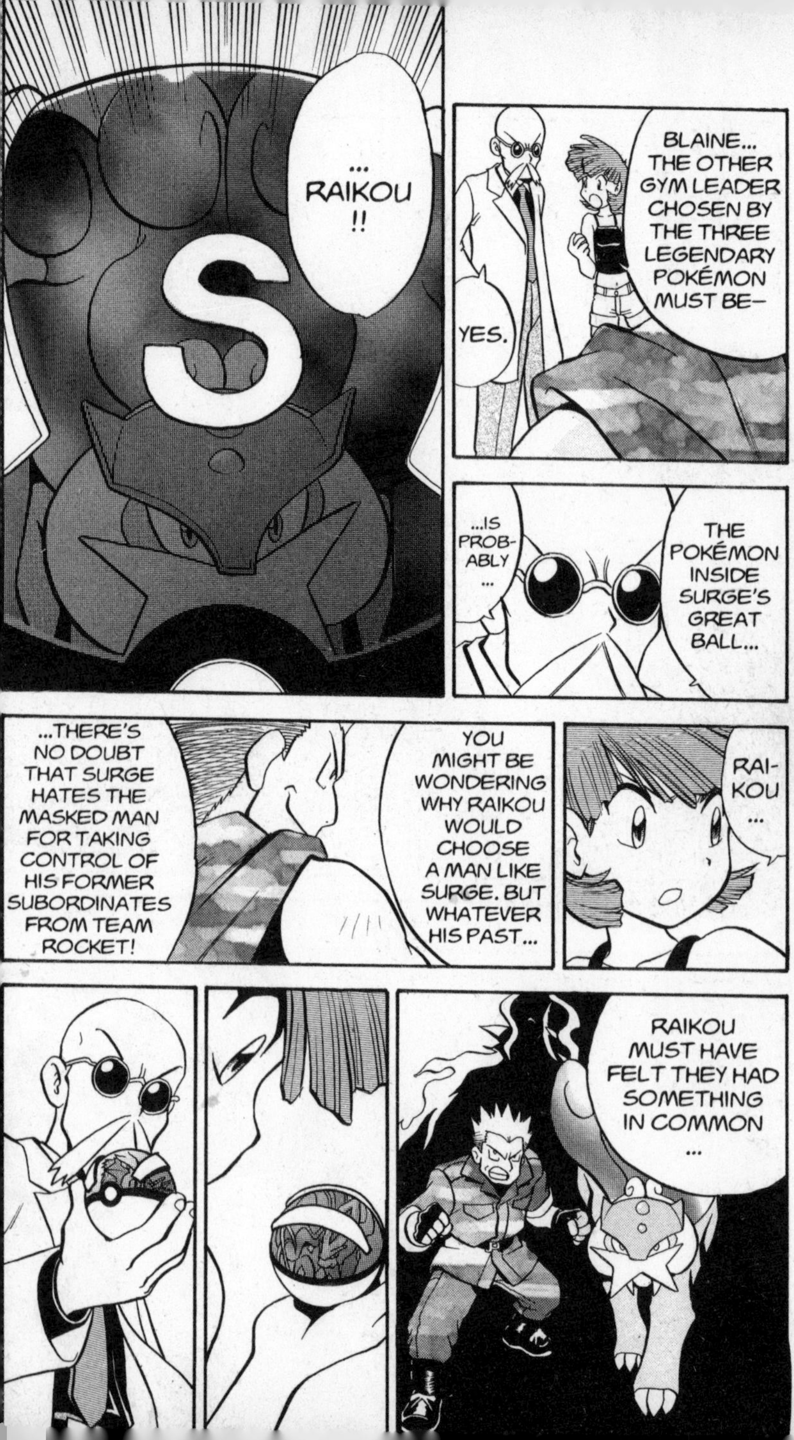
BLAINE... THE OTHER GYM LEADER CHOSEN BY THE THREE LEGENDARY POKÉMON MUST BE—
YES.
THE POKÉMON INSIDE SURGE'S GREAT BALL...
...IS PROBABLY ...
... RAIKOU !!
RAI-KOU ...
YOU MIGHT BE WONDERING WHY RAIKOU WOULD CHOOSE A MAN LIKE SURGE. BUT WHATEVER HIS PAST...
...THERE'S NO DOUBT THAT SURGE HATES THE MASKED MAN FOR TAKING CONTROL OF HIS FORMER SUBORDINATES FROM TEAM ROCKET!
RAIKOU MUST HAVE FELT THEY HAD SOMETHING IN COMMON ...

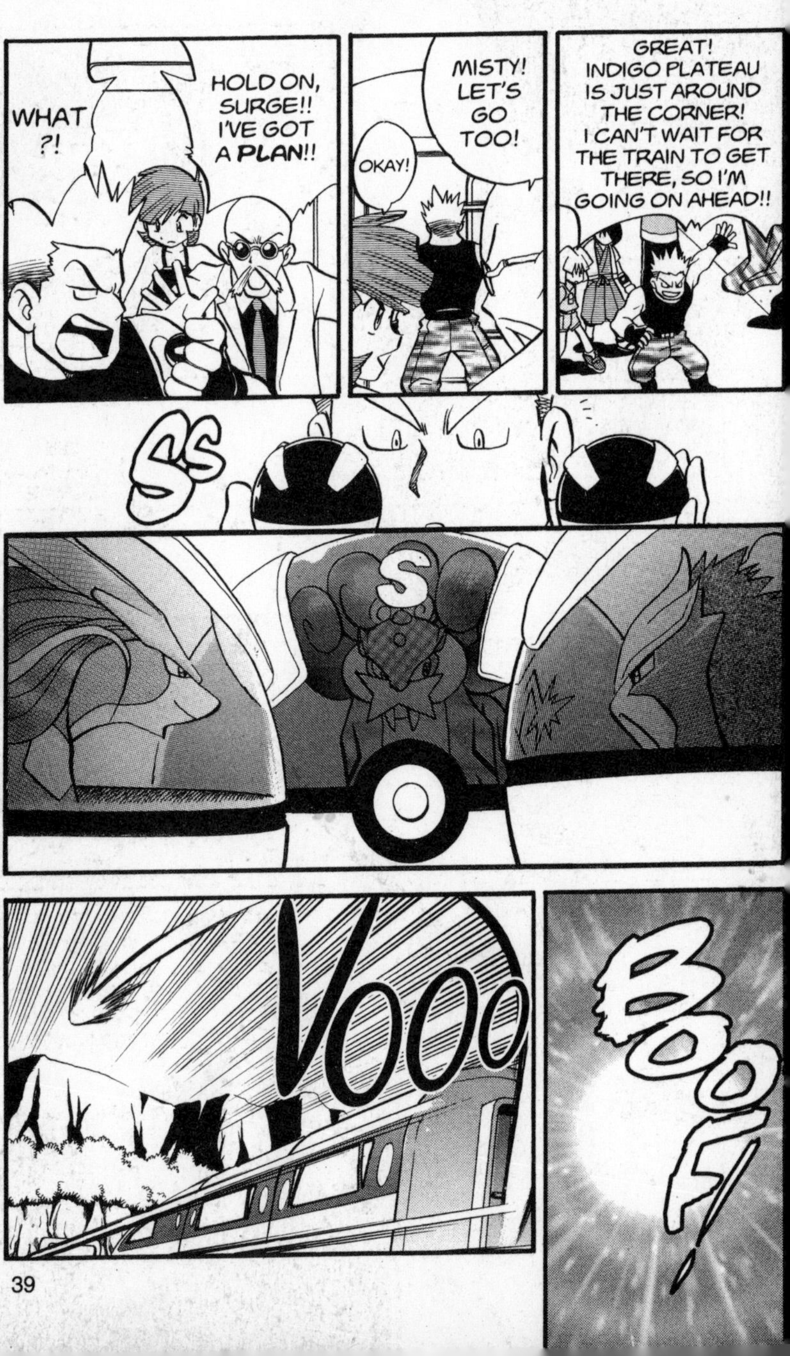
GREAT! INDIGO PLATEAU IS JUST AROUND THE CORNER! I CAN'T WAIT FOR THE TRAIN TO GET THERE, SO I'M GOING ON AHEAD!!
MISTY! LET'S GO TOO!
OKAY!
HOLD ON, SURGE!! I'VE GOT A PLAN!!
WHAT ?!
SS
S
BOOOF!
VOOO

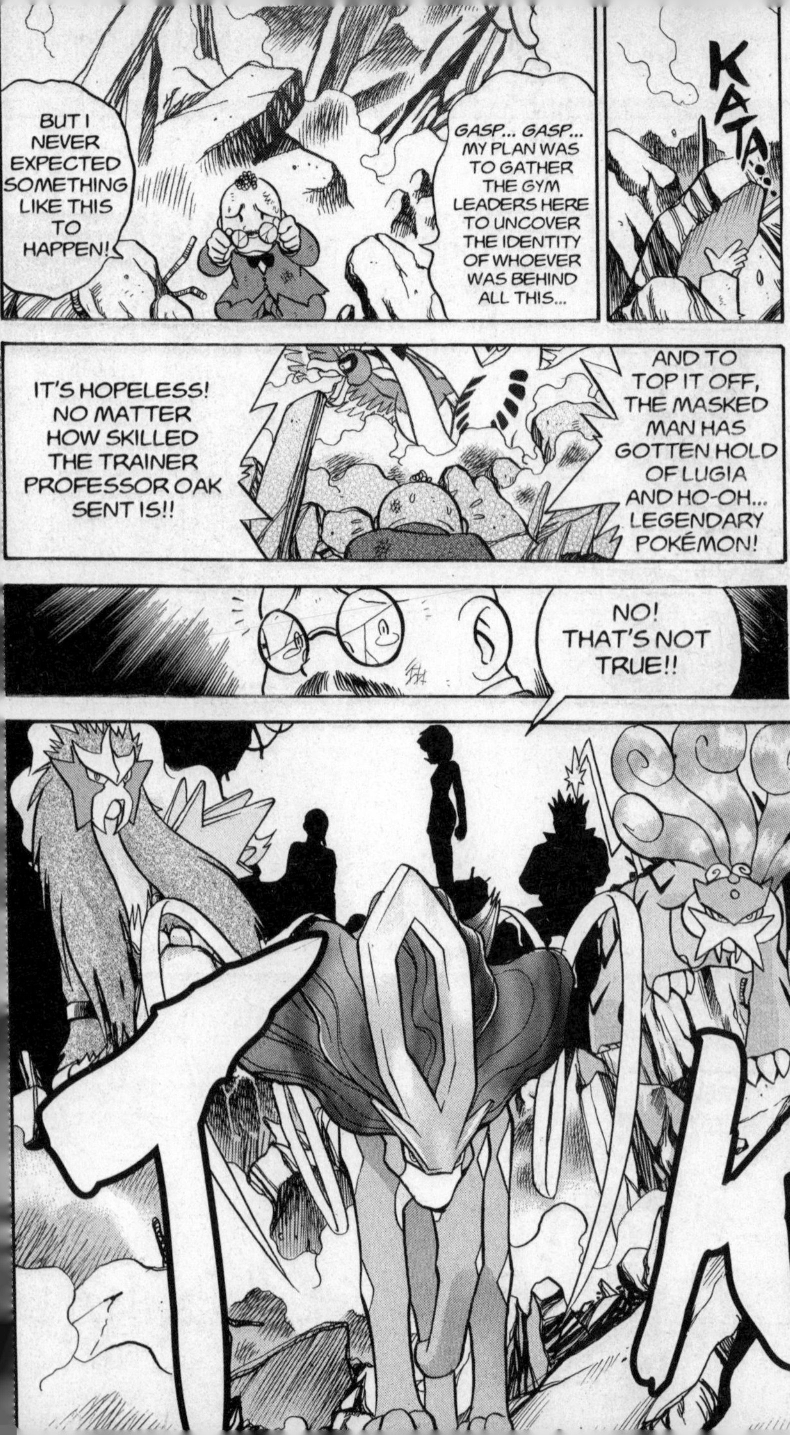
KATA...
GASP... GASP... MY PLAN WAS TO GATHER THE GYM LEADERS HERE TO UNCOVER THE IDENTITY OF WHOEVER WAS BEHIND ALL THIS...
BUT I NEVER EXPECTED SOMETHING LIKE THIS TO HAPPEN!
AND TO TOP IT OFF, THE MASKED MAN HAS GOTTEN HOLD OF LUGIA AND HO-OH... LEGENDARY POKÉMON!
IT'S HOPELESS! NO MATTER HOW SKILLED THE TRAINER PROFESSOR OAK SENT IS!!
NO! THAT'S NOT TRUE!!

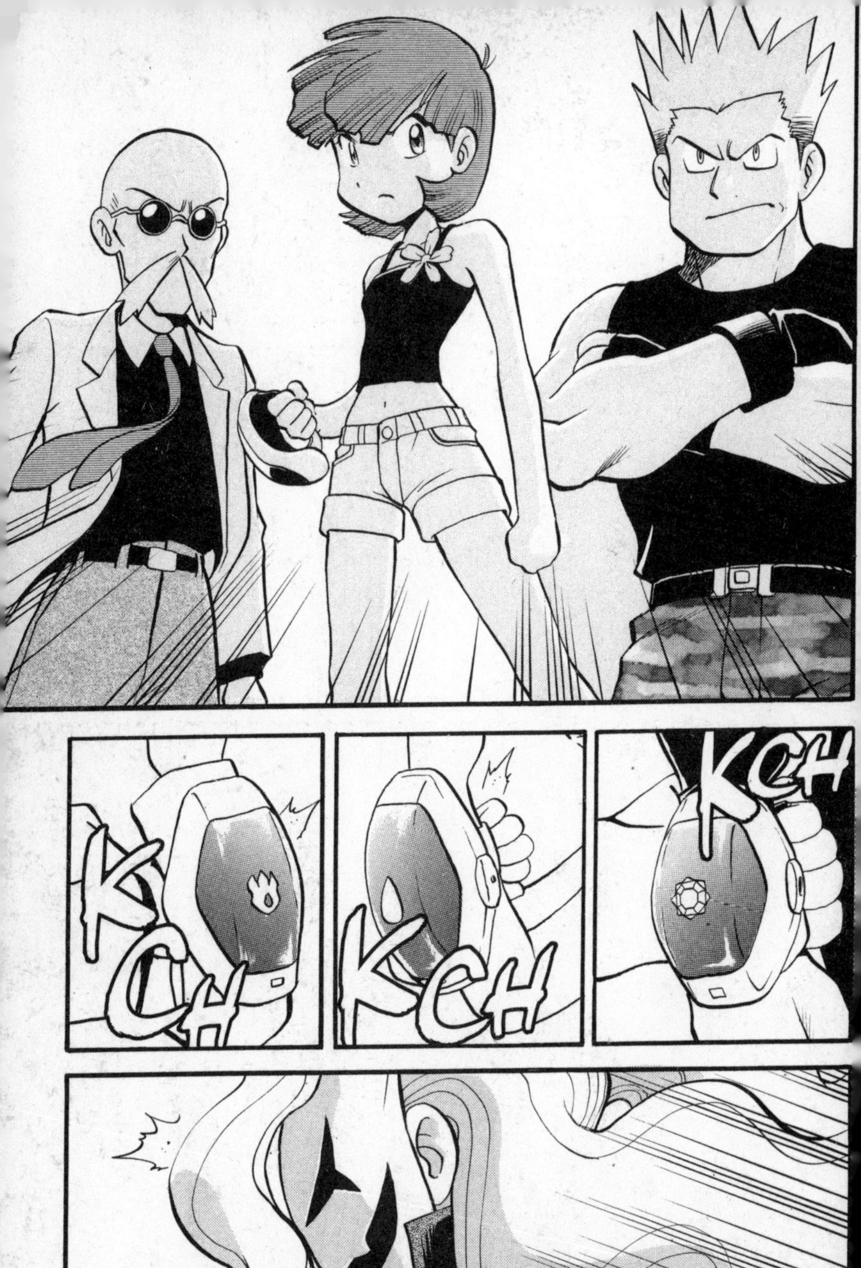
KCH
KCH
KCH

## (170) The Last Battle IV

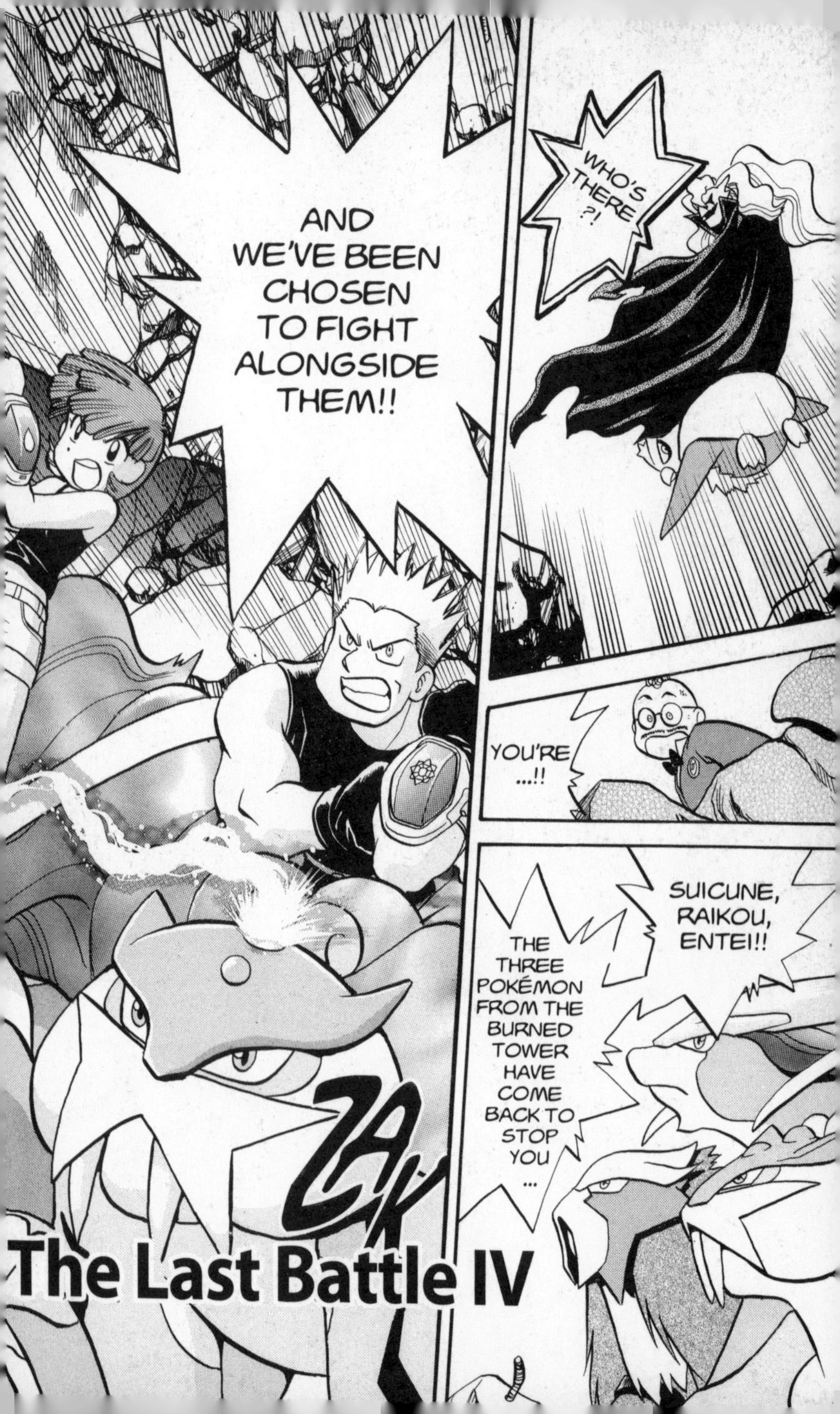
WHO'S THERE ?!
YOU'RE ...!!
SUICUNE, RAIKOU, ENTEI!!
THE THREE POKÉMON FROM THE BURNED TOWER HAVE COME BACK TO STOP YOU ...
AND WE'VE BEEN CHOSEN TO FIGHT ALONGSIDE THEM!!
ZAK

# The Last Battle IV

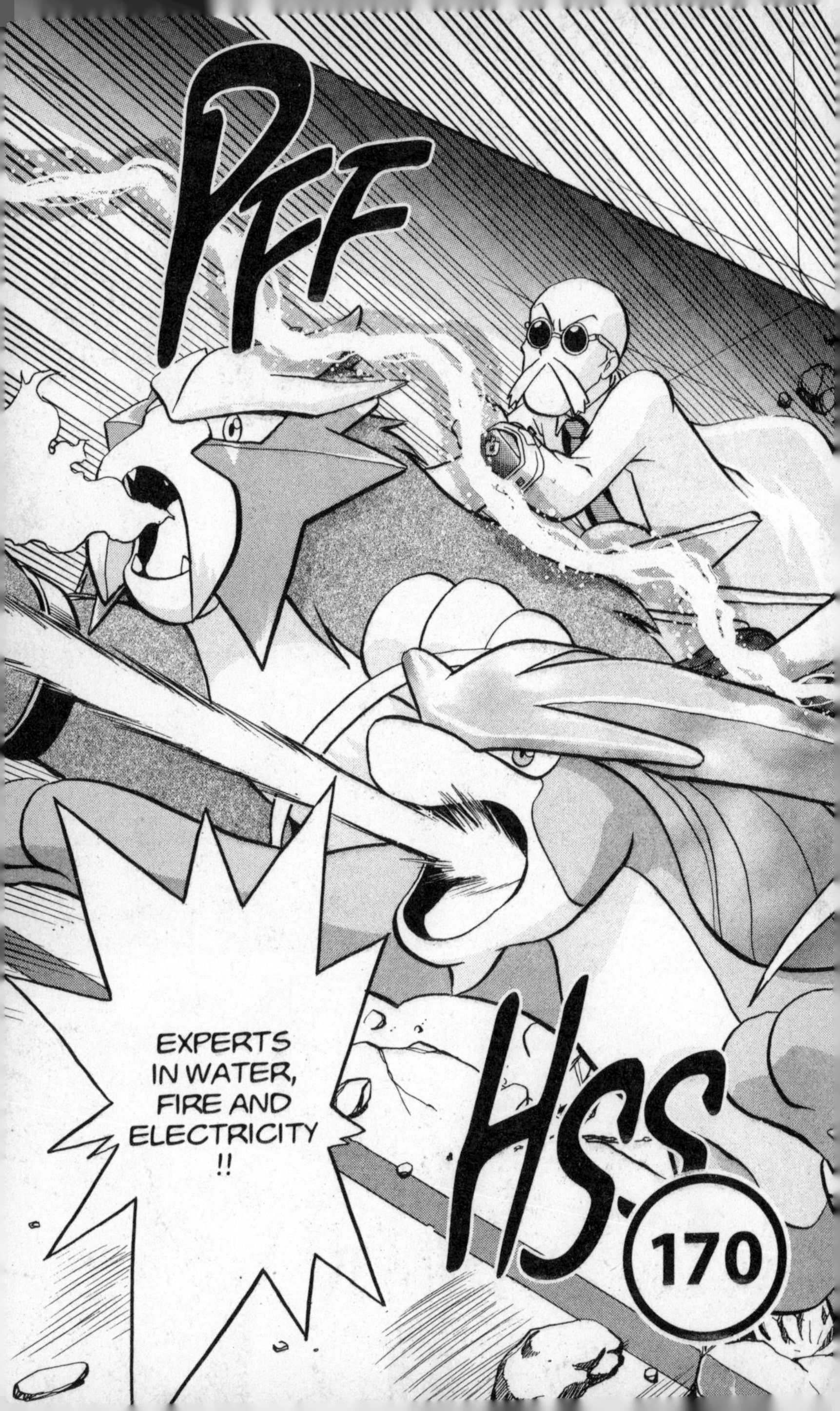
PFF
EXPERTS IN WATER, FIRE AND ELECTRICITY !!
HSS

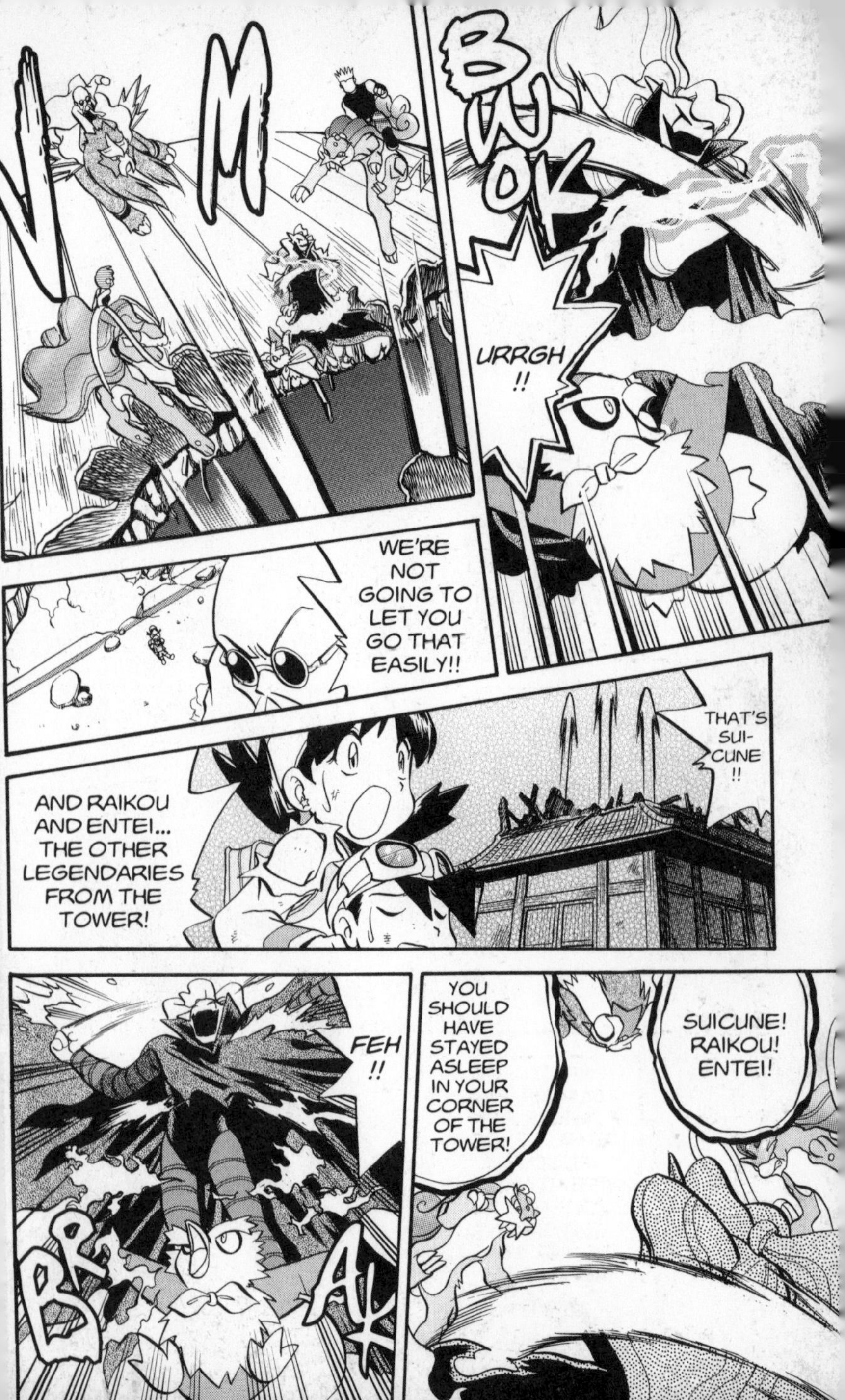
BWOK
URRGH!!
M
WE'RE NOT GOING TO LET YOU GO THAT EASILY!!
THAT'S SUI-CUNE!!
AND RAIKOU AND ENTEI... THE OTHER LEGENDARIES FROM THE TOWER!
SUICUNE! RAIKOU! ENTEI!
YOU SHOULD HAVE STAYED ASLEEP IN YOUR CORNER OF THE TOWER!
FEH!!
BRAK

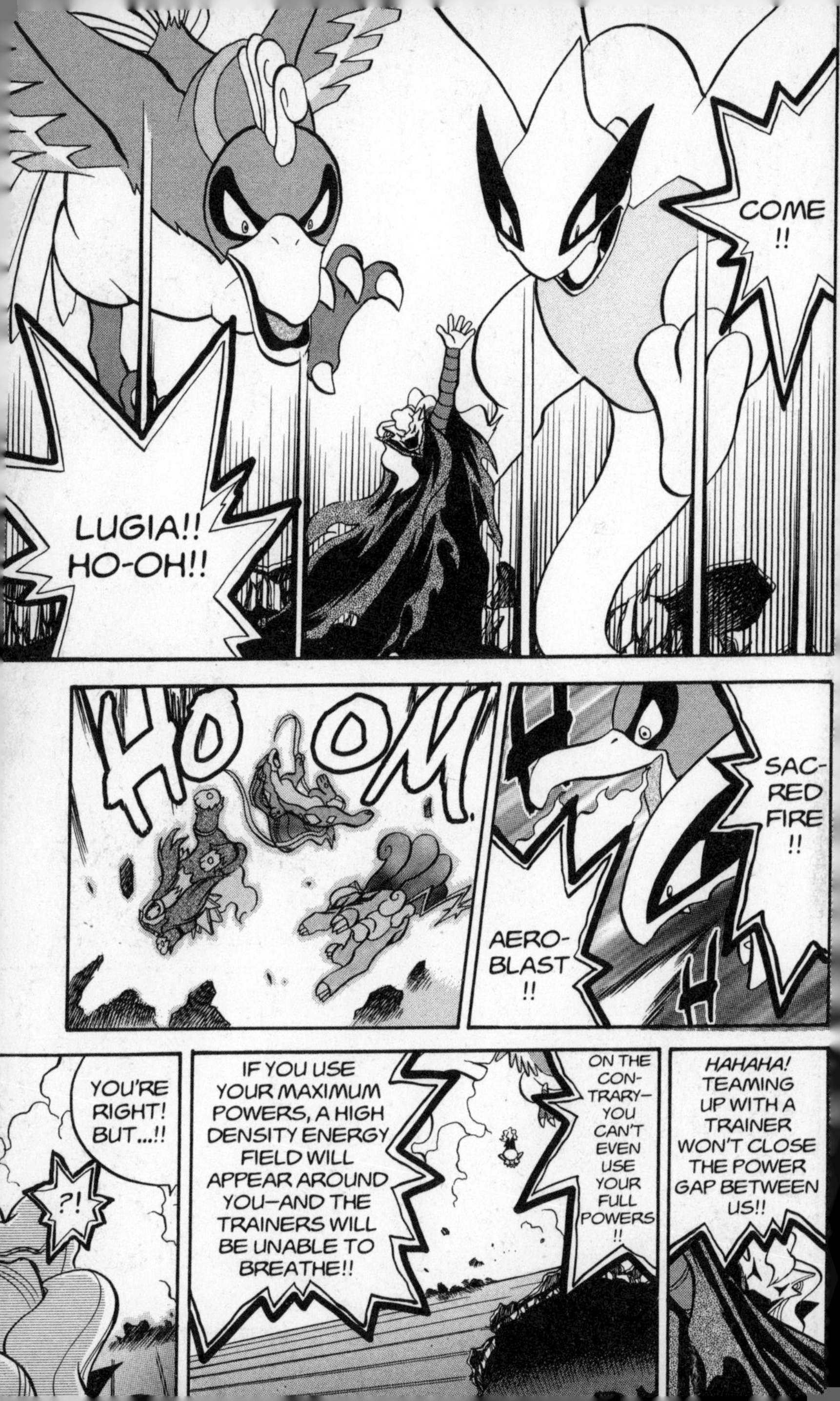
COME !!
LUGIA!! HO-OH!!
SAC-RED FIRE !!
AERO-BLAST !!
HOOM
HAHAHA! TEAMING UP WITH A TRAINER WON'T CLOSE THE POWER GAP BETWEEN US!!
ON THE CON-TRARY— YOU CAN'T EVEN USE YOUR FULL POWERS !!
IF YOU USE YOUR MAXIMUM POWERS, A HIGH DENSITY ENERGY FIELD WILL APPEAR AROUND YOU—AND THE TRAINERS WILL BE UNABLE TO BREATHE!!
YOU'RE RIGHT! BUT...!!
?!

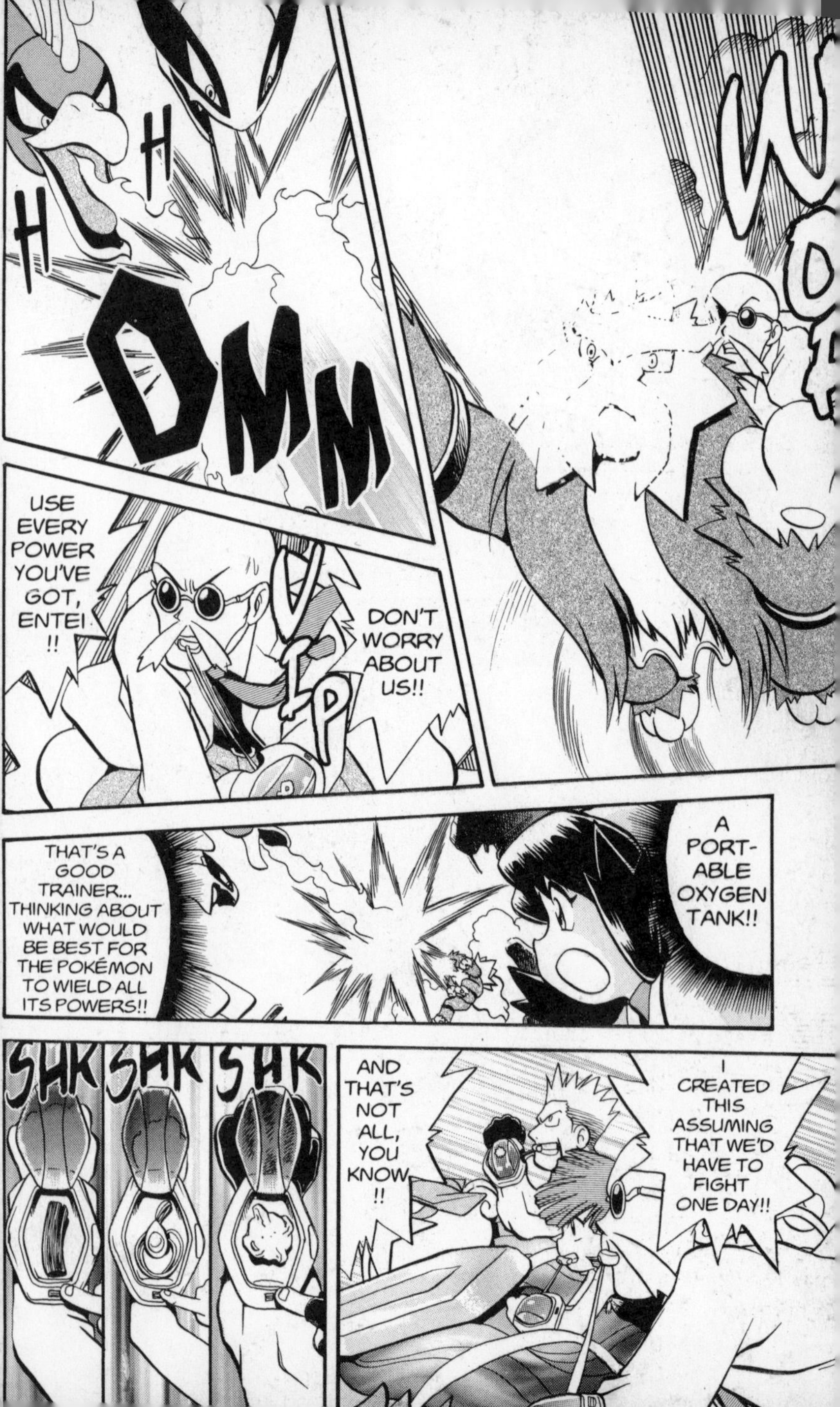
H
H
DMM
USE EVERY POWER YOU'VE GOT, ENTEI!!
DON'T WORRY ABOUT US!!
A PORT-ABLE OXYGEN TANK!!
THAT'S A GOOD TRAINER... THINKING ABOUT WHAT WOULD BE BEST FOR THE POKÉMON TO WIELD ALL ITS POWERS!!
I CREATED THIS ASSUMING THAT WE'D HAVE TO FIGHT ONE DAY!!
AND THAT'S NOT ALL, YOU KNOW!!
SHK
SHK
SHK

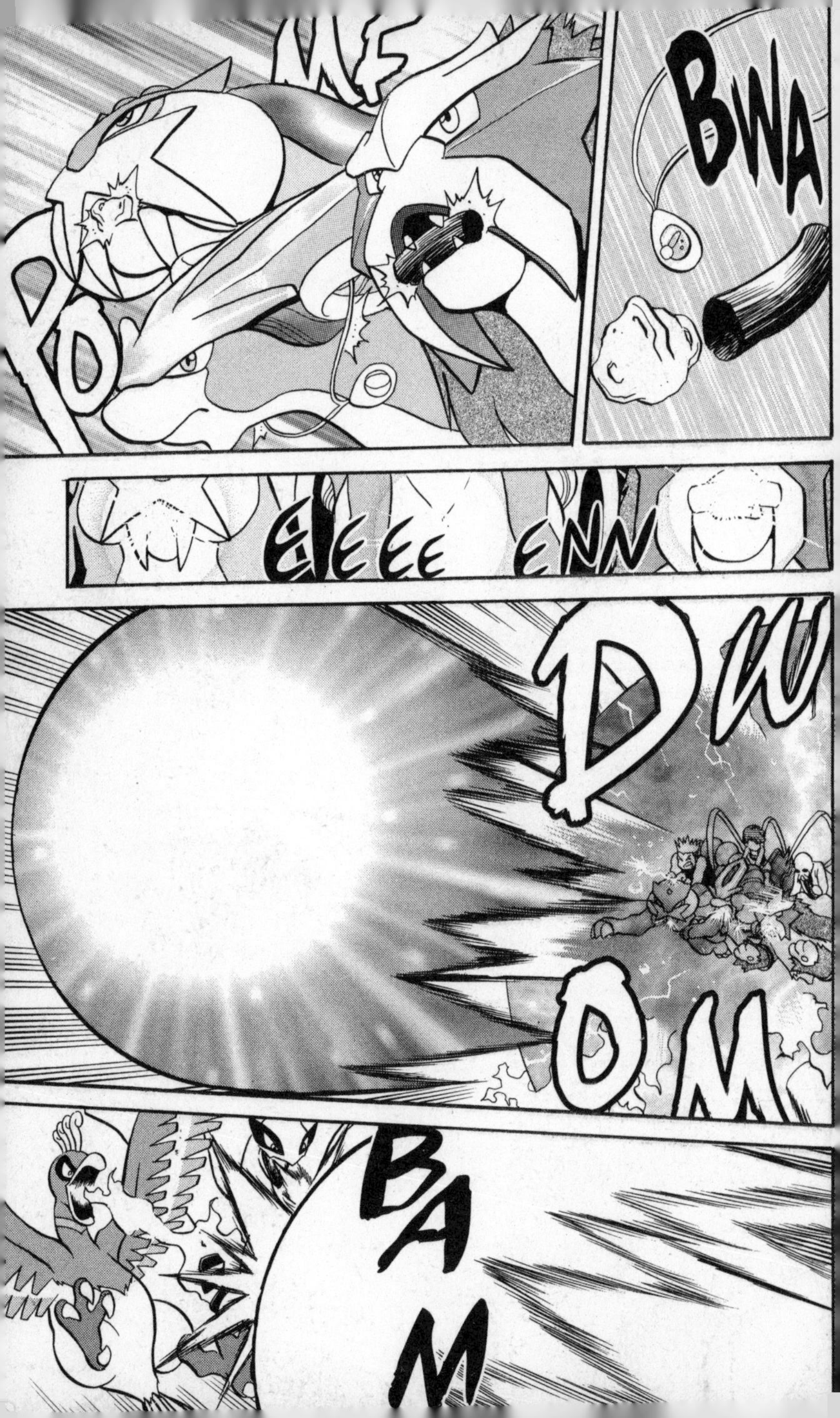
BWA
EEEE ENN
DW
OM
BAM

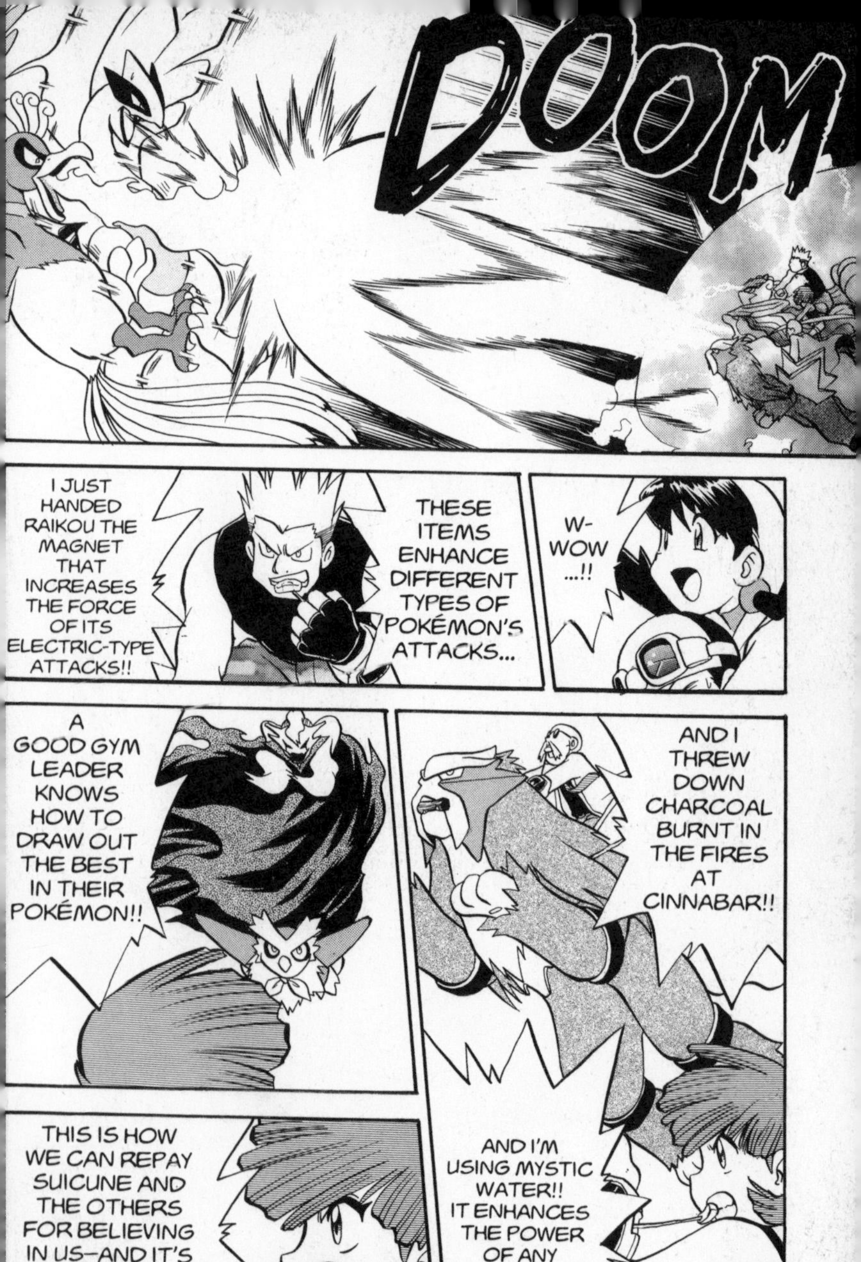
DOOM
W-WOW ...!!
THESE ITEMS ENHANCE DIFFERENT TYPES OF POKÉMON'S ATTACKS...
I JUST HANDED RAIKOU THE MAGNET THAT INCREASES THE FORCE OF ITS ELECTRIC-TYPE ATTACKS!!
AND I THREW DOWN CHARCOAL BURNT IN THE FIRES AT CINNABAR!!
A GOOD GYM LEADER KNOWS HOW TO DRAW OUT THE BEST IN THEIR POKÉMON!!
AND I'M USING MYSTIC WATER!! IT ENHANCES THE POWER OF ANY WATER-TYPE MOVES!!
THIS IS HOW WE CAN REPAY SUICUNE AND THE OTHERS FOR BELIEVING IN US—AND IT'S THE BEST WAY TO STOP YOU!!

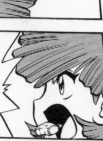

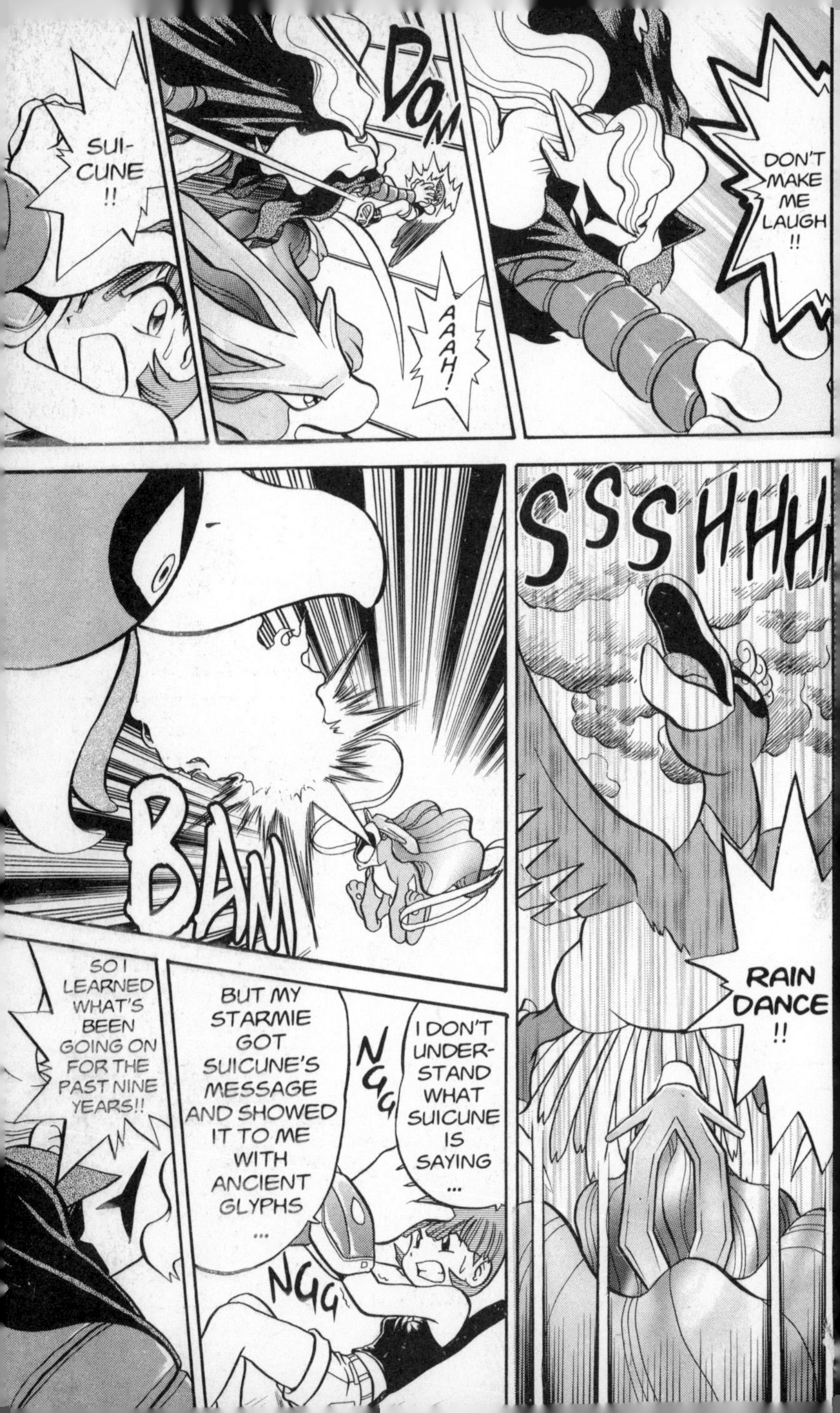

DON'T MAKE ME LAUGH!!
DOM
AAAAH!
SUI-CUNE!!
SSSHHHH
RAIN DANCE!!
BAM
I DON'T UNDER-STAND WHAT SUICUNE IS SAYING...
NGG
BUT MY STARMIE GOT SUICUNE'S MESSAGE AND SHOWED IT TO ME WITH ANCIENT GLYPHS...
NGG
SO I LEARNED WHAT'S BEEN GOING ON FOR THE PAST NINE YEARS!!

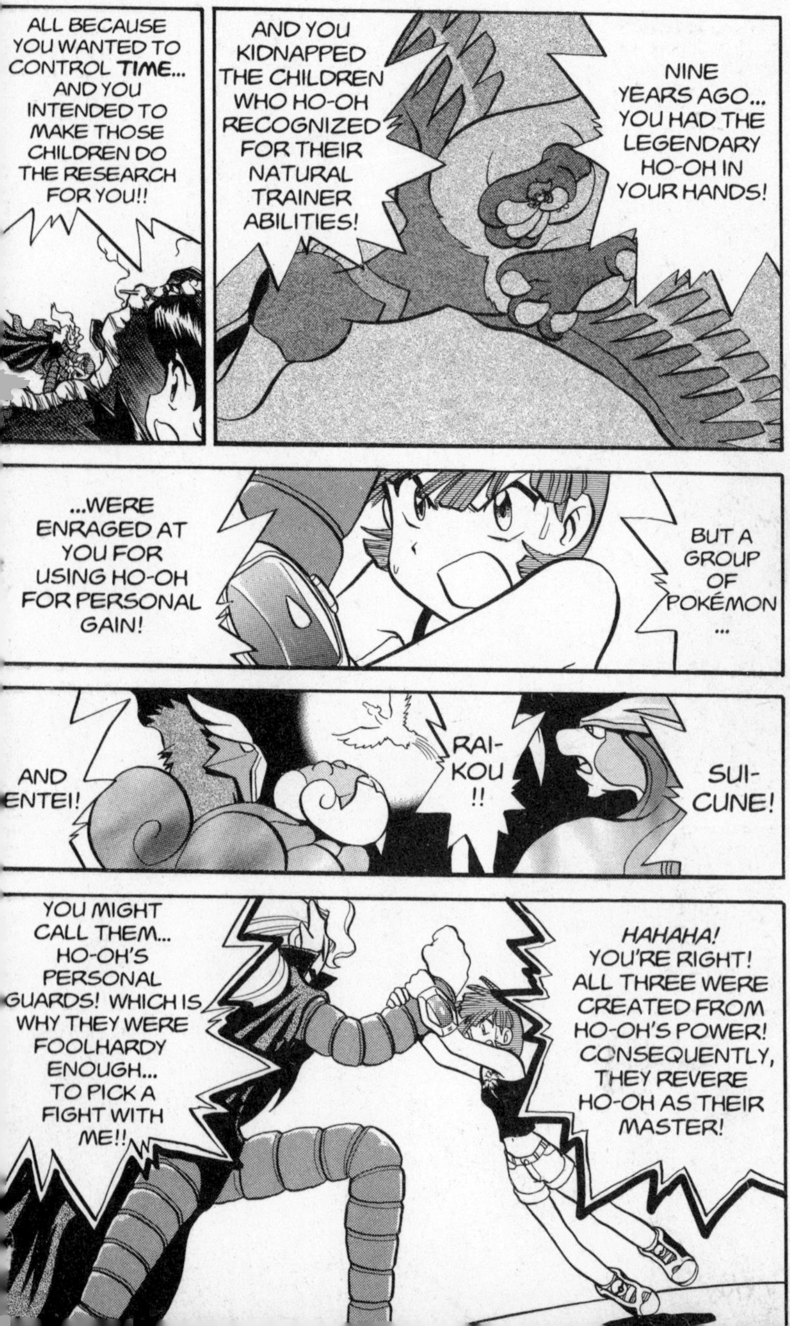
NINE YEARS AGO... YOU HAD THE LEGENDARY HO-OH IN YOUR HANDS!
AND YOU KIDNAPPED THE CHILDREN WHO HO-OH RECOGNIZED FOR THEIR NATURAL TRAINER ABILITIES!
ALL BECAUSE YOU WANTED TO CONTROL **TIME**... AND YOU INTENDED TO MAKE THOSE CHILDREN DO THE RESEARCH FOR YOU!!
BUT A GROUP OF POKÉMON...
...WERE ENRAGED AT YOU FOR USING HO-OH FOR PERSONAL GAIN!
SUI-CUNE!
RAI-KOU!!
AND ENTEI!
YOU MIGHT CALL THEM... HO-OH'S PERSONAL GUARDS! WHICH IS WHY THEY WERE FOOLHARDY ENOUGH... TO PICK A FIGHT WITH ME!!
*HAHAHA!* YOU'RE RIGHT! ALL THREE WERE CREATED FROM HO-OH'S POWER! CONSEQUENTLY, THEY REVERE HO-OH AS THEIR MASTER!

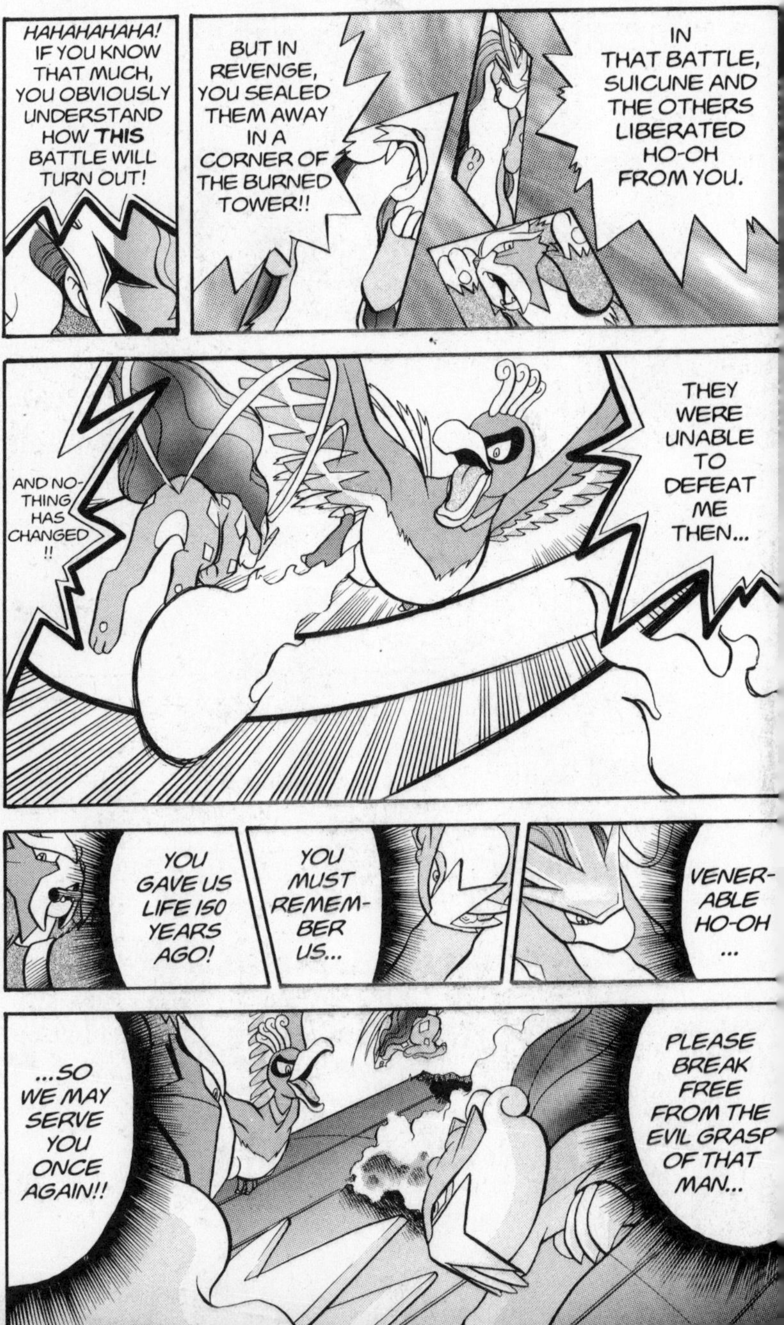
IN THAT BATTLE, SUICUNE AND THE OTHERS LIBERATED HO-OH FROM YOU.
BUT IN REVENGE, YOU SEALED THEM AWAY IN A CORNER OF THE BURNED TOWER!!
HAHAHAHAHA! IF YOU KNOW THAT MUCH, YOU OBVIOUSLY UNDERSTAND HOW **THIS** BATTLE WILL TURN OUT!
THEY WERE UNABLE TO DEFEAT ME THEN...
AND NO-THING HAS CHANGED!!
VENER-ABLE HO-OH ...
YOU MUST REMEM-BER US...
YOU GAVE US LIFE 150 YEARS AGO!
PLEASE BREAK FREE FROM THE EVIL GRASP OF THAT MAN...
...SO WE MAY SERVE YOU ONCE AGAIN!!

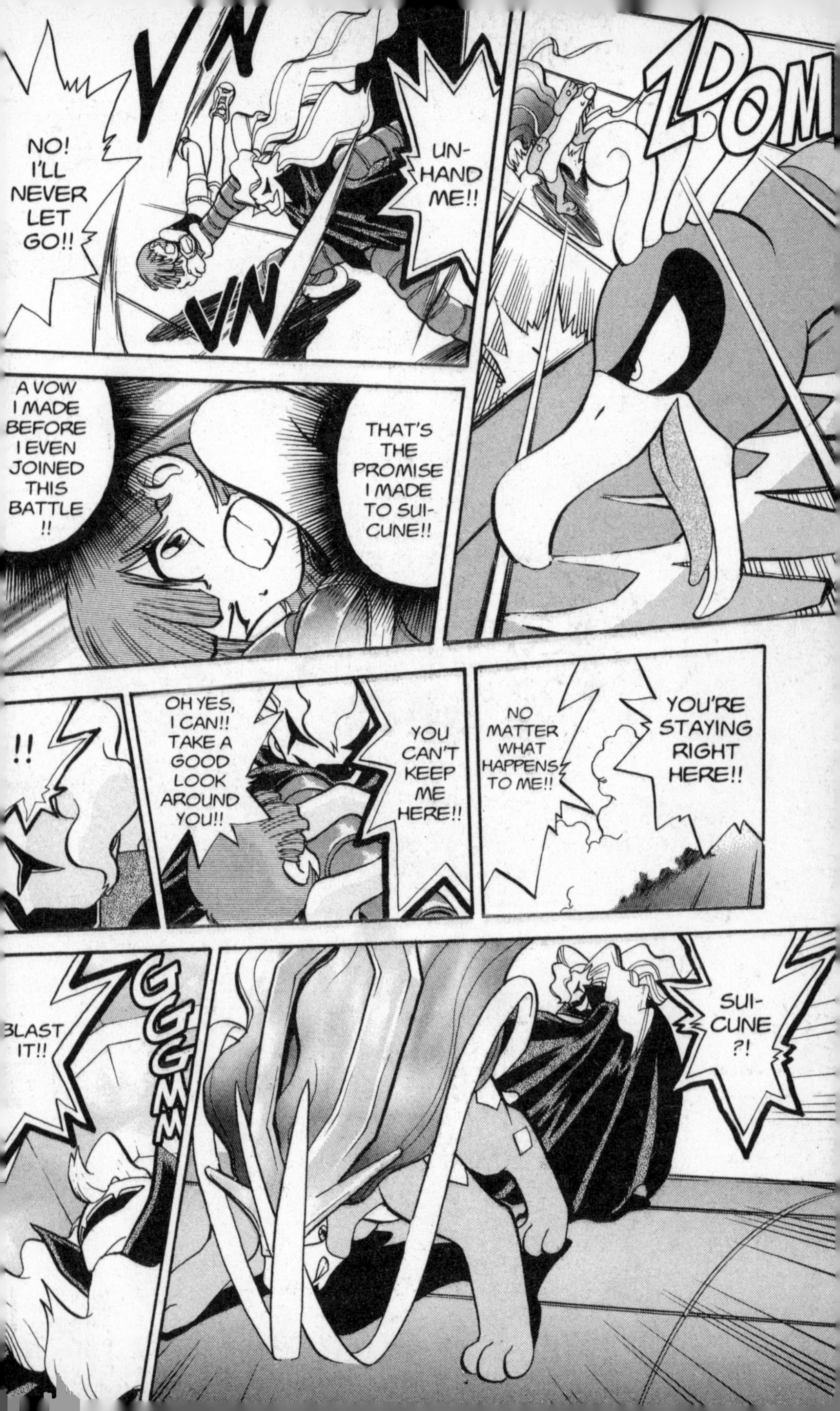
ZDOM
VN
UN-HAND ME!!
NO! I'LL NEVER LET GO!!
VN
THAT'S THE PROMISE I MADE TO SUI-CUNE!!
A VOW I MADE BEFORE I EVEN JOINED THIS BATTLE !!
YOU'RE STAYING RIGHT HERE!!
NO MATTER WHAT HAPPENS TO ME!!
YOU CAN'T KEEP ME HERE!!
OH YES, I CAN!! TAKE A GOOD LOOK AROUND YOU!!
!!
SUI-CUNE ?!
GGGMM
BLAST IT!!

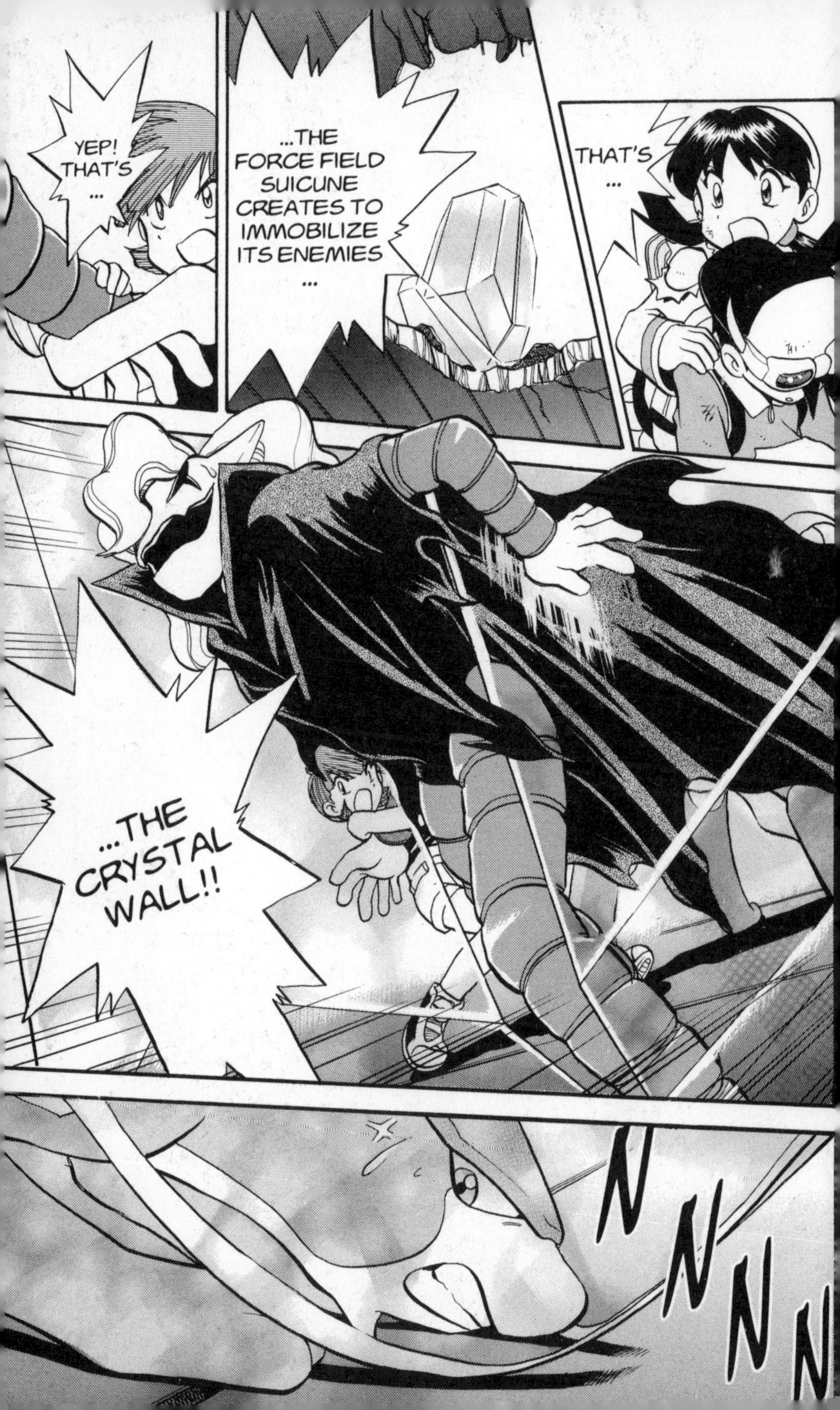
THAT'S ...
...THE FORCE FIELD SUICUNE CREATES TO IMMOBILIZE ITS ENEMIES ...
YEP! THAT'S ...
...THE CRYSTAL WALL!!
NNNNN

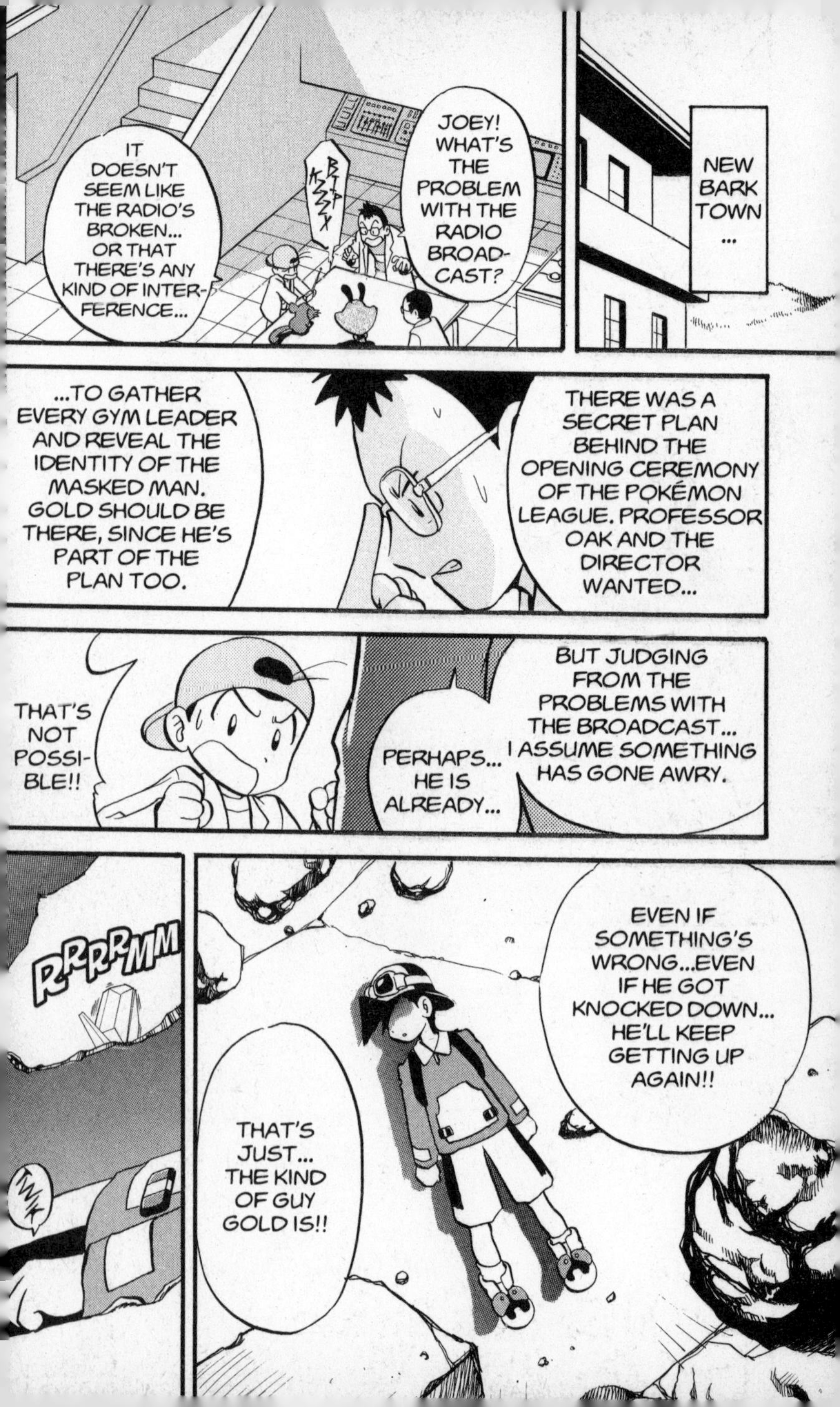
NEW BARK TOWN...
JOEY! WHAT'S THE PROBLEM WITH THE RADIO BROAD-CAST?
IT DOESN'T SEEM LIKE THE RADIO'S BROKEN... OR THAT THERE'S ANY KIND OF INTER-FERENCE...
THERE WAS A SECRET PLAN BEHIND THE OPENING CEREMONY OF THE POKÉMON LEAGUE. PROFESSOR OAK AND THE DIRECTOR WANTED...
...TO GATHER EVERY GYM LEADER AND REVEAL THE IDENTITY OF THE MASKED MAN. GOLD SHOULD BE THERE, SINCE HE'S PART OF THE PLAN TOO.
BUT JUDGING FROM THE PROBLEMS WITH THE BROADCAST... I ASSUME SOMETHING HAS GONE AWRY.
PERHAPS... HE IS ALREADY...
THAT'S NOT POSSI-BLE!!
EVEN IF SOMETHING'S WRONG...EVEN IF HE GOT KNOCKED DOWN... HE'LL KEEP GETTING UP AGAIN!!
THAT'S JUST... THE KIND OF GUY GOLD IS!!
RRRRMM

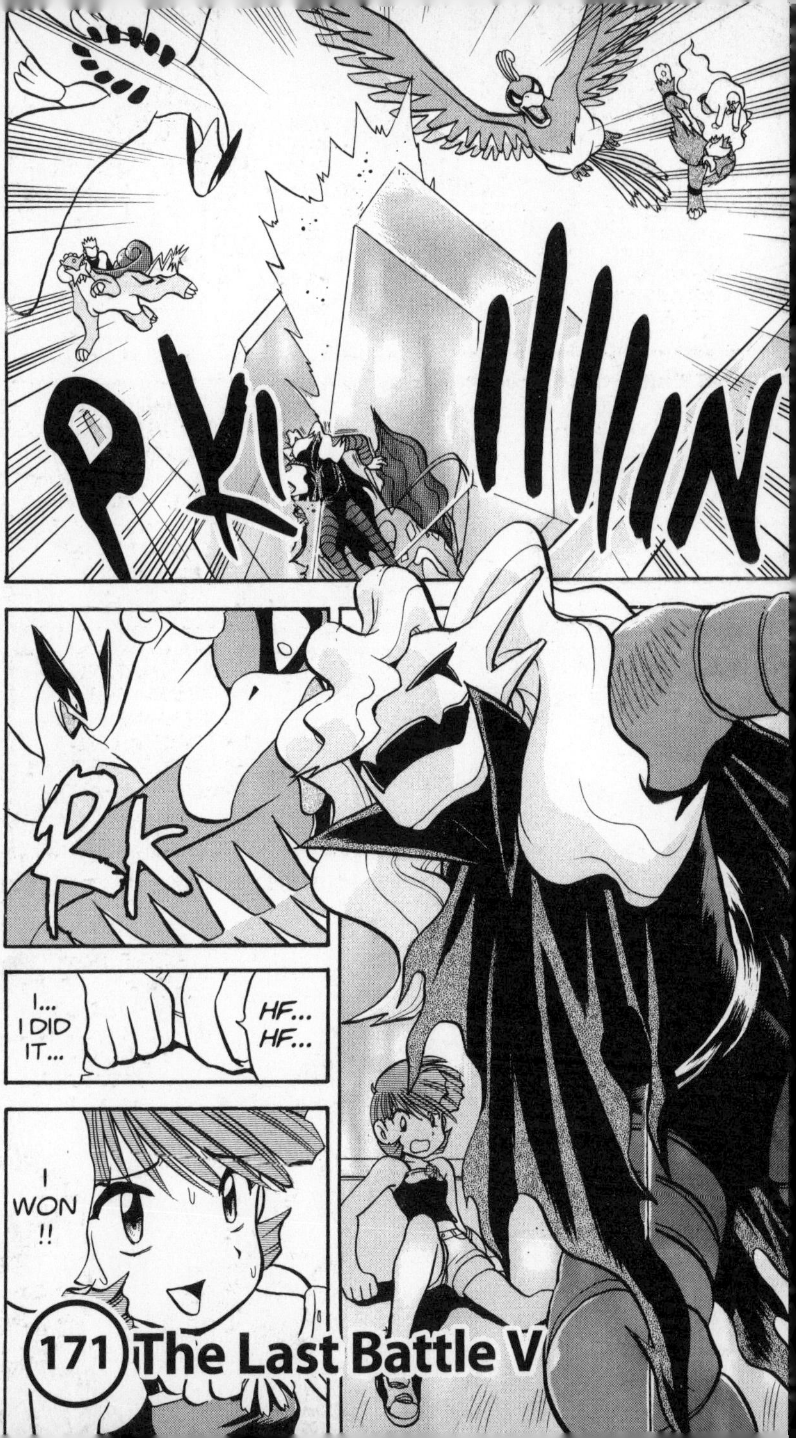
PKIIIIIIN
RK
HF... HF...
I... I DID IT...
I WON !!

## 171 The Last Battle V

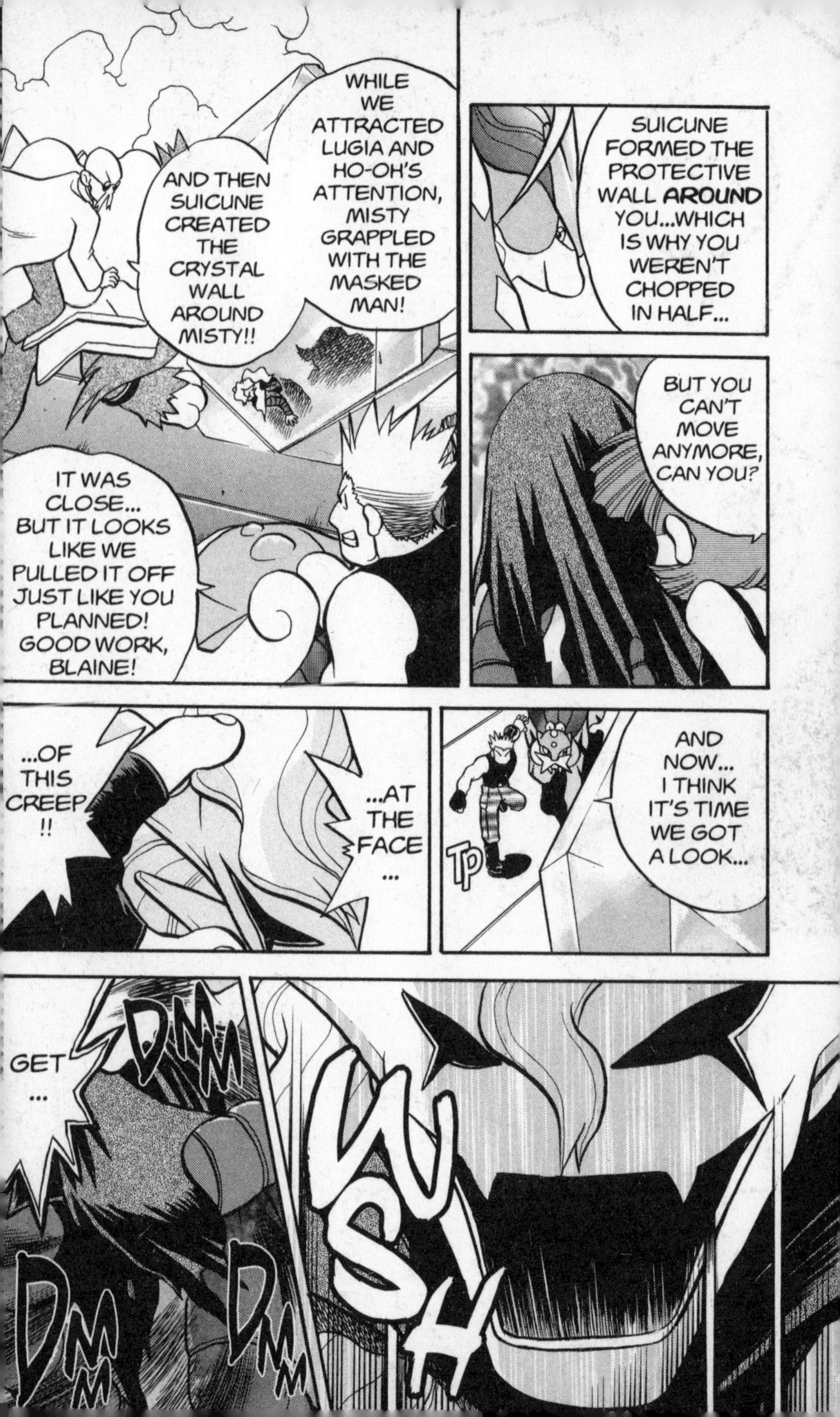

SUICUNE FORMED THE PROTECTIVE WALL **AROUND** YOU...WHICH IS WHY YOU WEREN'T CHOPPED IN HALF...
BUT YOU CAN'T MOVE ANYMORE, CAN YOU?
WHILE WE ATTRACTED LUGIA AND HO-OH'S ATTENTION, MISTY GRAPPLED WITH THE MASKED MAN!
AND THEN SUICUNE CREATED THE CRYSTAL WALL AROUND MISTY!!
IT WAS CLOSE... BUT IT LOOKS LIKE WE PULLED IT OFF JUST LIKE YOU PLANNED! GOOD WORK, BLAINE!
AND NOW... I THINK IT'S TIME WE GOT A LOOK...
Tp
...AT THE FACE...
...OF THIS CREEP!!
GET...
DMM
WUSH
DMM
DMM

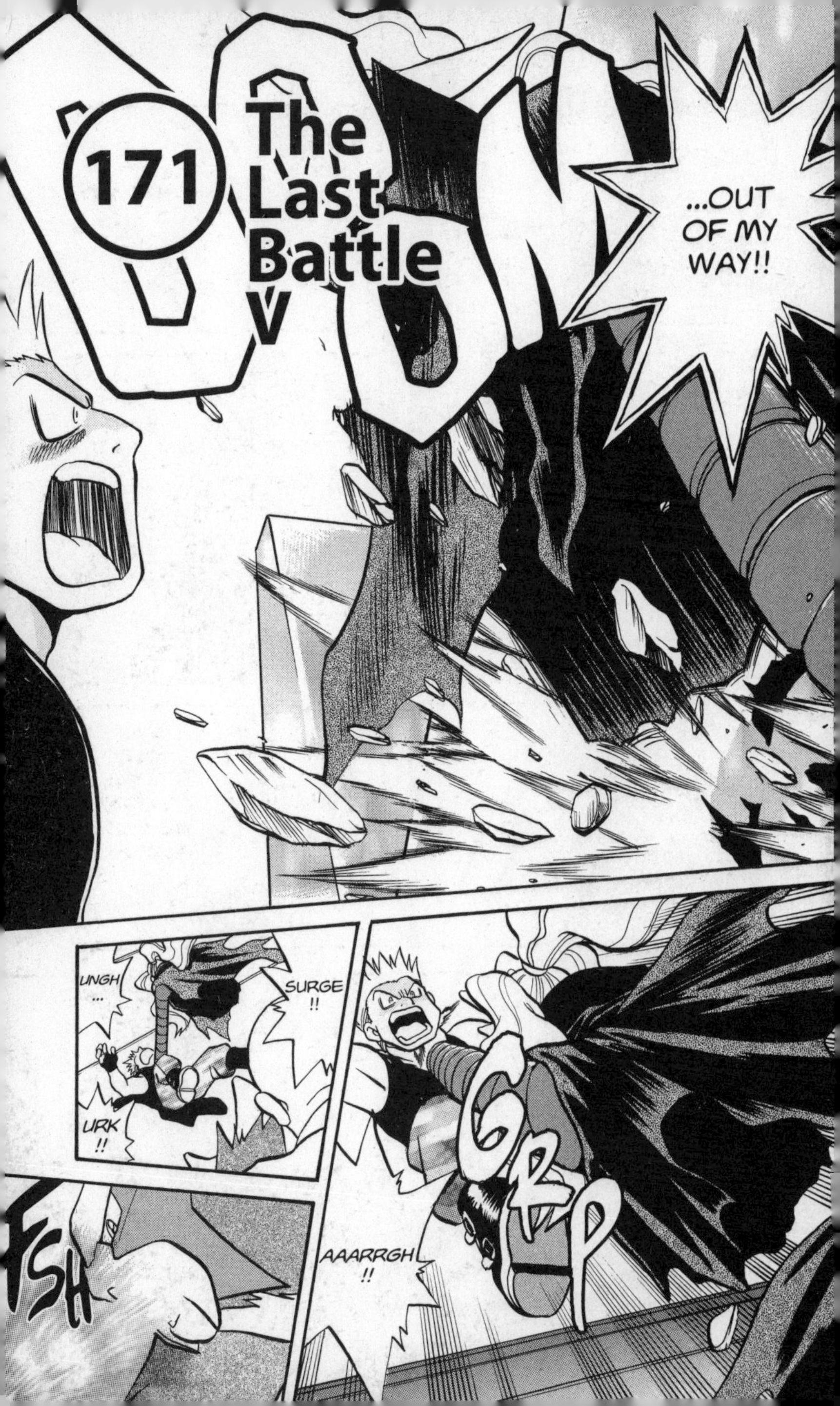
171 The Last Battle V
...OUT OF MY WAY!!
GRP
AAARRGH!!
SURGE!!
UNGH...
URK!!
FSH

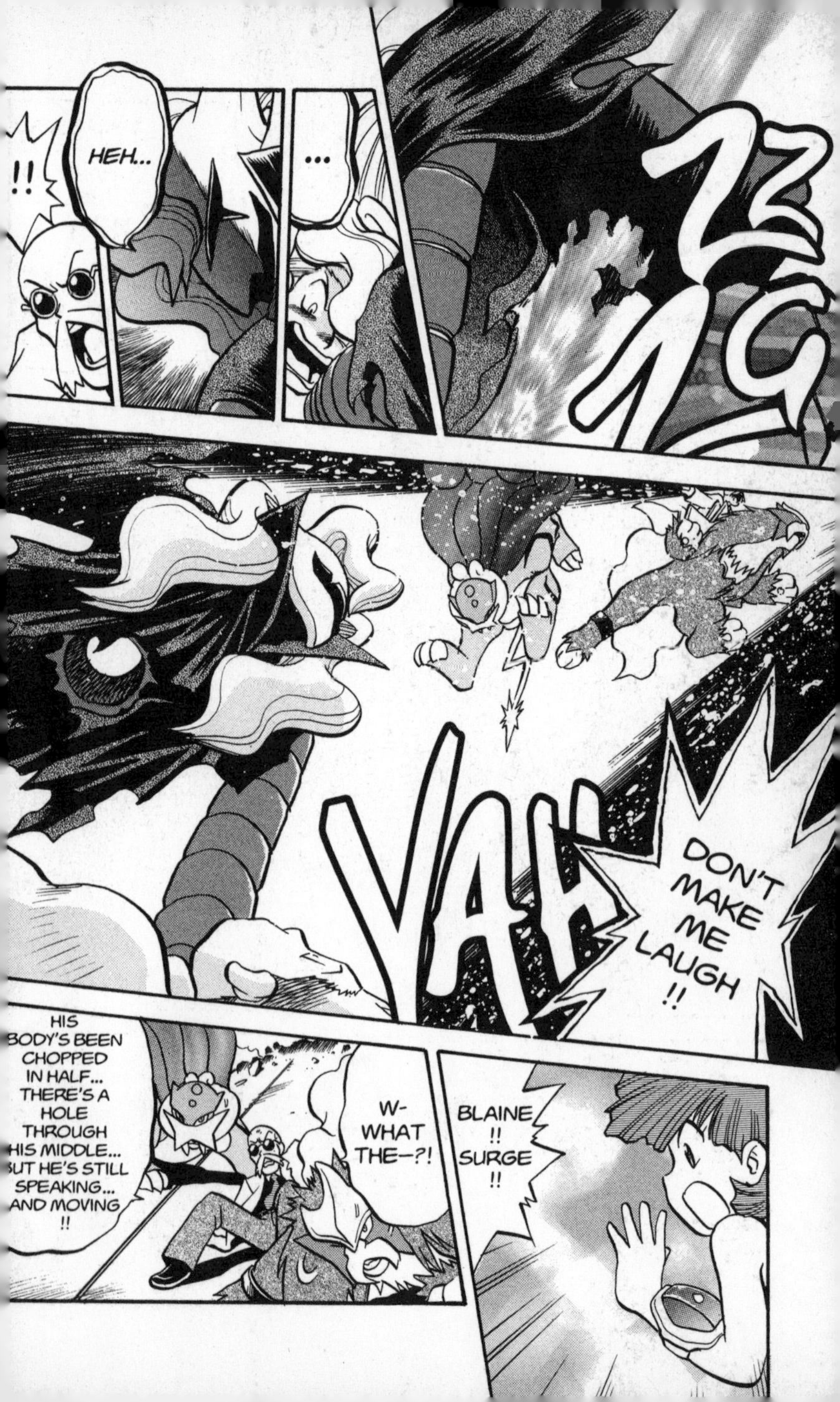
...
HEH...
!!
DON'T MAKE ME LAUGH !!
BLAINE!! SURGE!!
W-WHAT THE--?!
HIS BODY'S BEEN CHOPPED IN HALF... THERE'S A HOLE THROUGH HIS MIDDLE... BUT HE'S STILL SPEAKING... AND MOVING!!

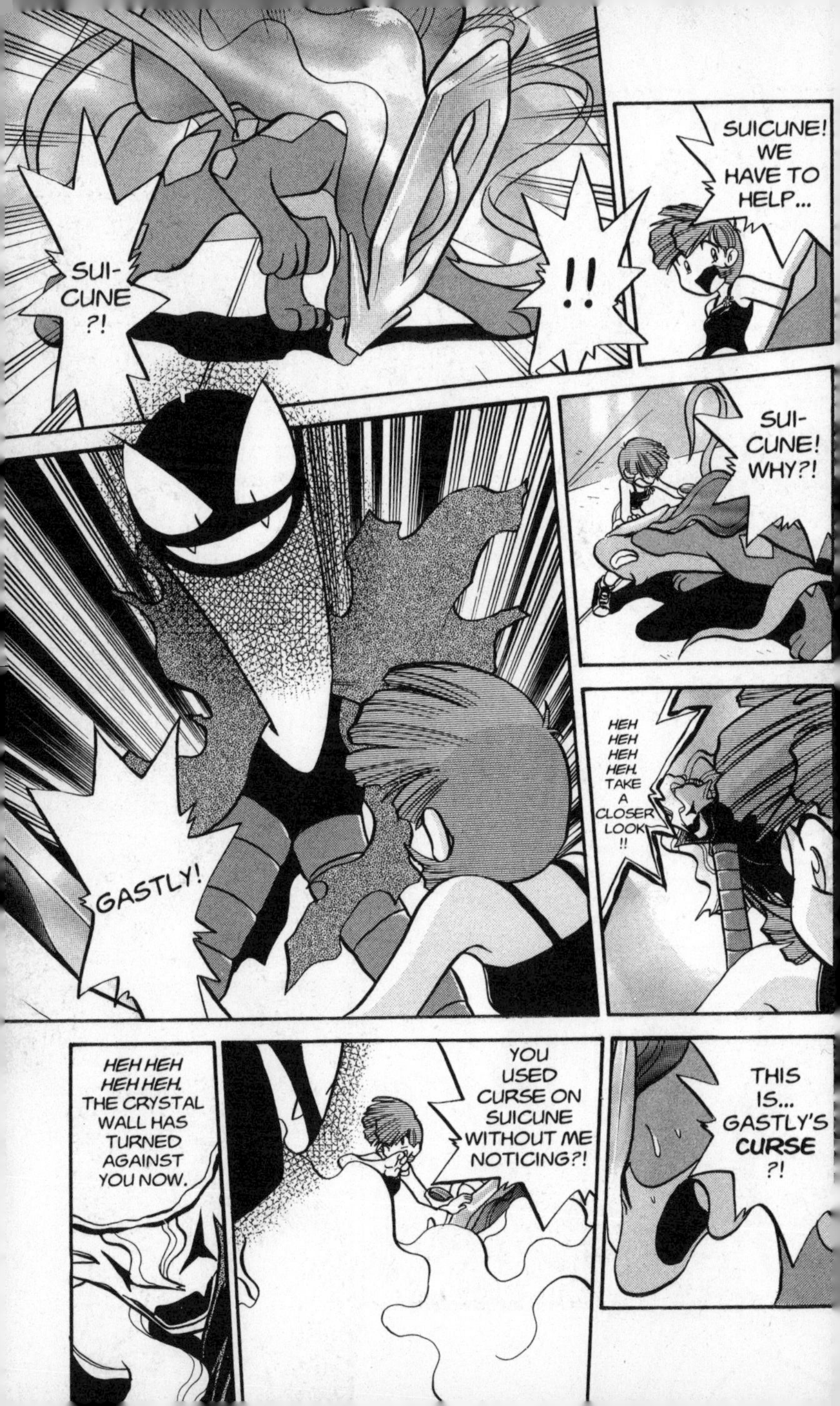
SUICUNE! WE HAVE TO HELP...
!!
SUI-CUNE ?!
SUI-CUNE! WHY?!
HEH HEH HEH HEH. TAKE A CLOSER LOOK !!
GASTLY!
THIS IS... GASTLY'S **CURSE** ?!
YOU USED CURSE ON SUICUNE WITHOUT ME NOTICING?!
HEH HEH HEH HEH. THE CRYSTAL WALL HAS TURNED AGAINST YOU NOW.

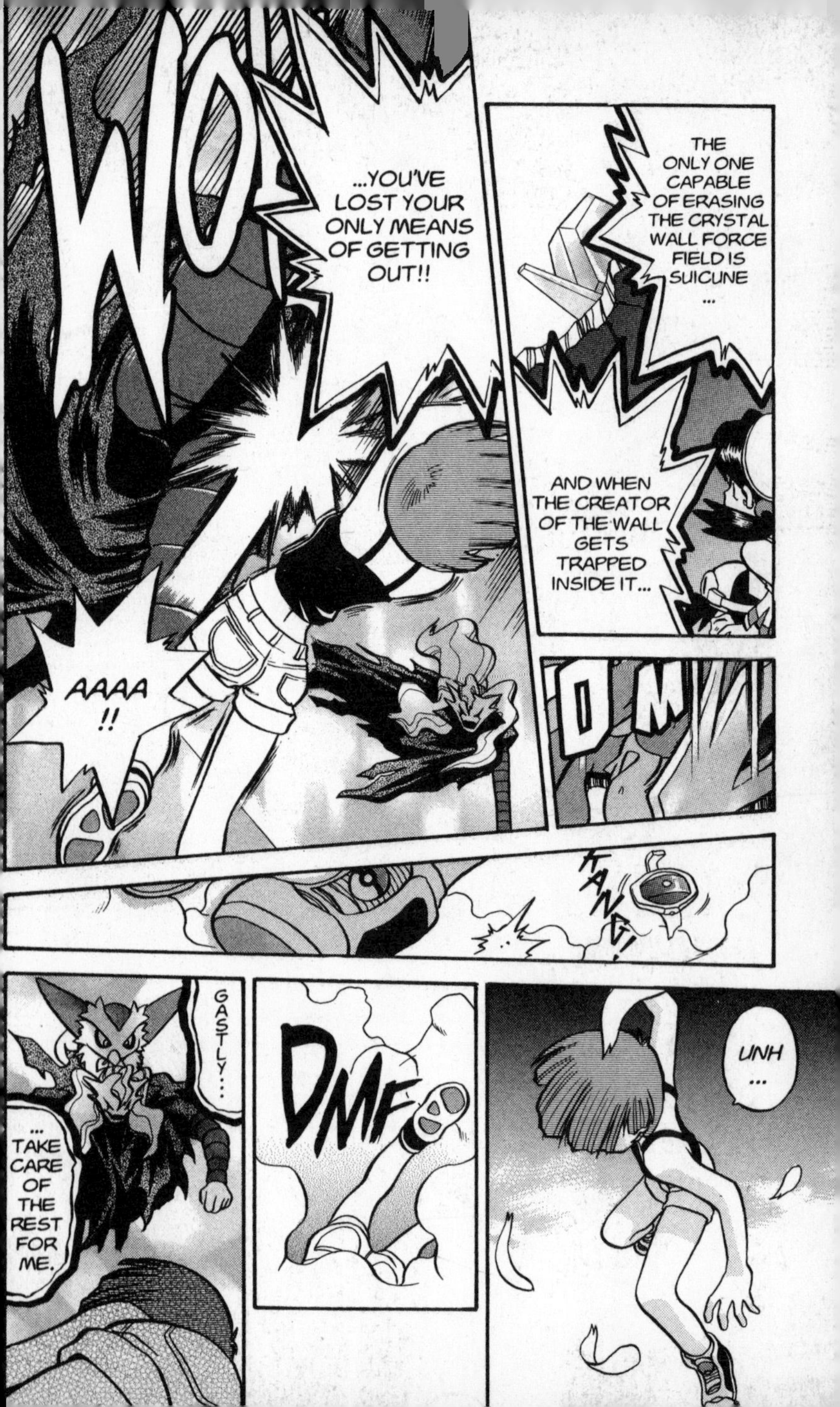
THE ONLY ONE CAPABLE OF ERASING THE CRYSTAL WALL FORCE FIELD IS SUICUNE ...
AND WHEN THE CREATOR OF THE WALL GETS TRAPPED INSIDE IT...
D M
WO
...YOU'VE LOST YOUR ONLY MEANS OF GETTING OUT!!
AAAA !!
KANG!
UNH ...
DMF
GASTLY...
... TAKE CARE OF THE REST FOR ME.

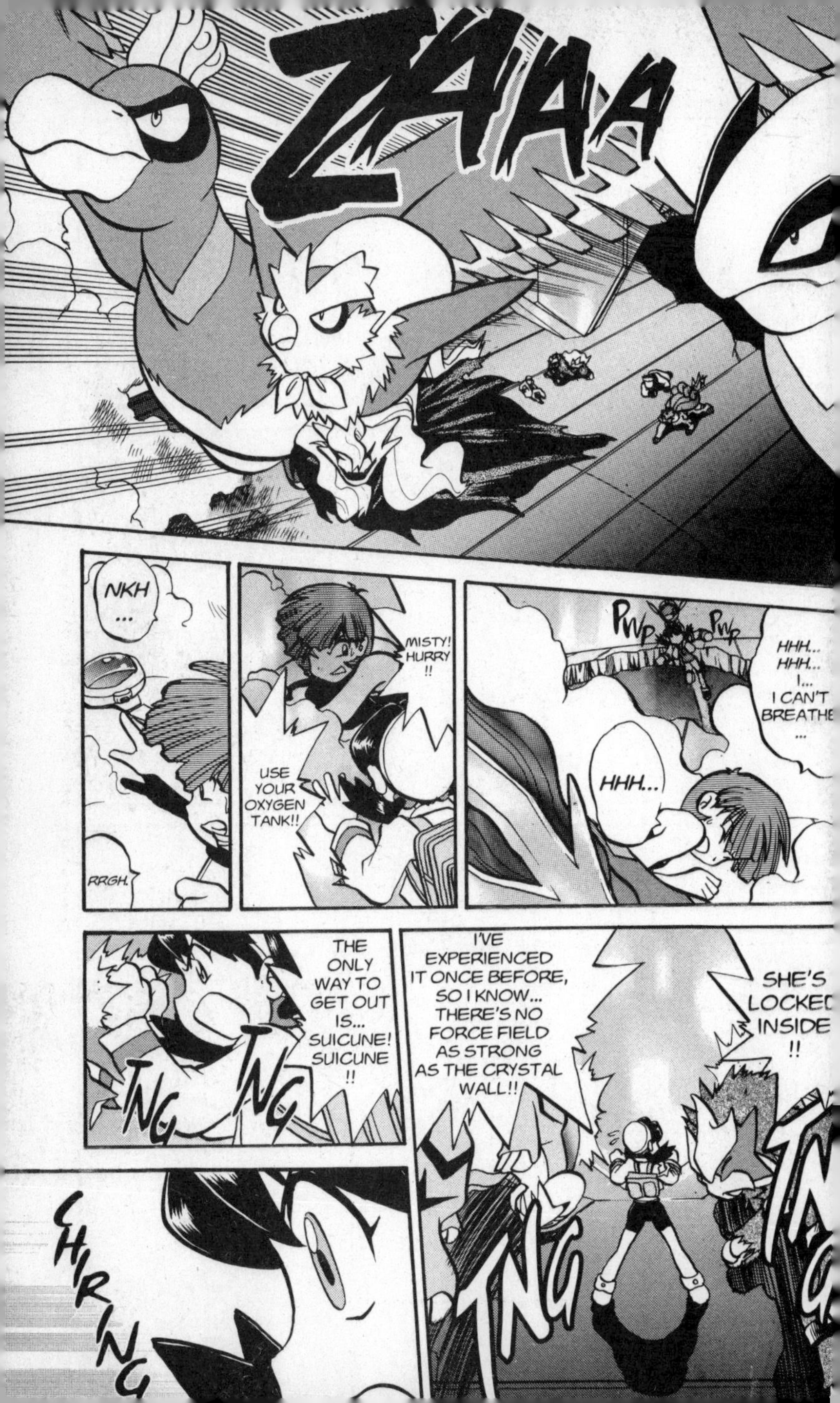
ZAAAA
PWP PWP
HHH... HHH... I... I CAN'T BREATHE...
HHH...
MISTY! HURRY!!
USE YOUR OXYGEN TANK!!
NKH...
RRGH.
SHE'S LOCKED INSIDE!!
I'VE EXPERIENCED IT ONCE BEFORE, SO I KNOW... THERE'S NO FORCE FIELD AS STRONG AS THE CRYSTAL WALL!!
TNG
THE ONLY WAY TO GET OUT IS... SUICUNE! SUICUNE!!
TNG TNG
CHIRING

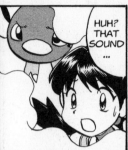

CHIRING
CHIRING
HUH? THAT SOUND ...
HH
THE AUTUMN WIND IS WISTFUL ...
SO HEART-RENDING ...
CHIRING
SOME-BODY ELSE IS INSIDE ...!!
THERE'S SOME-BODY BESIDES MISTY AND SUICUNE INSIDE THE CRYSTAL WALL!!

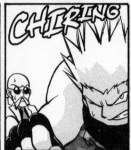

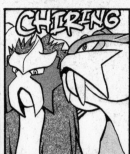

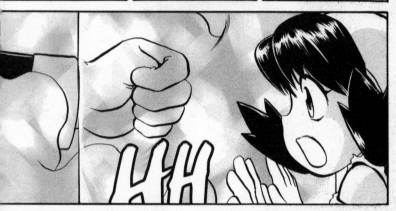

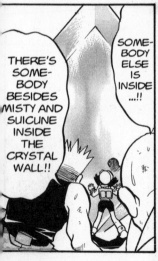

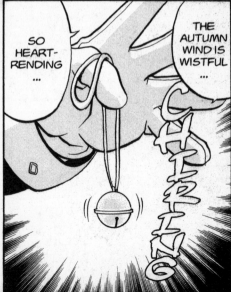

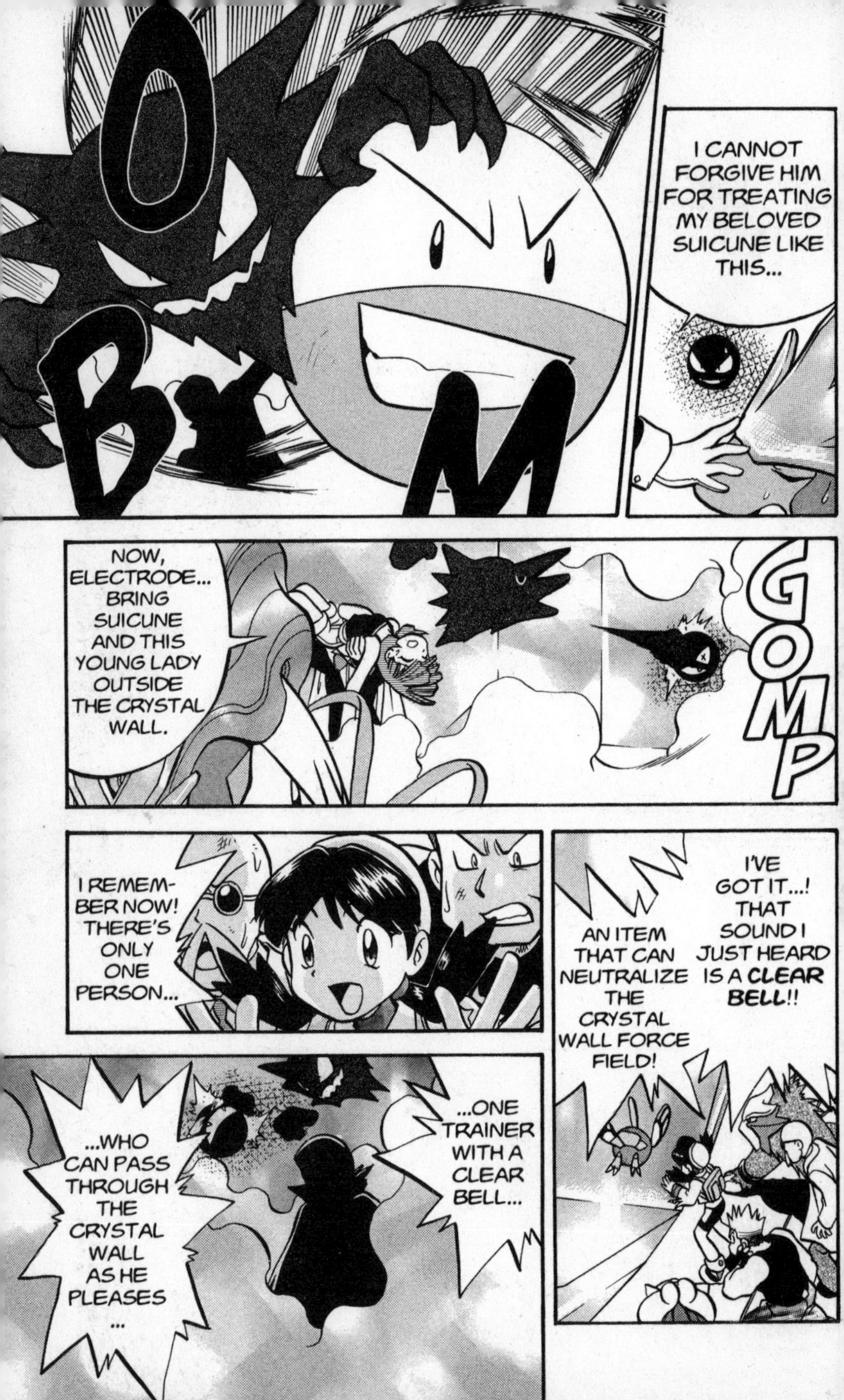
I CANNOT FORGIVE HIM FOR TREATING MY BELOVED SUICUNE LIKE THIS...
GOMP
NOW, ELECTRODE... BRING SUICUNE AND THIS YOUNG LADY OUTSIDE THE CRYSTAL WALL.
I'VE GOT IT...! THAT SOUND I JUST HEARD IS A **CLEAR BELL**!!
AN ITEM THAT CAN NEUTRALIZE THE CRYSTAL WALL FORCE FIELD!
I REMEM-BER NOW! THERE'S ONLY ONE PERSON...
...ONE TRAINER WITH A CLEAR BELL...
...WHO CAN PASS THROUGH THE CRYSTAL WALL AS HE PLEASES ...

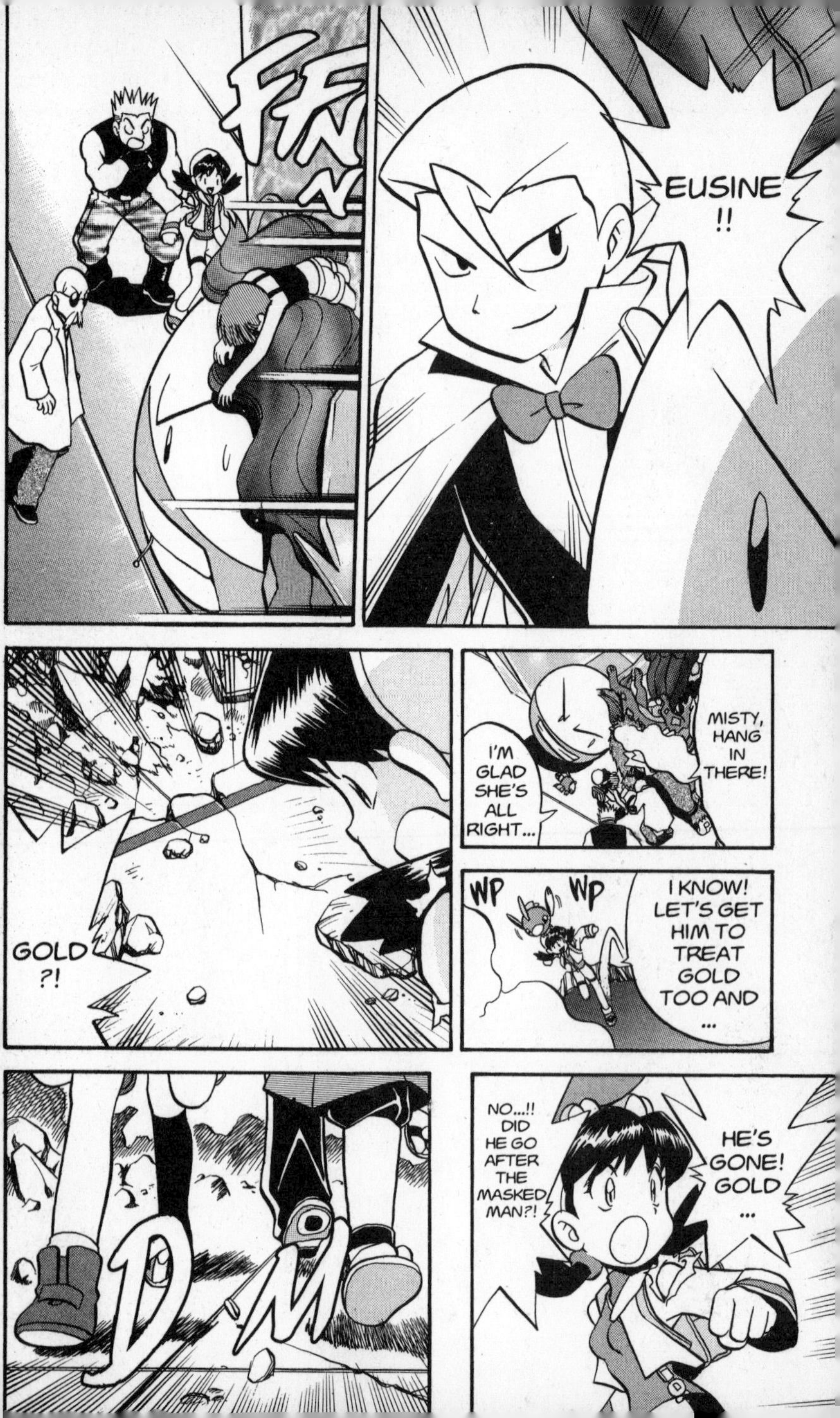
EUSINE !!
FFNN
MISTY, HANG IN THERE!
I'M GLAD SHE'S ALL RIGHT...
I KNOW! LET'S GET HIM TO TREAT GOLD TOO AND ...
WP WP
GOLD ?!
HE'S GONE! GOLD ...
NO...!! DID HE GO AFTER THE MASKED MAN?!
DM

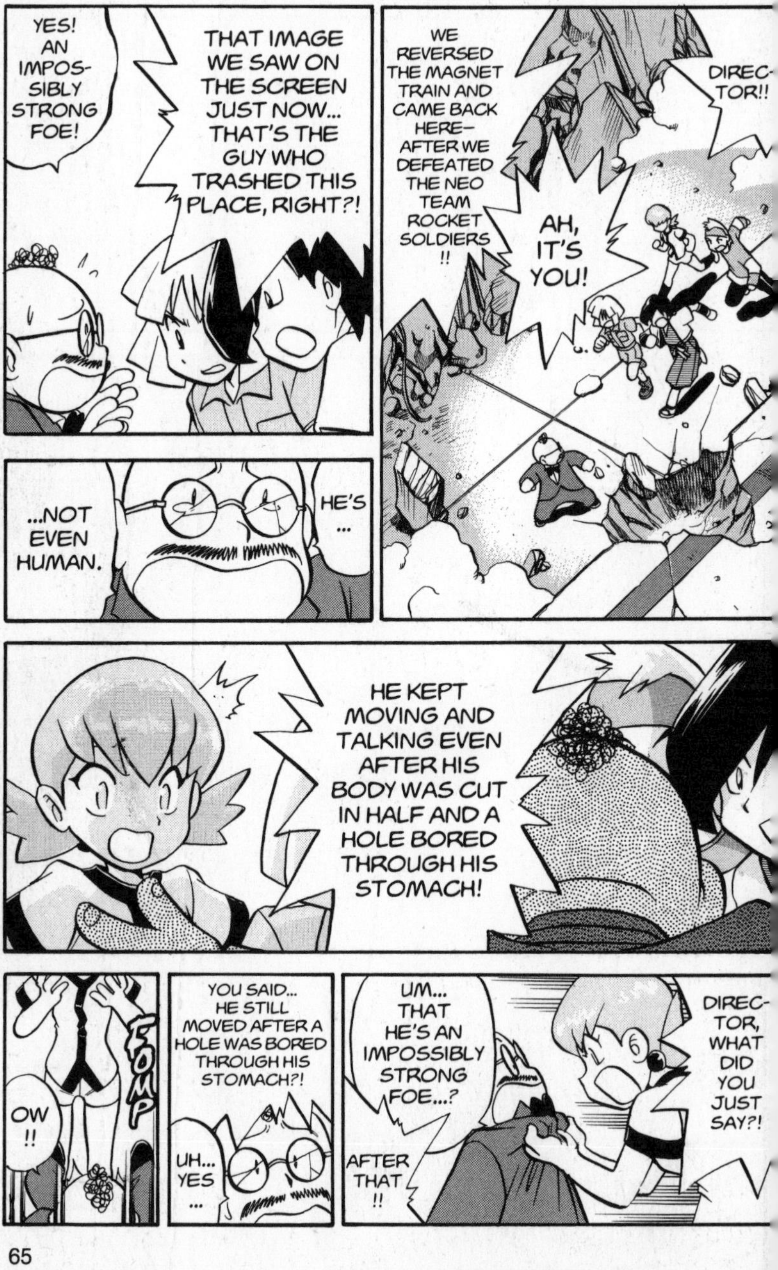
DIRECTOR!!
WE REVERSED THE MAGNET TRAIN AND CAME BACK HERE— AFTER WE DEFEATED THE NEO TEAM ROCKET SOLDIERS !!
AH, IT'S YOU!
THAT IMAGE WE SAW ON THE SCREEN JUST NOW... THAT'S THE GUY WHO TRASHED THIS PLACE, RIGHT?!
YES! AN IMPOS-SIBLY STRONG FOE!
HE'S ...
...NOT EVEN HUMAN.
HE KEPT MOVING AND TALKING EVEN AFTER HIS BODY WAS CUT IN HALF AND A HOLE BORED THROUGH HIS STOMACH!
DIREC-TOR, WHAT DID YOU JUST SAY?!
UM... THAT HE'S AN IMPOSSIBLY STRONG FOE...?
AFTER THAT !!
YOU SAID... HE STILL MOVED AFTER A HOLE WAS BORED THROUGH HIS STOMACH?!
UH... YES ...
FOMP
OW !!

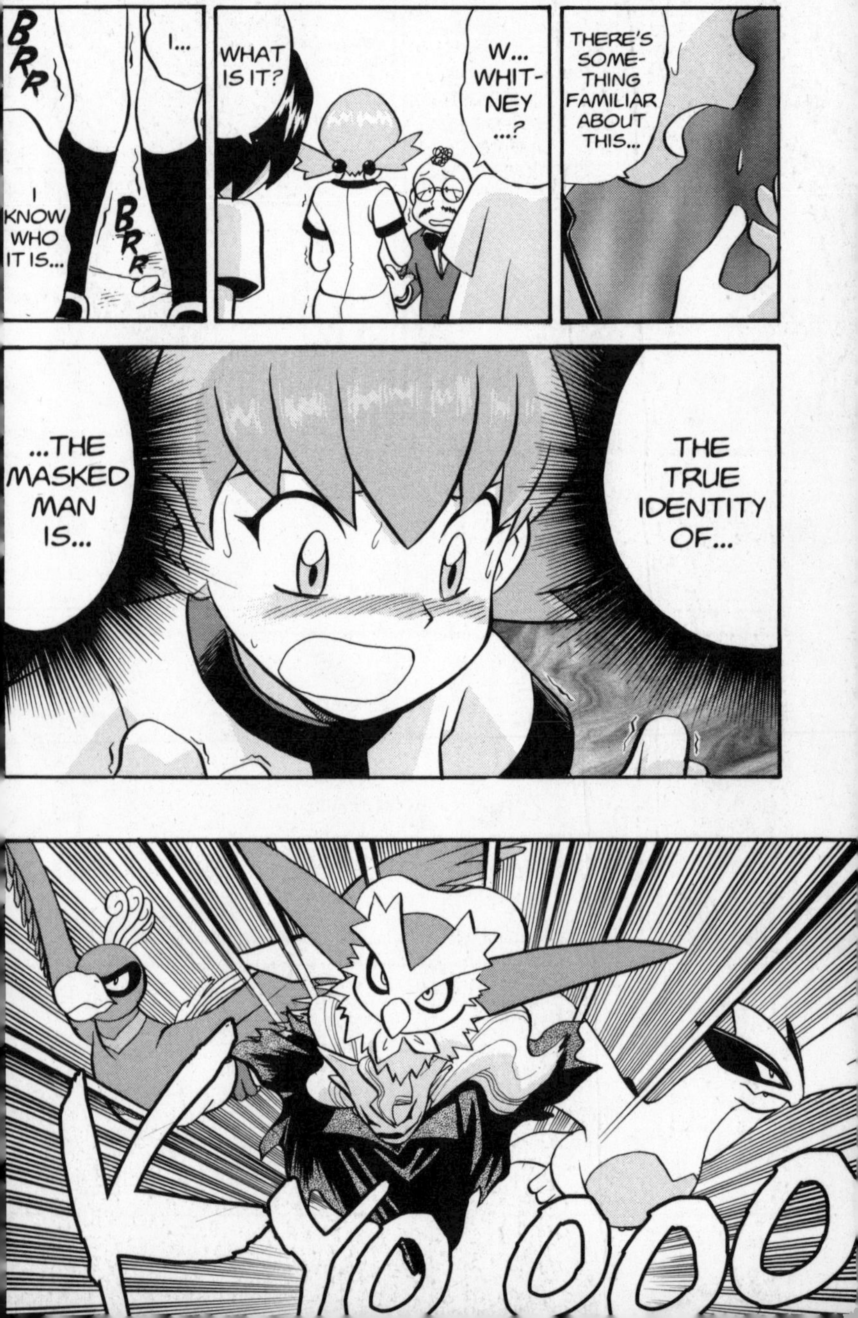
THERE'S SOME-THING FAMILIAR ABOUT THIS...
W... WHIT-NEY ...?
WHAT IS IT?
I...
BRR
I KNOW WHO IT IS...
BRR
THE TRUE IDENTITY OF...
...THE MASKED MAN IS...
KYOOOO

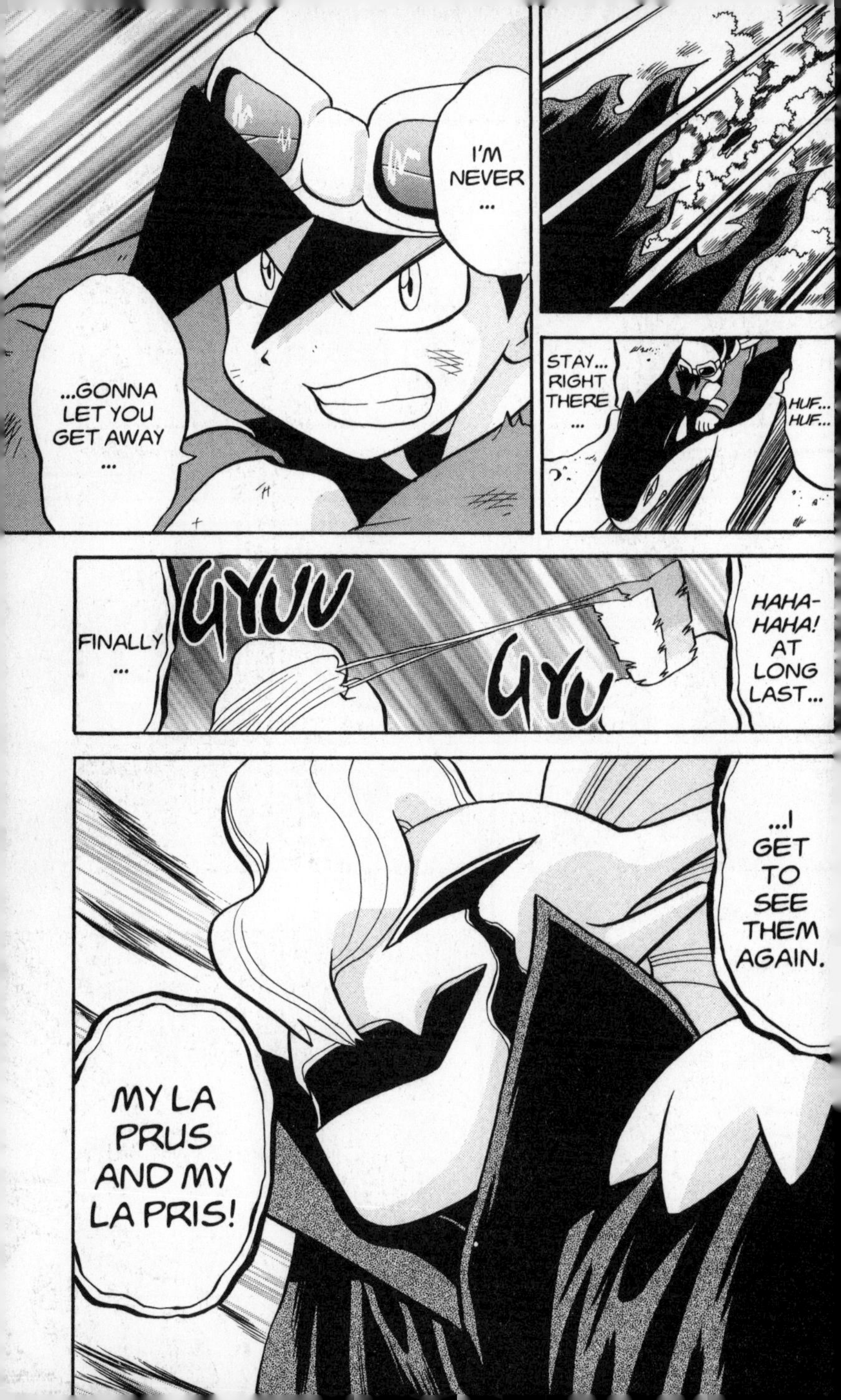
HUF... HUF...
STAY... RIGHT THERE...
I'M NEVER...
...GONNA LET YOU GET AWAY...
HAHA-HAHA! AT LONG LAST...
GYU
GYUU
FINALLY...
...I GET TO SEE THEM AGAIN.
MY LA PRUS AND MY LA PRIS!

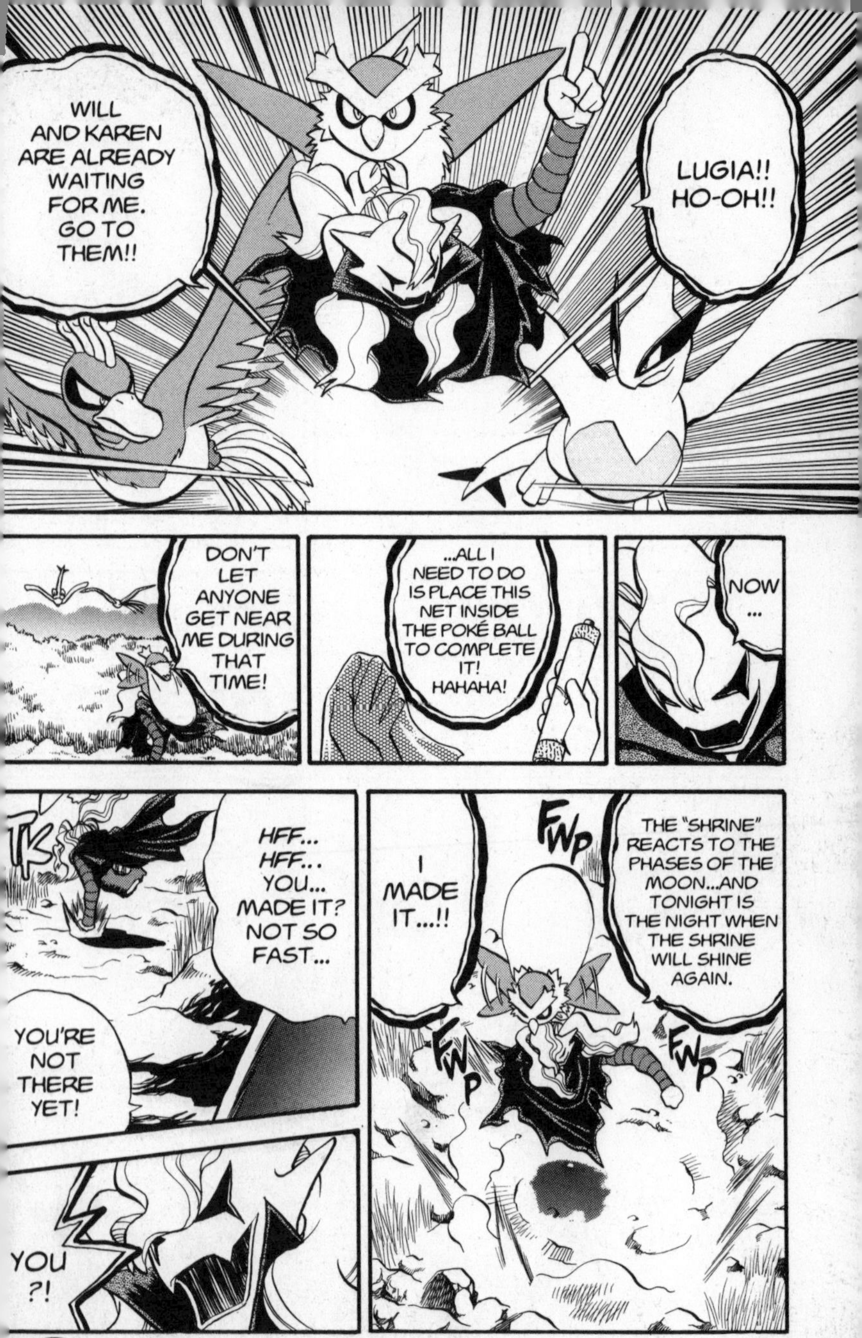
LUGIA!! HO-OH!!
WILL AND KAREN ARE ALREADY WAITING FOR ME. GO TO THEM!!
NOW ...
...ALL I NEED TO DO IS PLACE THIS NET INSIDE THE POKÉ BALL TO COMPLETE IT! HAHAHA!
DON'T LET ANYONE GET NEAR ME DURING THAT TIME!
THE "SHRINE" REACTS TO THE PHASES OF THE MOON...AND TONIGHT IS THE NIGHT WHEN THE SHRINE WILL SHINE AGAIN.
FWP
I MADE IT...!!
FWP
FWP
TK
HFF... HFF... YOU... MADE IT? NOT SO FAST...
YOU'RE NOT THERE YET!
YOU ?!

# (172) The Last Battle VI

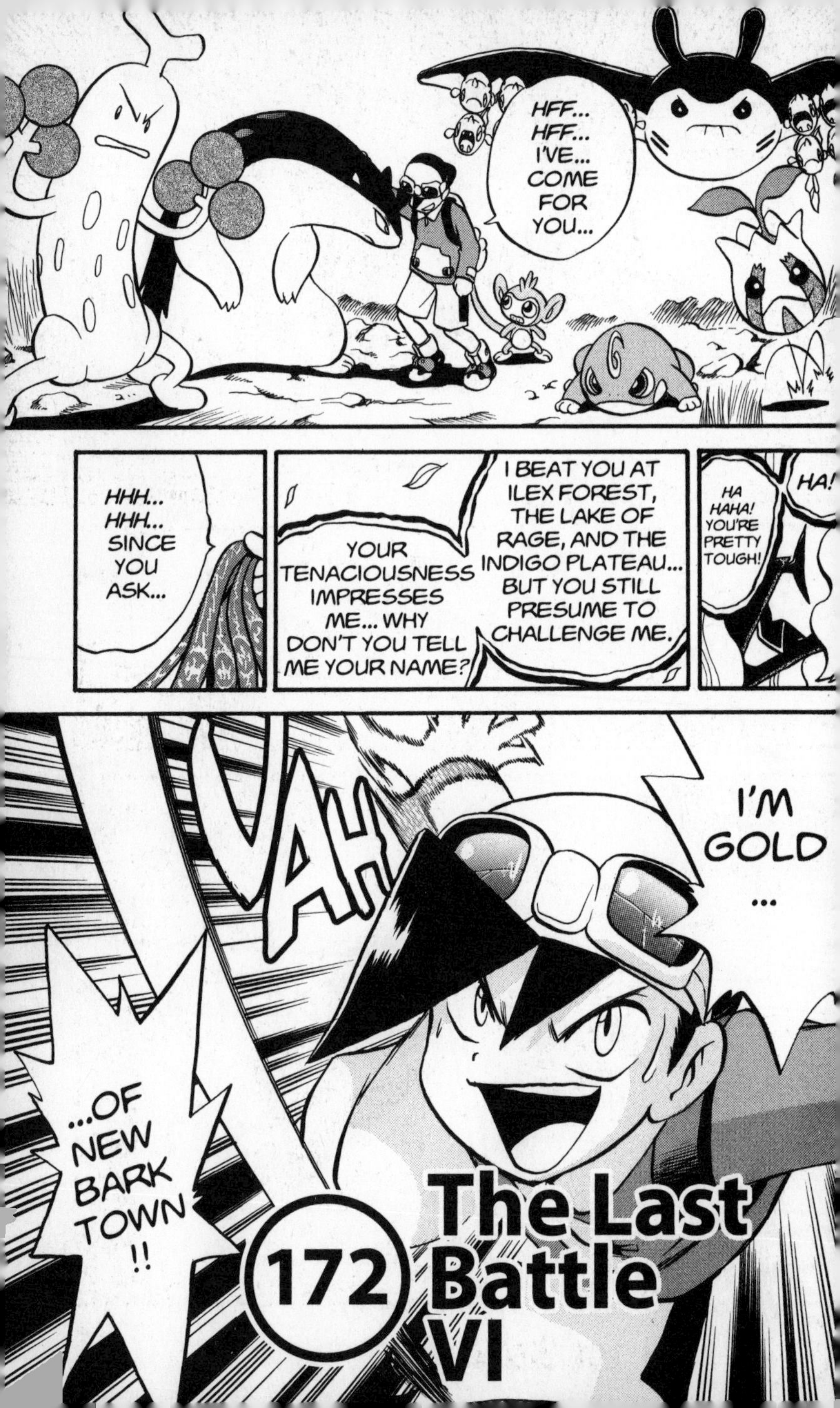
HFF... HFF... I'VE... COME FOR YOU...
HA!
HA HAHA! YOU'RE PRETTY TOUGH!
I BEAT YOU AT ILEX FOREST, THE LAKE OF RAGE, AND THE INDIGO PLATEAU... BUT YOU STILL PRESUME TO CHALLENGE ME.
YOUR TENACIOUSNESS IMPRESSES ME... WHY DON'T YOU TELL ME YOUR NAME?
HHH... HHH... SINCE YOU ASK...
I'M GOLD ...
...OF NEW BARK TOWN !!
172 The Last Battle VI

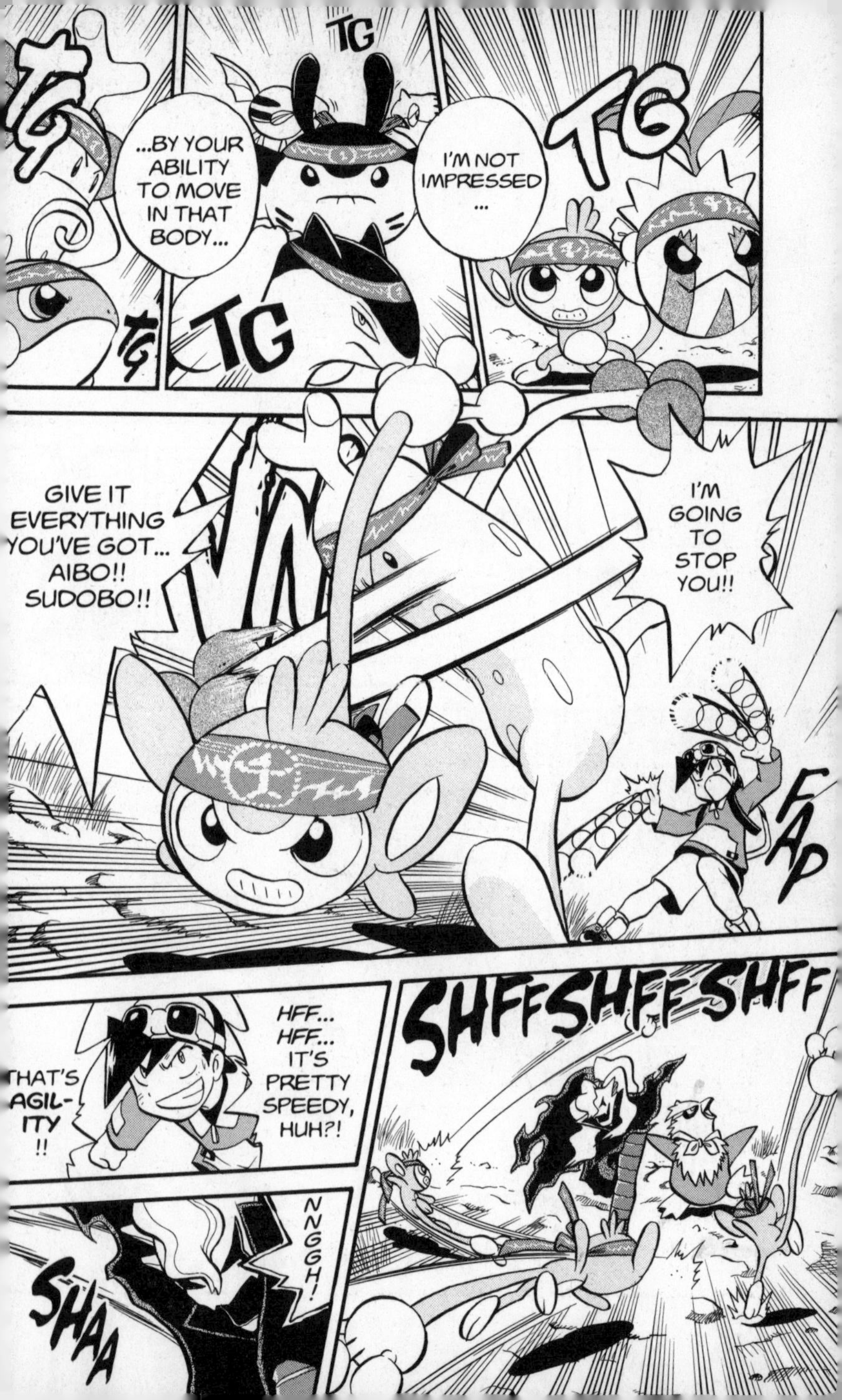
TG
I'M NOT IMPRESSED ...
TG
...BY YOUR ABILITY TO MOVE IN THAT BODY...
TG
TG
TG
I'M GOING TO STOP YOU!!
FAP
GIVE IT EVERYTHING YOU'VE GOT... AIBO!! SUDOBO!!
SHFF SHFF SHFF
HFF... HFF... IT'S PRETTY SPEEDY, HUH?!
THAT'S AGIL-ITY!!
NNGGH!
SHAA

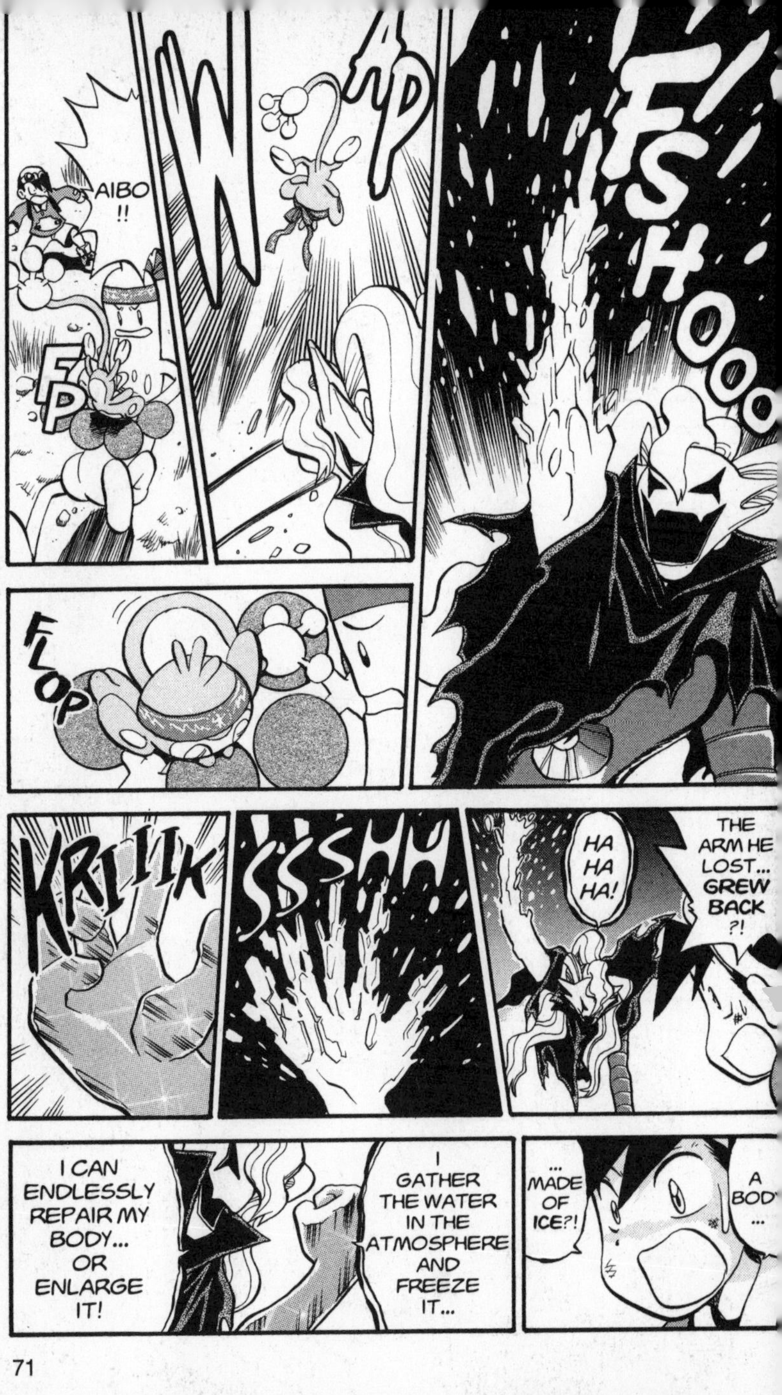
FISHOOO
WAP
AIBO !!
FP
FLOP
THE ARM HE LOST... GREW BACK ?!
HA HA HA!
SSSHH
KRIIIK
A BODY ...
... MADE OF ICE?!
I GATHER THE WATER IN THE ATMOSPHERE AND FREEZE IT...
I CAN ENDLESSLY REPAIR MY BODY... OR ENLARGE IT!

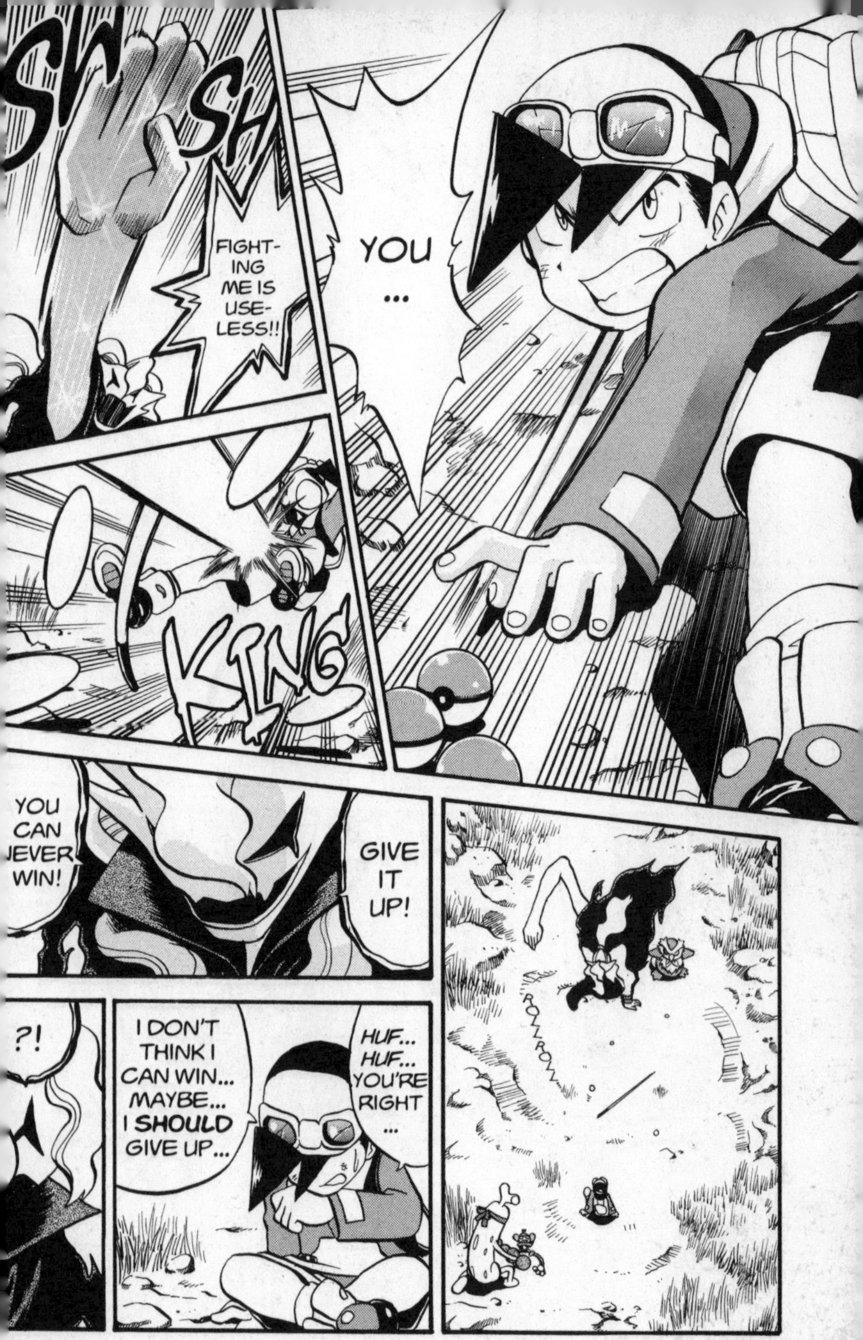
YOU ...
SHSH
FIGHTING ME IS USELESS!!
KING
ROLL ROLL
GIVE IT UP!
YOU CAN NEVER WIN!
HUF... HUF... YOU'RE RIGHT ...
I DON'T THINK I CAN WIN... MAYBE... I **SHOULD** GIVE UP...
?!

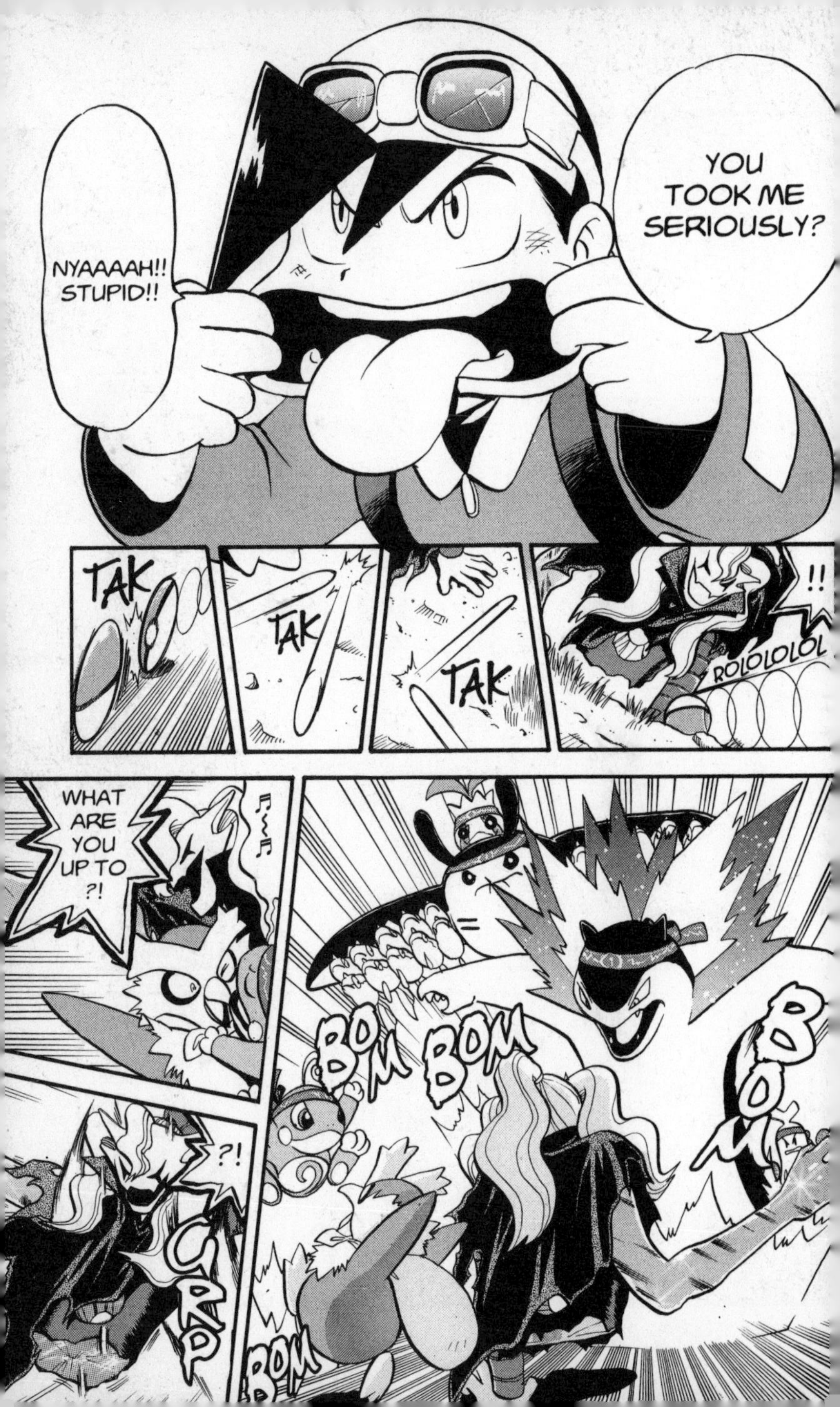
YOU TOOK ME SERIOUSLY?
NYAAAAH!! STUPID!!
!!
ROLOLOLOL
TAK
TAK
TAK
BOM BOM
BOM
BOM
WHAT ARE YOU UP TO ?!
?!

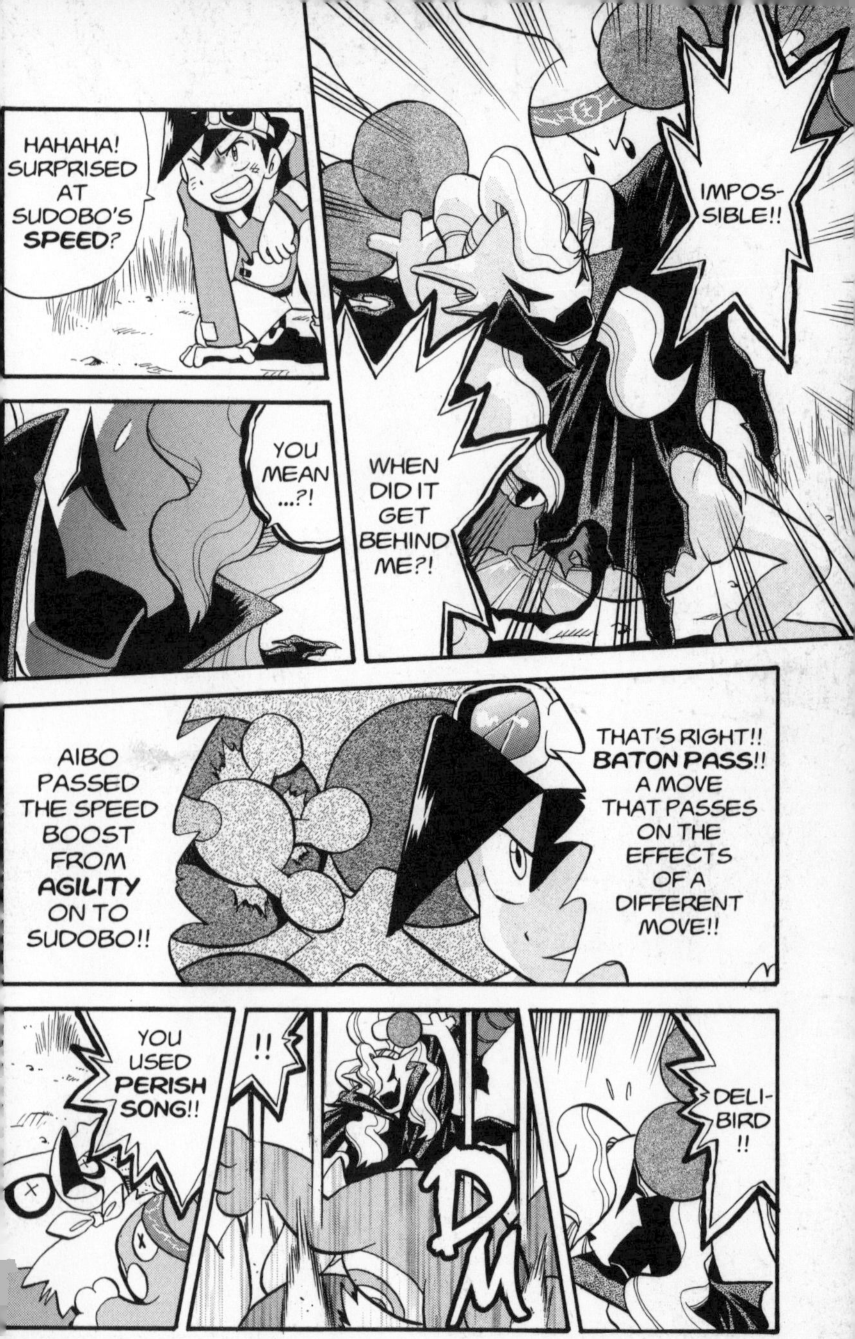
IMPOSSIBLE!!
WHEN DID IT GET BEHIND ME?!
HAHAHA! SURPRISED AT SUDOBO'S **SPEED**?
YOU MEAN ...?!
THAT'S RIGHT!! **BATON PASS**!! A MOVE THAT PASSES ON THE EFFECTS OF A DIFFERENT MOVE!!
AIBO PASSED THE SPEED BOOST FROM **AGILITY** ON TO SUDOBO!!
DELIBIRD!!
!!
DM
YOU USED **PERISH SONG**!!

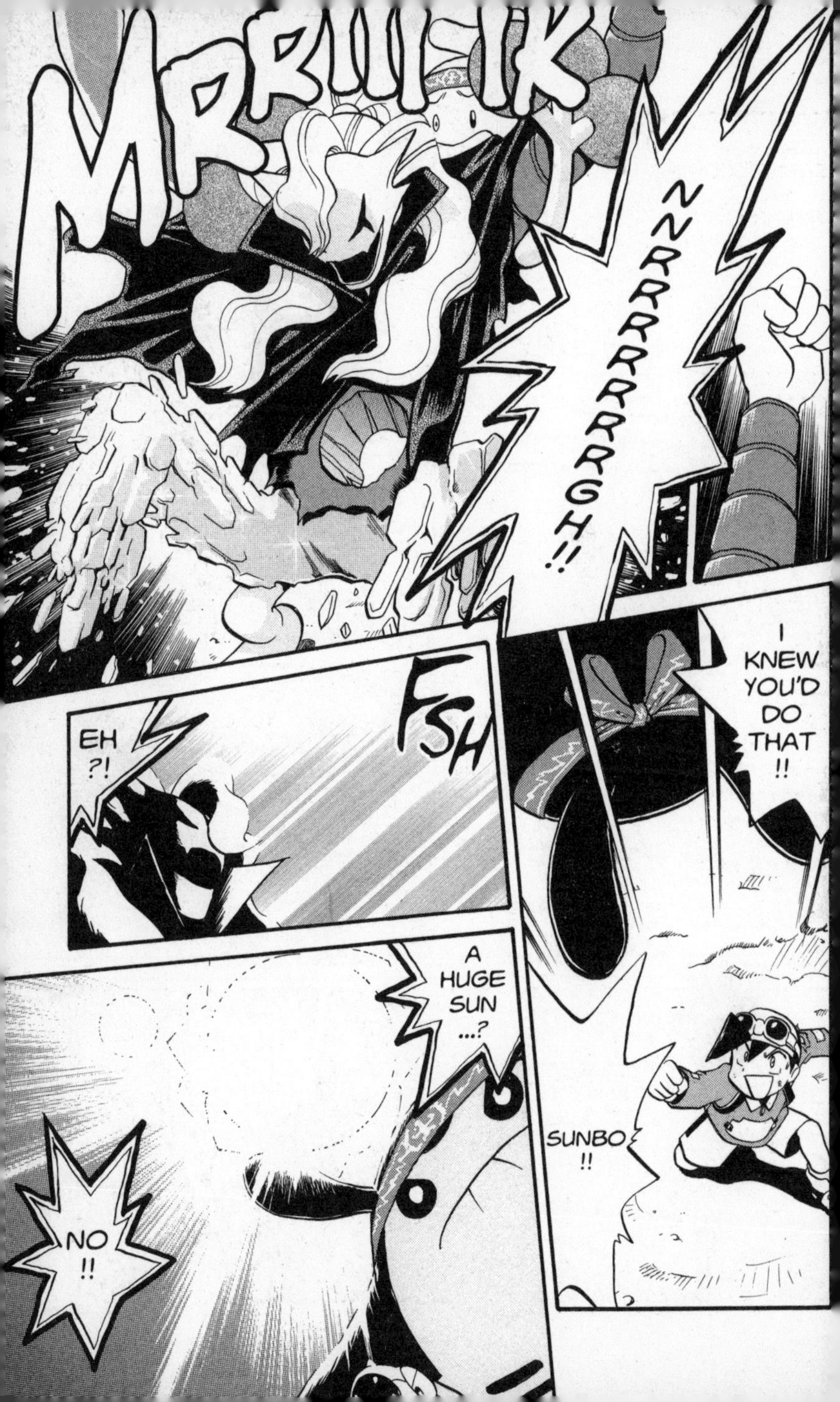
NNRRRRRRRRGH!!
MRRIIIK
I KNEW YOU'D DO THAT!!
SUNBO!!
FSH
EH?!
A HUGE SUN...?
NO!!

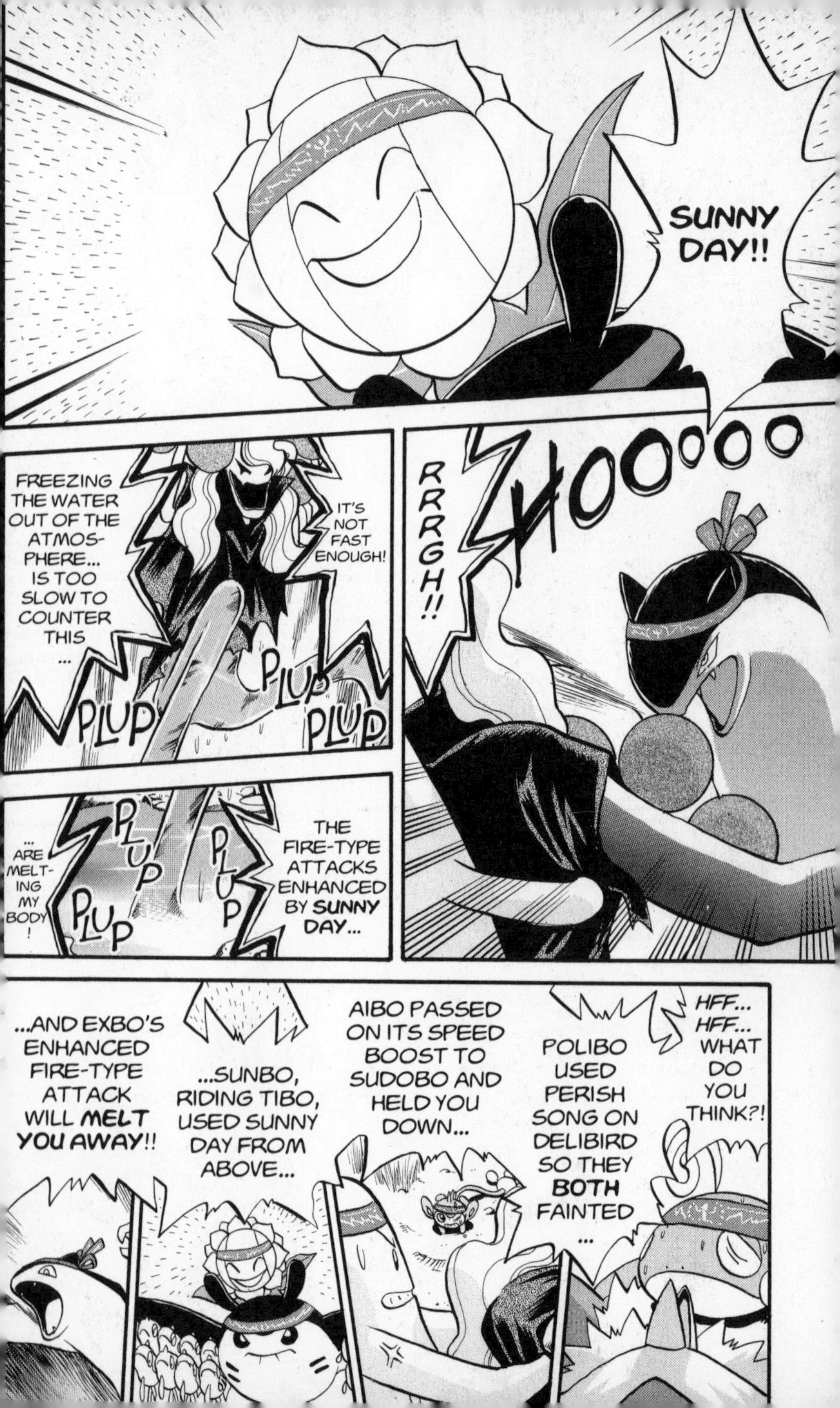
SUNNY DAY!!
ZHOOOOOO
RRRGH!!
IT'S NOT FAST ENOUGH!
FREEZING THE WATER OUT OF THE ATMOSPHERE... IS TOO SLOW TO COUNTER THIS...
PLUP
PLUP
PLUP
THE FIRE-TYPE ATTACKS ENHANCED BY SUNNY DAY...
PLUP
PLUP
PLUP
...ARE MELTING MY BODY!
HFF... HFF... WHAT DO YOU THINK?!
POLIBO USED PERISH SONG ON DELIBIRD SO THEY BOTH FAINTED...
AIBO PASSED ON ITS SPEED BOOST TO SUDOBO AND HELD YOU DOWN...
...SUNBO, RIDING TIBO, USED SUNNY DAY FROM ABOVE...
...AND EXBO'S ENHANCED FIRE-TYPE ATTACK WILL MELT YOU AWAY!!

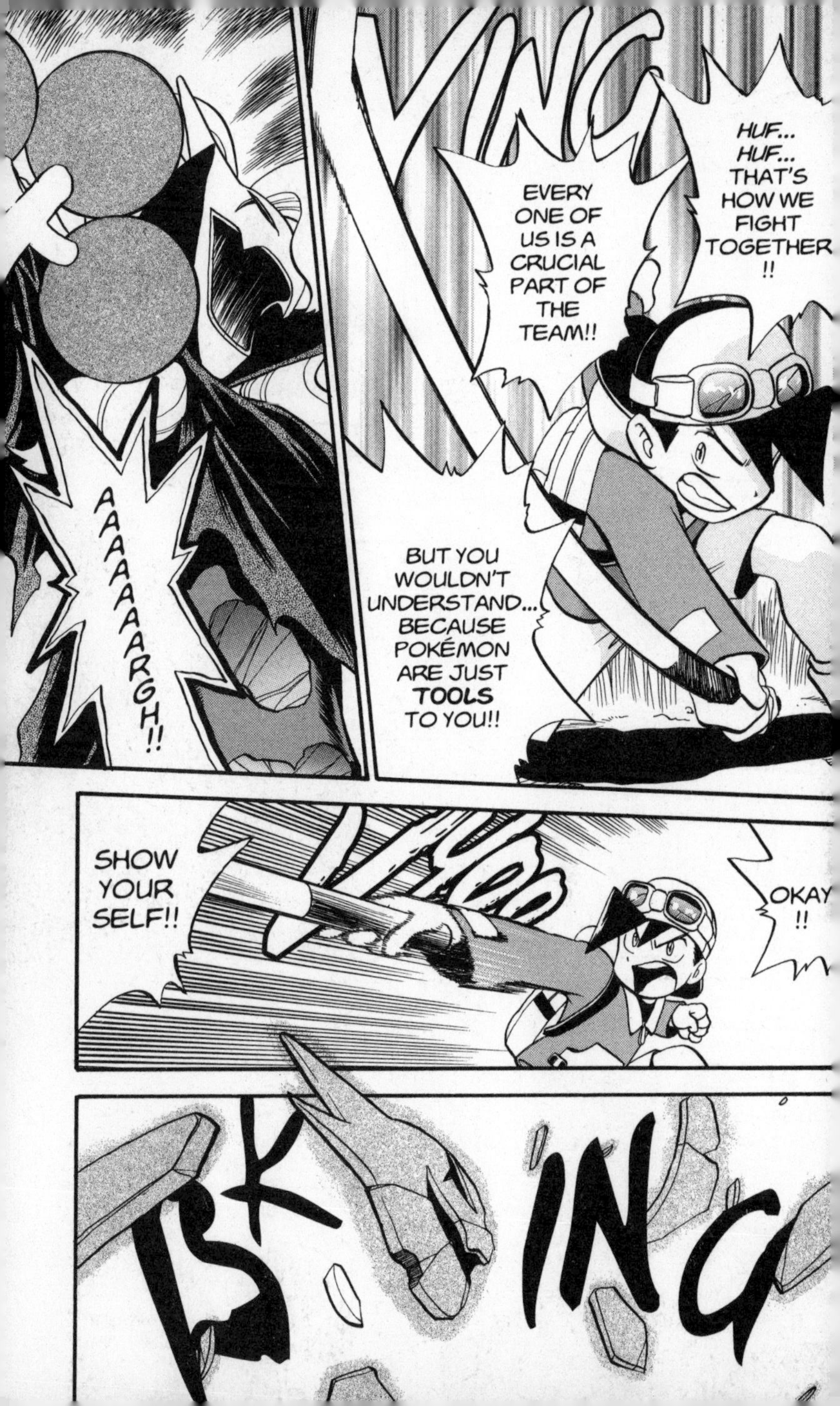
HUF... HUF... THAT'S HOW WE FIGHT TOGETHER !!
EVERY ONE OF US IS A CRUCIAL PART OF THE TEAM!!
BUT YOU WOULDN'T UNDERSTAND... BECAUSE POKÉMON ARE JUST **TOOLS** TO YOU!!
AAAAAAARGH!!
OKAY !!
SHOW YOUR SELF!!

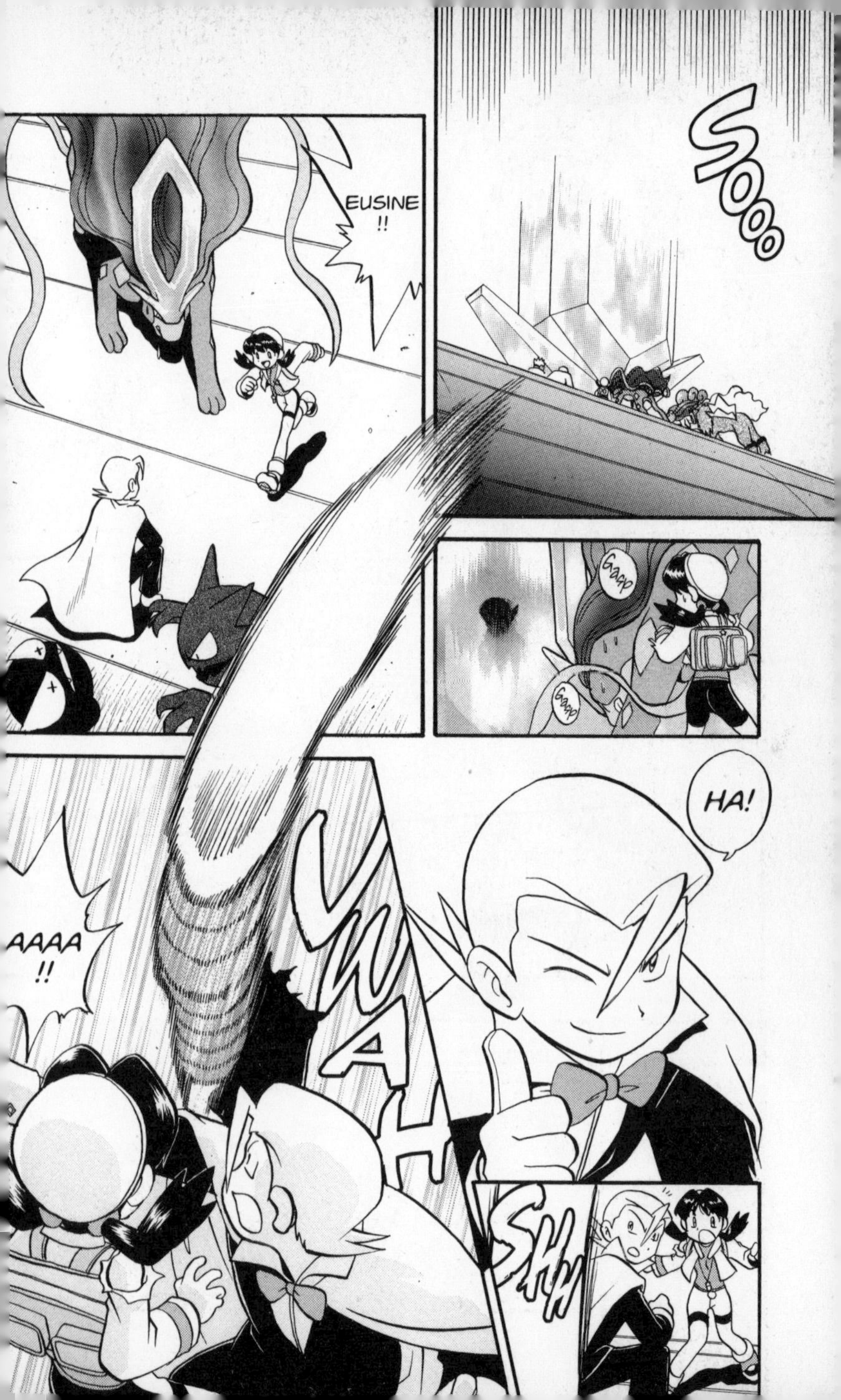
SOOO
EUSINE !!
Gasp
Gasp
HA!
UWAH
AAAA !!
SHH

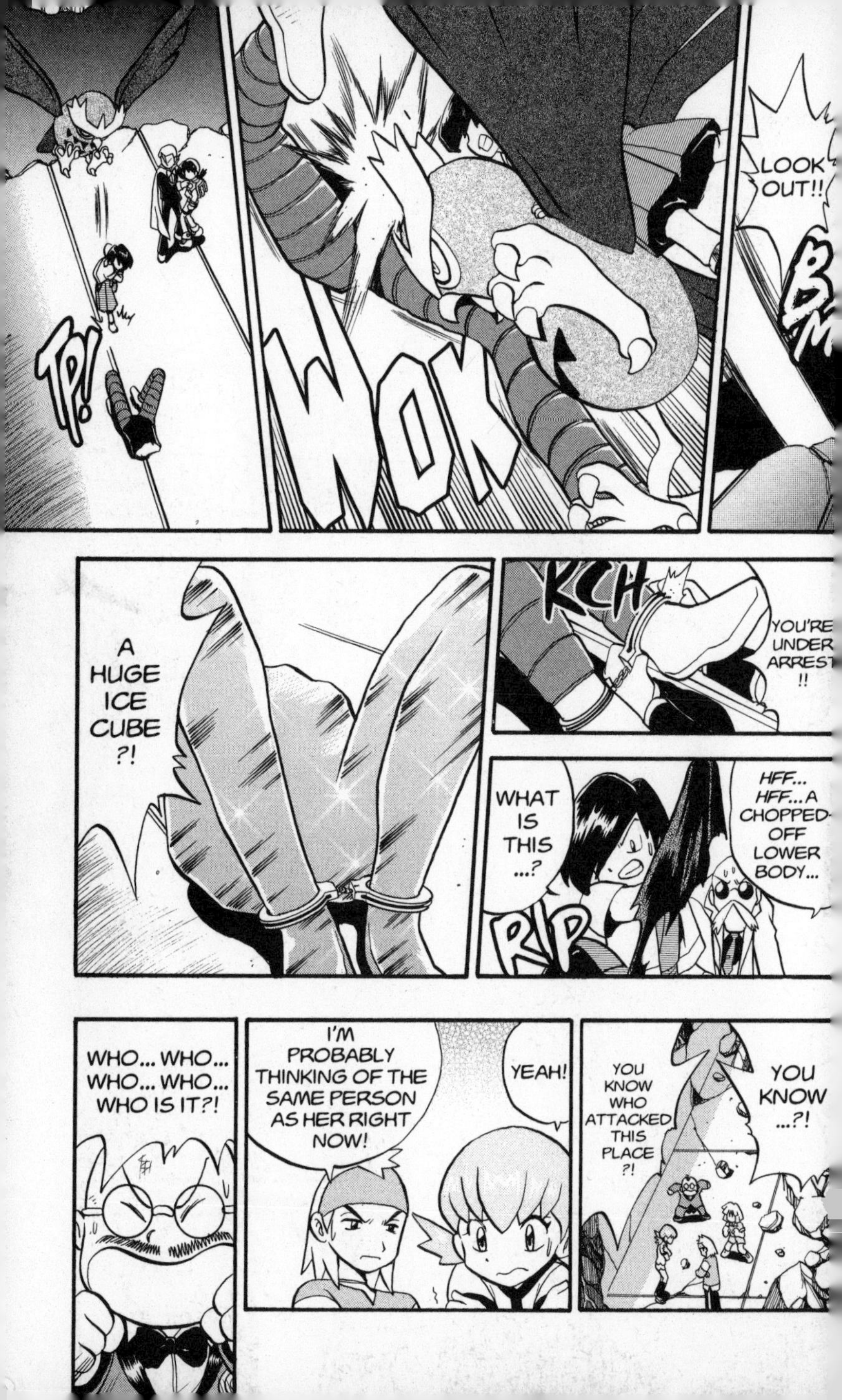
LOOK OUT!!
WOK
TP!
KCH
YOU'RE UNDER ARREST!!
HFF... HFF... A CHOPPED-OFF LOWER BODY...
WHAT IS THIS...?
RIP
A HUGE ICE CUBE?!
YOU KNOW...?!
YOU KNOW WHO ATTACKED THIS PLACE?!
YEAH!
I'M PROBABLY THINKING OF THE SAME PERSON AS HER RIGHT NOW!
WHO... WHO... WHO... WHO... WHO IS IT?!

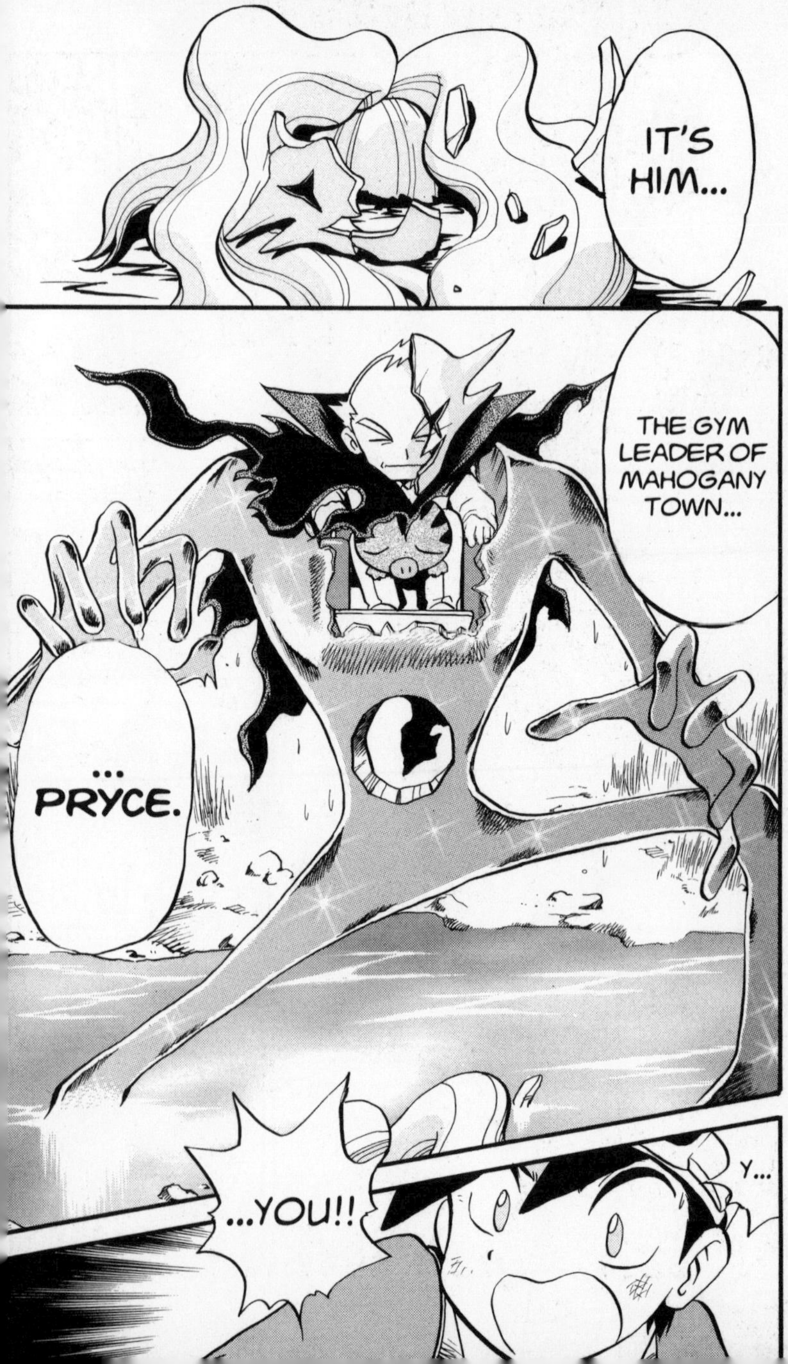
IT'S HIM...
THE GYM LEADER OF MAHOGANY TOWN...
... PRYCE.
Y...
...YOU!!

# 173 The Last Battle VIII

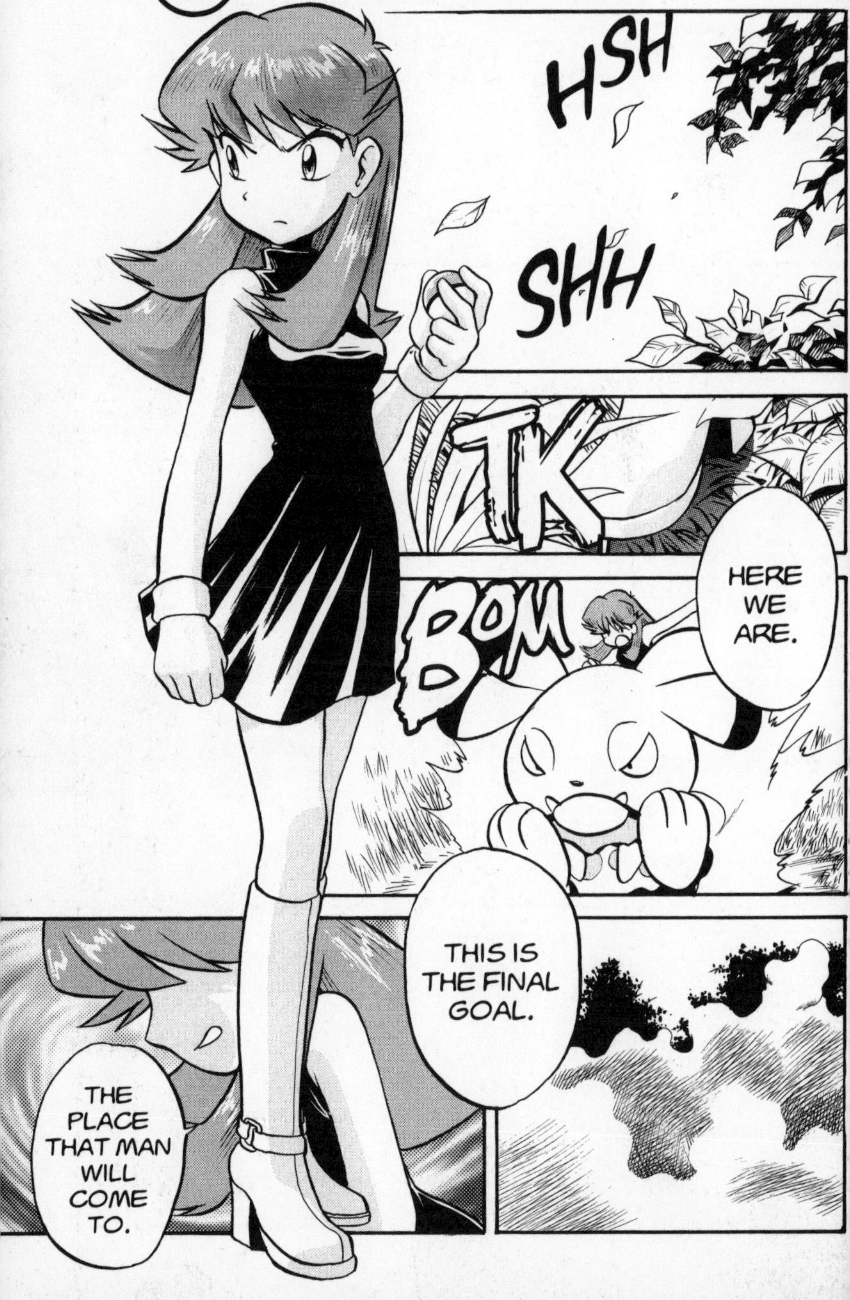
HSH
SHH
TK
BOM
HERE WE ARE.
THIS IS THE FINAL GOAL.
THE PLACE THAT MAN WILL COME TO.

# 173 The Last Battle VII

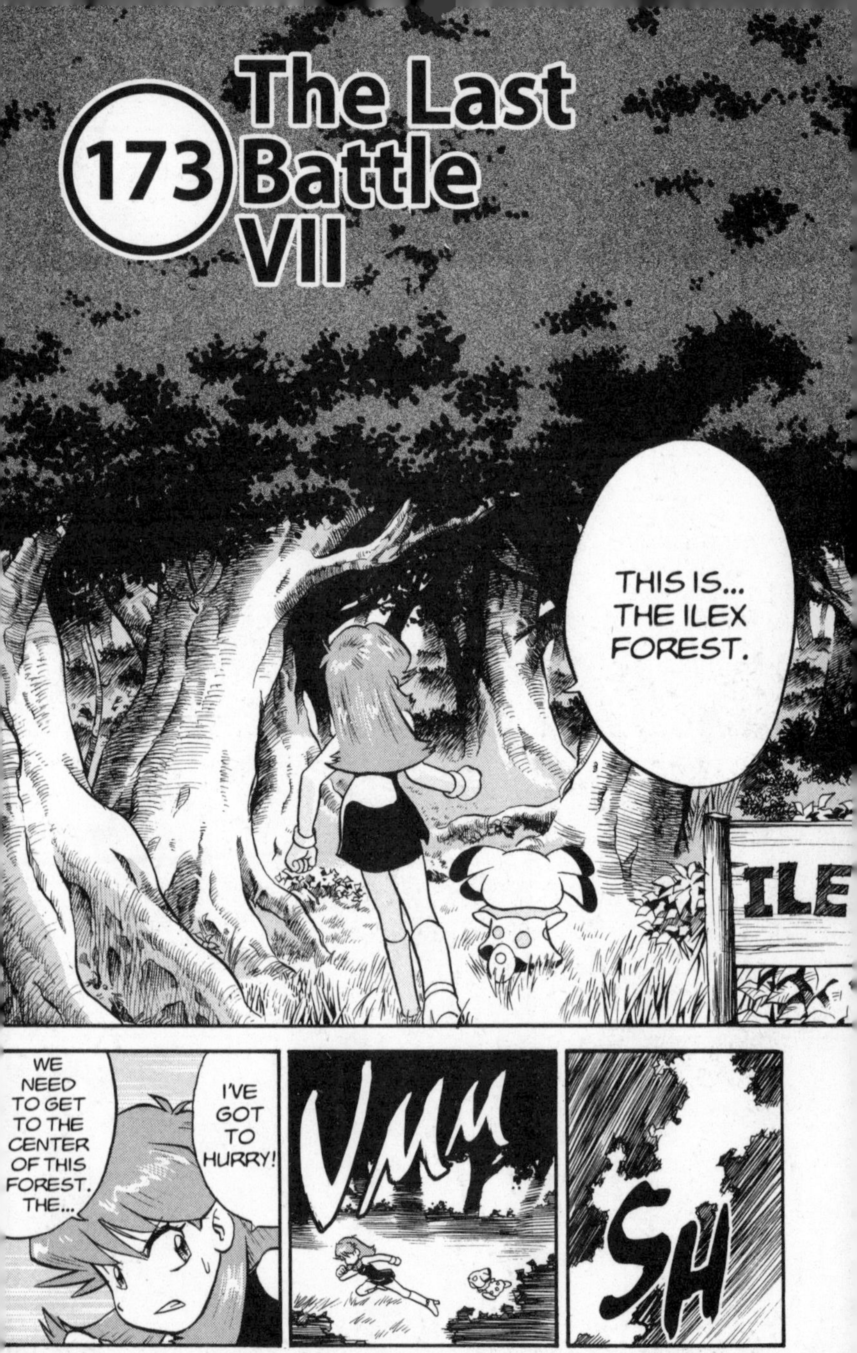
THIS IS... THE ILEX FOREST.
ILE
SH
VMM
I'VE GOT TO HURRY!
WE NEED TO GET TO THE CENTER OF THIS FOREST. THE...

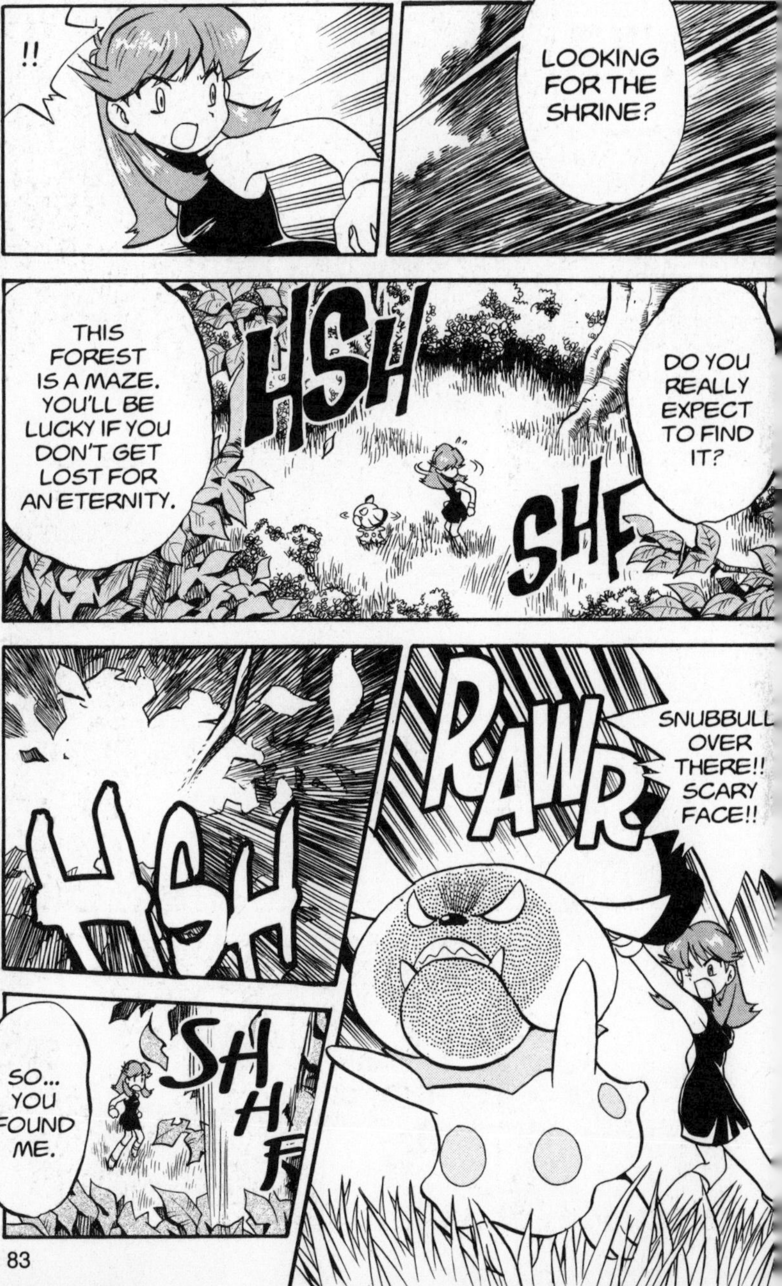
LOOKING FOR THE SHRINE?
!!
DO YOU REALLY EXPECT TO FIND IT?
HSH
SHF
THIS FOREST IS A MAZE. YOU'LL BE LUCKY IF YOU DON'T GET LOST FOR AN ETERNITY.
SNUBBULL OVER THERE!! SCARY FACE!!
RAWR
HSH
SHHF
SO... YOU FOUND ME.

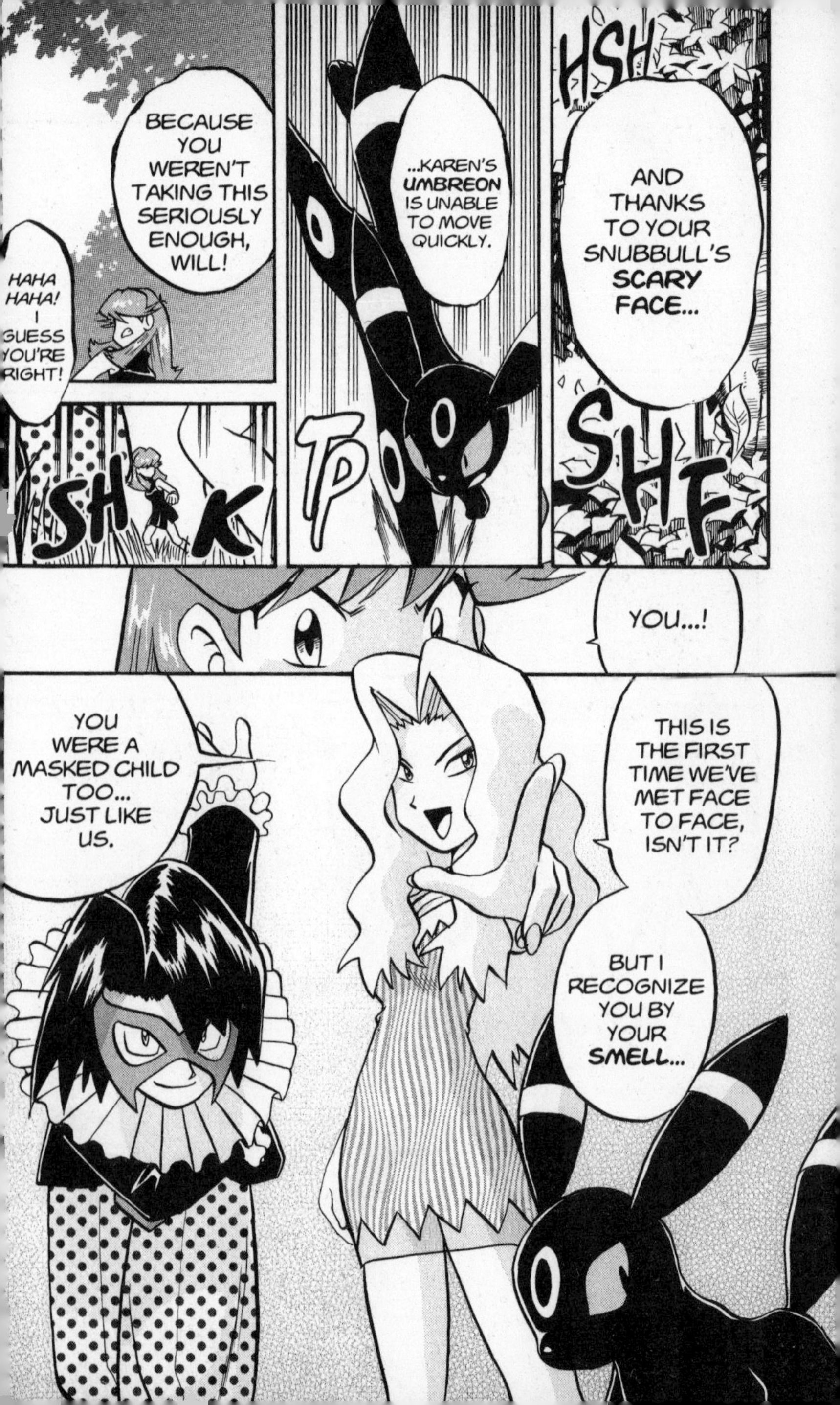
HSH
AND THANKS TO YOUR SNUBBULL'S **SCARY FACE**...
SHF
...KAREN'S **UMBREON** IS UNABLE TO MOVE QUICKLY.
TP
BECAUSE YOU WEREN'T TAKING THIS SERIOUSLY ENOUGH, WILL!
HAHA HAHA! I GUESS YOU'RE RIGHT!
SH K
YOU...!
THIS IS THE FIRST TIME WE'VE MET FACE TO FACE, ISN'T IT?
BUT I RECOGNIZE YOU BY YOUR **SMELL**...
YOU WERE A MASKED CHILD TOO... JUST LIKE US.

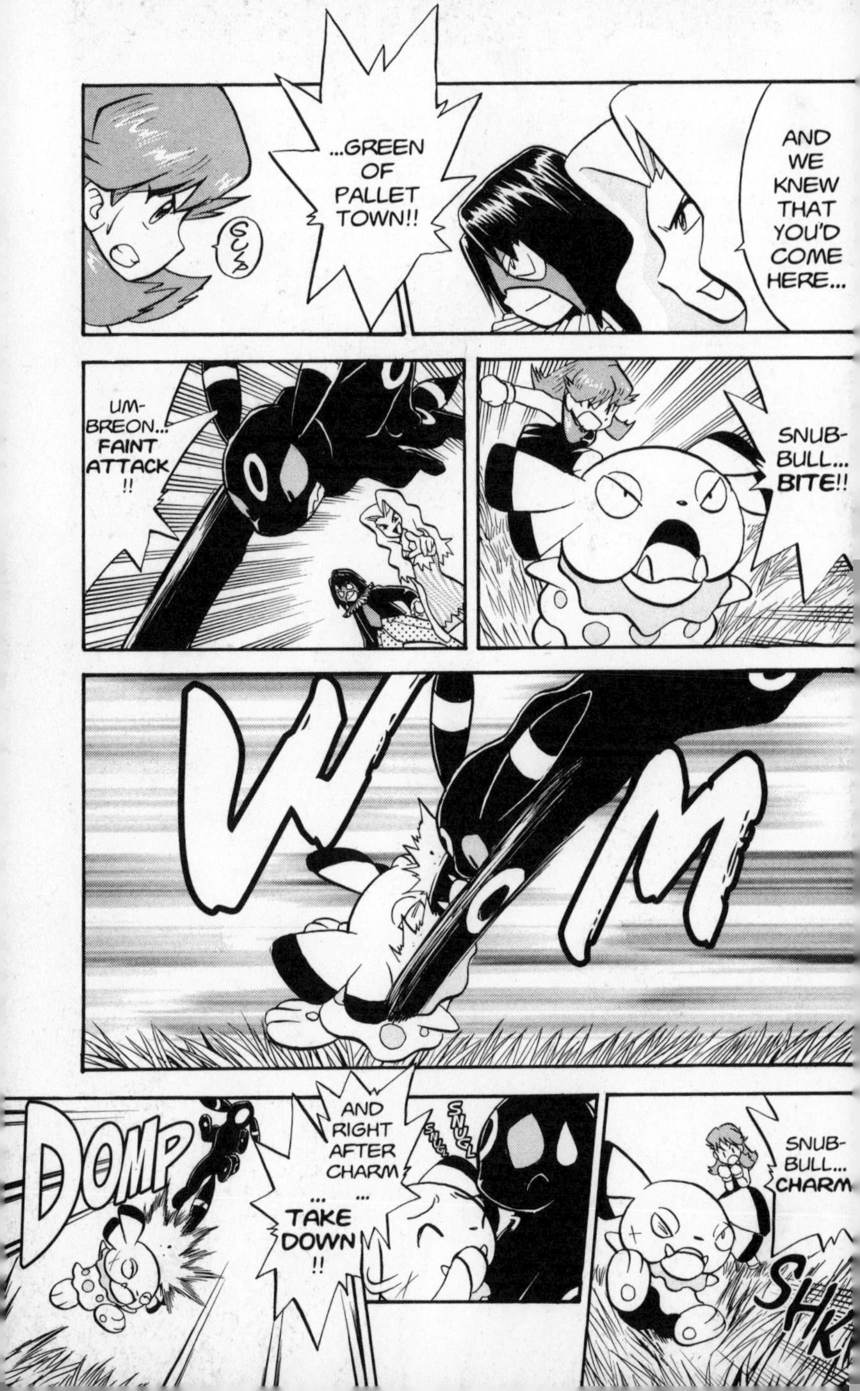
AND WE KNEW THAT YOU'D COME HERE...
...GREEN OF PALLET TOWN!!
GULP
SNUBBULL... BITE!!
UMBREON... FAINT ATTACK!!
WHOM
SNUBBULL... CHARM
SHK
SNUGL SNUGL
AND RIGHT AFTER CHARM... ...TAKE DOWN!!
DOMP

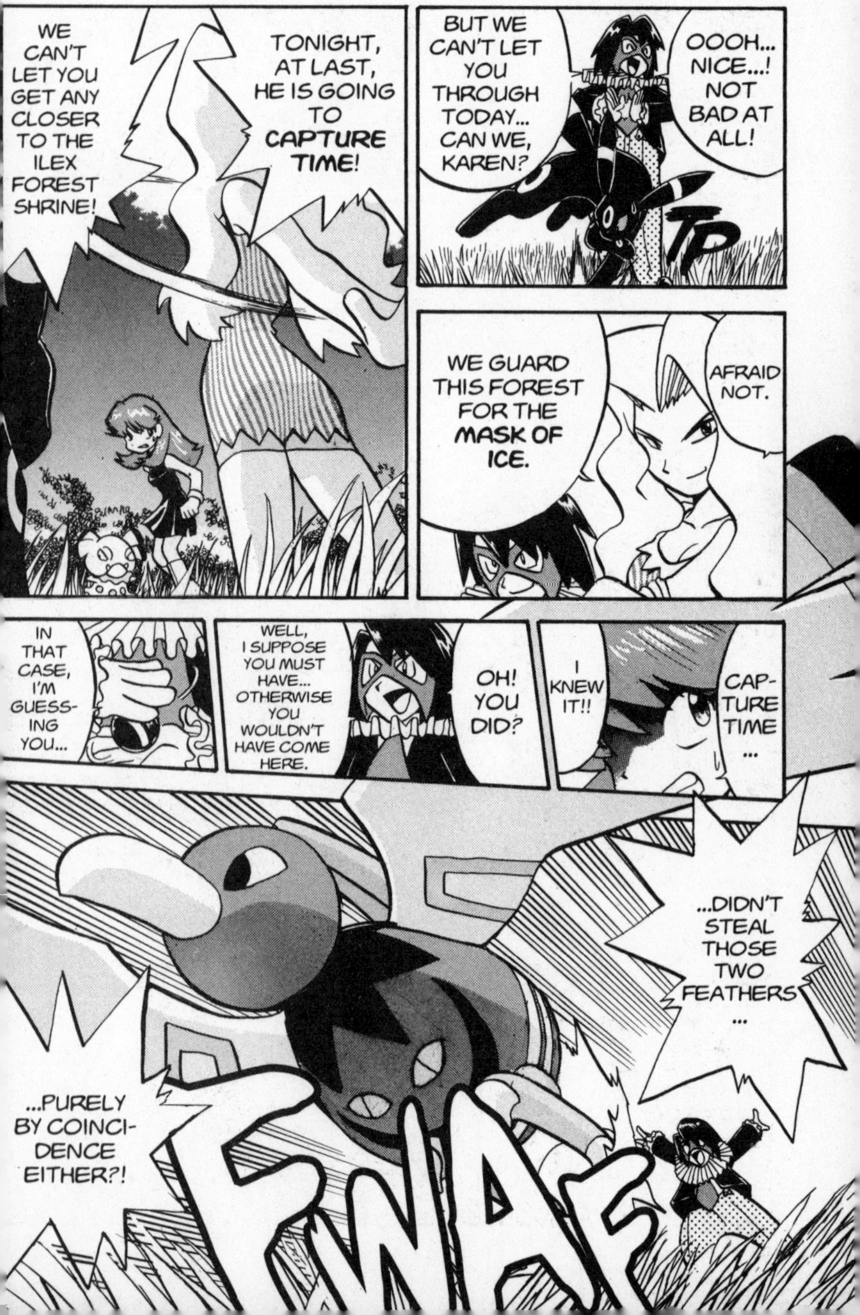
OOOH... NICE...! NOT BAD AT ALL!
BUT WE CAN'T LET YOU THROUGH TODAY... CAN WE, KAREN?
TP
AFRAID NOT.
WE GUARD THIS FOREST FOR THE MASK OF ICE.
TONIGHT, AT LAST, HE IS GOING TO CAPTURE TIME!
WE CAN'T LET YOU GET ANY CLOSER TO THE ILEX FOREST SHRINE!
CAP-TURE TIME ...
I KNEW IT!!
OH! YOU DID?
WELL, I SUPPOSE YOU MUST HAVE... OTHERWISE YOU WOULDN'T HAVE COME HERE.
IN THAT CASE, I'M GUESS-ING YOU...
...DIDN'T STEAL THOSE TWO FEATHERS ...
...PURELY BY COINCI-DENCE EITHER?!

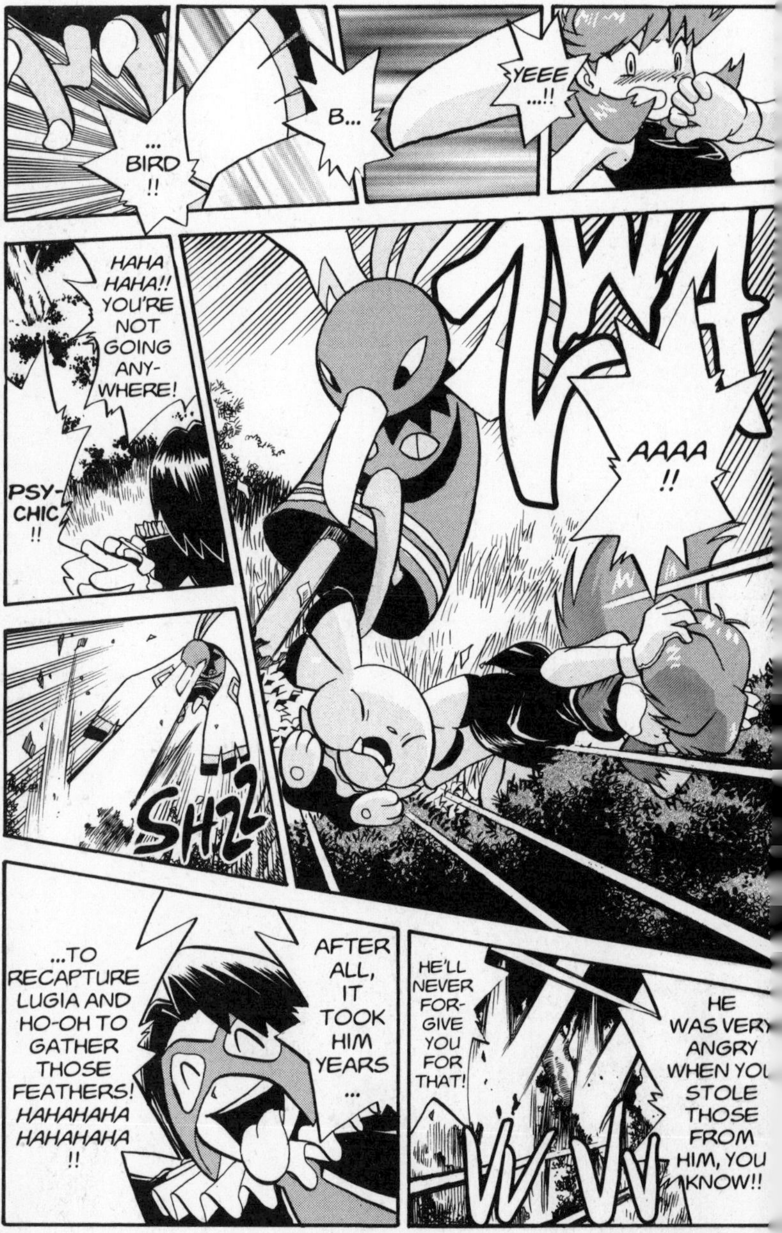
YEEE ...!!
B...
... BIRD !!
AAAA !!
HAHA HAHA!! YOU'RE NOT GOING ANY-WHERE!
PSY-CHIC !!
SHZZ
HE WAS VERY ANGRY WHEN YOU STOLE THOSE FROM HIM, YOU KNOW!!
HE'LL NEVER FOR-GIVE YOU FOR THAT!
AFTER ALL, IT TOOK HIM YEARS ...
...TO RECAPTURE LUGIA AND HO-OH TO GATHER THOSE FEATHERS! HAHAHAHA HAHAHAHA !!

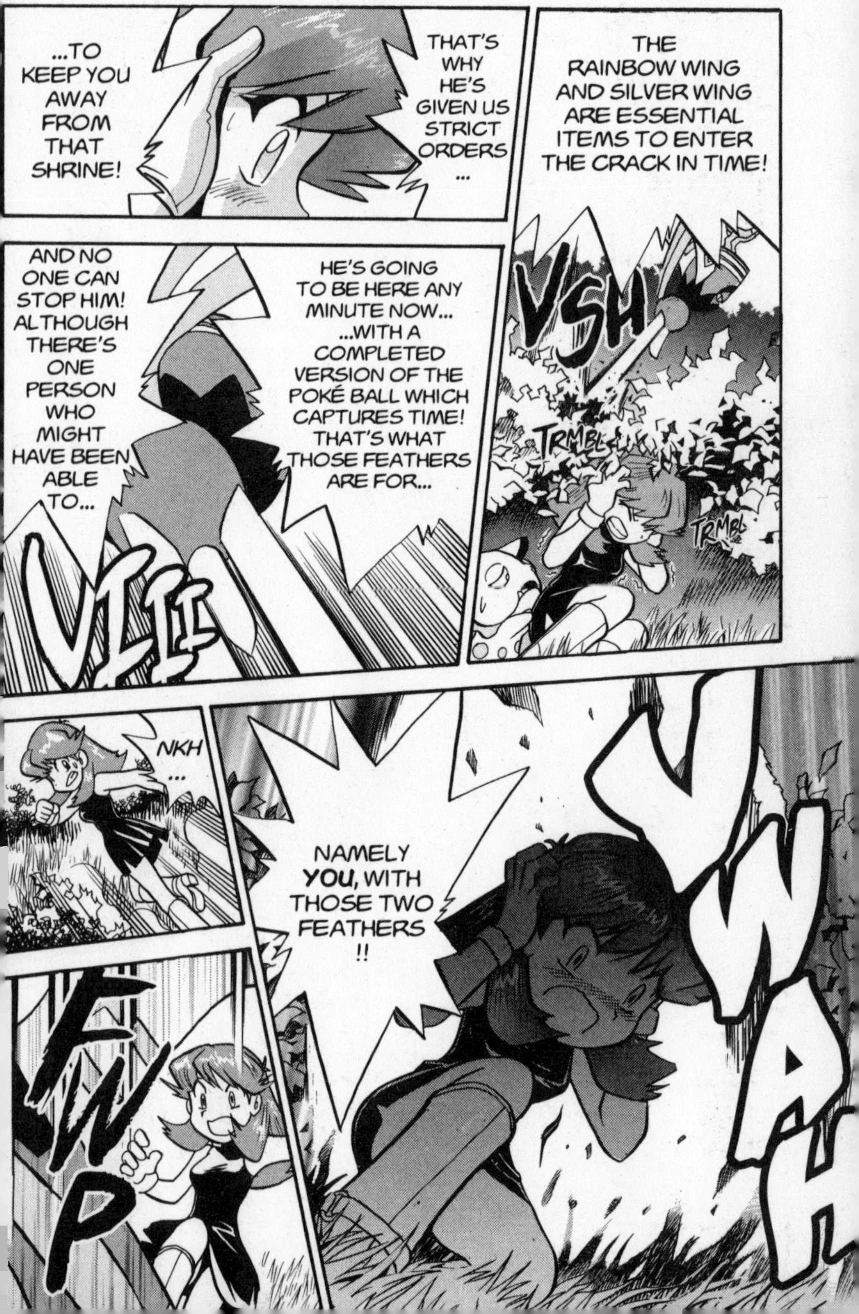
THE RAINBOW WING AND SILVER WING ARE ESSENTIAL ITEMS TO ENTER THE CRACK IN TIME!
THAT'S WHY HE'S GIVEN US STRICT ORDERS ...
...TO KEEP YOU AWAY FROM THAT SHRINE!
VSH
TRMBL
TRMBL
HE'S GOING TO BE HERE ANY MINUTE NOW... ...WITH A COMPLETED VERSION OF THE POKÉ BALL WHICH CAPTURES TIME! THAT'S WHAT THOSE FEATHERS ARE FOR...
AND NO ONE CAN STOP HIM! ALTHOUGH THERE'S ONE PERSON WHO MIGHT HAVE BEEN ABLE TO...
VIII
NAMELY **YOU**, WITH THOSE TWO FEATHERS !!
NKH ...
FWP

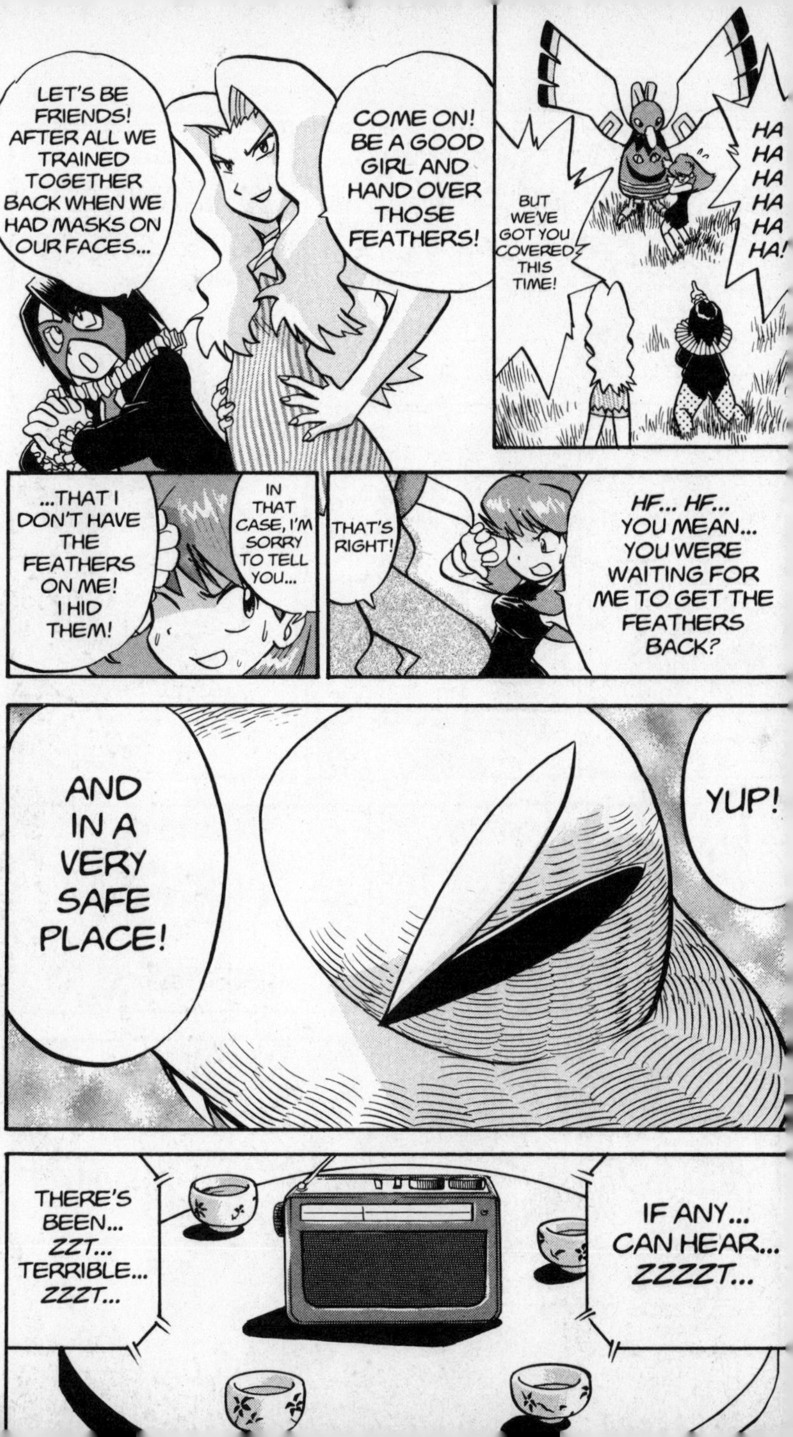
HA HA HA HA HA HA!
BUT WE'VE GOT YOU COVERED THIS TIME!
COME ON! BE A GOOD GIRL AND HAND OVER THOSE FEATHERS!
LET'S BE FRIENDS! AFTER ALL WE TRAINED TOGETHER BACK WHEN WE HAD MASKS ON OUR FACES...
HF... HF... YOU MEAN... YOU WERE WAITING FOR ME TO GET THE FEATHERS BACK?
THAT'S RIGHT!
IN THAT CASE, I'M SORRY TO TELL YOU...
...THAT I DON'T HAVE THE FEATHERS ON ME! I HID THEM!
YUP!
AND IN A VERY SAFE PLACE!
IF ANY... CAN HEAR... ZZZZT...
THERE'S BEEN... ZZT... TERRIBLE... ZZZT...

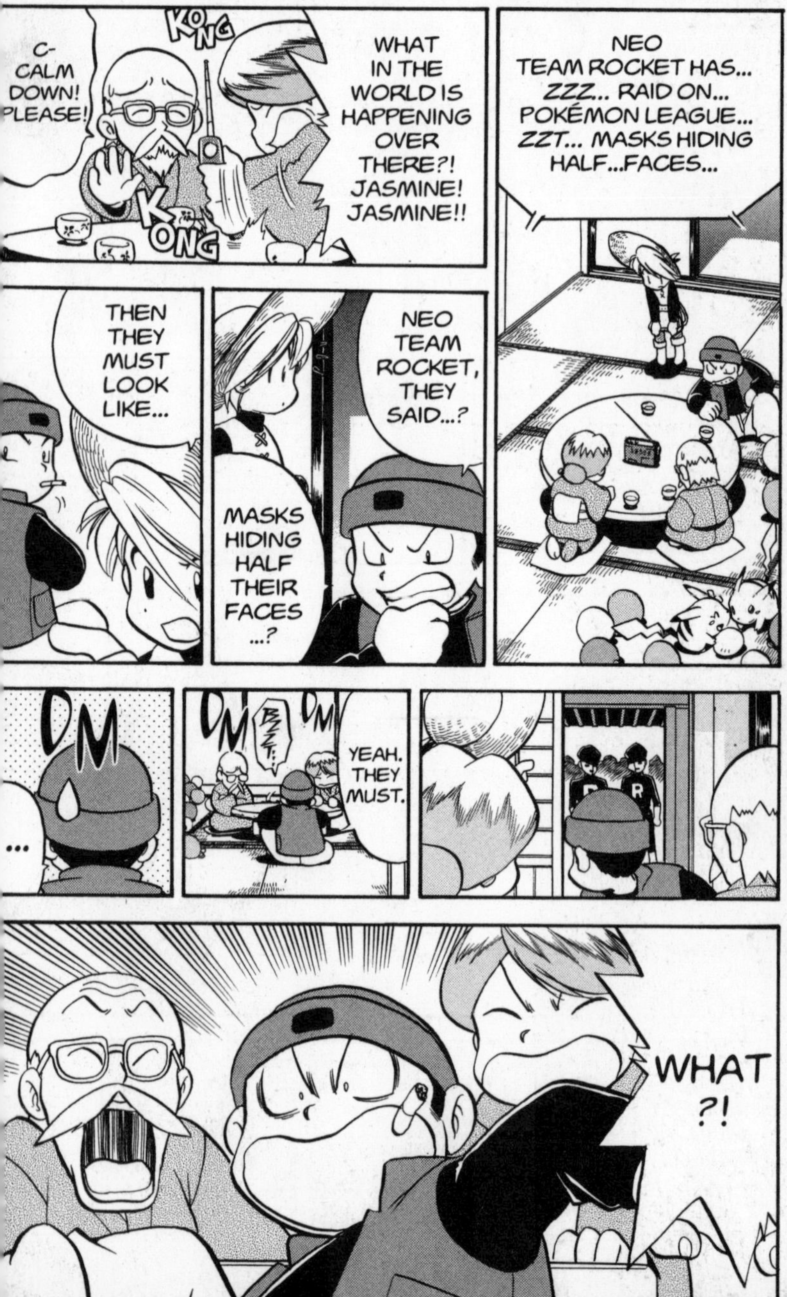
NEO TEAM ROCKET HAS... ZZZ... RAID ON... POKÉMON LEAGUE... ZZT... MASKS HIDING HALF...FACES...
WHAT IN THE WORLD IS HAPPENING OVER THERE?! JASMINE! JASMINE!!
KONG
C- CALM DOWN! PLEASE!
KONG
NEO TEAM ROCKET, THEY SAID...?
MASKS HIDING HALF THEIR FACES ...?
THEN THEY MUST LOOK LIKE...
DM
YEAH. THEY MUST.
BZZT!
DM
DM
...
WHAT ?!

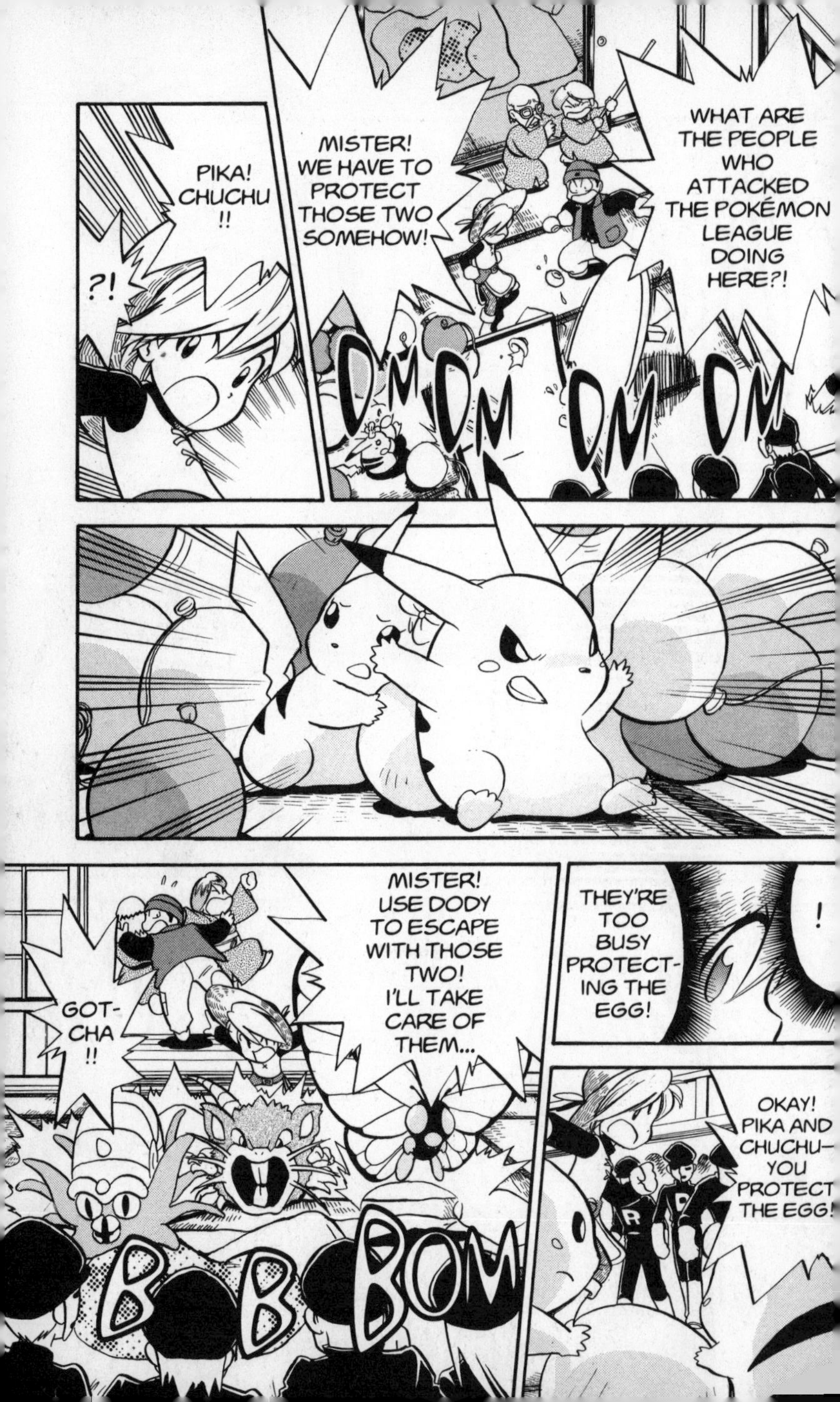
WHAT ARE THE PEOPLE WHO ATTACKED THE POKÉMON LEAGUE DOING HERE?!
MISTER! WE HAVE TO PROTECT THOSE TWO SOMEHOW!
DM DM DM DM
PIKA! CHUCHU !!
?!
!
THEY'RE TOO BUSY PROTECTING THE EGG!
OKAY! PIKA AND CHUCHU—YOU PROTECT THE EGG!
MISTER! USE DODY TO ESCAPE WITH THOSE TWO! I'LL TAKE CARE OF THEM...
GOT-CHA !!
B B BOM

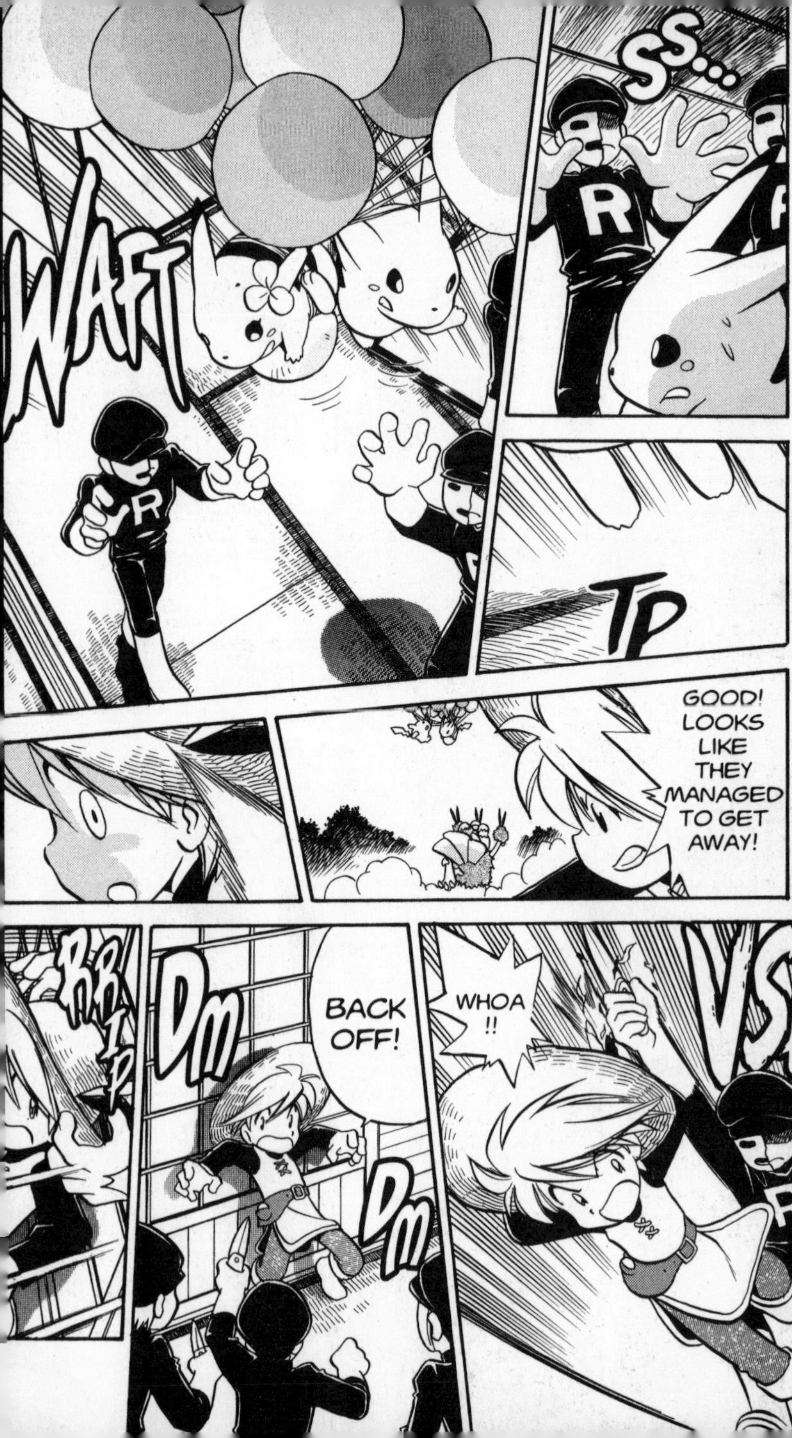
SS...
TP
WAFT
GOOD! LOOKS LIKE THEY MANAGED TO GET AWAY!
VSH
WHOA !!
BACK OFF!
Dm
Dm
RRIP

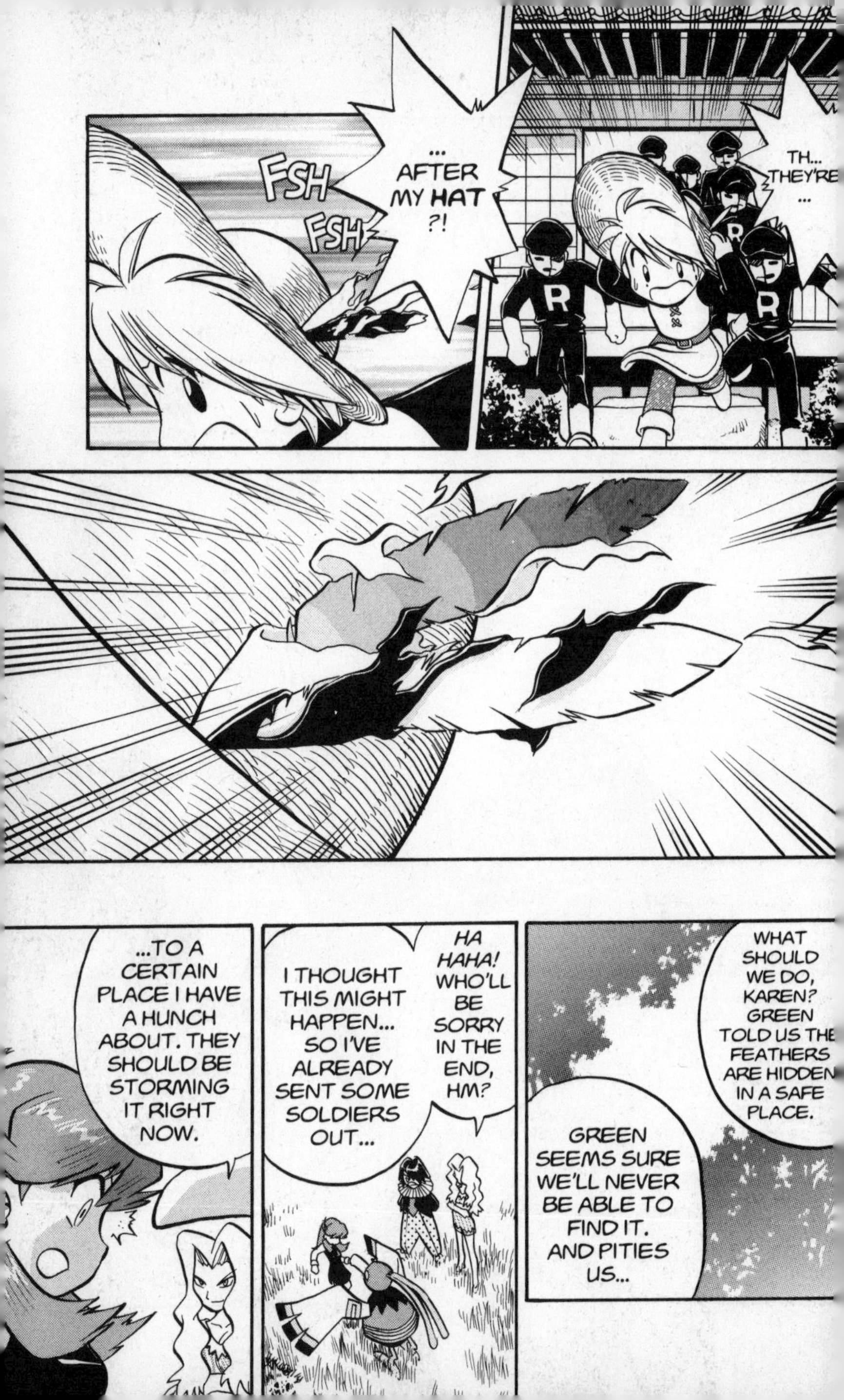
TH... THEY'RE ...
... AFTER MY HAT ?!
FSH
FSH
WHAT SHOULD WE DO, KAREN? GREEN TOLD US THE FEATHERS ARE HIDDEN IN A SAFE PLACE.
GREEN SEEMS SURE WE'LL NEVER BE ABLE TO FIND IT. AND PITIES US...
HA HAHA! WHO'LL BE SORRY IN THE END, HM?
I THOUGHT THIS MIGHT HAPPEN... SO I'VE ALREADY SENT SOME SOLDIERS OUT...
...TO A CERTAIN PLACE I HAVE A HUNCH ABOUT. THEY SHOULD BE STORMING IT RIGHT NOW.

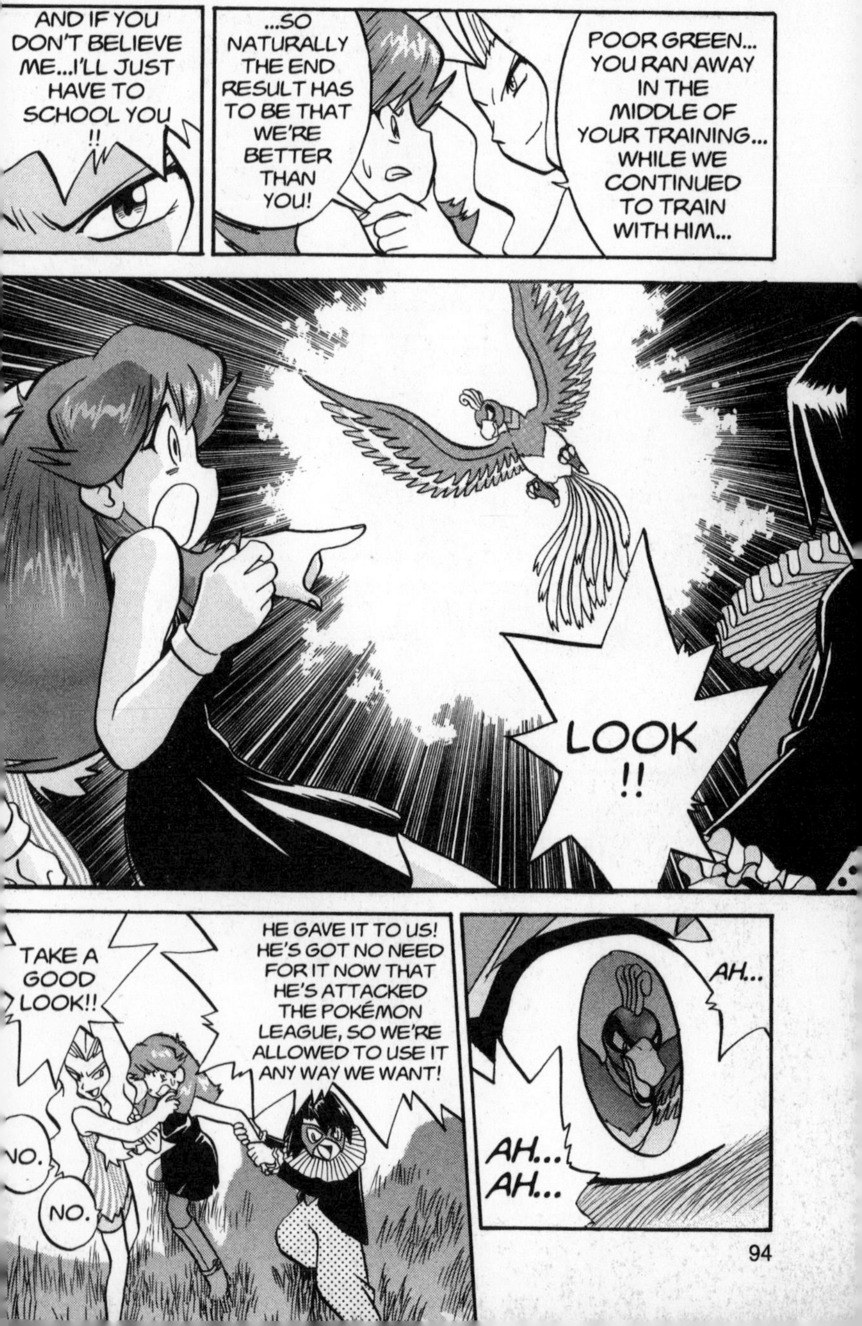
POOR GREEN... YOU RAN AWAY IN THE MIDDLE OF YOUR TRAINING... WHILE WE CONTINUED TO TRAIN WITH HIM...
...SO NATURALLY THE END RESULT HAS TO BE THAT WE'RE BETTER THAN YOU!
AND IF YOU DON'T BELIEVE ME...I'LL JUST HAVE TO SCHOOL YOU !!
LOOK !!
AH...
AH... AH...
HE GAVE IT TO US! HE'S GOT NO NEED FOR IT NOW THAT HE'S ATTACKED THE POKÉMON LEAGUE, SO WE'RE ALLOWED TO USE IT ANY WAY WE WANT!
TAKE A GOOD LOOK!!
NO.
NO.

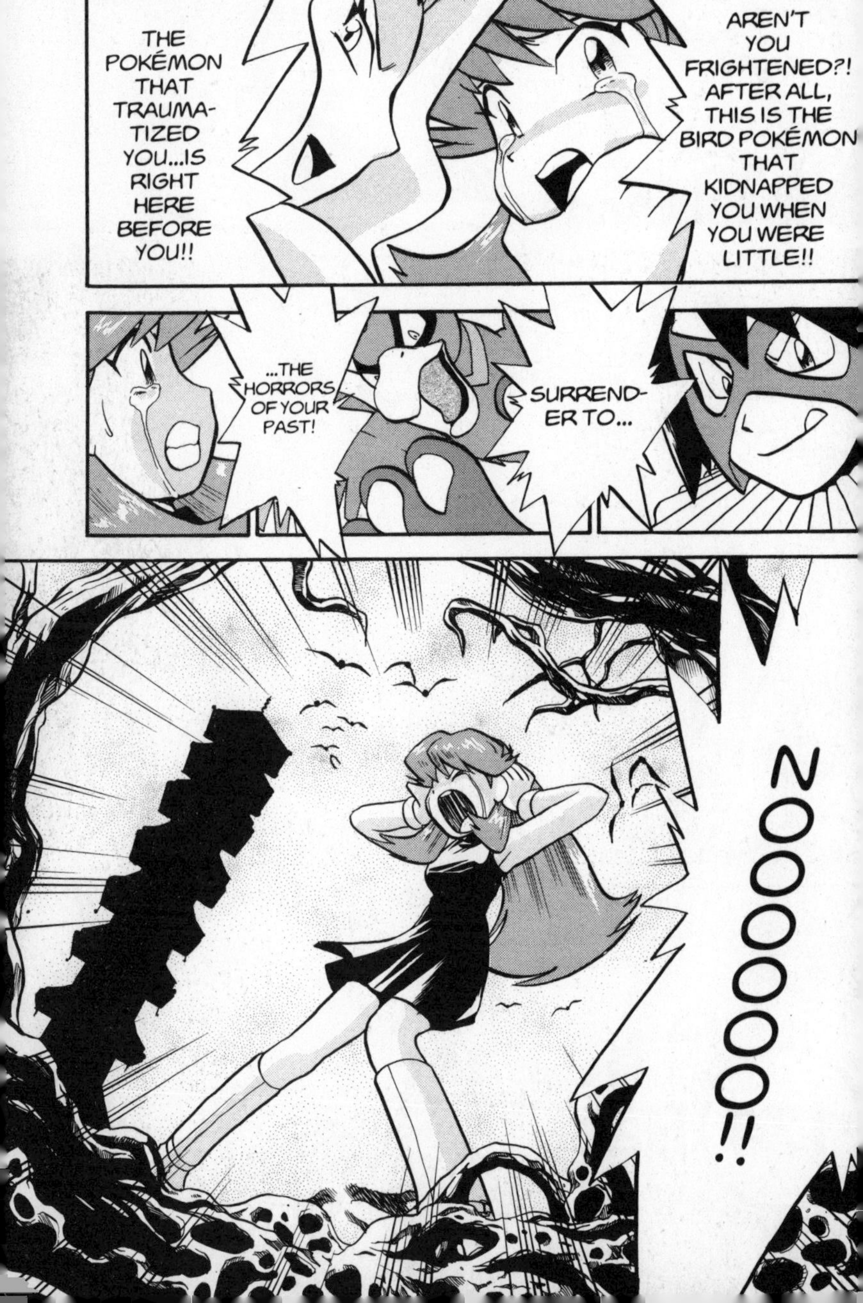

AREN'T YOU FRIGHTENED?! AFTER ALL, THIS IS THE BIRD POKÉMON THAT KIDNAPPED YOU WHEN YOU WERE LITTLE!!
THE POKÉMON THAT TRAUMA-TIZED YOU...IS RIGHT HERE BEFORE YOU!!
SURREND-ER TO...
...THE HORRORS OF YOUR PAST!
NOOOOOOO!!

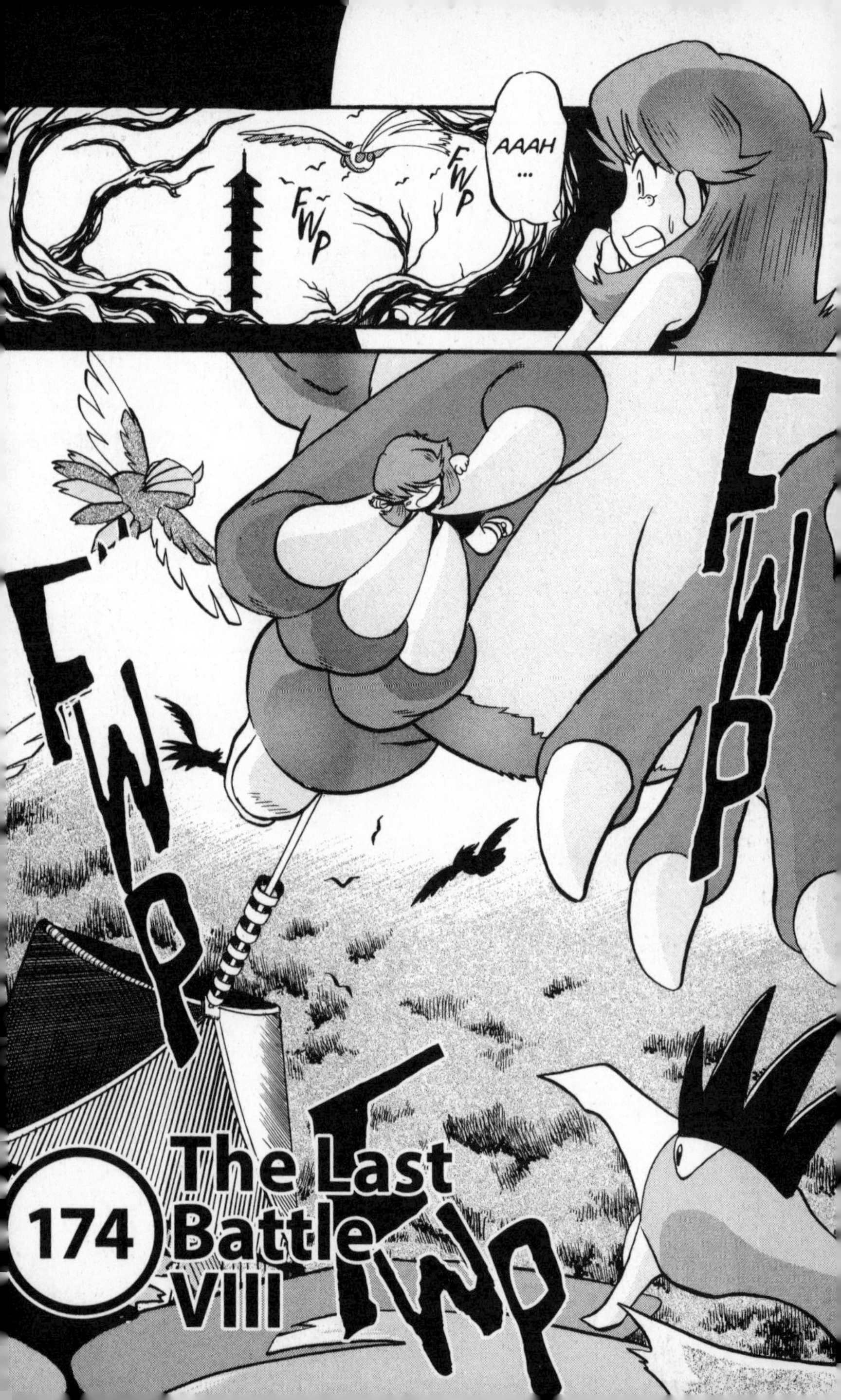
AAAH ...
FWP
FWP
FWP
FWP
FWP

# 174 The Last Battle VIII

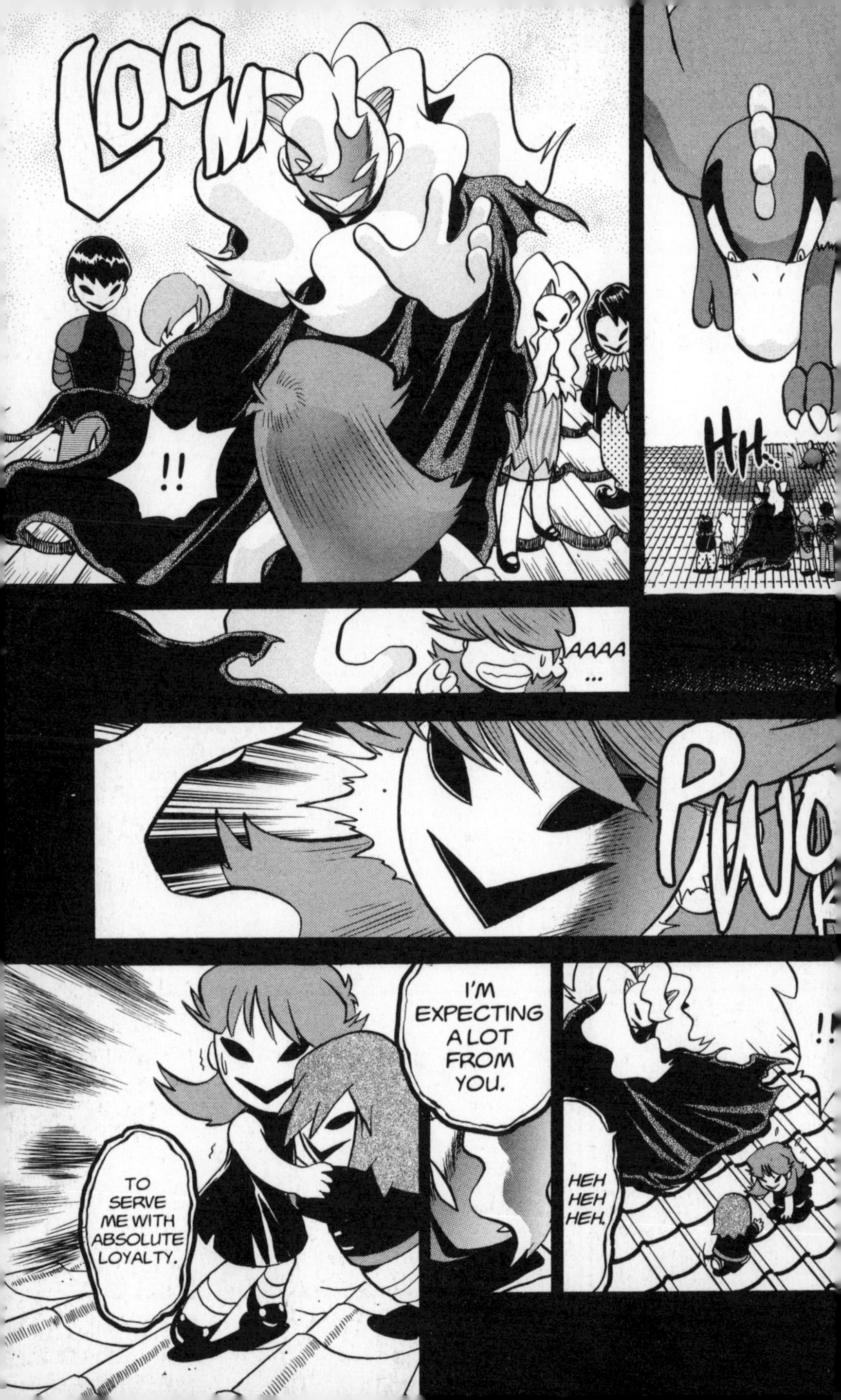
HH...
LOOM
!!
AAAA ...
PWO
!!
HEH HEH HEH.
I'M EXPECTING A LOT FROM YOU.
TO SERVE ME WITH ABSOLUTE LOYALTY.

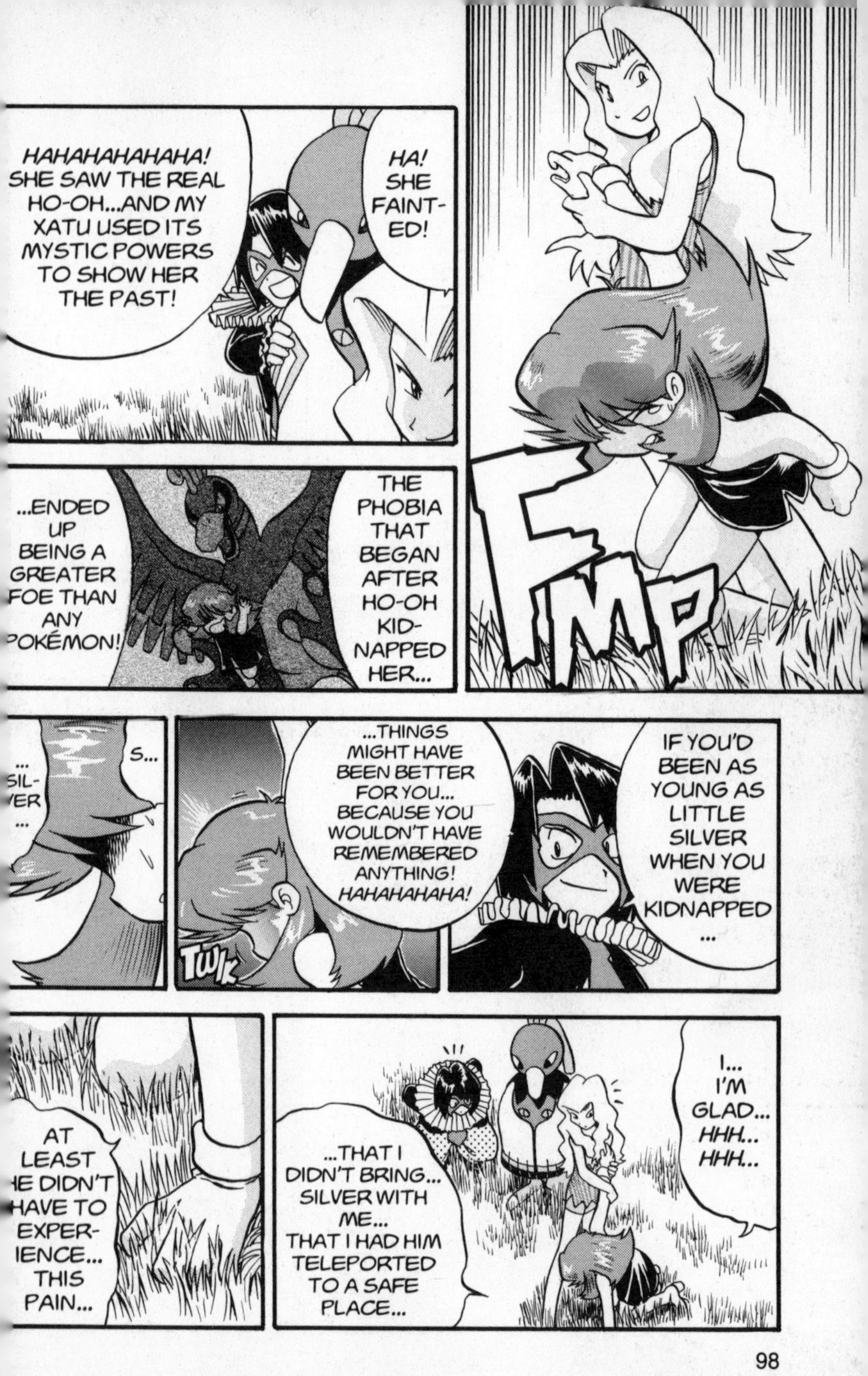
TMP
HA! SHE FAINT-ED!
HAHAHAHAHAHA! SHE SAW THE REAL HO-OH...AND MY XATU USED ITS MYSTIC POWERS TO SHOW HER THE PAST!
THE PHOBIA THAT BEGAN AFTER HO-OH KID-NAPPED HER...
...ENDED UP BEING A GREATER FOE THAN ANY POKÉMON!
IF YOU'D BEEN AS YOUNG AS LITTLE SILVER WHEN YOU WERE KIDNAPPED...
...THINGS MIGHT HAVE BEEN BETTER FOR YOU... BECAUSE YOU WOULDN'T HAVE REMEMBERED ANYTHING! HAHAHAHAHA!
TWK
S...
...SIL-VER...
I... I'M GLAD... HHH... HHH...
...THAT I DIDN'T BRING... SILVER WITH ME... THAT I HAD HIM TELEPORTED TO A SAFE PLACE...
AT LEAST HE DIDN'T HAVE TO EXPER-IENCE... THIS PAIN...

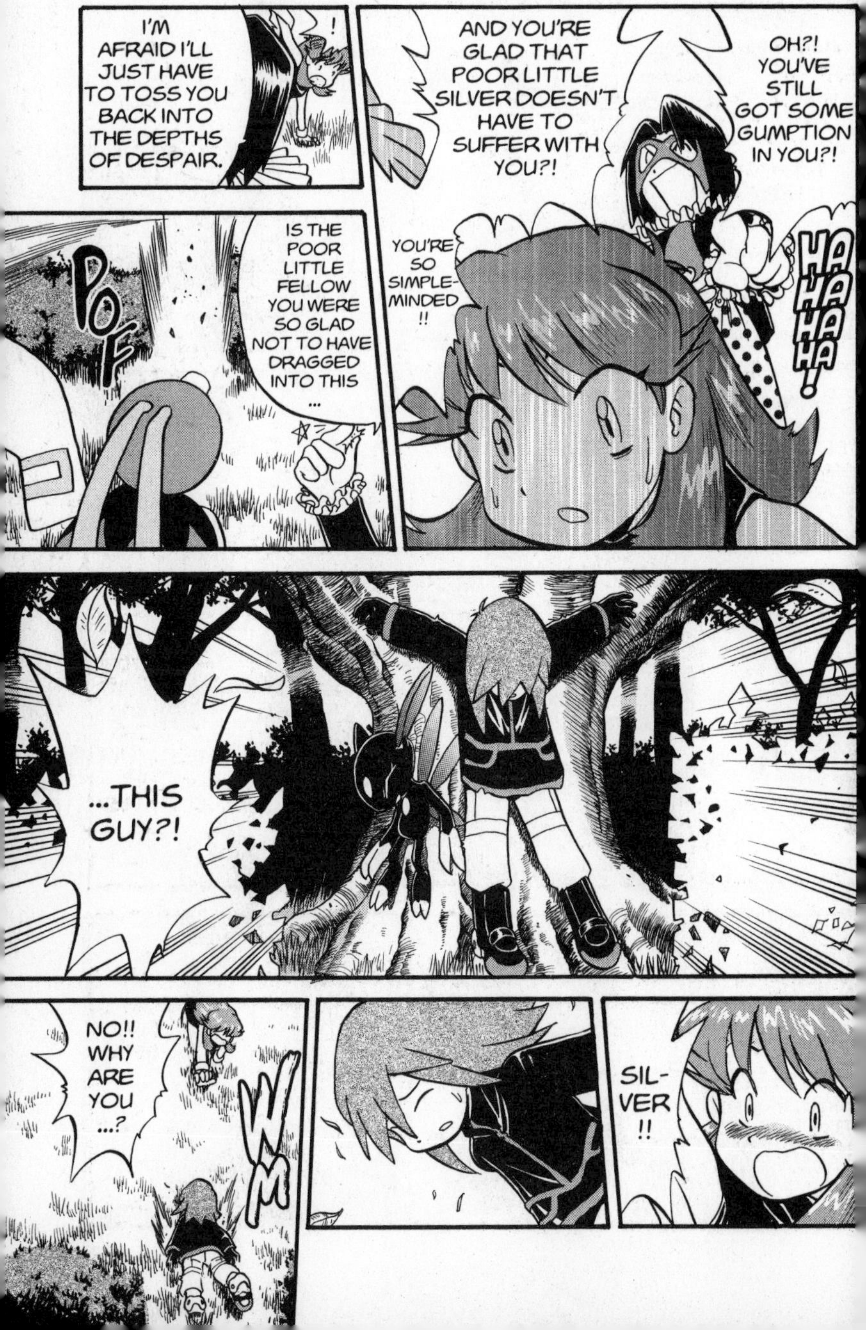
OH?! YOU'VE STILL GOT SOME GUMPTION IN YOU?!
AND YOU'RE GLAD THAT POOR LITTLE SILVER DOESN'T HAVE TO SUFFER WITH YOU?!
HA HA HA HA HA!
YOU'RE SO SIMPLE-MINDED!!
!
I'M AFRAID I'LL JUST HAVE TO TOSS YOU BACK INTO THE DEPTHS OF DESPAIR.
IS THE POOR LITTLE FELLOW YOU WERE SO GLAD NOT TO HAVE DRAGGED INTO THIS ...
POF
...THIS GUY?!
SIL-VER!!
WM
NO!! WHY ARE YOU ...?

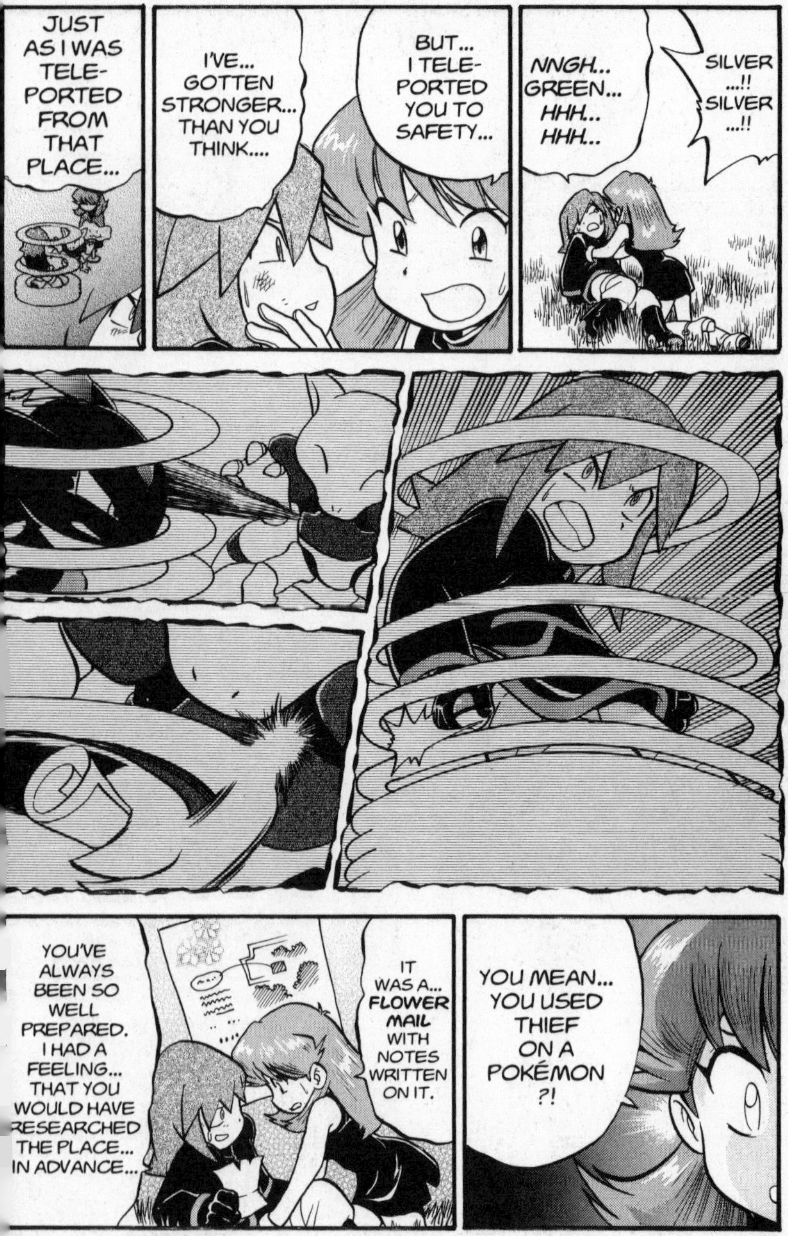
SILVER ...!! SILVER ...!!
NNGH... GREEN... HHH... HHH...
BUT... I TELE-PORTED YOU TO SAFETY...
I'VE... GOTTEN STRONGER... THAN YOU THINK....
JUST AS I WAS TELE-PORTED FROM THAT PLACE...
YOU MEAN... YOU USED THIEF ON A POKÉMON ?!
IT WAS A... **FLOWER MAIL** WITH NOTES WRITTEN ON IT.
YOU'VE ALWAYS BEEN SO WELL PREPARED. I HAD A FEELING... THAT YOU WOULD HAVE RESEARCHED THE PLACE... IN ADVANCE...

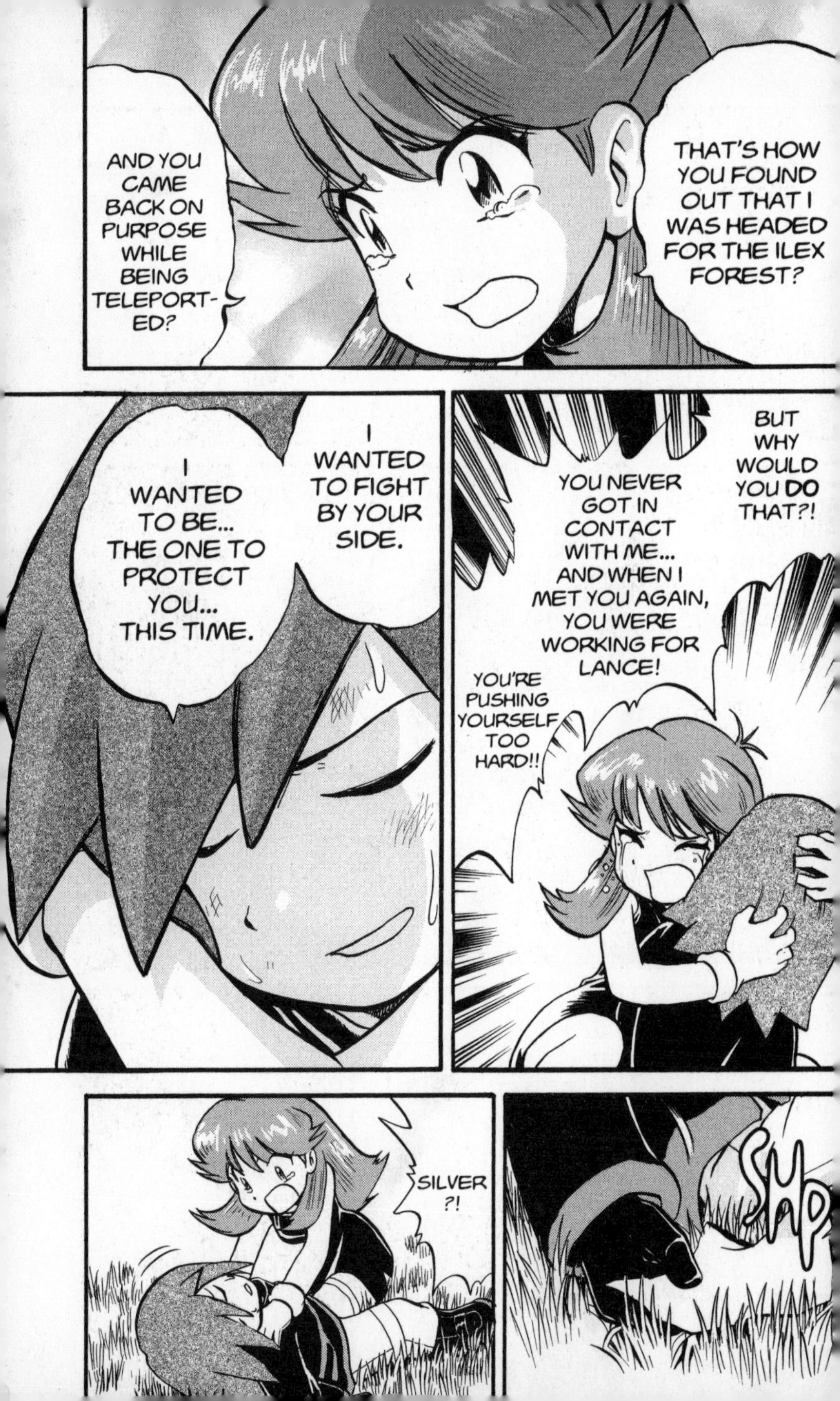
THAT'S HOW YOU FOUND OUT THAT I WAS HEADED FOR THE ILEX FOREST?
AND YOU CAME BACK ON PURPOSE WHILE BEING TELEPORT-ED?
BUT WHY WOULD YOU **DO** THAT?!
YOU NEVER GOT IN CONTACT WITH ME... AND WHEN I MET YOU AGAIN, YOU WERE WORKING FOR LANCE!
YOU'RE PUSHING YOURSELF TOO HARD!!
I WANTED TO FIGHT BY YOUR SIDE.
I WANTED TO BE... THE ONE TO PROTECT YOU... THIS TIME.
SHP
SILVER?!

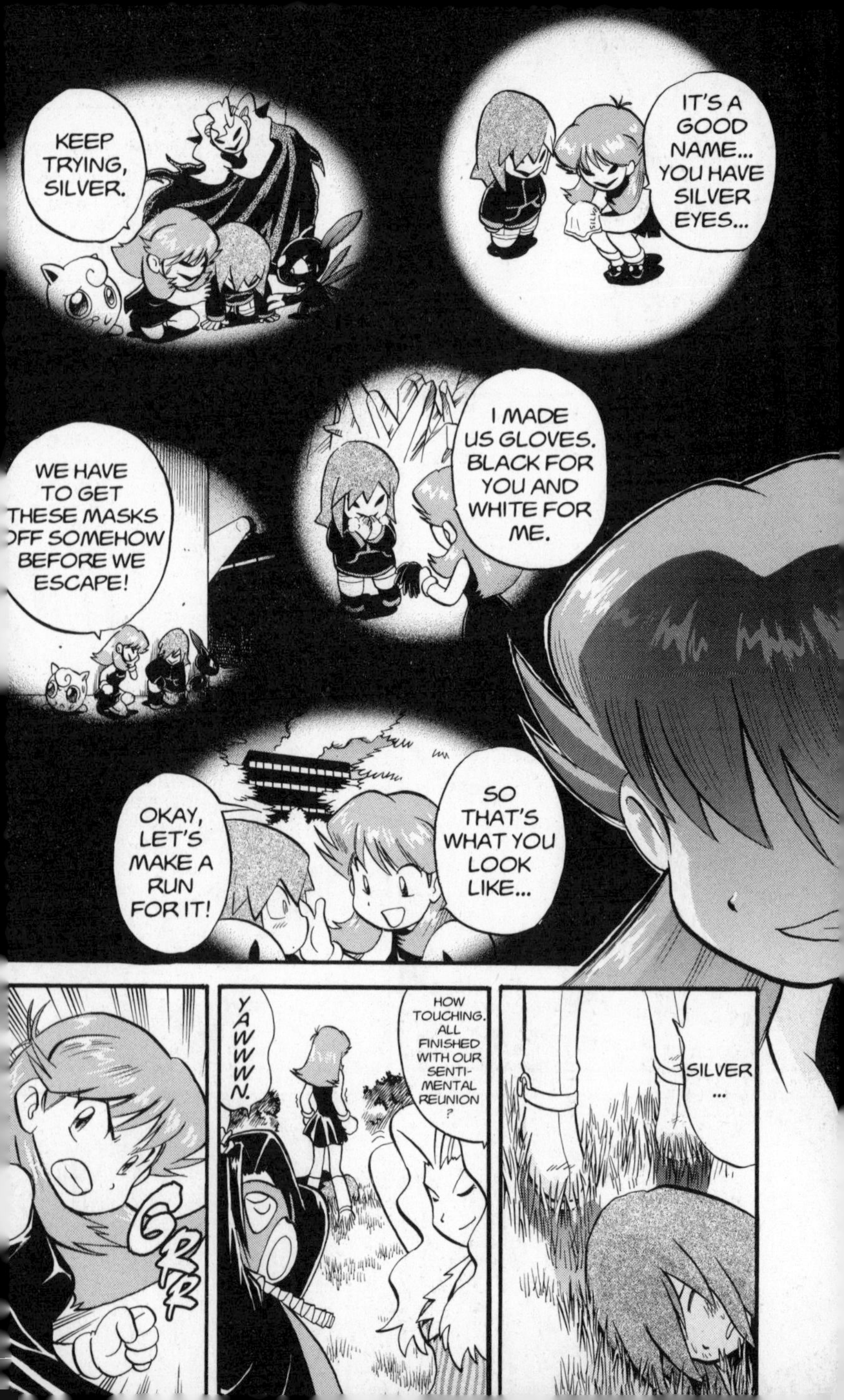
IT'S A GOOD NAME... YOU HAVE SILVER EYES...
KEEP TRYING, SILVER.
I MADE US GLOVES. BLACK FOR YOU AND WHITE FOR ME.
WE HAVE TO GET THESE MASKS OFF SOMEHOW BEFORE WE ESCAPE!
SO THAT'S WHAT YOU LOOK LIKE...
OKAY, LET'S MAKE A RUN FOR IT!
SILVER ...
HOW TOUCHING. ALL FINISHED WITH OUR SENTI-MENTAL REUNION?
YAWWWN.
GRR

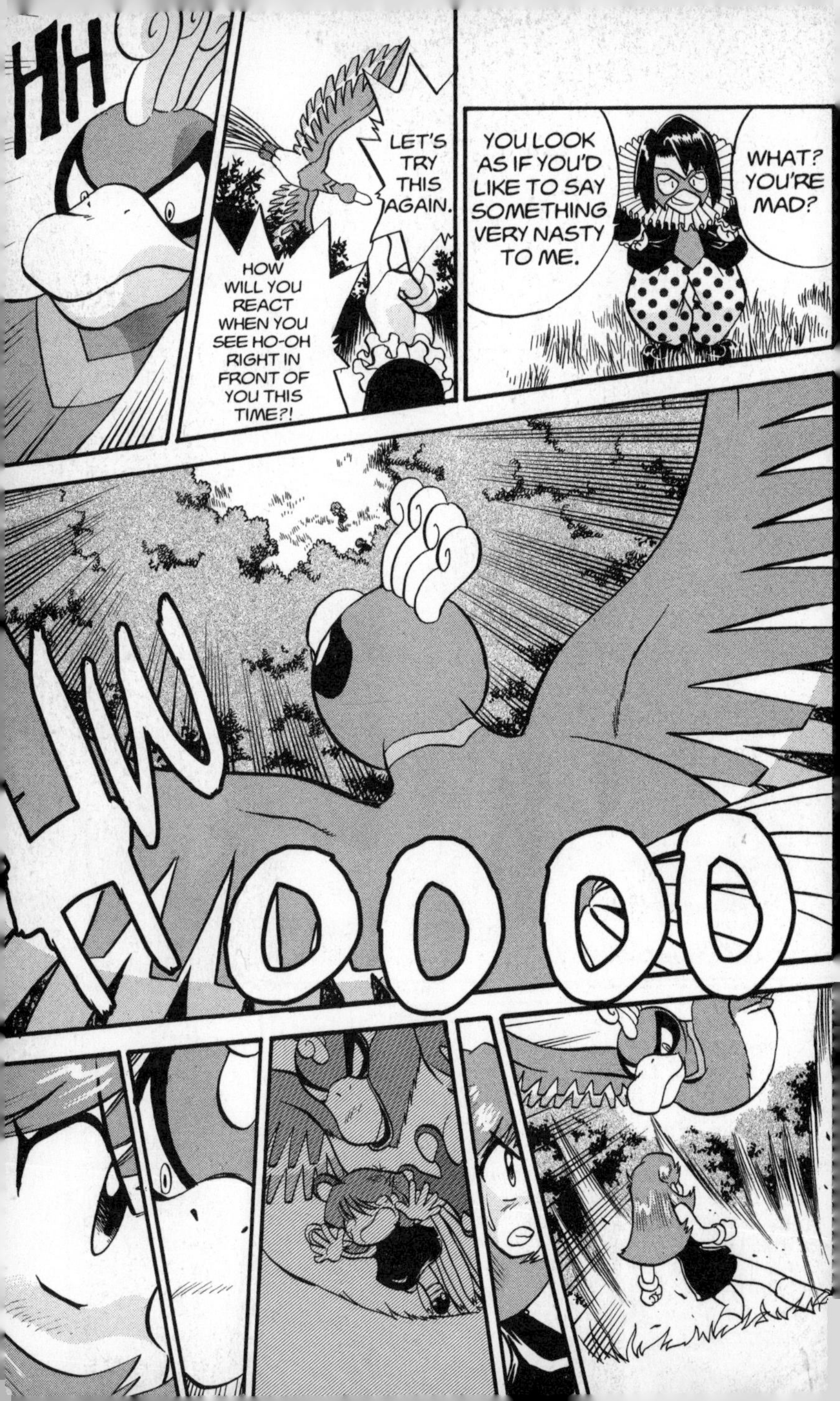
WHAT? YOU'RE MAD?
YOU LOOK AS IF YOU'D LIKE TO SAY SOMETHING VERY NASTY TO ME.
LET'S TRY THIS AGAIN.
HOW WILL YOU REACT WHEN YOU SEE HO-OH RIGHT IN FRONT OF YOU THIS TIME?!
HH
WHOOOO

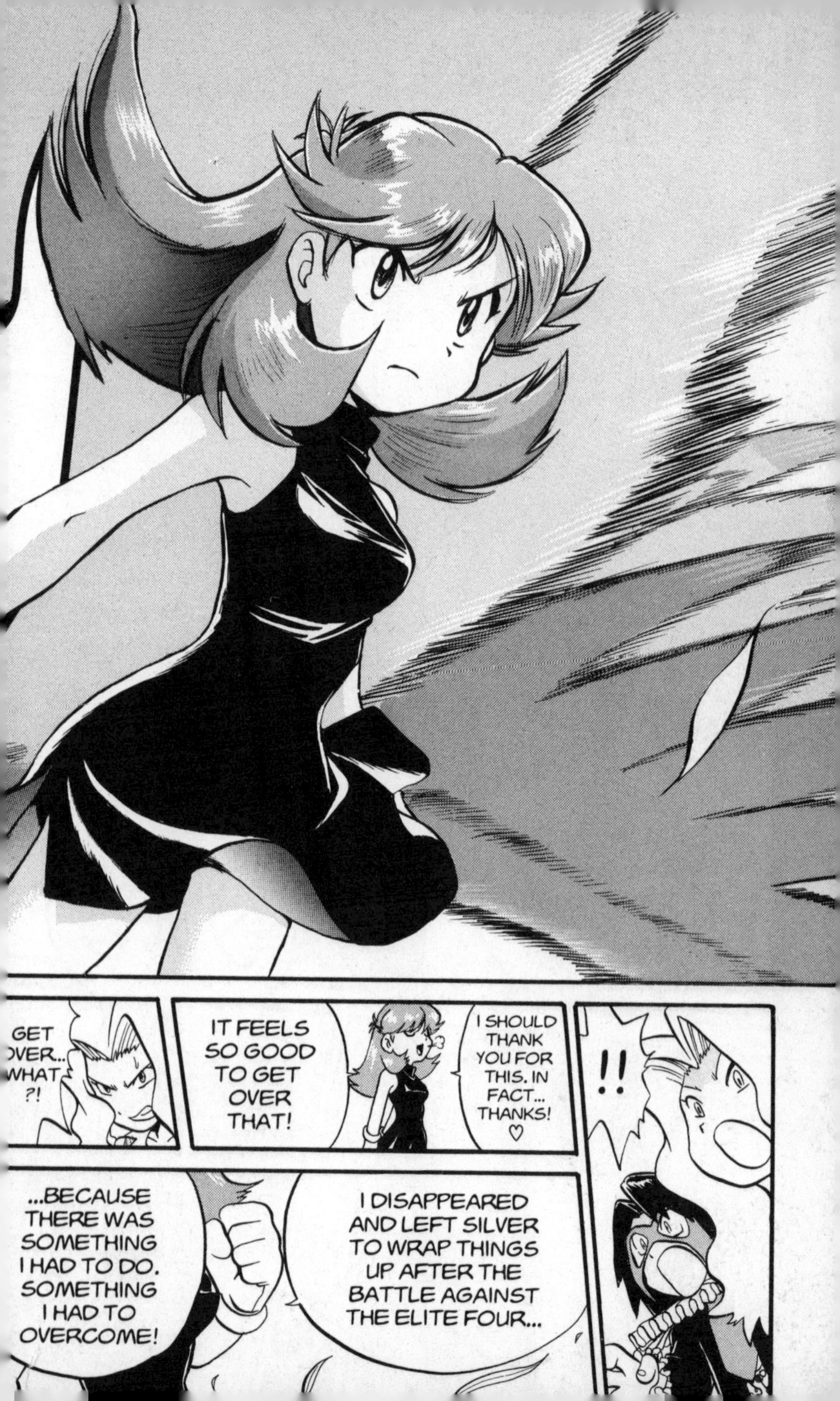
!!
I SHOULD THANK YOU FOR THIS. IN FACT... THANKS! ♡
IT FEELS SO GOOD TO GET OVER THAT!
GET VER... WHAT ?!
I DISAPPEARED AND LEFT SILVER TO WRAP THINGS UP AFTER THE BATTLE AGAINST THE ELITE FOUR...
...BECAUSE THERE WAS SOMETHING I HAD TO DO. SOMETHING I HAD TO OVERCOME!

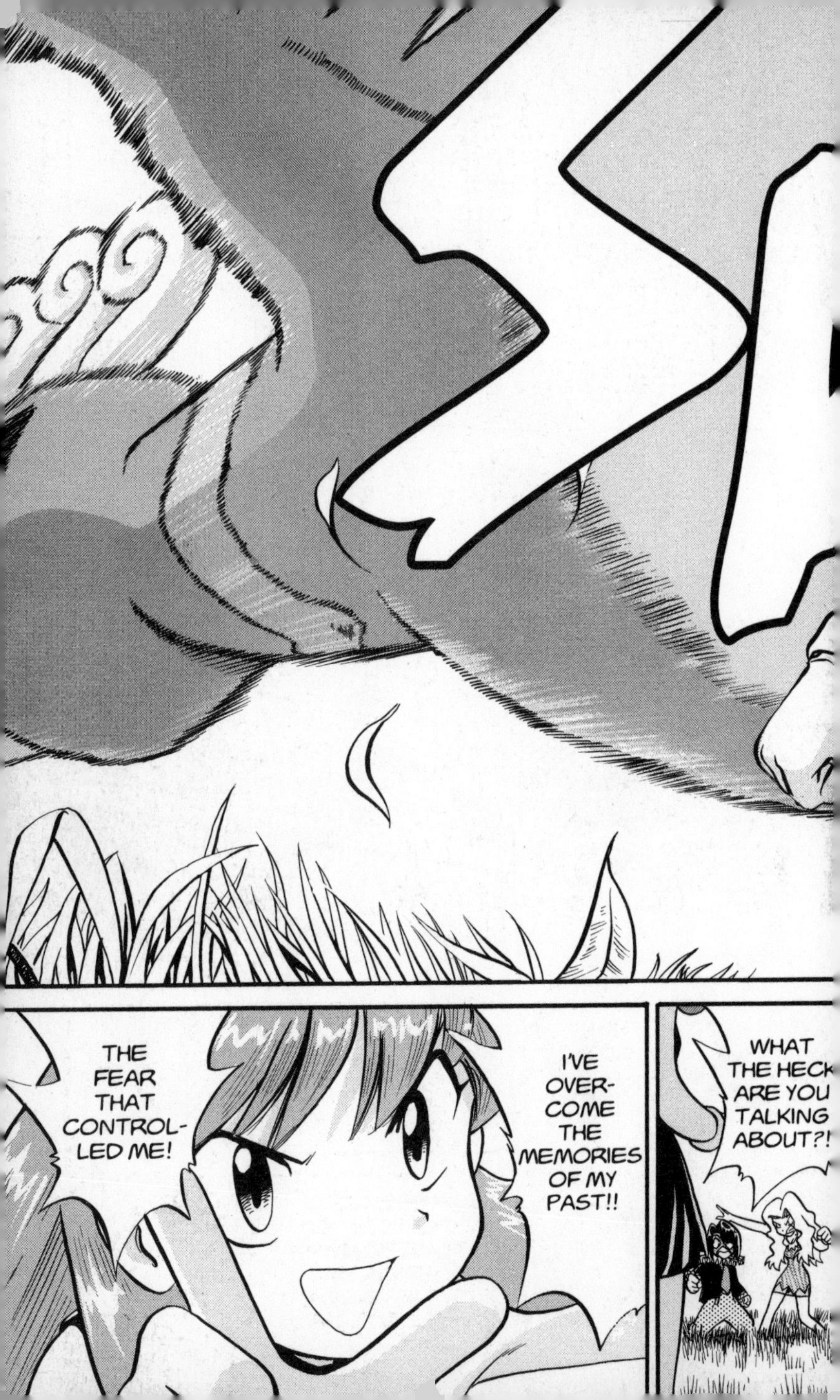
WHAT THE HECK ARE YOU TALKING ABOUT?!
I'VE OVER-COME THE MEMORIES OF MY PAST!!
THE FEAR THAT CONTROL-LED ME!

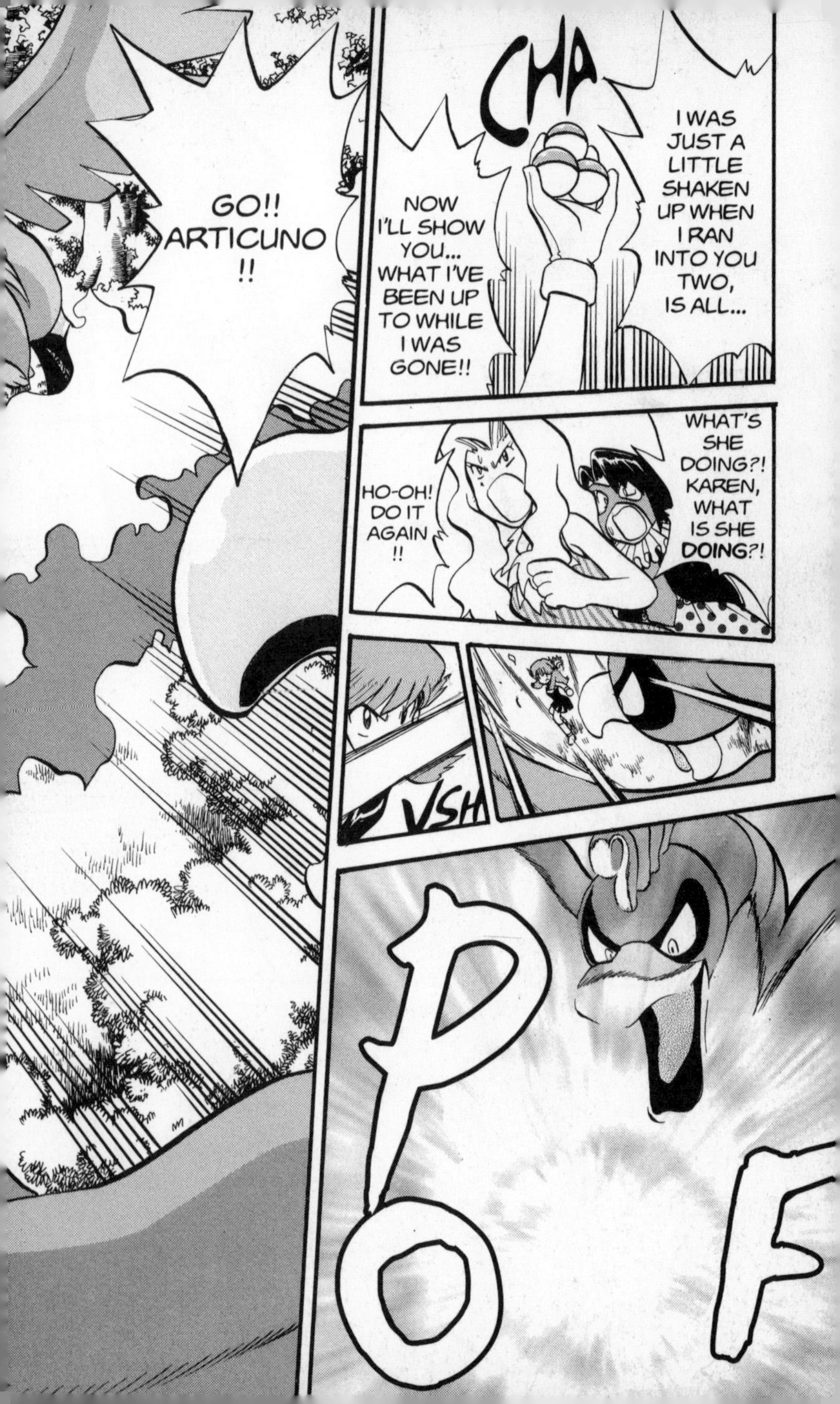
CHA
I WAS JUST A LITTLE SHAKEN UP WHEN I RAN INTO YOU TWO, IS ALL...
NOW I'LL SHOW YOU... WHAT I'VE BEEN UP TO WHILE I WAS GONE!!
WHAT'S SHE DOING?! KAREN, WHAT IS SHE DOING?!
HO-OH! DO IT AGAIN!!
VSH
POOF
GO!! ARTICUNO!!

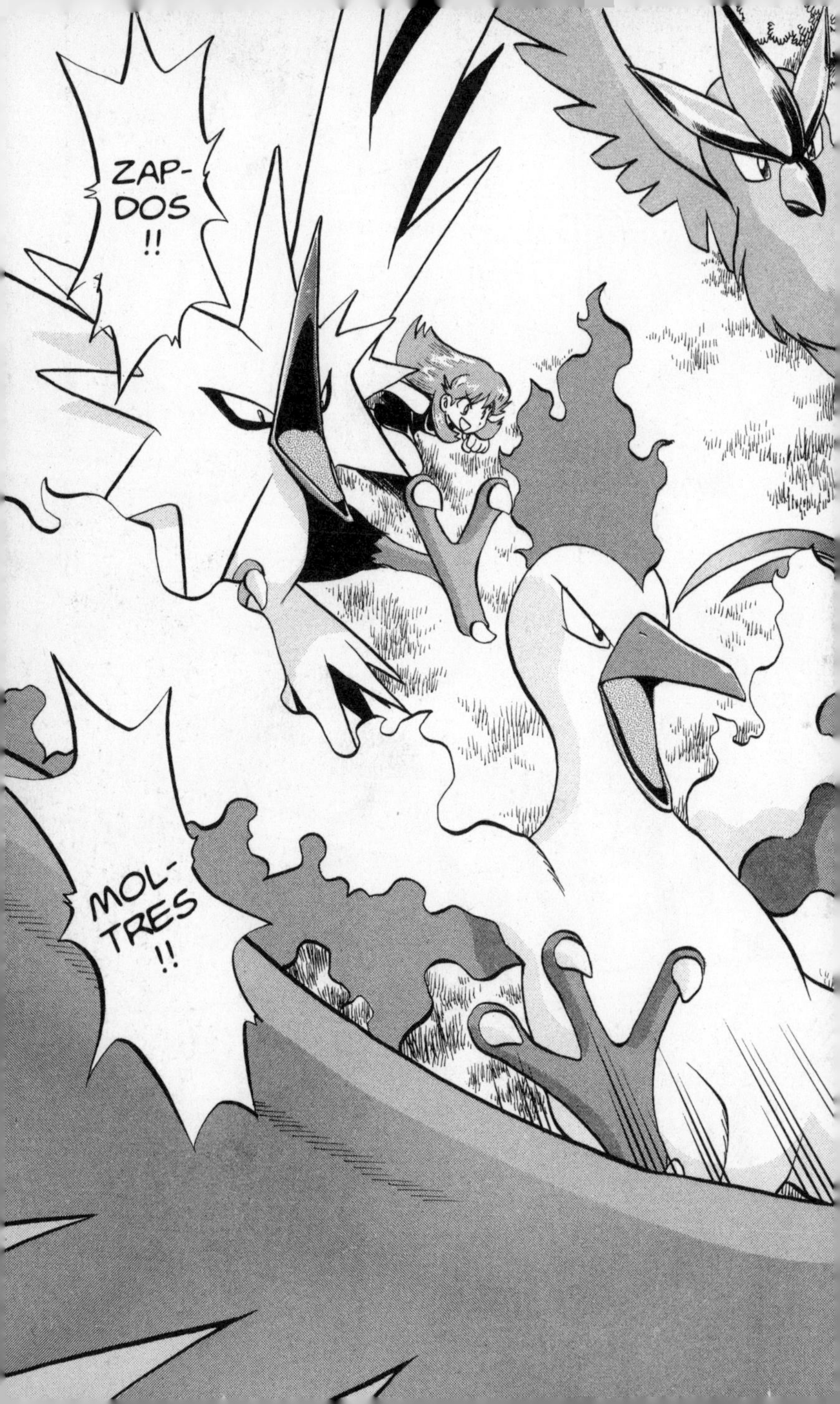
ZAP-
DOS
!!

MOL-
TRES
!!

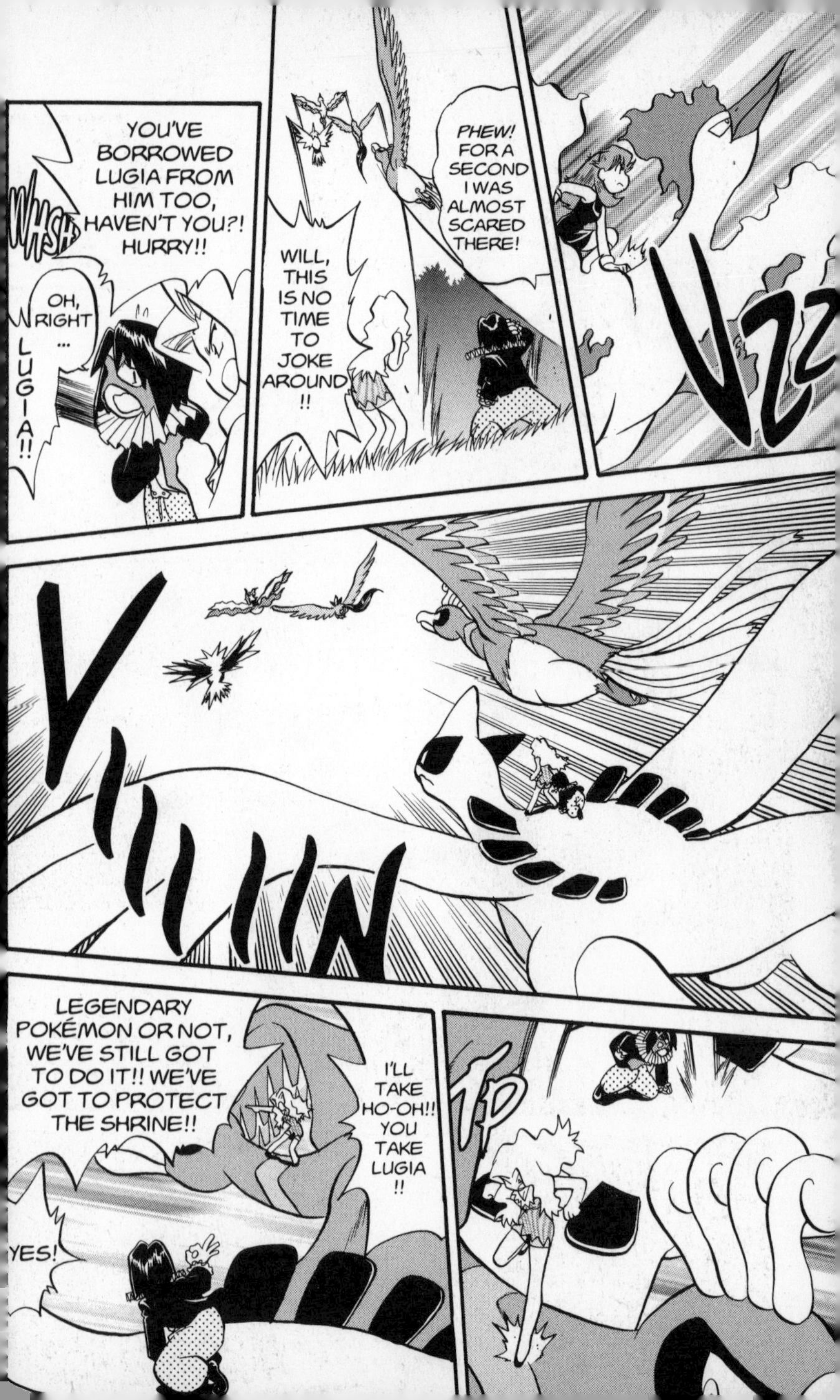
PHEW! FOR A SECOND I WAS ALMOST SCARED THERE!
WILL, THIS IS NO TIME TO JOKE AROUND!!
YOU'VE BORROWED LUGIA FROM HIM TOO, HAVEN'T YOU?! HURRY!!
WHSH
OH, RIGHT...
LUGIA!!
I'LL TAKE HO-OH!! YOU TAKE LUGIA!!
TP
LEGENDARY POKÉMON OR NOT, WE'VE STILL GOT TO DO IT!! WE'VE GOT TO PROTECT THE SHRINE!!
YES!

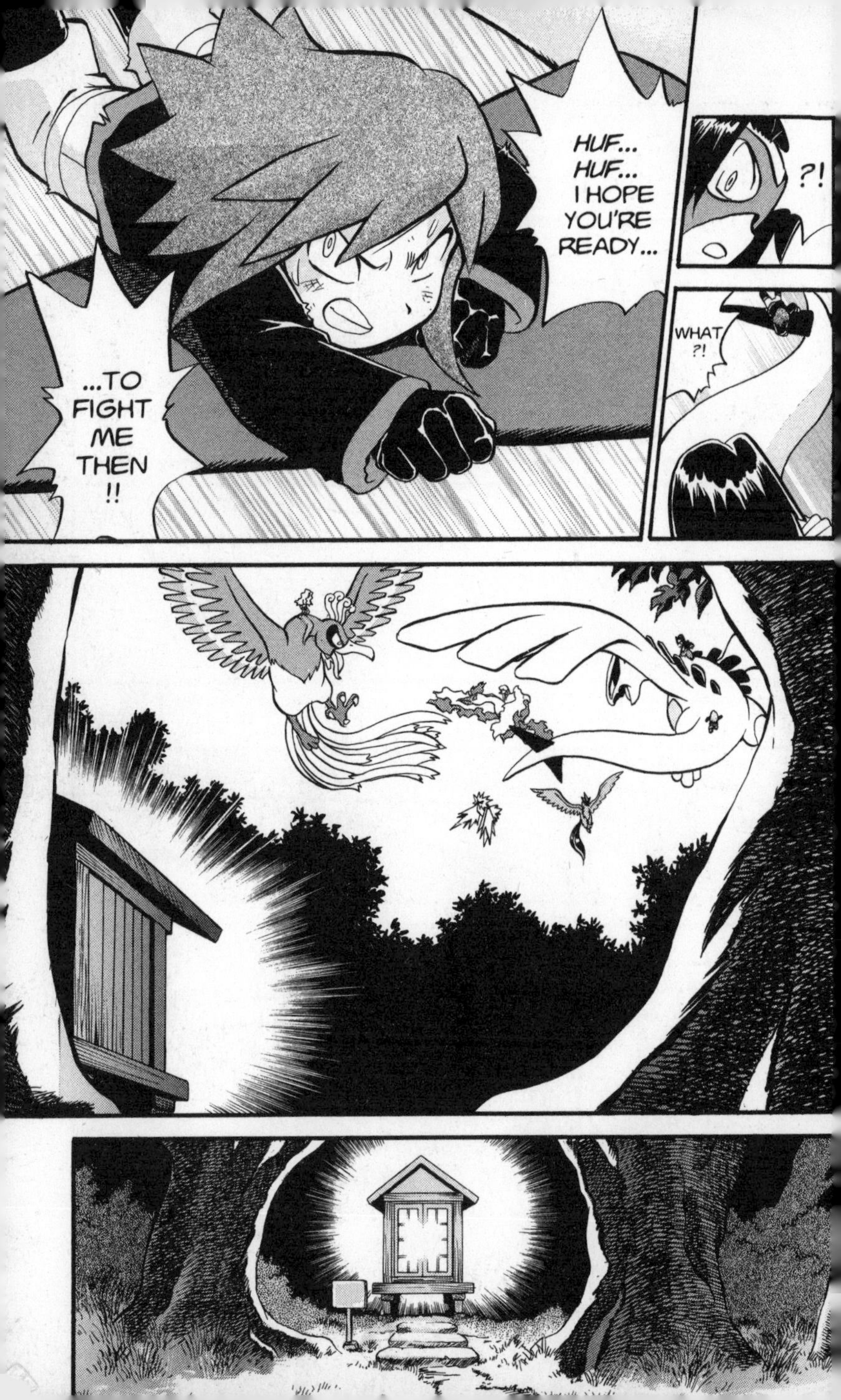
?!
WHAT ?!
HUF... HUF... I HOPE YOU'RE READY...
...TO FIGHT ME THEN !!

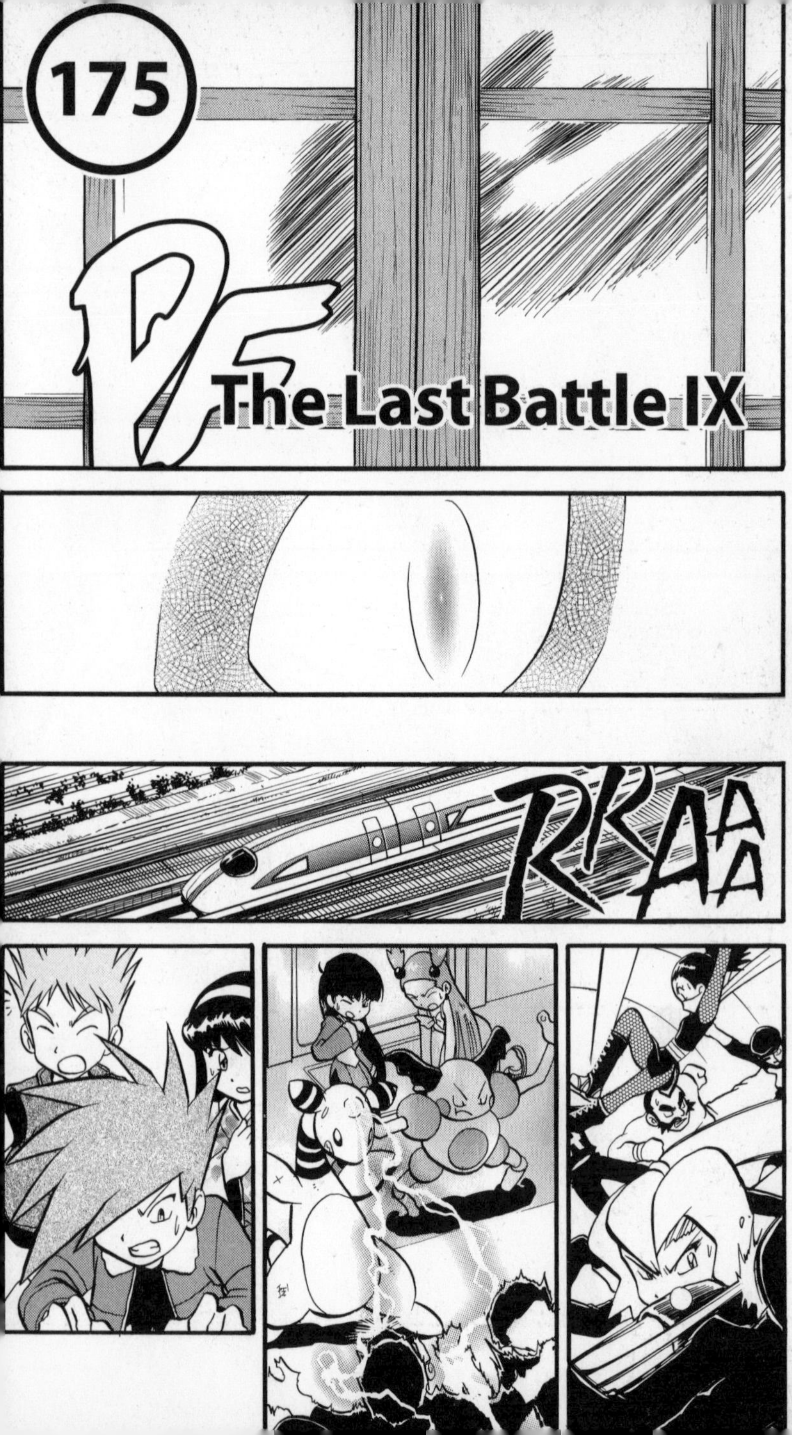
175
The Last Battle IX
RKAAA

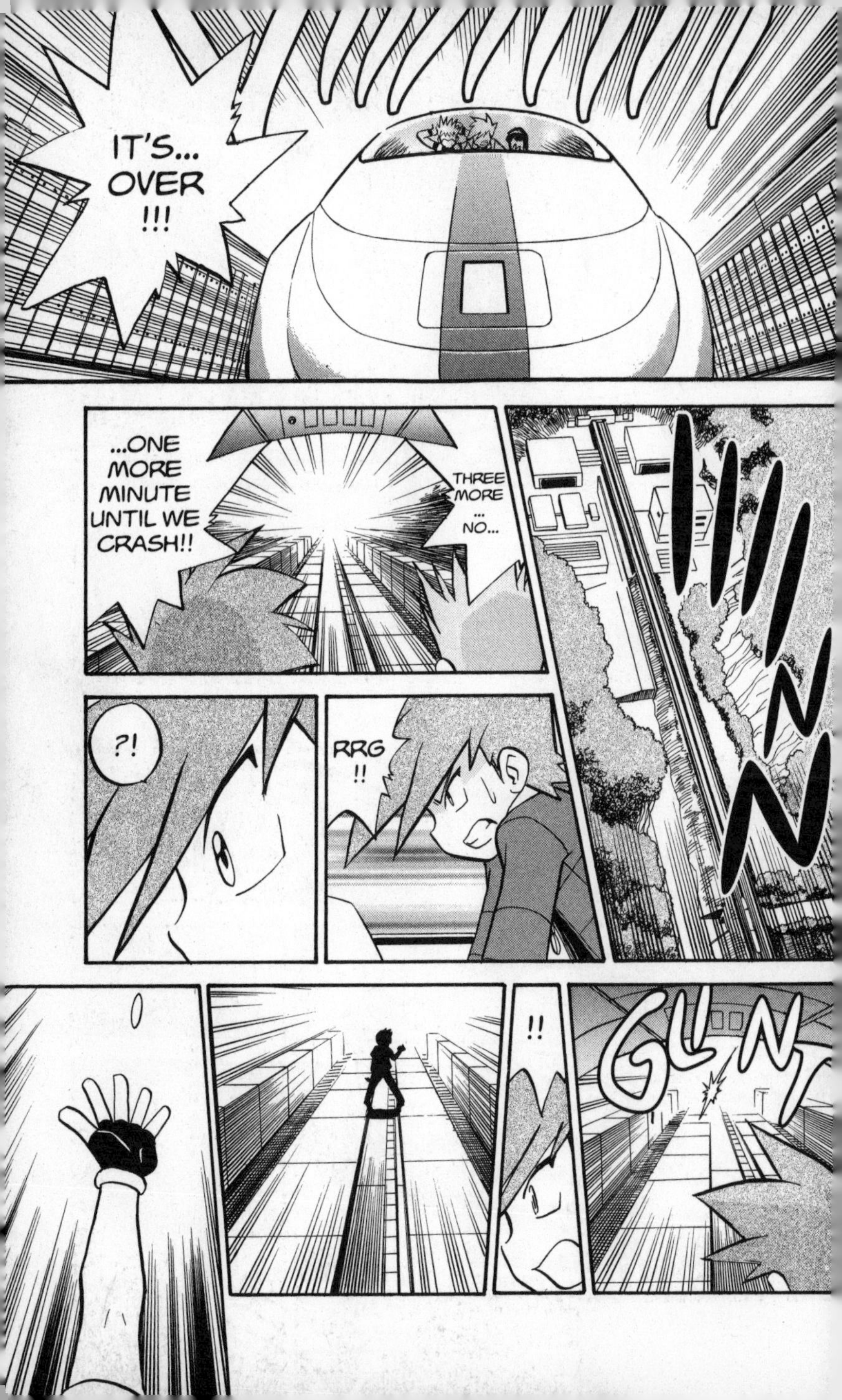
IT'S... OVER !!!
THREE MORE ... NO...
...ONE MORE MINUTE UNTIL WE CRASH!!
RRG !!
?!
GLINT
!!

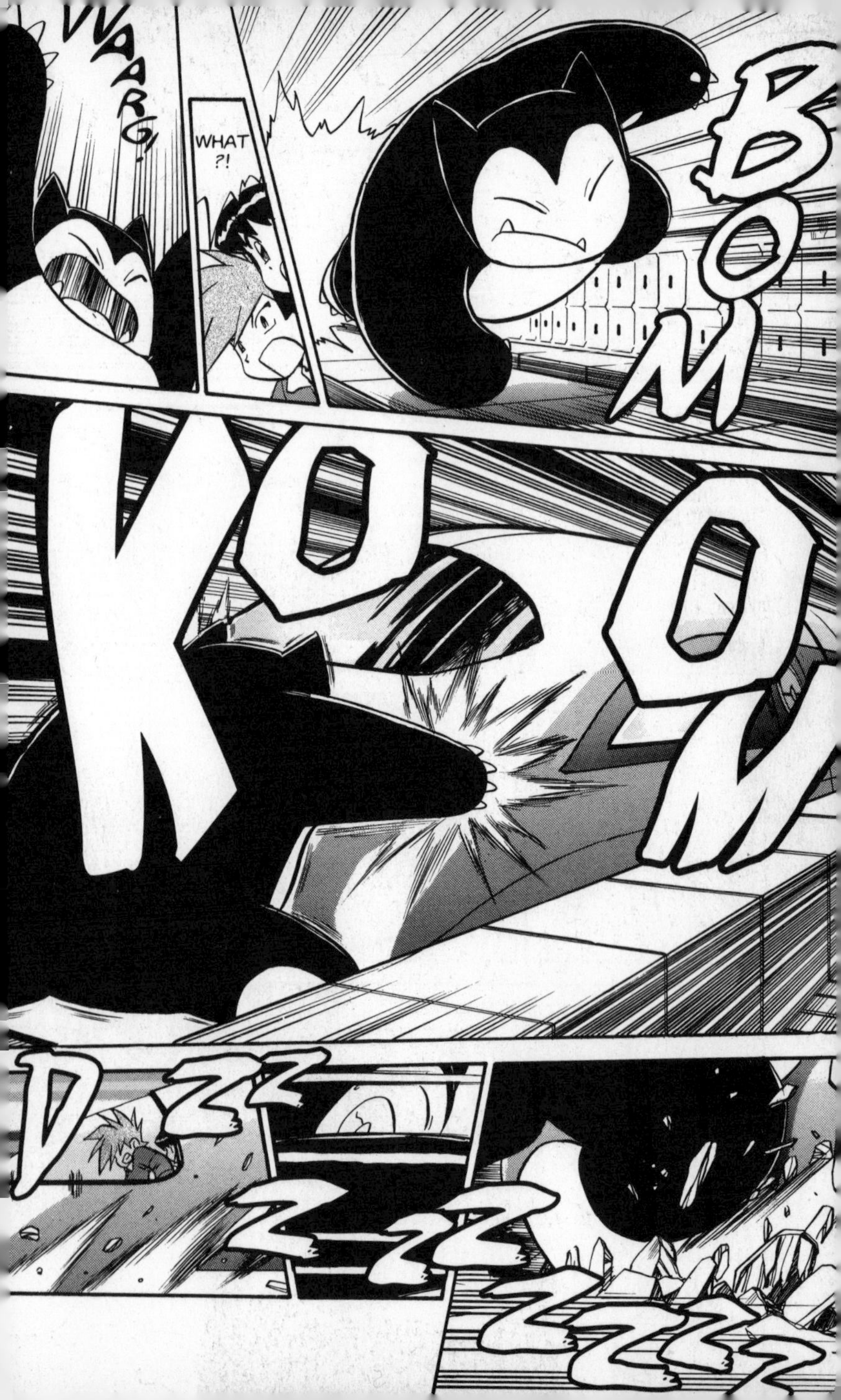
BOM
WHAT?!
VVAARG!
KOOM
DZZ
ZZZ
ZZZZZ

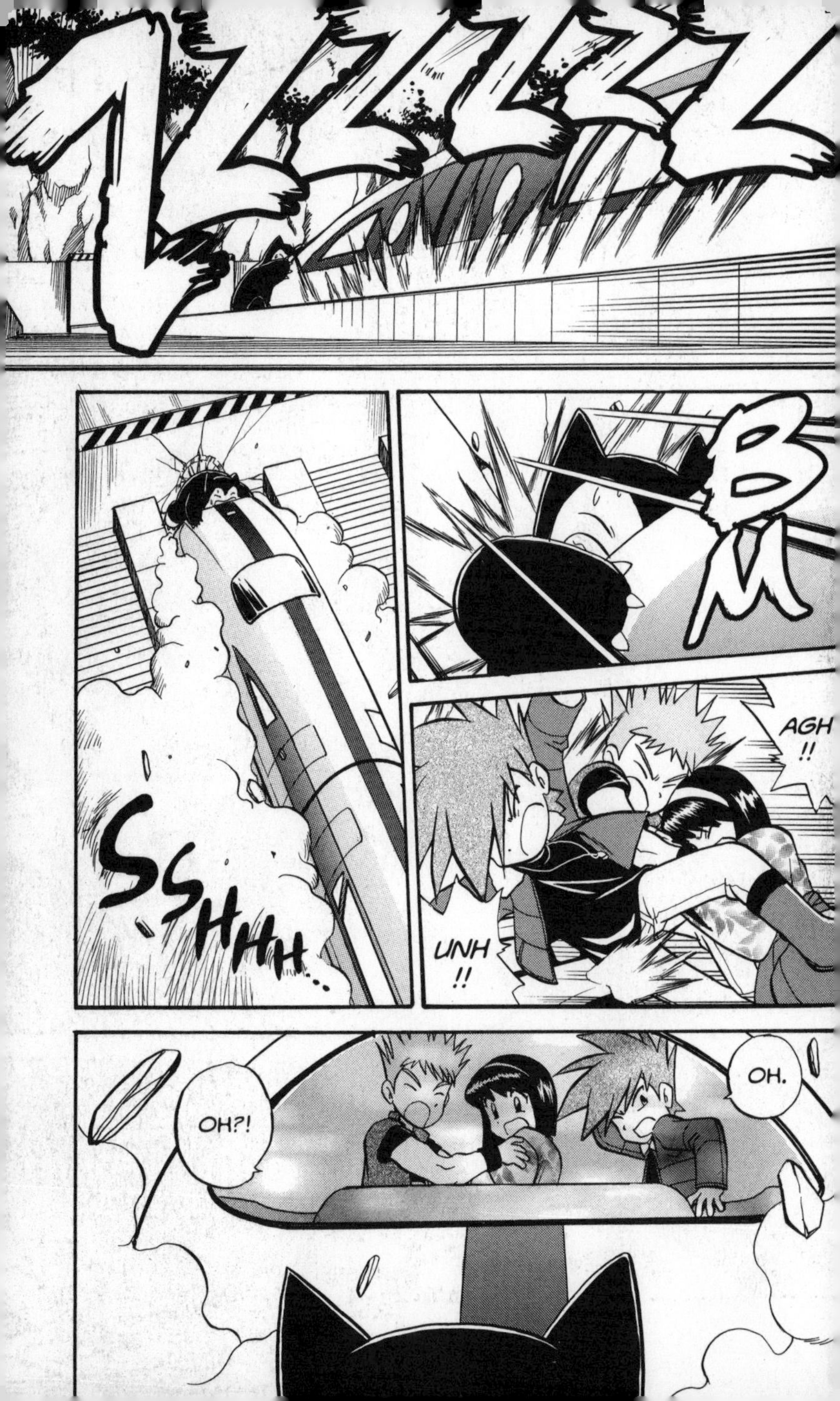

BM
AGH!!
UNH!!
SSHHH...
OH.
OH?!

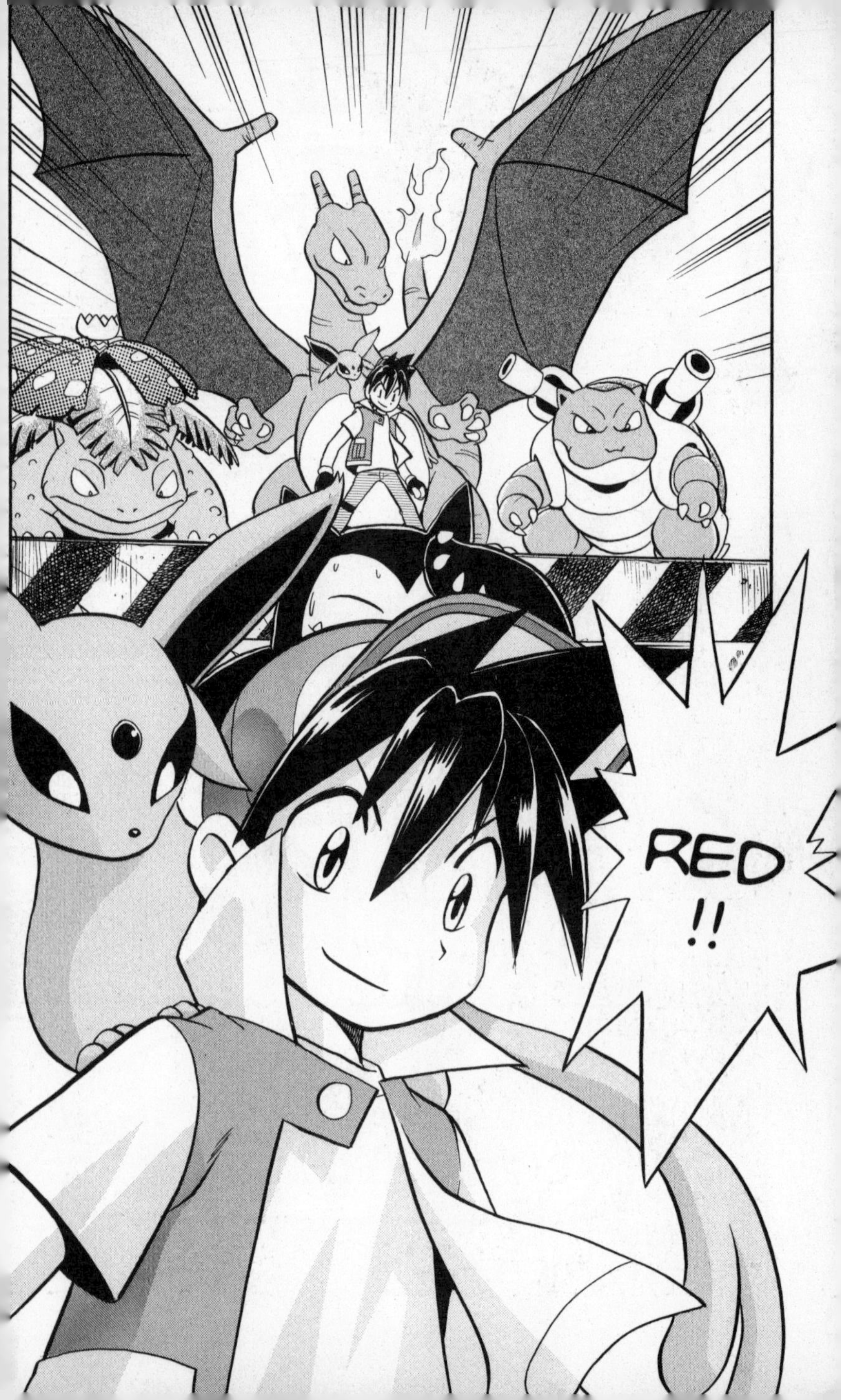
RED !!

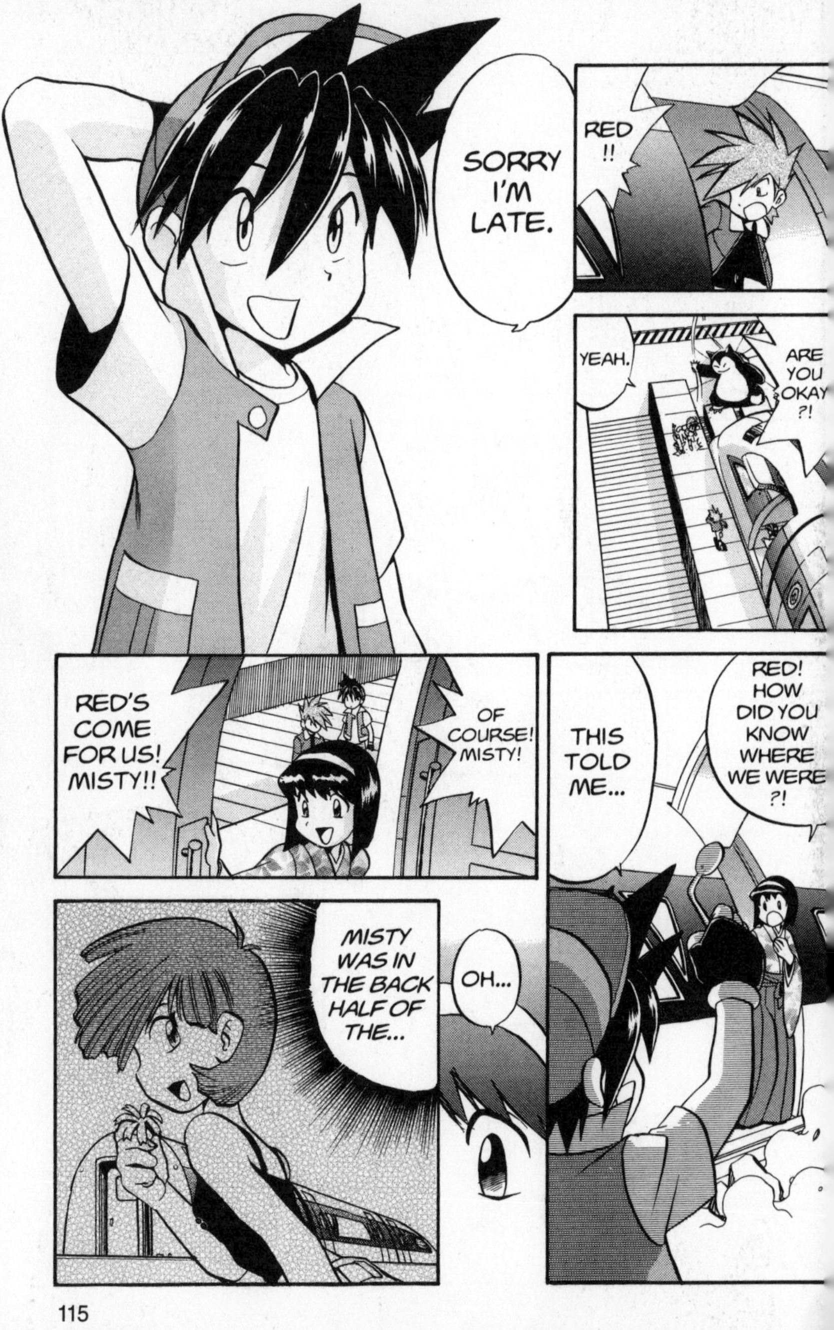
RED !!
ARE YOU OKAY ?!
YEAH.
SORRY I'M LATE.
RED! HOW DID YOU KNOW WHERE WE WERE ?!
THIS TOLD ME...
OF COURSE! MISTY!
RED'S COME FOR US! MISTY!!
OH...
MISTY WAS IN THE BACK HALF OF THE...

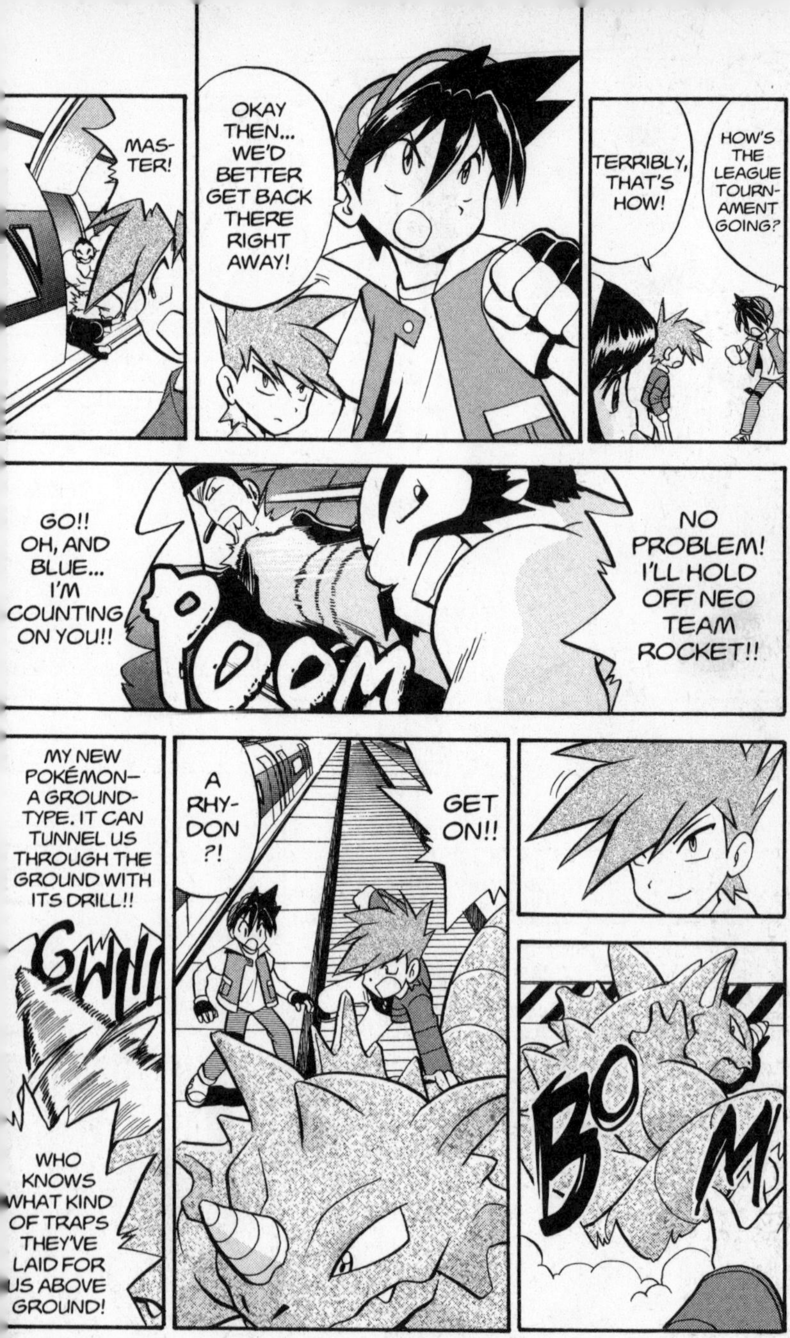
HOW'S THE LEAGUE TOURNAMENT GOING?
TERRIBLY, THAT'S HOW!
OKAY THEN... WE'D BETTER GET BACK THERE RIGHT AWAY!
MASTER!
NO PROBLEM! I'LL HOLD OFF NEO TEAM ROCKET!!
POOM
GO!! OH, AND BLUE... I'M COUNTING ON YOU!!
BOOM
GET ON!!
A RHYDON?!
MY NEW POKÉMON—A GROUND-TYPE. IT CAN TUNNEL US THROUGH THE GROUND WITH ITS DRILL!!
WHO KNOWS WHAT KIND OF TRAPS THEY'VE LAID FOR US ABOVE GROUND!

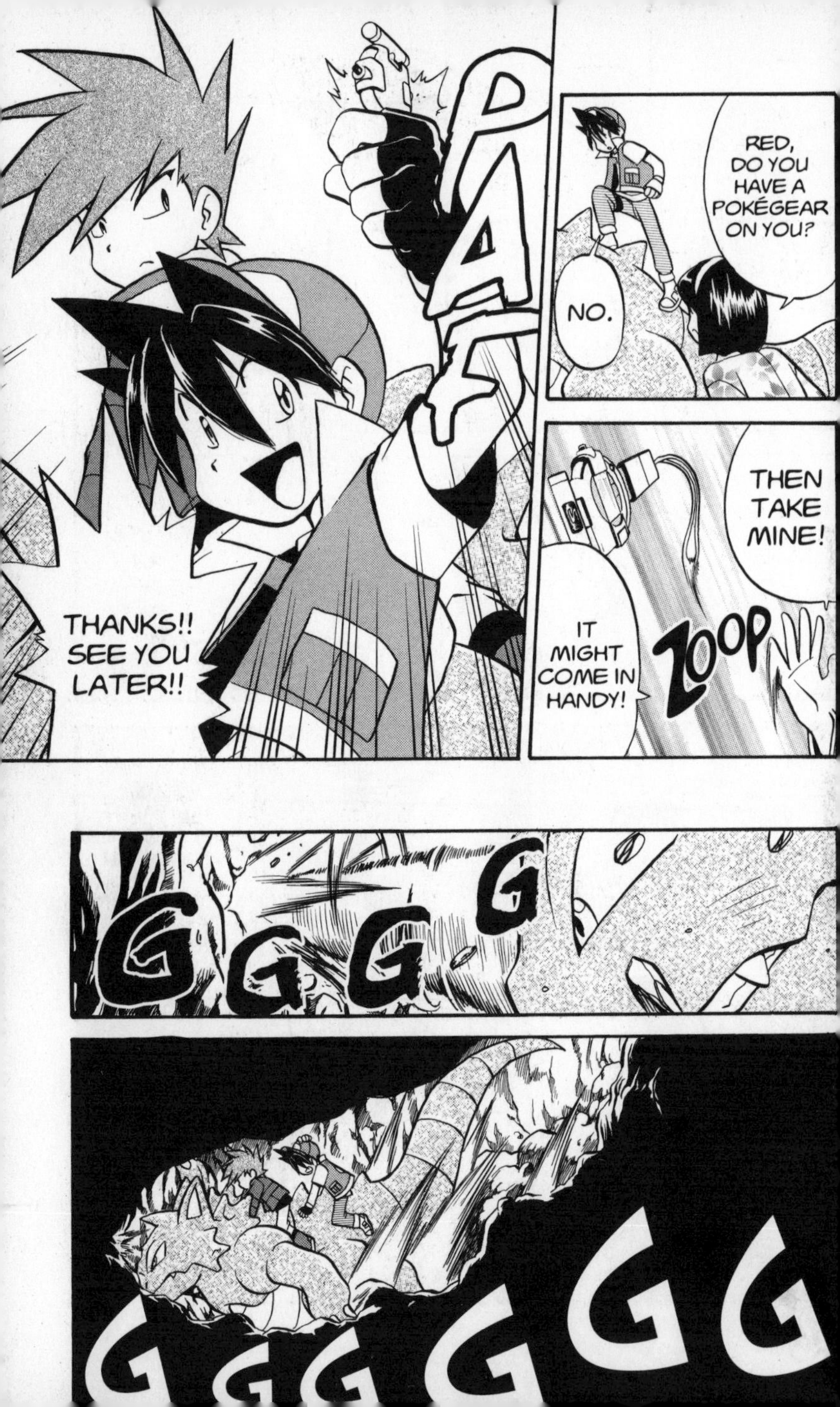
RED, DO YOU HAVE A POKÉGEAR ON YOU?
NO.
THEN TAKE MINE!
IT MIGHT COME IN HANDY!
ZOOP
PA
THANKS!! SEE YOU LATER!!
GGGG
GGGGGG

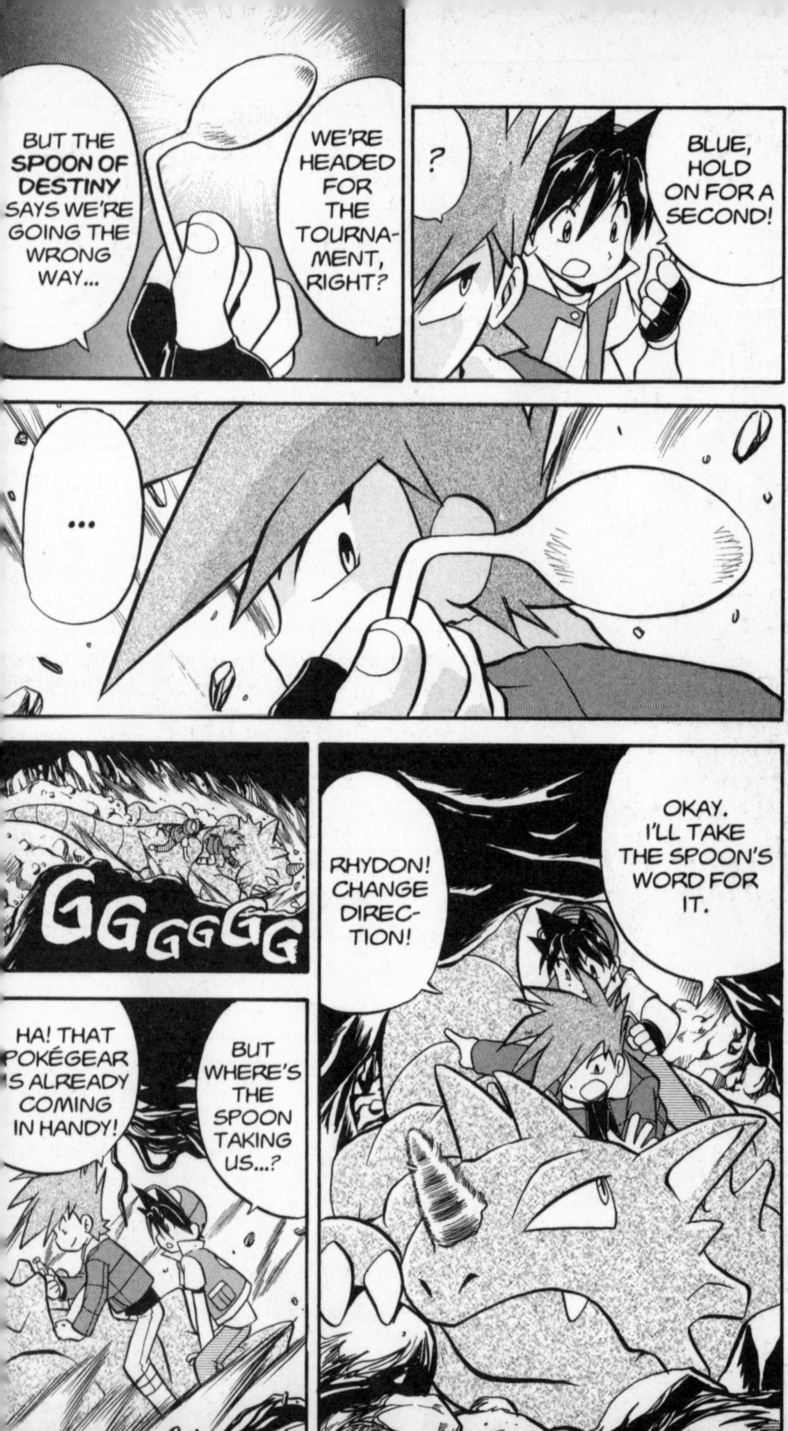
BLUE, HOLD ON FOR A SECOND!
?
WE'RE HEADED FOR THE TOURNAMENT, RIGHT?
BUT THE **SPOON OF DESTINY** SAYS WE'RE GOING THE WRONG WAY...
...
OKAY. I'LL TAKE THE SPOON'S WORD FOR IT.
RHYDON! CHANGE DIRECTION!
GGGGGG
BUT WHERE'S THE SPOON TAKING US...?
HA! THAT POKÉGEAR IS ALREADY COMING IN HANDY!

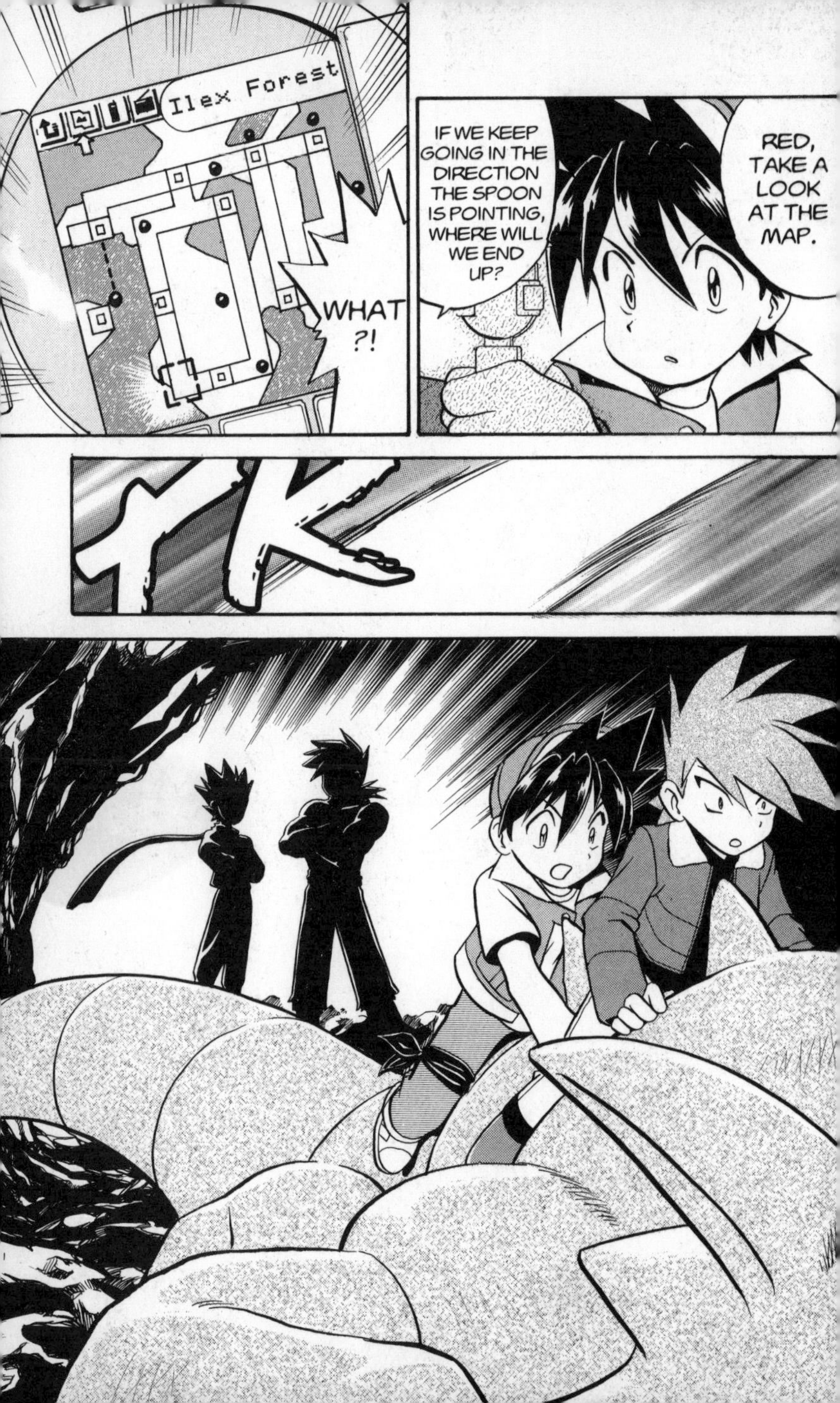
RED, TAKE A LOOK AT THE MAP.
IF WE KEEP GOING IN THE DIRECTION THE SPOON IS POINTING, WHERE WILL WE END UP?
Ilex Forest
WHAT ?!

# 176 The Last Battle X

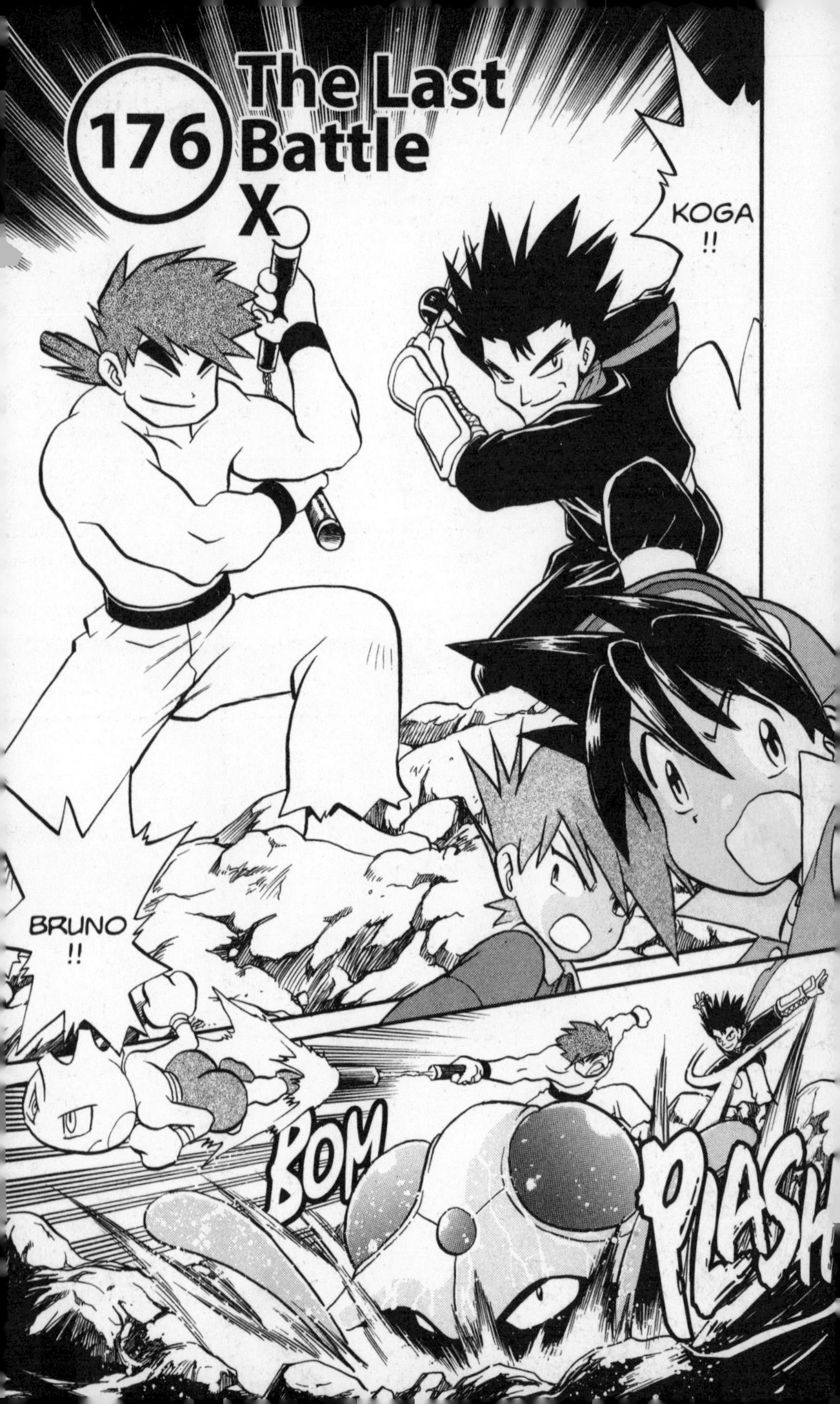
KOGA !!
BRUNO !!
PLASH
BOM

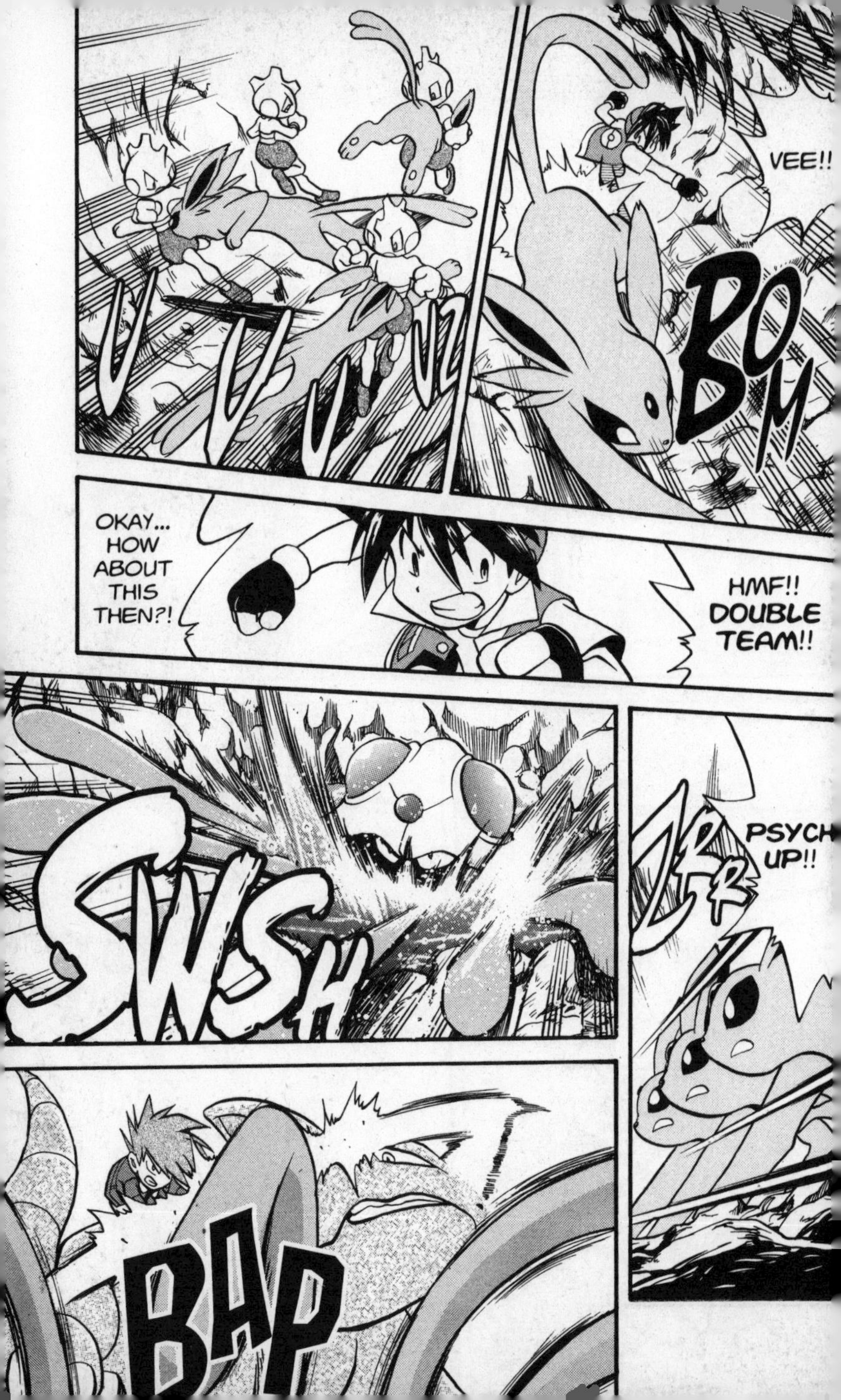
VEE!!
OKAY... HOW ABOUT THIS THEN?!
HMF!! DOUBLE TEAM!!
PSYCH UP!!
SWSH
BAP

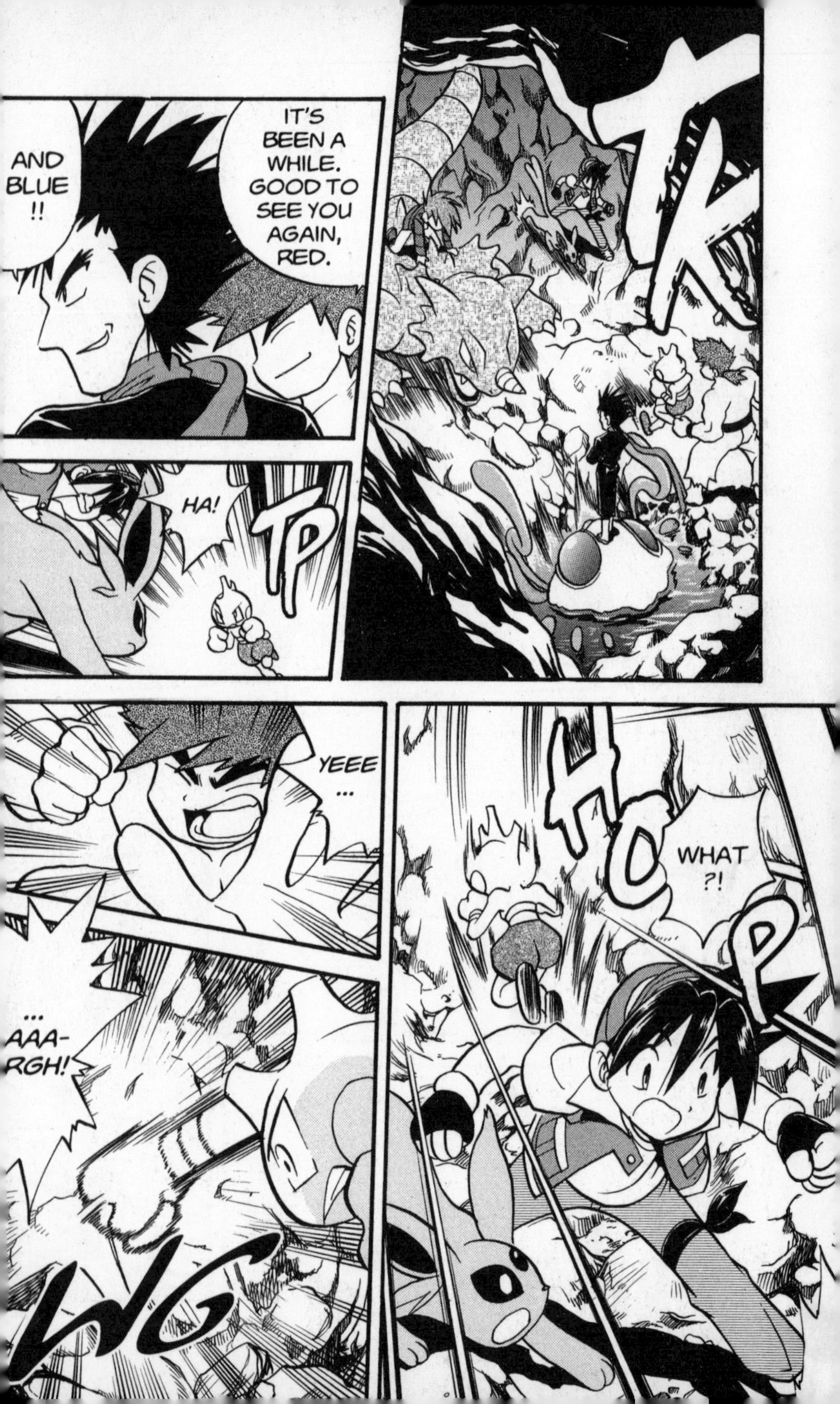
IT'S BEEN A WHILE. GOOD TO SEE YOU AGAIN, RED.
AND BLUE!!
HA!
HOP
WHAT?!
YEEE...
...AAA-RGH!

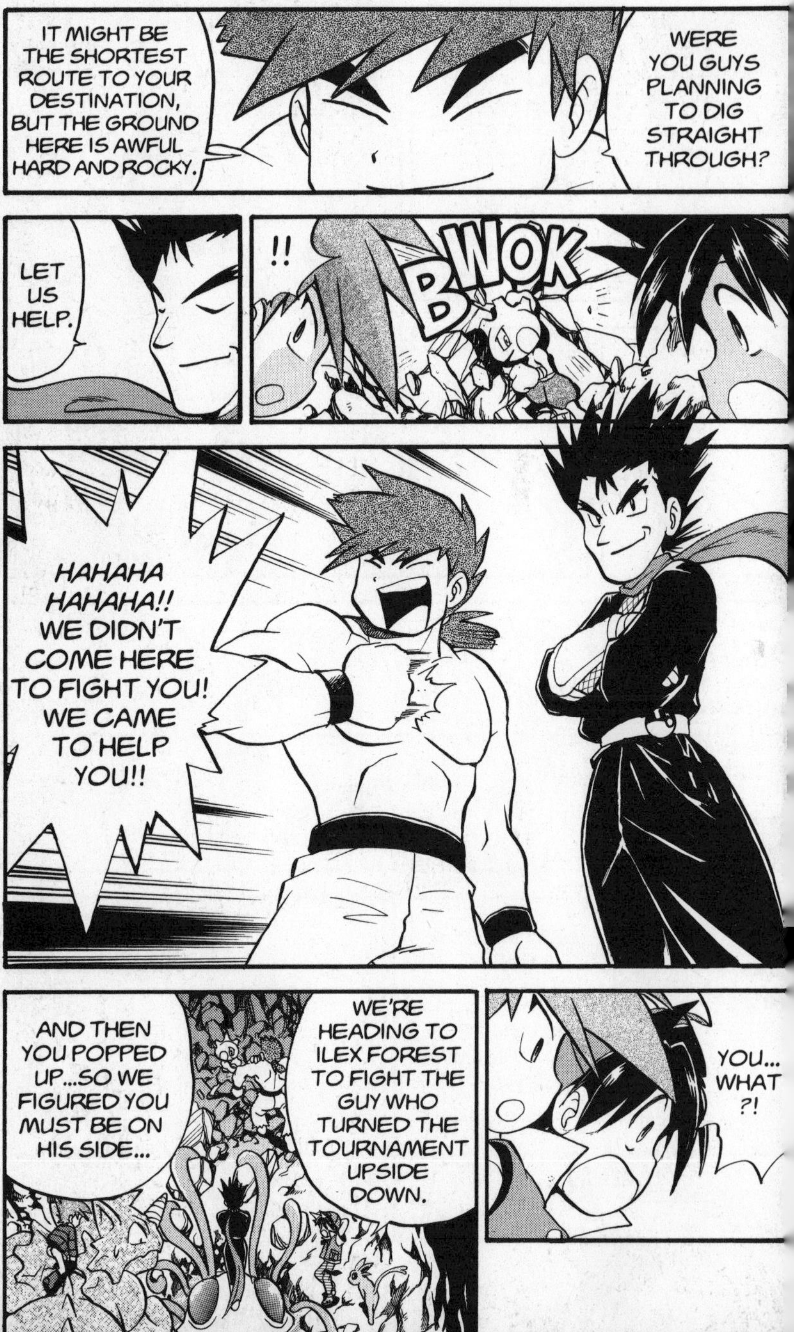
WERE YOU GUYS PLANNING TO DIG STRAIGHT THROUGH?
IT MIGHT BE THE SHORTEST ROUTE TO YOUR DESTINATION, BUT THE GROUND HERE IS AWFUL HARD AND ROCKY.
BWOK
!!
LET US HELP.
HAHAHA HAHAHA!! WE DIDN'T COME HERE TO FIGHT YOU! WE CAME TO HELP YOU!!
YOU... WHAT?!
WE'RE HEADING TO ILEX FOREST TO FIGHT THE GUY WHO TURNED THE TOURNAMENT UPSIDE DOWN.
AND THEN YOU POPPED UP...SO WE FIGURED YOU MUST BE ON HIS SIDE...

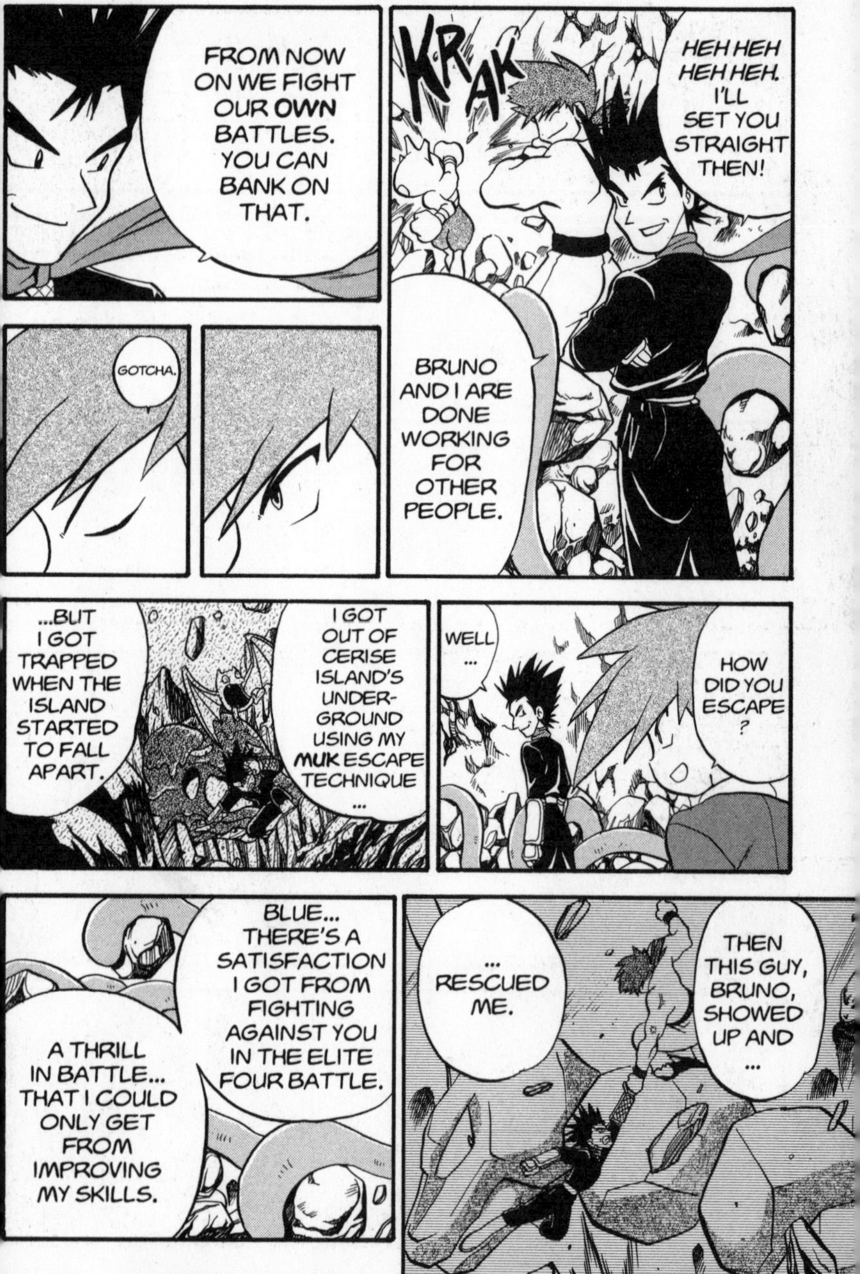
KRAK
HEH HEH HEH HEH. I'LL SET YOU STRAIGHT THEN!
BRUNO AND I ARE DONE WORKING FOR OTHER PEOPLE.
FROM NOW ON WE FIGHT OUR **OWN** BATTLES. YOU CAN BANK ON THAT.
GOTCHA.
HOW DID YOU ESCAPE?
WELL ...
I GOT OUT OF CERISE ISLAND'S UNDER-GROUND USING MY **MUK** ESCAPE TECHNIQUE ...
...BUT I GOT TRAPPED WHEN THE ISLAND STARTED TO FALL APART.
THEN THIS GUY, BRUNO, SHOWED UP AND ...
... RESCUED ME.
BLUE... THERE'S A SATISFACTION I GOT FROM FIGHTING AGAINST YOU IN THE ELITE FOUR BATTLE.
A THRILL IN BATTLE... THAT I COULD ONLY GET FROM IMPROVING MY SKILLS.

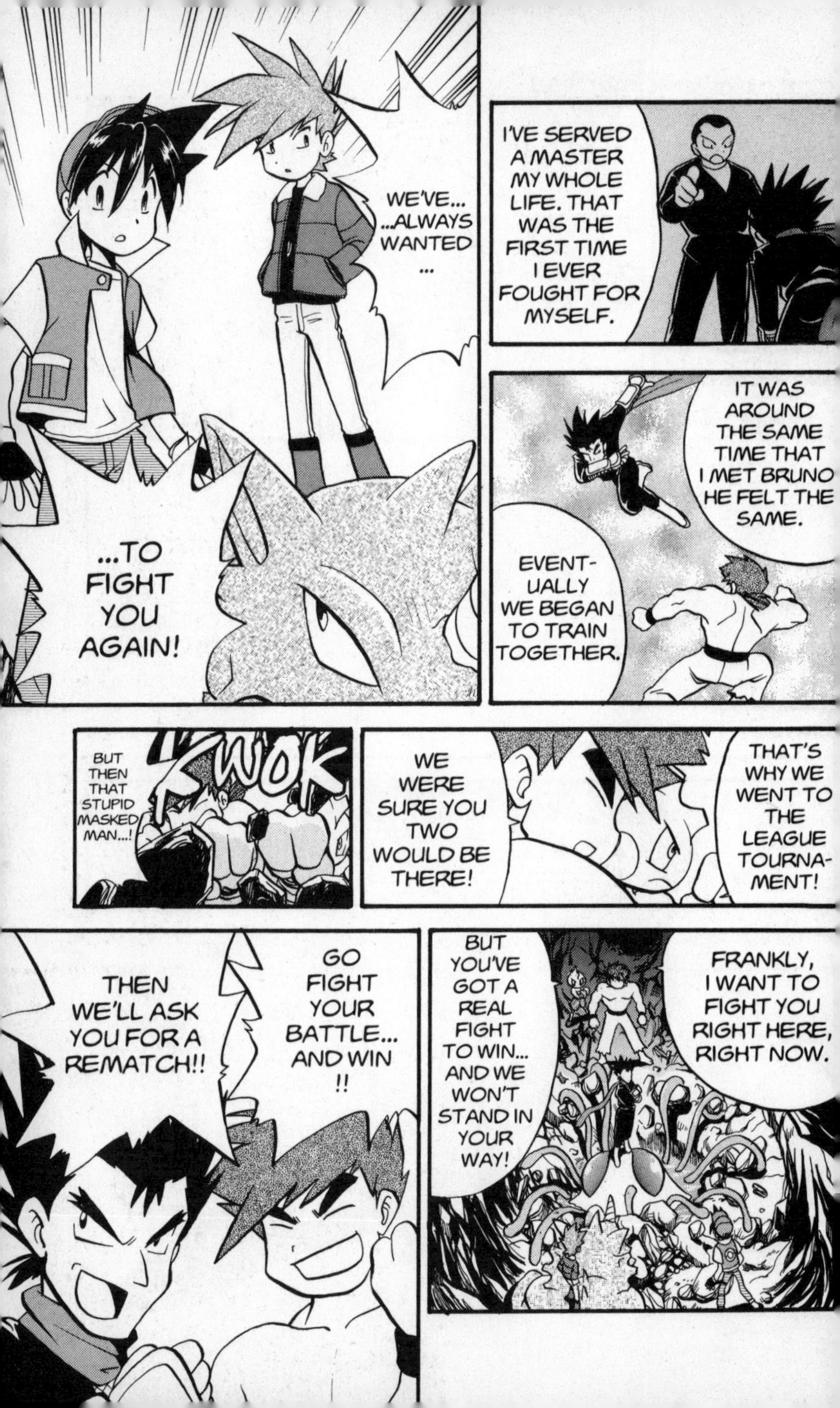
I'VE SERVED A MASTER MY WHOLE LIFE. THAT WAS THE FIRST TIME I EVER FOUGHT FOR MYSELF.
IT WAS AROUND THE SAME TIME THAT I MET BRUNO HE FELT THE SAME.
EVENT-UALLY WE BEGAN TO TRAIN TOGETHER.
WE'VE... ...ALWAYS WANTED ...
...TO FIGHT YOU AGAIN!
THAT'S WHY WE WENT TO THE LEAGUE TOURNA-MENT!
WE WERE SURE YOU TWO WOULD BE THERE!
BUT THEN THAT STUPID MASKED MAN...!
FRANKLY, I WANT TO FIGHT YOU RIGHT HERE, RIGHT NOW.
BUT YOU'VE GOT A REAL FIGHT TO WIN... AND WE WON'T STAND IN YOUR WAY!
GO FIGHT YOUR BATTLE... AND WIN !!
THEN WE'LL ASK YOU FOR A REMATCH!!

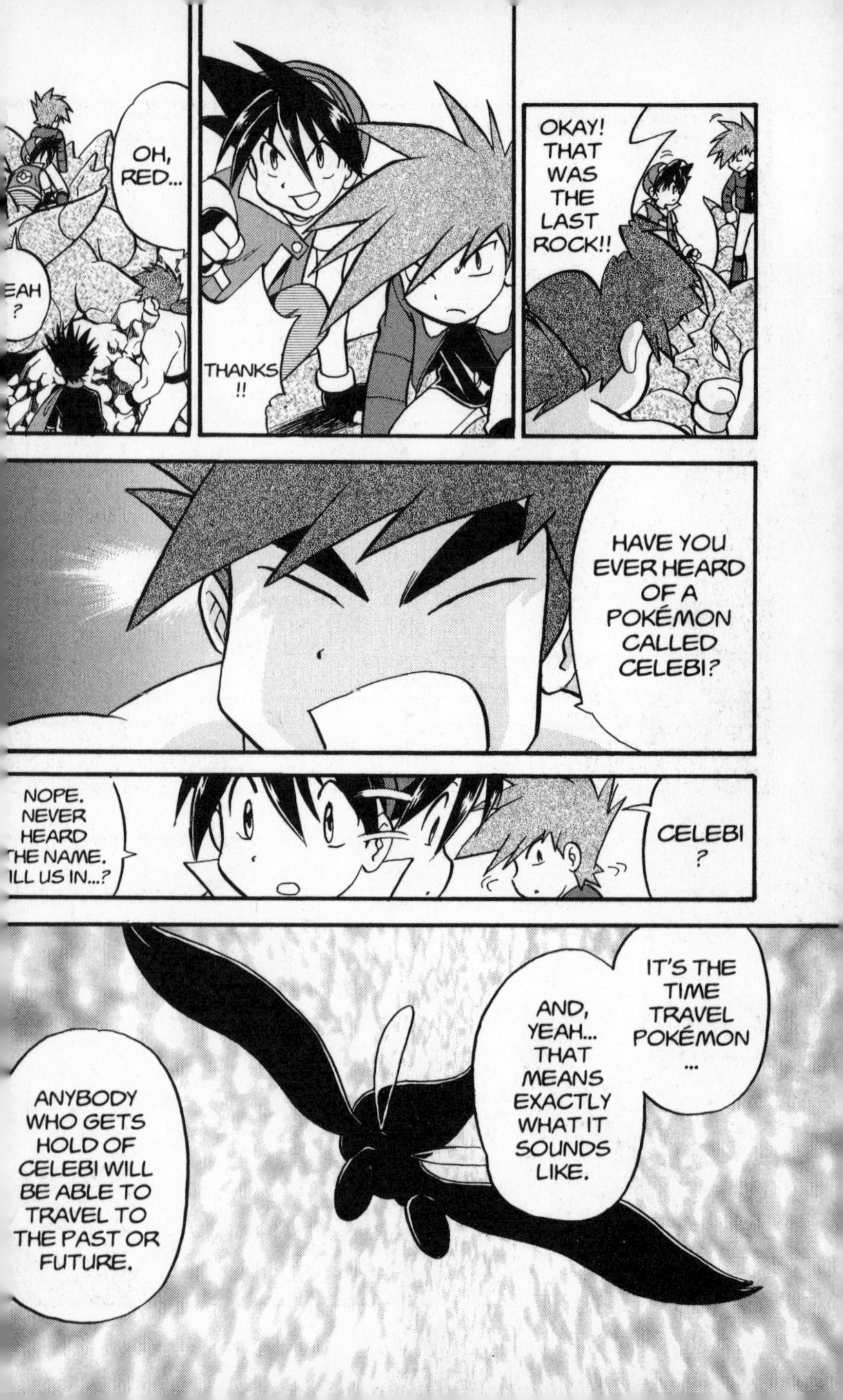
OKAY! THAT WAS THE LAST ROCK!!
THANKS !!
OH, RED...
EAH ?
HAVE YOU EVER HEARD OF A POKÉMON CALLED CELEBI?
CELEBI ?
NOPE. NEVER HEARD THE NAME. ILL US IN...?
IT'S THE TIME TRAVEL POKÉMON ...
AND, YEAH... THAT MEANS EXACTLY WHAT IT SOUNDS LIKE.
ANYBODY WHO GETS HOLD OF CELEBI WILL BE ABLE TO TRAVEL TO THE PAST OR FUTURE.

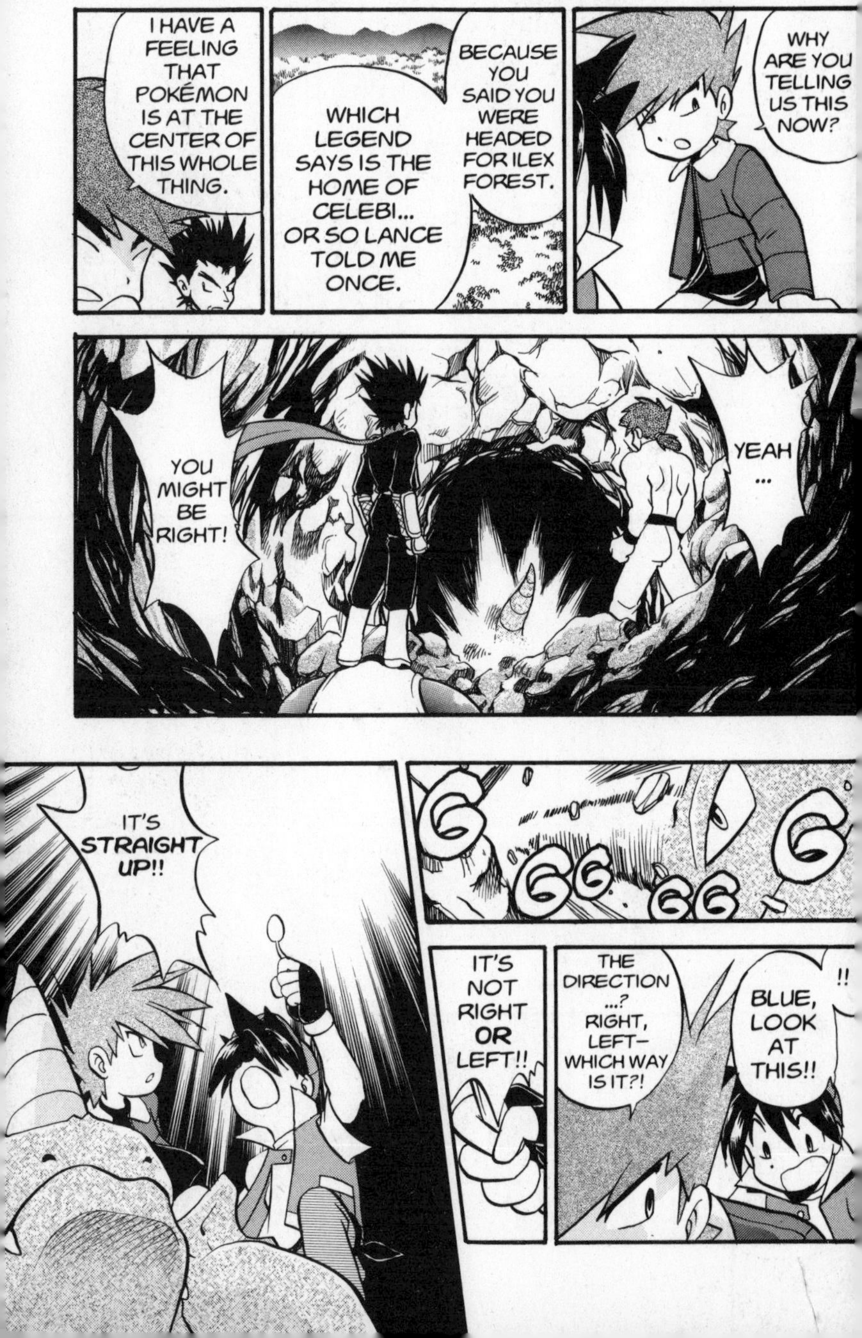
WHY ARE YOU TELLING US THIS NOW?
BECAUSE YOU SAID YOU WERE HEADED FOR ILEX FOREST.
WHICH LEGEND SAYS IS THE HOME OF CELEBI... OR SO LANCE TOLD ME ONCE.
I HAVE A FEELING THAT POKÉMON IS AT THE CENTER OF THIS WHOLE THING.
YEAH ...
YOU MIGHT BE RIGHT!
G
GG
GG
G
!!
BLUE, LOOK AT THIS!!
THE DIRECTION ...? RIGHT, LEFT— WHICH WAY IS IT?!
IT'S NOT RIGHT **OR** LEFT!!
IT'S **STRAIGHT UP!!**

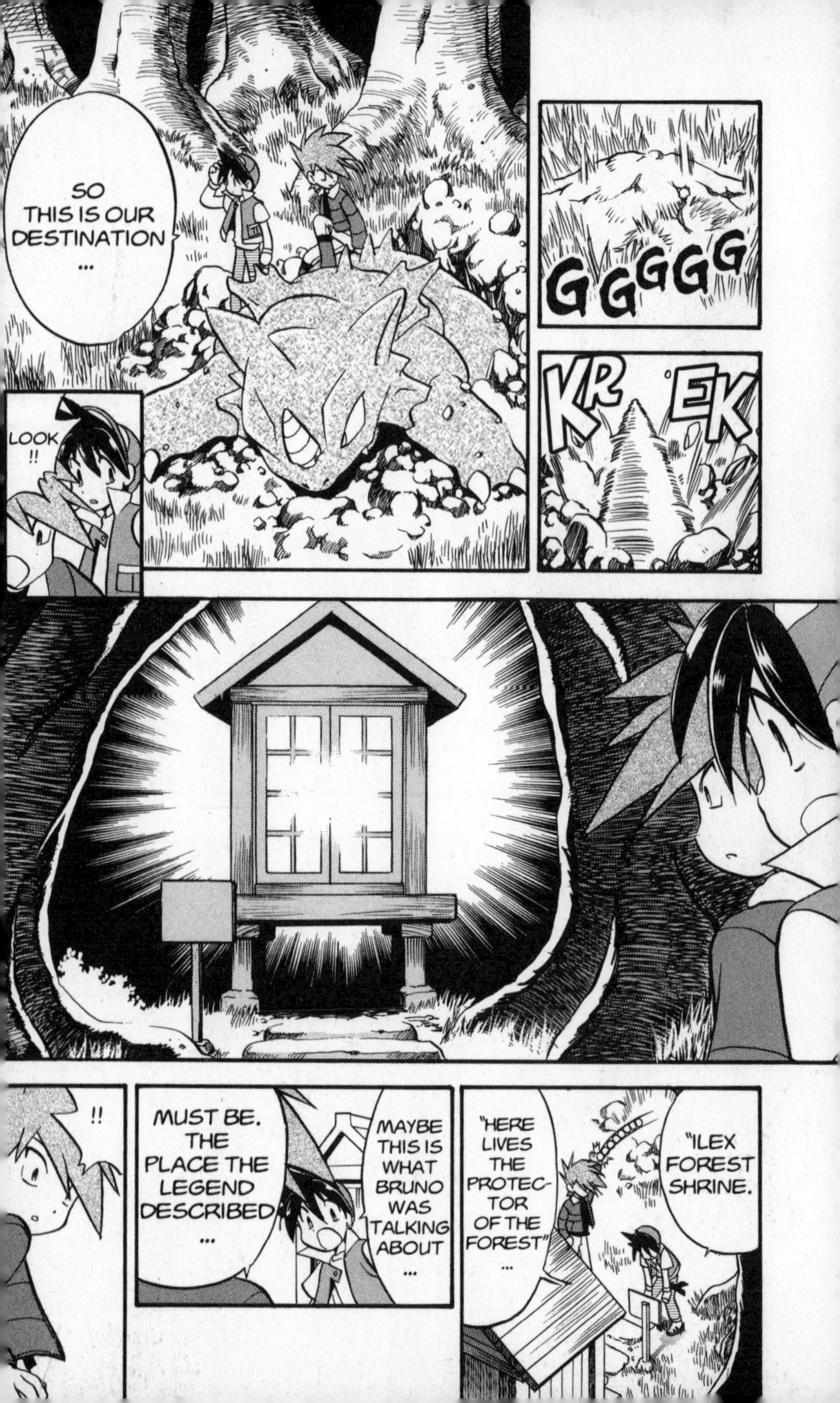
GGGGG
KREK
SO THIS IS OUR DESTINATION ...
LOOK !!
"ILEX FOREST SHRINE.
"HERE LIVES THE PROTECTOR OF THE FOREST" ...
MAYBE THIS IS WHAT BRUNO WAS TALKING ABOUT ...
MUST BE. THE PLACE THE LEGEND DESCRIBED ...
!!

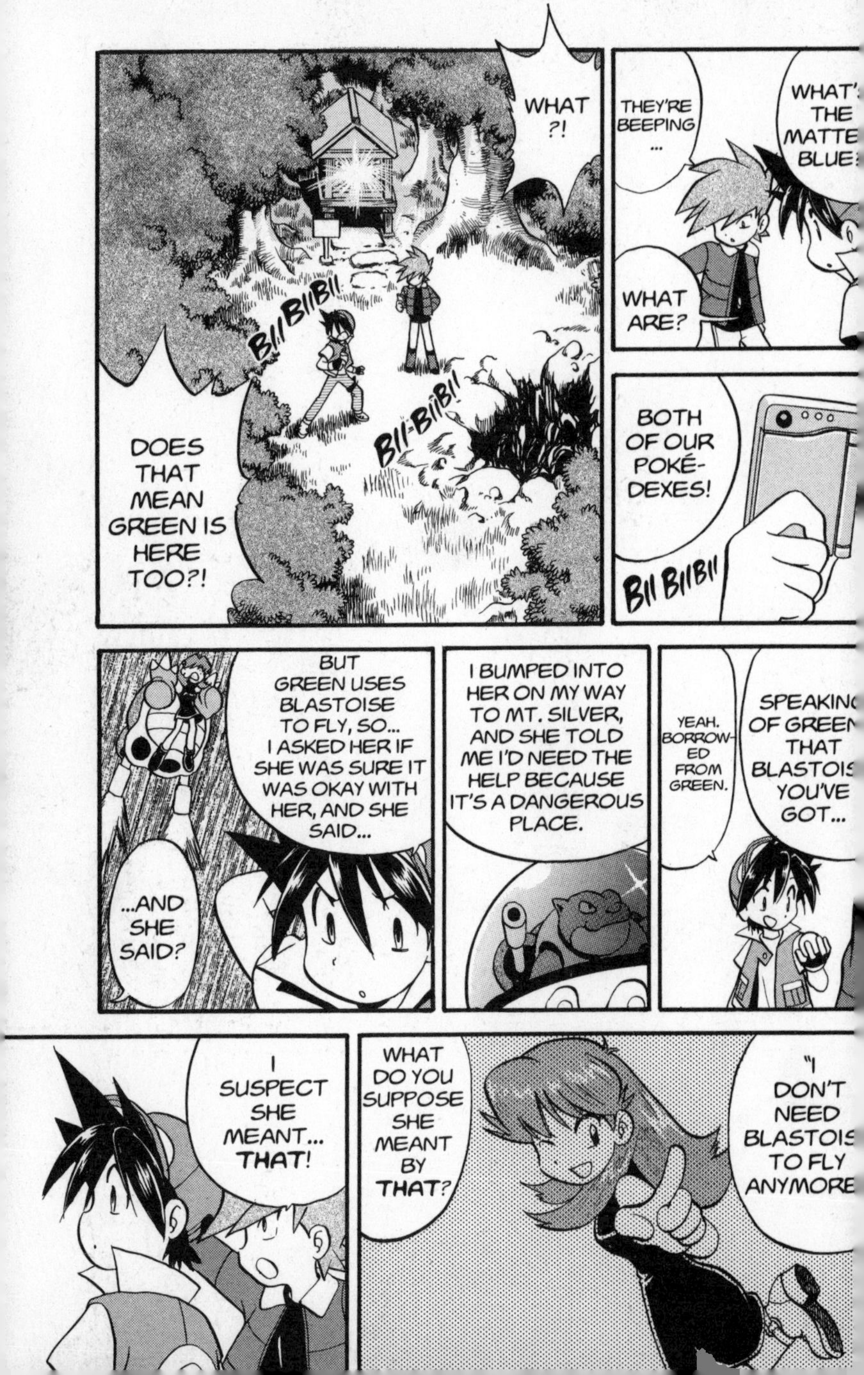
WHAT'S THE MATTE BLUE
THEY'RE BEEPING ...
WHAT ARE?
BOTH OF OUR POKÉ-DEXES!
BII BIIBII
WHAT ?!
BII BIIBII
BII-BIIBII!
DOES THAT MEAN GREEN IS HERE TOO?!
SPEAKING OF GREEN THAT BLASTOIS YOU'VE GOT...
YEAH. BORROW-ED FROM GREEN.
I BUMPED INTO HER ON MY WAY TO MT. SILVER, AND SHE TOLD ME I'D NEED THE HELP BECAUSE IT'S A DANGEROUS PLACE.
BUT GREEN USES BLASTOISE TO FLY, SO... I ASKED HER IF SHE WAS SURE IT WAS OKAY WITH HER, AND SHE SAID...
...AND SHE SAID?
"I DON'T NEED BLASTOIS TO FLY ANYMORE
WHAT DO YOU SUPPOSE SHE MEANT BY THAT?
I SUSPECT SHE MEANT... THAT!

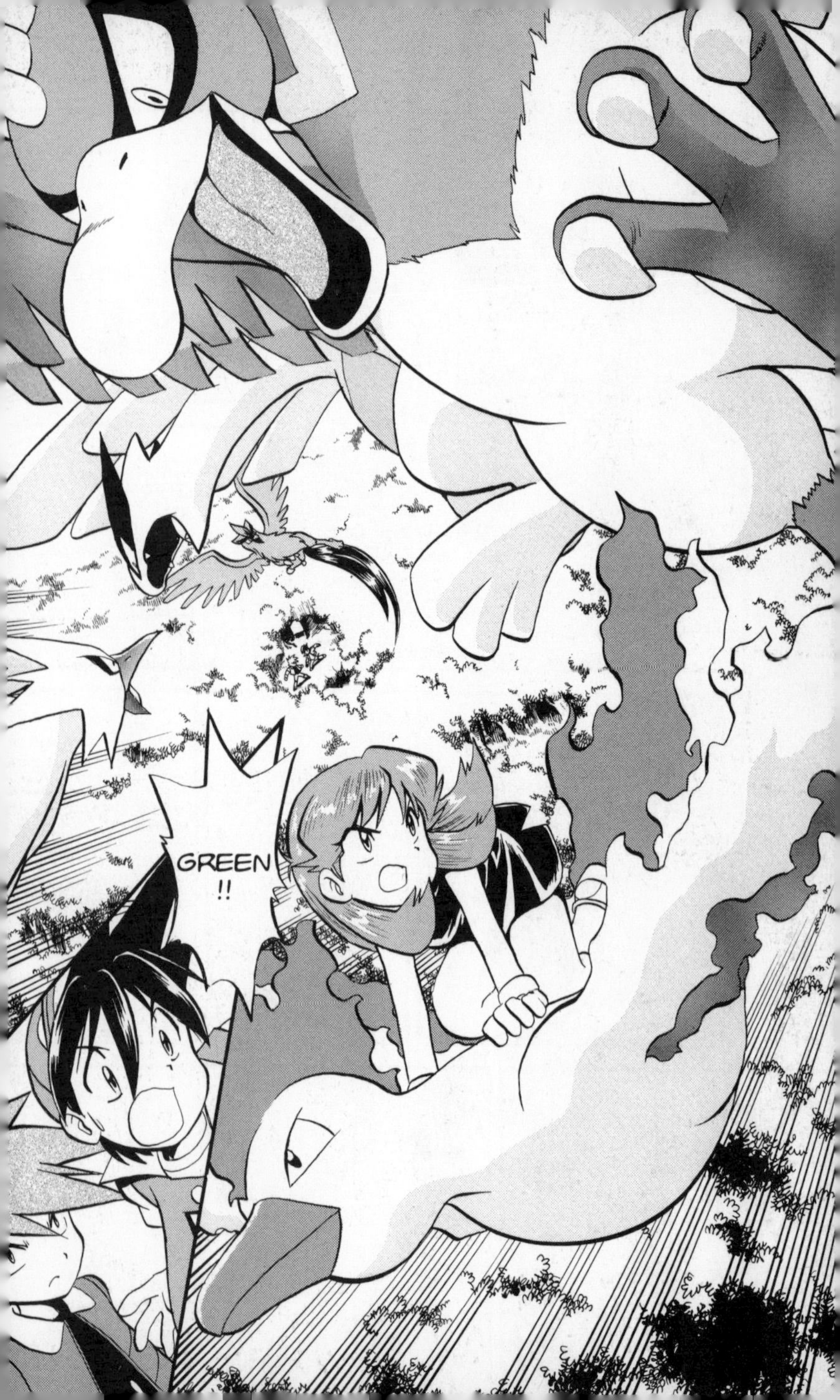
GREEN !!

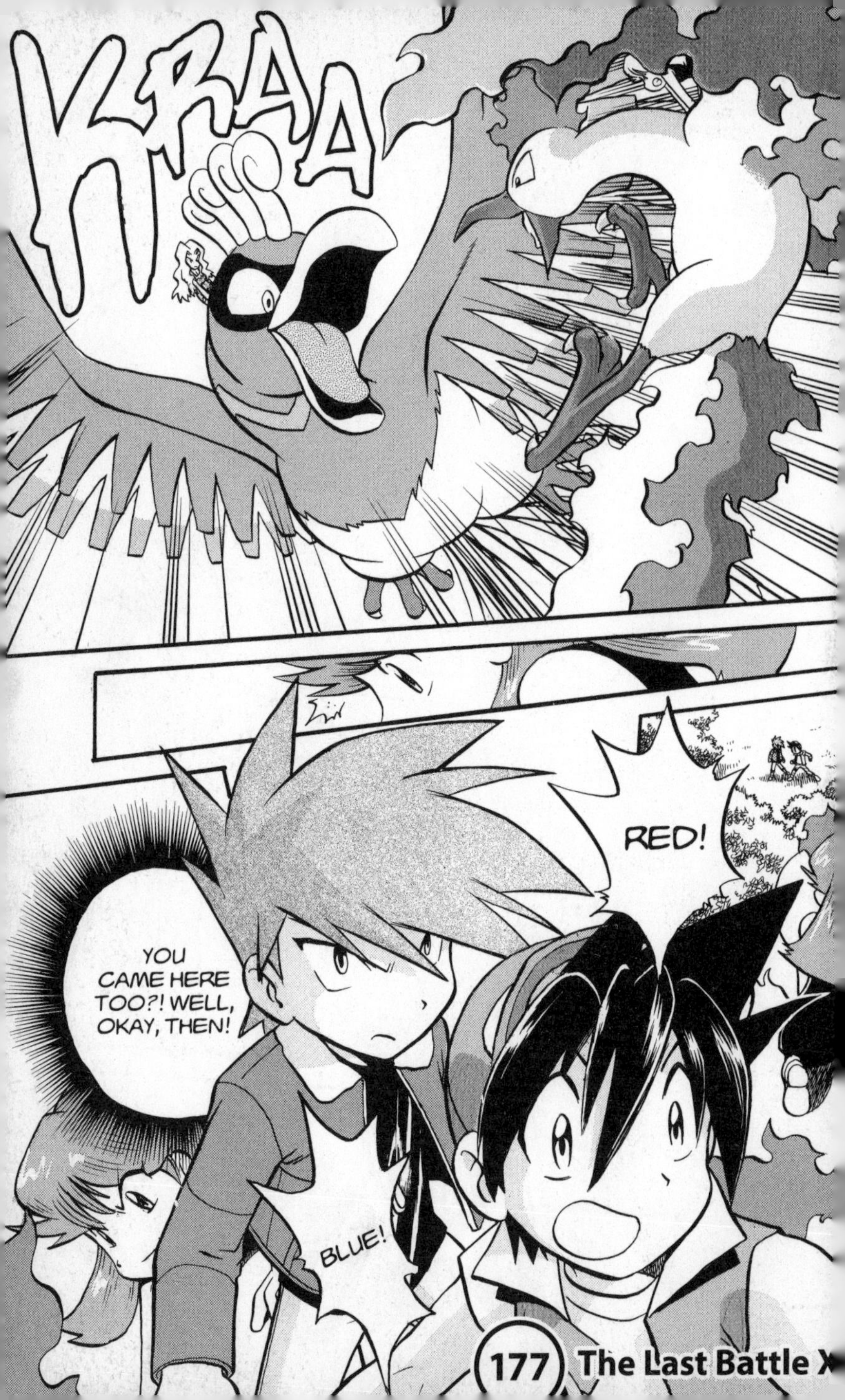
KRAA
RED!
YOU CAME HERE TOO?! WELL, OKAY, THEN!
BLUE!
177 The Last Battle X

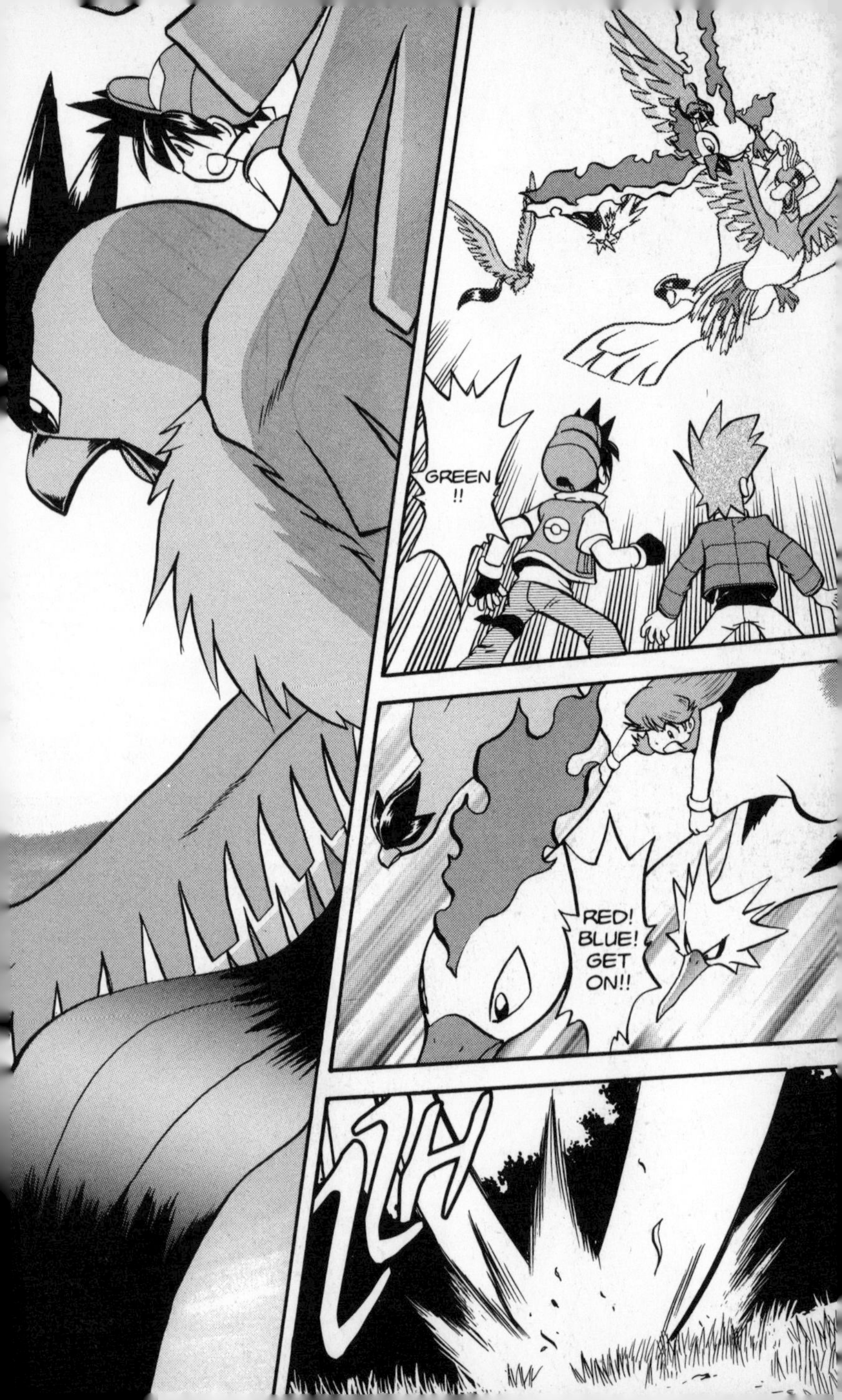
GREEN !!
RED! BLUE! GET ON!!

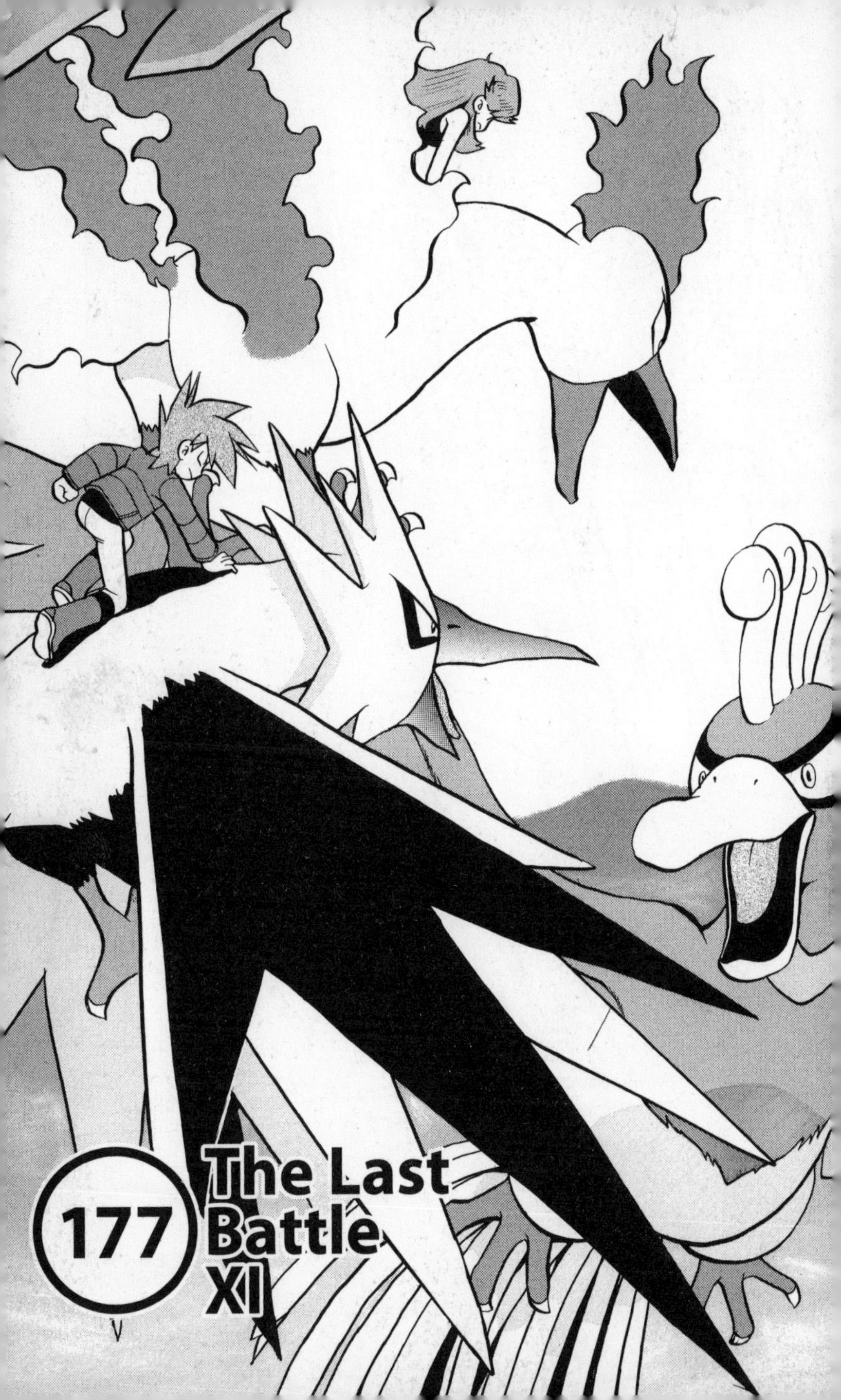
177
The Last Battle XI

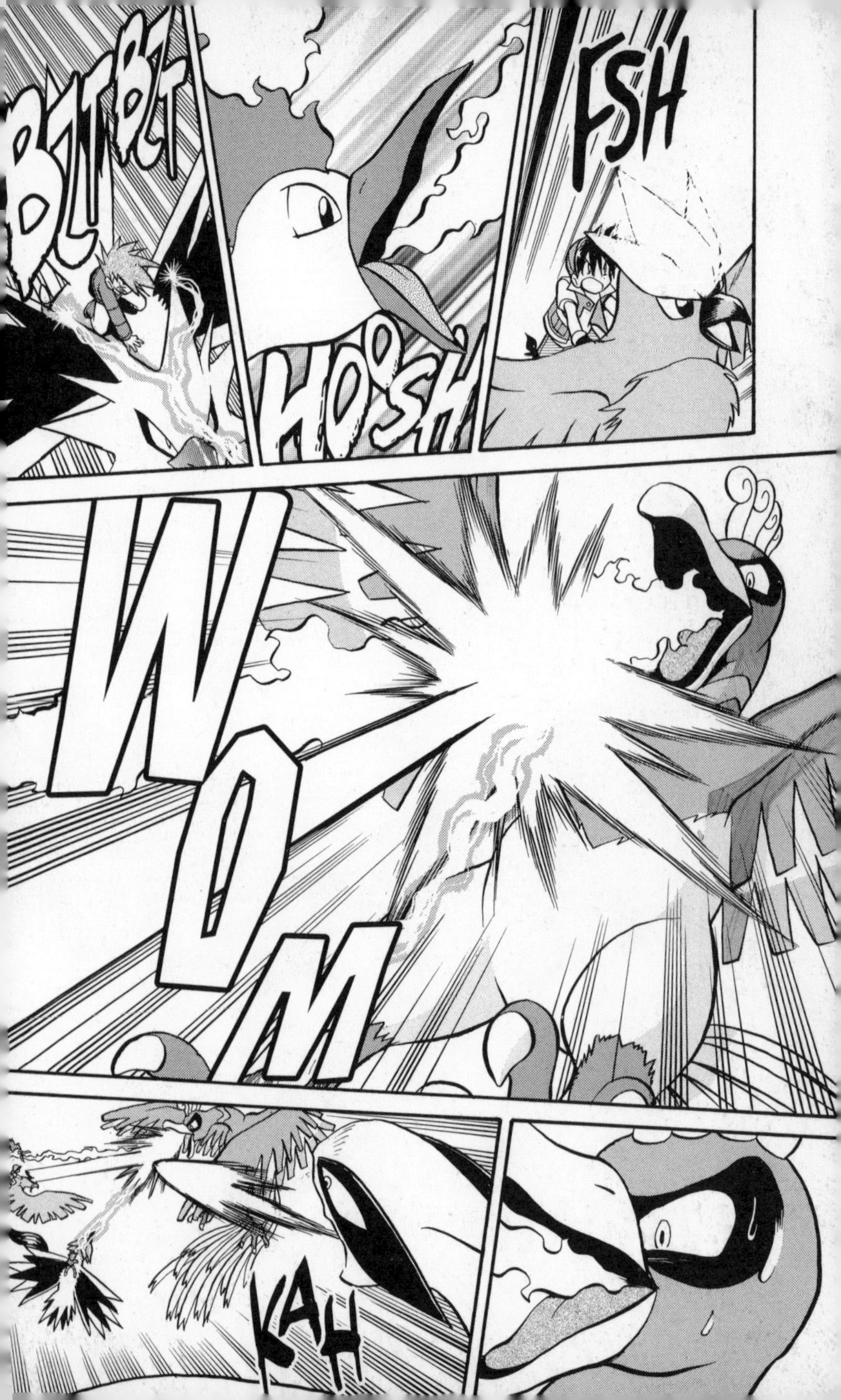
FSH
WHOOSH
BZT BZT
WOOM
KAH

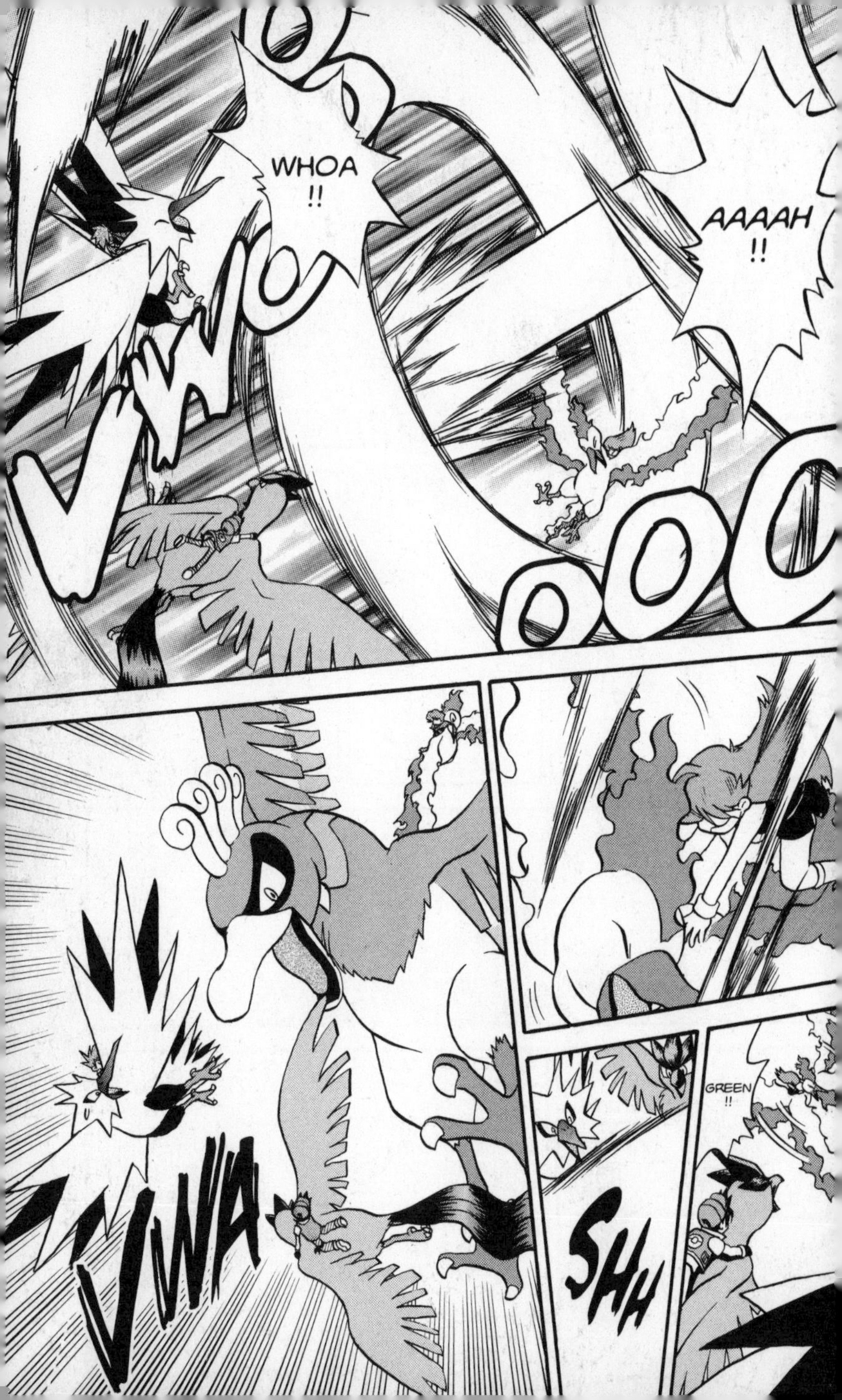
AAAAH!!
WHOA!!
GREEN!!
SHH
VWA

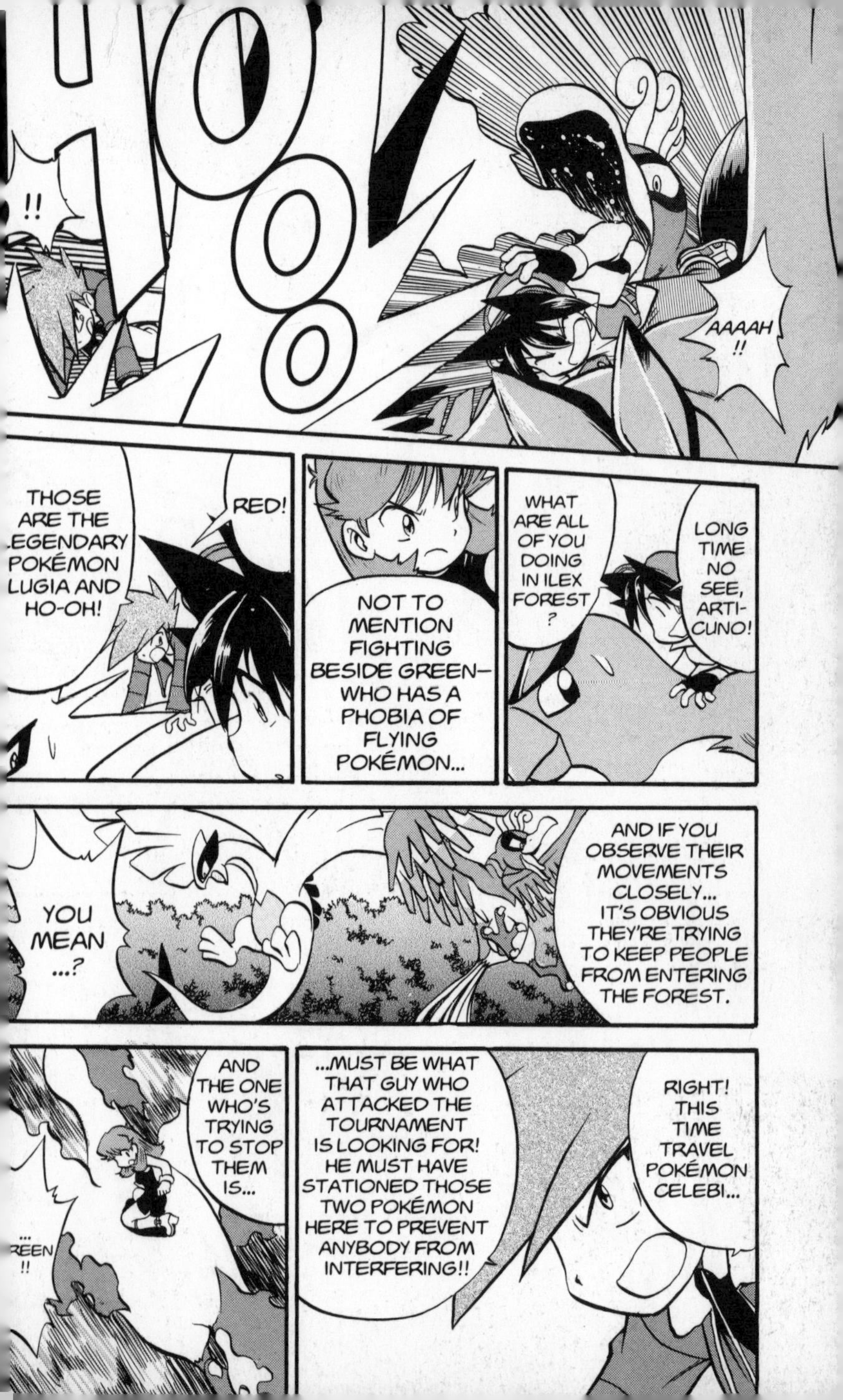
AAAAH !!
HOOOO
!!
LONG TIME NO SEE, ARTI-CUNO!
WHAT ARE ALL OF YOU DOING IN ILEX FOREST ?
NOT TO MENTION FIGHTING BESIDE GREEN— WHO HAS A PHOBIA OF FLYING POKÉMON...
RED!
THOSE ARE THE LEGENDARY POKÉMON LUGIA AND HO-OH!
AND IF YOU OBSERVE THEIR MOVEMENTS CLOSELY... IT'S OBVIOUS THEY'RE TRYING TO KEEP PEOPLE FROM ENTERING THE FOREST.
YOU MEAN ...?
RIGHT! THIS TIME TRAVEL POKÉMON CELEBI...
...MUST BE WHAT THAT GUY WHO ATTACKED THE TOURNAMENT IS LOOKING FOR! HE MUST HAVE STATIONED THOSE TWO POKÉMON HERE TO PREVENT ANYBODY FROM INTERFERING!!
AND THE ONE WHO'S TRYING TO STOP THEM IS...
... REEN !!

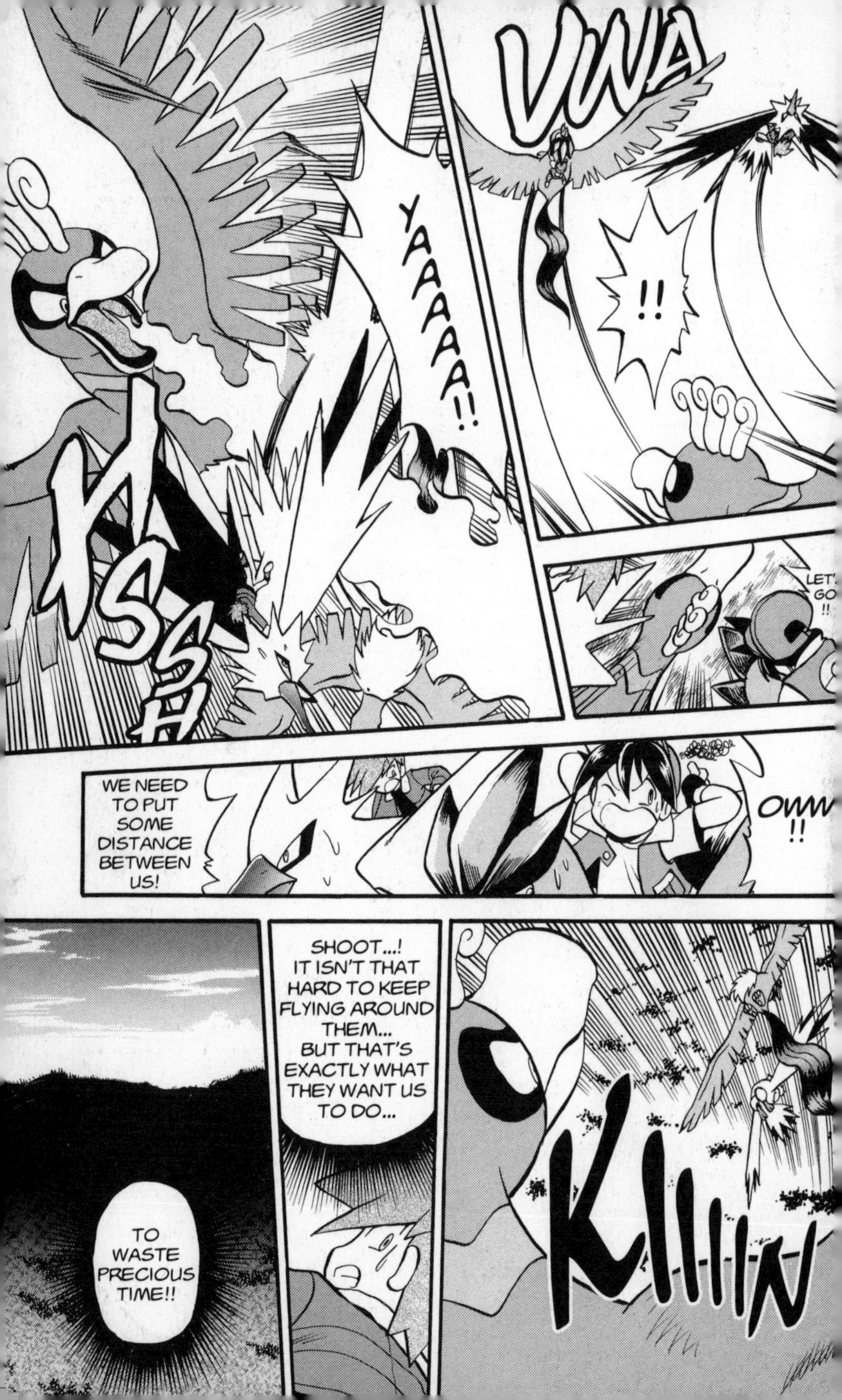
VWA
!!
YAAAAAA!!
WSSH
LET'S GO!!
OWW!!
WE NEED TO PUT SOME DISTANCE BETWEEN US!
KIIIIN
SHOOT...! IT ISN'T THAT HARD TO KEEP FLYING AROUND THEM... BUT THAT'S EXACTLY WHAT THEY WANT US TO DO...
TO WASTE PRECIOUS TIME!!

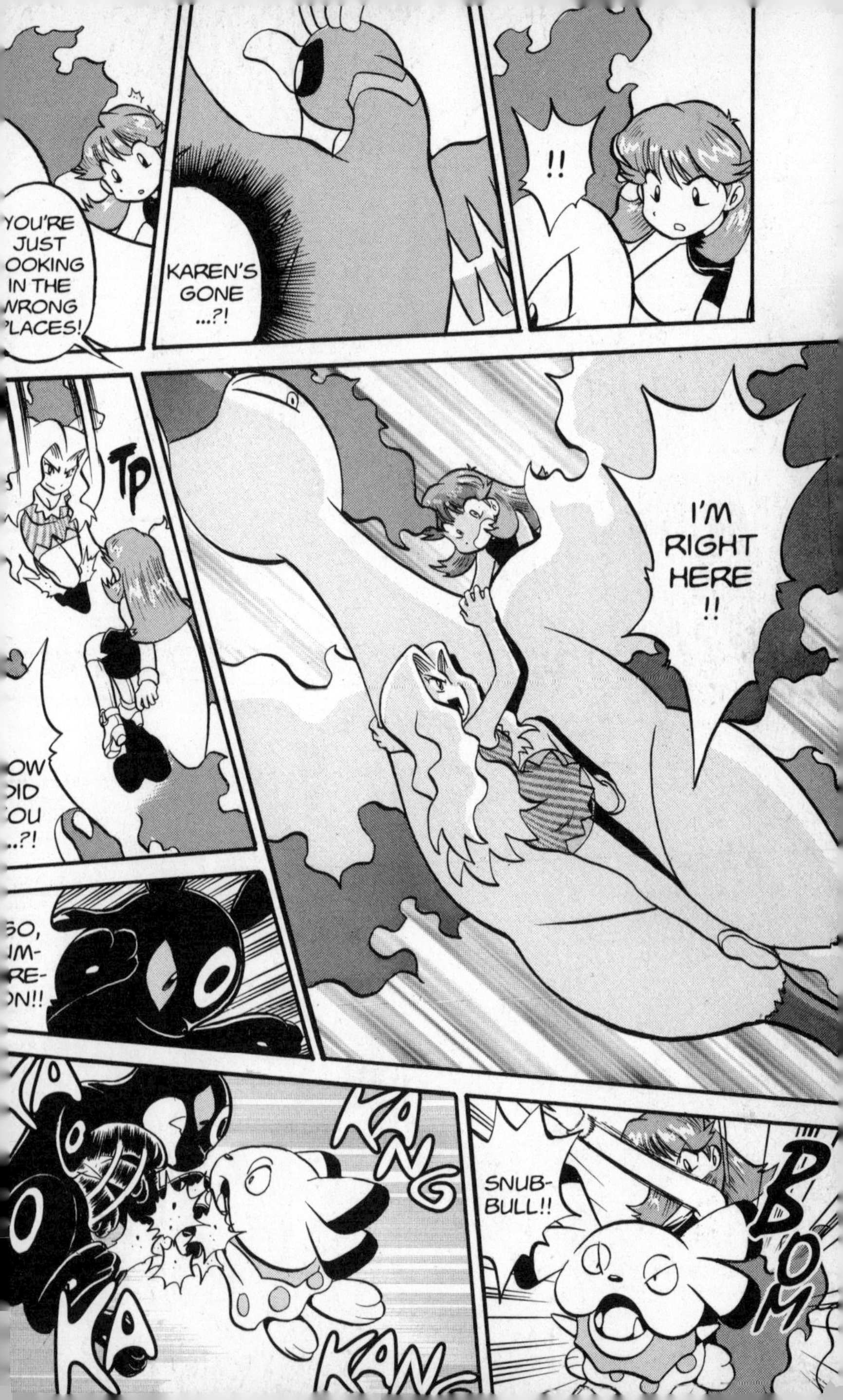
!!
KAREN'S GONE ...?!
YOU'RE JUST OOKING IN THE VRONG LACES!
I'M RIGHT HERE !!
TP
OW DID OU ...?!
SO, IM- RE- ON!!
SNUB- BULL!!
BOM
KANG
KANG

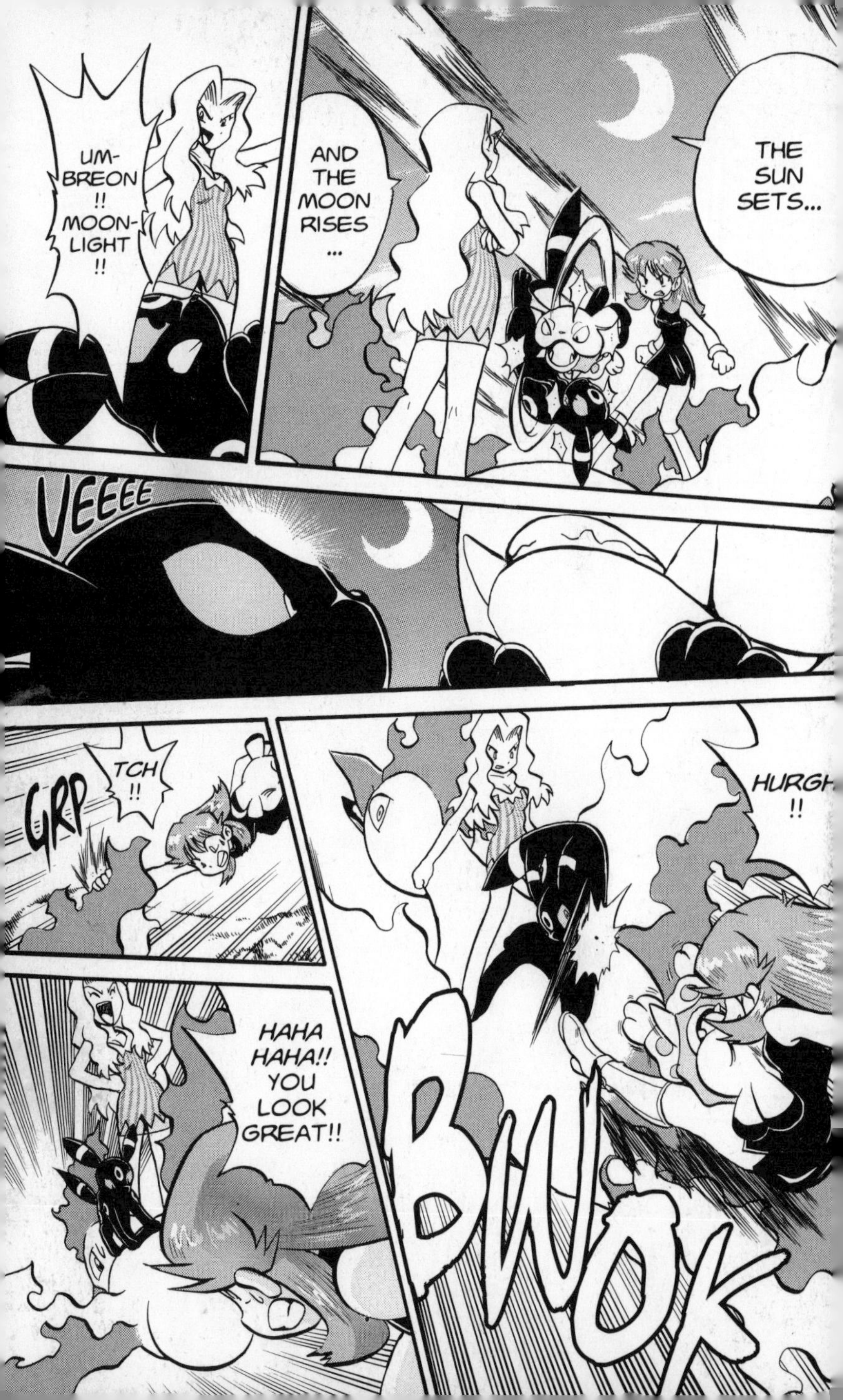
THE SUN SETS...
AND THE MOON RISES ...
UM-BREON!! MOON-LIGHT!!
VEEEE
HURGH!!
BWOK
TCH!!
GRP
HAHA HAHA!! YOU LOOK GREAT!!

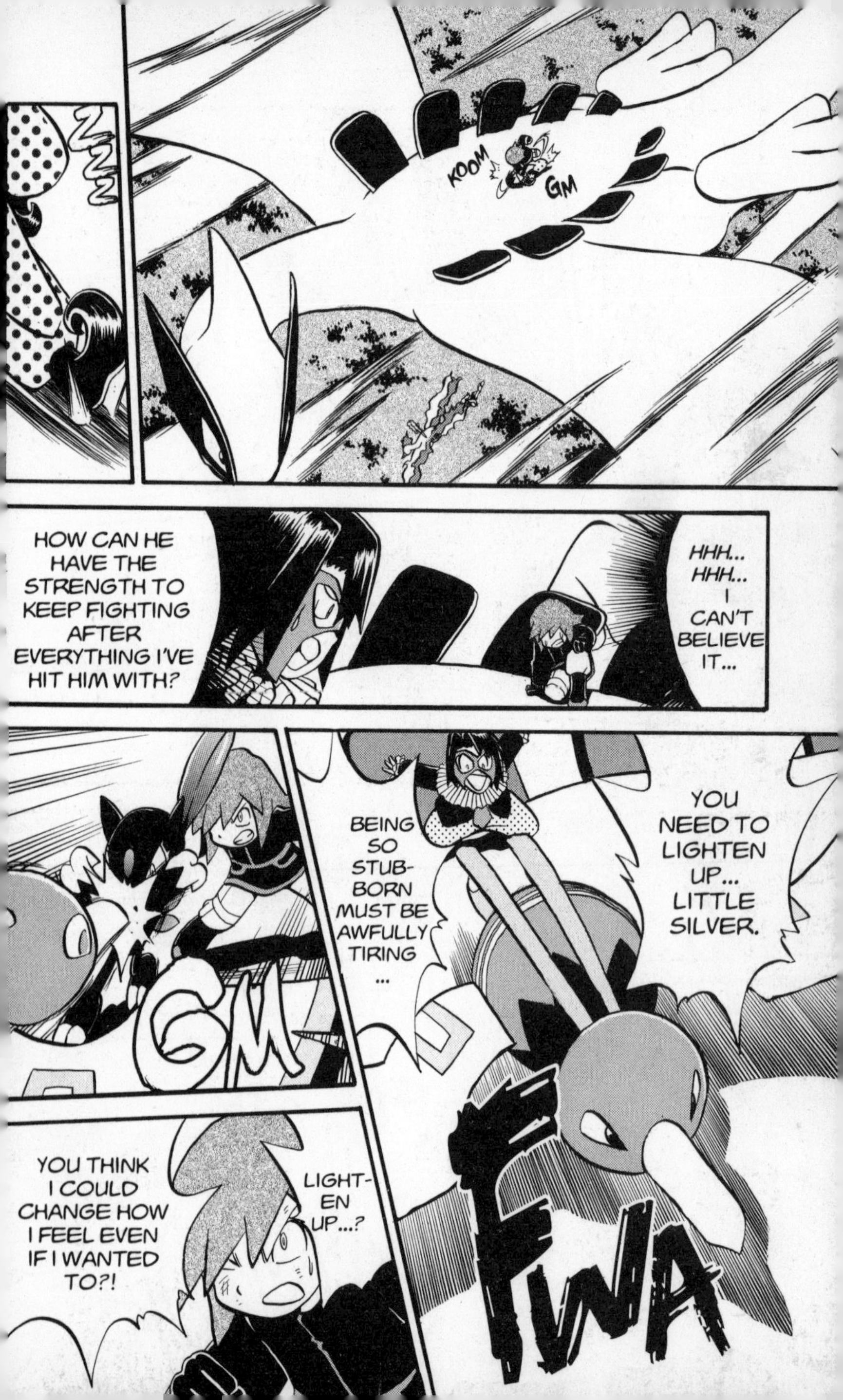

KOOM
GM
ZZZ
HHH... HHH... I CAN'T BELIEVE IT...
HOW CAN HE HAVE THE STRENGTH TO KEEP FIGHTING AFTER EVERYTHING I'VE HIT HIM WITH?
YOU NEED TO LIGHTEN UP... LITTLE SILVER.
BEING SO STUB-BORN MUST BE AWFULLY TIRING ...
FWA
GM
LIGHT-EN UP...?
YOU THINK I COULD CHANGE HOW I FEEL EVEN IF I WANTED TO?!

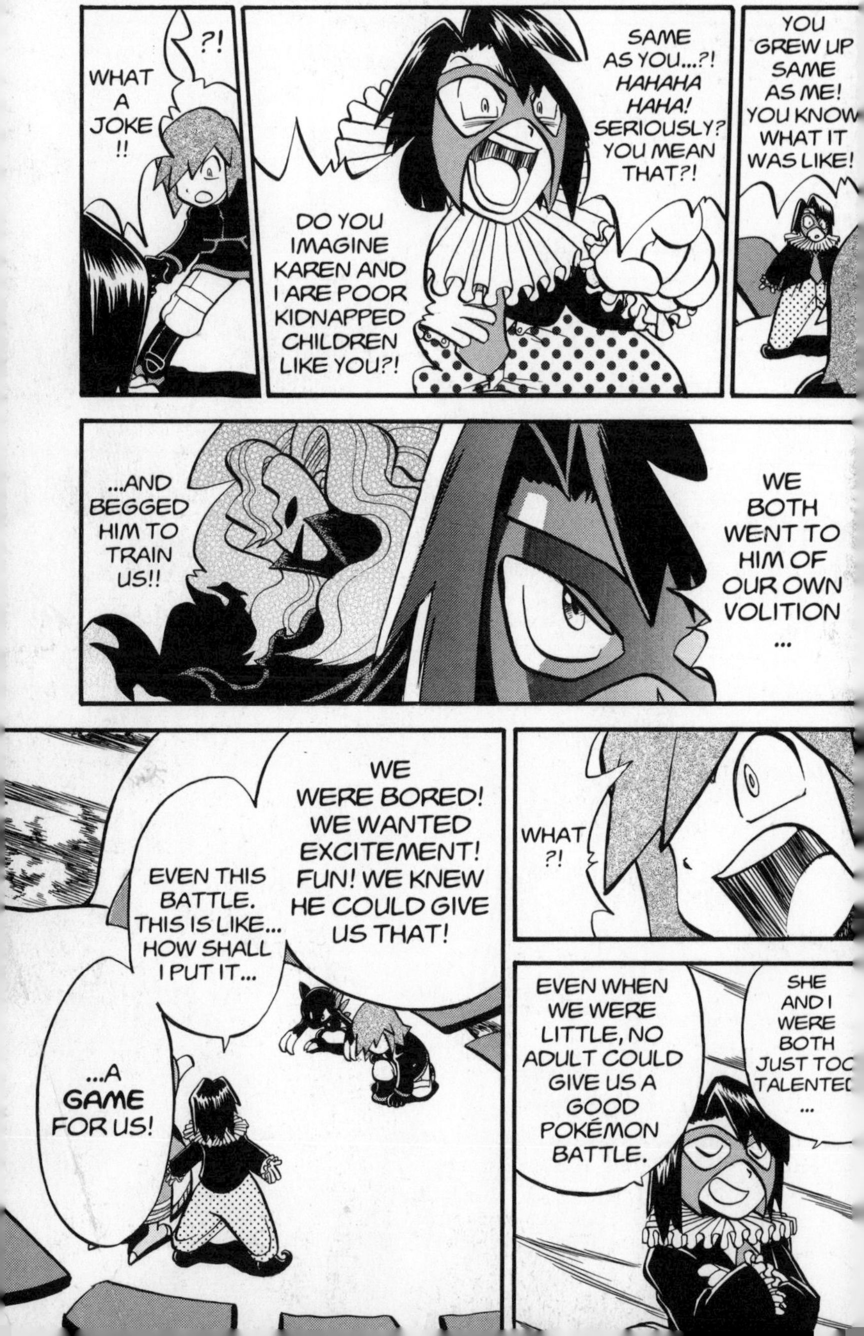

YOU GREW UP SAME AS ME! YOU KNOW WHAT IT WAS LIKE!
SAME AS YOU...?! *HAHAHA HAHA!* SERIOUSLY? YOU MEAN THAT?!
DO YOU IMAGINE KAREN AND I ARE POOR KIDNAPPED CHILDREN LIKE YOU?!
?!
WHAT A JOKE !!
WE BOTH WENT TO HIM OF OUR OWN VOLITION ...
...AND BEGGED HIM TO TRAIN US!!
WHAT ?!
SHE AND I WERE BOTH JUST TOO TALENTED ...
EVEN WHEN WE WERE LITTLE, NO ADULT COULD GIVE US A GOOD POKÉMON BATTLE.
WE WERE BORED! WE WANTED EXCITEMENT! FUN! WE KNEW HE COULD GIVE US THAT!
EVEN THIS BATTLE. THIS IS LIKE... HOW SHALL I PUT IT...
...A GAME FOR US!

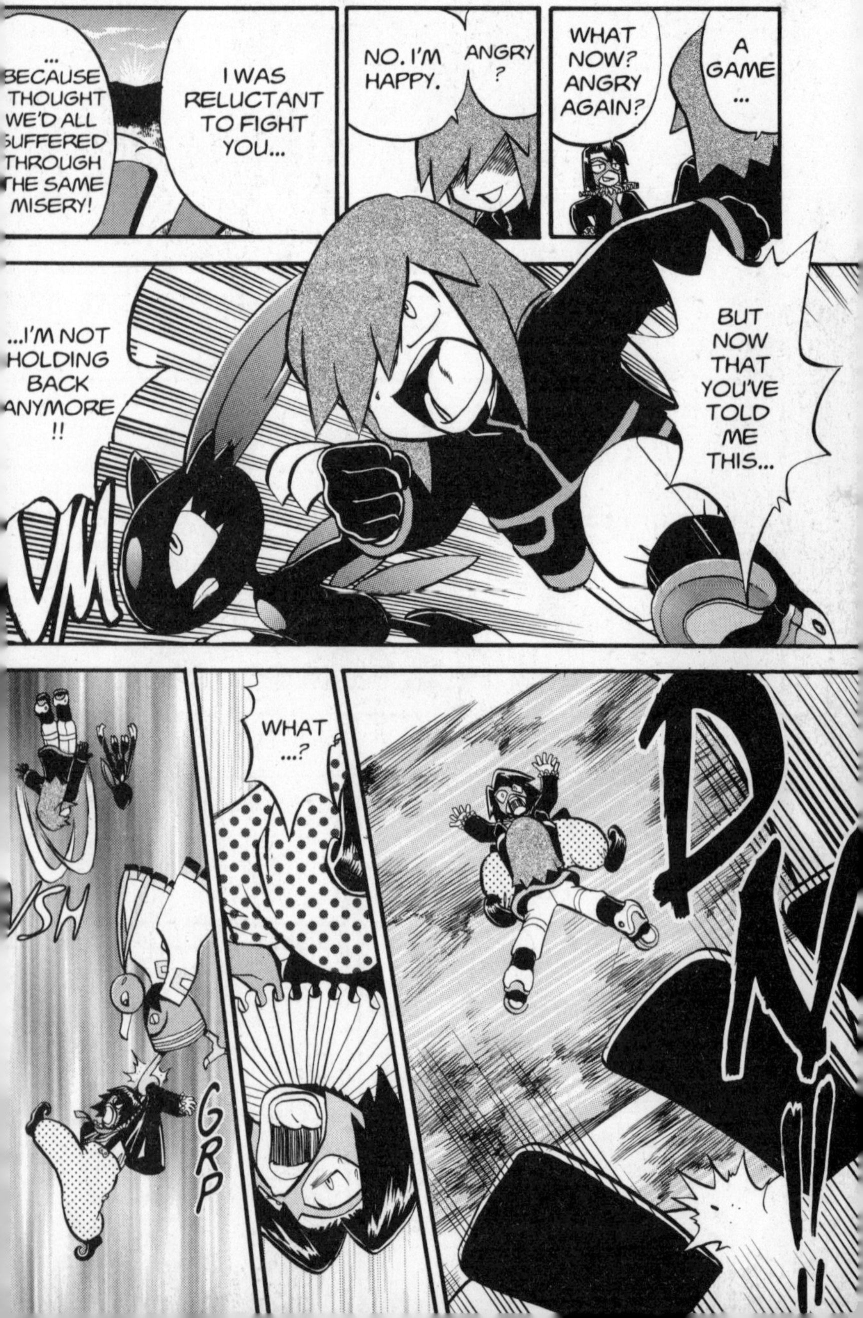
A GAME ...
WHAT NOW? ANGRY AGAIN?
ANGRY ?
NO. I'M HAPPY.
I WAS RELUCTANT TO FIGHT YOU...
... BECAUSE THOUGHT WE'D ALL UFFERED THROUGH THE SAME MISERY!
BUT NOW THAT YOU'VE TOLD ME THIS...
...I'M NOT HOLDING BACK ANYMORE !!
VM
WHAT ...?
GRP

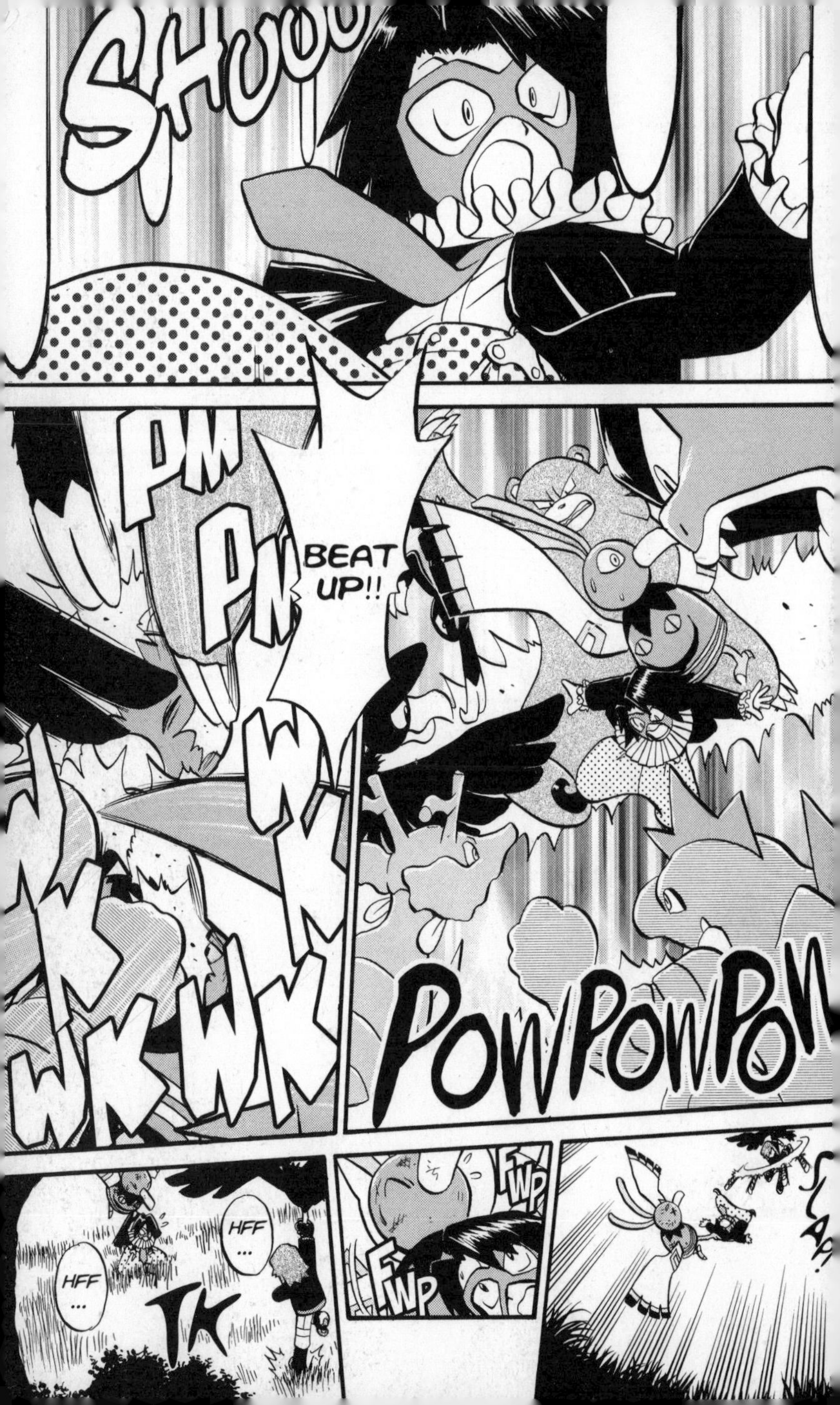
BEAT UP!!
POWPOWPOW
SLAP!
FWP
FWP
HFF ...
HFF ...

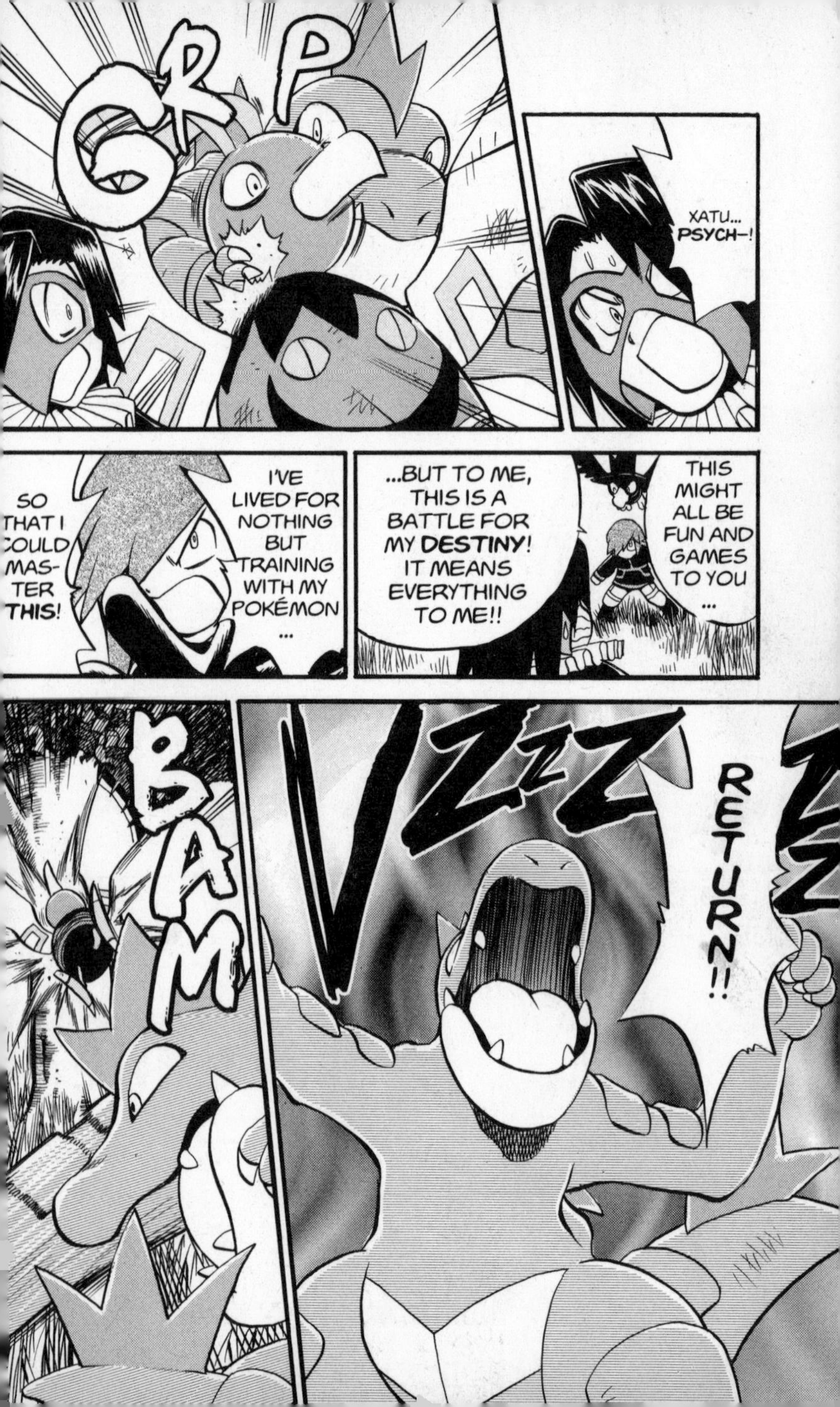
XATU... **PSYCH**—!
CRP
THIS MIGHT ALL BE FUN AND GAMES TO YOU...
...BUT TO ME, THIS IS A BATTLE FOR MY **DESTINY**! IT MEANS EVERYTHING TO ME!!
I'VE LIVED FOR NOTHING BUT TRAINING WITH MY POKÉMON...
SO THAT I COULD MASTER **THIS**!
VZZZ
RETURN!!
BAM

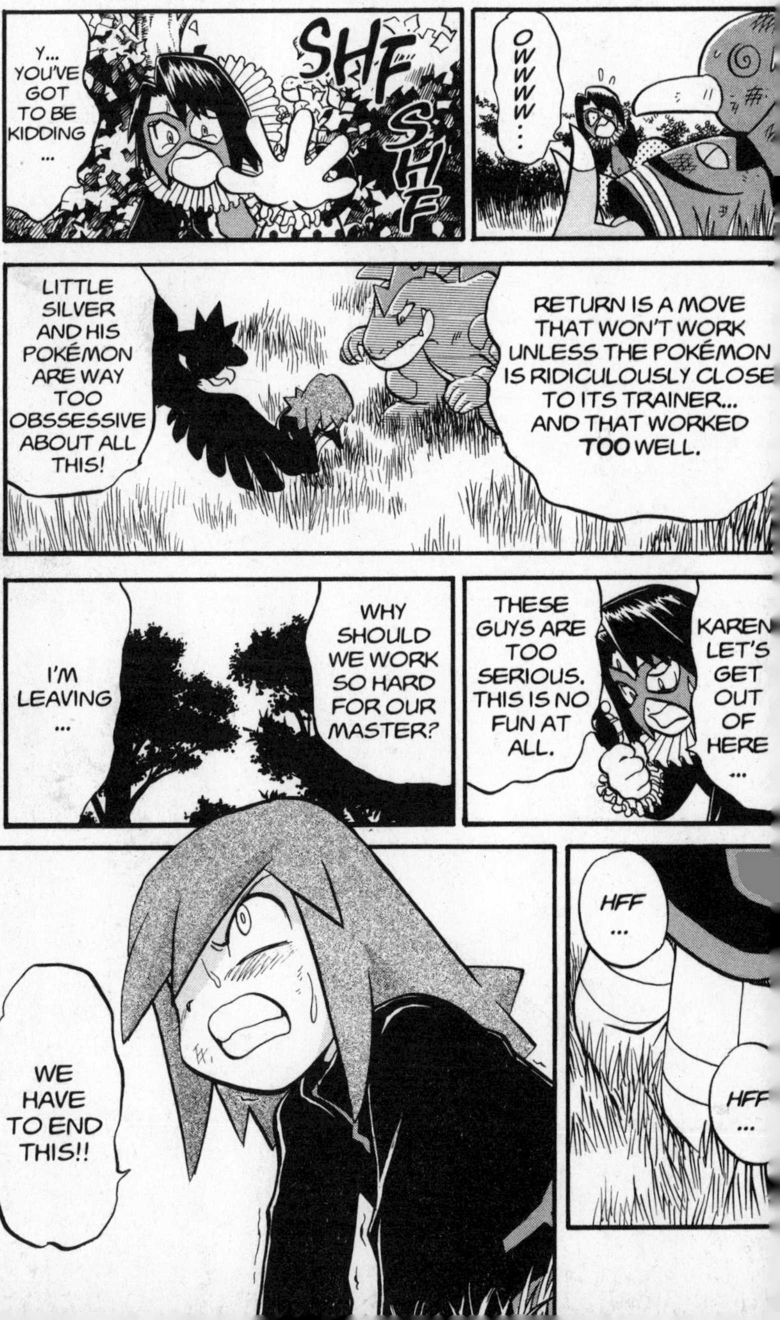
OWWWW...
Y... YOU'VE GOT TO BE KIDDING ...
SHF
SHF
RETURN IS A MOVE THAT WON'T WORK UNLESS THE POKÉMON IS RIDICULOUSLY CLOSE TO ITS TRAINER... AND THAT WORKED **TOO** WELL.
LITTLE SILVER AND HIS POKÉMON ARE WAY TOO OBSSESSIVE ABOUT ALL THIS!
KAREN LET'S GET OUT OF HERE ...
THESE GUYS ARE TOO SERIOUS. THIS IS NO FUN AT ALL.
WHY SHOULD WE WORK SO HARD FOR OUR MASTER?
I'M LEAVING ...
HFF ...
HFF ...
WE HAVE TO END THIS!!

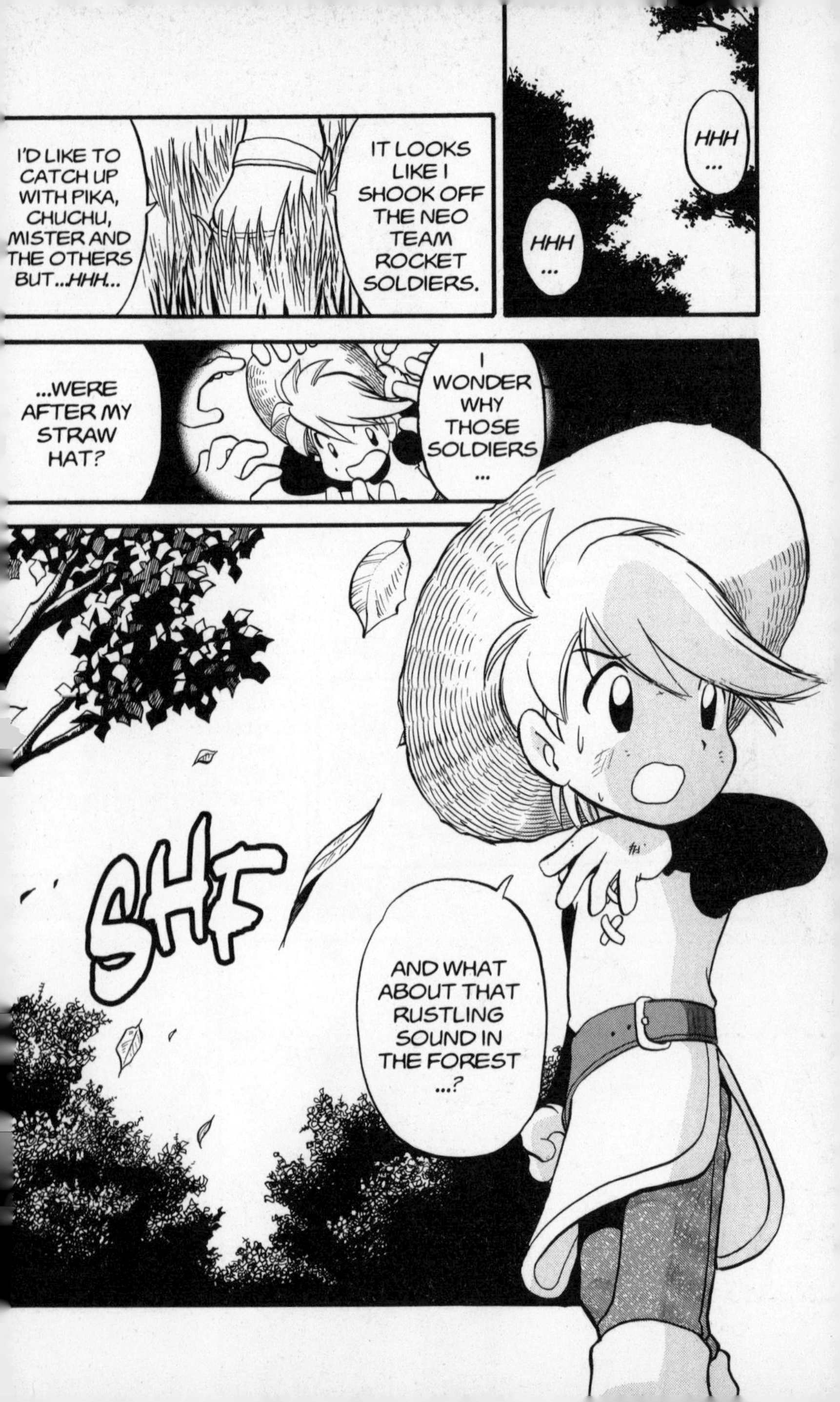
HHH...
HHH...
IT LOOKS LIKE I SHOOK OFF THE NEO TEAM ROCKET SOLDIERS.
I'D LIKE TO CATCH UP WITH PIKA, CHUCHU, MISTER AND THE OTHERS BUT...HHH...
I WONDER WHY THOSE SOLDIERS ...
...WERE AFTER MY STRAW HAT?
AND WHAT ABOUT THAT RUSTLING SOUND IN THE FOREST ...?
SHF

# 178 The Last Battle XII

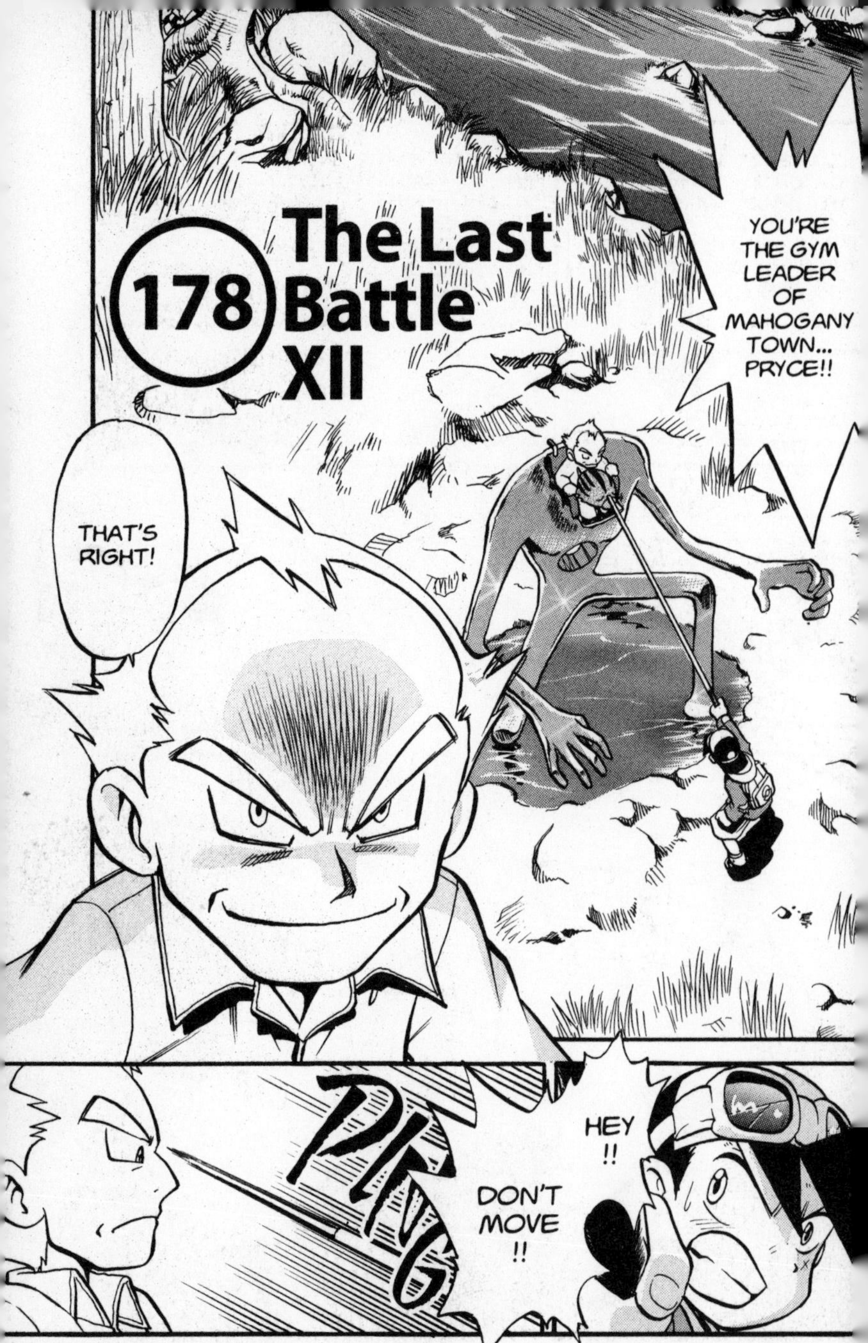
YOU'RE THE GYM LEADER OF MAHOGANY TOWN... PRYCE!!
THAT'S RIGHT!
HEY!!
DON'T MOVE!!
PING

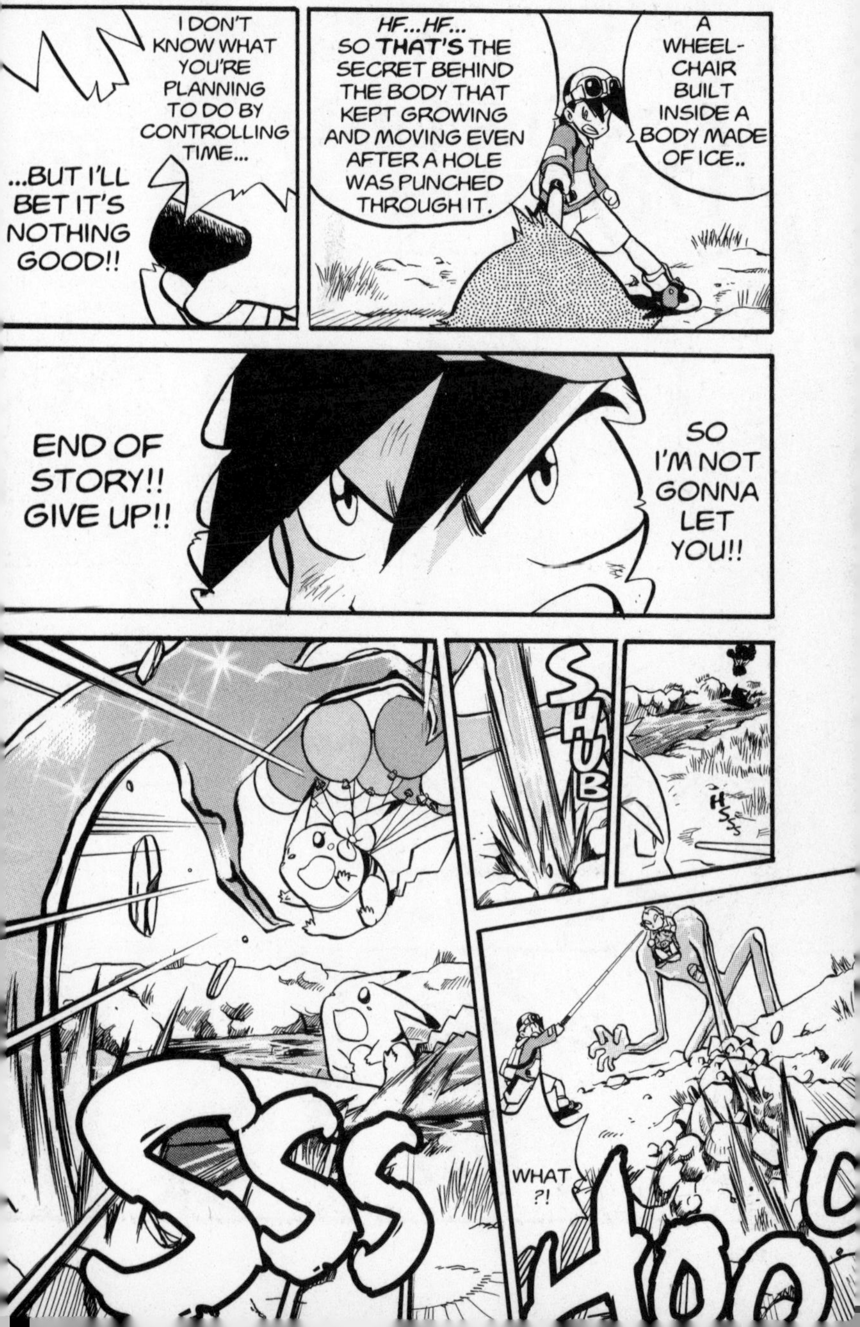
A WHEEL-CHAIR BUILT INSIDE A BODY MADE OF ICE..
HF...HF... SO THAT'S THE SECRET BEHIND THE BODY THAT KEPT GROWING AND MOVING EVEN AFTER A HOLE WAS PUNCHED THROUGH IT.
I DON'T KNOW WHAT YOU'RE PLANNING TO DO BY CONTROLLING TIME...
...BUT I'LL BET IT'S NOTHING GOOD!!
SO I'M NOT GONNA LET YOU!!
END OF STORY!! GIVE UP!!
HSSS
SHUB
WHAT ?!
SSS

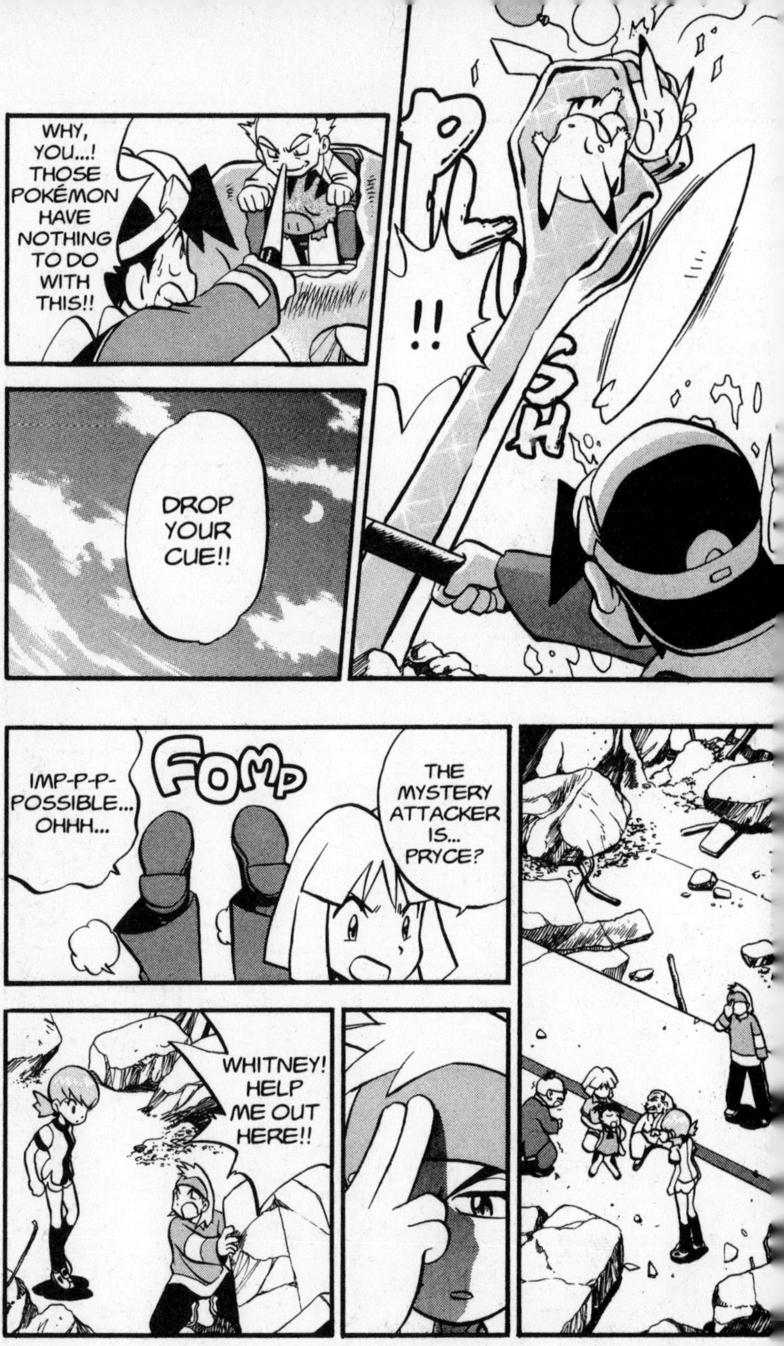
!!
WHY, YOU...! THOSE POKÉMON HAVE NOTHING TO DO WITH THIS!!
DROP YOUR CUE!!
THE MYSTERY ATTACKER IS... PRYCE?
FOMP
IMP-P-P-POSSIBLE... OHHH...
WHITNEY! HELP ME OUT HERE!!

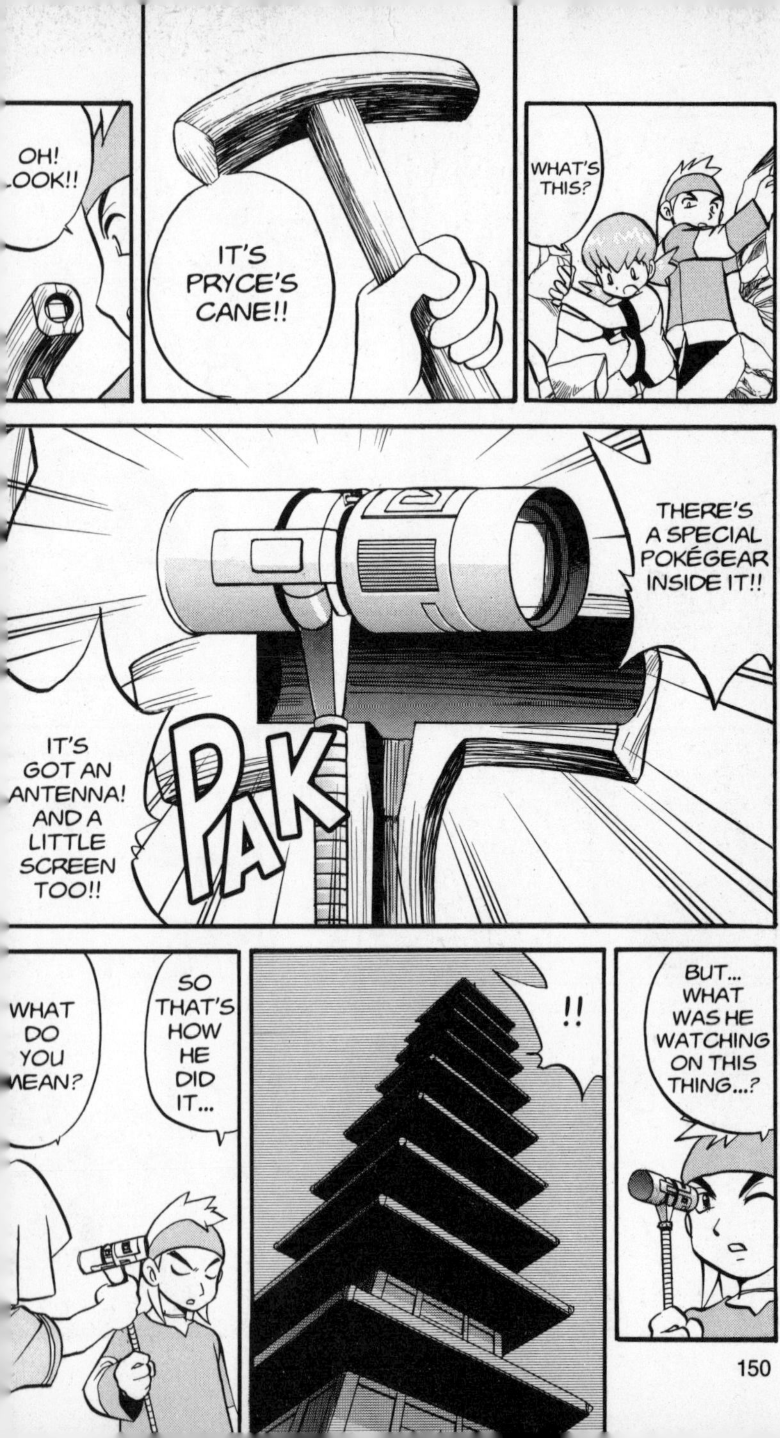
WHAT'S THIS?
IT'S PRYCE'S CANE!!
OH! LOOK!!
THERE'S A SPECIAL POKÉGEAR INSIDE IT!!
PAK
IT'S GOT AN ANTENNA! AND A LITTLE SCREEN TOO!!
BUT... WHAT WAS HE WATCHING ON THIS THING...?
!!
SO THAT'S HOW HE DID IT...
WHAT DO YOU MEAN?

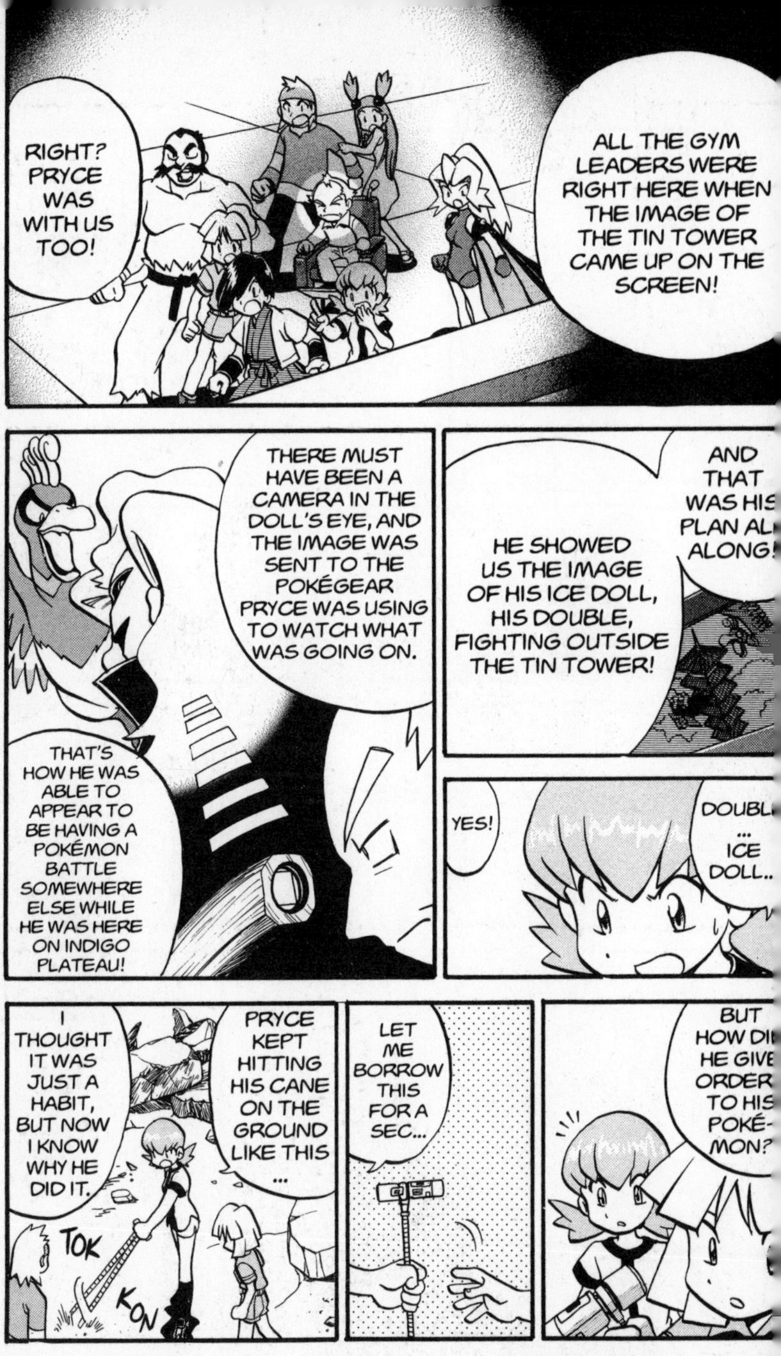
ALL THE GYM LEADERS WERE RIGHT HERE WHEN THE IMAGE OF THE TIN TOWER CAME UP ON THE SCREEN!
RIGHT? PRYCE WAS WITH US TOO!
AND THAT WAS HIS PLAN AL ALONG!
HE SHOWED US THE IMAGE OF HIS ICE DOLL, HIS DOUBLE, FIGHTING OUTSIDE THE TIN TOWER!
DOUBL ... ICE DOLL...
YES!
THERE MUST HAVE BEEN A CAMERA IN THE DOLL'S EYE, AND THE IMAGE WAS SENT TO THE POKÉGEAR PRYCE WAS USING TO WATCH WHAT WAS GOING ON.
THAT'S HOW HE WAS ABLE TO APPEAR TO BE HAVING A POKÉMON BATTLE SOMEWHERE ELSE WHILE HE WAS HERE ON INDIGO PLATEAU!
BUT HOW DI HE GIVE ORDER TO HIS POKÉ-MON?
LET ME BORROW THIS FOR A SEC...
PRYCE KEPT HITTING HIS CANE ON THE GROUND LIKE THIS ...
I THOUGHT IT WAS JUST A HABIT, BUT NOW I KNOW WHY HE DID IT.
TOK
KON

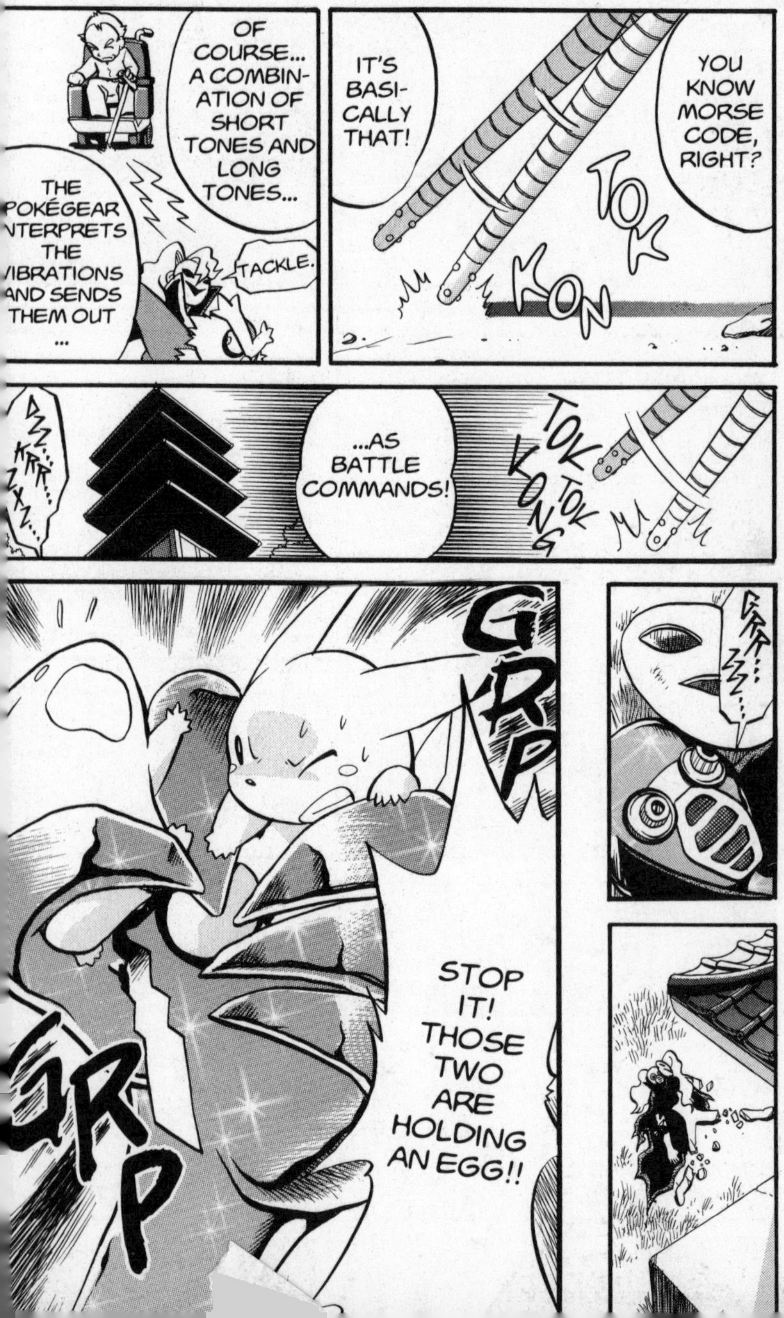
YOU KNOW MORSE CODE, RIGHT?
IT'S BASICALLY THAT!
TOK
KON
OF COURSE... A COMBINATION OF SHORT TONES AND LONG TONES...
TACKLE.
THE POKÉGEAR INTERPRETS THE VIBRATIONS AND SENDS THEM OUT ...
TOK TOK
KONG
...AS BATTLE COMMANDS!
GRRR... ZZZ...
GRP
STOP IT! THOSE TWO ARE HOLDING AN EGG!!
GRP

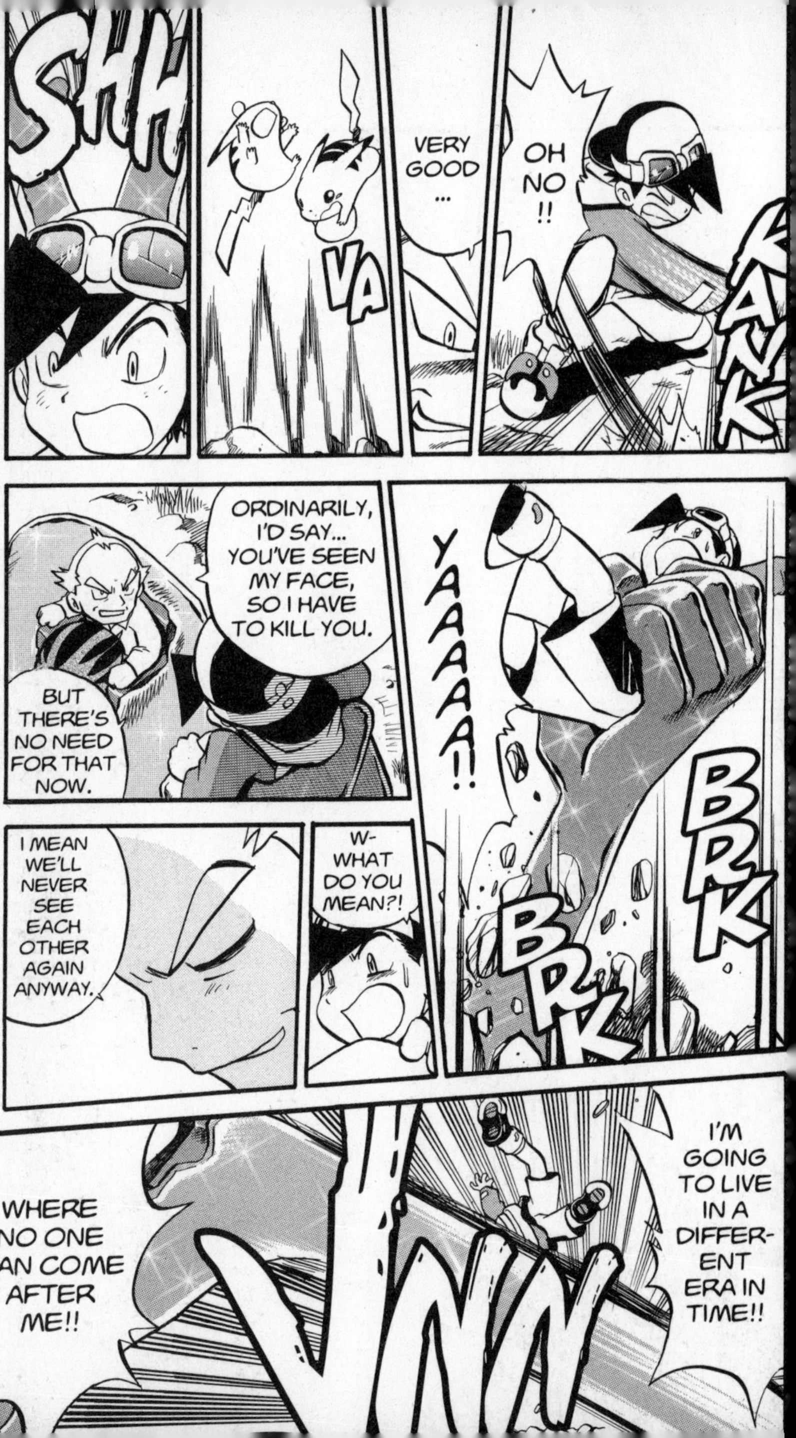
OH NO !!
KANK
VERY GOOD ...
VA
SHH
YAAAAA!!
BRK
BRK
ORDINARILY, I'D SAY... YOU'VE SEEN MY FACE, SO I HAVE TO KILL YOU.
BUT THERE'S NO NEED FOR THAT NOW.
W- WHAT DO YOU MEAN?!
I MEAN WE'LL NEVER SEE EACH OTHER AGAIN ANYWAY.
I'M GOING TO LIVE IN A DIFFER-ENT ERA IN TIME!!
VNN
WHERE NO ONE CAN COME AFTER ME!!

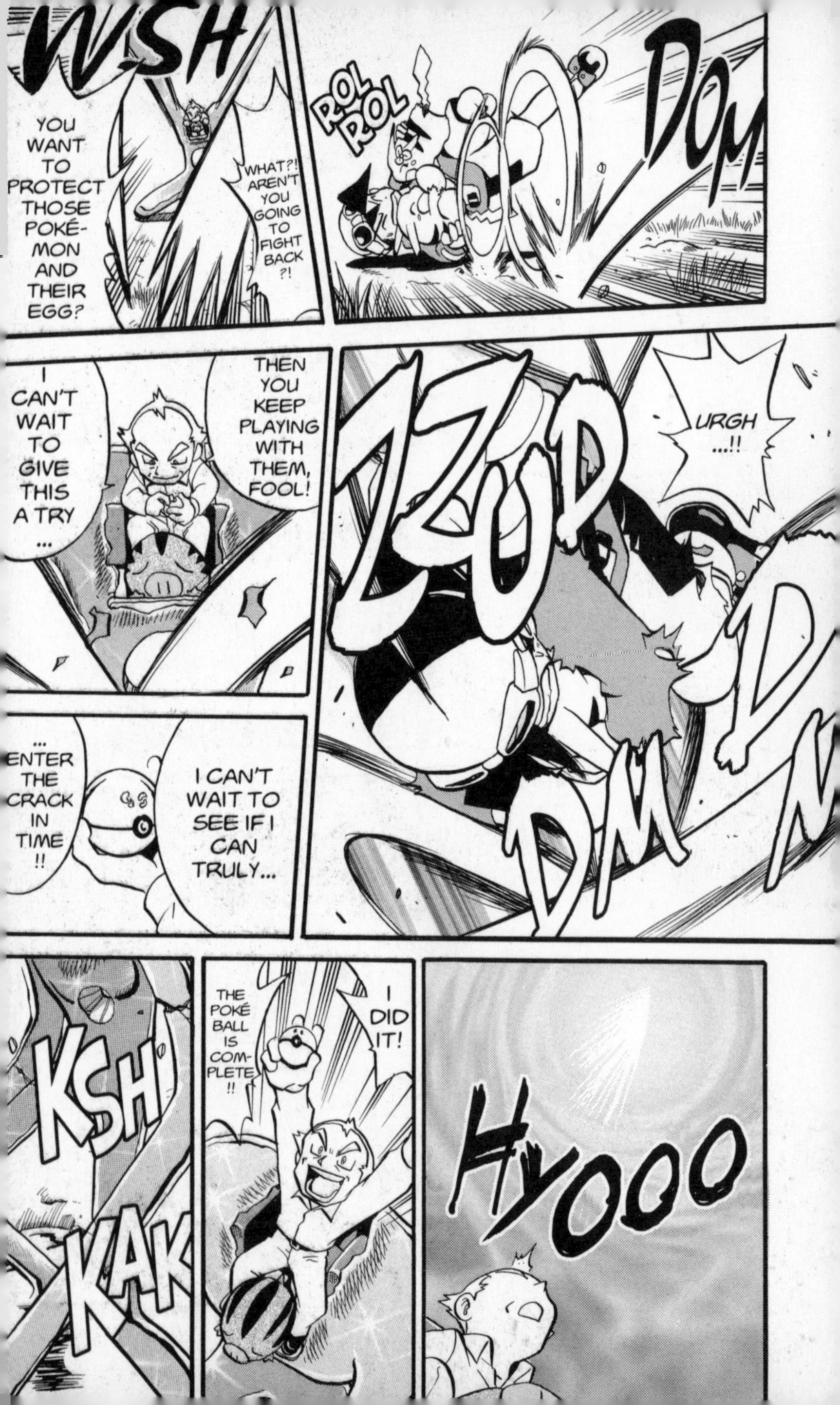
ROL ROL
DOM
WSH
WHAT?! AREN'T YOU GOING TO FIGHT BACK?!
YOU WANT TO PROTECT THOSE POKÉ-MON AND THEIR EGG?
ZZOP
URGH ...!!
DMM
THEN YOU KEEP PLAYING WITH THEM, FOOL!
I CAN'T WAIT TO GIVE THIS A TRY ...
I CAN'T WAIT TO SEE IF I CAN TRULY...
... ENTER THE CRACK IN TIME !!
HYOOO
I DID IT!
THE POKÉ BALL IS COM-PLETE !!
KSH
KAK

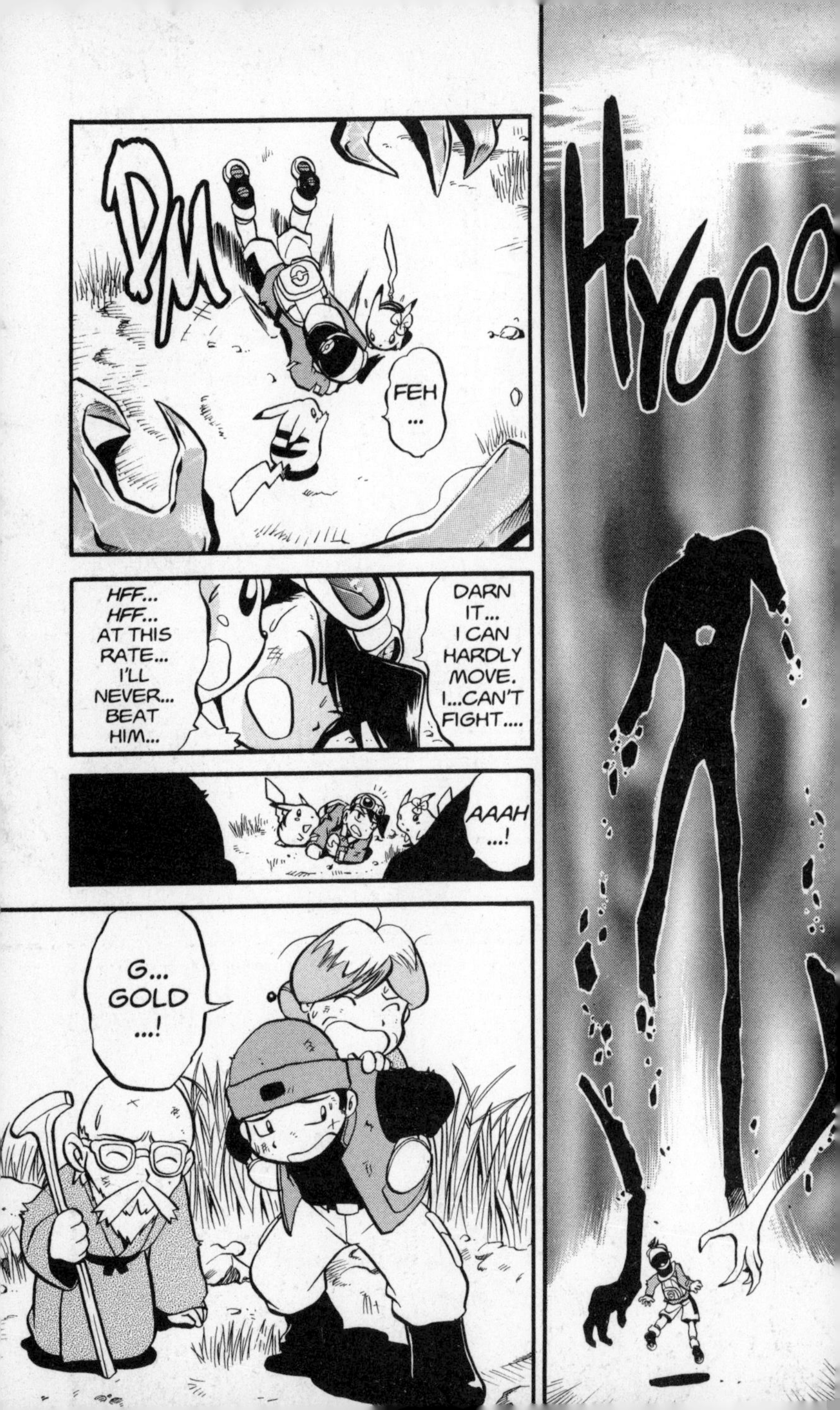
HYOOO
DM
FEH ...
DARN IT... I CAN HARDLY MOVE. I...CAN'T FIGHT....
HFF... HFF... AT THIS RATE... I'LL NEVER... BEAT HIM...
AAAH ...!
G... GOLD ...!

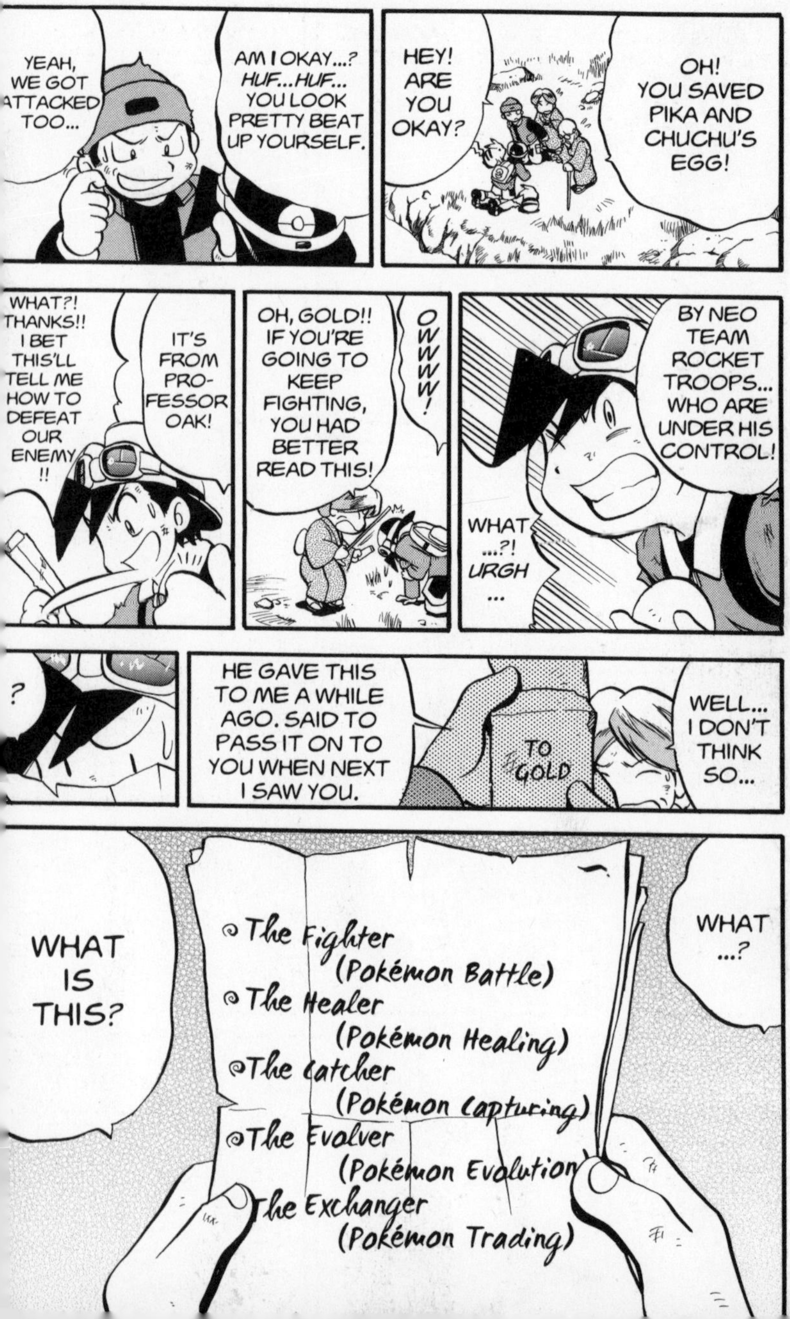
OH! YOU SAVED PIKA AND CHUCHU'S EGG!
HEY! ARE YOU OKAY?
AM I OKAY...? *HUF...HUF...* YOU LOOK PRETTY BEAT UP YOURSELF.
YEAH, WE GOT ATTACKED TOO...
BY NEO TEAM ROCKET TROOPS... WHO ARE UNDER HIS CONTROL!
WHAT ...?! URGH ...
OWWWW!
OH, GOLD!! IF YOU'RE GOING TO KEEP FIGHTING, YOU HAD BETTER READ THIS!
IT'S FROM PRO-FESSOR OAK!
WHAT?! THANKS!! I BET THIS'LL TELL ME HOW TO DEFEAT OUR ENEMY!!
WELL... I DON'T THINK SO...
TO GOLD
HE GAVE THIS TO ME A WHILE AGO. SAID TO PASS IT ON TO YOU WHEN NEXT I SAW YOU.
?
WHAT ...?
The Fighter (Pokémon Battle)
The Healer (Pokémon Healing)
The Catcher (Pokémon Capturing)
The Evolver (Pokémon Evolution)
The Exchanger (Pokémon Trading)
WHAT IS THIS?

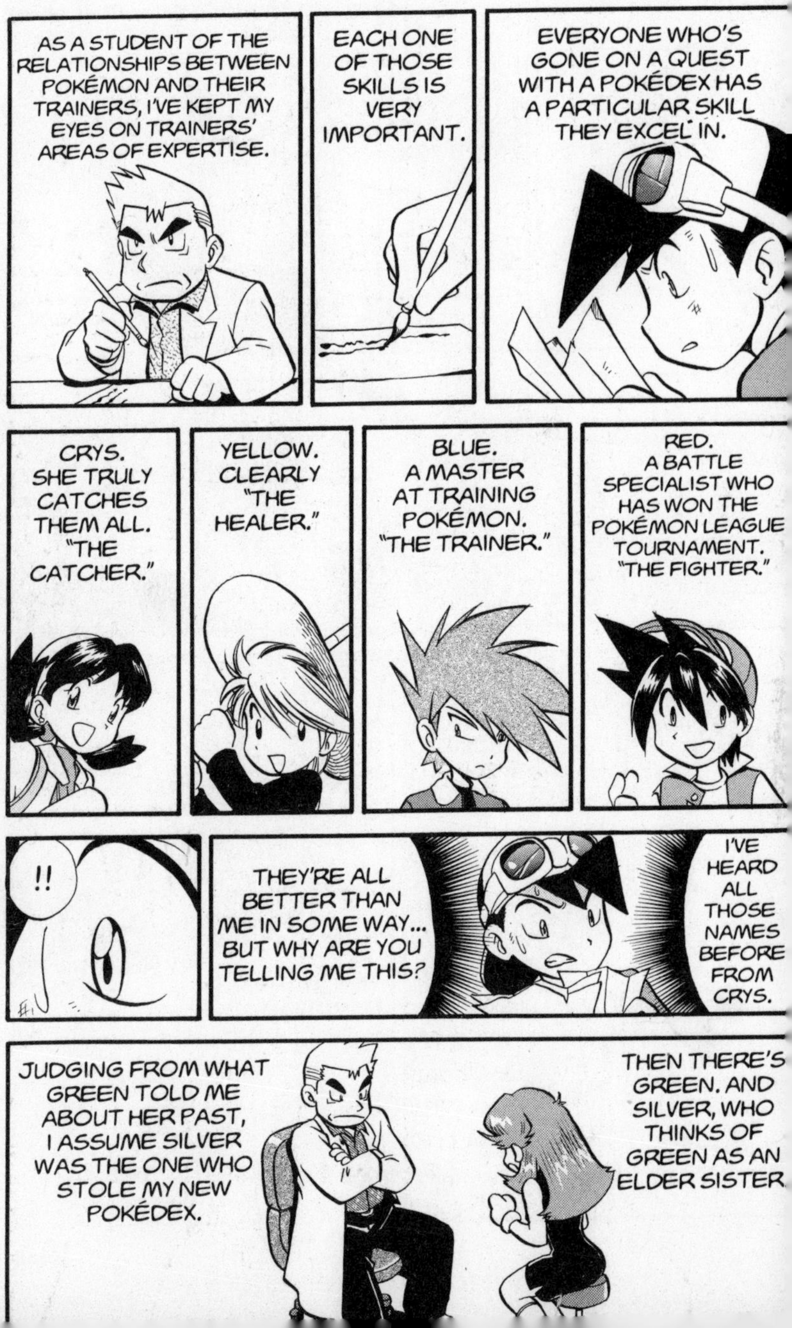
EVERYONE WHO'S GONE ON A QUEST WITH A POKÉDEX HAS A PARTICULAR SKILL THEY EXCEL IN.
EACH ONE OF THOSE SKILLS IS VERY IMPORTANT.
AS A STUDENT OF THE RELATIONSHIPS BETWEEN POKÉMON AND THEIR TRAINERS, I'VE KEPT MY EYES ON TRAINERS' AREAS OF EXPERTISE.
RED. A BATTLE SPECIALIST WHO HAS WON THE POKÉMON LEAGUE TOURNAMENT. "THE FIGHTER."
BLUE. A MASTER AT TRAINING POKÉMON. "THE TRAINER."
YELLOW. CLEARLY "THE HEALER."
CRYS. SHE TRULY CATCHES THEM ALL. "THE CATCHER."
I'VE HEARD ALL THOSE NAMES BEFORE FROM CRYS.
THEY'RE ALL BETTER THAN ME IN SOME WAY... BUT WHY ARE YOU TELLING ME THIS?
!!
THEN THERE'S GREEN. AND SILVER, WHO THINKS OF GREEN AS AN ELDER SISTER
JUDGING FROM WHAT GREEN TOLD ME ABOUT HER PAST, I ASSUME SILVER WAS THE ONE WHO STOLE MY NEW POKÉDEX.

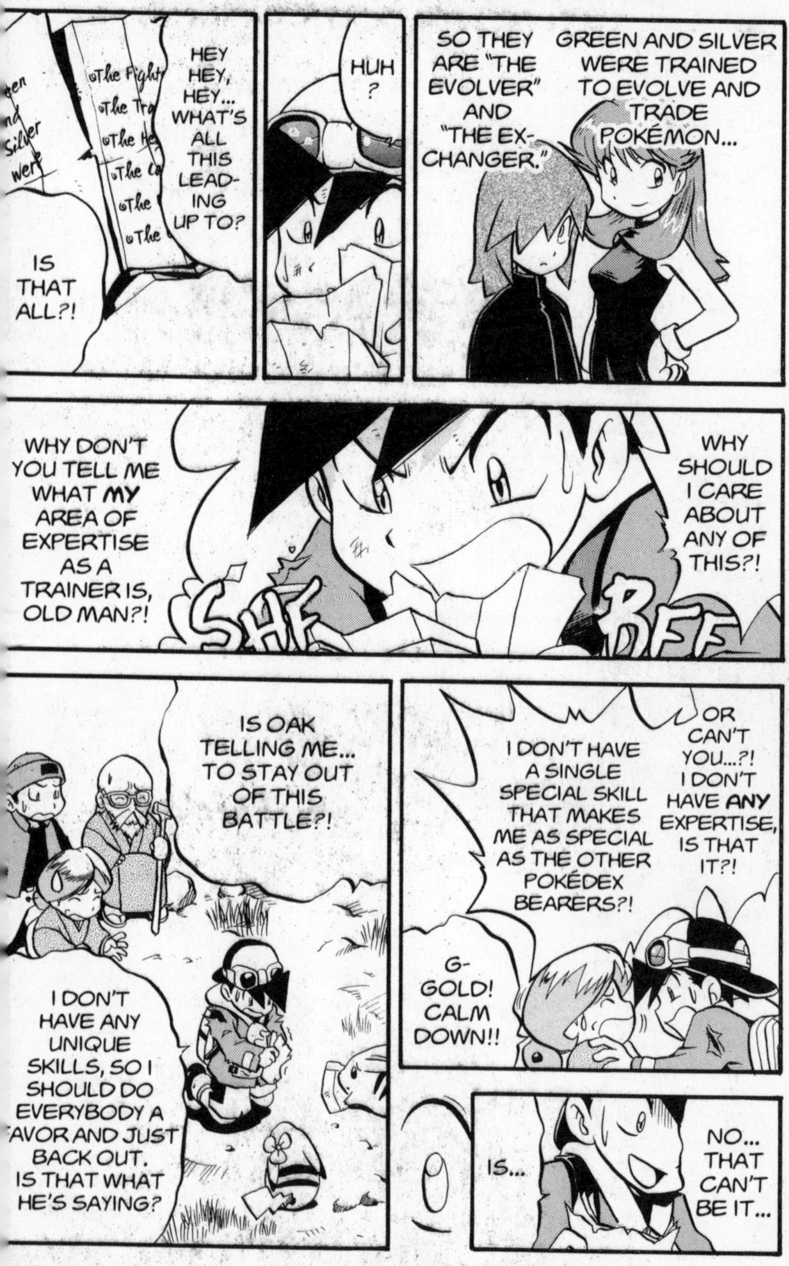
GREEN AND SILVER WERE TRAINED TO EVOLVE AND TRADE POKÉMON...
SO THEY ARE "THE EVOLVER" AND "THE EX-CHANGER."
HUH?
HEY HEY, HEY... WHAT'S ALL THIS LEADING UP TO?
IS THAT ALL?!
WHY SHOULD I CARE ABOUT ANY OF THIS?!
WHY DON'T YOU TELL ME WHAT **MY** AREA OF EXPERTISE AS A TRAINER IS, OLD MAN?!
SHF
BFF
OR CAN'T YOU...?! I DON'T HAVE **ANY** EXPERTISE, IS THAT IT?!
I DON'T HAVE A SINGLE SPECIAL SKILL THAT MAKES ME AS SPECIAL AS THE OTHER POKÉDEX BEARERS?!
G-GOLD! CALM DOWN!!
NO... THAT CAN'T BE IT...
IS...
IS OAK TELLING ME... TO STAY OUT OF THIS BATTLE?!
I DON'T HAVE ANY UNIQUE SKILLS, SO I SHOULD DO EVERYBODY A FAVOR AND JUST BACK OUT. IS THAT WHAT HE'S SAYING?

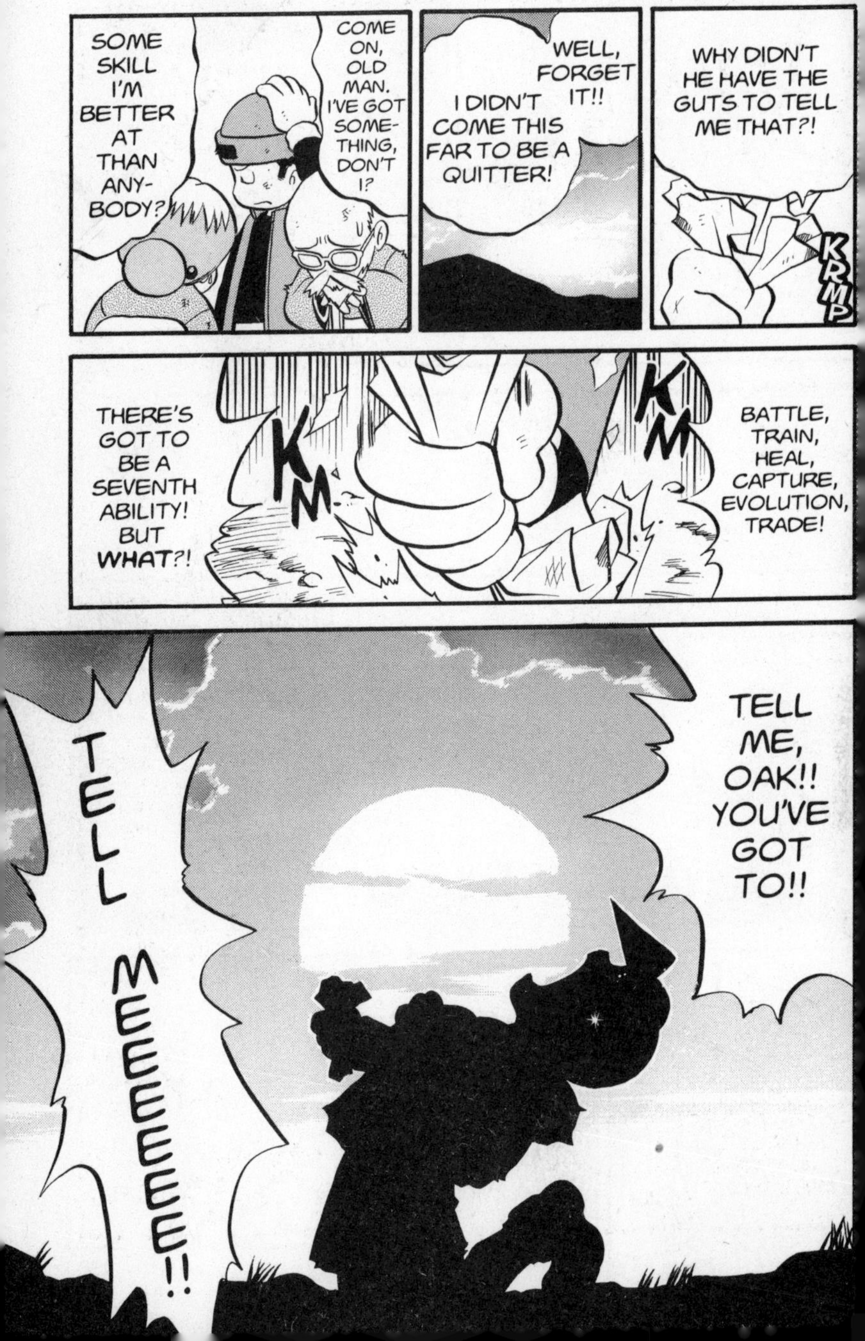
WHY DIDN'T HE HAVE THE GUTS TO TELL ME THAT?!
KRMP
WELL, FORGET IT!!
I DIDN'T COME THIS FAR TO BE A QUITTER!
COME ON, OLD MAN. I'VE GOT SOME-THING, DON'T I?
SOME SKILL I'M BETTER AT THAN ANY-BODY?
BATTLE, TRAIN, HEAL, CAPTURE, EVOLUTION, TRADE!
KM
KM
THERE'S GOT TO BE A SEVENTH ABILITY! BUT **WHAT**?!
TELL ME, OAK!! YOU'VE GOT TO!!
TELL MEEEEEEE!!

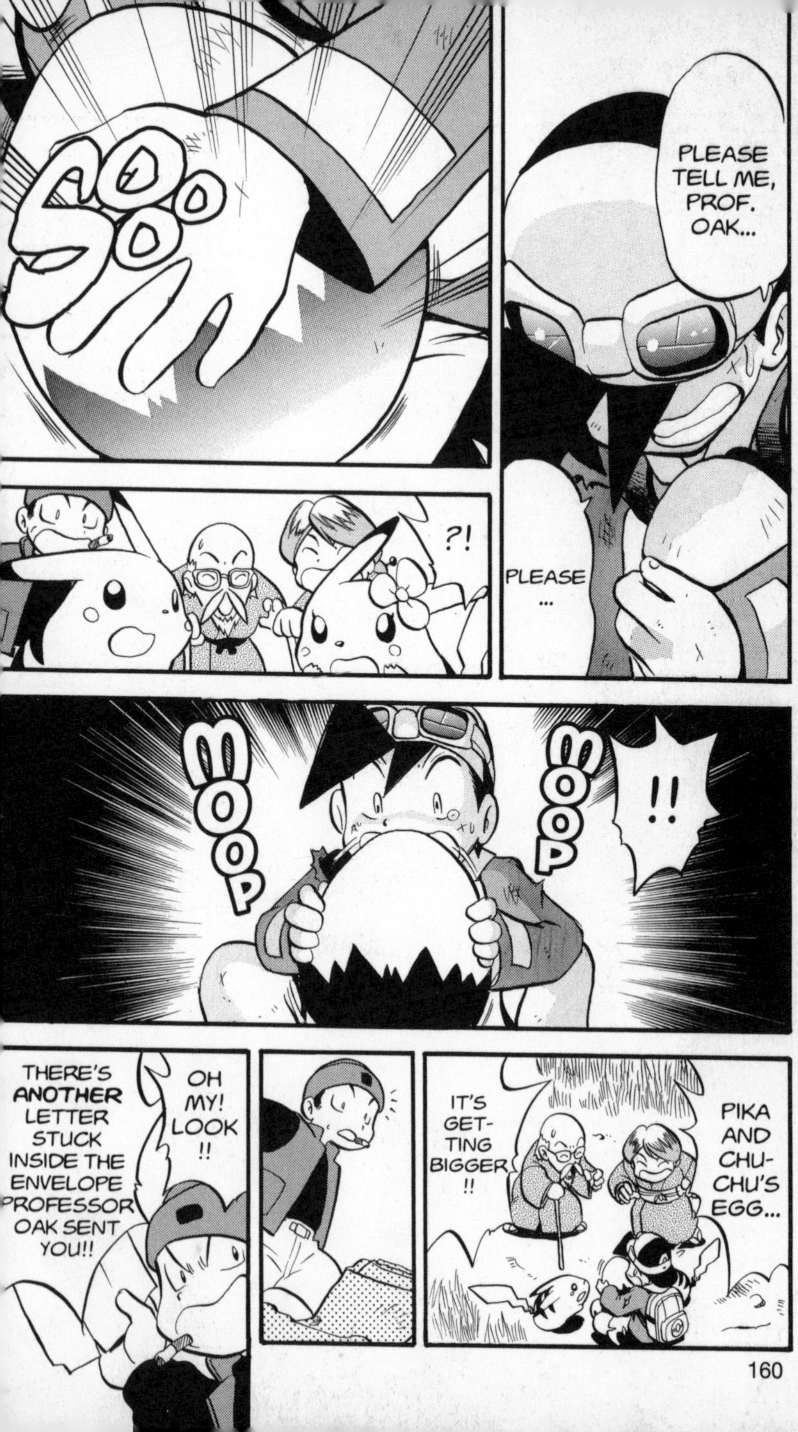
PLEASE TELL ME, PROF. OAK...
SQOO
PLEASE ...
?!
!!
MOOOP
MOOOP
PIKA AND CHU-CHU'S EGG...
IT'S GET-TING BIGGER!!
OH MY! LOOK!!
THERE'S **ANOTHER** LETTER STUCK INSIDE THE ENVELOPE PROFESSOR OAK SENT YOU!!

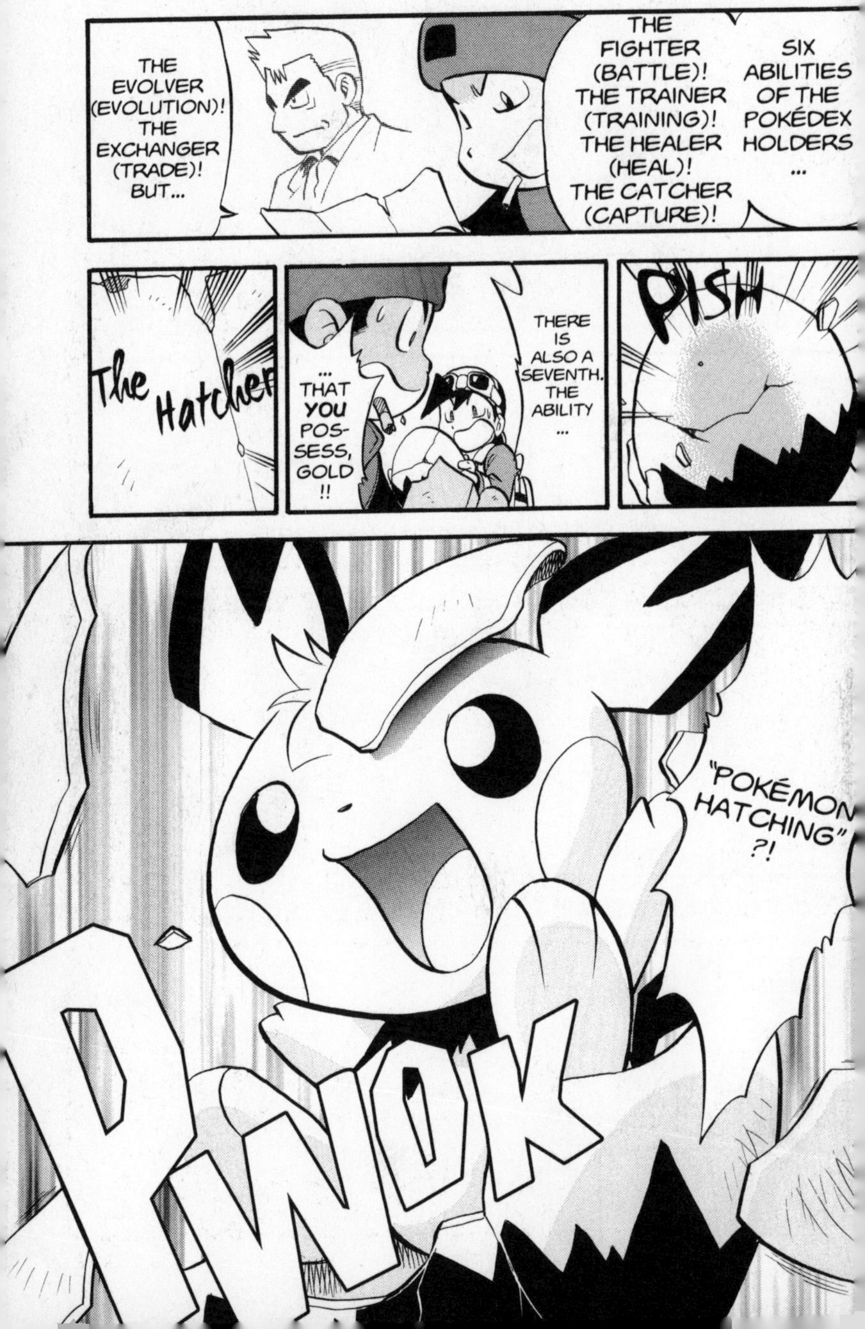
SIX ABILITIES OF THE POKÉDEX HOLDERS ...
THE FIGHTER (BATTLE)! THE TRAINER (TRAINING)! THE HEALER (HEAL)! THE CATCHER (CAPTURE)!
THE EVOLVER (EVOLUTION)! THE EXCHANGER (TRADE)! BUT...
PISH
THERE IS ALSO A SEVENTH. THE ABILITY ...
... THAT **YOU** POSSESS, GOLD !!
The Hatcher
"POKÉMON HATCHING" ?!
PWOK

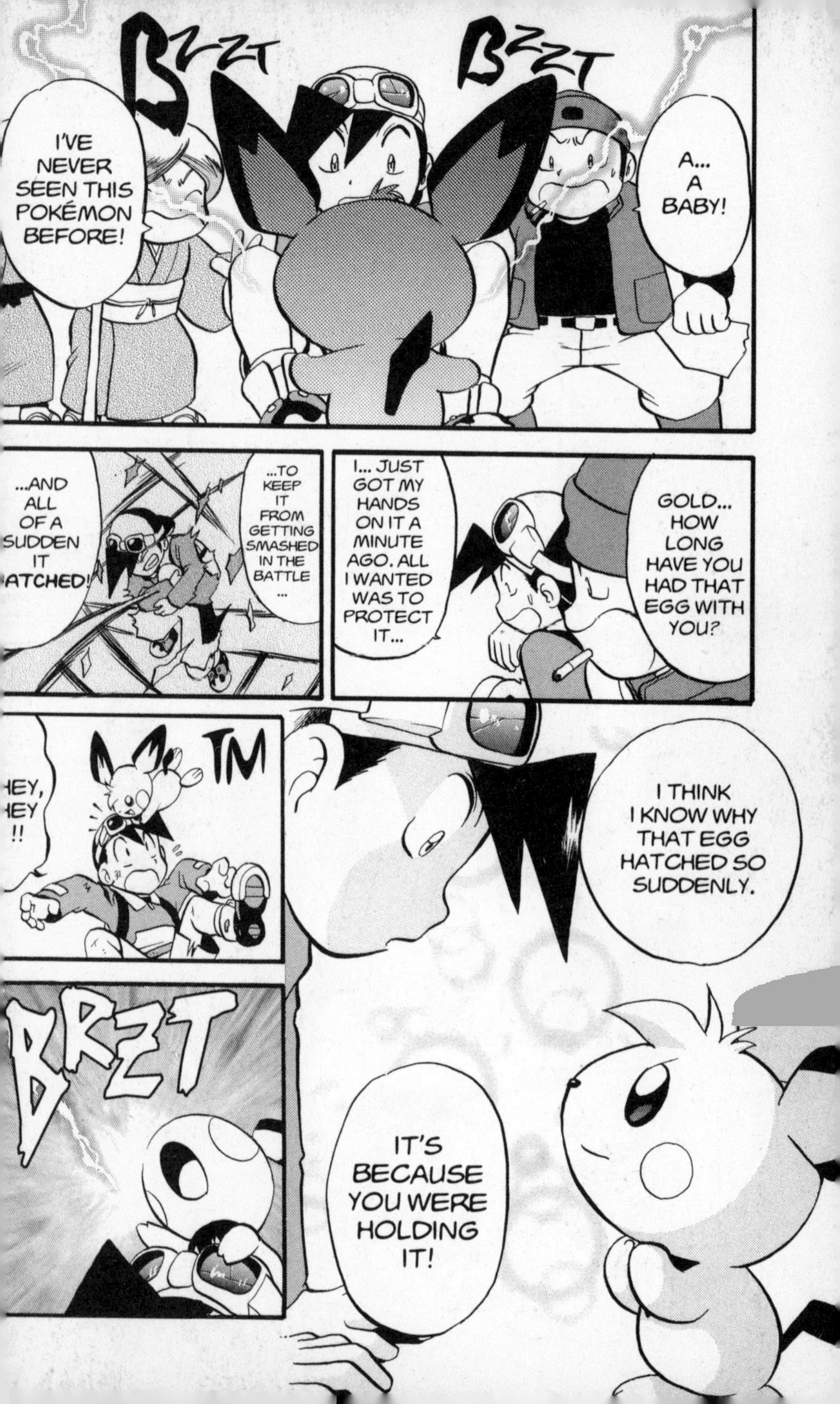
BZZT
BZZT
A... A BABY!
I'VE NEVER SEEN THIS POKÉMON BEFORE!
GOLD... HOW LONG HAVE YOU HAD THAT EGG WITH YOU?
I... JUST GOT MY HANDS ON IT A MINUTE AGO. ALL I WANTED WAS TO PROTECT IT...
...TO KEEP IT FROM GETTING SMASHED IN THE BATTLE ...
...AND ALL OF A SUDDEN IT ATCHED!
I THINK I KNOW WHY THAT EGG HATCHED SO SUDDENLY.
IT'S BECAUSE YOU WERE HOLDING IT!
TM
EY, EY !!
BRZT

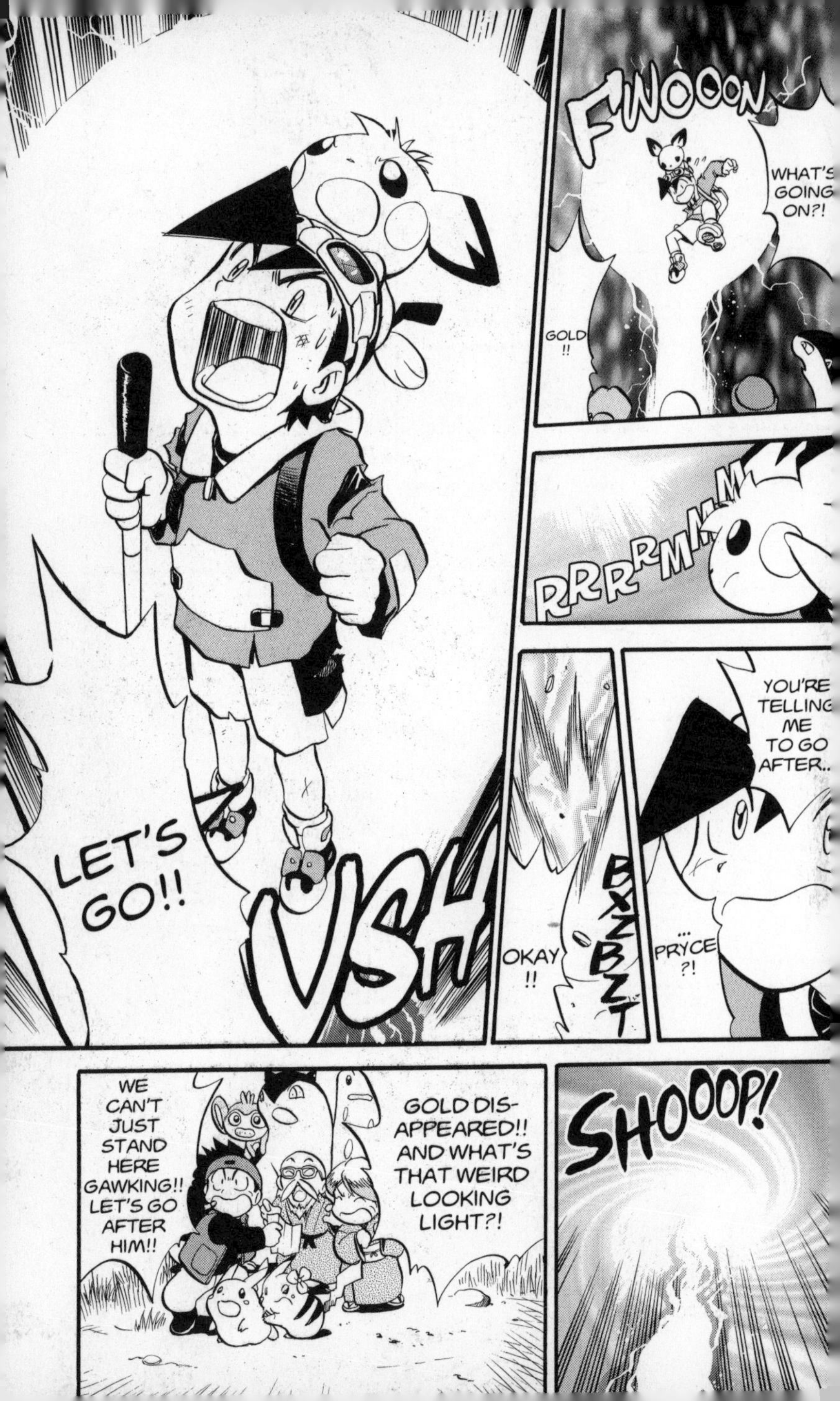
FWOOON
WHAT'S GOING ON?!
GOLD!!
RRRRMMM
YOU'RE TELLING ME TO GO AFTER...
...PRYCE?!
BXZBZT
OKAY!!
LET'S GO!!
VSH
SHOOOP!
GOLD DIS-APPEARED!! AND WHAT'S THAT WEIRD LOOKING LIGHT?!
WE CAN'T JUST STAND HERE GAWKING!! LET'S GO AFTER HIM!!

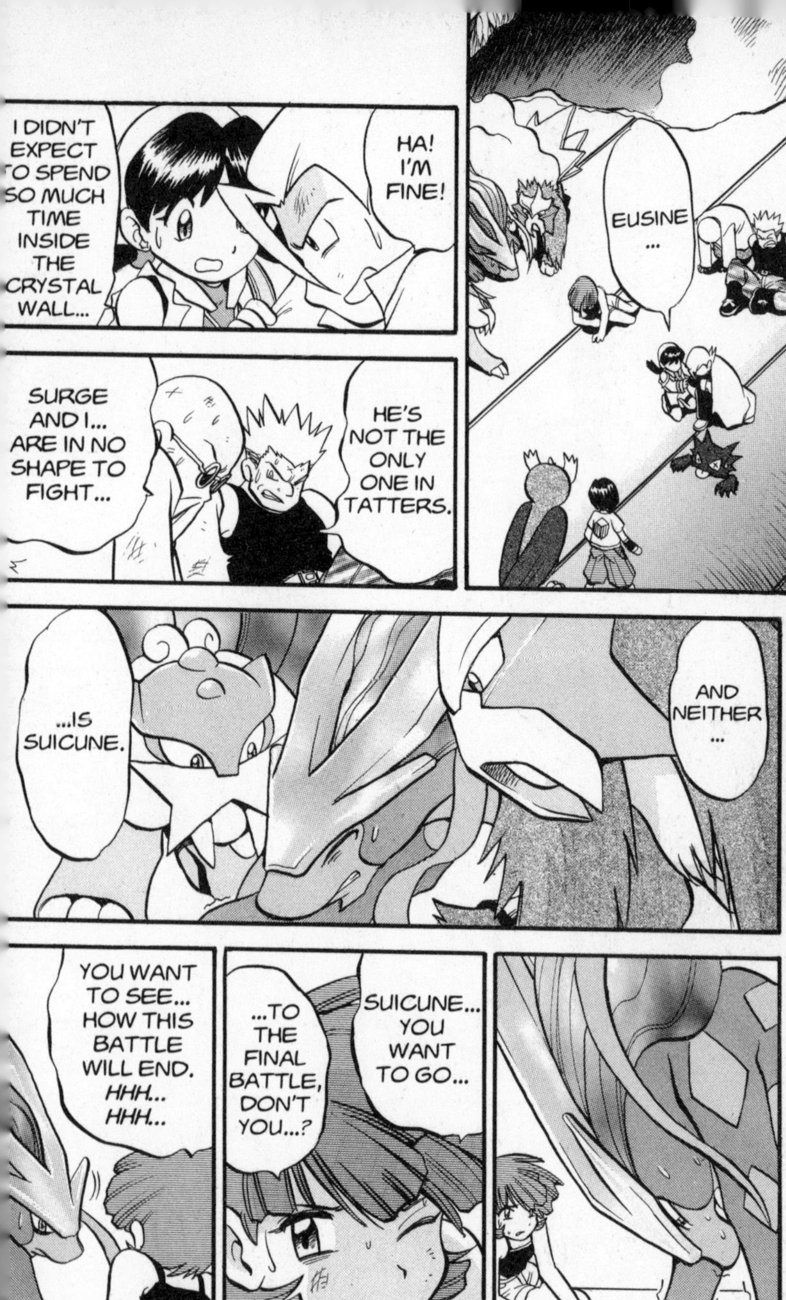
EUSINE...
HA! I'M FINE!
I DIDN'T EXPECT TO SPEND SO MUCH TIME INSIDE THE CRYSTAL WALL...
HE'S NOT THE ONLY ONE IN TATTERS.
SURGE AND I... ARE IN NO SHAPE TO FIGHT...
AND NEITHER...
...IS SUICUNE.
SUICUNE... YOU WANT TO GO...
...TO THE FINAL BATTLE, DON'T YOU...?
YOU WANT TO SEE... HOW THIS BATTLE WILL END. *HHH... HHH...*

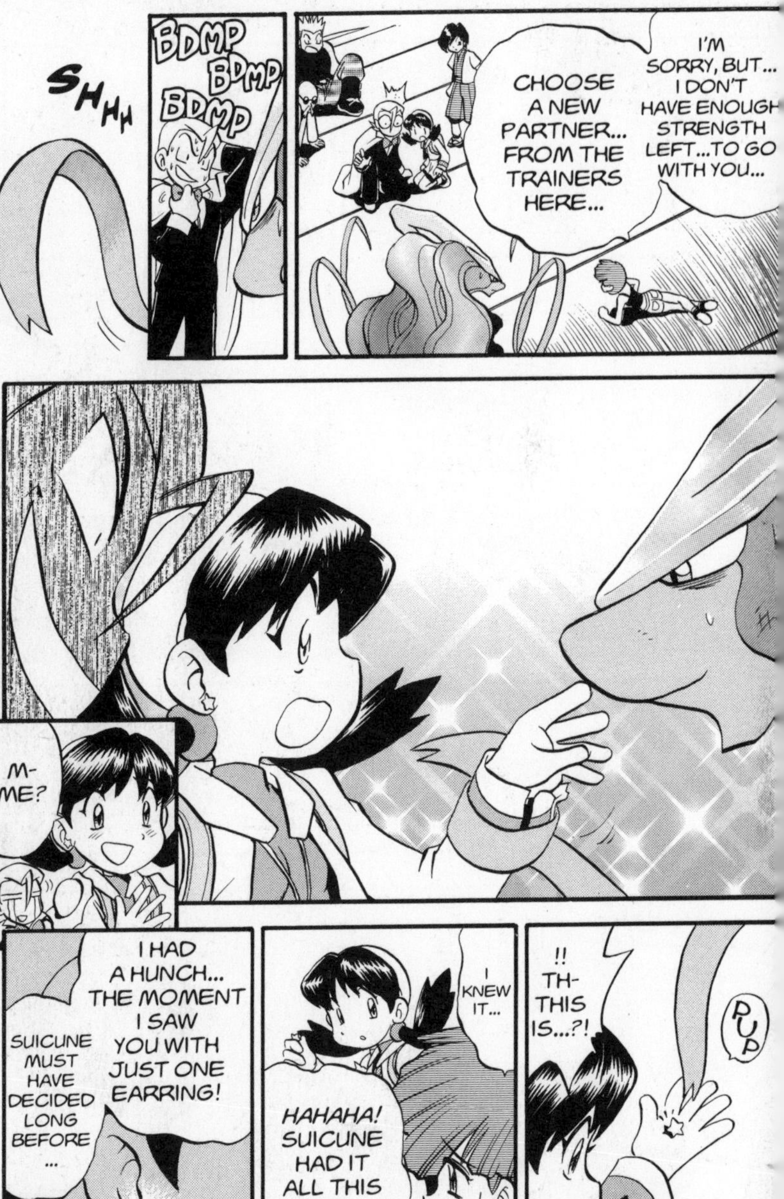
I'M SORRY, BUT... I DON'T HAVE ENOUGH STRENGTH LEFT...TO GO WITH YOU...
CHOOSE A NEW PARTNER... FROM THE TRAINERS HERE...
BDMP BDMP BDMP
SHHH
M-ME?
PUP
!! TH-THIS IS...?!
I KNEW IT...
HAHAHA! SUICUNE HAD IT ALL THIS TIME...
I HAD A HUNCH... THE MOMENT I SAW YOU WITH JUST ONE EARRING!
SUICUNE MUST HAVE DECIDED LONG BEFORE ...

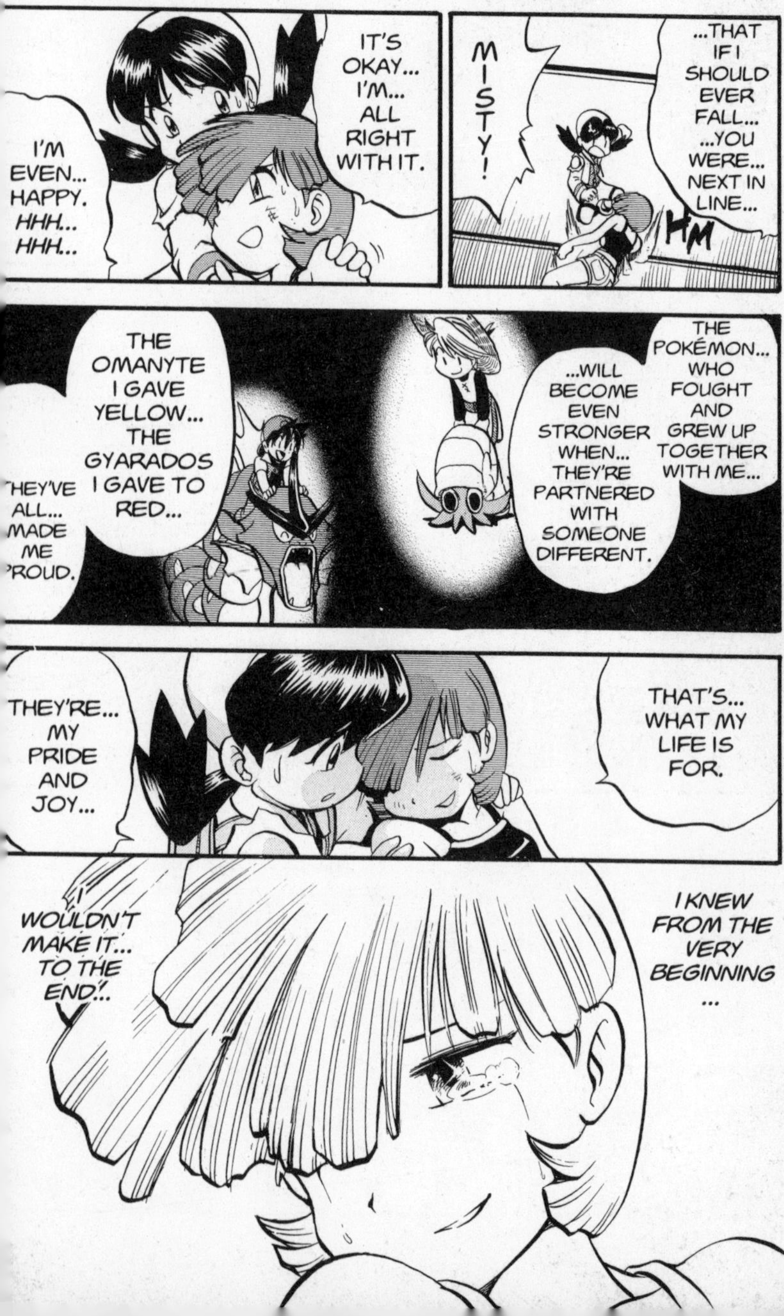
...THAT IF I SHOULD EVER FALL... ...YOU WERE... NEXT IN LINE...
MISTY!
HM
IT'S OKAY... I'M... ALL RIGHT WITH IT.
I'M EVEN... HAPPY. HHH... HHH...
THE POKÉMON... WHO FOUGHT AND GREW UP TOGETHER WITH ME...
...WILL BECOME EVEN STRONGER WHEN... THEY'RE PARTNERED WITH SOMEONE DIFFERENT.
THE OMANYTE I GAVE YELLOW... THE GYARADOS I GAVE TO RED...
THEY'VE ALL... MADE ME PROUD.
THAT'S... WHAT MY LIFE IS FOR.
THEY'RE... MY PRIDE AND JOY...
I KNEW FROM THE VERY BEGINNING ...
I WOULDN'T MAKE IT... TO THE END...

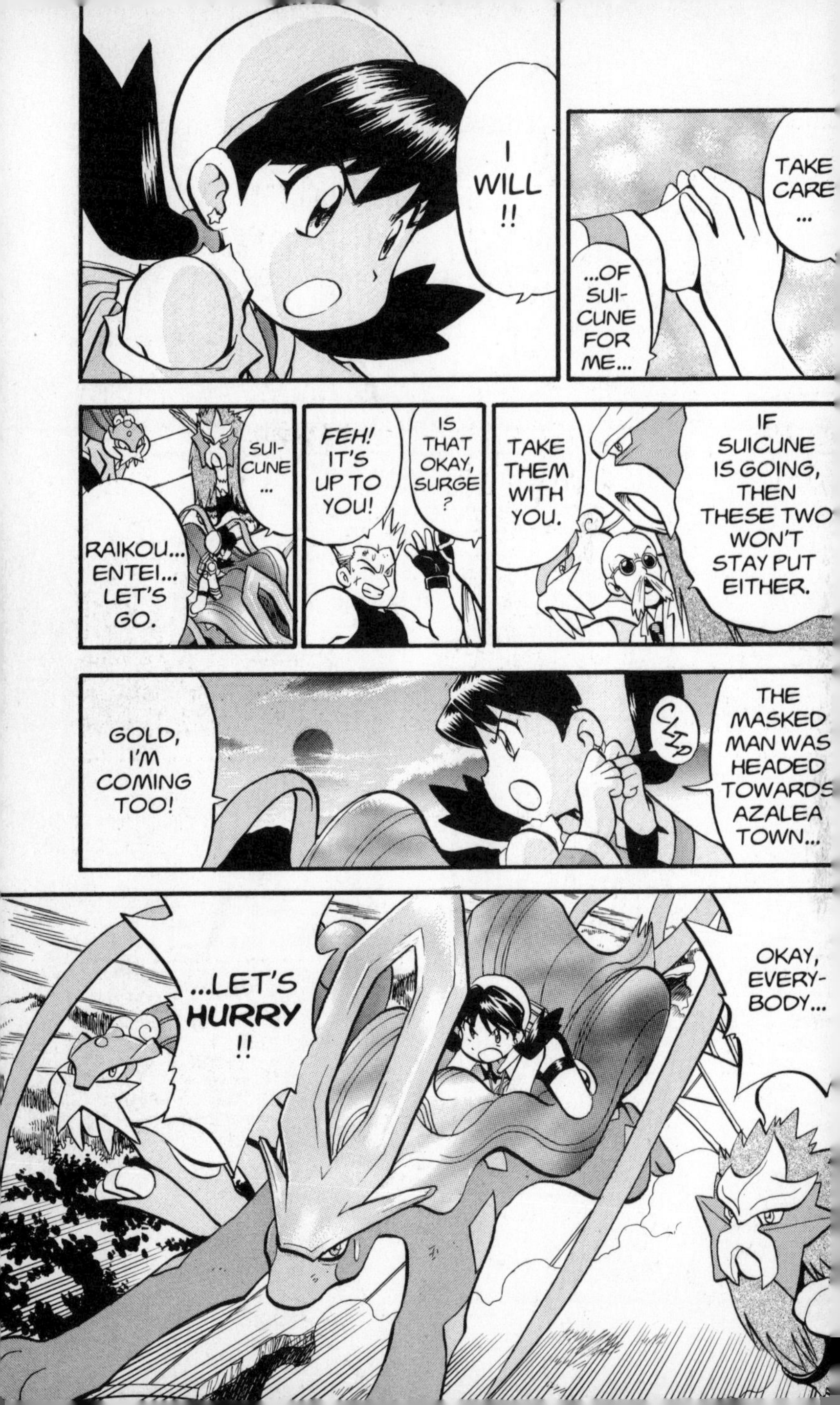
TAKE CARE ...
...OF SUI-CUNE FOR ME...
I WILL !!
IF SUICUNE IS GOING, THEN THESE TWO WON'T STAY PUT EITHER.
TAKE THEM WITH YOU.
IS THAT OKAY, SURGE?
FEH! IT'S UP TO YOU!
SUI-CUNE ...
RAIKOU... ENTEI... LET'S GO.
THE MASKED MAN WAS HEADED TOWARDS AZALEA TOWN...
CLIP
GOLD, I'M COMING TOO!
OKAY, EVERY-BODY...
...LET'S HURRY !!

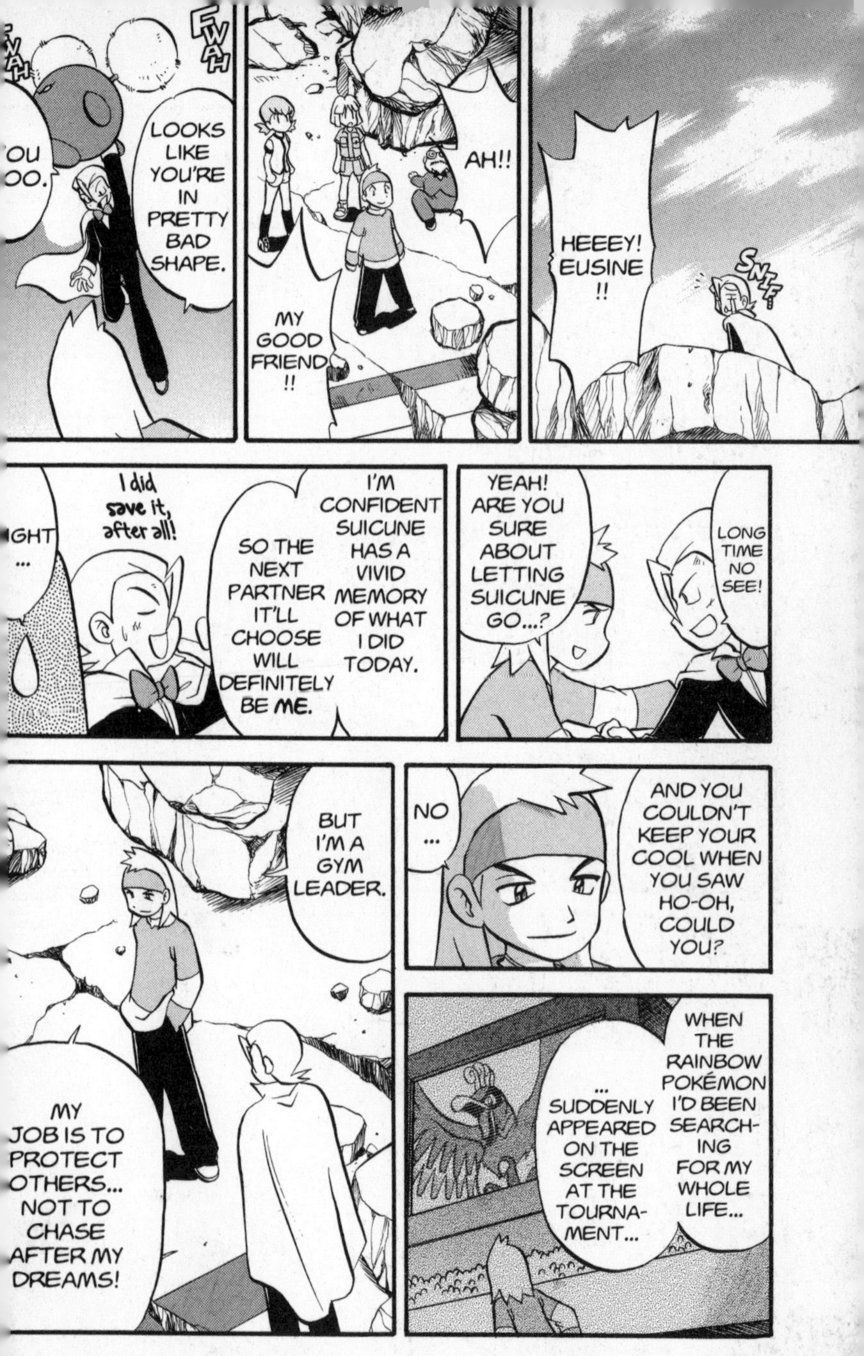
HEEEY! EUSINE !!
SNIFF
AH!!
MY GOOD FRIEND !!
FWAH
FWAH
LOOKS LIKE YOU'RE IN PRETTY BAD SHAPE.
LONG TIME NO SEE!
YEAH! ARE YOU SURE ABOUT LETTING SUICUNE GO...?
I'M CONFIDENT SUICUNE HAS A VIVID MEMORY OF WHAT I DID TODAY.
SO THE NEXT PARTNER IT'LL CHOOSE WILL DEFINITELY BE ME.
I did save it, after all!
AND YOU COULDN'T KEEP YOUR COOL WHEN YOU SAW HO-OH, COULD YOU?
NO ...
WHEN THE RAINBOW POKÉMON I'D BEEN SEARCH-ING FOR MY WHOLE LIFE...
... SUDDENLY APPEARED ON THE SCREEN AT THE TOURNA-MENT...
BUT I'M A GYM LEADER.
MY JOB IS TO PROTECT OTHERS... NOT TO CHASE AFTER MY DREAMS!

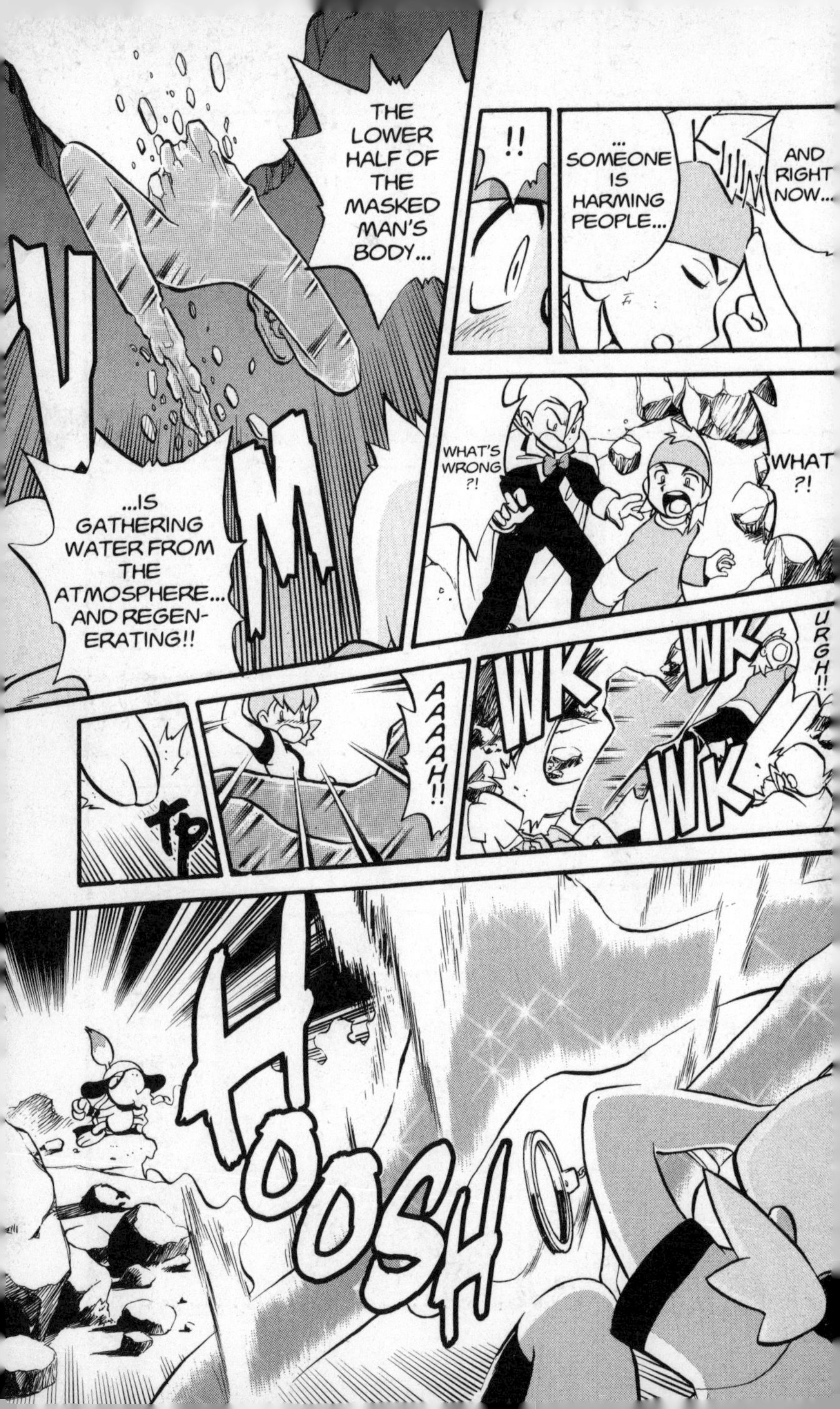

AND RIGHT NOW...
...SOMEONE IS HARMING PEOPLE...
!!
WHAT?!
WHAT'S WRONG?!
THE LOWER HALF OF THE MASKED MAN'S BODY...
...IS GATHERING WATER FROM THE ATMOSPHERE... AND REGENERATING!!
URGH!!
WK
WK
WK
AAAAH!!
TP
WHOOSH

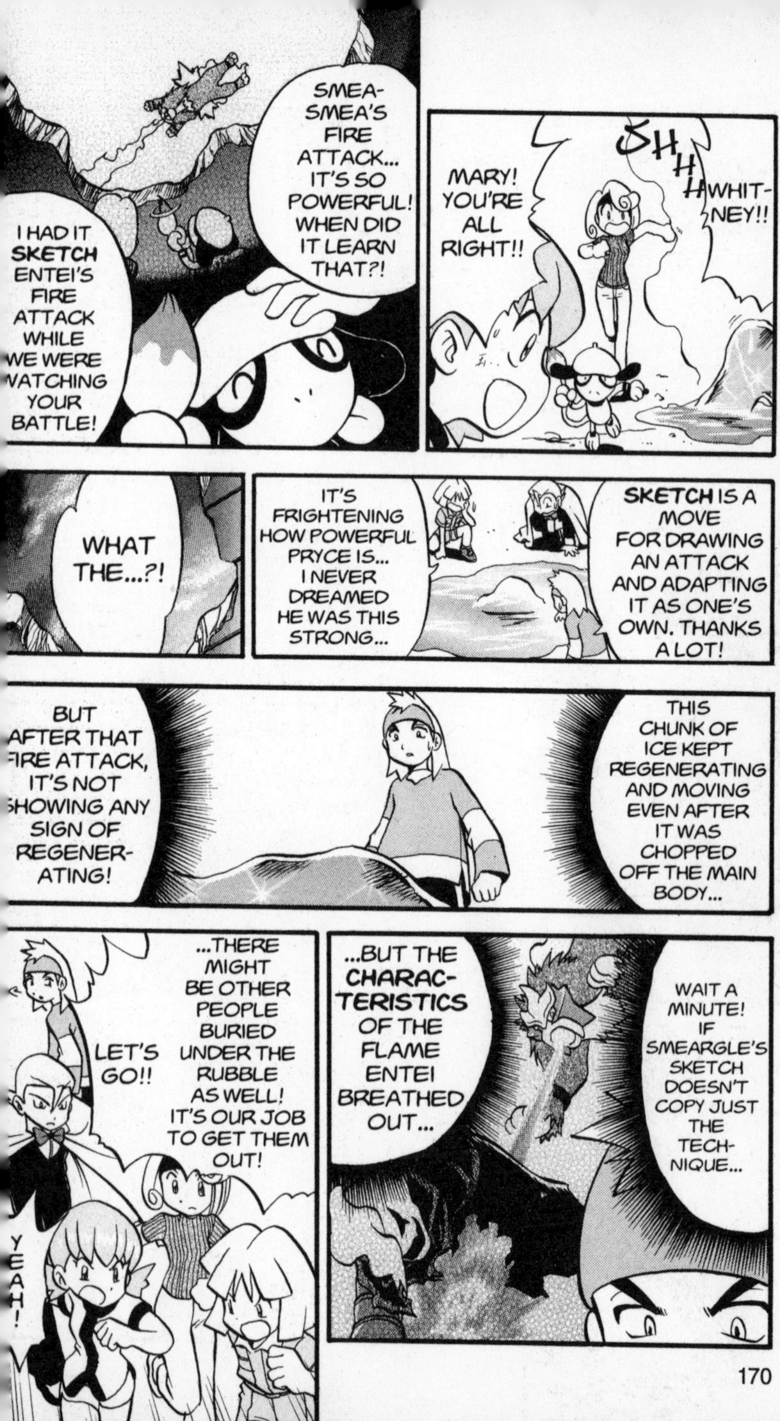
SHHH
WHITNEY!!
MARY! YOU'RE ALL RIGHT!!
SMEA-SMEA'S FIRE ATTACK... IT'S SO POWERFUL! WHEN DID IT LEARN THAT?!
I HAD IT SKETCH ENTEI'S FIRE ATTACK WHILE WE WERE WATCHING YOUR BATTLE!
SKETCH IS A MOVE FOR DRAWING AN ATTACK AND ADAPTING IT AS ONE'S OWN. THANKS A LOT!
IT'S FRIGHTENING HOW POWERFUL PRYCE IS... I NEVER DREAMED HE WAS THIS STRONG...
WHAT THE...?!
THIS CHUNK OF ICE KEPT REGENERATING AND MOVING EVEN AFTER IT WAS CHOPPED OFF THE MAIN BODY...
BUT AFTER THAT FIRE ATTACK, IT'S NOT SHOWING ANY SIGN OF REGENER-ATING!
WAIT A MINUTE! IF SMEARGLE'S SKETCH DOESN'T COPY JUST THE TECH-NIQUE...
...BUT THE CHARAC-TERISTICS OF THE FLAME ENTEI BREATHED OUT...
...THERE MIGHT BE OTHER PEOPLE BURIED UNDER THE RUBBLE AS WELL! IT'S OUR JOB TO GET THEM OUT!
LET'S GO!!
YEAH!

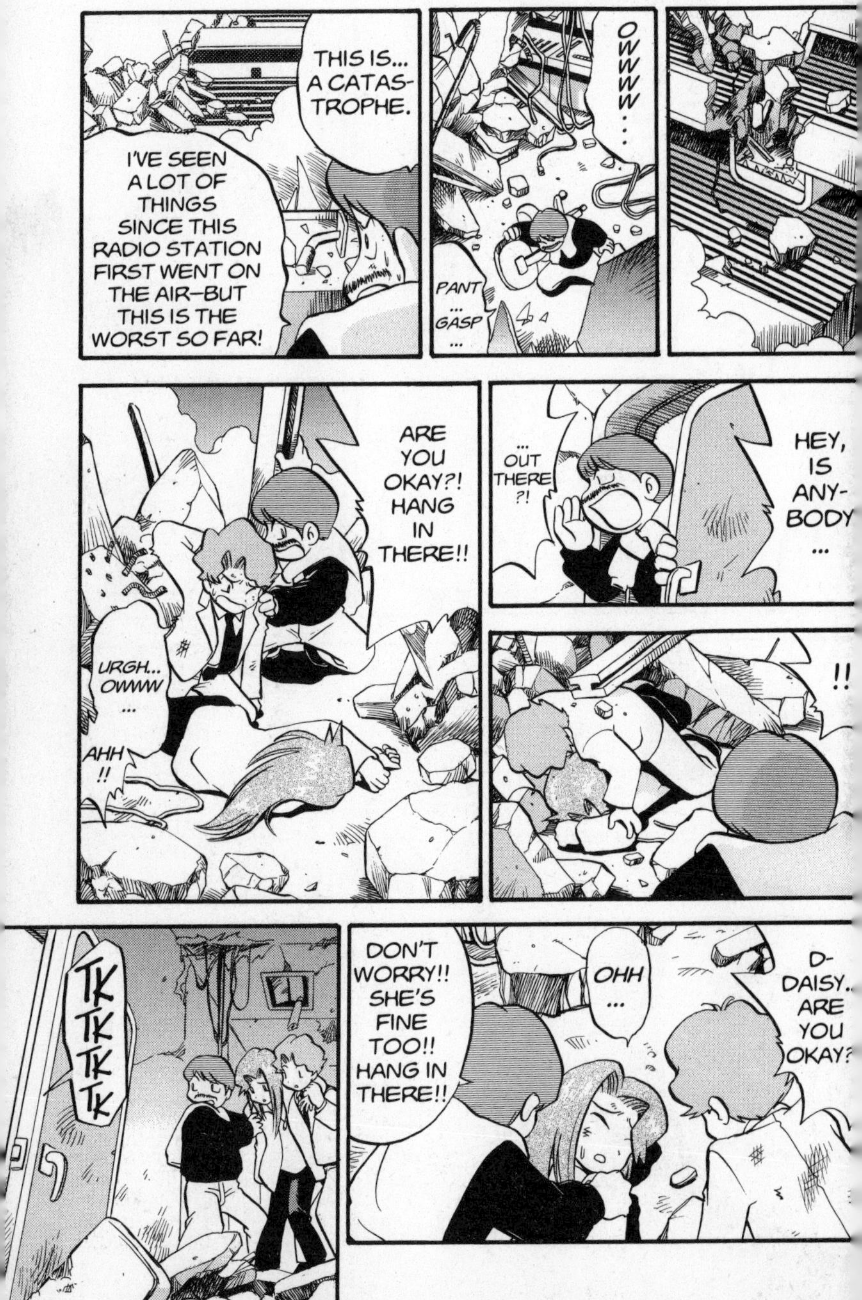
OWWWW...
PANT... GASP...
THIS IS... A CATASTROPHE.
I'VE SEEN A LOT OF THINGS SINCE THIS RADIO STATION FIRST WENT ON THE AIR—BUT THIS IS THE WORST SO FAR!
HEY, IS ANYBODY...
...OUT THERE?!
!!
ARE YOU OKAY?! HANG IN THERE!!
URGH... OWWW...
AHH!!
D-DAISY... ARE YOU OKAY?
OHH...
DON'T WORRY!! SHE'S FINE TOO!! HANG IN THERE!!
TK TK TK TK TK

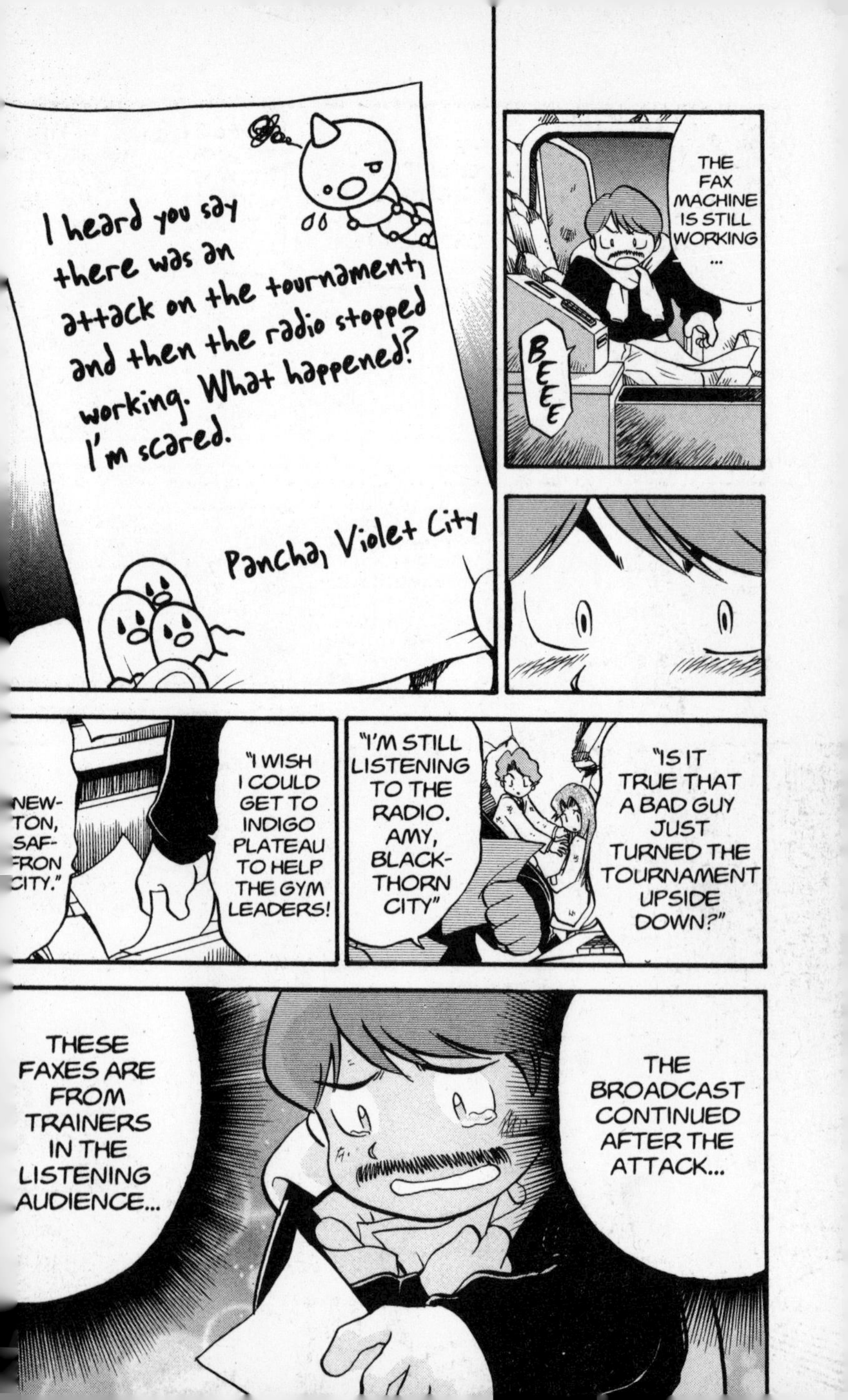
THE FAX MACHINE IS STILL WORKING...
BEEE
I heard you say there was an attack on the tournament, and then the radio stopped working. What happened? I'm scared.
Pancha, Violet City
"IS IT TRUE THAT A BAD GUY JUST TURNED THE TOURNAMENT UPSIDE DOWN?"
"I'M STILL LISTENING TO THE RADIO. AMY, BLACKTHORN CITY"
"I WISH I COULD GET TO INDIGO PLATEAU TO HELP THE GYM LEADERS!
NEWTON, SAFFRON CITY."
THE BROADCAST CONTINUED AFTER THE ATTACK...
THESE FAXES ARE FROM TRAINERS IN THE LISTENING AUDIENCE...

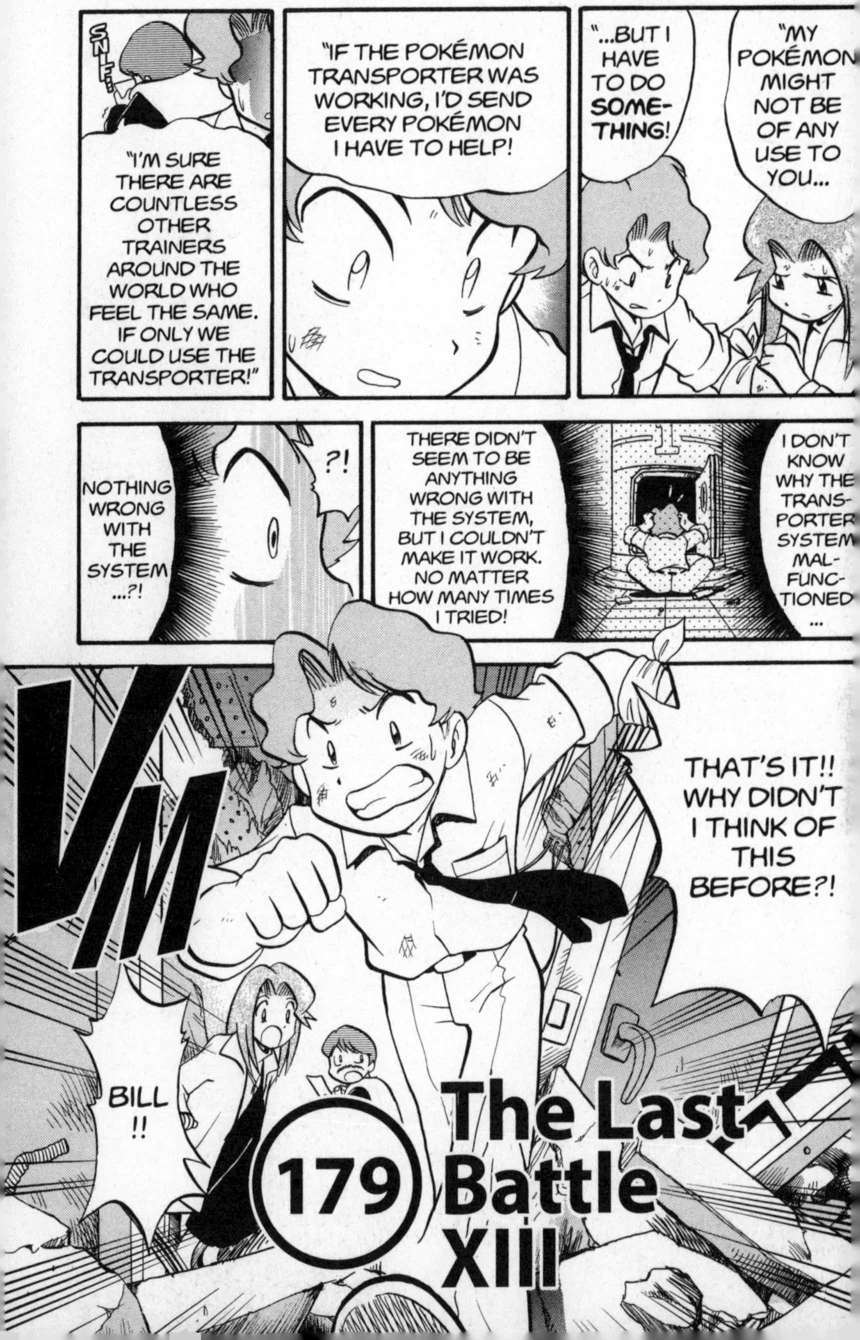
"MY POKÉMON MIGHT NOT BE OF ANY USE TO YOU...
"...BUT I HAVE TO DO SOME-THING!
"IF THE POKÉMON TRANSPORTER WAS WORKING, I'D SEND EVERY POKÉMON I HAVE TO HELP!
SNIFF...
"I'M SURE THERE ARE COUNTLESS OTHER TRAINERS AROUND THE WORLD WHO FEEL THE SAME. IF ONLY WE COULD USE THE TRANSPORTER!"
I DON'T KNOW WHY THE TRANS-PORTER SYSTEM MAL-FUNC-TIONED...
THERE DIDN'T SEEM TO BE ANYTHING WRONG WITH THE SYSTEM, BUT I COULDN'T MAKE IT WORK. NO MATTER HOW MANY TIMES I TRIED!
?!
NOTHING WRONG WITH THE SYSTEM ...?!
THAT'S IT!! WHY DIDN'T I THINK OF THIS BEFORE?!
VM
BILL !!
179 The Last Battle XIII

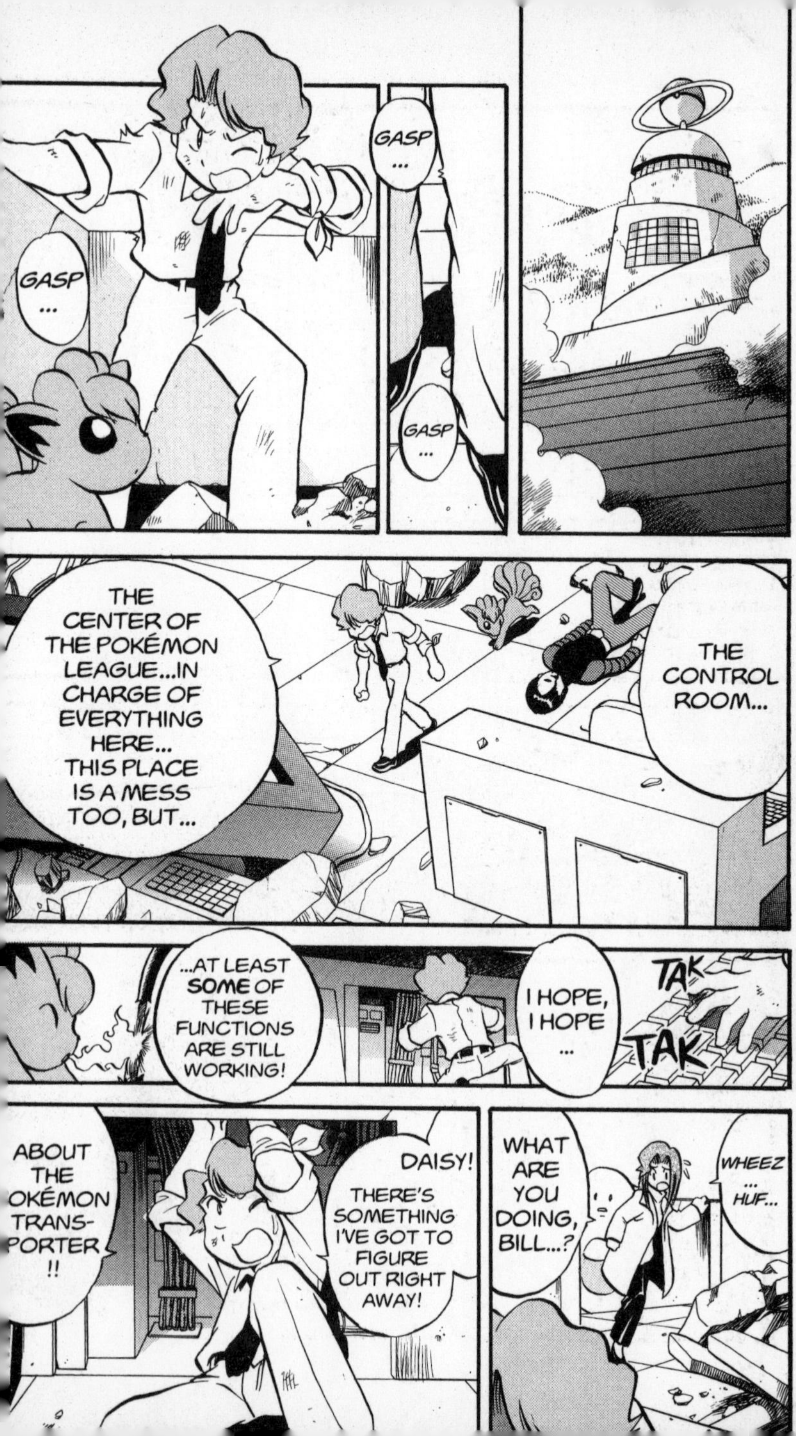
GASP ...
GASP ...
GASP ...
THE CONTROL ROOM...
THE CENTER OF THE POKÉMON LEAGUE...IN CHARGE OF EVERYTHING HERE... THIS PLACE IS A MESS TOO, BUT...
TAK
TAK
I HOPE, I HOPE ...
...AT LEAST SOME OF THESE FUNCTIONS ARE STILL WORKING!
WHEEZ ... HUF...
WHAT ARE YOU DOING, BILL...?
DAISY!
THERE'S SOMETHING I'VE GOT TO FIGURE OUT RIGHT AWAY!
ABOUT THE OKÉMON TRANS-PORTER !!

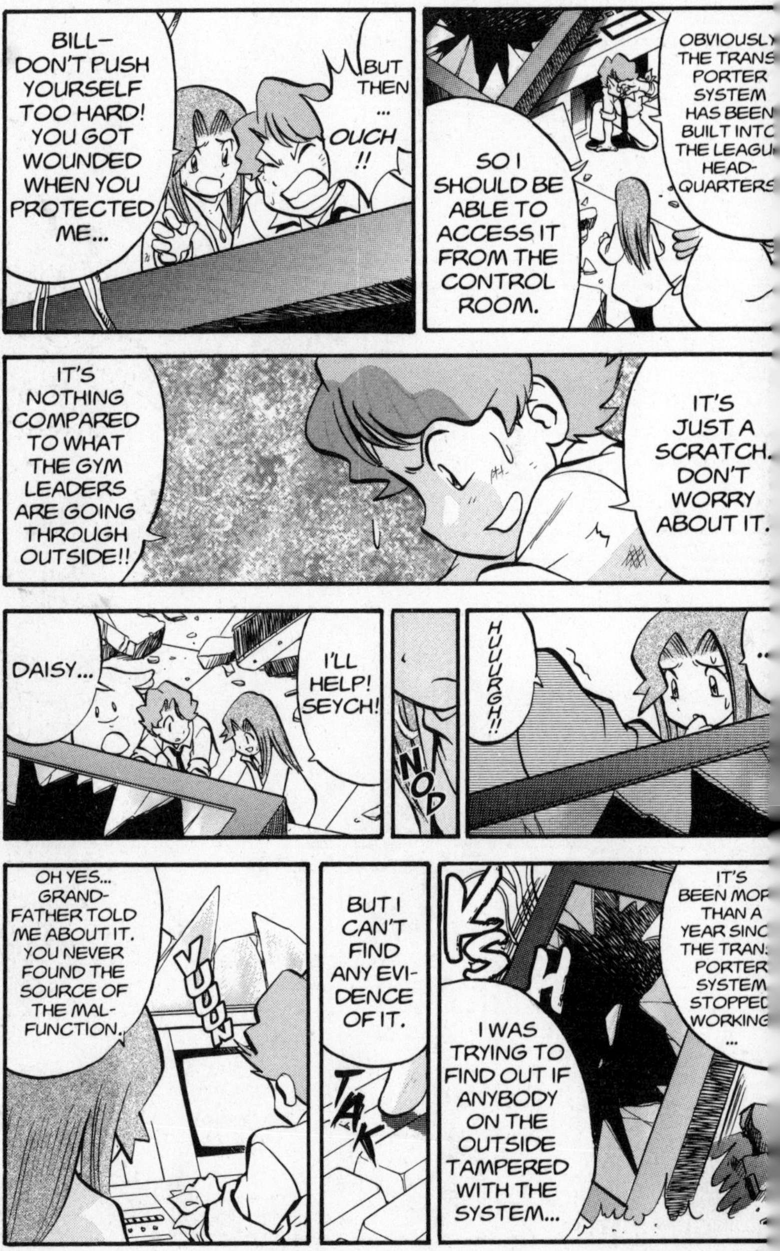
OBVIOUSL THE TRANS PORTER SYSTEM HAS BEEN BUILT INTO THE LEAGU HEAD-QUARTERS
SO I SHOULD BE ABLE TO ACCESS IT FROM THE CONTROL ROOM.
BUT THEN ...
OUCH !!
BILL— DON'T PUSH YOURSELF TOO HARD! YOU GOT WOUNDED WHEN YOU PROTECTED ME...
IT'S JUST A SCRATCH. DON'T WORRY ABOUT IT.
IT'S NOTHING COMPARED TO WHAT THE GYM LEADERS ARE GOING THROUGH OUTSIDE!!
HUUURGH!!
NOD
I'LL HELP! SEYCH!
DAISY...
IT'S BEEN MOR THAN A YEAR SINC THE TRANS PORTER SYSTEM STOPPED WORKING ...
KSSH
I WAS TRYING TO FIND OUT IF ANYBODY ON THE OUTSIDE TAMPERED WITH THE SYSTEM...
BUT I CAN'T FIND ANY EVI-DENCE OF IT.
TAK
OH YES... GRAND-FATHER TOLD ME ABOUT IT. YOU NEVER FOUND THE SOURCE OF THE MAL-FUNCTION.
VUUUN

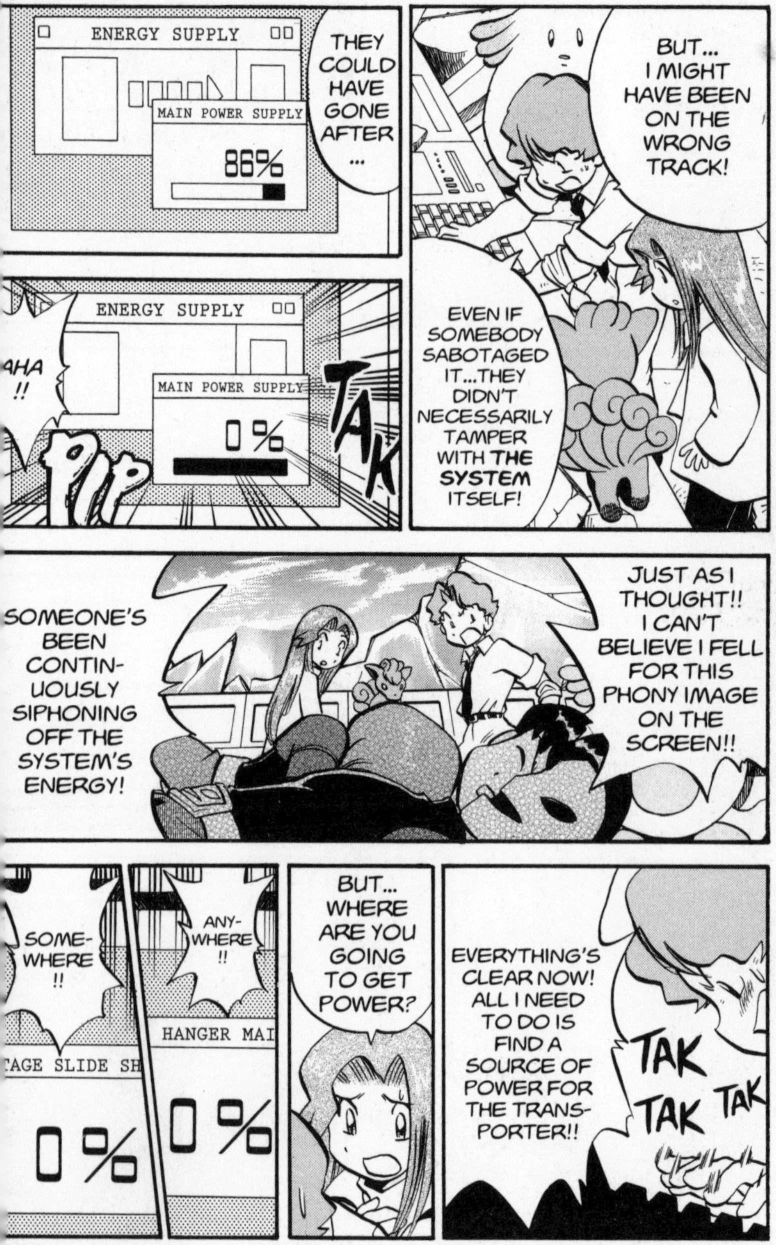
BUT... I MIGHT HAVE BEEN ON THE WRONG TRACK!
EVEN IF SOMEBODY SABOTAGED IT...THEY DIDN'T NECESSARILY TAMPER WITH THE SYSTEM ITSELF!
THEY COULD HAVE GONE AFTER ...
ENERGY SUPPLY
MAIN POWER SUPPLY
86%
ENERGY SUPPLY
MAIN POWER SUPPLY
0 %
TAK
PIP
AHA !!
JUST AS I THOUGHT!! I CAN'T BELIEVE I FELL FOR THIS PHONY IMAGE ON THE SCREEN!!
SOMEONE'S BEEN CONTIN-UOUSLY SIPHONING OFF THE SYSTEM'S ENERGY!
EVERYTHING'S CLEAR NOW! ALL I NEED TO DO IS FIND A SOURCE OF POWER FOR THE TRANS-PORTER!!
TAK TAK TAK
BUT... WHERE ARE YOU GOING TO GET POWER?
ANY-WHERE !!
HANGER MAI
0 %
SOME-WHERE !!
TAGE SLIDE SH
0 %

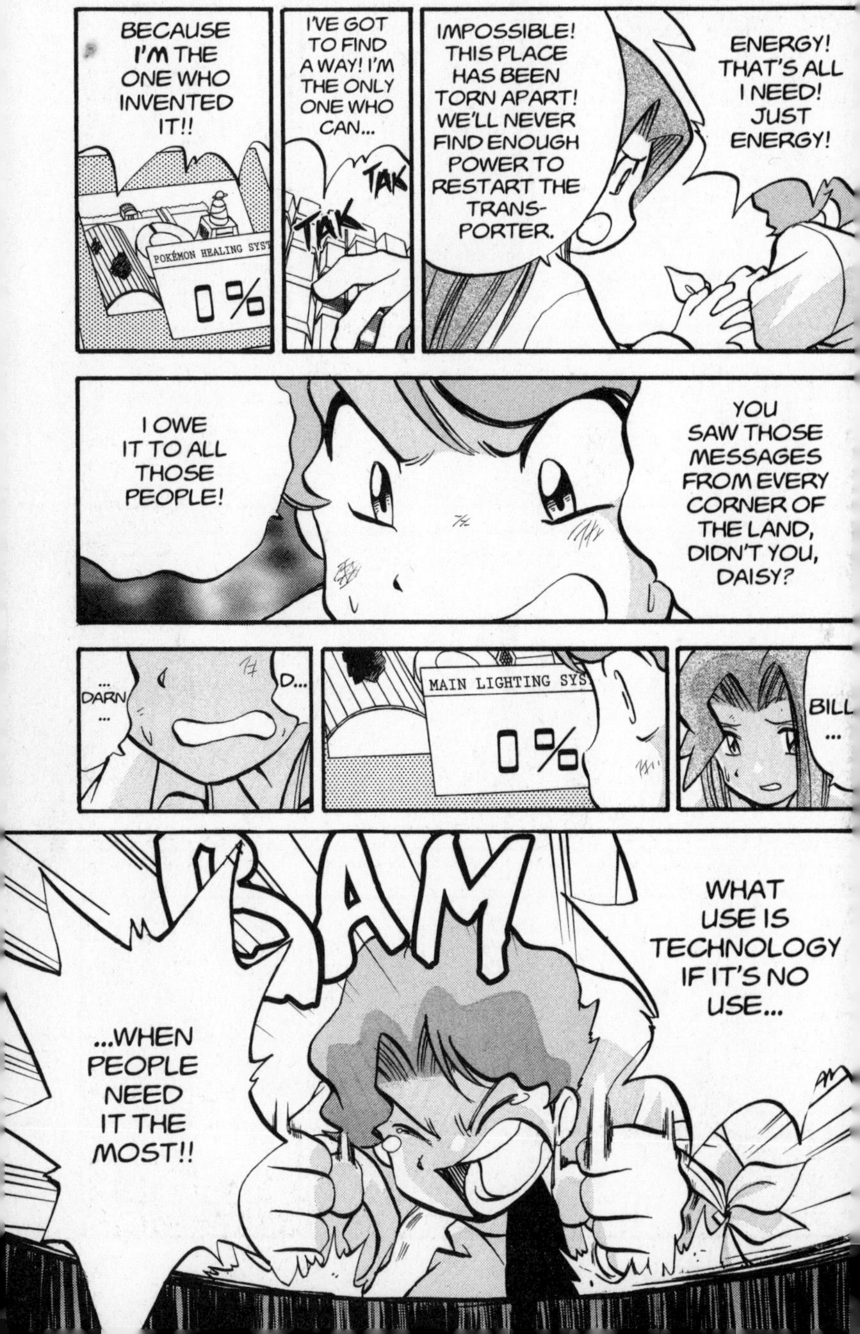
ENERGY! THAT'S ALL I NEED! JUST ENERGY!
IMPOSSIBLE! THIS PLACE HAS BEEN TORN APART! WE'LL NEVER FIND ENOUGH POWER TO RESTART THE TRANS-PORTER.
I'VE GOT TO FIND A WAY! I'M THE ONLY ONE WHO CAN...
TAK
TAK
BECAUSE I'M THE ONE WHO INVENTED IT!!
POKÉMON HEALING SYST
0%
YOU SAW THOSE MESSAGES FROM EVERY CORNER OF THE LAND, DIDN'T YOU, DAISY?
I OWE IT TO ALL THOSE PEOPLE!
BILL...
MAIN LIGHTING SYS
0%
D...
...DARN...
BAM
WHAT USE IS TECHNOLOGY IF IT'S NO USE...
...WHEN PEOPLE NEED IT THE MOST!!

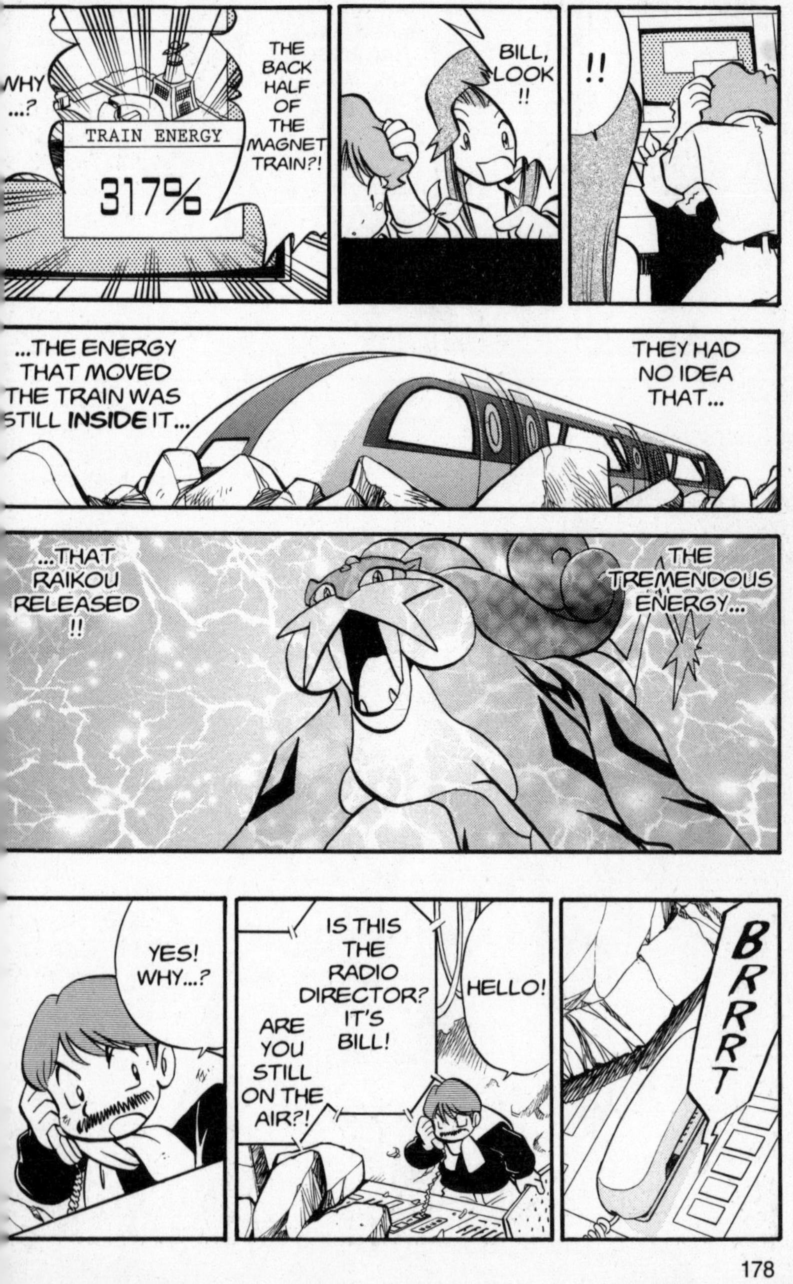
!!
BILL, LOOK !!
THE BACK HALF OF THE MAGNET TRAIN?!
WHY ...?
TRAIN ENERGY
317%
THEY HAD NO IDEA THAT...
...THE ENERGY THAT MOVED THE TRAIN WAS STILL **INSIDE** IT...
THE TREMENDOUS ENERGY...
...THAT RAIKOU RELEASED !!
BRRRT
HELLO!
IS THIS THE RADIO DIRECTOR? IT'S BILL!
ARE YOU STILL ON THE AIR?!
YES! WHY...?

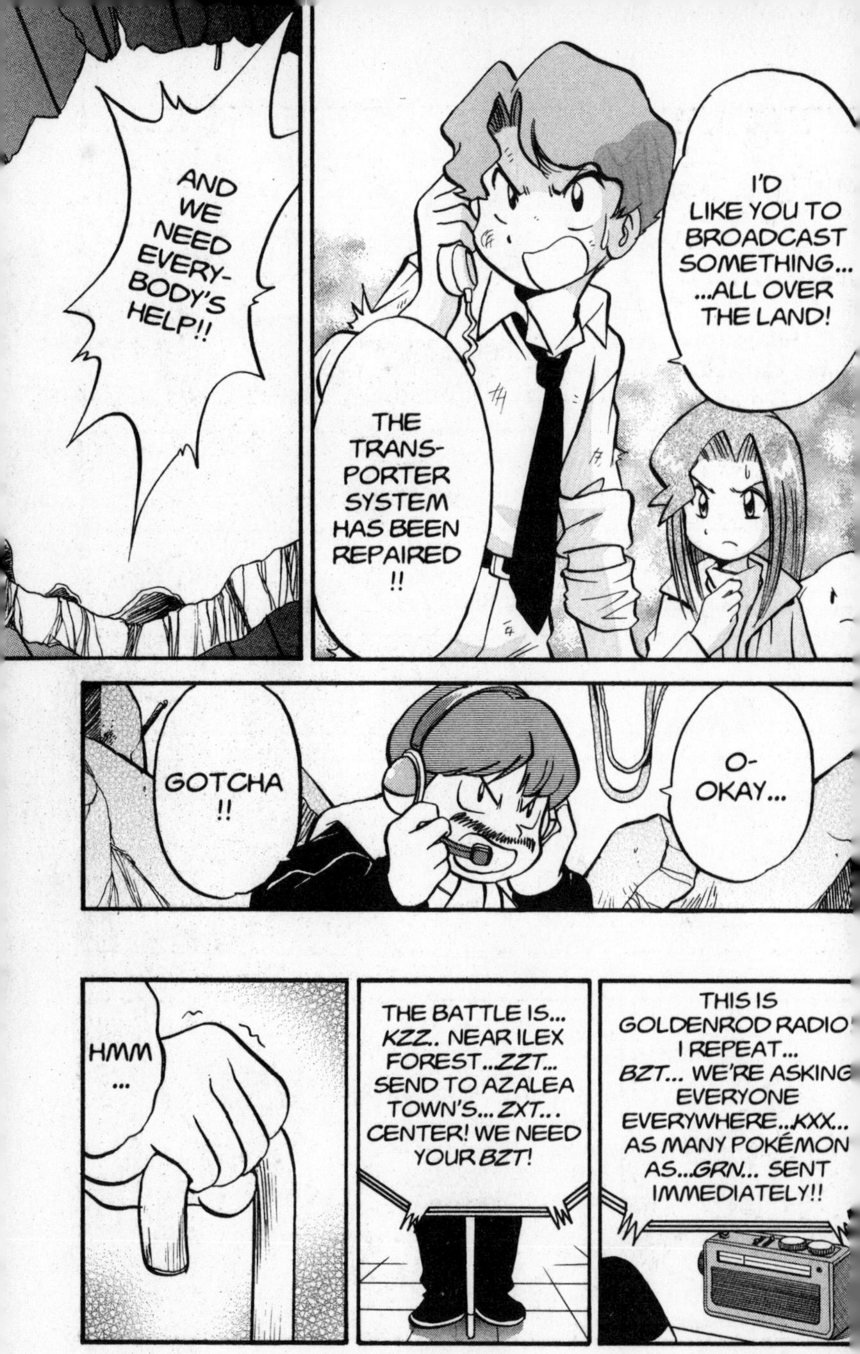
I'D LIKE YOU TO BROADCAST SOMETHING... ...ALL OVER THE LAND!
THE TRANS-PORTER SYSTEM HAS BEEN REPAIRED!!
AND WE NEED EVERY-BODY'S HELP!!
O-OKAY...
GOTCHA!!
THIS IS GOLDENROD RADIO! I REPEAT... *BZT*... WE'RE ASKING EVERYONE EVERYWHERE...*KXX*... AS MANY POKÉMON AS...*GRN*... SENT IMMEDIATELY!!
THE BATTLE IS... *KZZ*.. NEAR ILEX FOREST...*ZZT*... SEND TO AZALEA TOWN'S... *ZXT*... CENTER! WE NEED YOUR *BZT*!
HMM...

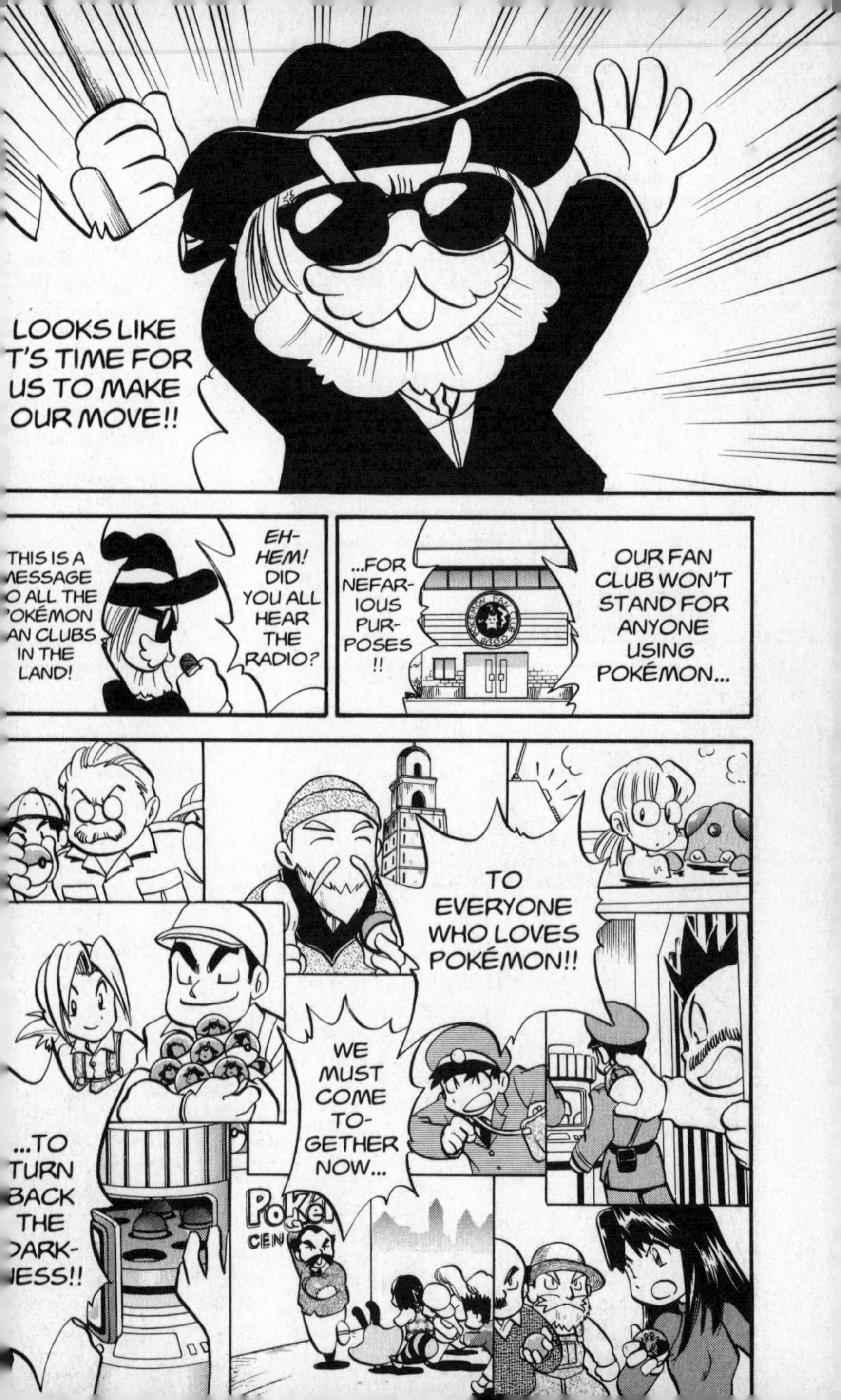

LOOKS LIKE T'S TIME FOR US TO MAKE OUR MOVE!!
OUR FAN CLUB WON'T STAND FOR ANYONE USING POKÉMON...
...FOR NEFARIOUS PURPOSES!!
EH-HEM! DID YOU ALL HEAR THE RADIO?
THIS IS A MESSAGE O ALL THE 'OKÉMON AN CLUBS IN THE LAND!
TO EVERYONE WHO LOVES POKÉMON!!
WE MUST COME TOGETHER NOW...
...TO TURN BACK THE DARKNESS!!
PoKé CEN

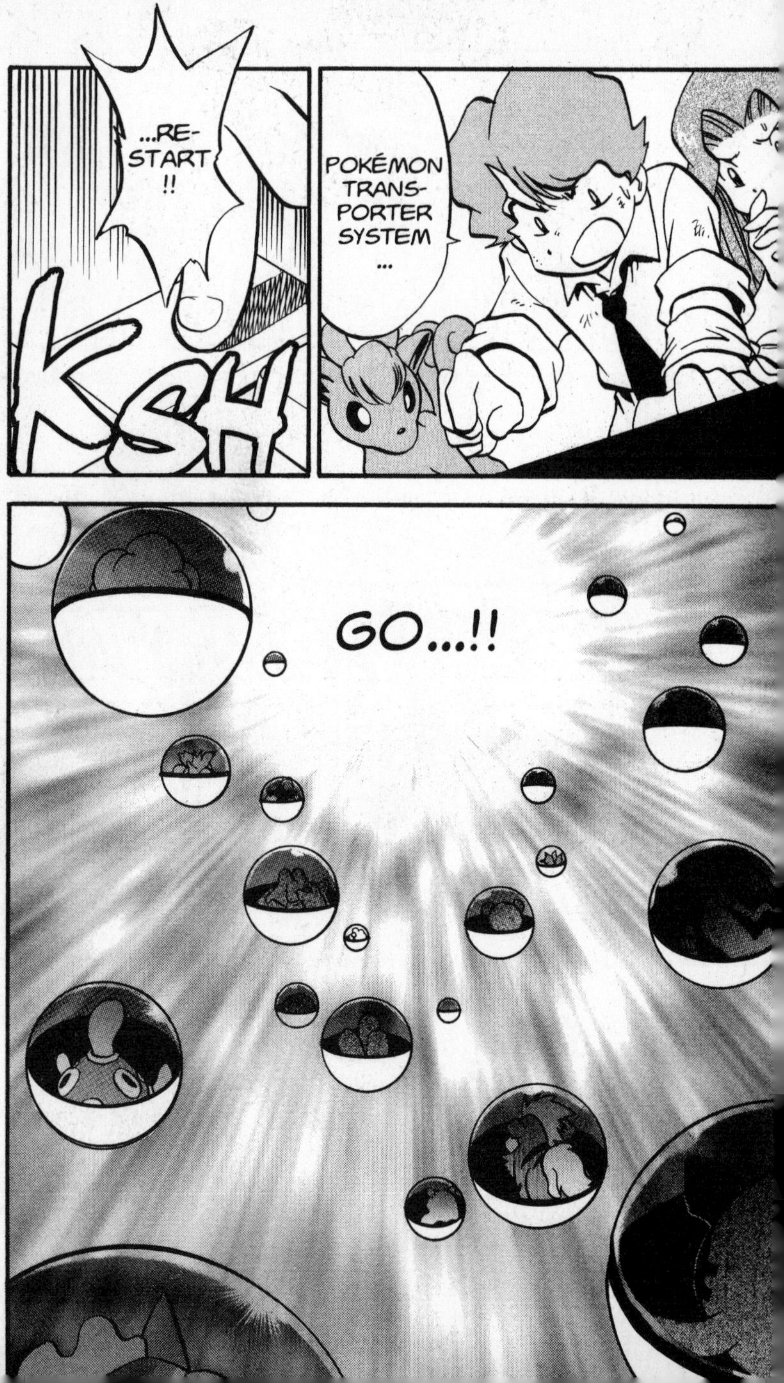
POKÉMON TRANSPORTER SYSTEM ...
...RE-START !!
KSH
GO...!!

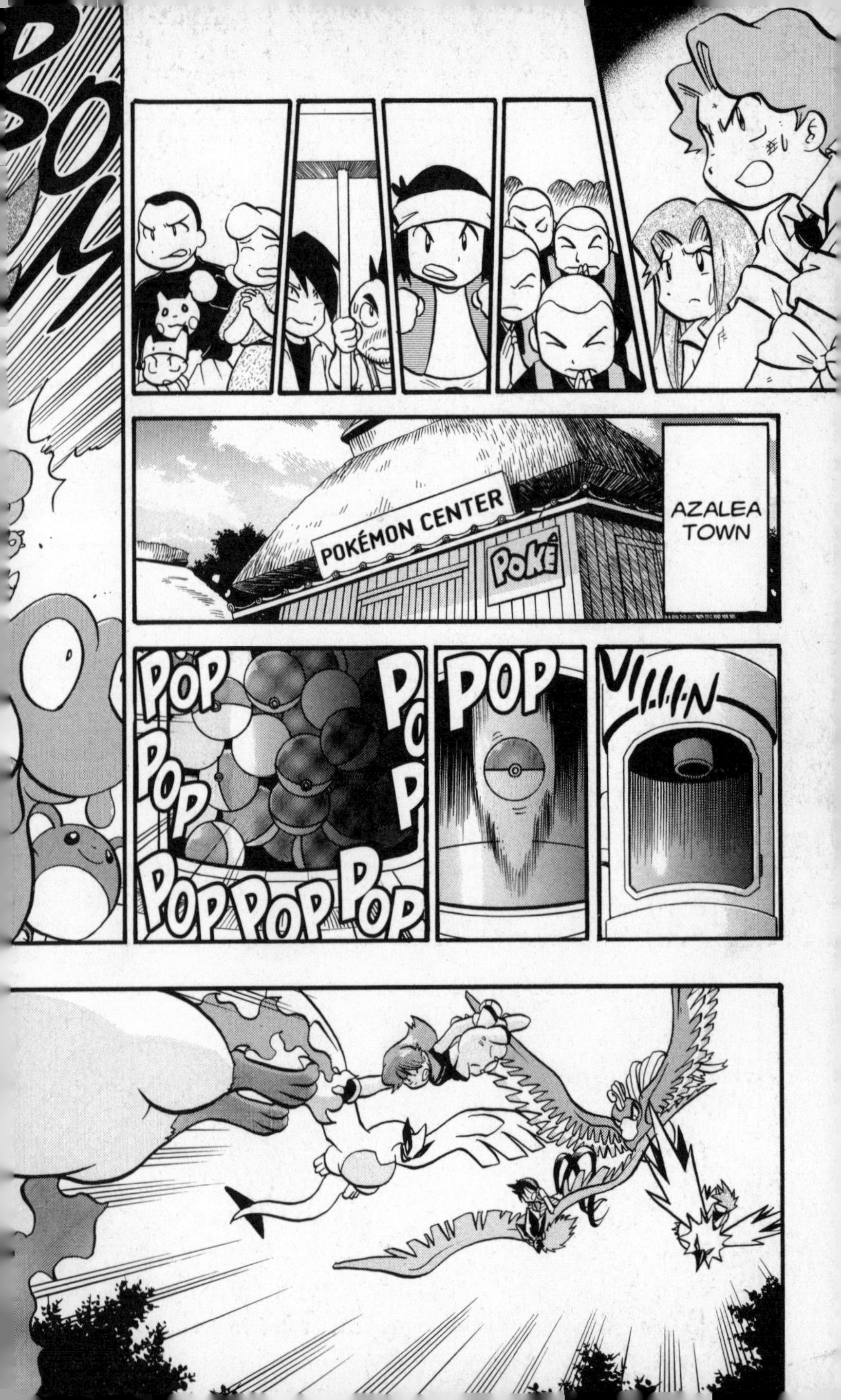

AZALEA TOWN
POKÉMON CENTER
POKé
VIIIN
POP
POP
POP
POP
POP POP POP
POP
BOOM

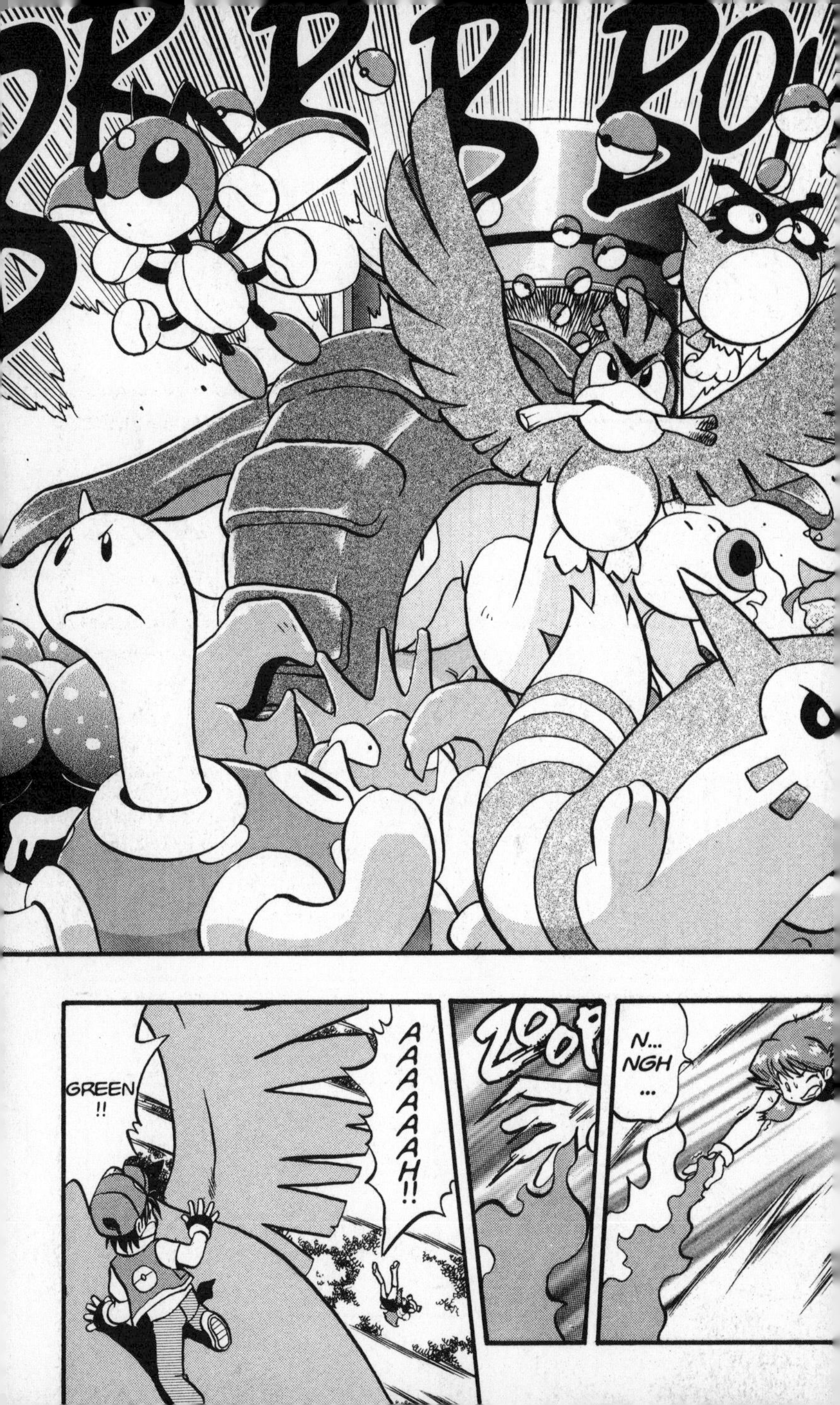
N... NGH ...
ZOOP
AAAAAAAH!!
GREEN !!

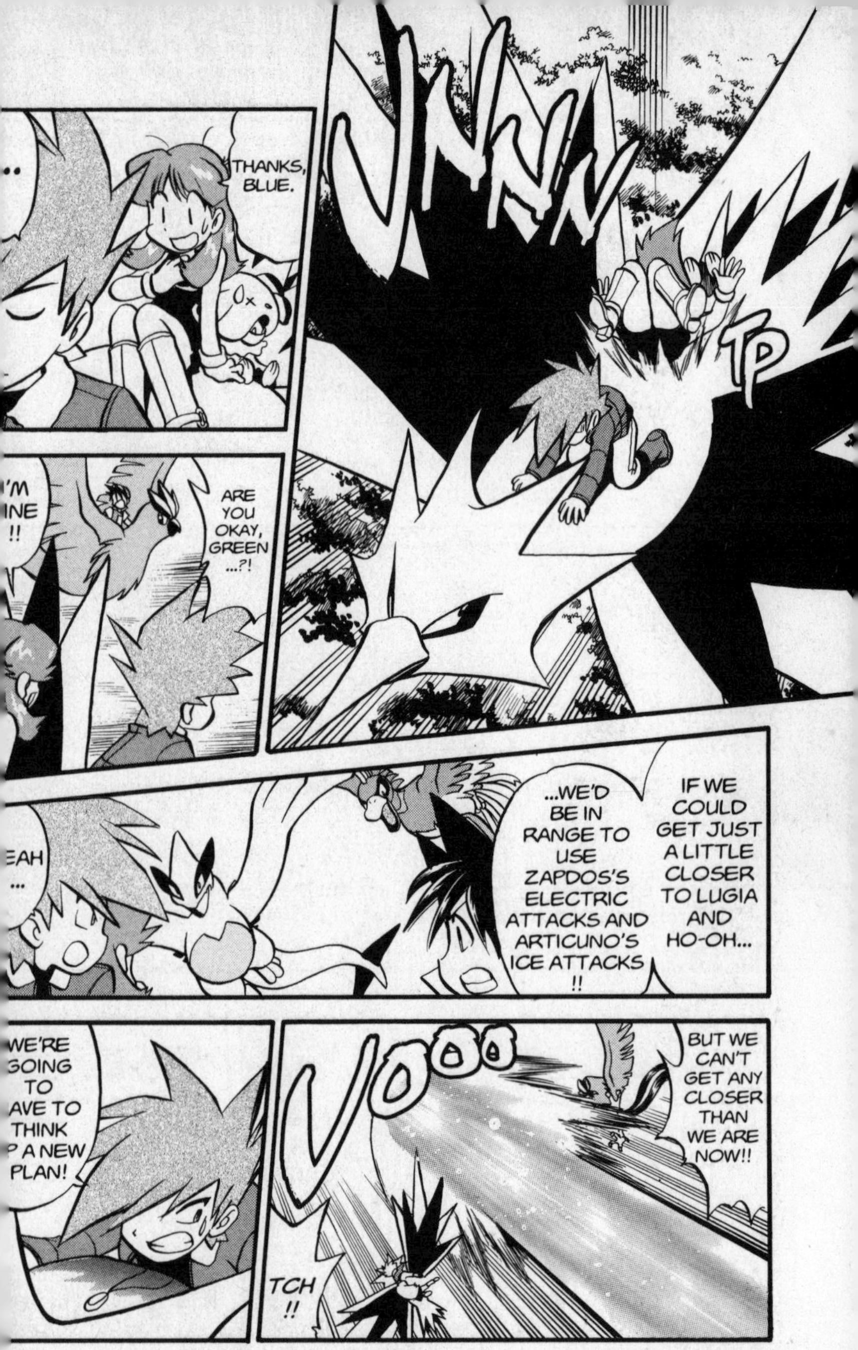
JNNN
TP
THANKS, BLUE.
..
ARE YOU OKAY, GREEN ...?!
'M INE !!
IF WE COULD GET JUST A LITTLE CLOSER TO LUGIA AND HO-OH...
...WE'D BE IN RANGE TO USE ZAPDOS'S ELECTRIC ATTACKS AND ARTICUNO'S ICE ATTACKS !!
EAH ...
VOOO
BUT WE CAN'T GET ANY CLOSER THAN WE ARE NOW!!
TCH !!
WE'RE GOING TO AVE TO THINK P A NEW PLAN!

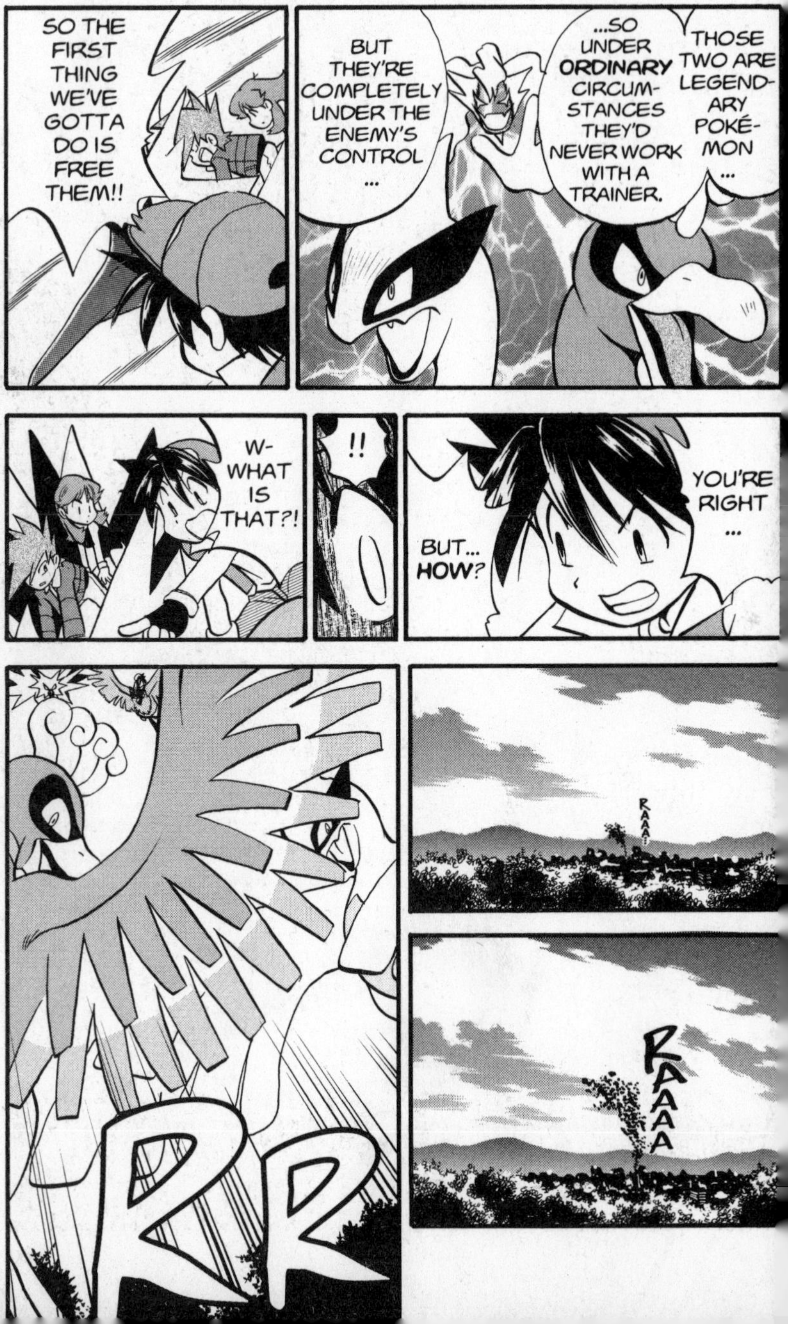
THOSE TWO ARE LEGENDARY POKÉMON...
...SO UNDER **ORDINARY** CIRCUMSTANCES THEY'D NEVER WORK WITH A TRAINER.
BUT THEY'RE COMPLETELY UNDER THE ENEMY'S CONTROL...
SO THE FIRST THING WE'VE GOTTA DO IS FREE THEM!!
YOU'RE RIGHT...
BUT... **HOW**?
!!
W-WHAT IS THAT?!
RAAA!
RAAAA
RR

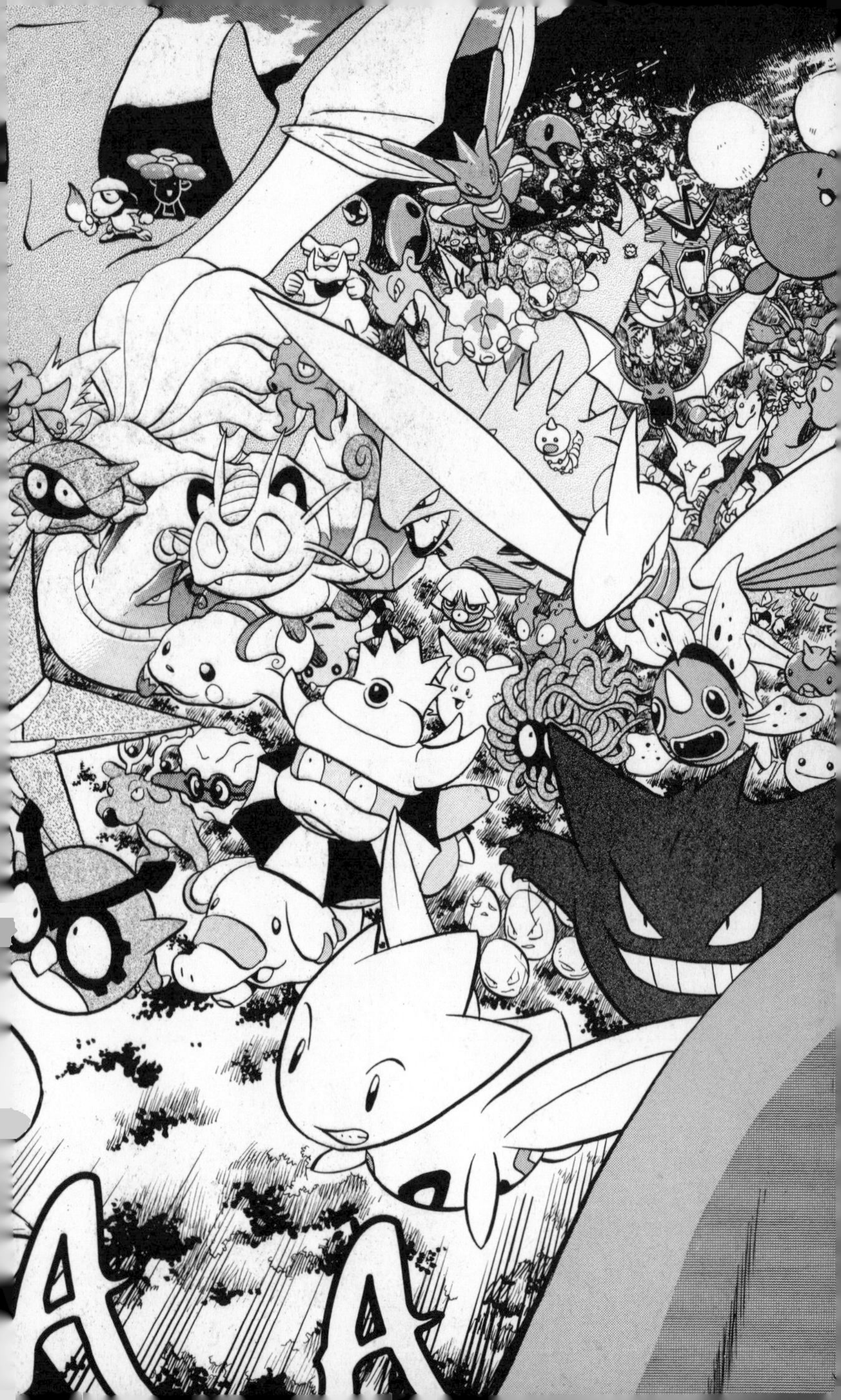

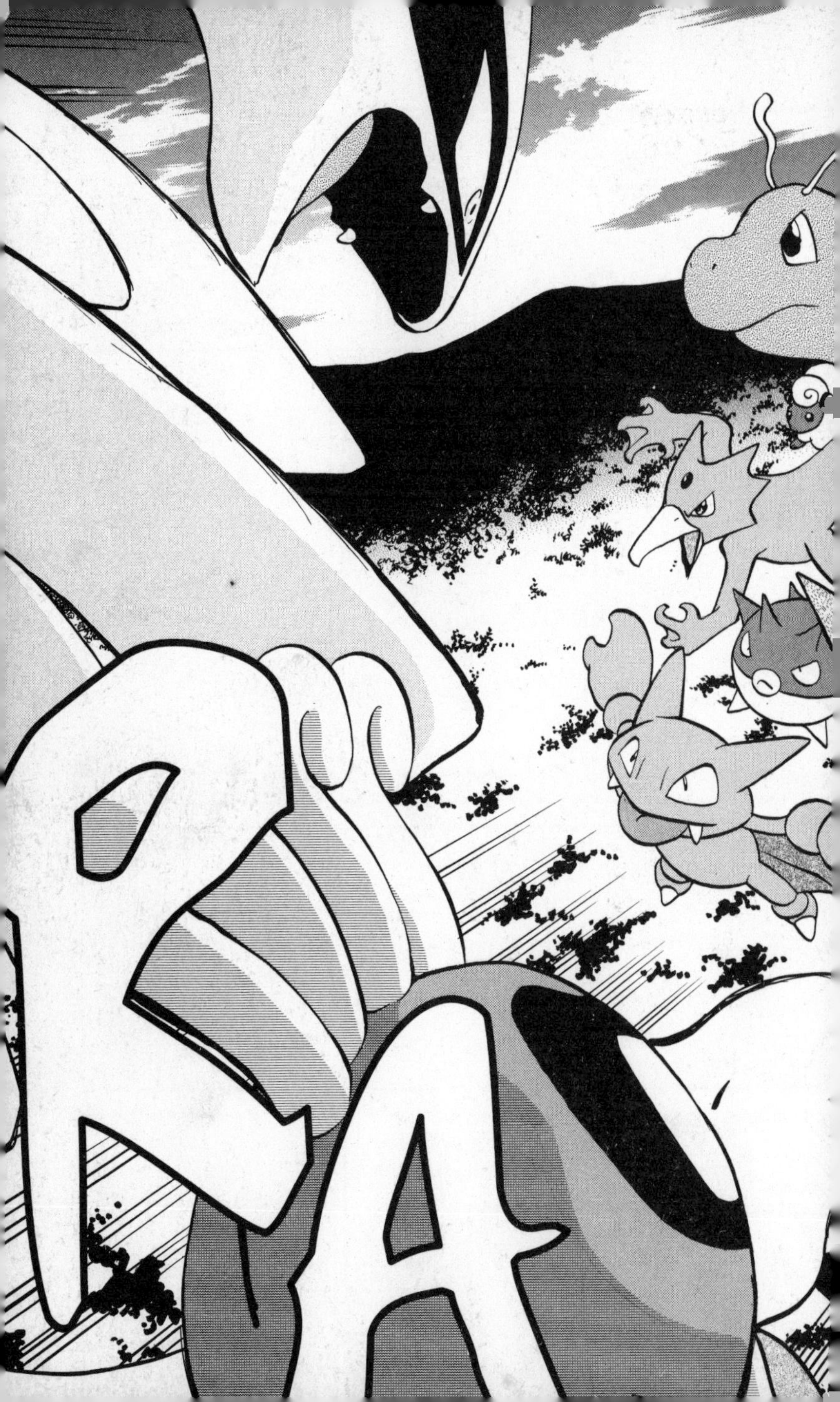

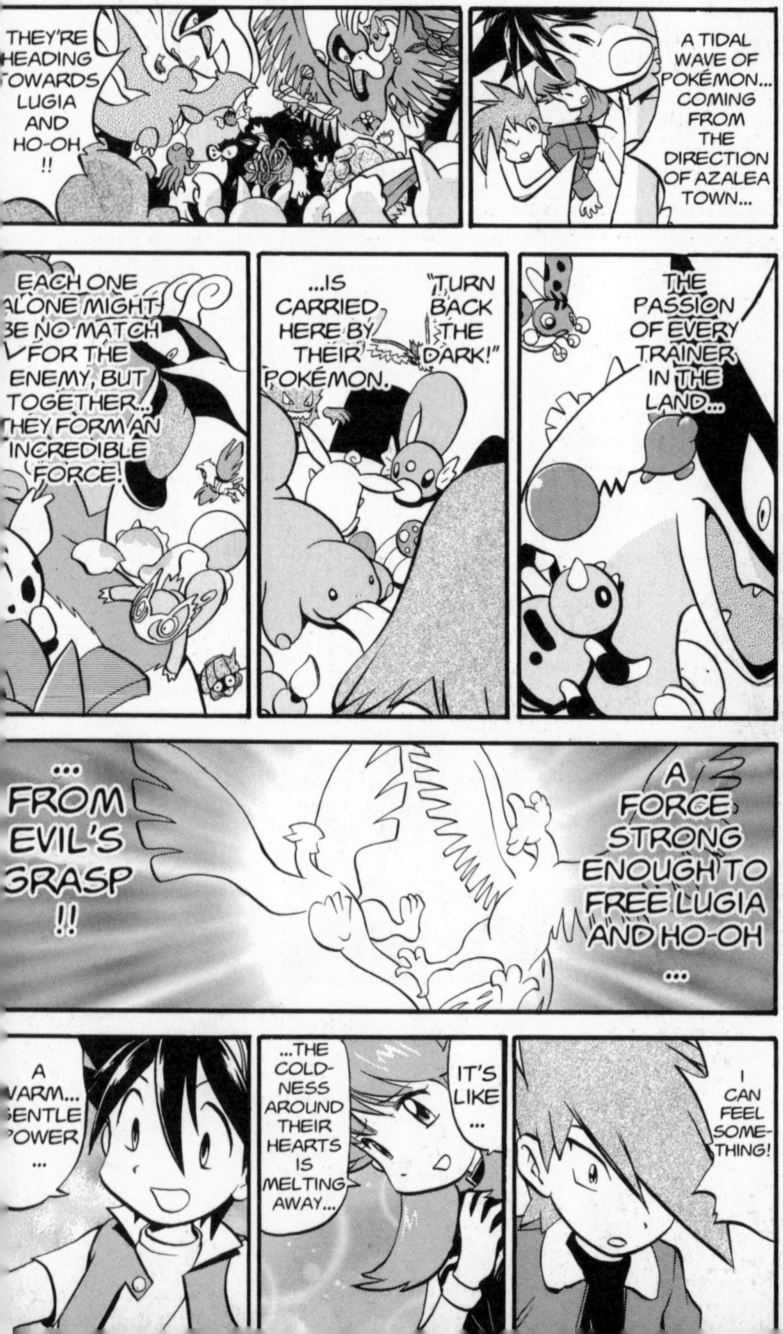
A TIDAL WAVE OF POKÉMON... COMING FROM THE DIRECTION OF AZALEA TOWN...
THEY'RE HEADING TOWARDS LUGIA AND HO-OH !!
THE PASSION OF EVERY TRAINER IN THE LAND...
"TURN BACK THE DARK!"
...IS CARRIED HERE BY THEIR POKÉMON.
EACH ONE ALONE MIGHT BE NO MATCH FOR THE ENEMY, BUT TOGETHER... THEY FORM AN INCREDIBLE FORCE!
A FORCE STRONG ENOUGH TO FREE LUGIA AND HO-OH ...
... FROM EVIL'S GRASP !!
I CAN FEEL SOME-THING!
IT'S LIKE ...
...THE COLDNESS AROUND THEIR HEARTS IS MELTING AWAY...
A WARM... GENTLE POWER ...

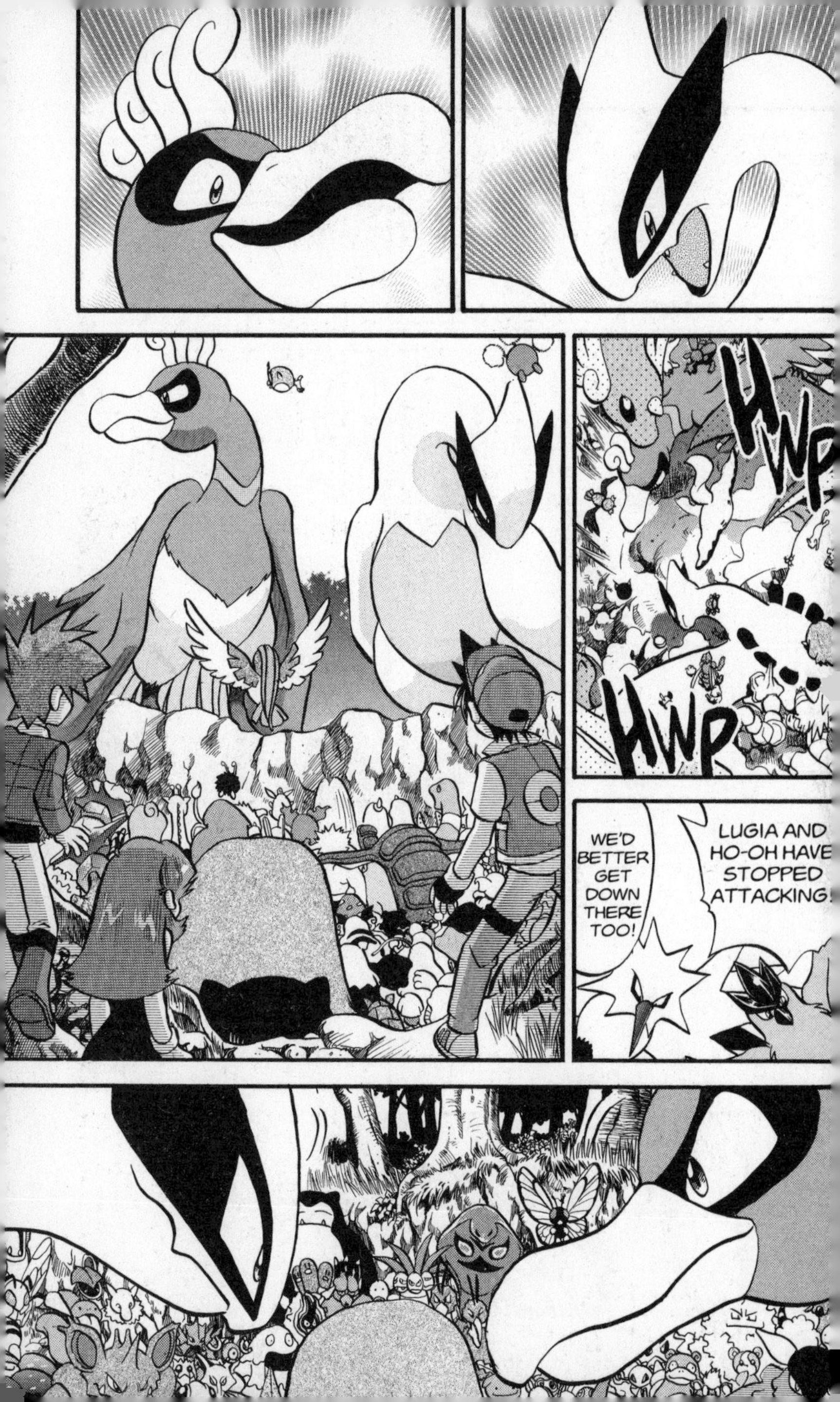
HWP
HWP
LUGIA AND HO-OH HAVE STOPPED ATTACKING!
WE'D BETTER GET DOWN THERE TOO!

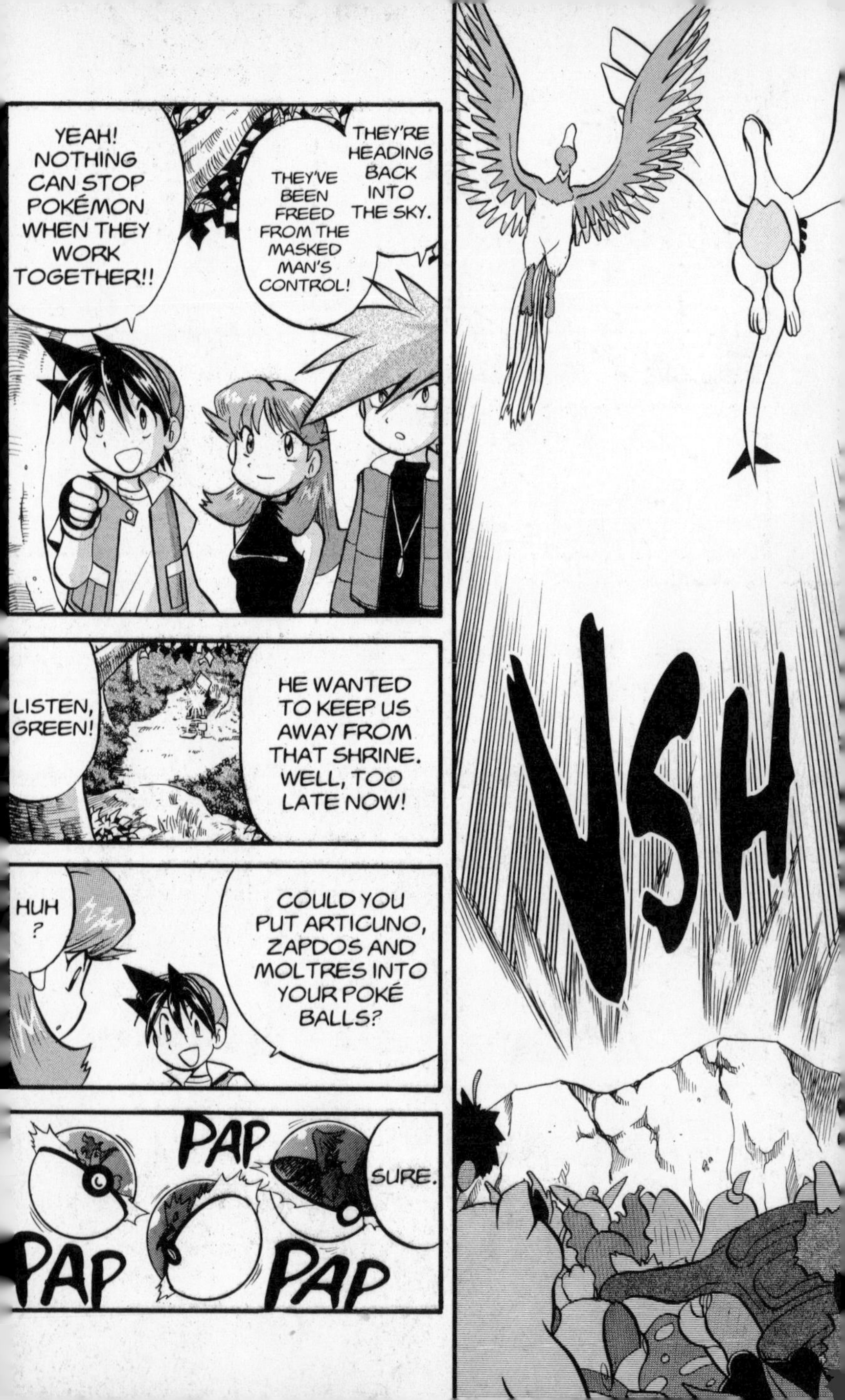
VSH
THEY'RE HEADING BACK INTO THE SKY.
THEY'VE BEEN FREED FROM THE MASKED MAN'S CONTROL!
YEAH! NOTHING CAN STOP POKÉMON WHEN THEY WORK TOGETHER!!
HE WANTED TO KEEP US AWAY FROM THAT SHRINE. WELL, TOO LATE NOW!
LISTEN, GREEN!
COULD YOU PUT ARTICUNO, ZAPDOS AND MOLTRES INTO YOUR POKÉ BALLS?
HUH ?
SURE.
PAP
PAP
PAP

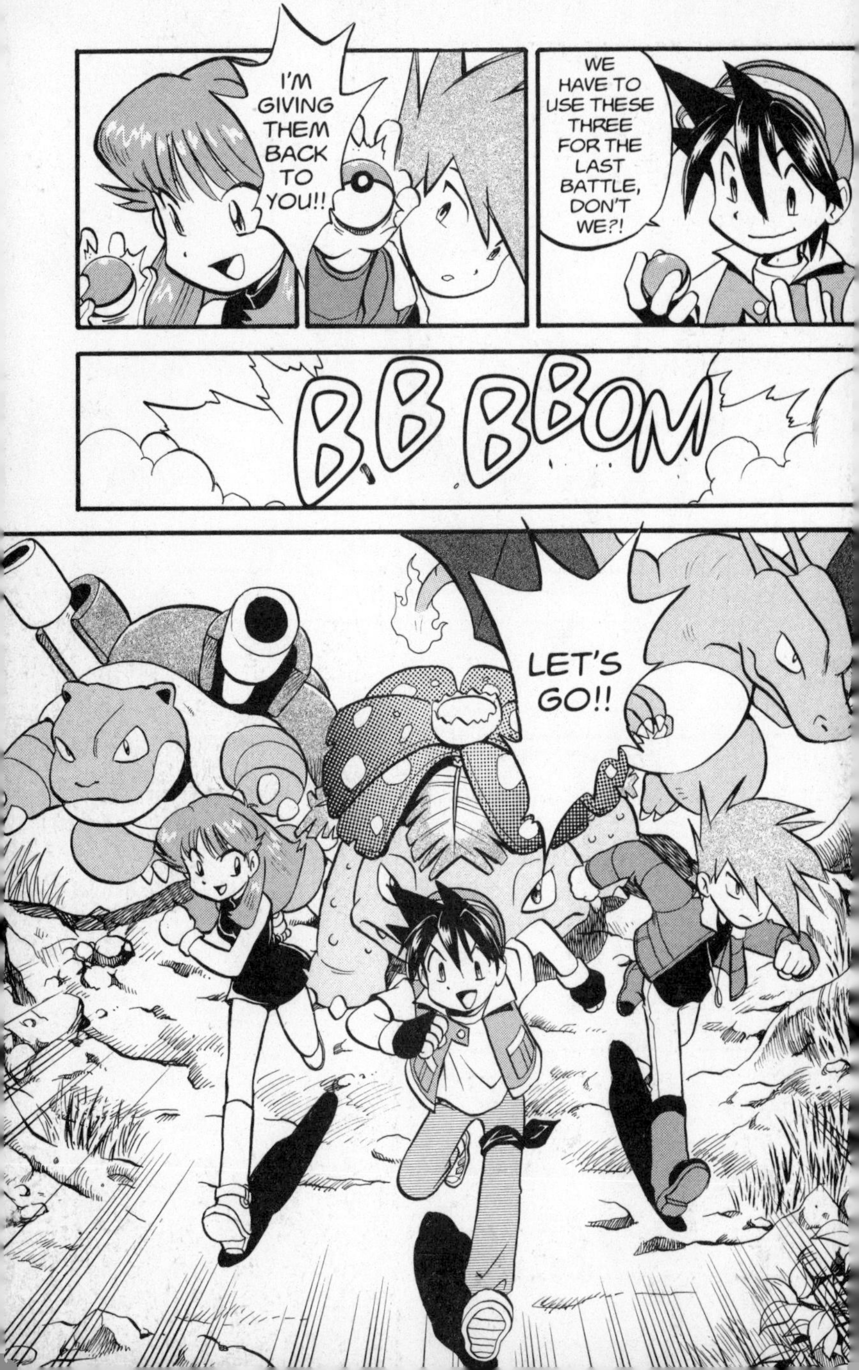
WE HAVE TO USE THESE THREE FOR THE LAST BATTLE, DON'T WE?!
I'M GIVING THEM BACK TO YOU!!
B B BBOM
LET'S GO!!

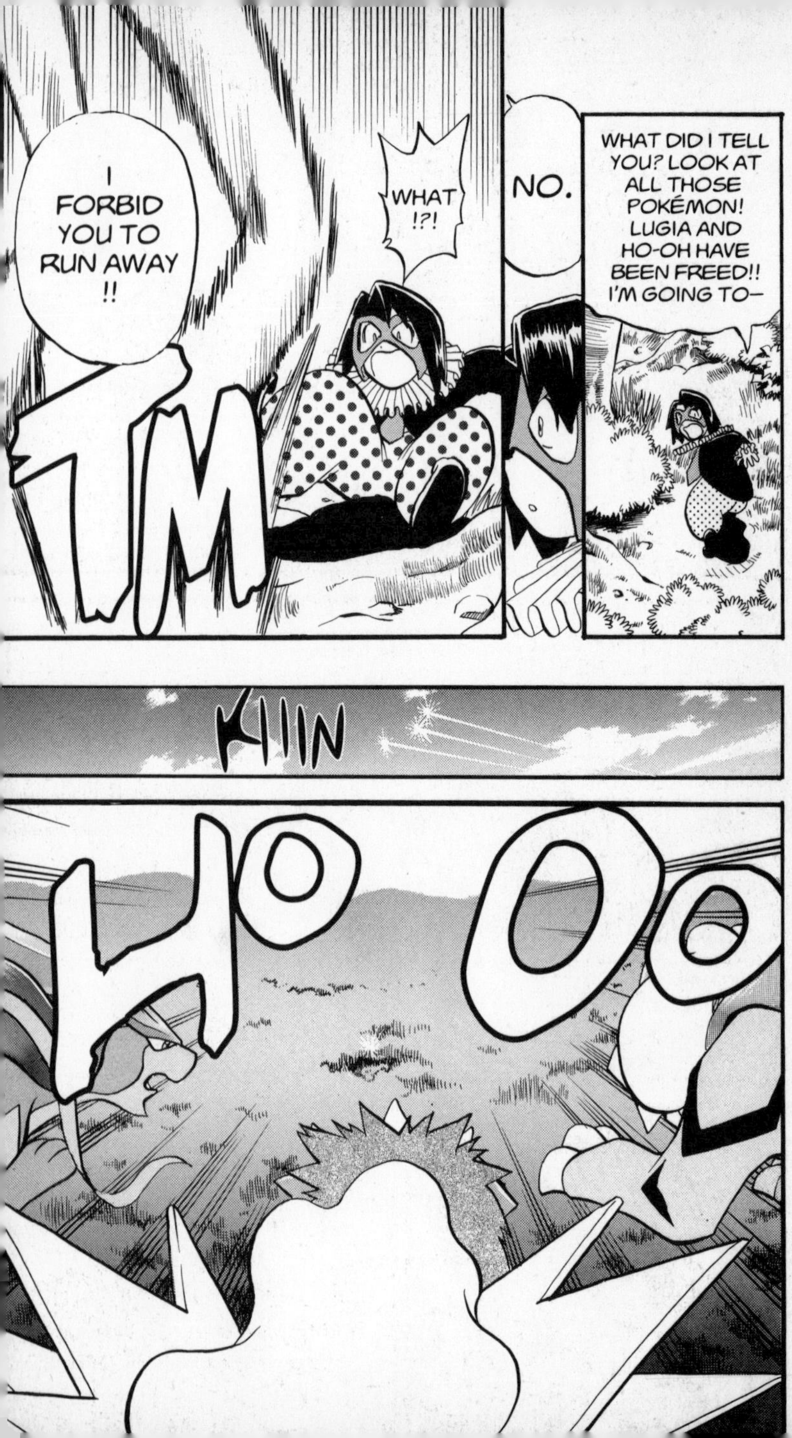

WHAT DID I TELL YOU? LOOK AT ALL THOSE POKÉMON! LUGIA AND HO-OH HAVE BEEN FREED!! I'M GOING TO—
NO.
WHAT !?!
I FORBID YOU TO RUN AWAY !!
TM
KIIN
HOOO

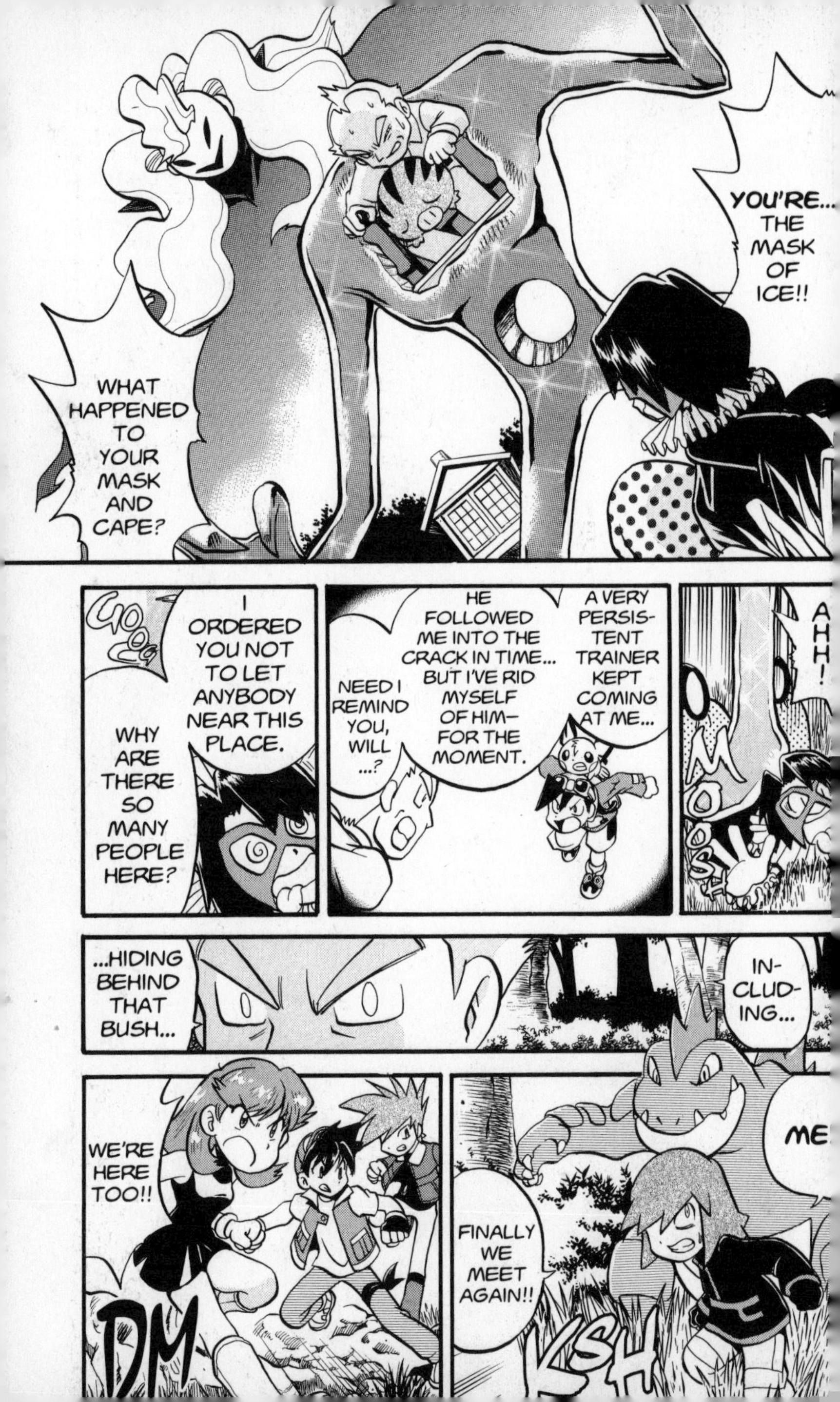
YOU'RE... THE MASK OF ICE!!
WHAT HAPPENED TO YOUR MASK AND CAPE?
AHH!
A VERY PERSIS-TENT TRAINER KEPT COMING AT ME...
HE FOLLOWED ME INTO THE CRACK IN TIME... BUT I'VE RID MYSELF OF HIM— FOR THE MOMENT.
NEED I REMIND YOU, WILL ...?
I ORDERED YOU NOT TO LET ANYBODY NEAR THIS PLACE.
WHY ARE THERE SO MANY PEOPLE HERE?
IN-CLUD-ING...
...HIDING BEHIND THAT BUSH...
ME
FINALLY WE MEET AGAIN!!
KSH
WE'RE HERE TOO!!
DM

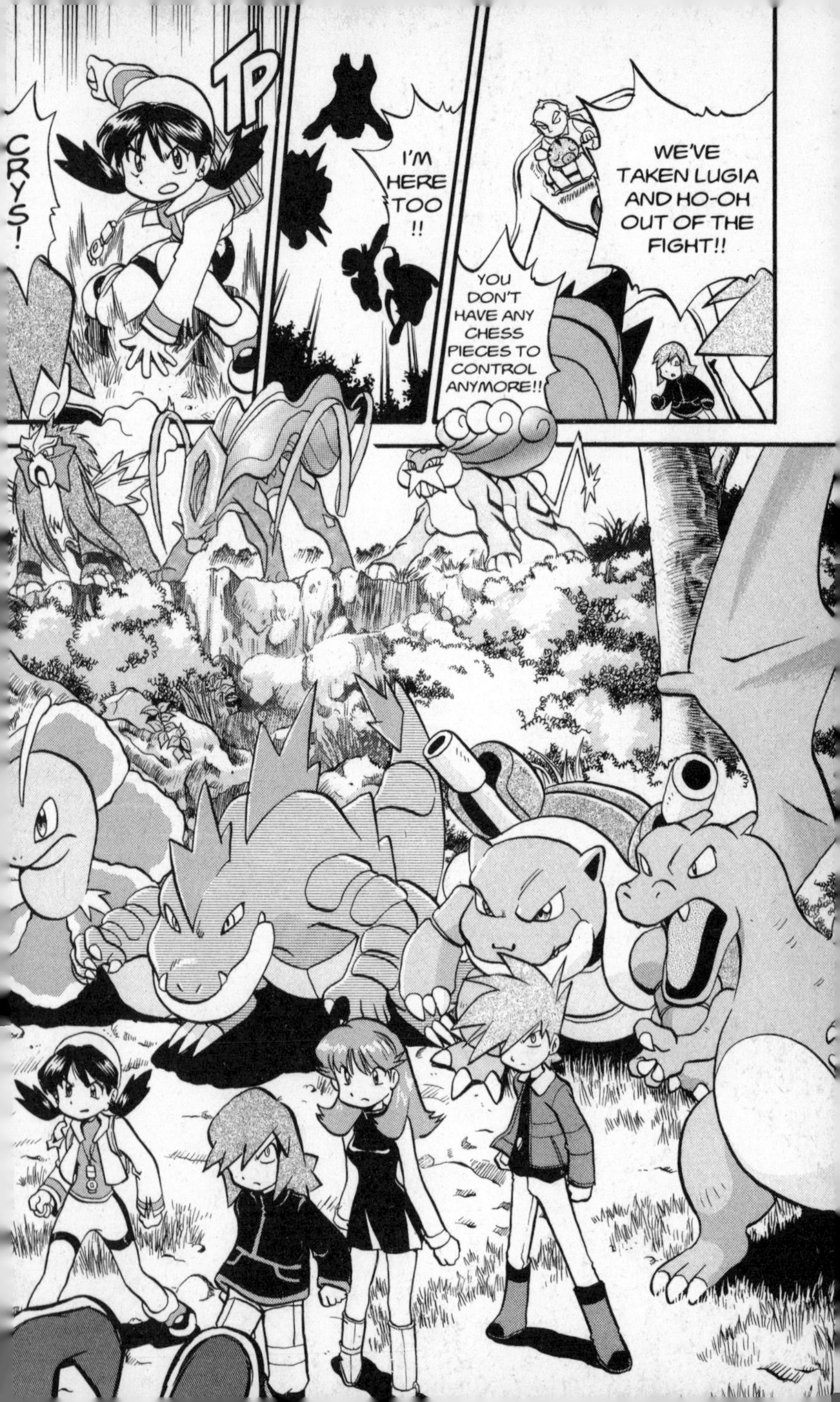
WE'VE TAKEN LUGIA AND HO-OH OUT OF THE FIGHT!!
YOU DON'T HAVE ANY CHESS PIECES TO CONTROL ANYMORE!!
I'M HERE TOO!!
TP
CRYS!

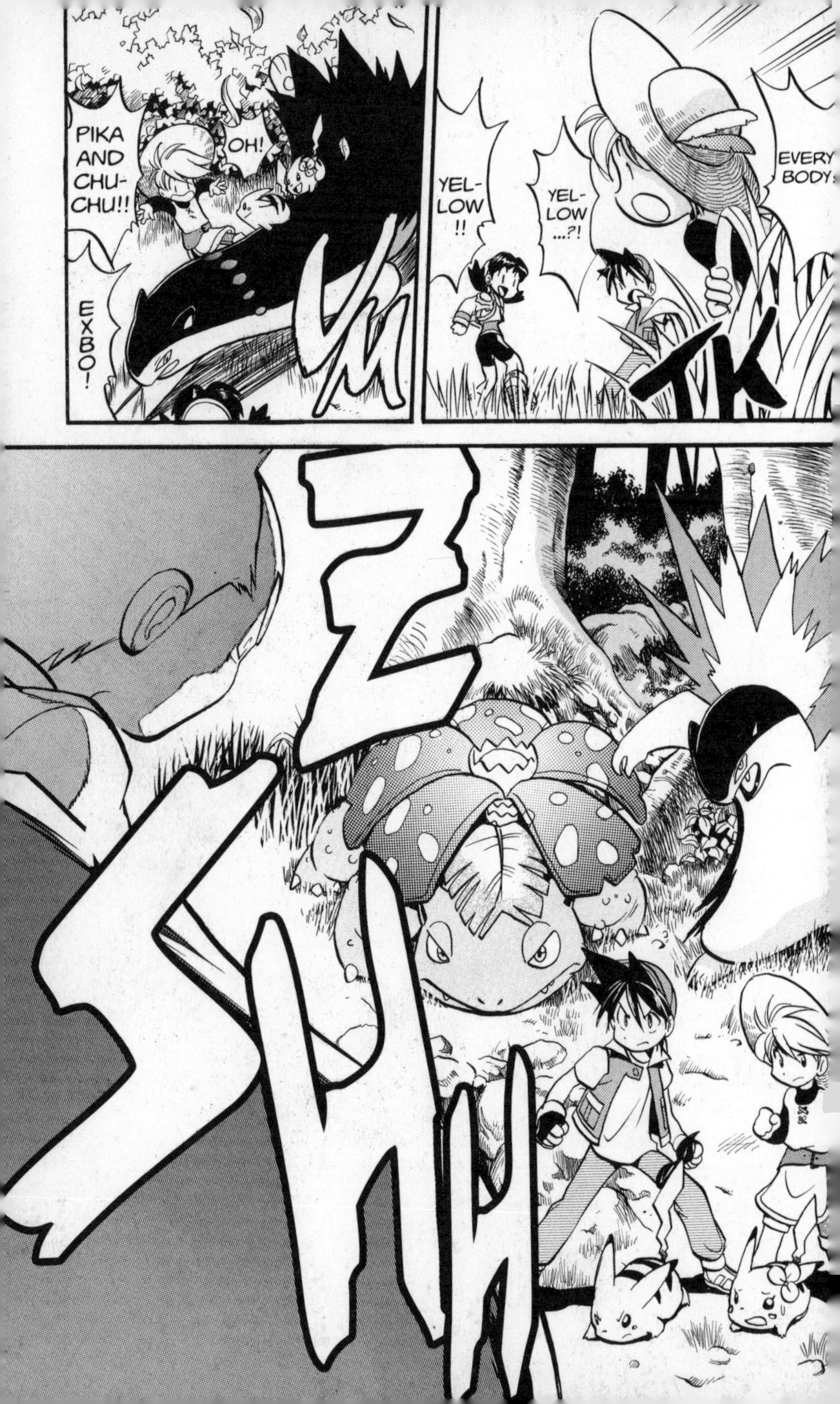
EVERY BODY
YEL-LOW ...?!
YEL-LOW !!
TK
OH!
PIKA AND CHU-CHU!!
EXBO!

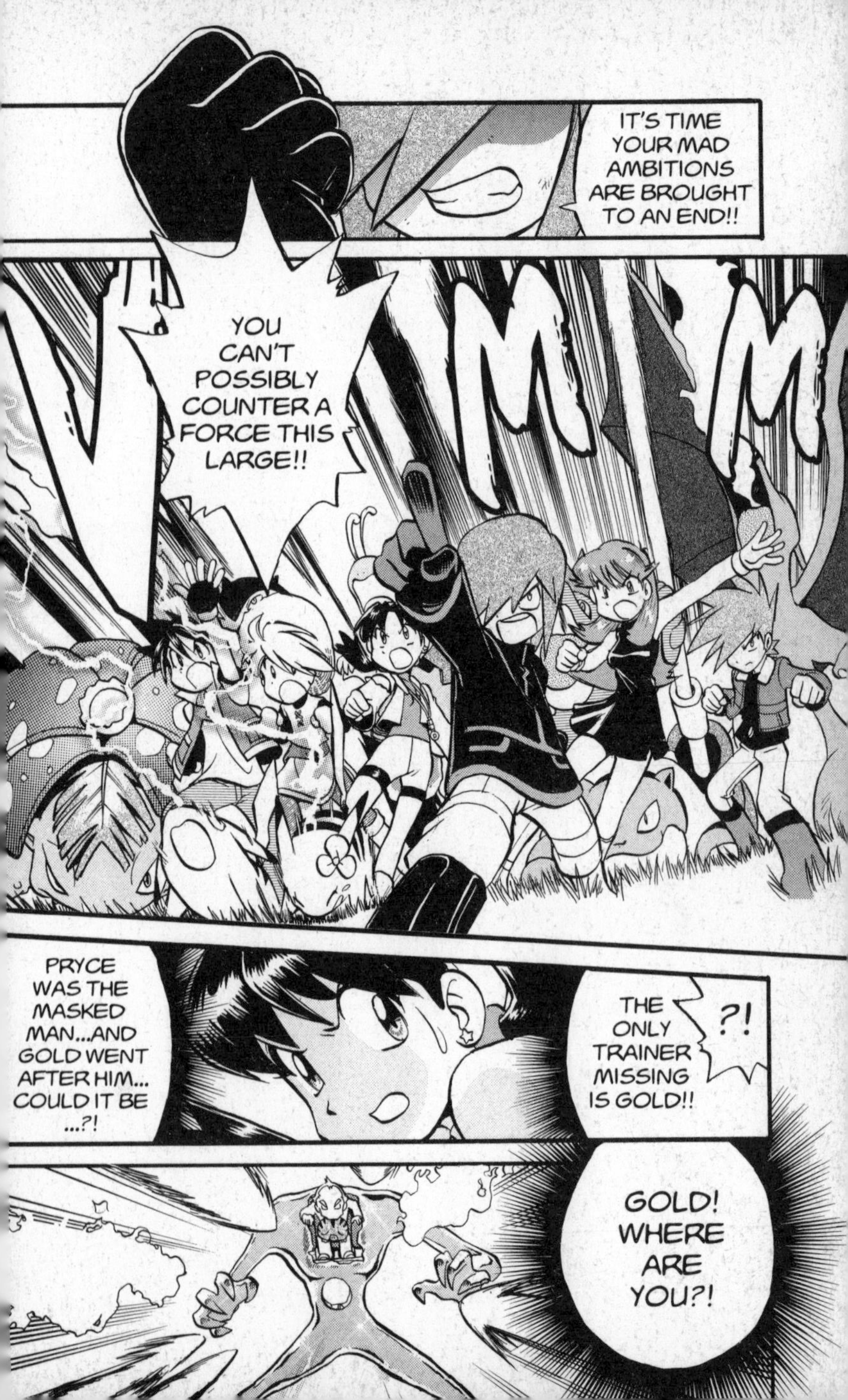
IT'S TIME YOUR MAD AMBITIONS ARE BROUGHT TO AN END!!
YOU CAN'T POSSIBLY COUNTER A FORCE THIS LARGE!!
THE ONLY TRAINER MISSING IS GOLD!!
?!
PRYCE WAS THE MASKED MAN...AND GOLD WENT AFTER HIM... COULD IT BE ...?!
GOLD! WHERE ARE YOU?!

TO BE CONTINUED

# ADVENTURE ROUTE MAP 14

FOLLOW OUR POKÉDEX HOLDERS FROM THE INDIGO PLATEAU TO ILEX FOREST—WHERE THE FINAL BATTLE WILL BE FOUGHT!

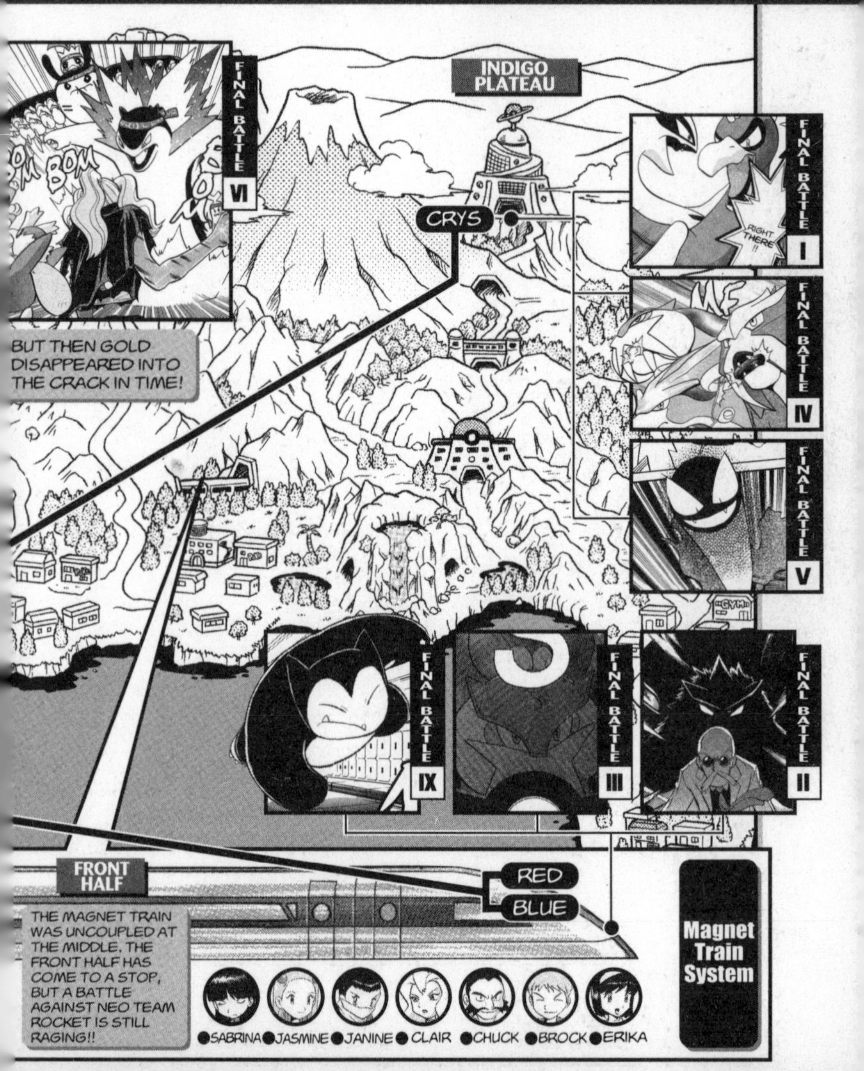
INDIGO PLATEAU
FINAL BATTLE I
RIGHT THERE!!
FINAL BATTLE IV
FINAL BATTLE V
FINAL BATTLE VI
BOM
CRYS
BUT THEN GOLD DISAPPEARED INTO THE CRACK IN TIME!
GYM
FINAL BATTLE II
FINAL BATTLE III
FINAL BATTLE IX
FRONT HALF
RED
BLUE
Magnet Train System
THE MAGNET TRAIN WAS UNCOUPLED AT THE MIDDLE. THE FRONT HALF HAS COME TO A STOP, BUT A BATTLE AGAINST NEO TEAM ROCKET IS STILL RAGING!!
SABRINA
JASMINE
JANINE
CLAIR
CHUCK
BROCK
ERIKA

# "GOTTA CATCH 'EM ALL!!"
## ADVENTURE ROUTE MAP 14

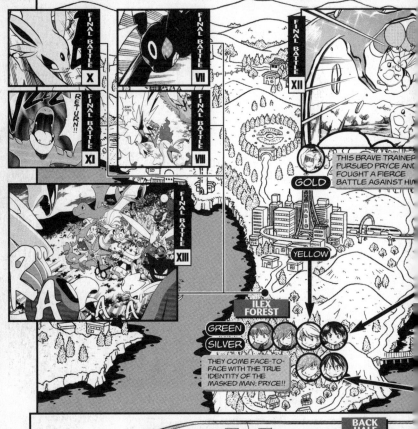

FINAL BATTLE X

FINAL BATTLE VII

FINAL BATTLE XI

RETURN!!

FINAL BATTLE VIII

FINAL BATTLE XIII

FINAL BATTLE XII

THIS BRAVE TRAINER PURSUED PRYCE AND FOUGHT A FIERCE BATTLE AGAINST HIM

GOLD

YELLOW

ILEX FOREST

GREEN

SILVER

THEY COME FACE-TO-FACE WITH THE TRUE IDENTITY OF THE MASKED MAN: PRYCE!!

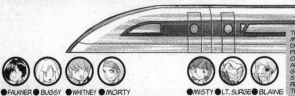

BACK HALF

THE BACK HALF OF THE MAGNET TRAIN WAS DRIVEN BACK TO INDIGO PLATEAU. THE PARTNERS OF THE THREE LEGENDARY POKÉMON AND THE GYM LEADERS RIDING IT STAYED BEHIND TO RESCUE THE PEOPLE THERE.

● FALKNER ● BUGSY ● WHITNEY ● MORTY

● MISTY ● LT. SURGE ● BLAINE

# This is the Masked Man!

## BONUS INFO 1

MASK · OF · ICE PERFECT DATA

~An Analysis in Five Parts~

THE TRUE IDENTITY OF THE MASKED MAN HAS FINALLY BEEN REVEALED. LET'S TAKE A CLOSER LOOK AT PRYCE, THE ICE EXPERT!

### 01 Goal

PRYCE'S GOAL IS TO CAPTURE THE TIME TRAVEL POKÉMON CELEBI IN ORDER TO CONTROL TIME. KIDNAPPING CHILDREN AND CONTROLLING THE SOLDIERS OF NEO TEAM ROCKET WERE NOTHING BUT MEANS TO THAT END!

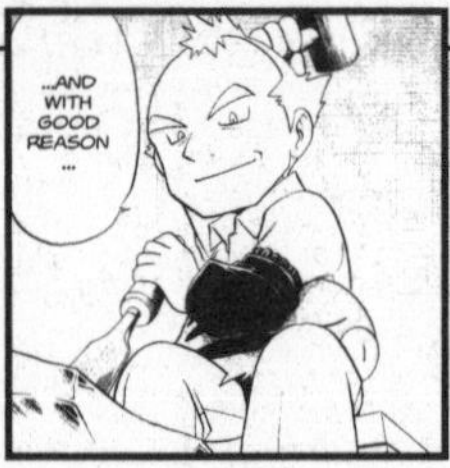

...AND WITH GOOD REASON ...


▲ SUICUNE INSTINCTIVELY SENSED WHAT KIND OF A MAN PRYCE WAS AND AVOIDED HIM.

### 02 Double

PRYCE IS AN OLD MAN WHO RARELY GOES OUTSIDE, SO HE CARVED AN ICE DOLL AS A DOUBLE TO CARRY OUT HIS PLANS. THE DOLL LED HIS ICE-TYPE POKÉMON IN BATTLES AND CAPTURES.

PRYCE ◀ ▼ WAS EVEN ABLE TO CAPTURE A LEGENDARY POKÉMON WITHOUT BEING PRESENT IN PERSON! (ADV. 149 AND OTHERS)

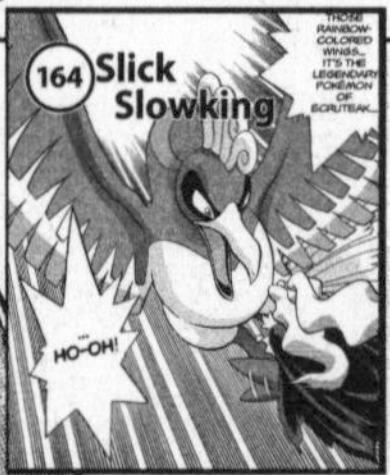

164 Slick Slowking
THOSE RAINBOW-COLORED WINGS... IT'S THE LEGENDARY POKÉMON OF ECRUTEAK...
...HO-OH!


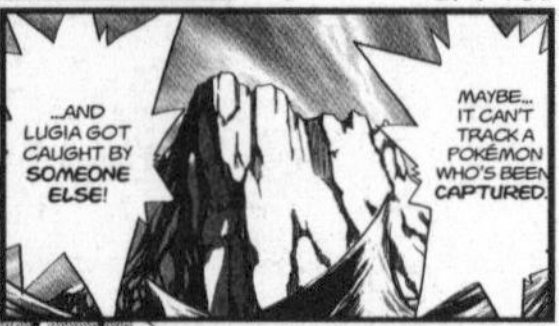

MAYBE... IT CAN'T TRACK A POKÉMON WHO'S BEEN CAPTURED.
...AND LUGIA GOT CAUGHT BY SOMEONE ELSE!


### 03 Equipment

THIS MECHANICAL CANE WAS PRYCE'S TOOL TO CONTROL HIS ICE DOLL DOUBLE. A SPECIAL POKÉGEAR HAS BEEN IMPLANTED INSIDE IT, ENABLING PRYCE TO SEE WHATEVER HIS DOUBLE SEES. PRYCE INGENIOUSLY SENT ORDERS TO HIS POKÉMON BY TAPPING THE TIP OF THE CANE ON THE FLOOR. (SEE ADV. 178)

◀ BY COMBINING SHORT AND LONG TONES, HE COMMUNICATES THROUGH A SORT OF MORSE CODE. HE NEVER SPEAKS HIS ORDERS.

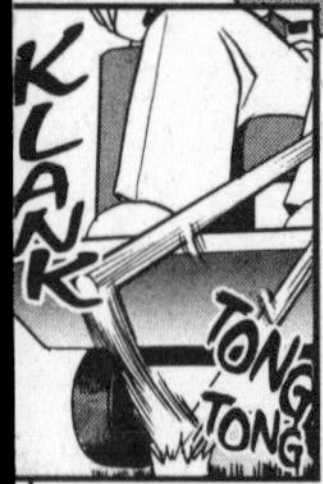

KLANK
TONG TONG TONG


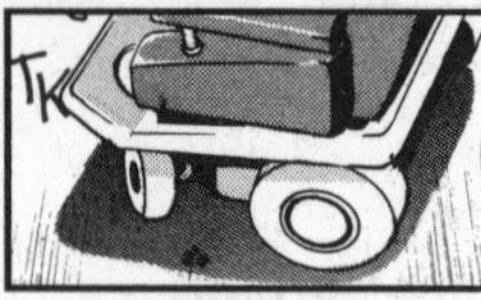

TK


A WHEELCHAIR WITH SPECIAL NON-SLIP TIRES. THERE'S ANOTHER SECRET GIMMICK IN THOSE TIRES YET TO BE REVEALED!

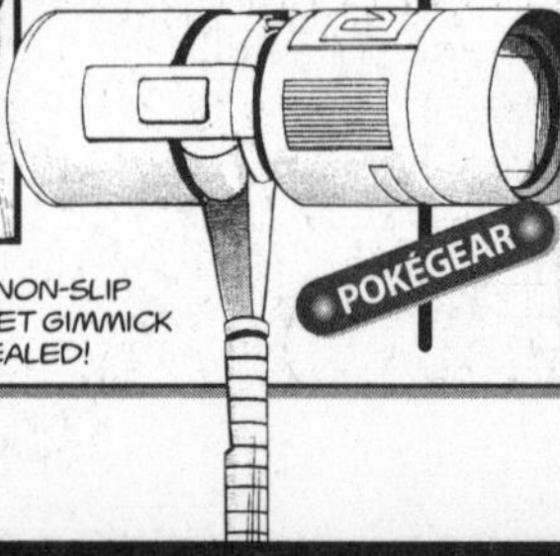

POKÉGEAR

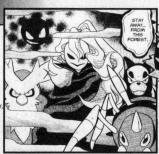

STAY AWAY... FROM THIS FOREST.

PRYCE'S CELEBI-CAPTURING TEAM INCLUDES TYPES THAT ARE NOT HIS SPECIALTY. (SEE ADV. 103)

## 04 Poké-mon

VERY LITTLE IS KNOWN ABOUT CELEBI, THE POKÉMON PRYCE IS AFTER, BUT IT SEEMS TO BE A GRASS-TYPE OR PSYCHIC-TYPE POKÉMON; THEREFORE, PRYCE BRINGS FIRE-, ICE-, POISON-TYPE AND FLYING-TYPE POKÉMON WITH HIM BECAUSE THEY ARE STRONG AGAINST GRASS-TYPE POKÉMON, AND BUG-, GHOST- AND DARK-TYPE POKÉMON BECAUSE THEY ARE STRONG AGAINST PSYCHIC-TYPE POKÉMON.

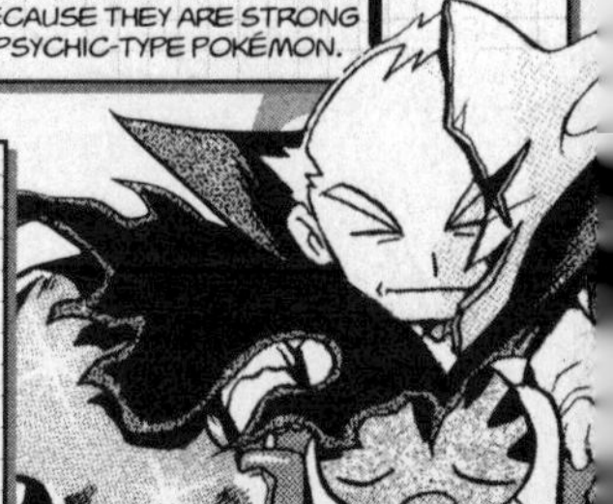

## 05 Body

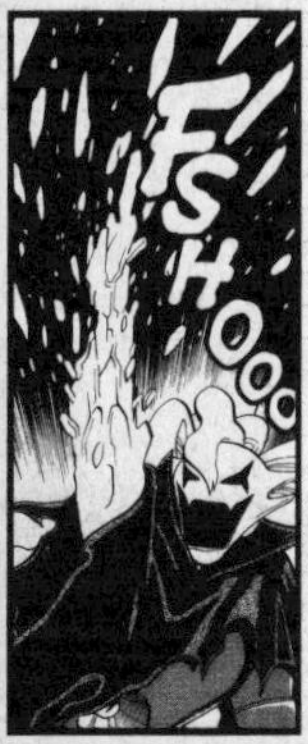

FSHOOO

PRYCE DRAWS ON THE WATER IN THE ATMOSPHERE TO CREATE HIS BODY DOUBLE. WHENEVER HE NEEDS TO GO OUT HIMSELF, HE COVERS HIS WHEELCHAIR WITH ICE AND WEARS A CAPE OVER IT TO HIDE HIS BODY...CREATING AN EVERLASTING ICE WALL THAT CAN REGENERATE ITSELF EVEN IF PARTS OF HIS BODY ARE DESTROYED! (SEE ADV. 172)

PRYCE'S SIZE VARIED EVERY TIME HE APPEARED, WHICH MADE IT HARDER FOR PEOPLE TO FIGURE OUT HIS IDENTITY.

## COMPLETE! THE POKÉ BALL THAT CAPTURES TIME!!

A SPECIAL POKÉ BALL PRYCE CREATED TO CAPTURE CELEBI, WITH A CAPTURE NET WOVEN OUT OF THE RAINBOW WING AND SILVER WING. HE MIGHT BE ABLE TO TAKE CONTROL OF TIME YET!

HYOOO

▶ WITH THE AID OF THESE TWO FEATHERS, HE WAS ABLE TO OPEN THE "CRACK IN TIME". (SEE ADV. 178)

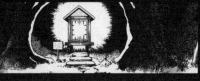

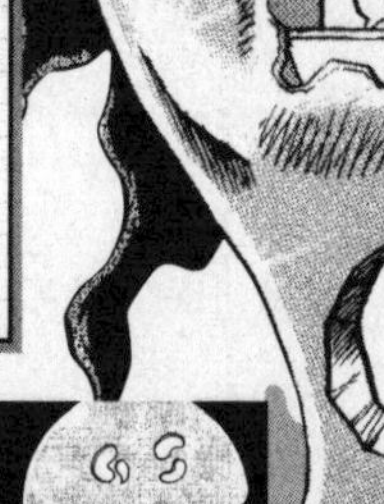

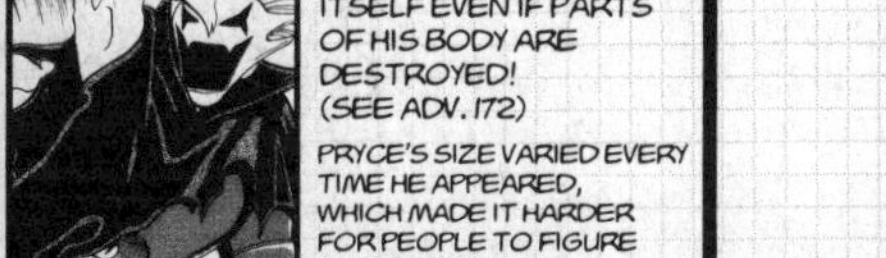

▲THE ILEX FOREST SHRINE, WHICH CELEBI USES AS AN ENTRANCE TO OUR WORLD.

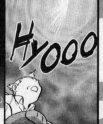

MINI TOPIC 2

SPECIAL TRAINERS PERFECT DATA

# The Special Abilities of the Pokédex Holders!!

~ An Analysis in Seven Parts ~

THE SEVEN TRAINERS WHO RECEIVED POKÉDEXES FROM PROFESSOR OAK. EACH OF THEM HAS A UNIQUE AREA OF EXPERTISE. AND THOSE EXPERTISES ARE...?!

## 01 The Fighter

RED. A FIGHTING GENIUS WITH A NATURAL INSTINCT FOR COMBAT AND STRATEGY WHO HAS WON THE POKÉMON LEAGUE TOURNAMENT. HIS SPECIAL ABILITY IS POKÉMON BATTLE!!

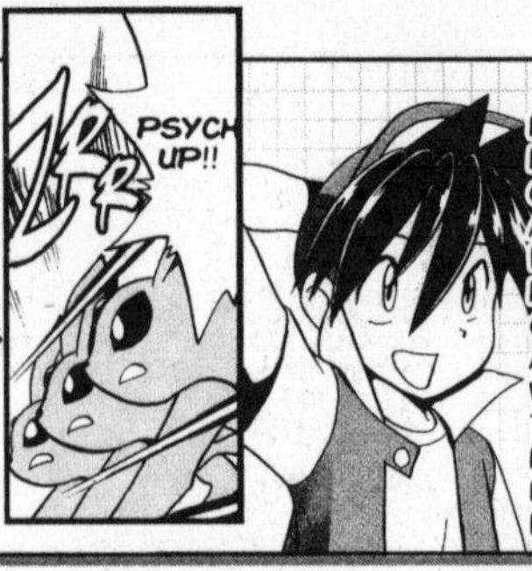

PSYCH UP!!
ZRR


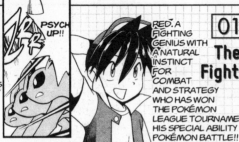

A ▶ UNIQUE TACTIC IN WHICH HE USES HIS OPPONENTS' ATTACKS AGAINST THEM.

## 02 The Trainer

YOU'LL NEVER FIND ANYBODY AS GOOD AS BLUE WHEN IT COMES TO TRAINING POKÉMON. HIS POKÉMON TRAINING ABILITY WAS ATTAINED THROUGH HARD PRACTICE!

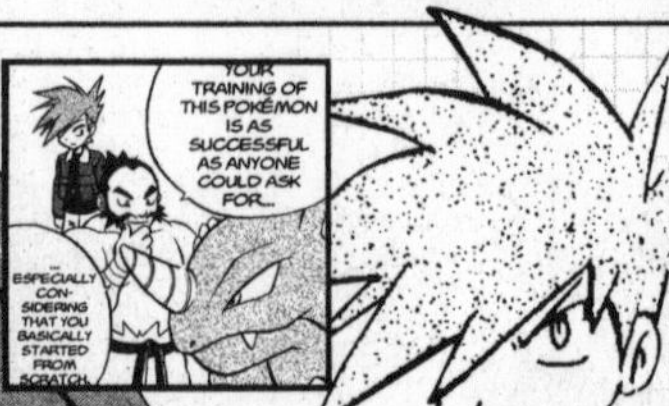

YOUR TRAINING OF THIS POKÉMON IS AS SUCCESSFUL AS ANYONE COULD ASK FOR...
...ESPECIALLY CONSIDERING THAT YOU BASICALLY STARTED FROM SCRATCH.


▲ HE PARTICIPATED IN THE TOURNAMENT WITH A TEAM HE HAD NEWLY TRAINED. HIS MASTER THINKS HIGHLY OF HIM TOO. (SEE ADV. 162)

## 03 The Healer

YELLOW. THE WIELDER OF A GENTLE POWER WHICH CAN HEAL AND CHEER UP WOUNDED POKÉMON. THIS POKÉMON HEALING ABILITY WAS BESTOWED UPON HER BY THE VIRIDIAN FOREST.

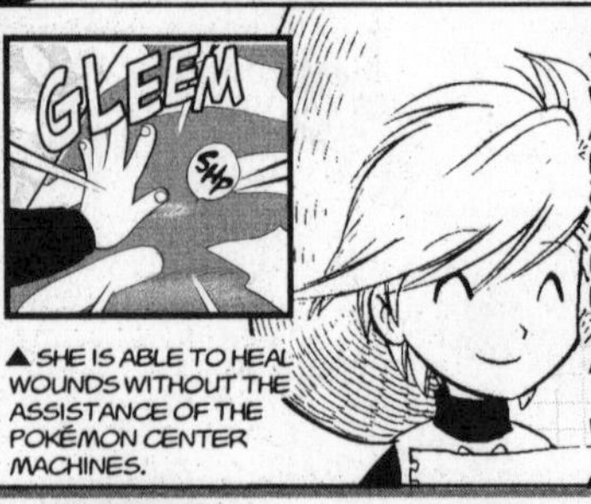

GLEEM
SHP


▲ SHE IS ABLE TO HEAL WOUNDS WITHOUT THE ASSISTANCE OF THE POKÉMON CENTER MACHINES.

## 04 The Catcher

CRYS. HER SKILLS AS A CAPTURE SPECIALIST ARE LEGENDARY. SHE MASTERED HER POKÉMON CAPTURING SKILL BY TRAINING FROM HER EARLY CHILDHOOD ON!

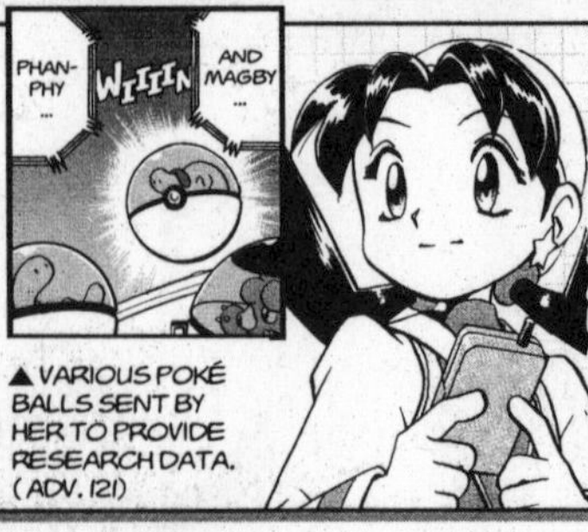

AND MAGBY...
WIIIIN
PHANPHY...


▲ VARIOUS POKÉ BALLS SENT BY HER TO PROVIDE RESEARCH DATA. (ADV. 121)

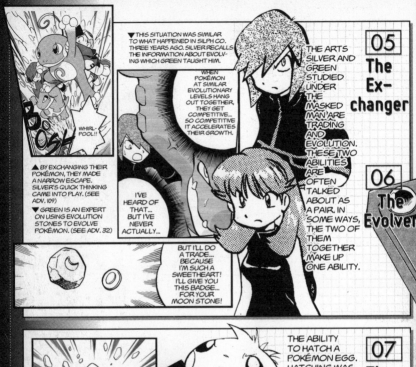

## 05 The Ex-changer

## 06 The Evolver

THE ARTS SILVER AND GREEN STUDIED UNDER THE MASKED MAN ARE TRADING AND EVOLUTION. THESE TWO ABILITIES ARE OFTEN TALKED ABOUT AS A PAIR. IN SOME WAYS, THE TWO OF THEM TOGETHER MAKE UP ONE ABILITY.

▼THIS SITUATION WAS SIMILAR TO WHAT HAPPENED IN SILPH CO. THREE YEARS AGO. SILVER RECALLS THE INFORMATION ABOUT EVOLVING WHICH GREEN TAUGHT HIM.

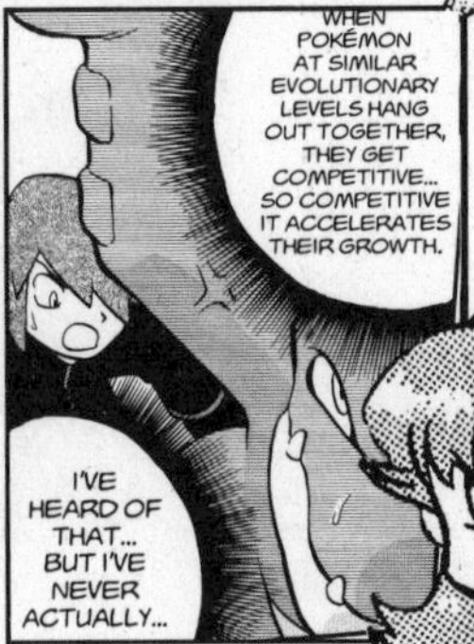

WHEN POKéMON AT SIMILAR EVOLUTIONARY LEVELS HANG OUT TOGETHER, THEY GET COMPETITIVE... SO COMPETITIVE IT ACCELERATES THEIR GROWTH.
I'VE HEARD OF THAT... BUT I'VE NEVER ACTUALLY...


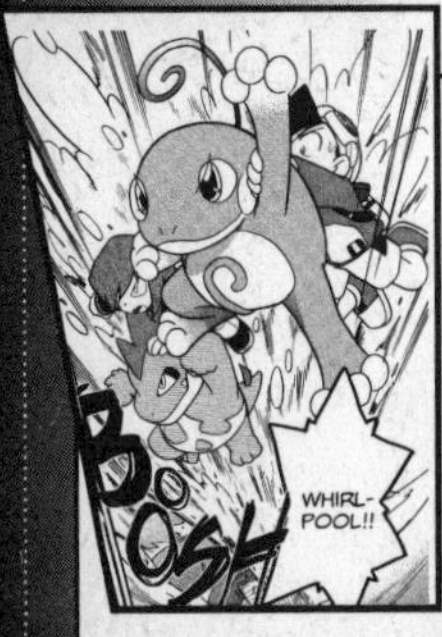

WHIRL-POOL!!
BOOSH


▲BY EXCHANGING THEIR POKéMON, THEY MADE A NARROW ESCAPE. SILVER'S QUICK THINKING CAME INTO PLAY. (SEE ADV. 109)

▼GREEN IS AN EXPERT ON USING EVOLUTION STONES TO EVOLVE POKéMON. (SEE ADV. 32)

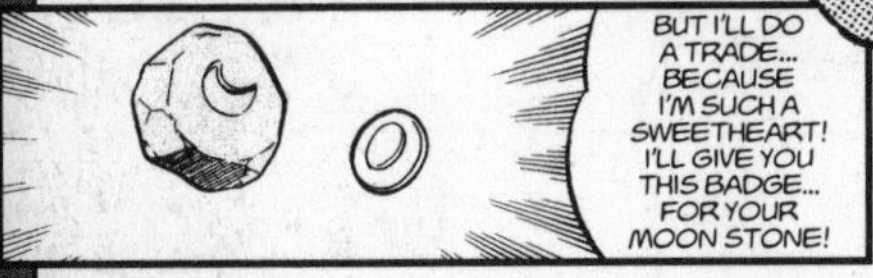

BUT I'LL DO A TRADE... BECAUSE I'M SUCH A SWEETHEART! I'LL GIVE YOU THIS BADGE... FOR YOUR MOON STONE!


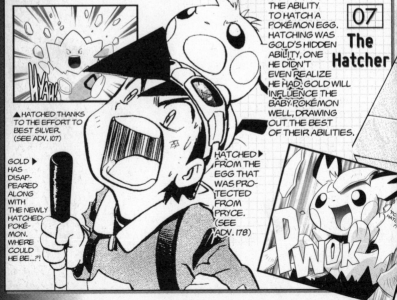

## 07 The Hatcher

THE ABILITY TO HATCH A POKéMON EGG. HATCHING WAS GOLD'S HIDDEN ABILITY, ONE HE DIDN'T EVEN REALIZE HE HAD. GOLD WILL INFLUENCE THE BABY POKéMON WELL, DRAWING OUT THE BEST OF THEIR ABILITIES.

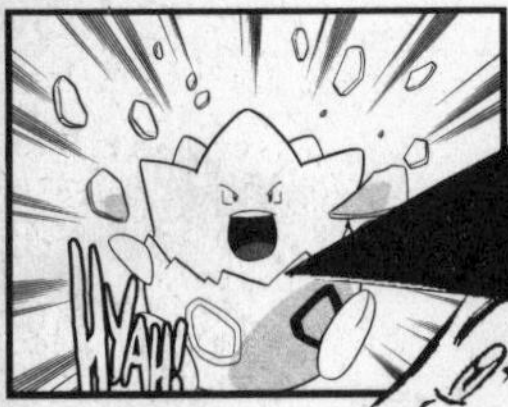

HYAH!


▲HATCHED THANKS TO THE EFFORT TO BEST SILVER. (SEE ADV. 107)

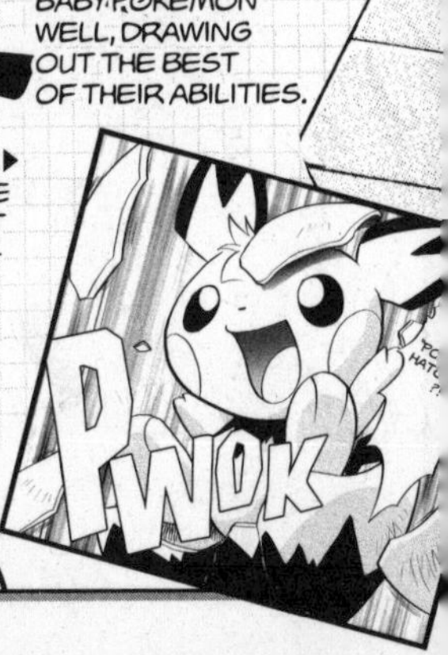

PWOK


HATCHED▶ FROM THE EGG THAT WAS PROTECTED FROM PRYCE. (SEE ADV. 178)

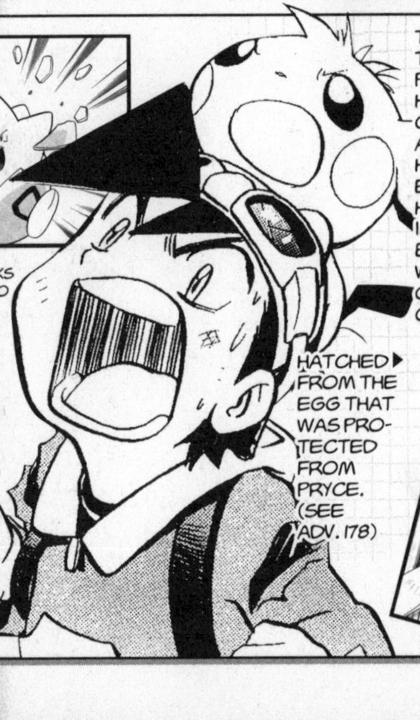

GOLD▶ HAS DISAPPEARED ALONG WITH THE NEWLY HATCHED POKéMON. WHERE COULD HE BE...?!

# The Last Battle XIV

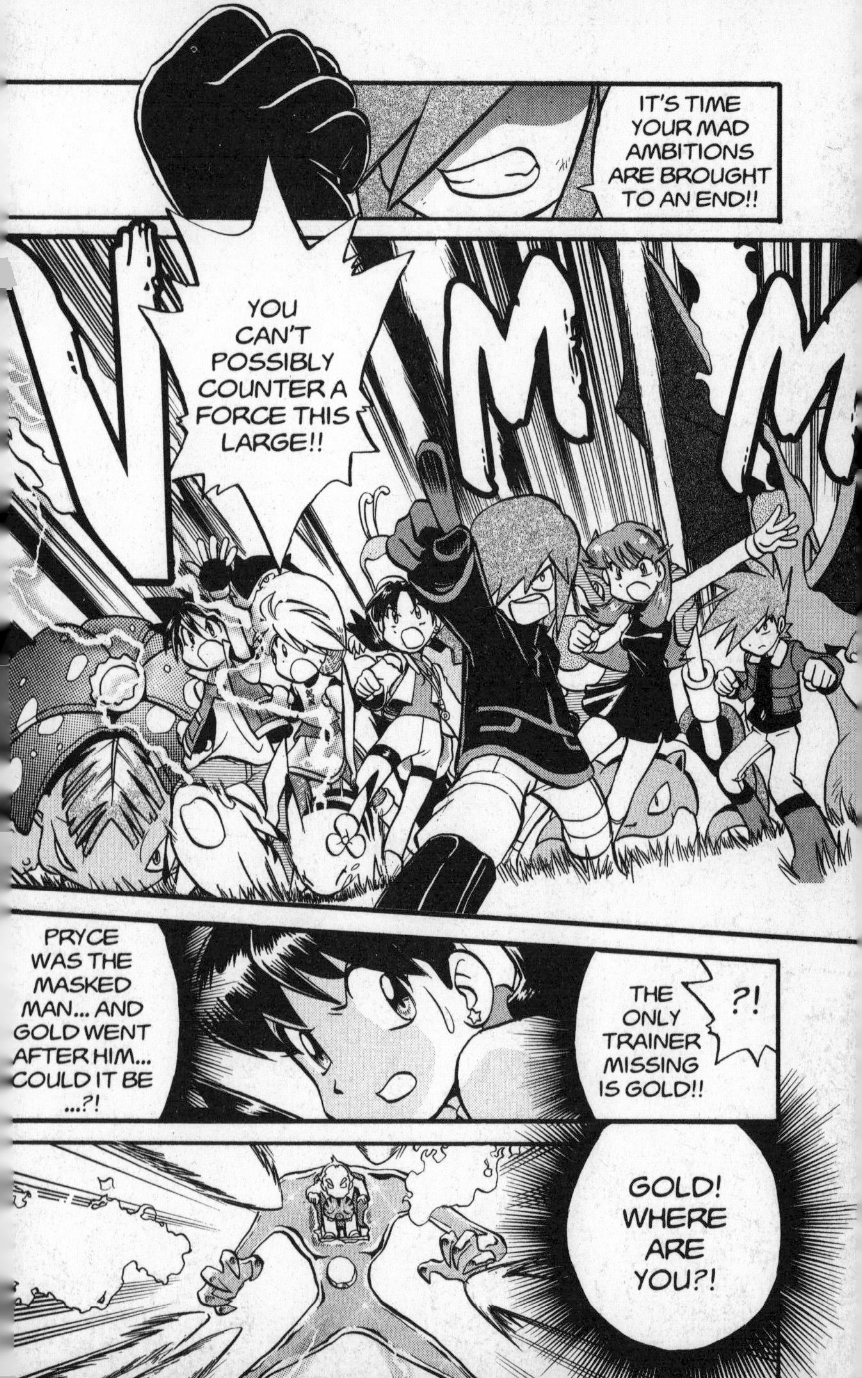
IT'S TIME YOUR MAD AMBITIONS ARE BROUGHT TO AN END!!
VMMM
YOU CAN'T POSSIBLY COUNTER A FORCE THIS LARGE!!
THE ONLY TRAINER MISSING IS GOLD!!
?!
PRYCE WAS THE MASKED MAN... AND GOLD WENT AFTER HIM... COULD IT BE ...?!
GOLD! WHERE ARE YOU?!

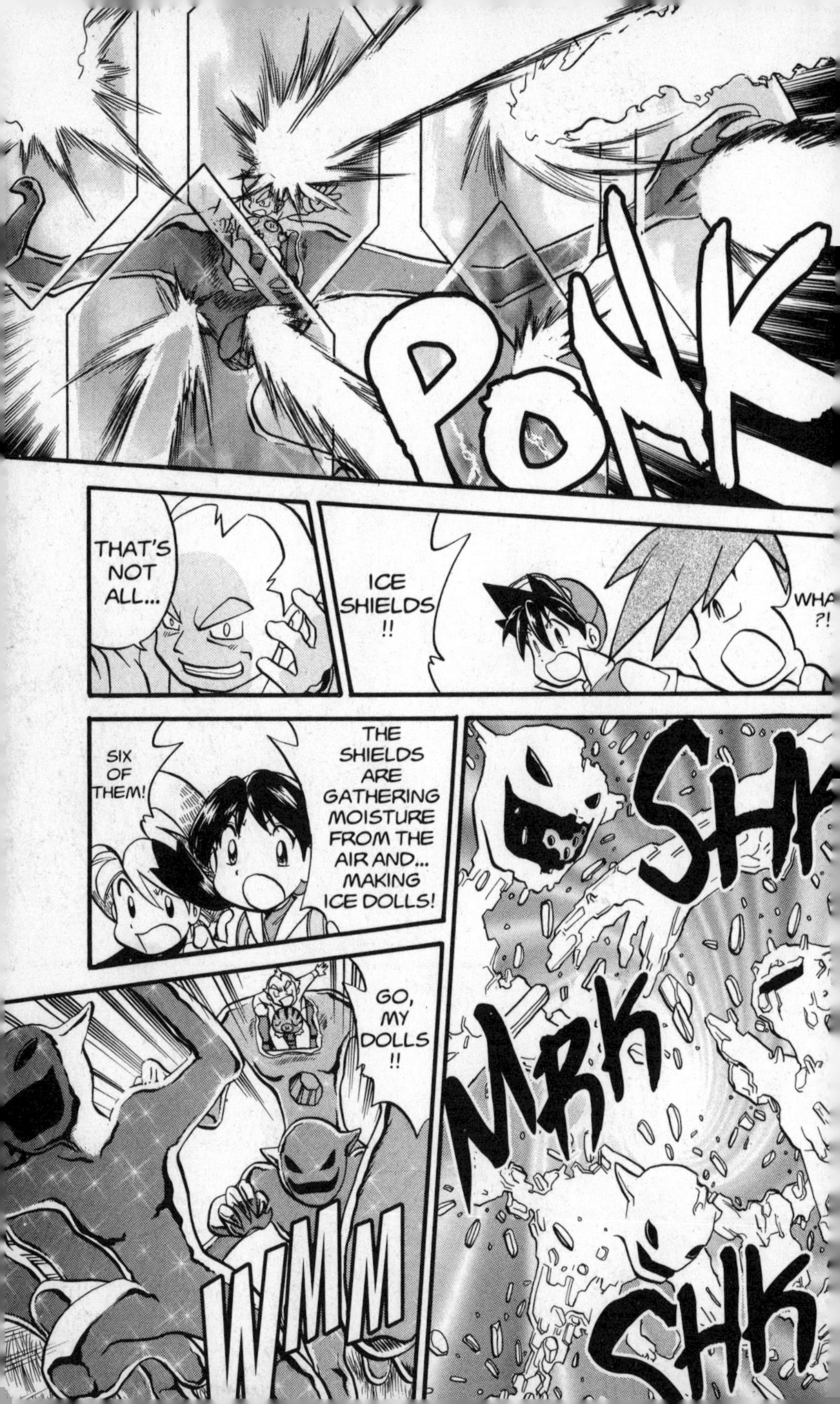

PONK
WHA ?!
ICE SHIELDS !!
THAT'S NOT ALL...
SH
MRK
SHK
THE SHIELDS ARE GATHERING MOISTURE FROM THE AIR AND... MAKING ICE DOLLS!
SIX OF THEM!
GO, MY DOLLS !!
WMM

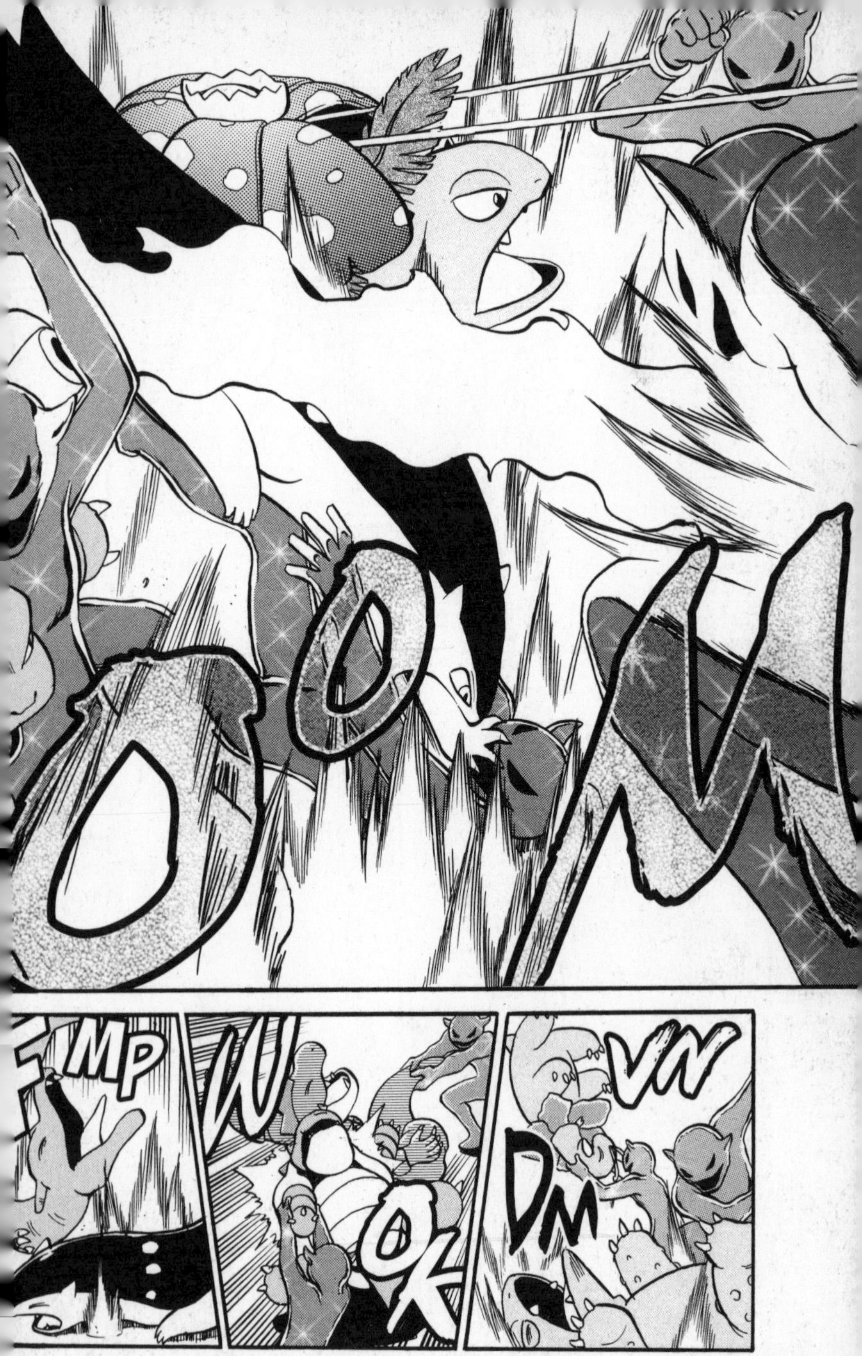
DOM
VN
DM
W
OK
FMP

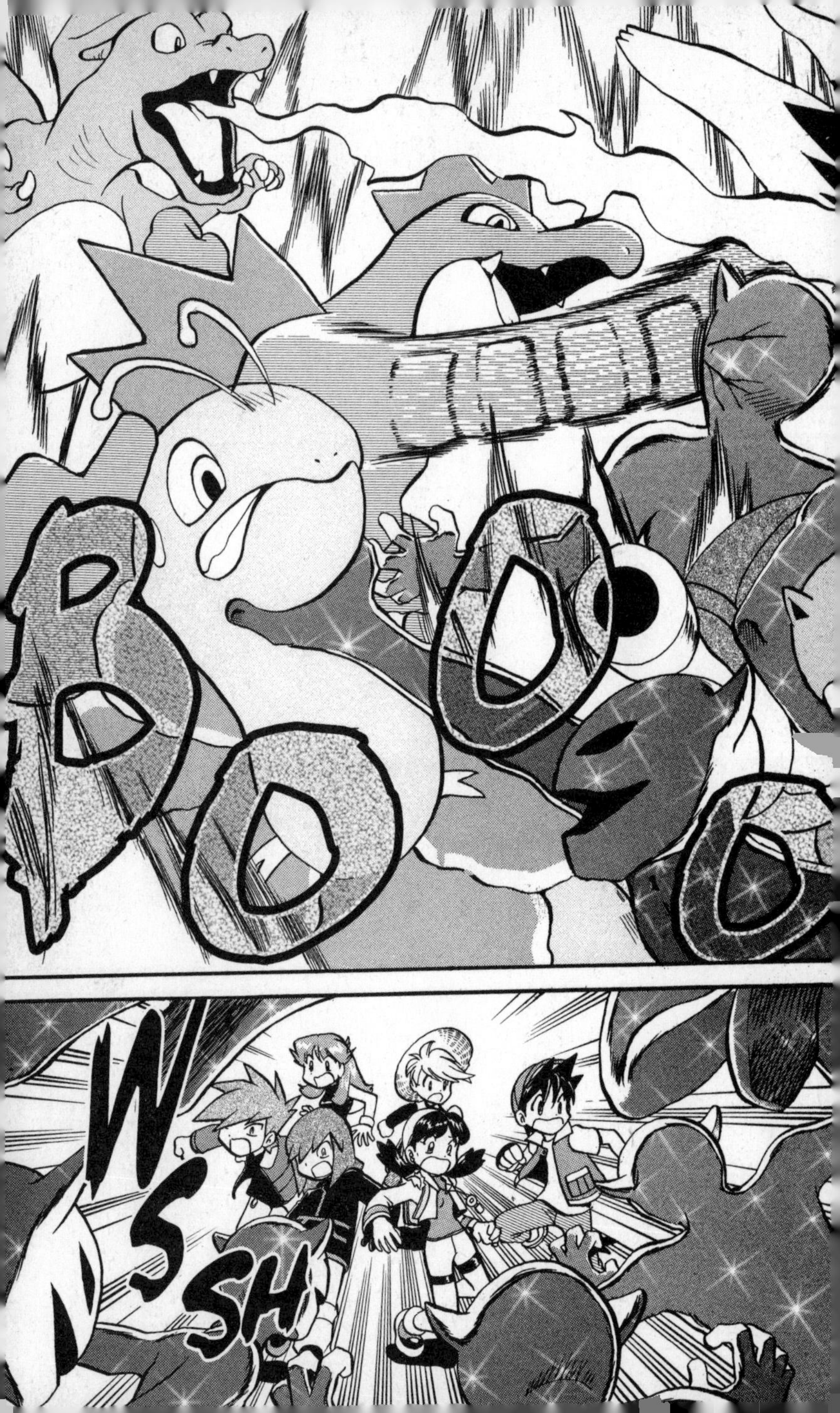
BOOOM
WSSH

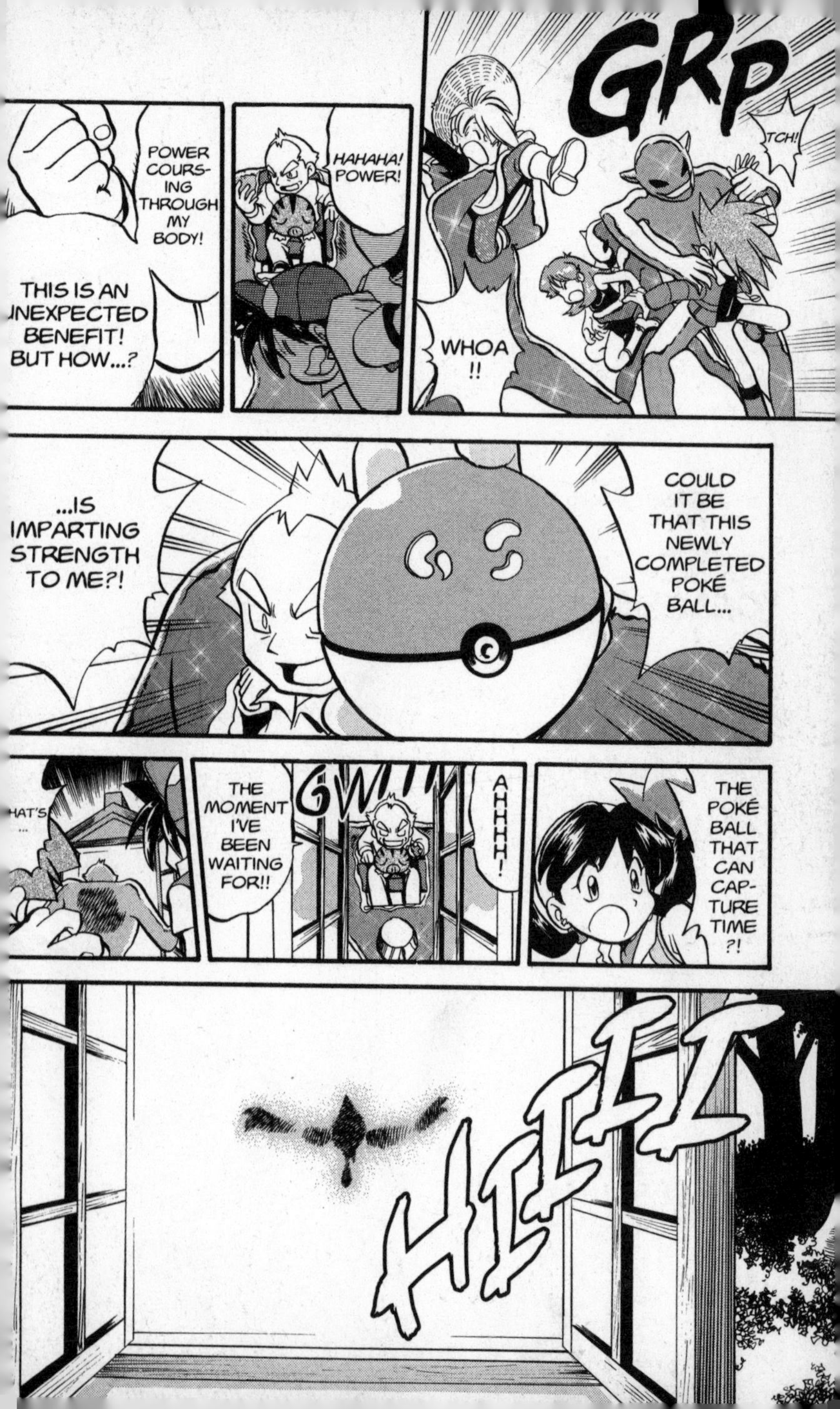
GRP
TCH!
WHOA !!
HAHAHA! POWER!
POWER COURSING THROUGH MY BODY!
THIS IS AN UNEXPECTED BENEFIT! BUT HOW...?
COULD IT BE THAT THIS NEWLY COMPLETED POKÉ BALL...
...IS IMPARTING STRENGTH TO ME?!
THE POKÉ BALL THAT CAN CAPTURE TIME ?!
AHHHH!
GWIII
THE MOMENT I'VE BEEN WAITING FOR!!
HAT'S ...
HIIIIY

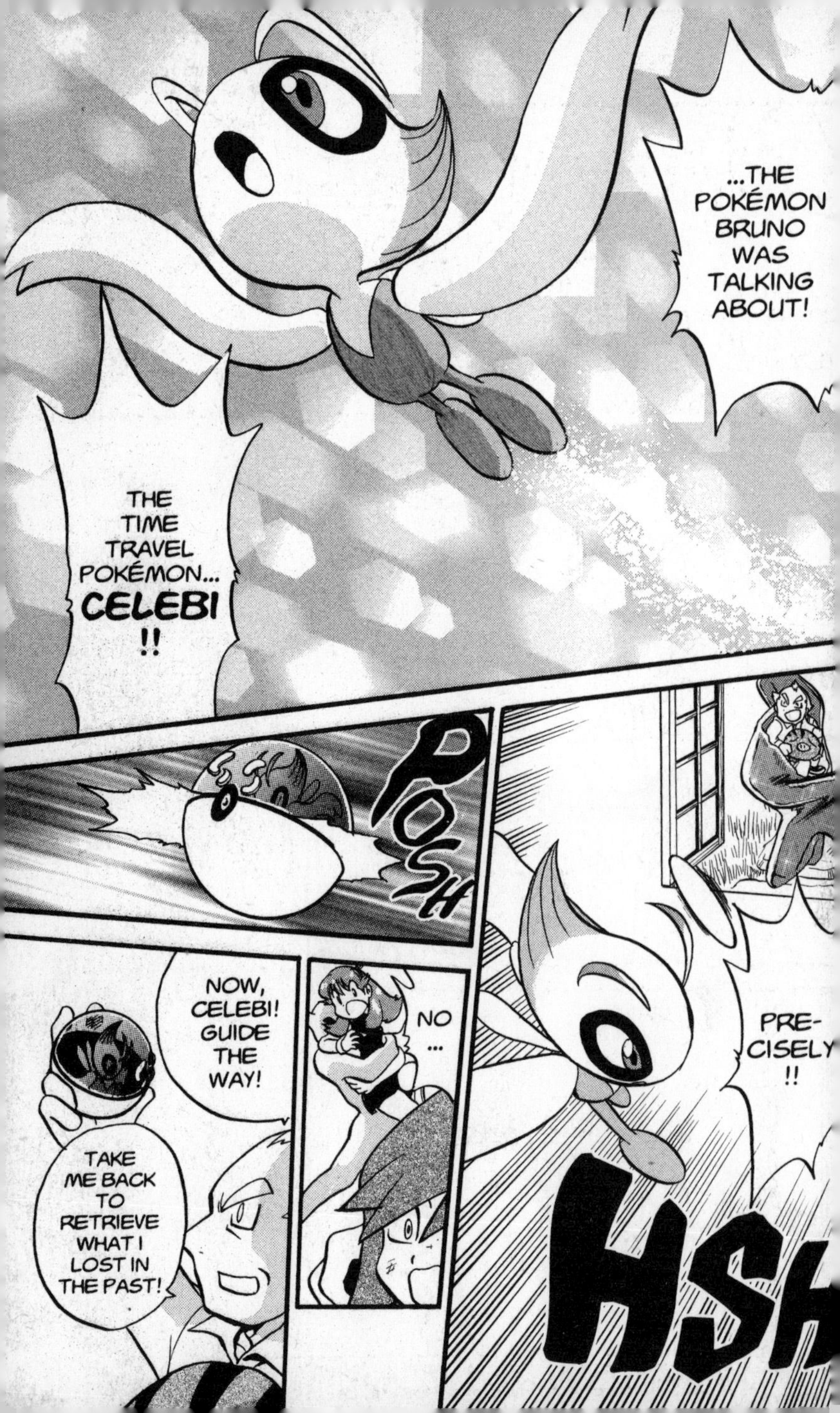
...THE POKÉMON BRUNO WAS TALKING ABOUT!
THE TIME TRAVEL POKÉMON... **CELEBI** !!
PRE-CISELY !!
HSH
POSH
NO ...
NOW, CELEBI! GUIDE THE WAY!
TAKE ME BACK TO RETRIEVE WHAT I LOST IN THE PAST!

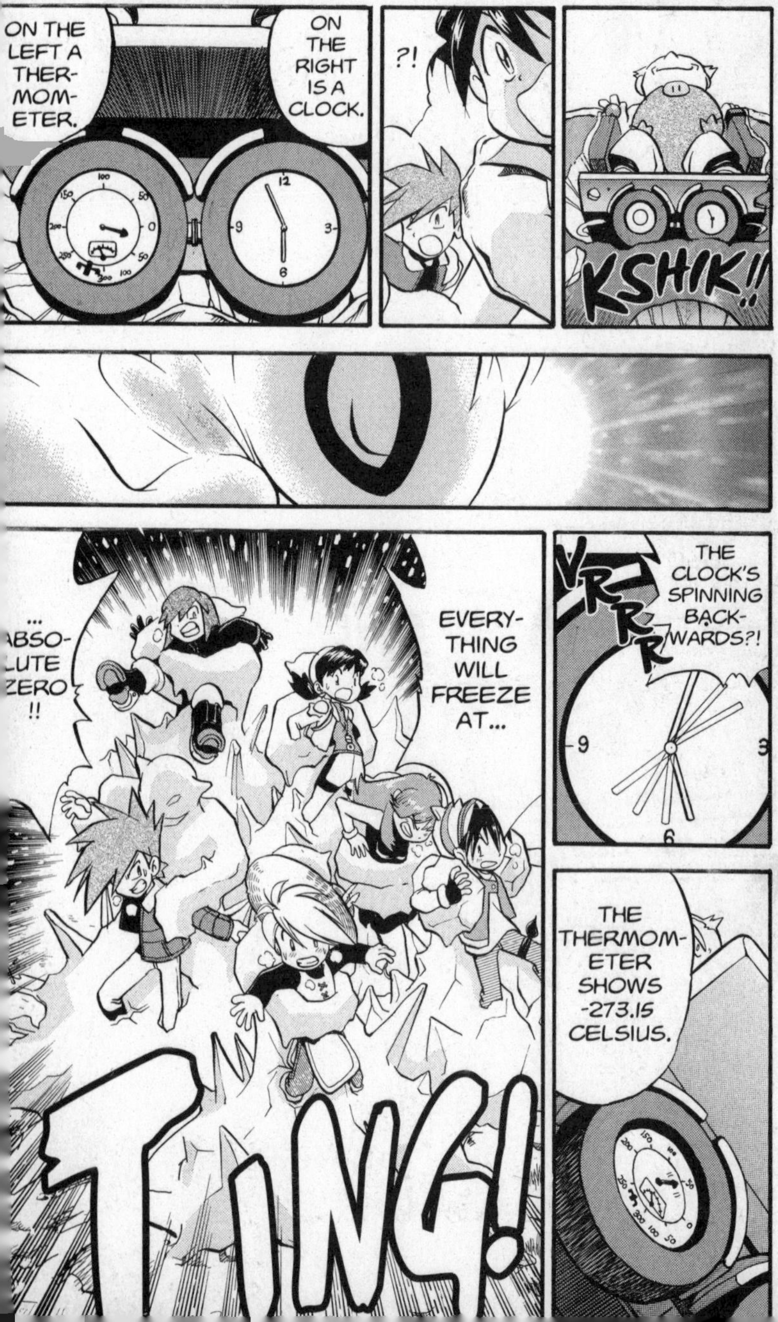
KSHIK!!
?!
ON THE RIGHT IS A CLOCK.
ON THE LEFT A THER-MOM-ETER.
VRRRR
THE CLOCK'S SPINNING BACK-WARDS?!
THE THERMOM-ETER SHOWS -273.15 CELSIUS.
EVERY-THING WILL FREEZE AT...
...ABSO-LUTE ZERO!!
TING!

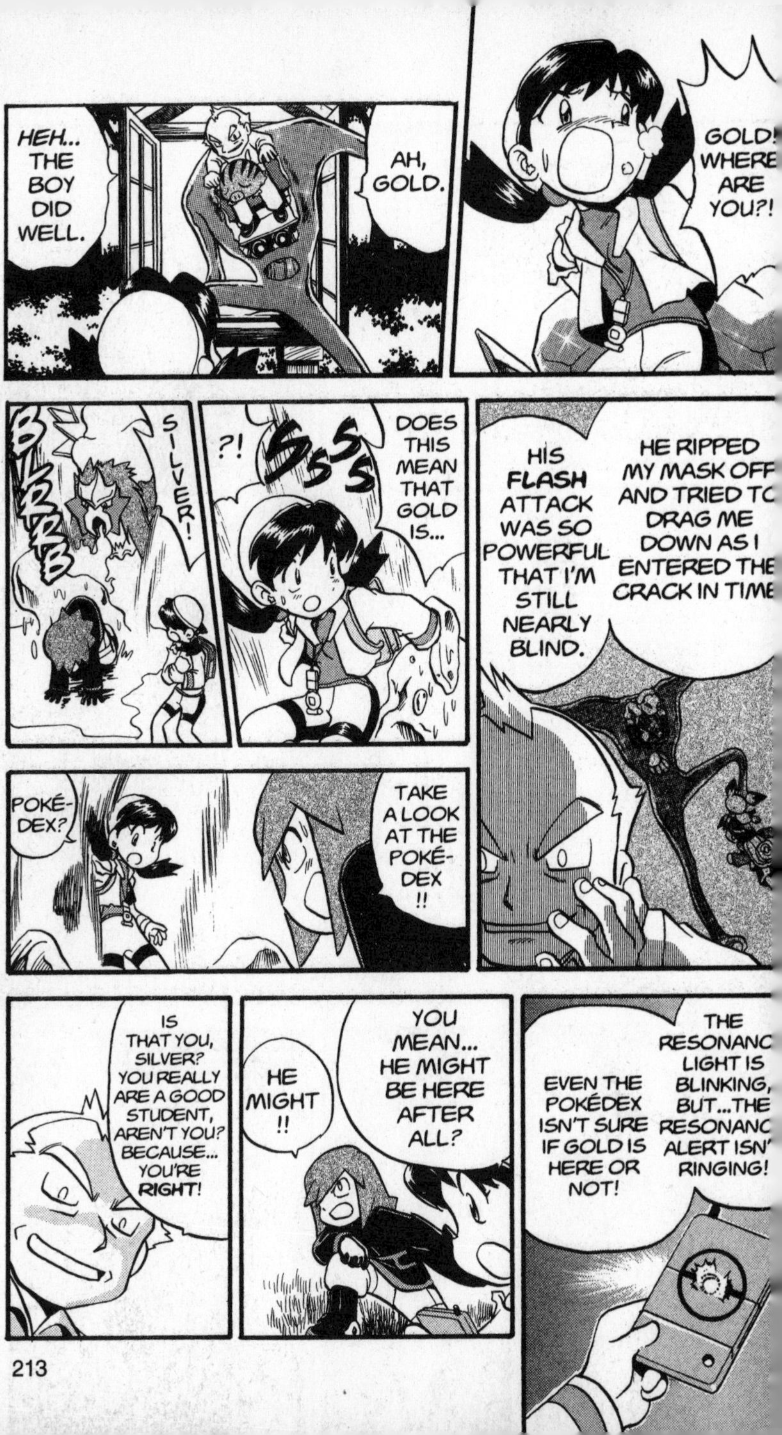

GOLD! WHERE ARE YOU?!
AH, GOLD.
HEH... THE BOY DID WELL.
HE RIPPED MY MASK OFF AND TRIED TO DRAG ME DOWN AS I ENTERED THE CRACK IN TIME
HIS FLASH ATTACK WAS SO POWERFUL THAT I'M STILL NEARLY BLIND.
DOES THIS MEAN THAT GOLD IS...
SSSS
?!
SILVER!
BLRRRB
TAKE A LOOK AT THE POKÉDEX!!
POKÉDEX?
THE RESONANC LIGHT IS BLINKING, BUT...THE RESONANC ALERT ISN' RINGING!
EVEN THE POKÉDEX ISN'T SURE IF GOLD IS HERE OR NOT!
YOU MEAN... HE MIGHT BE HERE AFTER ALL?
HE MIGHT!!
IS THAT YOU, SILVER? YOU REALLY ARE A GOOD STUDENT, AREN'T YOU? BECAUSE... YOU'RE RIGHT!

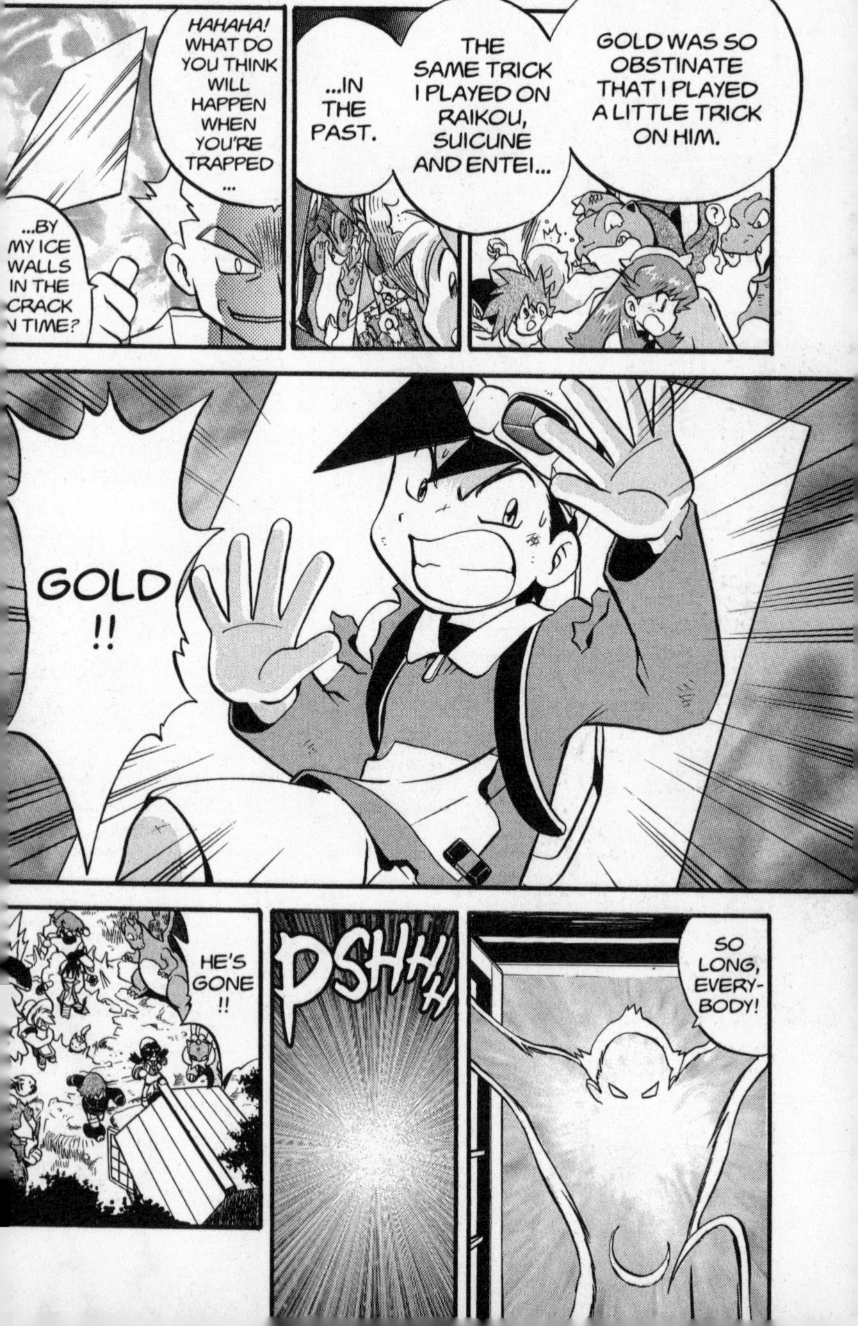
GOLD WAS SO OBSTINATE THAT I PLAYED A LITTLE TRICK ON HIM.
THE SAME TRICK I PLAYED ON RAIKOU, SUICUNE AND ENTEI...
...IN THE PAST.
HAHAHA! WHAT DO YOU THINK WILL HAPPEN WHEN YOU'RE TRAPPED ...
...BY MY ICE WALLS IN THE CRACK N TIME?
GOLD !!
SO LONG, EVERY-BODY!
PSHHH
HE'S GONE !!

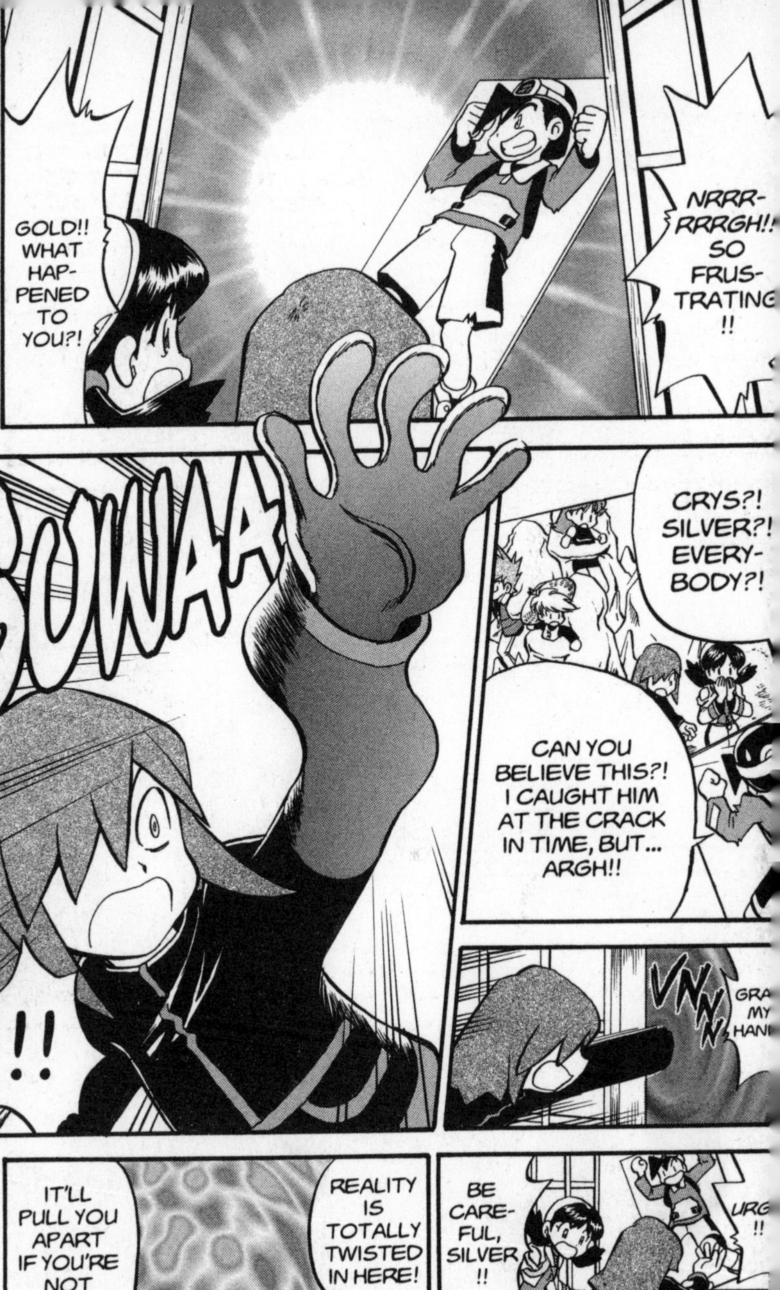
NRRR-RRRGH!! SO FRUS-TRATING!!
GOLD!! WHAT HAP-PENED TO YOU?!
CRYS?! SILVER?! EVERY-BODY?!
CAN YOU BELIEVE THIS?! I CAUGHT HIM AT THE CRACK IN TIME, BUT... ARGH!!
VNNN
GRA MY HAN
GUWAA
!!
URG !!
BE CARE-FUL, SILVER !!
REALITY IS TOTALLY TWISTED IN HERE!
IT'LL PULL YOU APART IF YOU'RE NOT CAREFUL!!

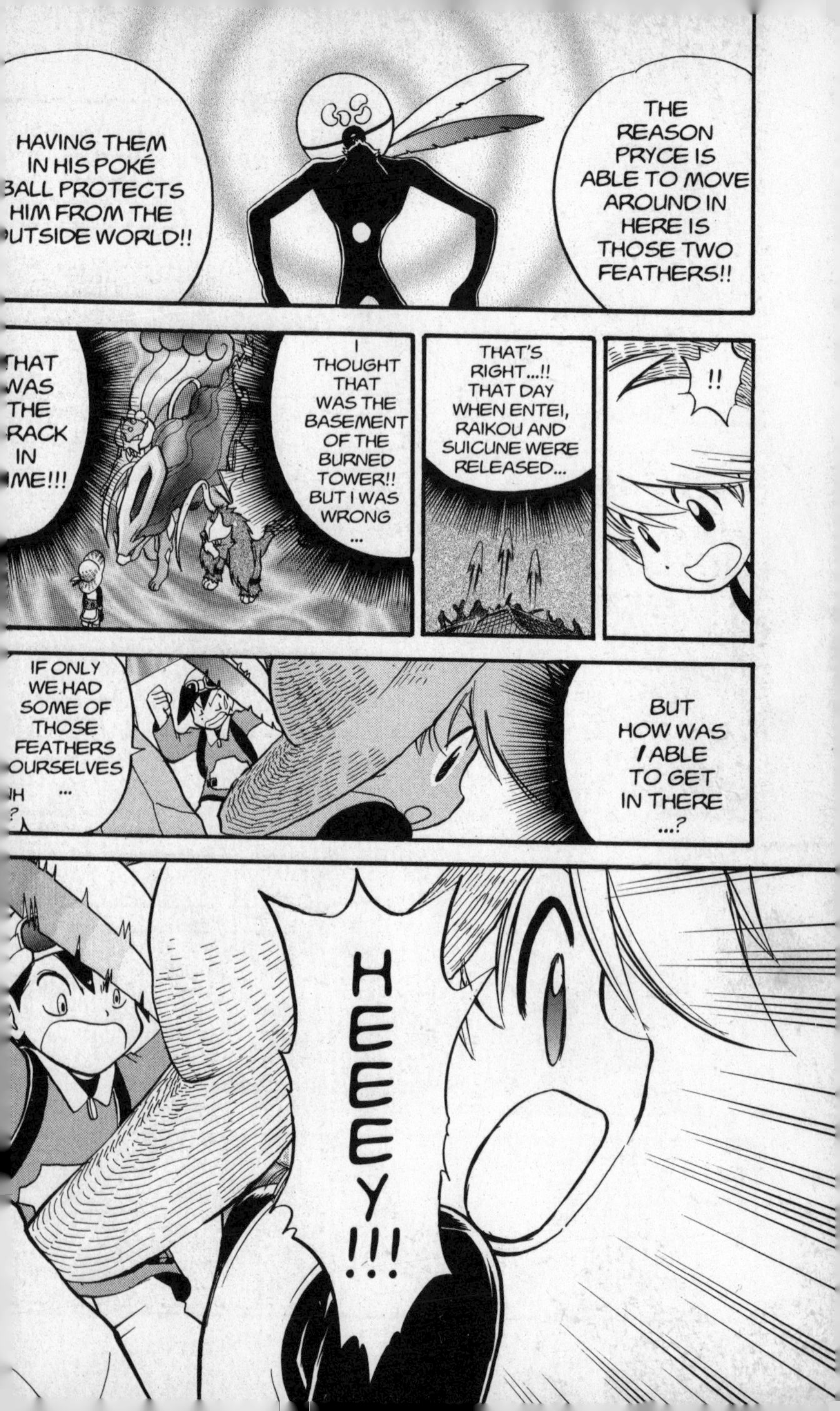
THE REASON PRYCE IS ABLE TO MOVE AROUND IN HERE IS THOSE TWO FEATHERS!!
HAVING THEM IN HIS POKÉ BALL PROTECTS HIM FROM THE OUTSIDE WORLD!!
!!
THAT'S RIGHT...!! THAT DAY WHEN ENTEI, RAIKOU AND SUICUNE WERE RELEASED...
I THOUGHT THAT WAS THE BASEMENT OF THE BURNED TOWER!! BUT I WAS WRONG ...
THAT WAS THE CRACK IN TIME!!!
BUT HOW WAS I ABLE TO GET IN THERE ...?
IF ONLY WE HAD SOME OF THOSE FEATHERS OURSELVES ...
HEEEEY!!!

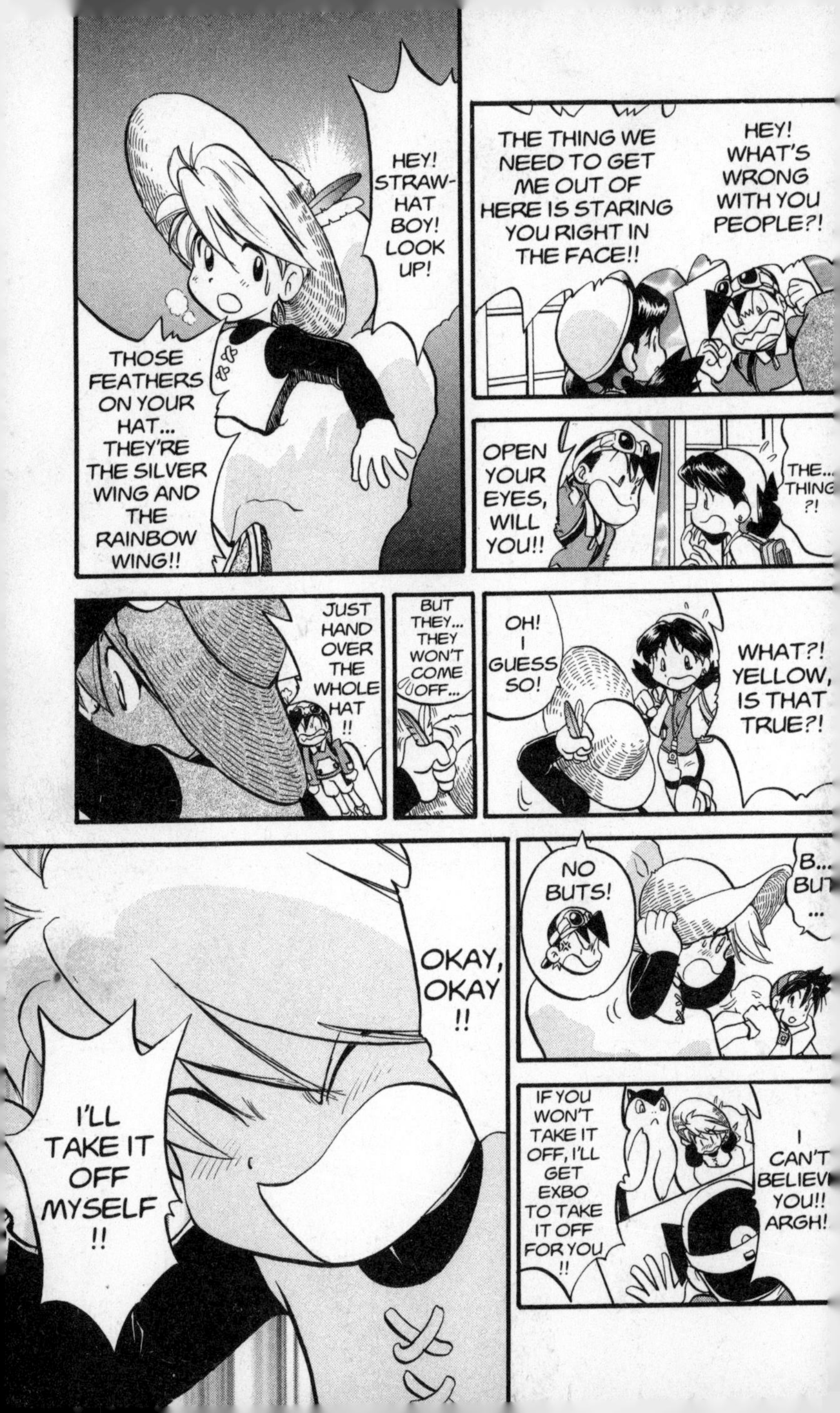
HEY! WHAT'S WRONG WITH YOU PEOPLE?!
THE THING WE NEED TO GET ME OUT OF HERE IS STARING YOU RIGHT IN THE FACE!!
THE... THING ?!
OPEN YOUR EYES, WILL YOU!!
HEY! STRAW-HAT BOY! LOOK UP!
THOSE FEATHERS ON YOUR HAT... THEY'RE THE SILVER WING AND THE RAINBOW WING!!
WHAT?! YELLOW, IS THAT TRUE?!
OH! I GUESS SO!
BUT THEY... THEY WON'T COME OFF...
JUST HAND OVER THE WHOLE HAT !!
B... BUT ...
NO BUTS!
I CAN'T BELIEV YOU!! ARGH!
IF YOU WON'T TAKE IT OFF, I'LL GET EXBO TO TAKE IT OFF FOR YOU !!
OKAY, OKAY !!
I'LL TAKE IT OFF MYSELF !!

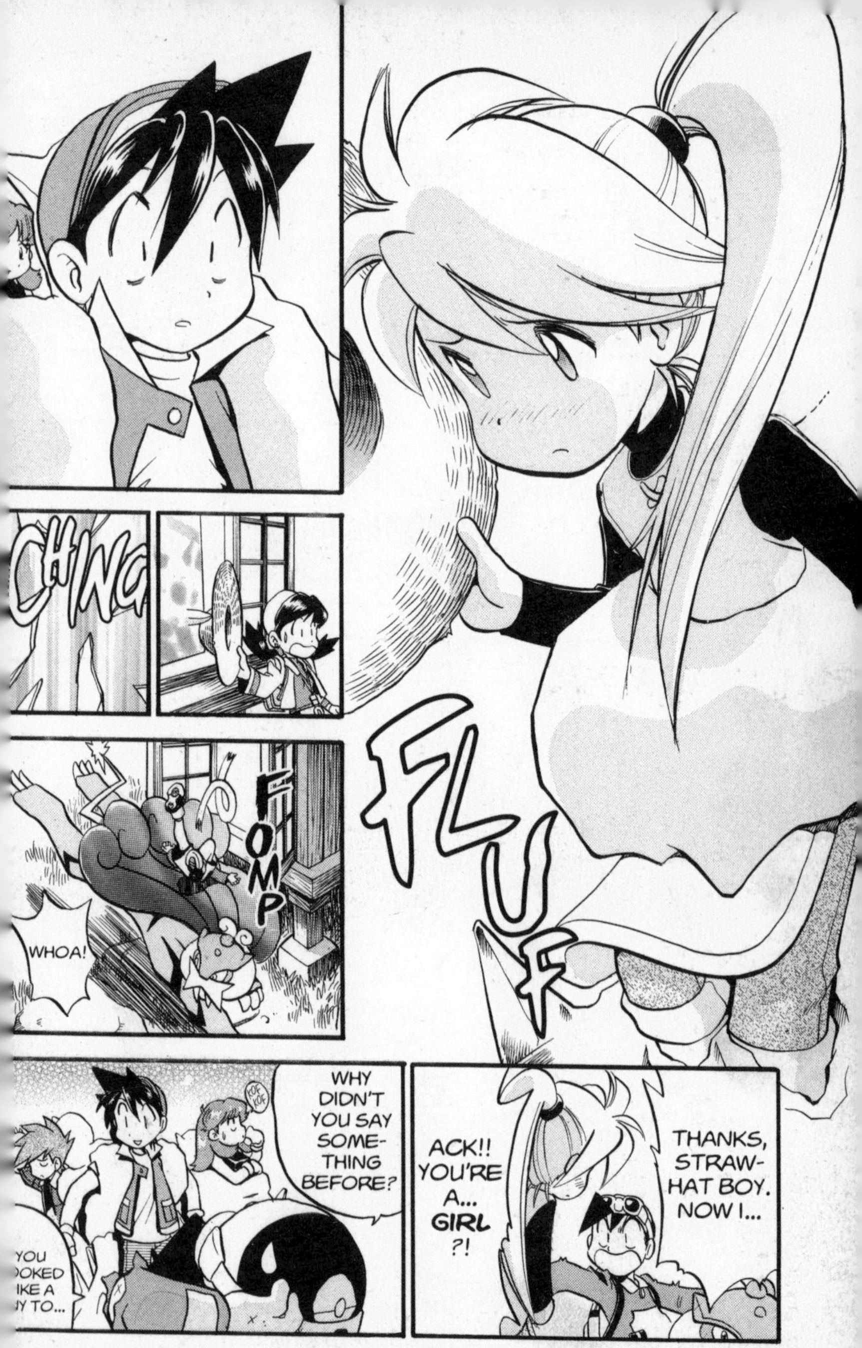
FLUF
CHING
FOMP
WHOA!
THANKS, STRAW-HAT BOY. NOW I...
ACK!! YOU'RE A... GIRL?!
WHY DIDN'T YOU SAY SOME-THING BEFORE?
KOF KOF
YOU OOKED IKE A Y TO...

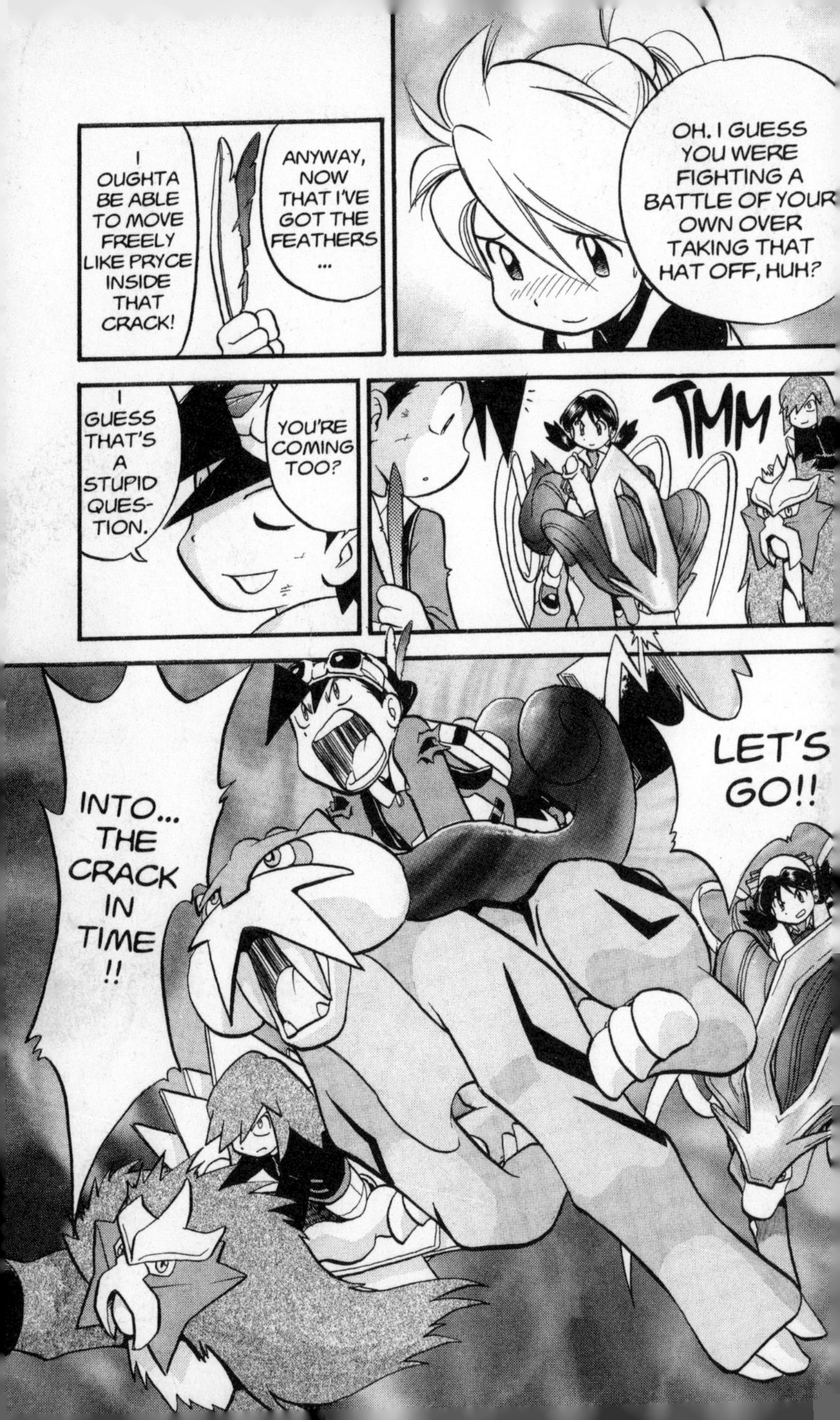
OH. I GUESS YOU WERE FIGHTING A BATTLE OF YOUR OWN OVER TAKING THAT HAT OFF, HUH?
ANYWAY, NOW THAT I'VE GOT THE FEATHERS...
I OUGHTA BE ABLE TO MOVE FREELY LIKE PRYCE INSIDE THAT CRACK!
TMM
YOU'RE COMING TOO?
I GUESS THAT'S A STUPID QUES-TION.
LET'S GO!!
INTO... THE CRACK IN TIME!!

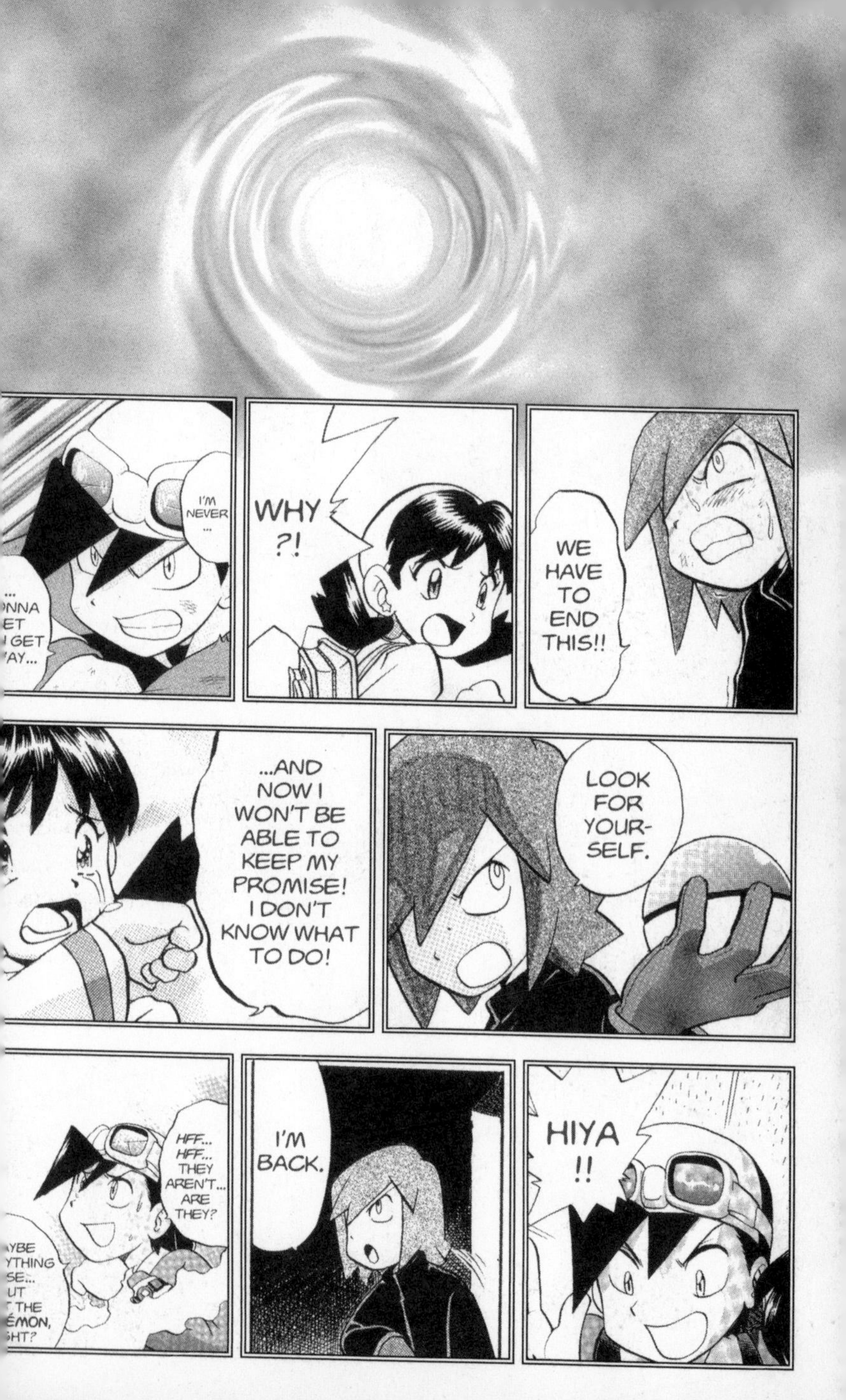
WE HAVE TO END THIS!!
WHY ?!
I'M NEVER ...
... ONNA ET GET AY...
LOOK FOR YOUR-SELF.
...AND NOW I WON'T BE ABLE TO KEEP MY PROMISE! I DON'T KNOW WHAT TO DO!
HIYA !!
I'M BACK.
HFF... HFF... THEY AREN'T... ARE THEY?
AYBE YTHING SE... UT T THE ÉMON, GHT?

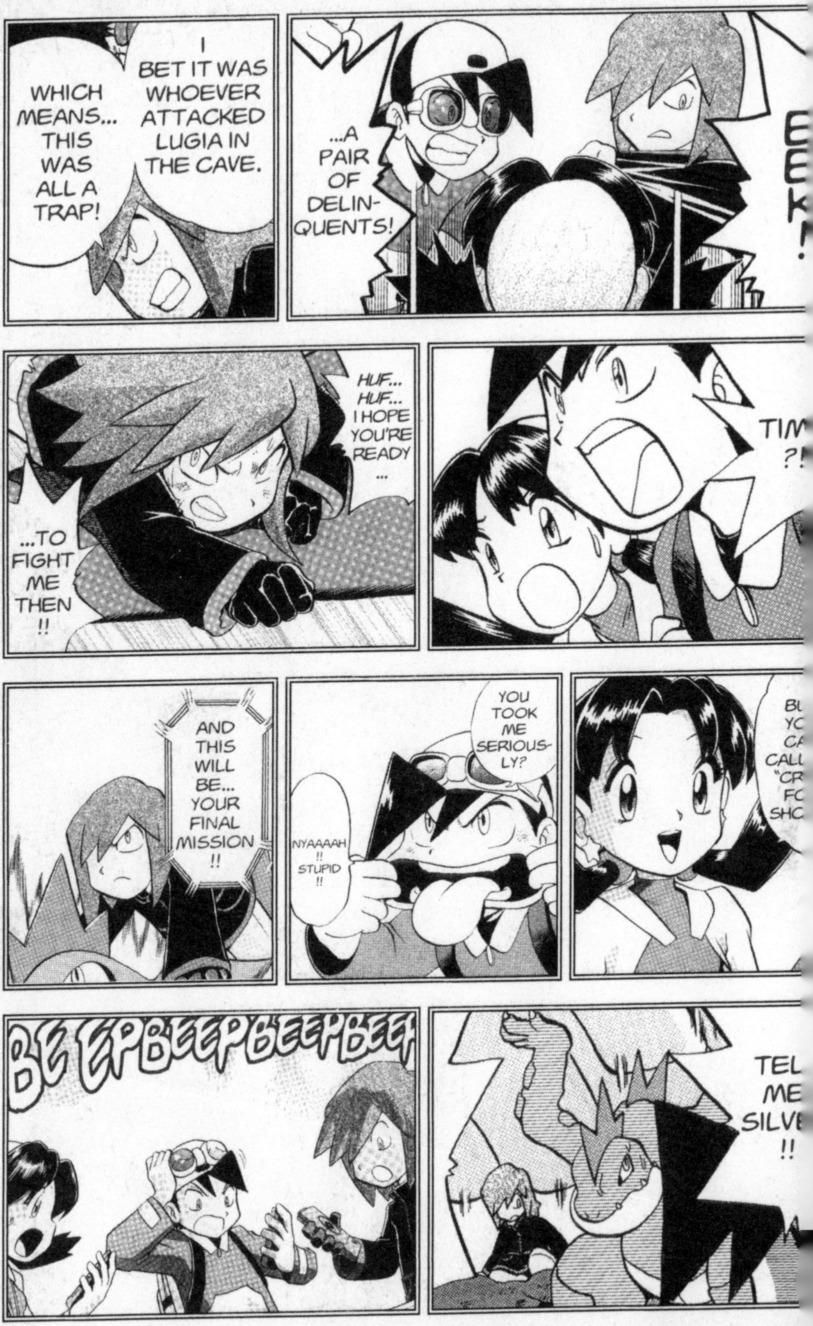
EEEK!
...A PAIR OF DELIN-QUENTS!
I BET IT WAS WHOEVER ATTACKED LUGIA IN THE CAVE.
WHICH MEANS... THIS WAS ALL A TRAP!
TIM ?!
HUF... HUF... I HOPE YOU'RE READY ...
...TO FIGHT ME THEN !!
BU YO CA CALL "CR FO SHO
YOU TOOK ME SERIOUS-LY?
NYAAAAH !! STUPID !!
AND THIS WILL BE... YOUR FINAL MISSION !!
TEL ME SILVE !!
BEEPBEEPBEEPBEE

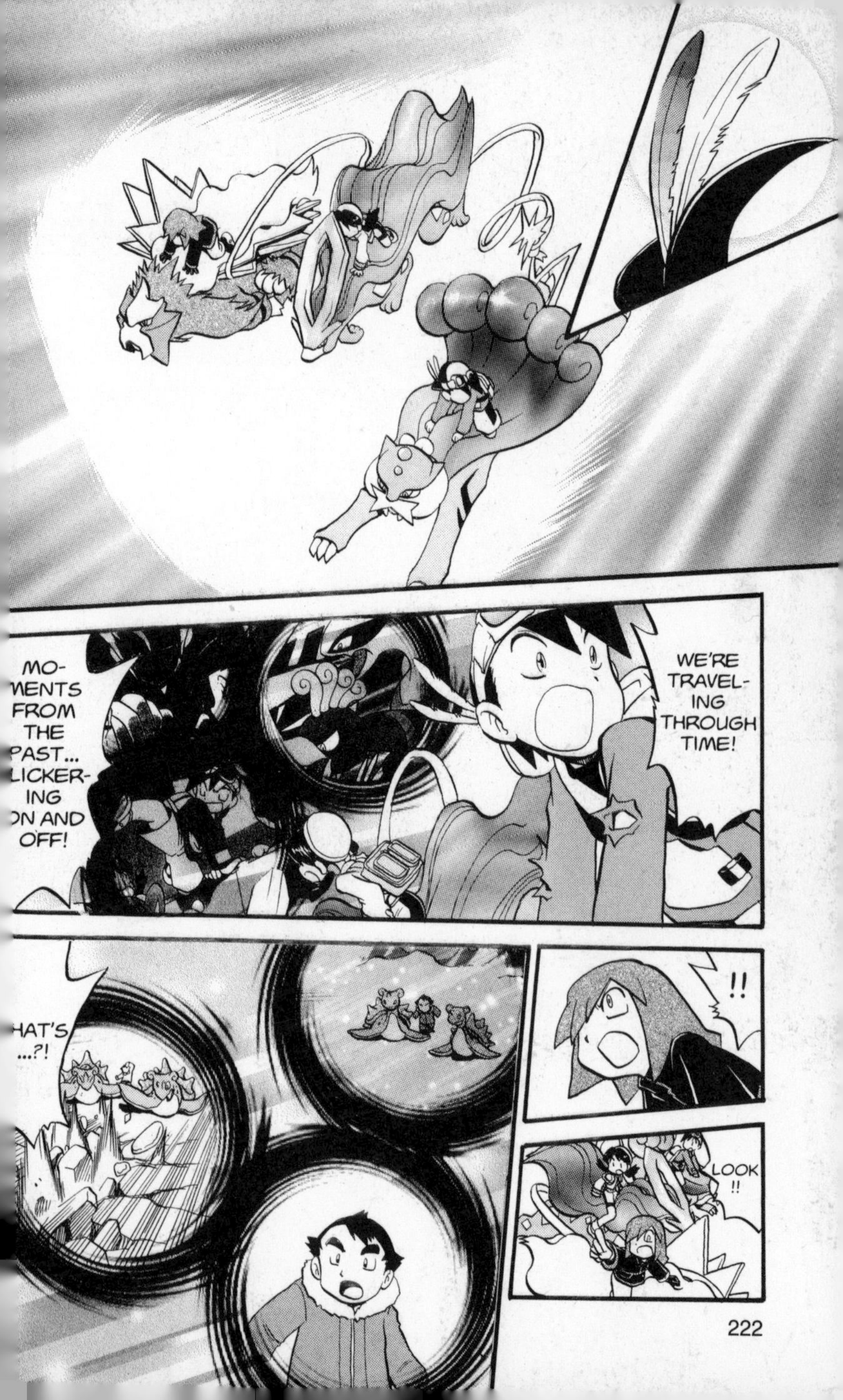
WE'RE TRAVEL- ING THROUGH TIME!
MO- MENTS FROM THE PAST... LICKER- ING ON AND OFF!
!!
LOOK !!
HAT'S ...?!

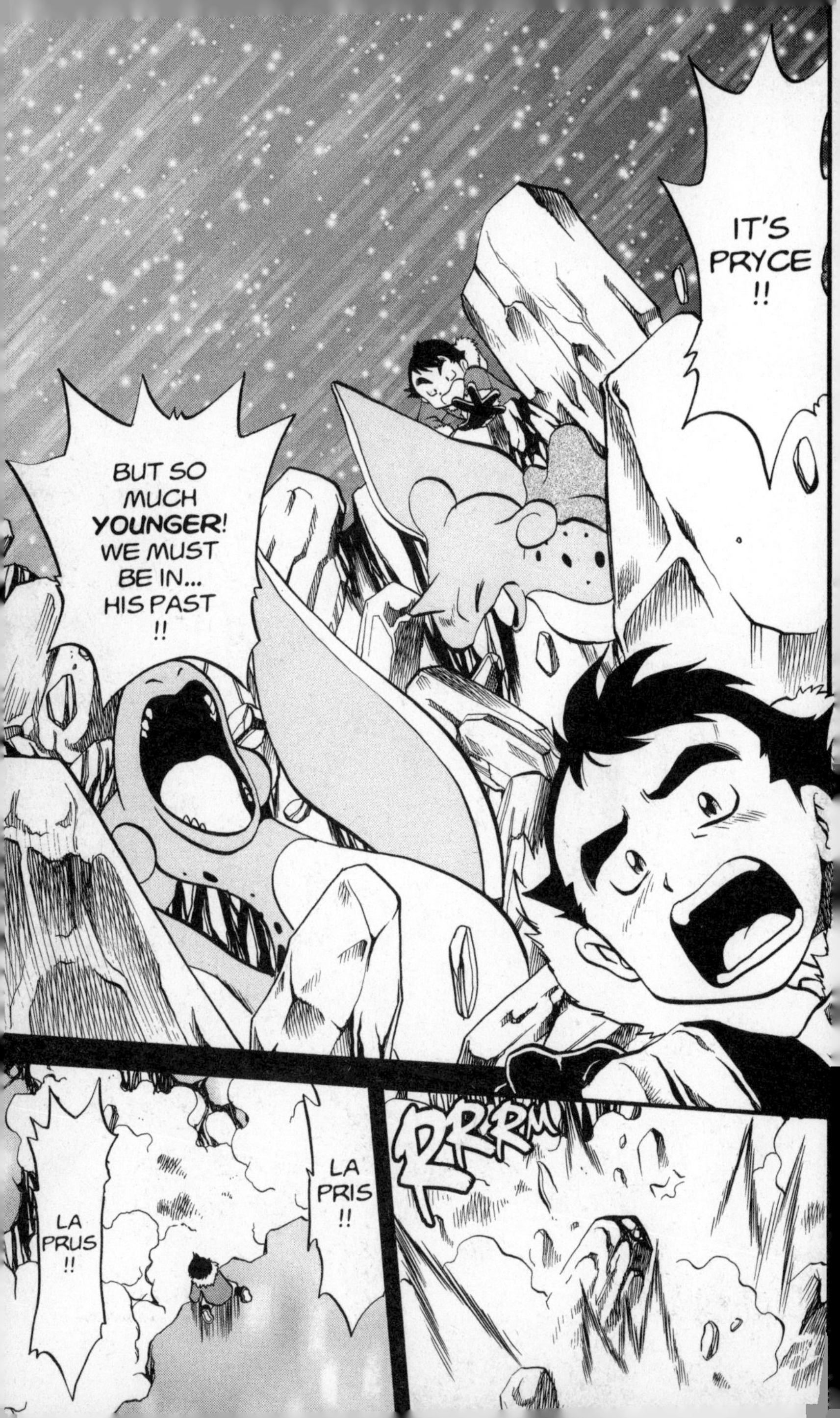
IT'S PRYCE !!
BUT SO MUCH YOUNGER! WE MUST BE IN... HIS PAST !!
RRRM
LA PRIS !!
LA PRUS !!

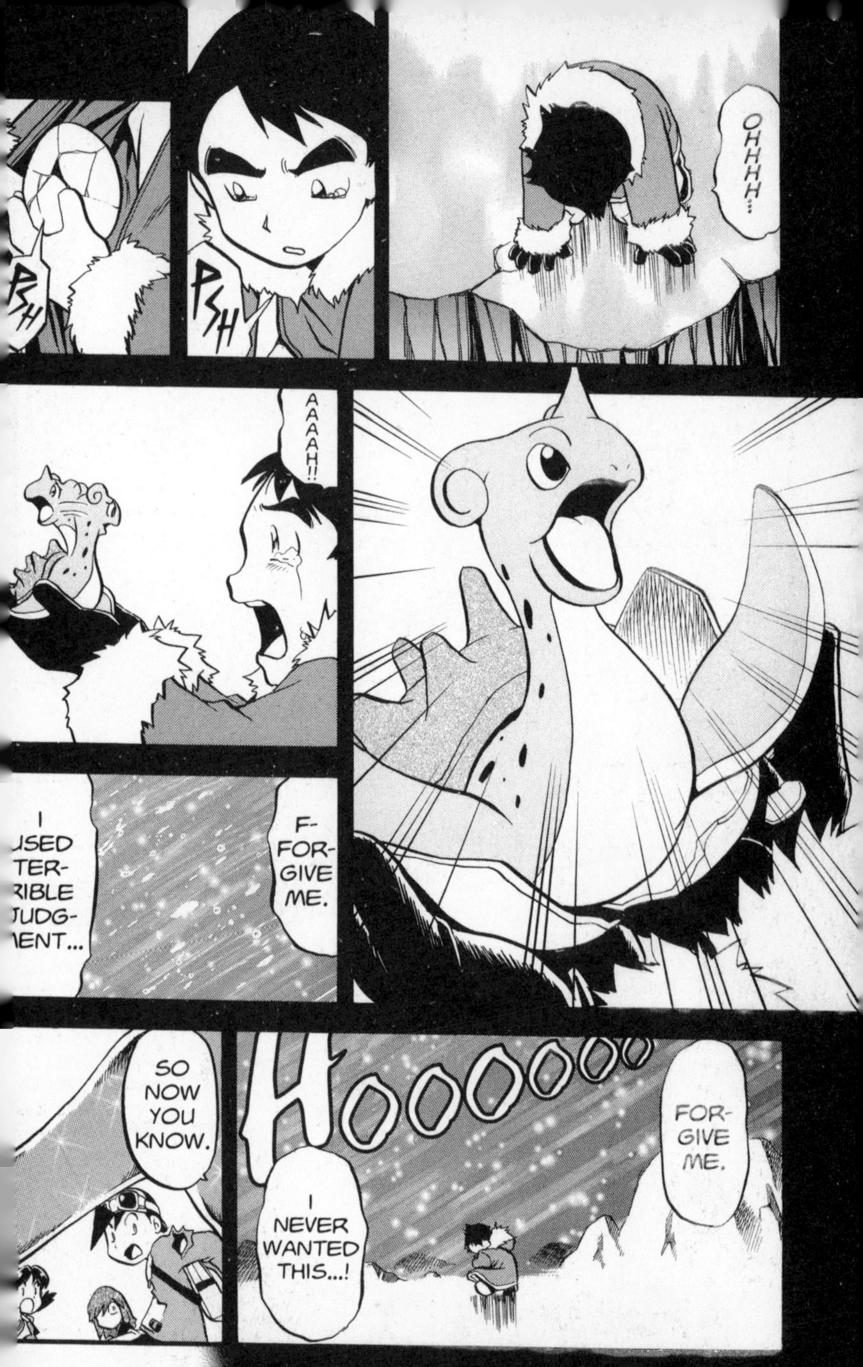
OHHHH...
PSH
PSH
AAAAH!!
F-FOR-GIVE ME.
I USED TER-RIBLE JUDG-MENT...
FOR-GIVE ME.
HOOOOOOO
I NEVER WANTED THIS...!
SO NOW YOU KNOW.

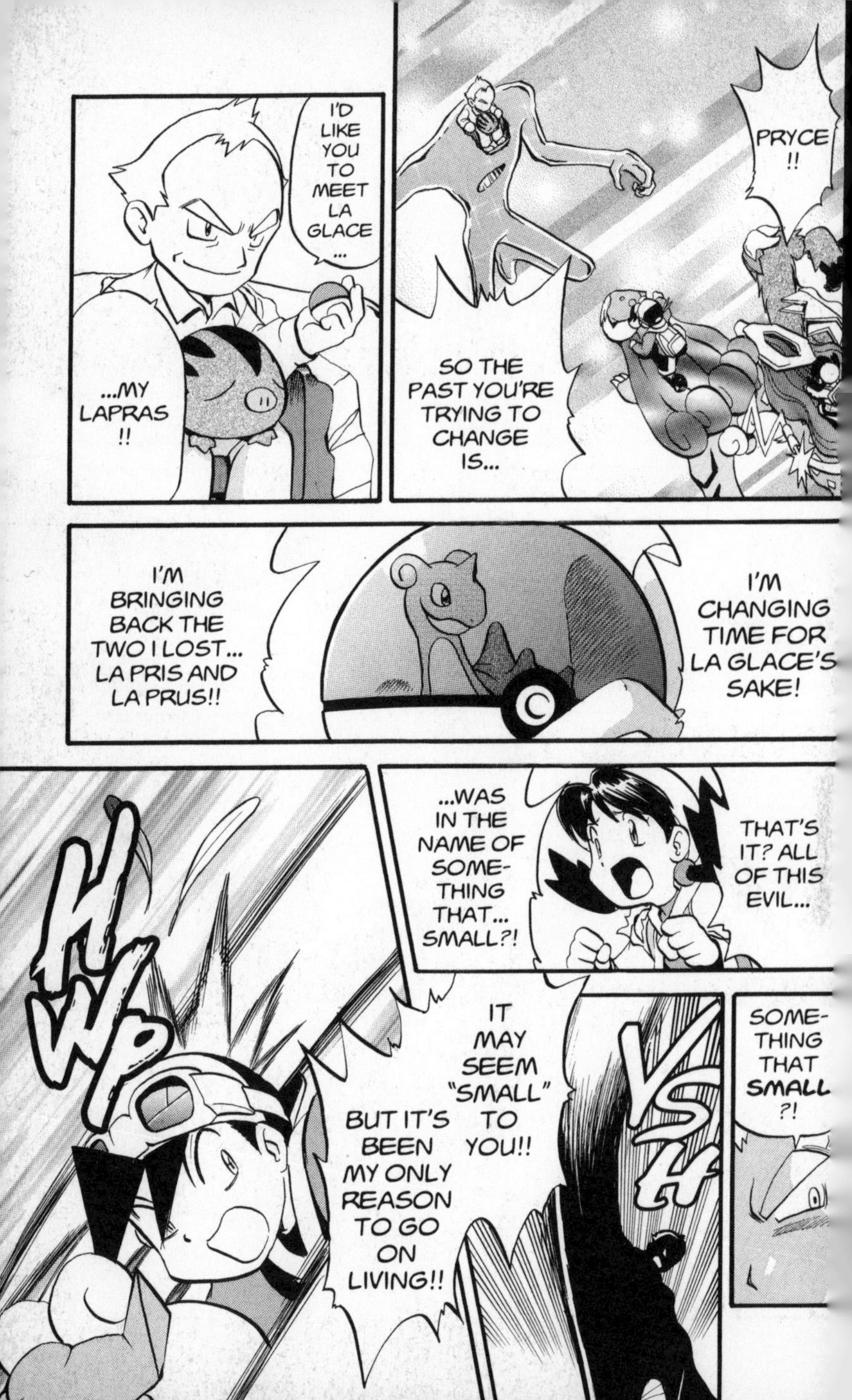
PRYCE!!
SO THE PAST YOU'RE TRYING TO CHANGE IS...
I'D LIKE YOU TO MEET LA GLACE...
...MY LAPRAS!!
I'M CHANGING TIME FOR LA GLACE'S SAKE!
I'M BRINGING BACK THE TWO I LOST... LA PRIS AND LA PRUS!!
THAT'S IT? ALL OF THIS EVIL...
...WAS IN THE NAME OF SOME-THING THAT... SMALL?!
SOME-THING THAT SMALL?!
VSH
HWP
IT MAY SEEM "SMALL" TO YOU!!
BUT IT'S BEEN MY ONLY REASON TO GO ON LIVING!!

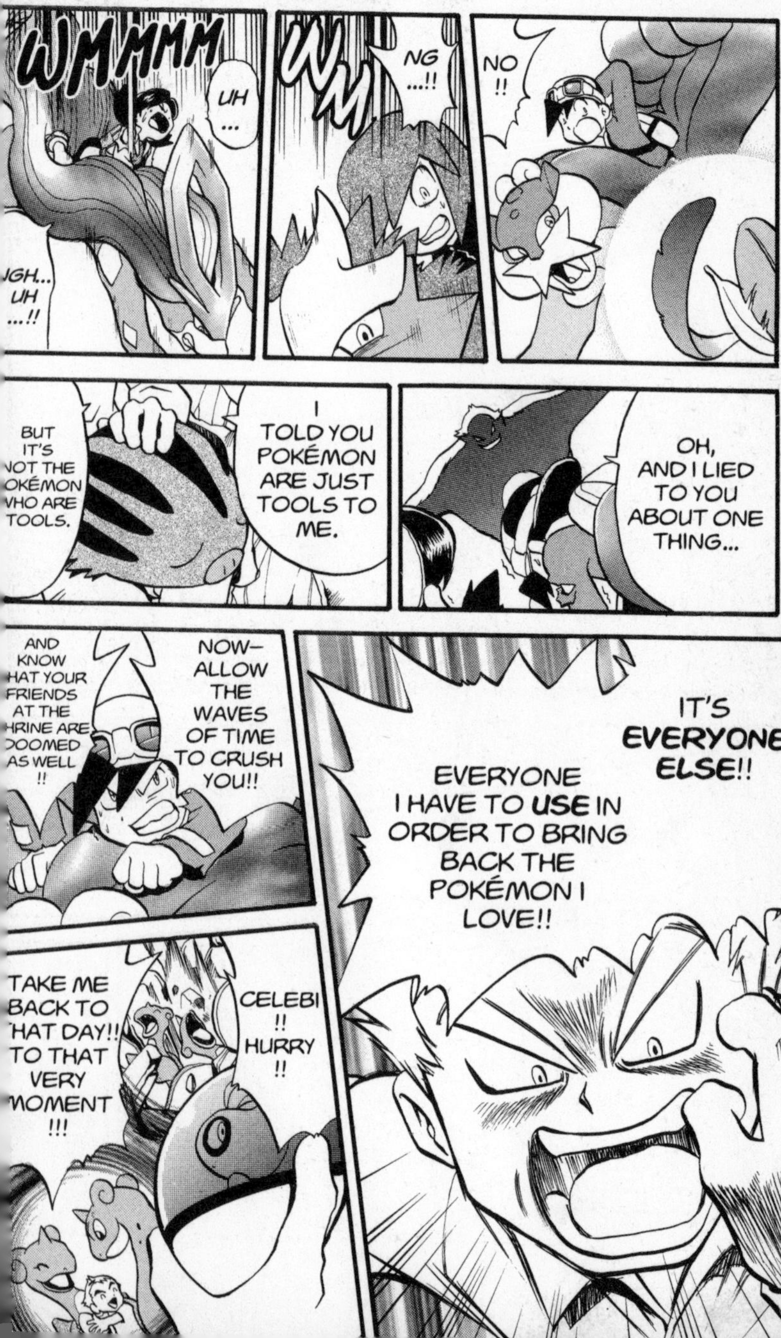
NO !!
WM
NG ...!!
WMMMM
UH ...
GH... UH ...!!
OH, AND I LIED TO YOU ABOUT ONE THING...
I TOLD YOU POKÉMON ARE JUST TOOLS TO ME.
BUT IT'S NOT THE OKÉMON WHO ARE TOOLS.
IT'S EVERYONE ELSE!!
EVERYONE I HAVE TO USE IN ORDER TO BRING BACK THE POKÉMON I LOVE!!
NOW— ALLOW THE WAVES OF TIME TO CRUSH YOU!!
AND KNOW HAT YOUR FRIENDS AT THE HRINE ARE OOMED AS WELL !!
CELEBI !! HURRY !!
TAKE ME BACK TO HAT DAY!! TO THAT VERY MOMENT !!!

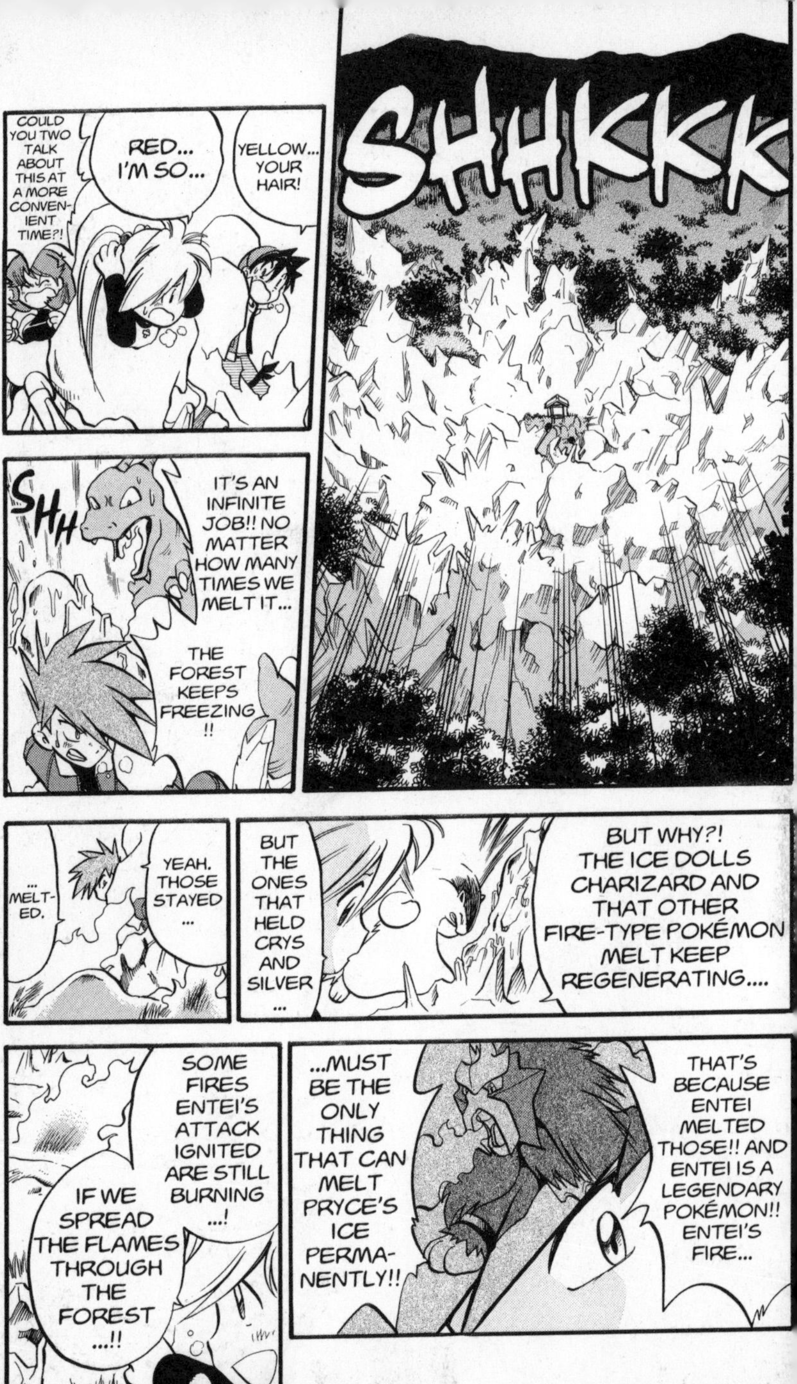
SHHKKK
YELLOW... YOUR HAIR!
RED... I'M SO...
COULD YOU TWO TALK ABOUT THIS AT A MORE CONVEN-IENT TIME?!
IT'S AN INFINITE JOB!! NO MATTER HOW MANY TIMES WE MELT IT...
SHH
THE FOREST KEEPS FREEZING!!
BUT WHY?! THE ICE DOLLS CHARIZARD AND THAT OTHER FIRE-TYPE POKÉMON MELT KEEP REGENERATING....
BUT THE ONES THAT HELD CRYS AND SILVER...
YEAH. THOSE STAYED...
...MELT-ED.
THAT'S BECAUSE ENTEI MELTED THOSE!! AND ENTEI IS A LEGENDARY POKÉMON!! ENTEI'S FIRE...
...MUST BE THE ONLY THING THAT CAN MELT PRYCE'S ICE PERMA-NENTLY!!
SOME FIRES ENTEI'S ATTACK IGNITED ARE STILL BURNING...!
IF WE SPREAD THE FLAMES THROUGH THE FOREST....!!

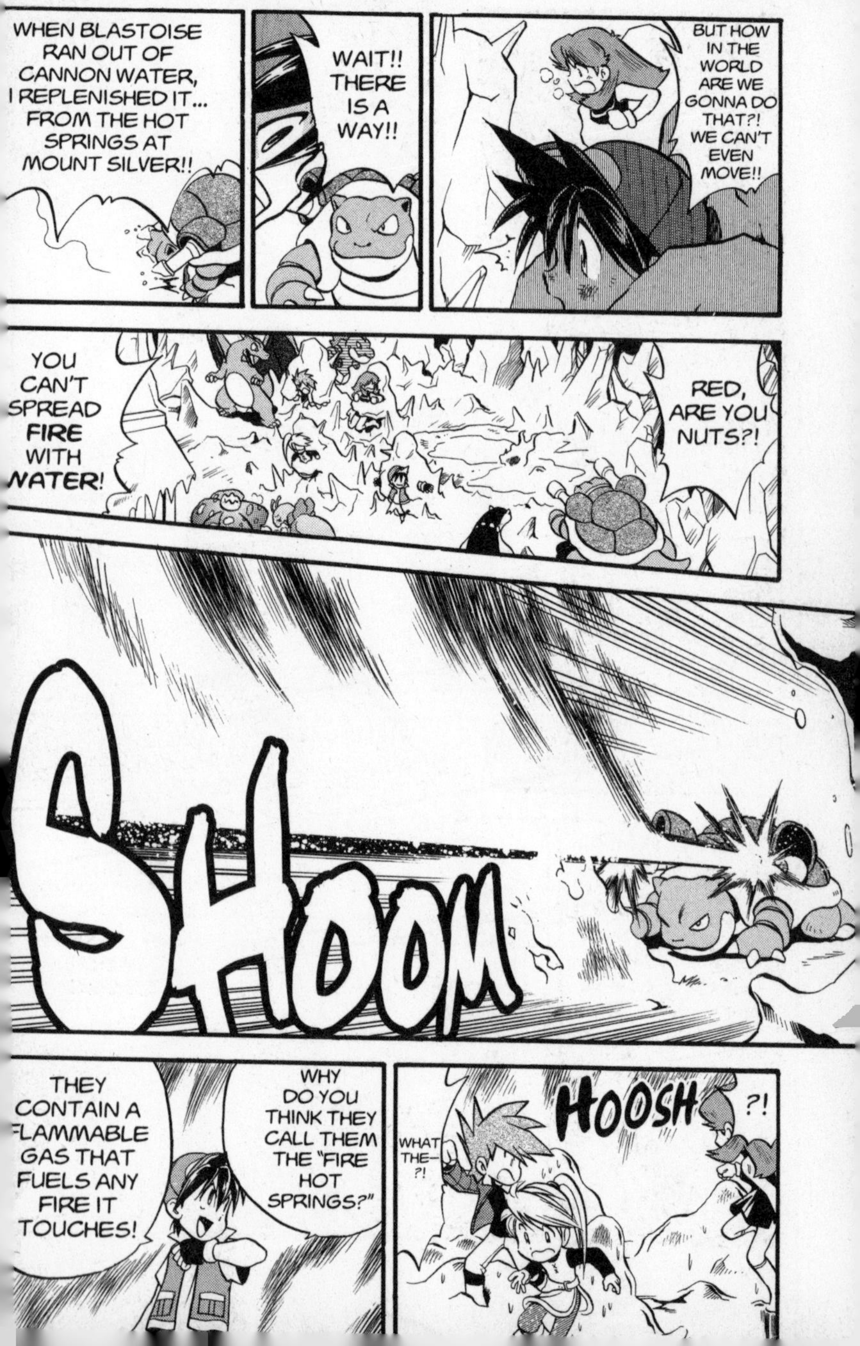

BUT HOW IN THE WORLD ARE WE GONNA DO THAT?! WE CAN'T EVEN MOVE!!
WAIT!! THERE IS A WAY!!
WHEN BLASTOISE RAN OUT OF CANNON WATER, I REPLENISHED IT... FROM THE HOT SPRINGS AT MOUNT SILVER!!
RED, ARE YOU NUTS?!
YOU CAN'T SPREAD FIRE WITH WATER!
SHOOM
HOOSH
?!
WHAT THE—?!
WHY DO YOU THINK THEY CALL THEM THE "FIRE HOT SPRINGS?"
THEY CONTAIN A FLAMMABLE GAS THAT FUELS ANY FIRE IT TOUCHES!

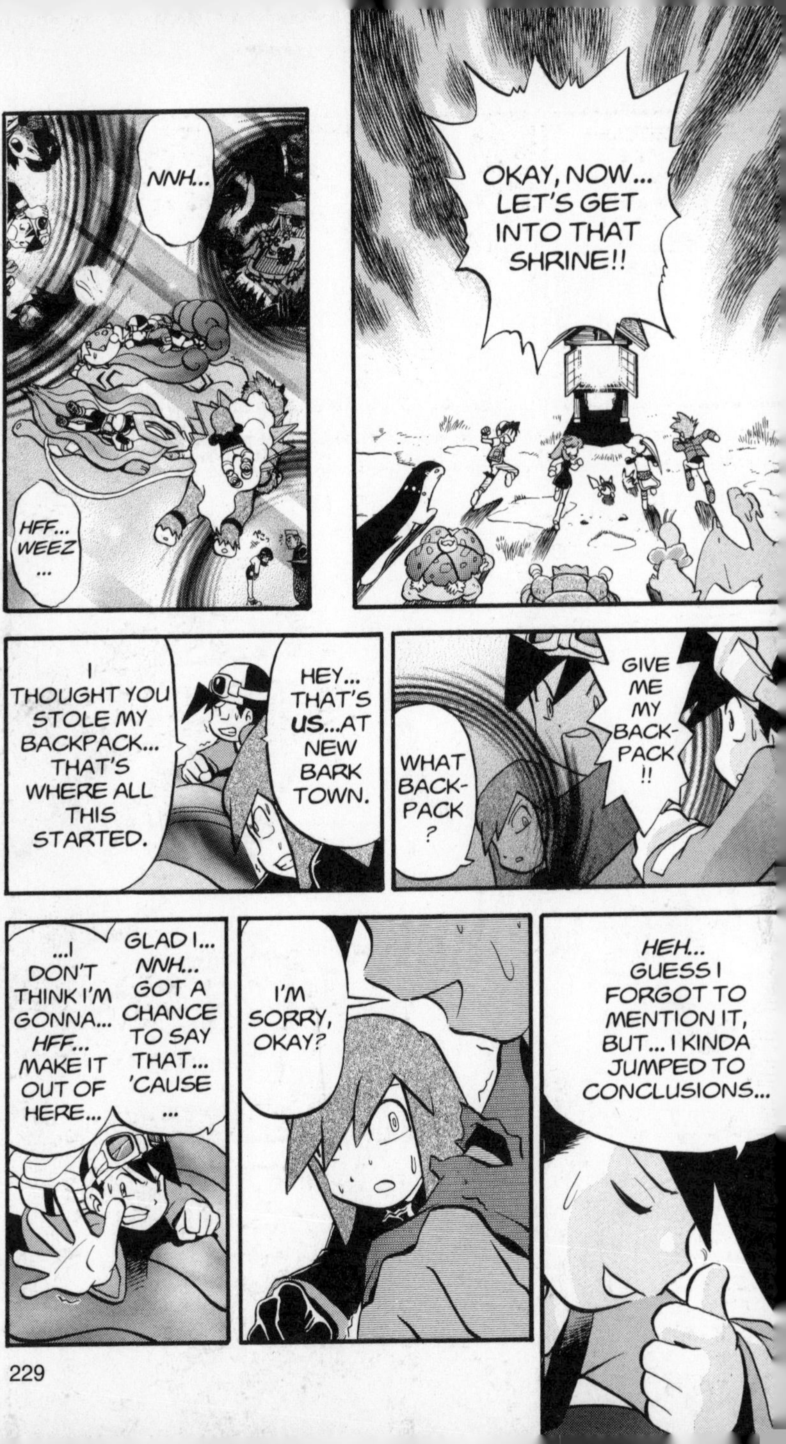
OKAY, NOW... LET'S GET INTO THAT SHRINE!!
NNH...
HFF... WEEZ ...
GIVE ME MY BACK-PACK !!
WHAT BACK-PACK ?
HEY... THAT'S **US**...AT NEW BARK TOWN.
I THOUGHT YOU STOLE MY BACKPACK... THAT'S WHERE ALL THIS STARTED.
*HEH...* GUESS I FORGOT TO MENTION IT, BUT... I KINDA JUMPED TO CONCLUSIONS...
I'M SORRY, OKAY?
GLAD I... *NNH...* GOT A CHANCE TO SAY THAT... 'CAUSE ...
...I DON'T THINK I'M GONNA... *HFF...* MAKE IT OUT OF HERE...

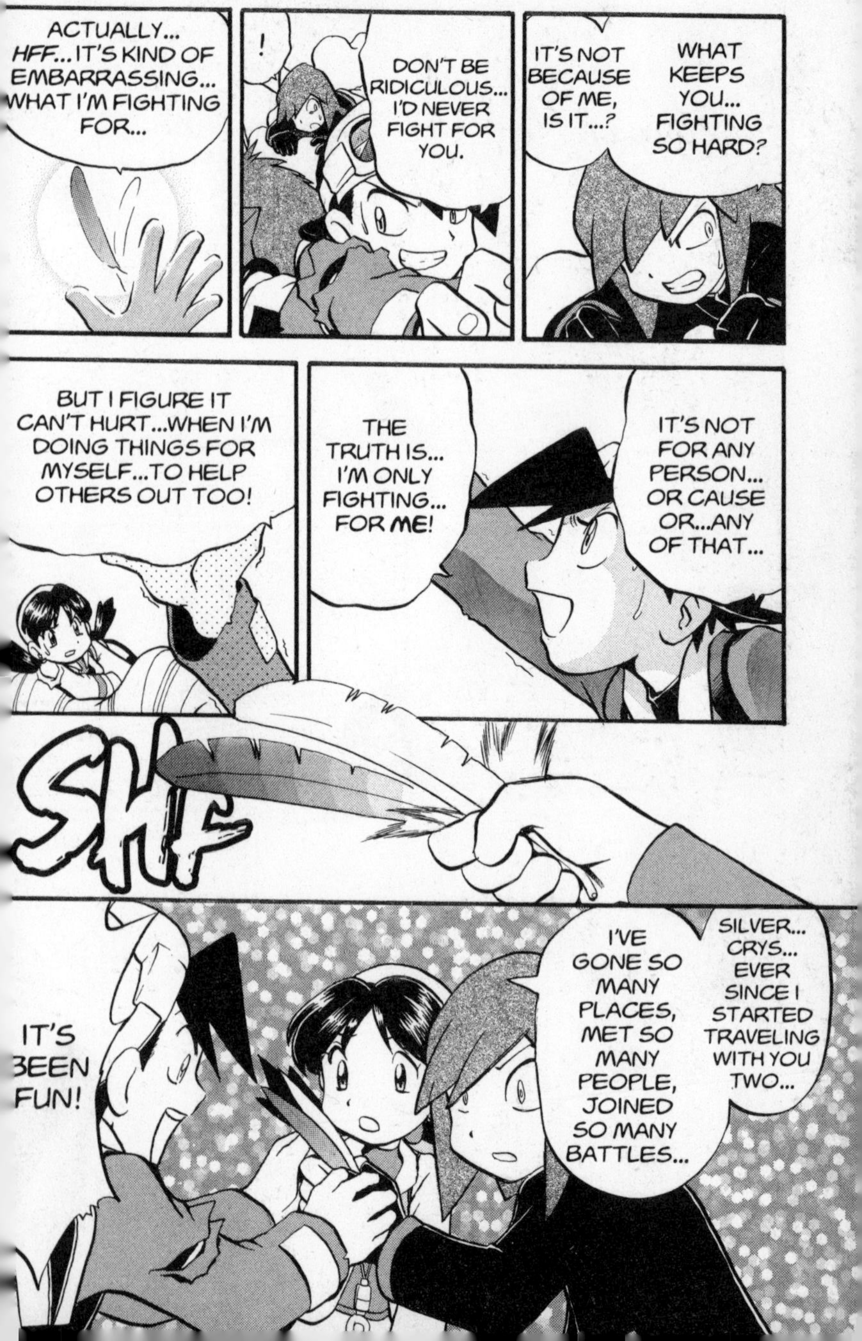
WHAT KEEPS YOU... FIGHTING SO HARD?
IT'S NOT BECAUSE OF ME, IS IT...?
DON'T BE RIDICULOUS... I'D NEVER FIGHT FOR YOU.
!
ACTUALLY... *HFF*... IT'S KIND OF EMBARRASSING... WHAT I'M FIGHTING FOR...
IT'S NOT FOR ANY PERSON... OR CAUSE OR... ANY OF THAT...
THE TRUTH IS... I'M ONLY FIGHTING... FOR **ME**!
BUT I FIGURE IT CAN'T HURT... WHEN I'M DOING THINGS FOR MYSELF... TO HELP OTHERS OUT TOO!
SHF
SILVER... CRYS... EVER SINCE I STARTED TRAVELING WITH YOU TWO...
I'VE GONE SO MANY PLACES, MET SO MANY PEOPLE, JOINED SO MANY BATTLES...
IT'S BEEN FUN!

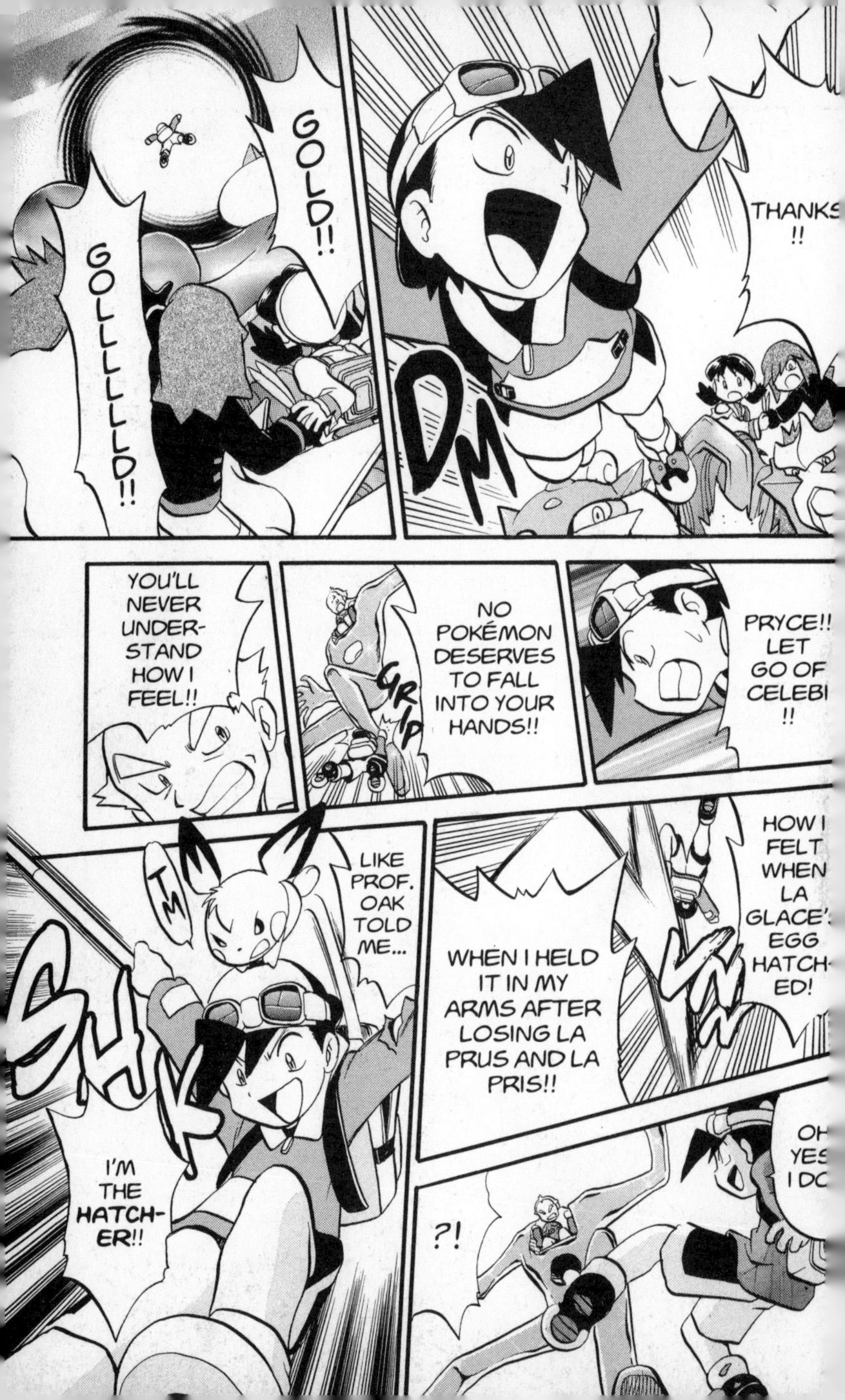
THANKS!!
DM
GOLD!!
GOLLLLLLLD!!
PRYCE!! LET GO OF CELEBI!!
NO POKÉMON DESERVES TO FALL INTO YOUR HANDS!!
GRIP
YOU'LL NEVER UNDER-STAND HOW I FEEL!!
HOW I FELT WHEN LA GLACE'S EGG HATCH-ED!
WHEN I HELD IT IN MY ARMS AFTER LOSING LA PRUS AND LA PRIS!!
OH YES I DO
?!
LIKE PROF. OAK TOLD ME...
TM
SHUK
I'M THE HATCH-ER!!

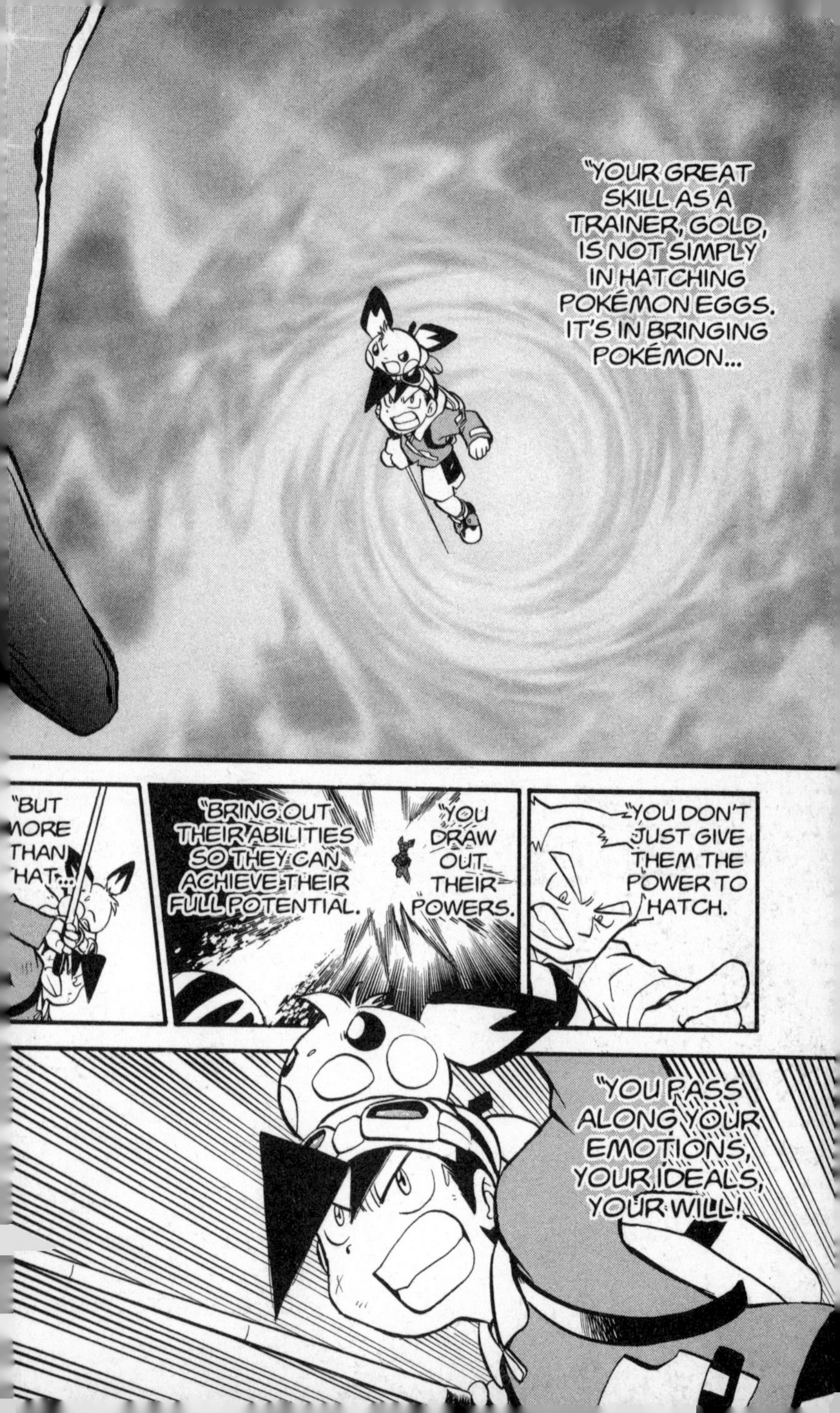
"YOUR GREAT SKILL AS A TRAINER, GOLD, IS NOT SIMPLY IN HATCHING POKÉMON EGGS. IT'S IN BRINGING POKÉMON...
"YOU DON'T JUST GIVE THEM THE POWER TO HATCH.
"YOU DRAW OUT THEIR POWERS.
"BRING OUT THEIR ABILITIES SO THEY CAN ACHIEVE THEIR FULL POTENTIAL.
"BUT MORE THAN THAT...
"YOU PASS ALONG YOUR EMOTIONS, YOUR IDEALS, YOUR WILL!

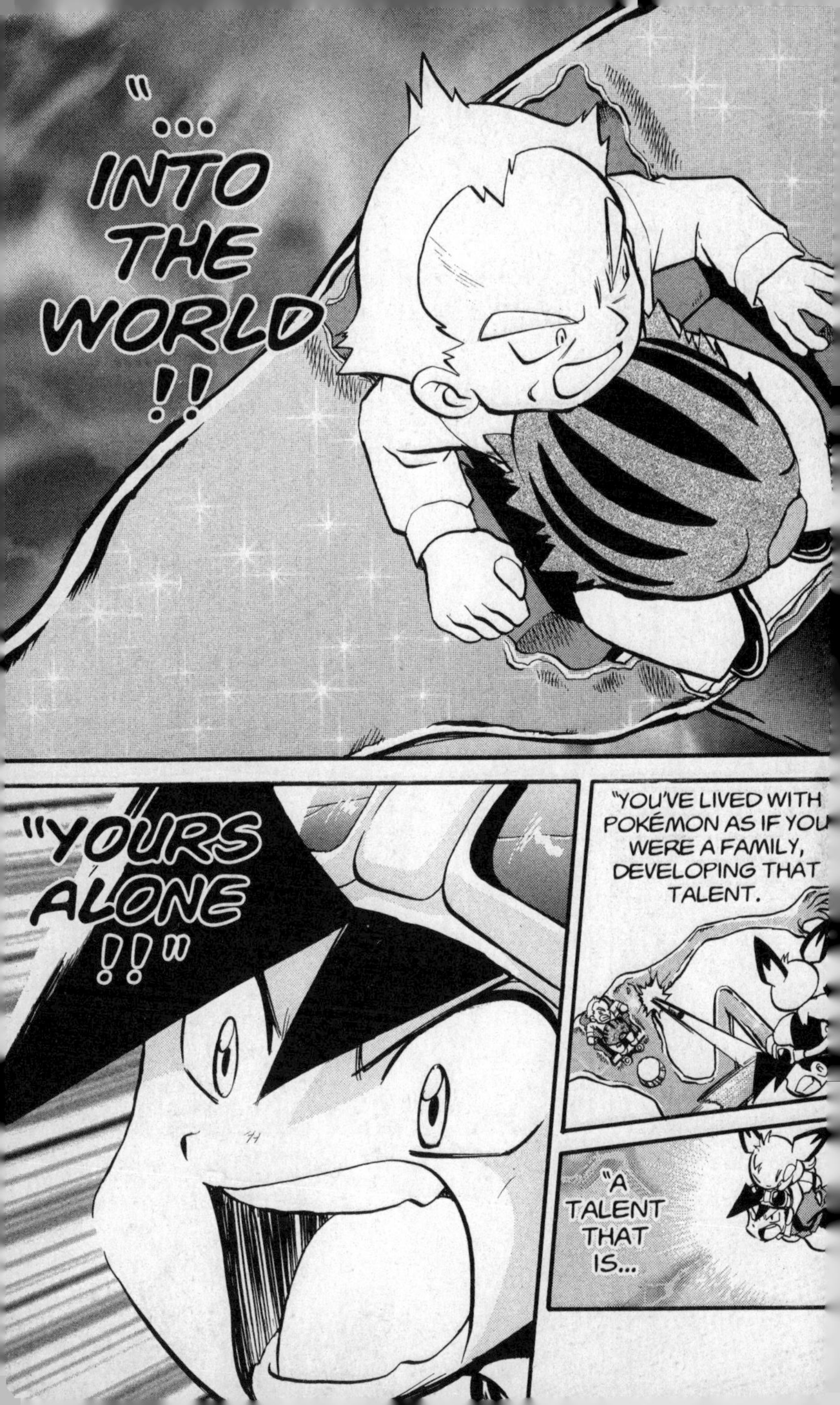
"...INTO THE WORLD!!
"YOU'VE LIVED WITH POKÉMON AS IF YOU WERE A FAMILY, DEVELOPING THAT TALENT.
"A TALENT THAT IS...
"YOURS ALONE!!"

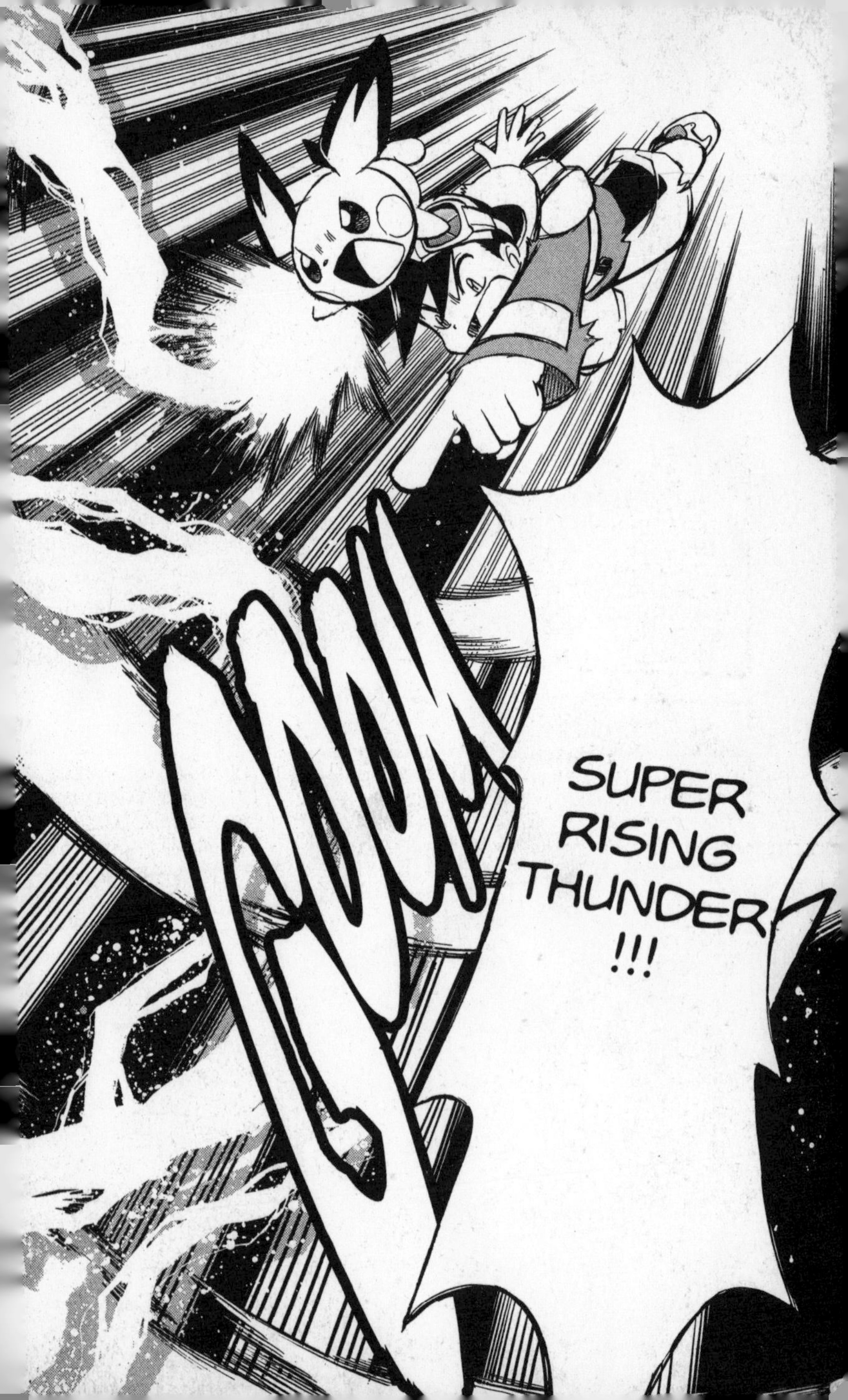
SUPER RISING THUNDER !!!

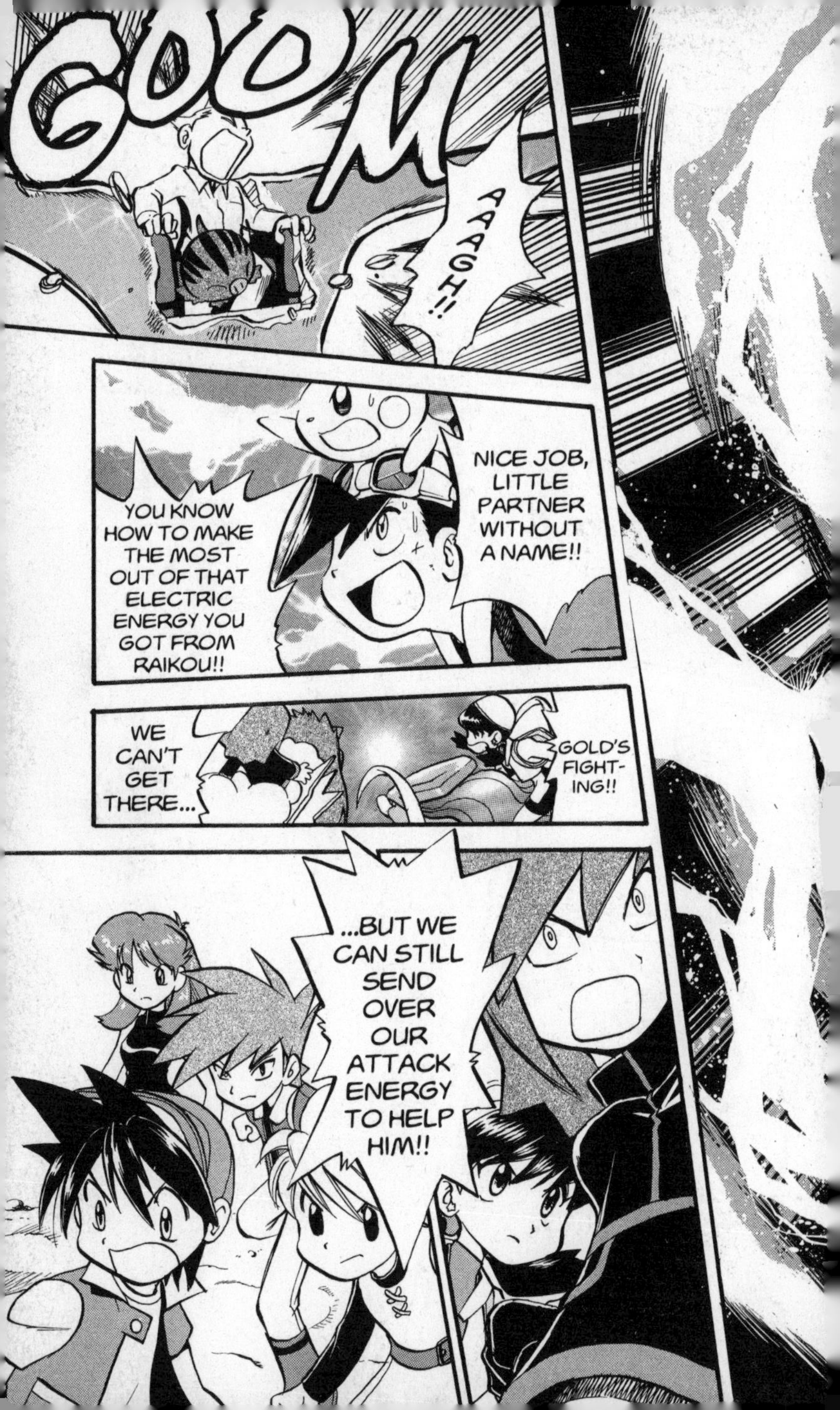
GOOOM
AAAAGH!!
NICE JOB, LITTLE PARTNER WITHOUT A NAME!!
YOU KNOW HOW TO MAKE THE MOST OUT OF THAT ELECTRIC ENERGY YOU GOT FROM RAIKOU!!
GOLD'S FIGHT-ING!!
WE CAN'T GET THERE...
...BUT WE CAN STILL SEND OVER OUR ATTACK ENERGY TO HELP HIM!!

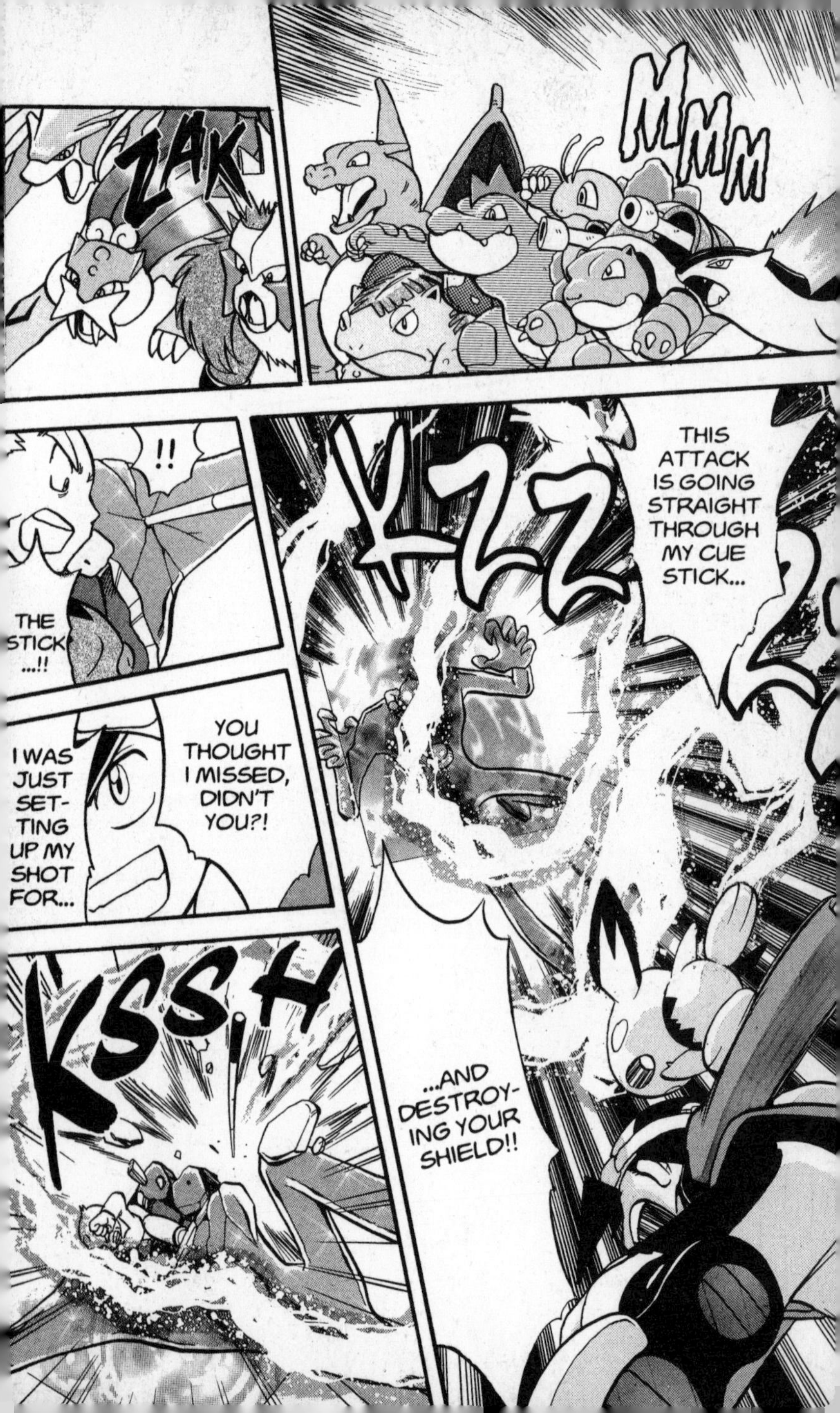
MMMM
ZAK
XZZZ
THIS ATTACK IS GOING STRAIGHT THROUGH MY CUE STICK...
...AND DESTROYING YOUR SHIELD!!
!!
THE STICK ...!!
YOU THOUGHT I MISSED, DIDN'T YOU?!
I WAS JUST SET-TING UP MY SHOT FOR...
KSSH

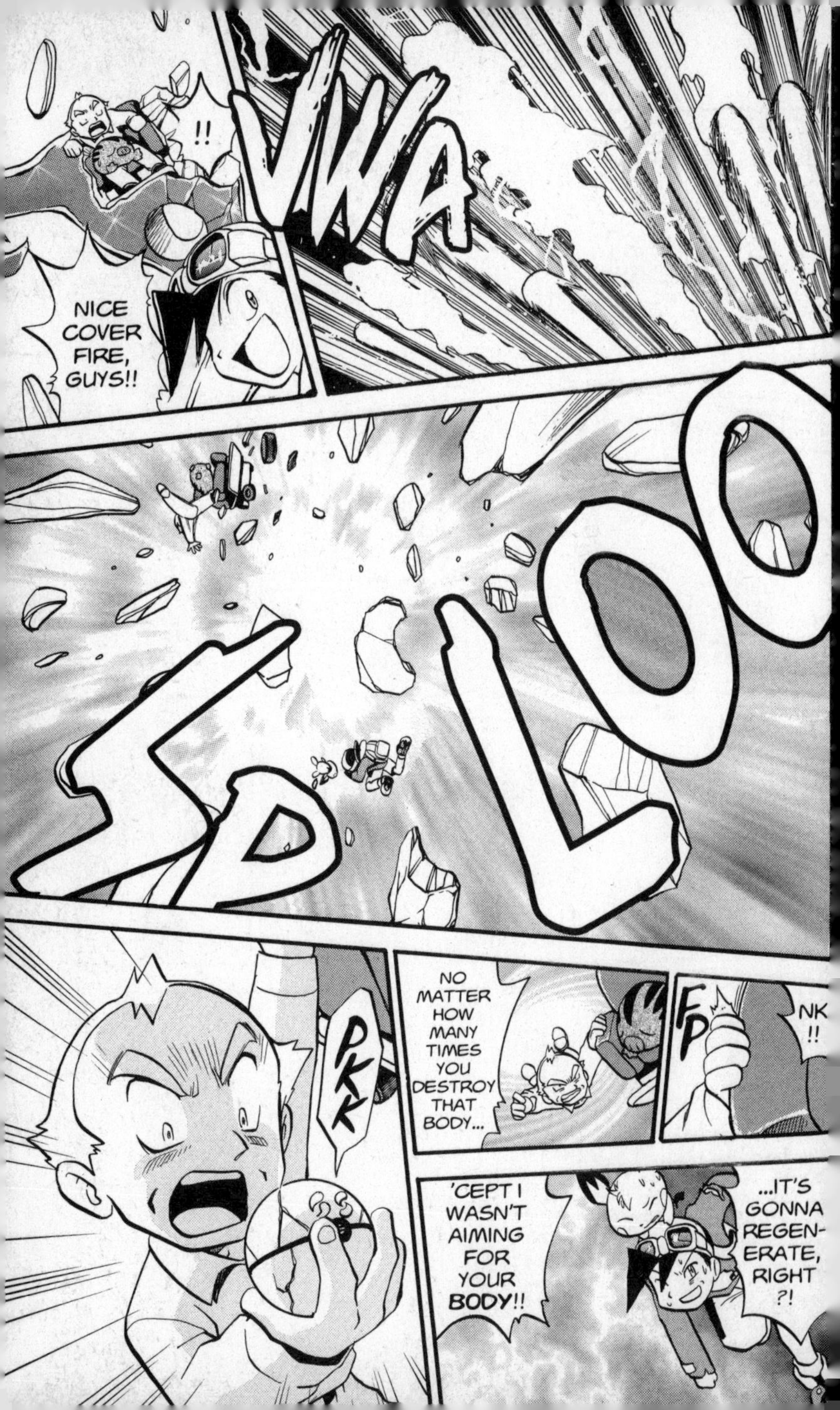
VWA
!!
NICE COVER FIRE, GUYS!!
SPLOO
FP
NK!!
NO MATTER HOW MANY TIMES YOU DESTROY THAT BODY...
...IT'S GONNA REGEN-ERATE, RIGHT?!
'CEPT I WASN'T AIMING FOR YOUR BODY!!
PKK

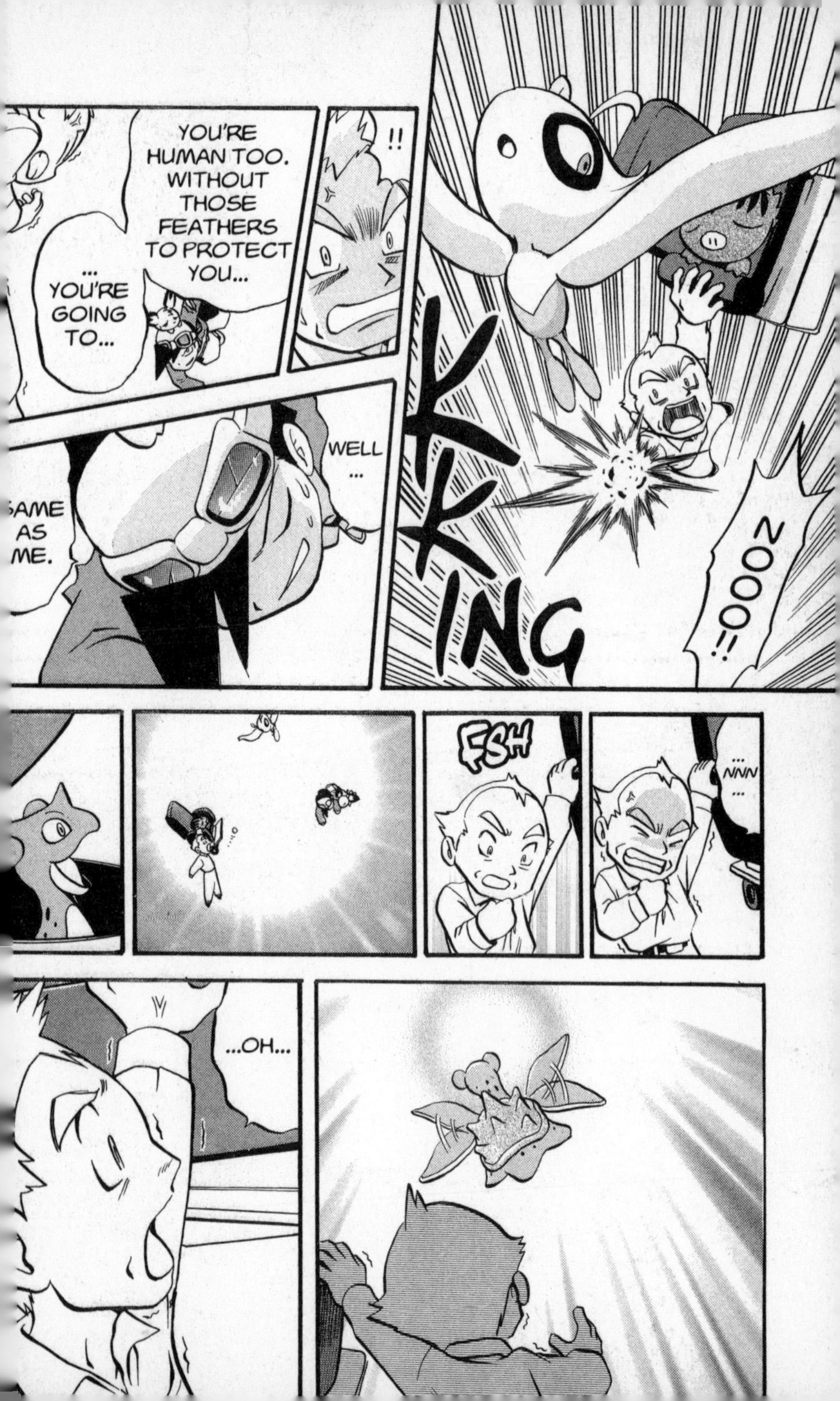
KKING
NOOOO!!
!!
YOU'RE HUMAN TOO. WITHOUT THOSE FEATHERS TO PROTECT YOU...
...YOU'RE GOING TO...
WELL...
SAME AS ME.
...NNN...
FSH
...OH...

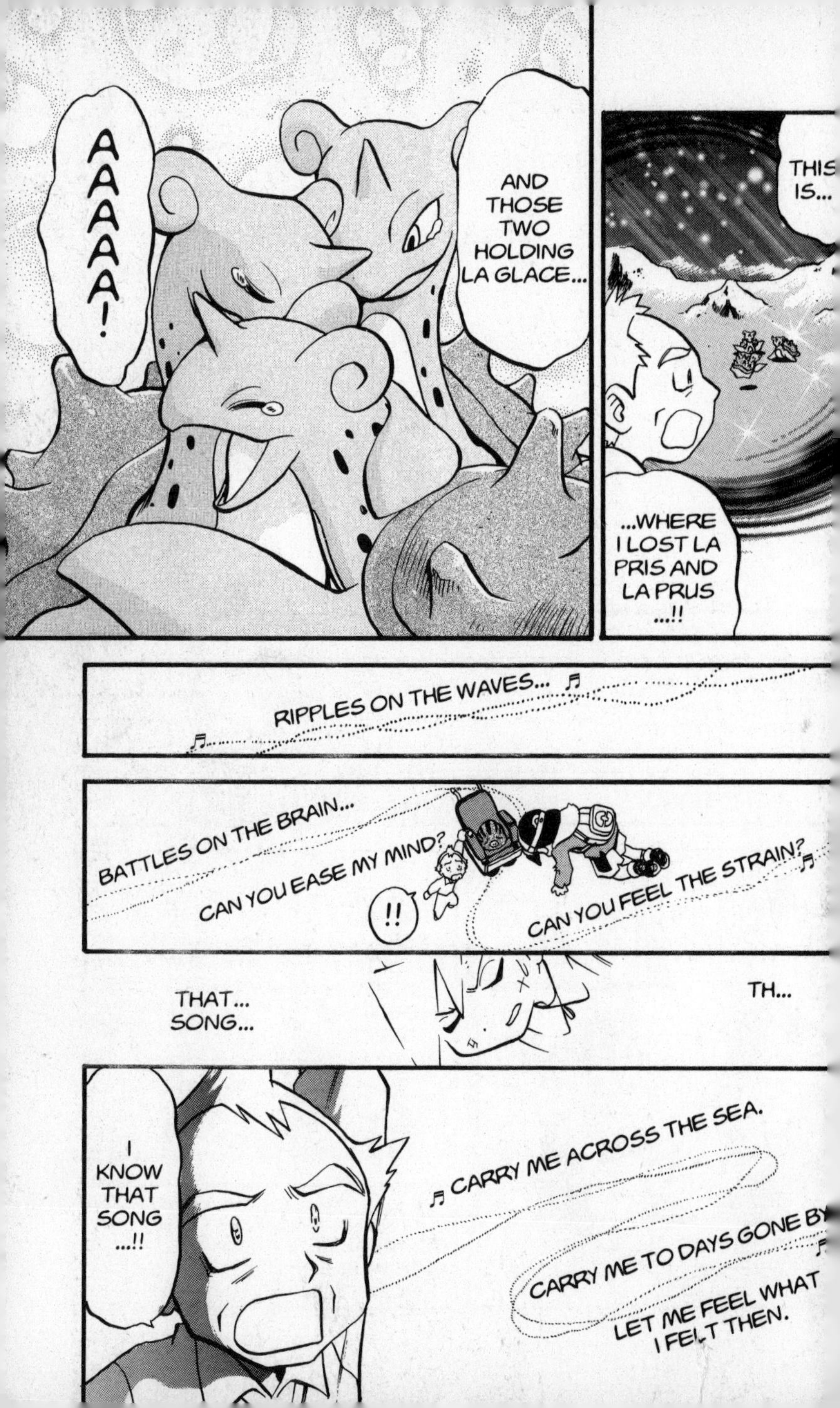
THIS IS...
...WHERE I LOST LA PRIS AND LA PRUS ...!!
AND THOSE TWO HOLDING LA GLACE...
AAAAA!
RIPPLES ON THE WAVES... ♬
BATTLES ON THE BRAIN...
CAN YOU EASE MY MIND?
CAN YOU FEEL THE STRAIN? ♬
!!
TH...
THAT... SONG...
♬ CARRY ME ACROSS THE SEA.
CARRY ME TO DAYS GONE BY
LET ME FEEL WHAT I FELT THEN.
I KNOW THAT SONG ...!!

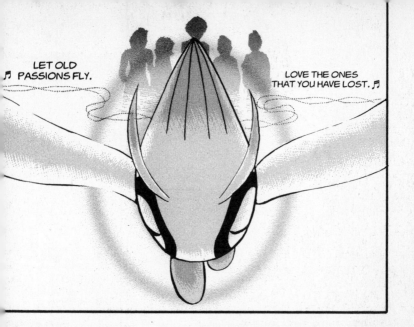

LOVE THE ONES THAT YOU HAVE LOST. ♬
♬ LET OLD PASSIONS FLY.
ARE YOU SERIOUS, OLD LADY?!
HE MAN WHO WRECKED THE TOURNAMENT... THE MASTERMIND BEHIND EVERYTHING... **YOU'VE KNOWN HIM FOR YEARS?!**
I HAD A HUNCH WHEN I SAW A SHADOW DISAPPEAR INTO THE SKY ON THE WAY HERE.
AND AFTER GOLD CALLED HIS NAME...I KNEW I WAS RIGHT.
LOOK AT THIS PHOTO.
WE WERE YOUNG THEN... OUR FUTURES SEEMED SO BRIGHT...
AGA-THA ...
SAM-UEL...
THAT'S ME IN THE MIDDLE...
URT ON HE EFT ...

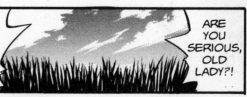

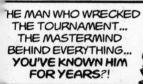

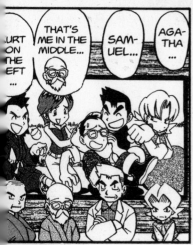

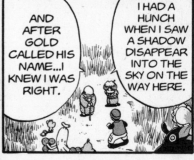

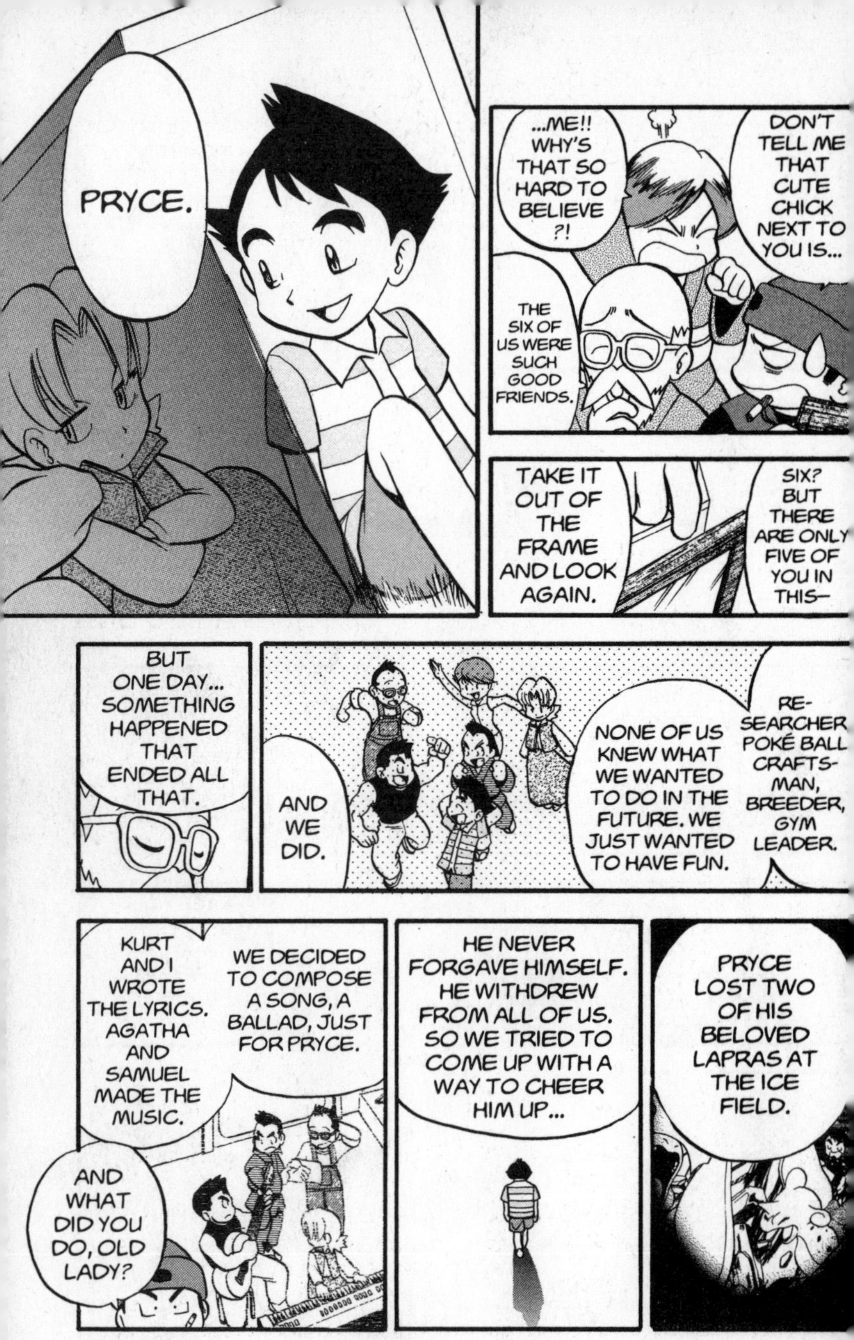
DON'T TELL ME THAT CUTE CHICK NEXT TO YOU IS...
...ME!! WHY'S THAT SO HARD TO BELIEVE ?!
THE SIX OF US WERE SUCH GOOD FRIENDS.
SIX? BUT THERE ARE ONLY FIVE OF YOU IN THIS—
TAKE IT OUT OF THE FRAME AND LOOK AGAIN.
PRYCE.
RE-SEARCHER POKÉ BALL CRAFTS-MAN, BREEDER, GYM LEADER.
NONE OF US KNEW WHAT WE WANTED TO DO IN THE FUTURE. WE JUST WANTED TO HAVE FUN.
AND WE DID.
BUT ONE DAY... SOMETHING HAPPENED THAT ENDED ALL THAT.
PRYCE LOST TWO OF HIS BELOVED LAPRAS AT THE ICE FIELD.
HE NEVER FORGAVE HIMSELF. HE WITHDREW FROM ALL OF US. SO WE TRIED TO COME UP WITH A WAY TO CHEER HIM UP...
WE DECIDED TO COMPOSE A SONG, A BALLAD, JUST FOR PRYCE.
KURT AND I WROTE THE LYRICS. AGATHA AND SAMUEL MADE THE MUSIC.
AND WHAT DID YOU DO, OLD LADY?

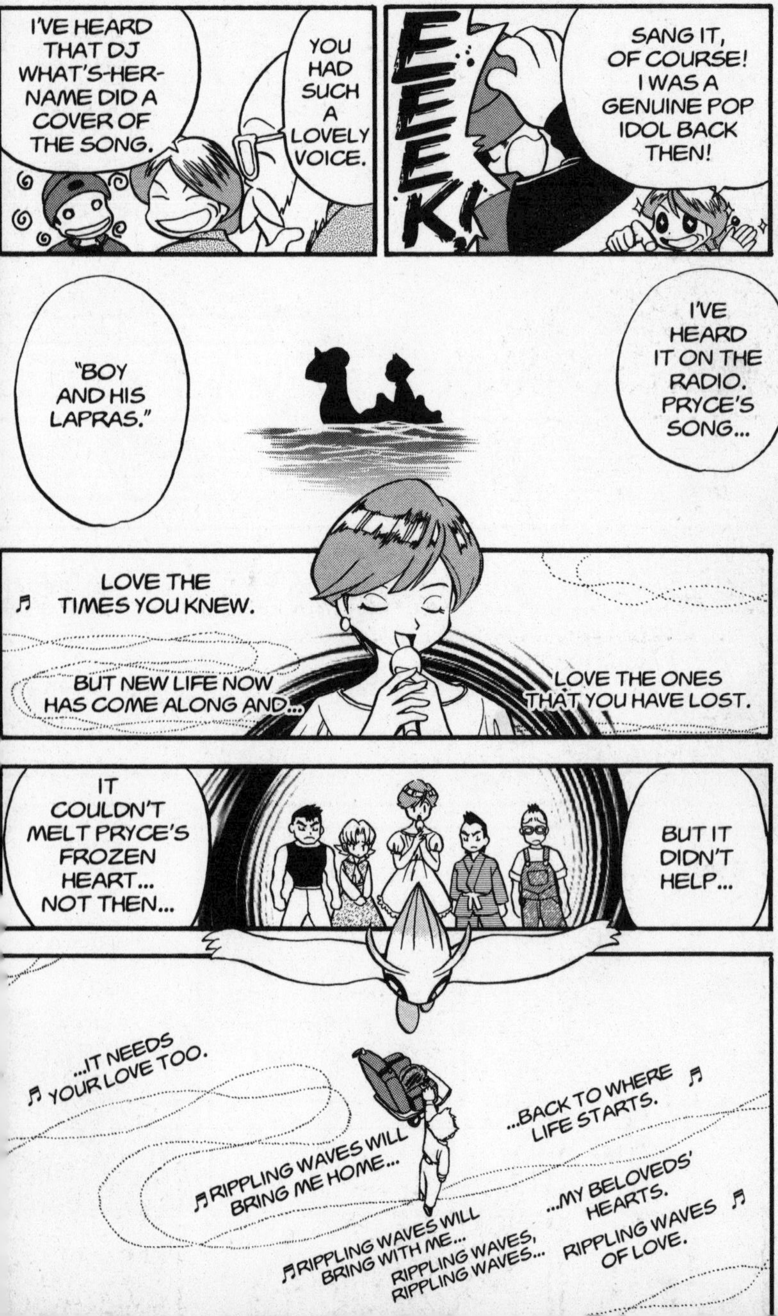
SANG IT, OF COURSE! I WAS A GENUINE POP IDOL BACK THEN!
EEEEK!
YOU HAD SUCH A LOVELY VOICE.
I'VE HEARD THAT DJ WHAT'S-HER-NAME DID A COVER OF THE SONG.
I'VE HEARD IT ON THE RADIO. PRYCE'S SONG...
"BOY AND HIS LAPRAS."
♬ LOVE THE TIMES YOU KNEW.
LOVE THE ONES THAT YOU HAVE LOST.
BUT NEW LIFE NOW HAS COME ALONG AND...
BUT IT DIDN'T HELP...
IT COULDN'T MELT PRYCE'S FROZEN HEART... NOT THEN...
...IT NEEDS YOUR LOVE TOO. ♬
♬ RIPPLING WAVES WILL BRING ME HOME...
...BACK TO WHERE LIFE STARTS. ♬
♬ RIPPLING WAVES WILL BRING WITH ME...
...MY BELOVEDS' HEARTS.
RIPPLING WAVES, RIPPLING WAVES...
RIPPLING WAVES OF LOVE. ♬

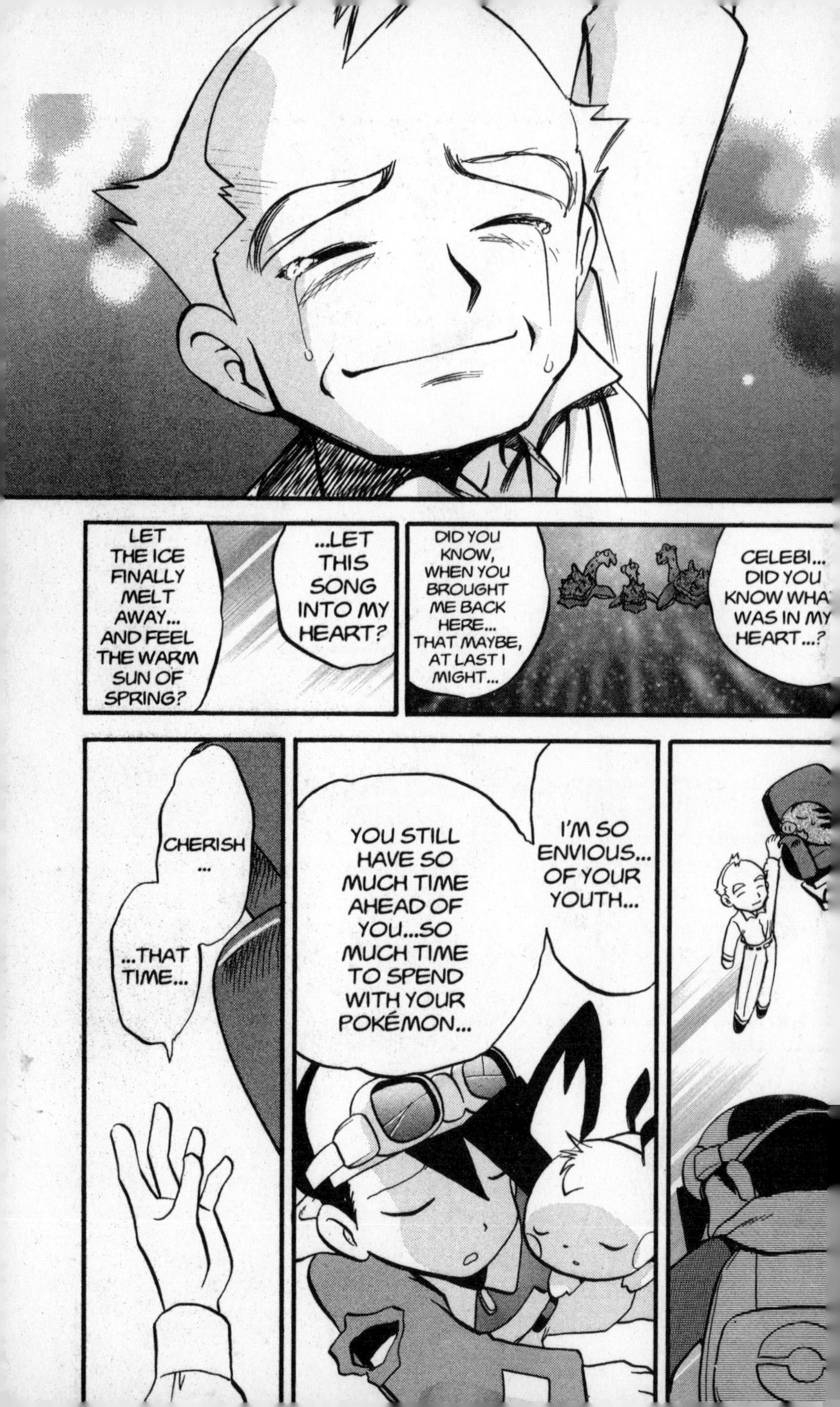
CELEBI... DID YOU KNOW WHAT WAS IN MY HEART...?
DID YOU KNOW, WHEN YOU BROUGHT ME BACK HERE... THAT MAYBE, AT LAST I MIGHT...
...LET THIS SONG INTO MY HEART?
LET THE ICE FINALLY MELT AWAY... AND FEEL THE WARM SUN OF SPRING?
I'M SO ENVIOUS... OF YOUR YOUTH...
YOU STILL HAVE SO MUCH TIME AHEAD OF YOU...SO MUCH TIME TO SPEND WITH YOUR POKÉMON...
CHERISH...
...THAT TIME...

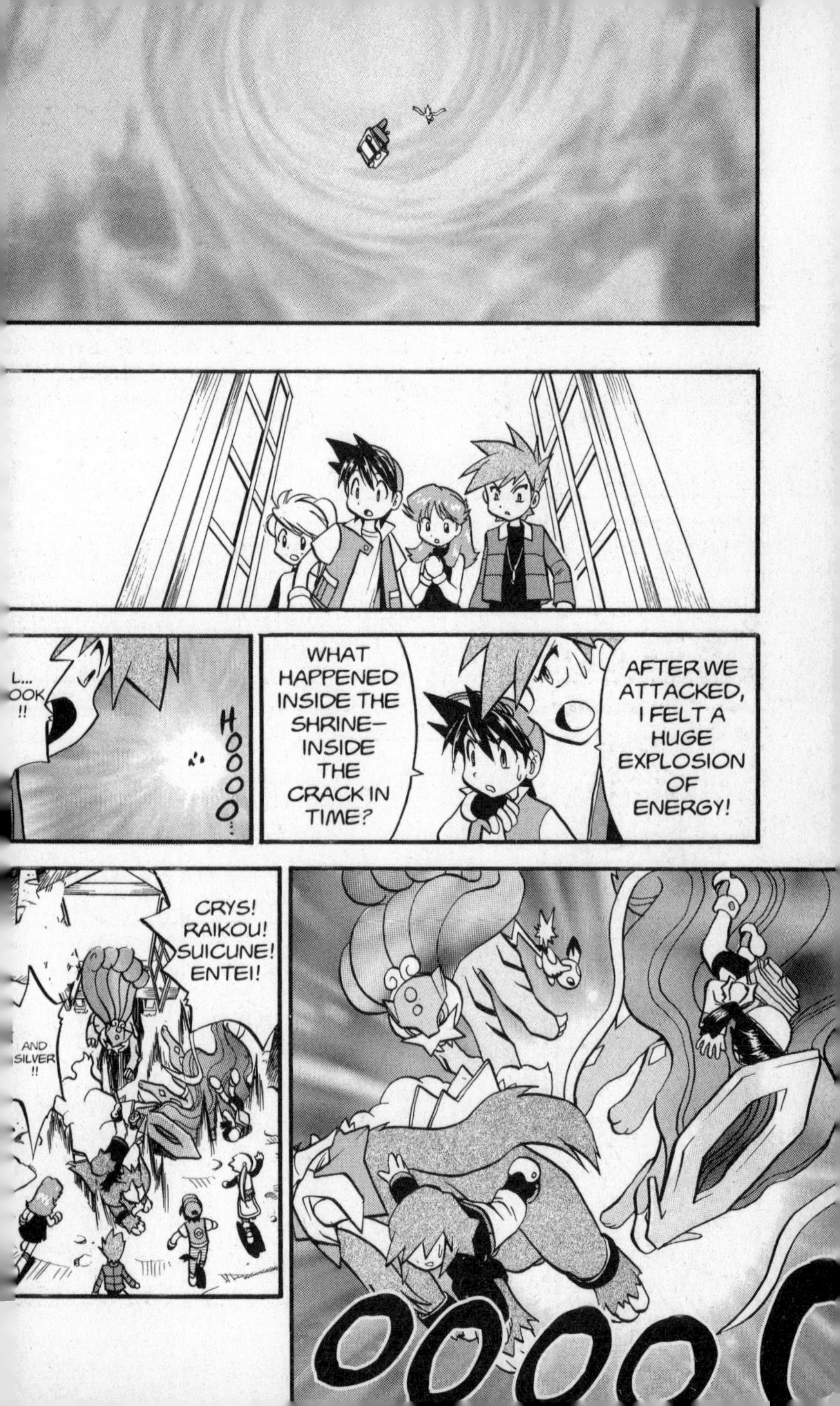
AFTER WE ATTACKED, I FELT A HUGE EXPLOSION OF ENERGY!
WHAT HAPPENED INSIDE THE SHRINE— INSIDE THE CRACK IN TIME?
L... OOK !!
HOOOO...
OOOO
CRYS! RAIKOU! SUICUNE! ENTEI!
AND SILVER !!

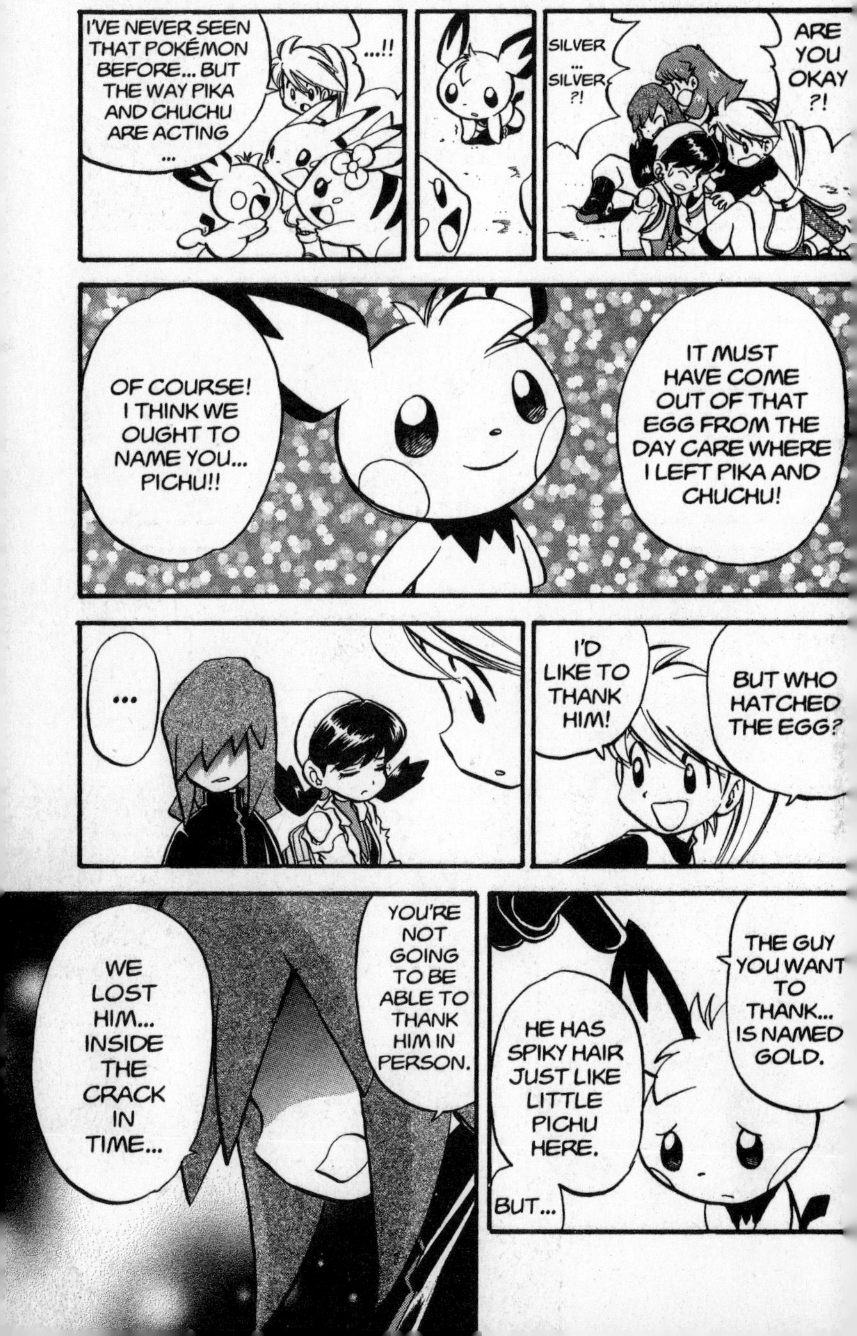
ARE YOU OKAY?!
SILVER... SILVER?!
...!!
I'VE NEVER SEEN THAT POKÉMON BEFORE... BUT THE WAY PIKA AND CHUCHU ARE ACTING...
IT MUST HAVE COME OUT OF THAT EGG FROM THE DAY CARE WHERE I LEFT PIKA AND CHUCHU!
OF COURSE! I THINK WE OUGHT TO NAME YOU... PICHU!!
BUT WHO HATCHED THE EGG?
I'D LIKE TO THANK HIM!
...
THE GUY YOU WANT TO THANK... IS NAMED GOLD.
HE HAS SPIKY HAIR JUST LIKE LITTLE PICHU HERE.
BUT...
YOU'RE NOT GOING TO BE ABLE TO THANK HIM IN PERSON.
WE LOST HIM... INSIDE THE CRACK IN TIME...

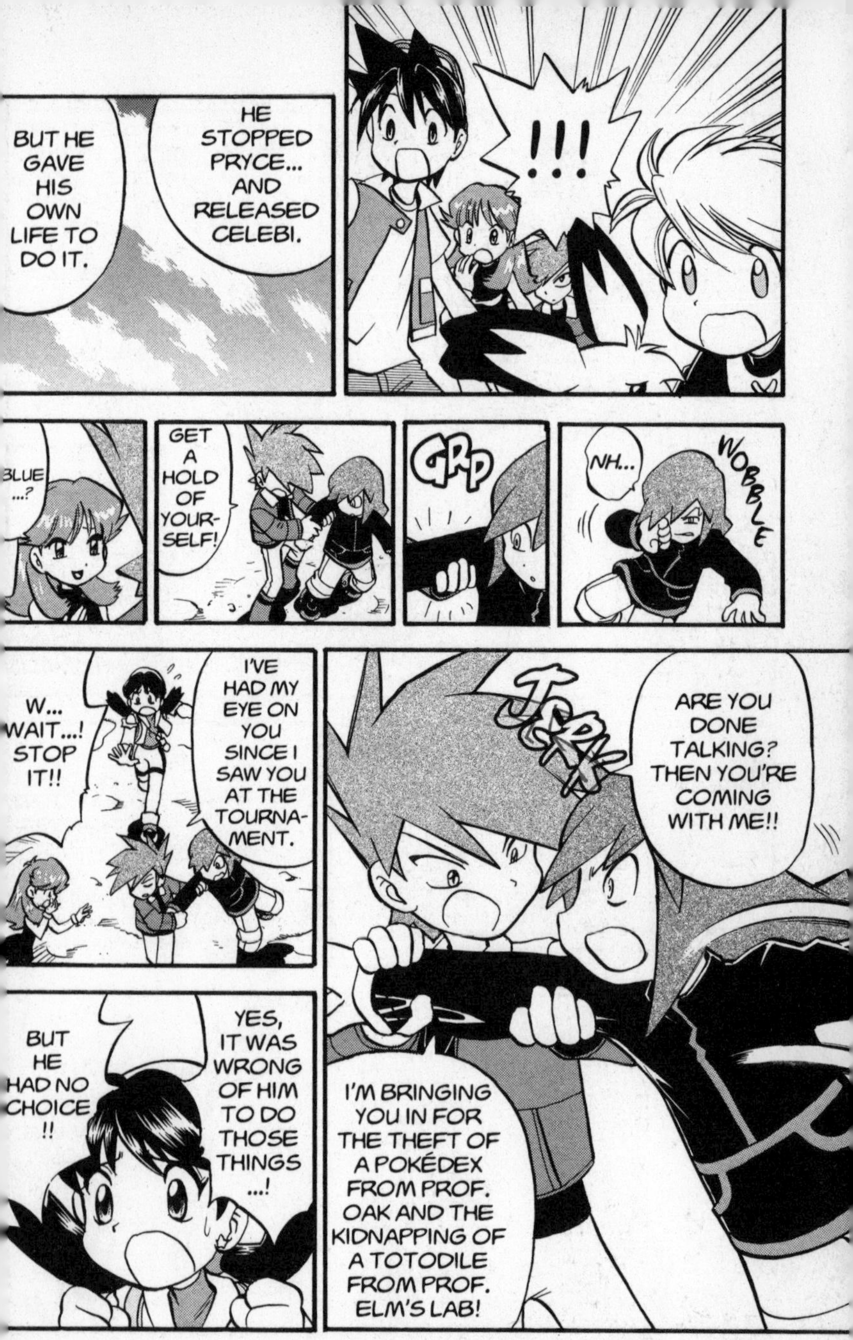
!!!
HE STOPPED PRYCE... AND RELEASED CELEBI.
BUT HE GAVE HIS OWN LIFE TO DO IT.
WOBBLE
NH...
GRP
GET A HOLD OF YOURSELF!
BLUE ...?
ARE YOU DONE TALKING? THEN YOU'RE COMING WITH ME!!
I'M BRINGING YOU IN FOR THE THEFT OF A POKÉDEX FROM PROF. OAK AND THE KIDNAPPING OF A TOTODILE FROM PROF. ELM'S LAB!
I'VE HAD MY EYE ON YOU SINCE I SAW YOU AT THE TOURNAMENT.
W... WAIT...! STOP IT!!
YES, IT WAS WRONG OF HIM TO DO THOSE THINGS...!
BUT HE HAD NO CHOICE!!

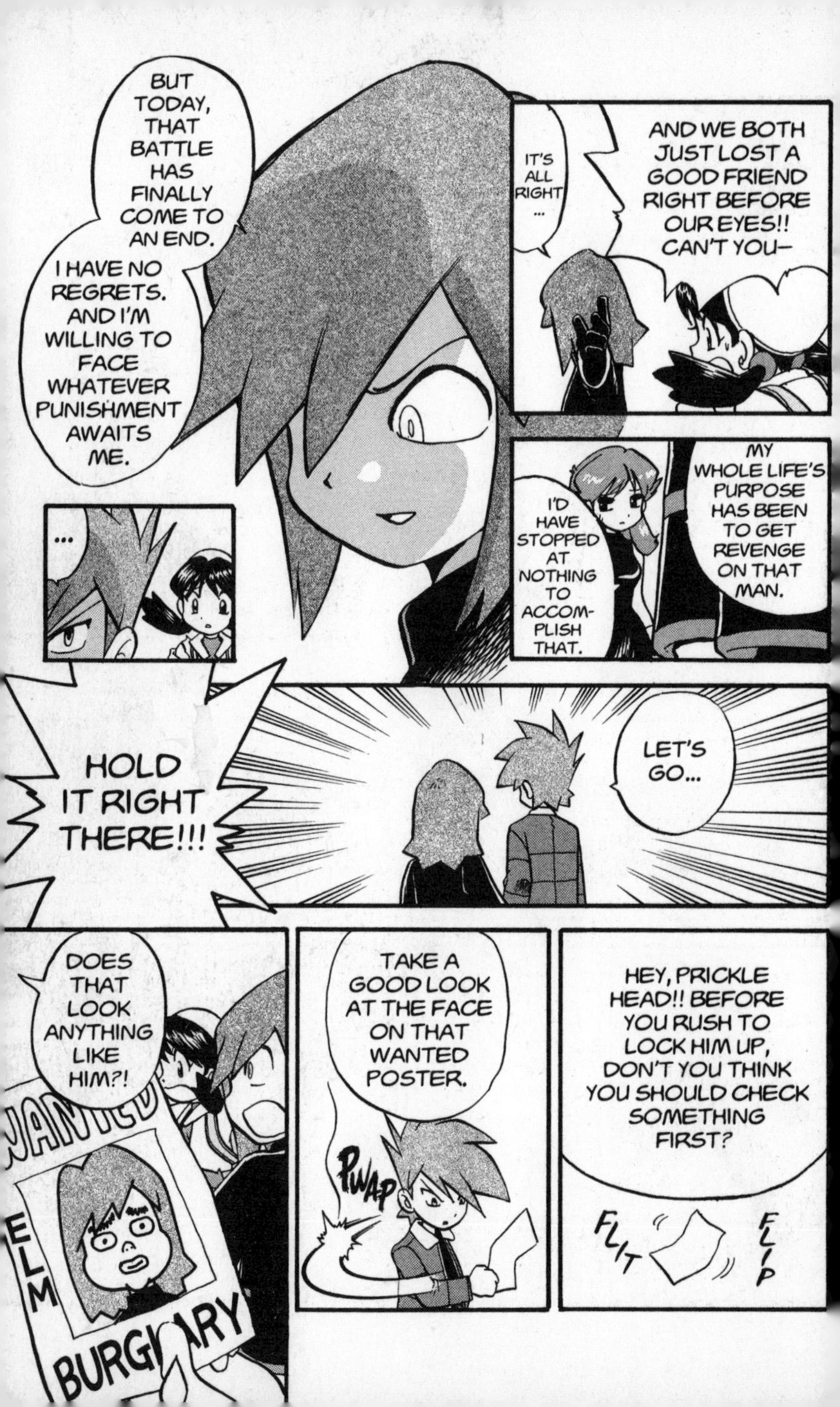
AND WE BOTH JUST LOST A GOOD FRIEND RIGHT BEFORE OUR EYES!! CAN'T YOU–
IT'S ALL RIGHT...
MY WHOLE LIFE'S PURPOSE HAS BEEN TO GET REVENGE ON THAT MAN.
I'D HAVE STOPPED AT NOTHING TO ACCOMPLISH THAT.
BUT TODAY, THAT BATTLE HAS FINALLY COME TO AN END.
I HAVE NO REGRETS. AND I'M WILLING TO FACE WHATEVER PUNISHMENT AWAITS ME.
...
LET'S GO...
HOLD IT RIGHT THERE!!!
HEY, PRICKLE HEAD!! BEFORE YOU RUSH TO LOCK HIM UP, DON'T YOU THINK YOU SHOULD CHECK SOMETHING FIRST?
FLIT
FLIP
TAKE A GOOD LOOK AT THE FACE ON THAT WANTED POSTER.
PWAP
DOES THAT LOOK ANYTHING LIKE HIM?!
ELM

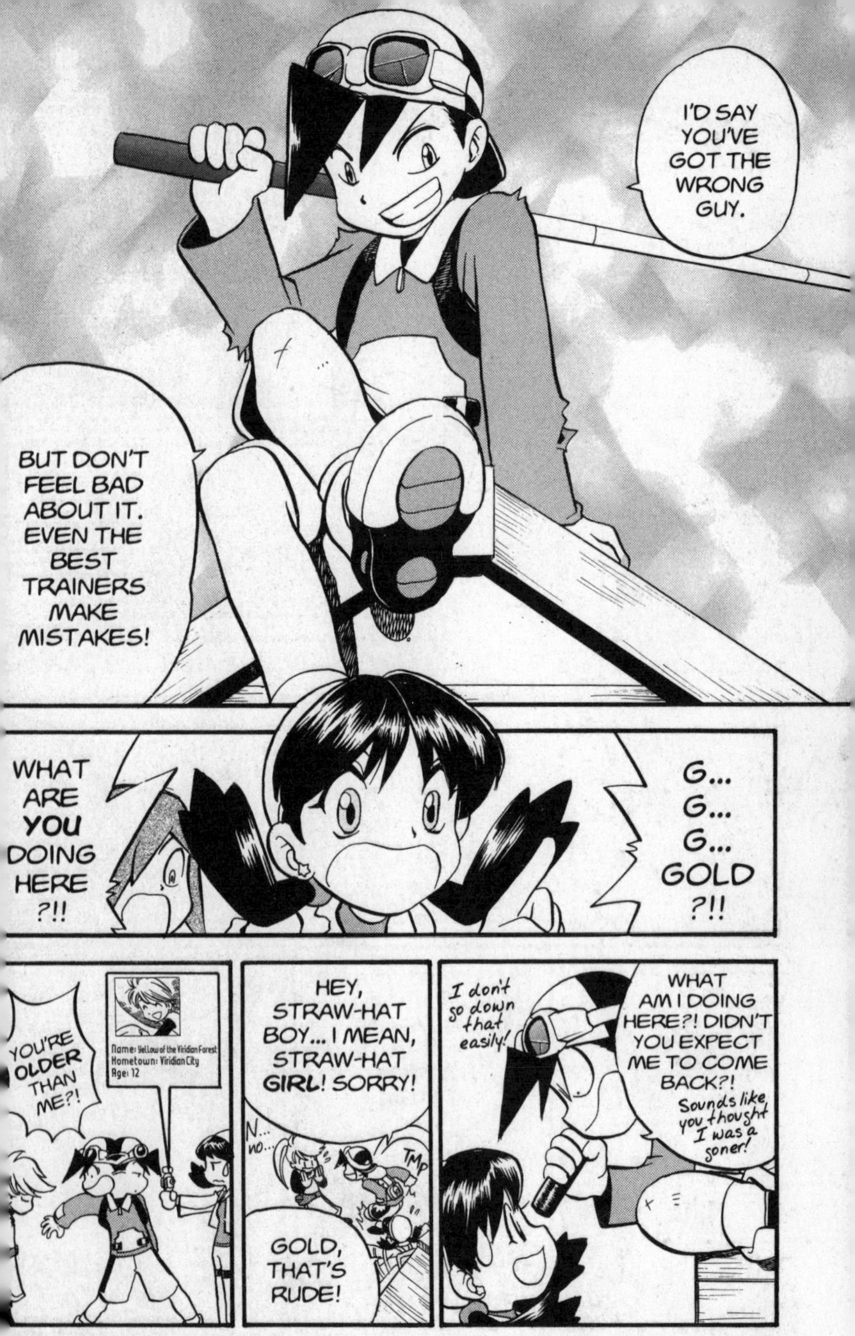
I'D SAY YOU'VE GOT THE WRONG GUY.
BUT DON'T FEEL BAD ABOUT IT. EVEN THE BEST TRAINERS MAKE MISTAKES!
G... G... G... GOLD ?!!
WHAT ARE **YOU** DOING HERE ?!!
WHAT AM I DOING HERE?! DIDN'T YOU EXPECT ME TO COME BACK?!
I don't go down that easily!
Sounds like you thought I was a goner!
HEY, STRAW-HAT BOY... I MEAN, STRAW-HAT **GIRL**! SORRY!
N... no...
TMP
GOLD, THAT'S RUDE!
Name: Yellow of the Viridian Forest
Hometown: Viridian City
Age: 12
YOU'RE **OLDER** THAN ME?!

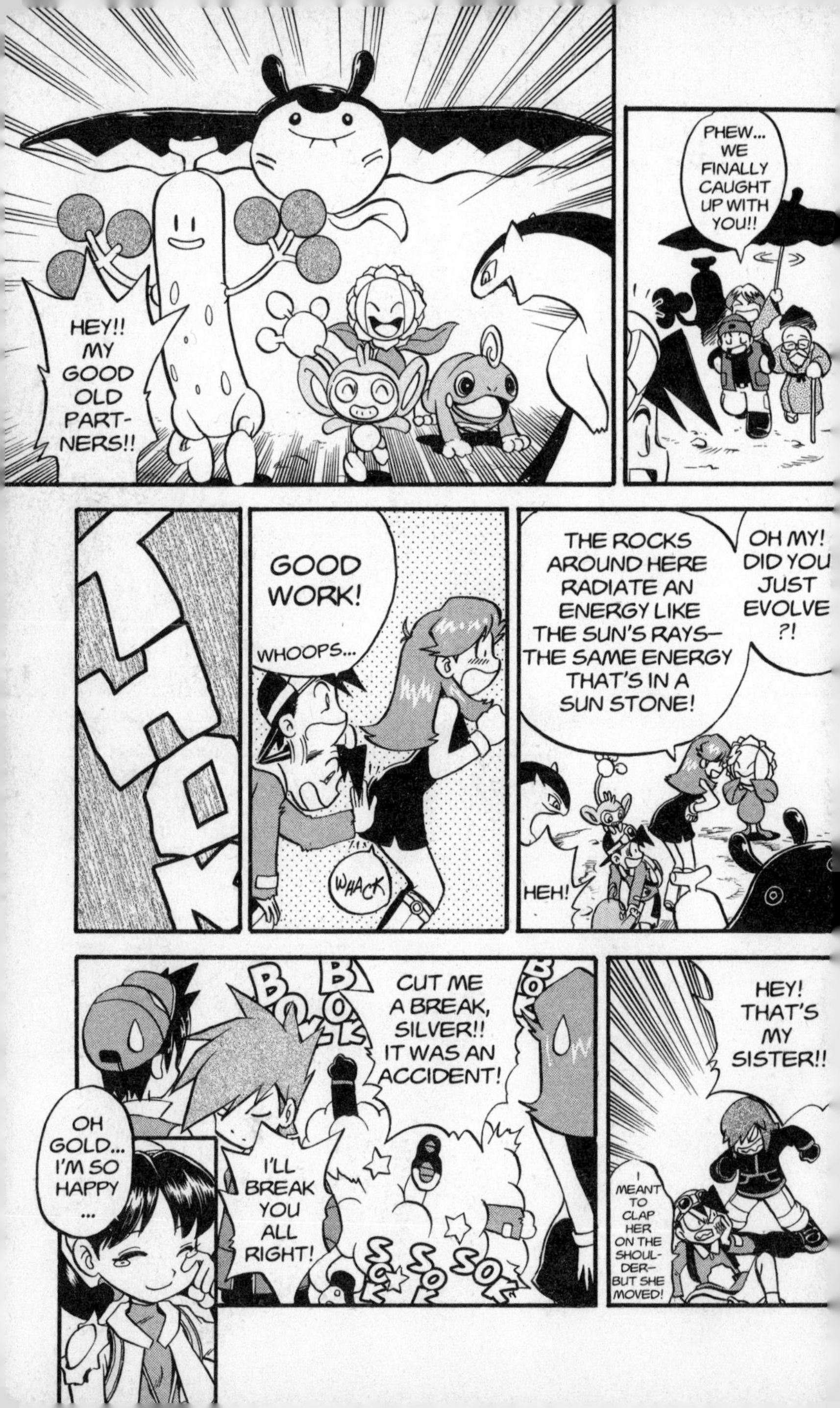
PHEW... WE FINALLY CAUGHT UP WITH YOU!!
HEY!! MY GOOD OLD PARTNERS!!
OH MY! DID YOU JUST EVOLVE?!
THE ROCKS AROUND HERE RADIATE AN ENERGY LIKE THE SUN'S RAYS—THE SAME ENERGY THAT'S IN A SUN STONE!
HEH!
GOOD WORK!
WHOOPS...
WHACK
HEY! THAT'S MY SISTER!!
I MEANT TO CLAP HER ON THE SHOUL-DER—BUT SHE MOVED!
BOK
BOK
BOK
CUT ME A BREAK, SILVER!! IT WAS AN ACCIDENT!
I'LL BREAK YOU ALL RIGHT!
SOK SOK SOK
OH GOLD... I'M SO HAPPY...

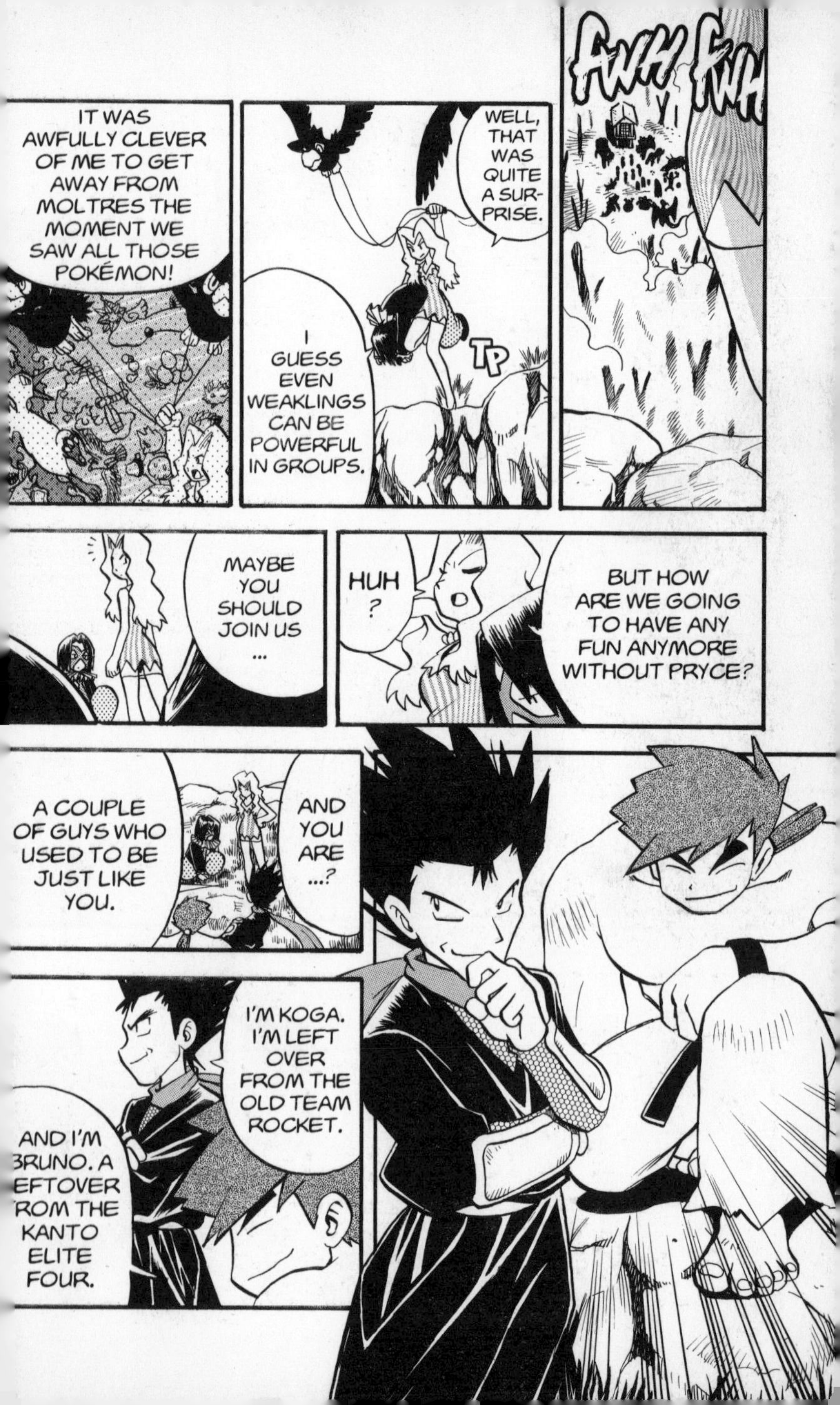
FWH FWH
WELL, THAT WAS QUITE A SURPRISE.
TP
I GUESS EVEN WEAKLINGS CAN BE POWERFUL IN GROUPS.
IT WAS AWFULLY CLEVER OF ME TO GET AWAY FROM MOLTRES THE MOMENT WE SAW ALL THOSE POKÉMON!
BUT HOW ARE WE GOING TO HAVE ANY FUN ANYMORE WITHOUT PRYCE?
HUH?
MAYBE YOU SHOULD JOIN US ...
AND YOU ARE ...?
A COUPLE OF GUYS WHO USED TO BE JUST LIKE YOU.
I'M KOGA. I'M LEFT OVER FROM THE OLD TEAM ROCKET.
AND I'M 3RUNO. A EFTOVER ROM THE KANTO ELITE FOUR.

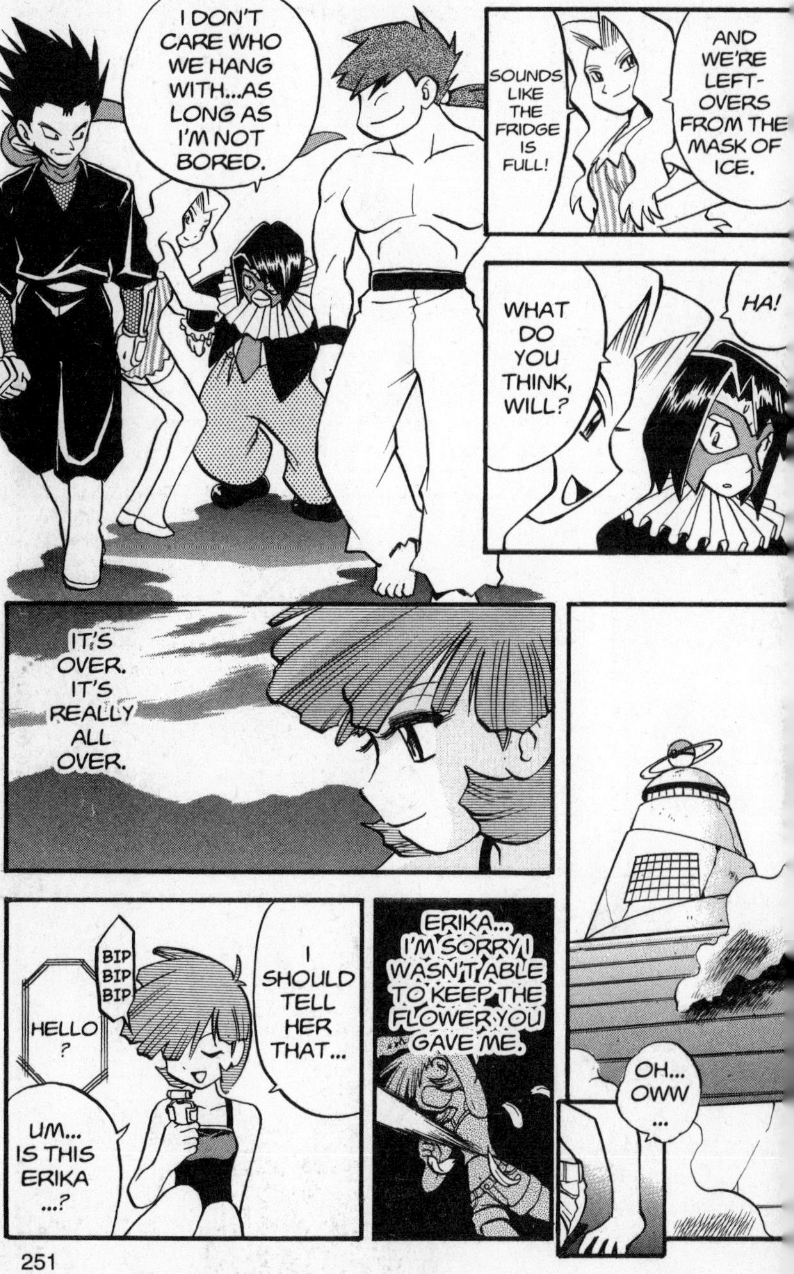
AND WE'RE LEFT-OVERS FROM THE MASK OF ICE.
SOUNDS LIKE THE FRIDGE IS FULL!
HA!
WHAT DO YOU THINK, WILL?
I DON'T CARE WHO WE HANG WITH...AS LONG AS I'M NOT BORED.
OH... OWW ...
IT'S OVER. IT'S REALLY ALL OVER.
ERIKA... I'M SORRY I WASN'T ABLE TO KEEP THE FLOWER YOU GAVE ME.
I SHOULD TELL HER THAT...
BIP BIP BIP
HELLO ?
UM... IS THIS ERIKA ...?

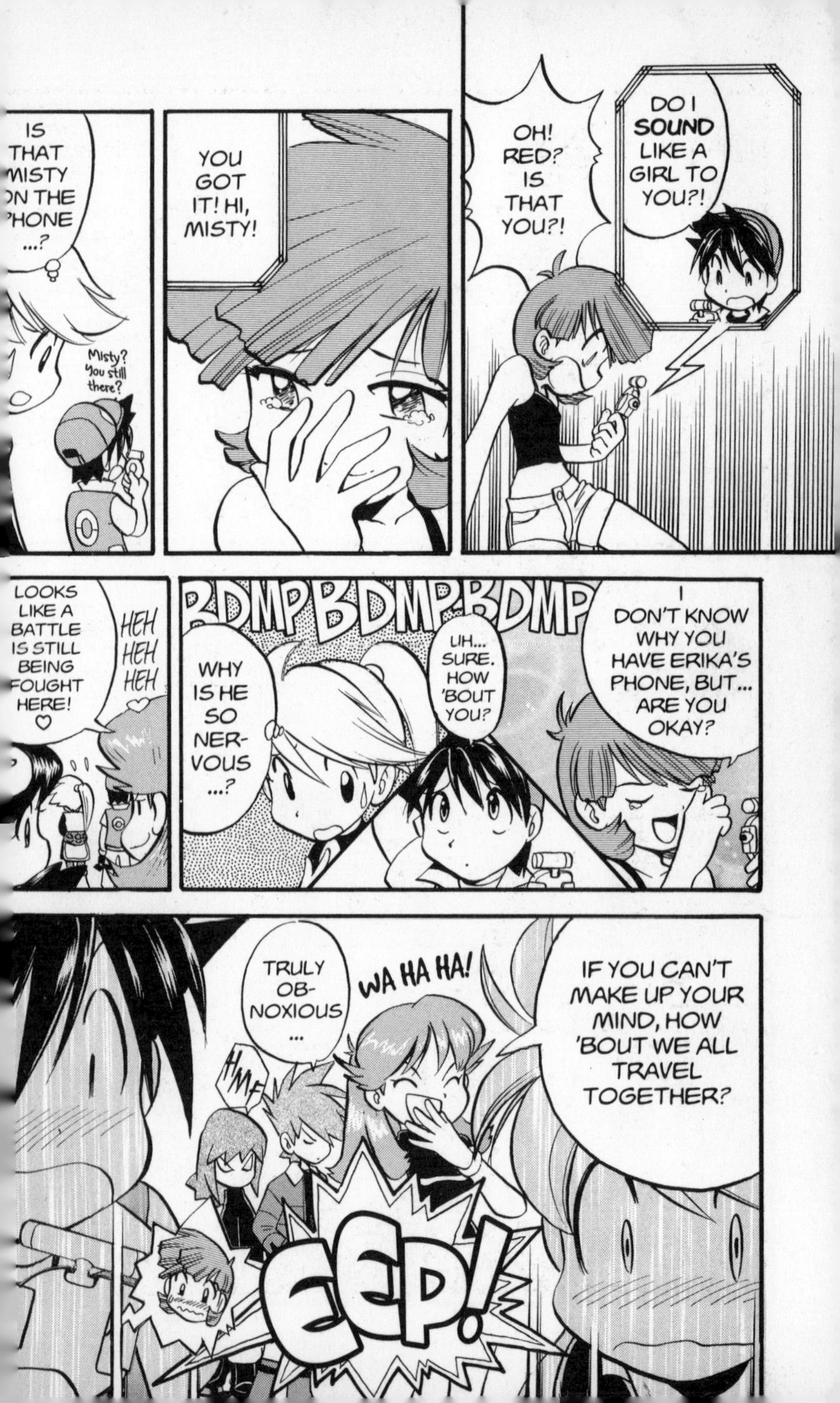
IS THAT MISTY ON THE PHONE ...?
Misty? You still there?
YOU GOT IT! HI, MISTY!
OH! RED? IS THAT YOU?!
DO I **SOUND** LIKE A GIRL TO YOU?!
LOOKS LIKE A BATTLE IS STILL BEING FOUGHT HERE! ♡
HEH HEH HEH
BDMP BDMP BDMP
WHY IS HE SO NER-VOUS ...?
UH... SURE. HOW 'BOUT YOU?
I DON'T KNOW WHY YOU HAVE ERIKA'S PHONE, BUT... ARE YOU OKAY?
TRULY OB-NOXIOUS ...
HMF
WA HA HA!
IF YOU CAN'T MAKE UP YOUR MIND, HOW 'BOUT WE ALL TRAVEL TOGETHER?
EEP!

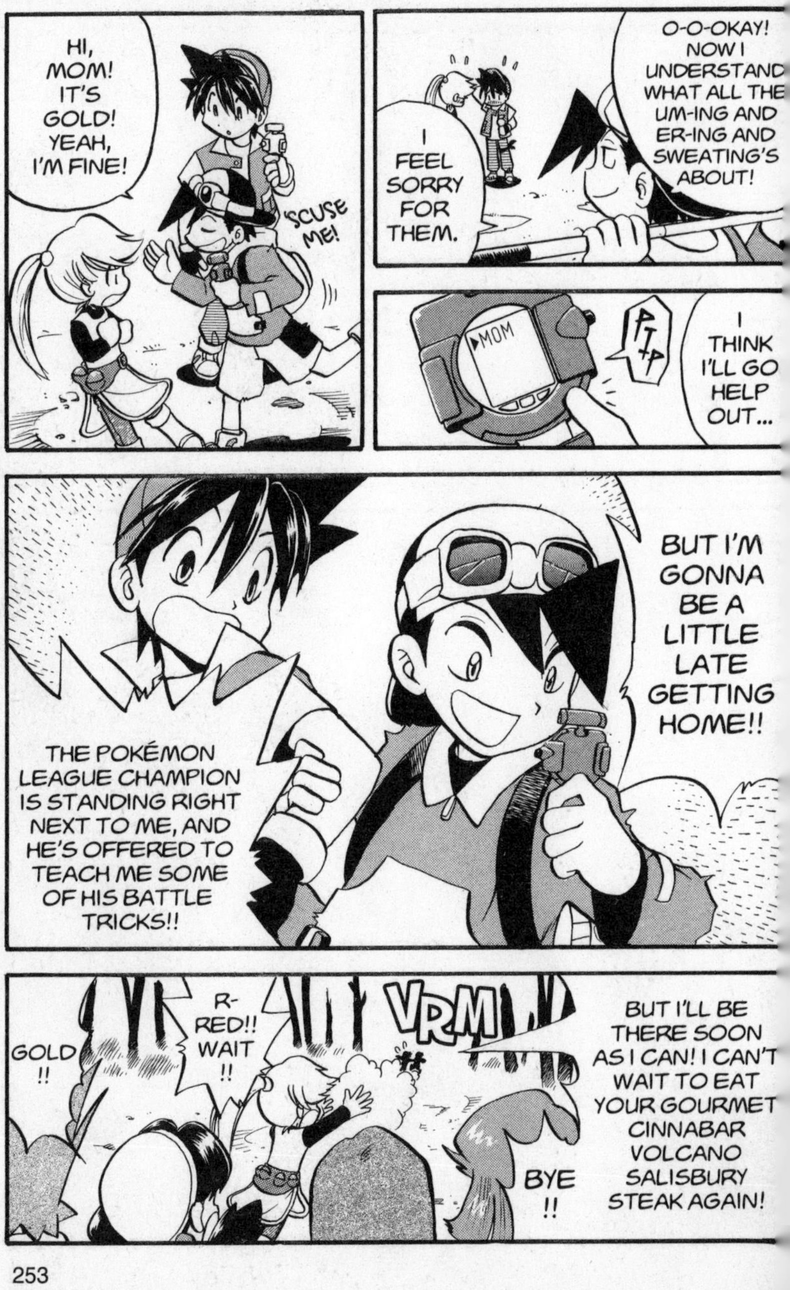
O-O-OKAY! NOW I UNDERSTAND WHAT ALL THE UM-ING AND ER-ING AND SWEATING'S ABOUT!
I FEEL SORRY FOR THEM.
I THINK I'LL GO HELP OUT...
PIP
MOM
HI, MOM! IT'S GOLD! YEAH, I'M FINE!
'SCUSE ME!
BUT I'M GONNA BE A LITTLE LATE GETTING HOME!!
THE POKÉMON LEAGUE CHAMPION IS STANDING RIGHT NEXT TO ME, AND HE'S OFFERED TO TEACH ME SOME OF HIS BATTLE TRICKS!!
BUT I'LL BE THERE SOON AS I CAN! I CAN'T WAIT TO EAT YOUR GOURMET CINNABAR VOLCANO SALISBURY STEAK AGAIN!
VRM
BYE !!
R-RED!! WAIT !!
GOLD !!

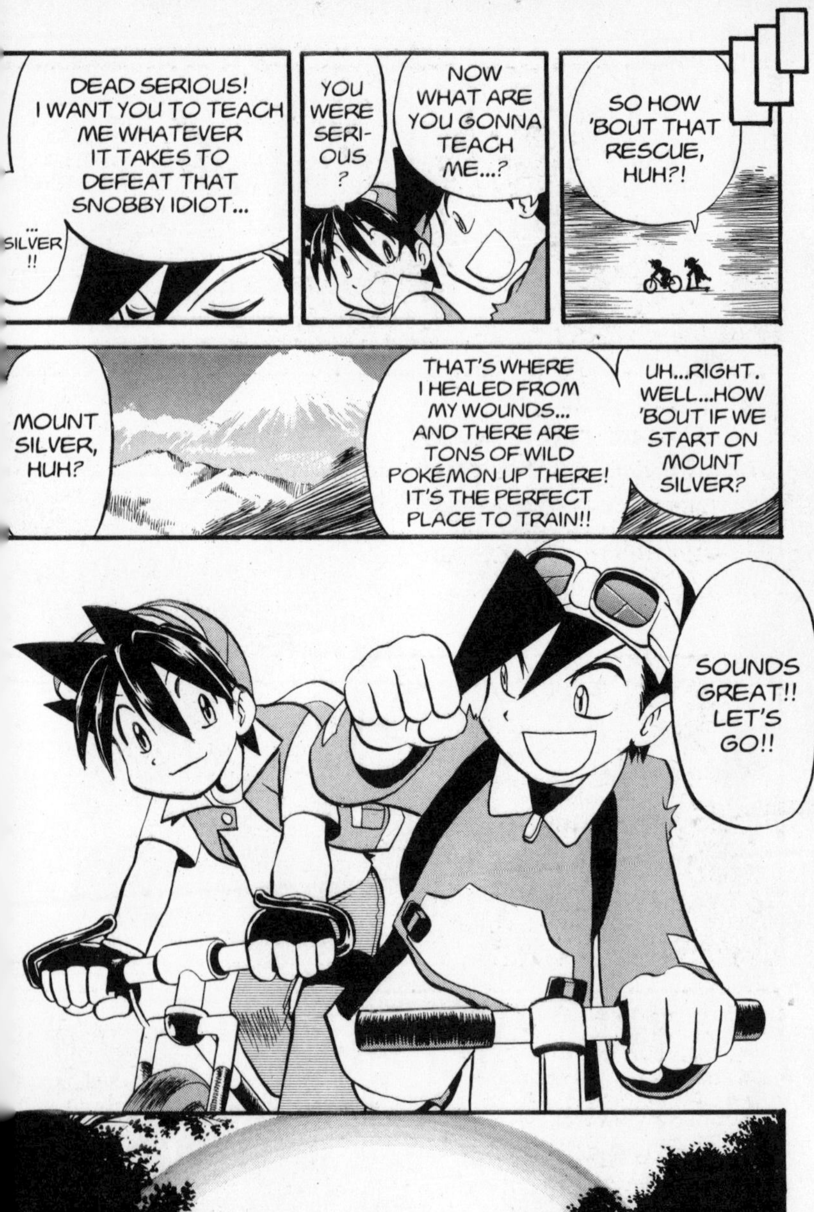
SO HOW 'BOUT THAT RESCUE, HUH?!
NOW WHAT ARE YOU GONNA TEACH ME...?
YOU WERE SERI-OUS?
DEAD SERIOUS! I WANT YOU TO TEACH ME WHATEVER IT TAKES TO DEFEAT THAT SNOBBY IDIOT...
...SILVER!!
UH...RIGHT. WELL...HOW 'BOUT IF WE START ON MOUNT SILVER?
THAT'S WHERE I HEALED FROM MY WOUNDS... AND THERE ARE TONS OF WILD POKÉMON UP THERE! IT'S THE PERFECT PLACE TO TRAIN!!
MOUNT SILVER, HUH?
SOUNDS GREAT!! LET'S GO!!

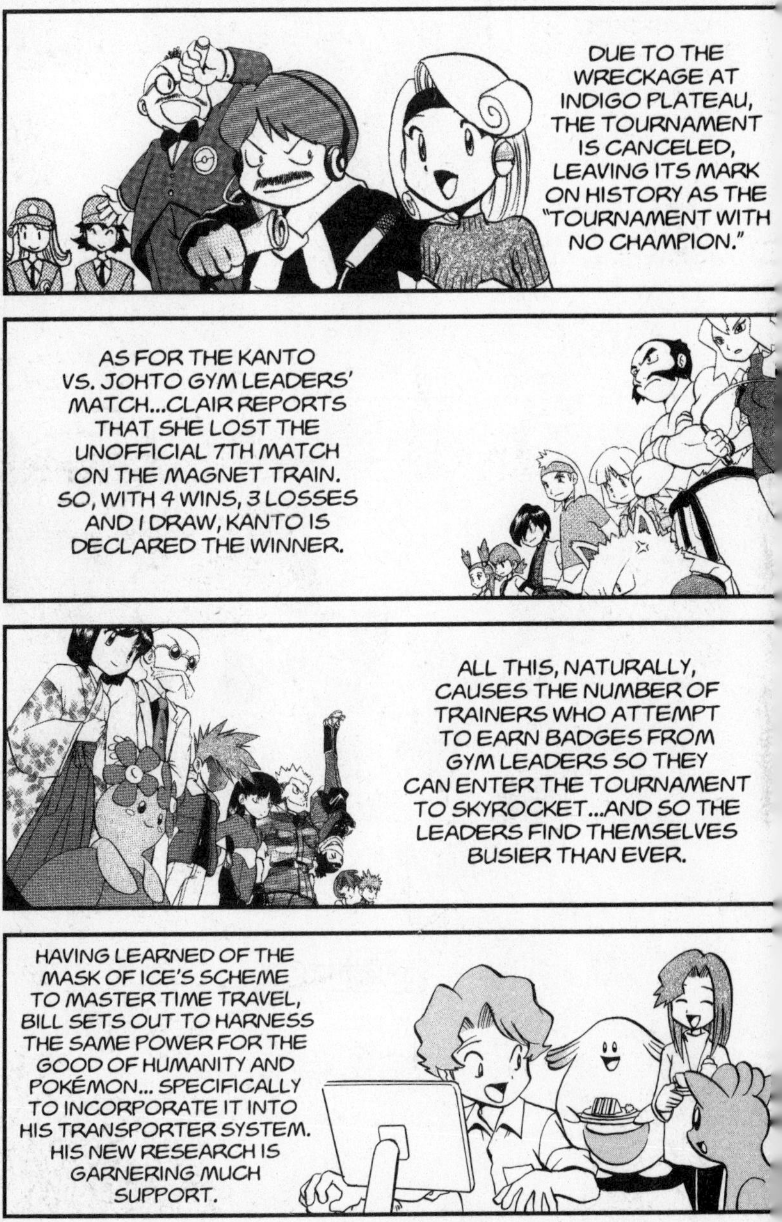
DUE TO THE WRECKAGE AT INDIGO PLATEAU, THE TOURNAMENT IS CANCELED, LEAVING ITS MARK ON HISTORY AS THE "TOURNAMENT WITH NO CHAMPION."
AS FOR THE KANTO VS. JOHTO GYM LEADERS' MATCH...CLAIR REPORTS THAT SHE LOST THE UNOFFICIAL 7TH MATCH ON THE MAGNET TRAIN. SO, WITH 4 WINS, 3 LOSSES AND 1 DRAW, KANTO IS DECLARED THE WINNER.
ALL THIS, NATURALLY, CAUSES THE NUMBER OF TRAINERS WHO ATTEMPT TO EARN BADGES FROM GYM LEADERS SO THEY CAN ENTER THE TOURNAMENT TO SKYROCKET...AND SO THE LEADERS FIND THEMSELVES BUSIER THAN EVER.
HAVING LEARNED OF THE MASK OF ICE'S SCHEME TO MASTER TIME TRAVEL, BILL SETS OUT TO HARNESS THE SAME POWER FOR THE GOOD OF HUMANITY AND POKéMON... SPECIFICALLY TO INCORPORATE IT INTO HIS TRANSPORTER SYSTEM. HIS NEW RESEARCH IS GARNERING MUCH SUPPORT.

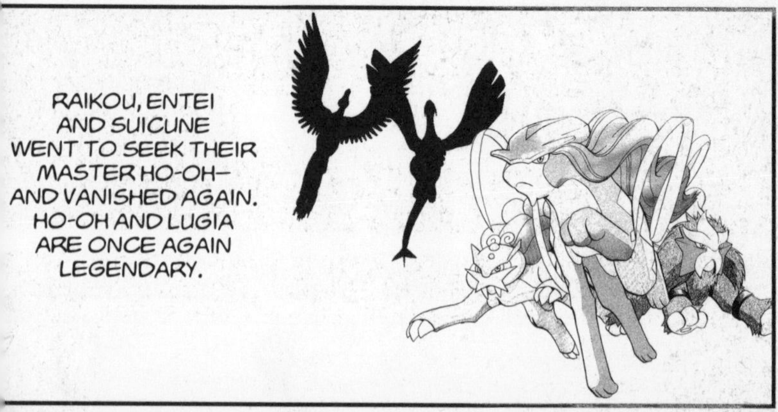
RAIKOU, ENTEI AND SUICUNE WENT TO SEEK THEIR MASTER HO-OH—AND VANISHED AGAIN. HO-OH AND LUGIA ARE ONCE AGAIN LEGENDARY.

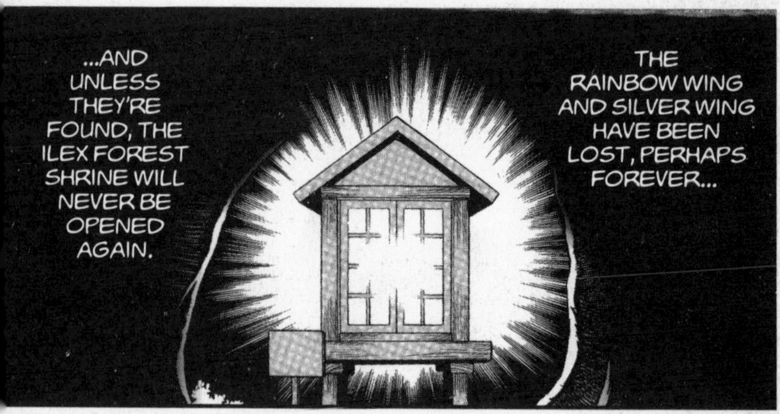
THE RAINBOW WING AND SILVER WING HAVE BEEN LOST, PERHAPS FOREVER...
...AND UNLESS THEY'RE FOUND, THE ILEX FOREST SHRINE WILL NEVER BE OPENED AGAIN.

SO THE STORY OF THE MASK OF ICE WHO SHOOK THE JOHTO AND KANTO REGIONS TO THEIR BEDROCK COMES TO A CLOSE.

AND NOW...

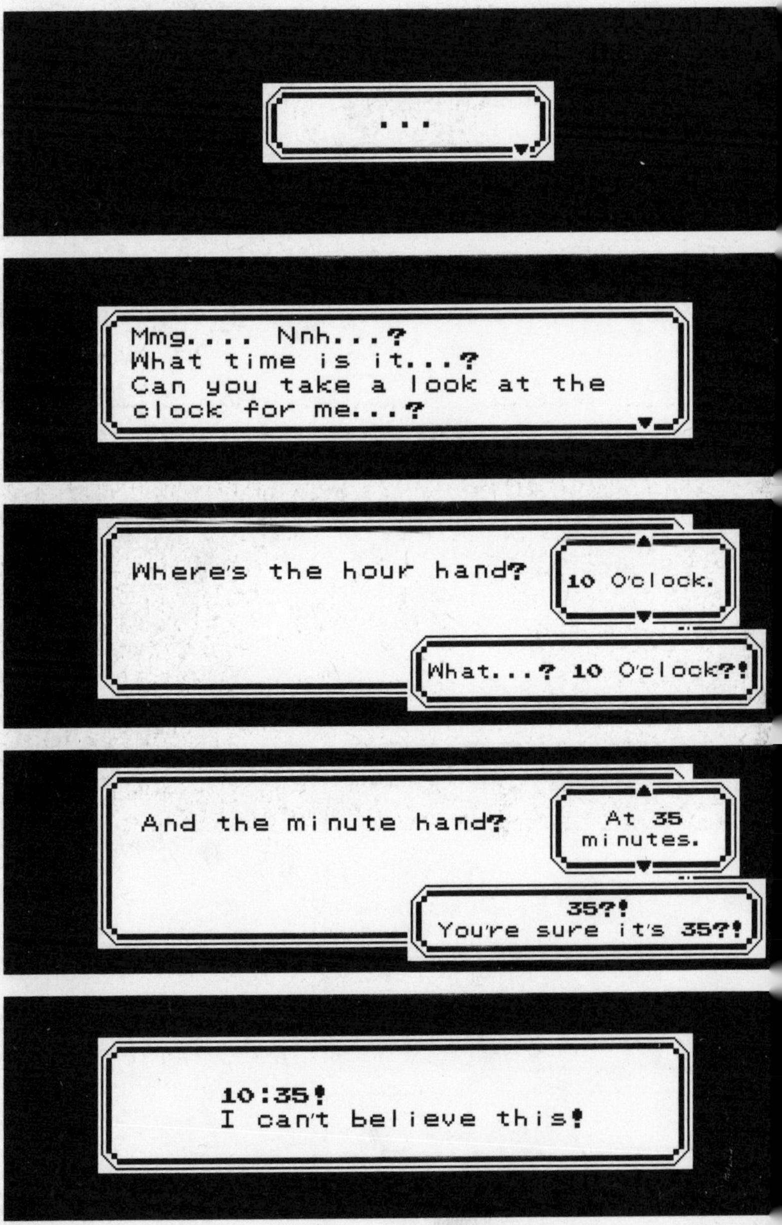
...
Mmg.... Nnh...? What time is it...? Can you take a look at the clock for me...?
Where's the hour hand?
10 O'clock.
What...? 10 O'clock?!
And the minute hand?
At 35 minutes.
35?! You're sure it's 35?!
10:35! I can't believe this!

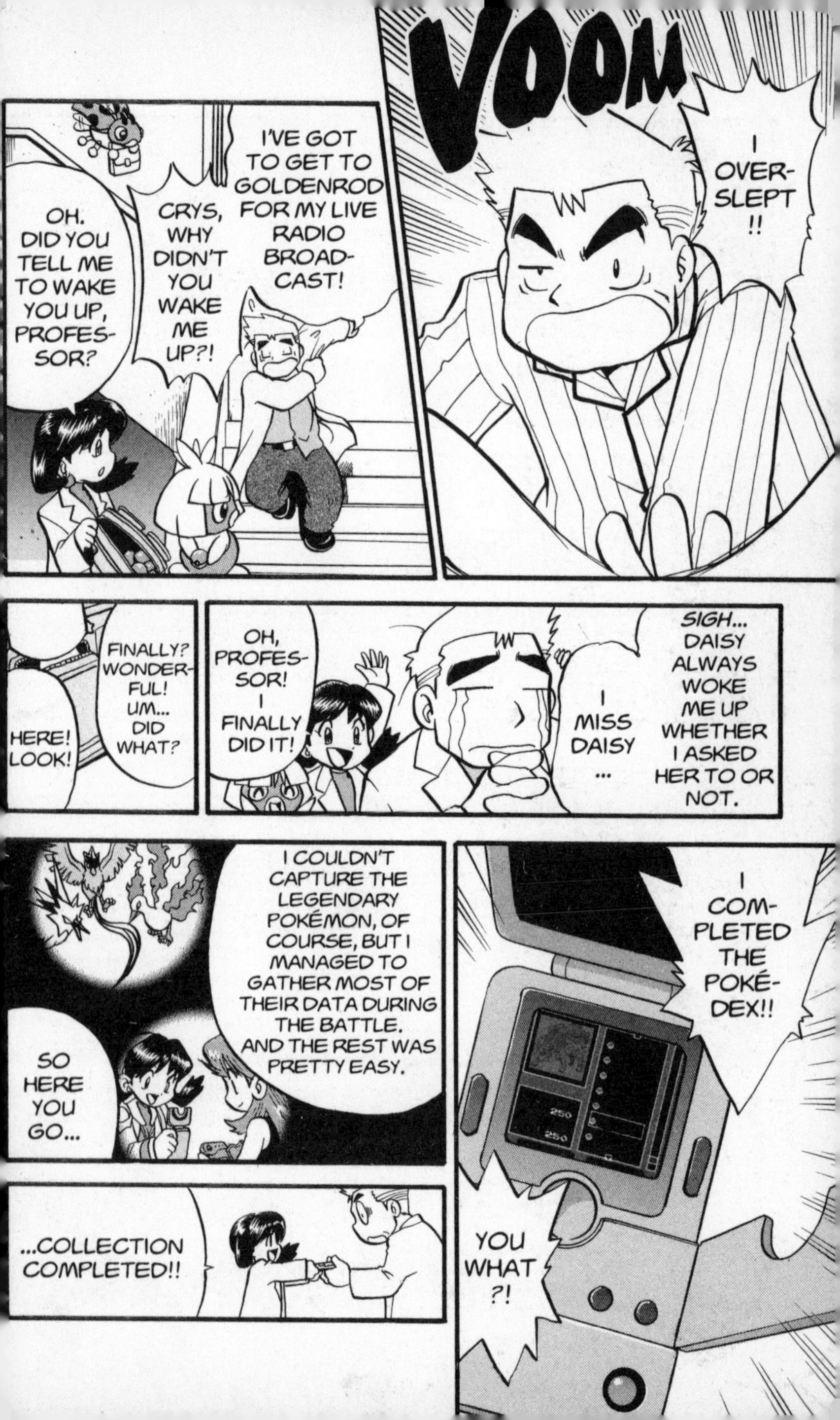
VOOM
I OVERSLEPT!!
I'VE GOT TO GET TO GOLDENROD FOR MY LIVE RADIO BROADCAST!
CRYS, WHY DIDN'T YOU WAKE ME UP?!
OH. DID YOU TELL ME TO WAKE YOU UP, PROFESSOR?
SIGH... DAISY ALWAYS WOKE ME UP WHETHER I ASKED HER TO OR NOT.
I MISS DAISY...
OH, PROFESSOR! I FINALLY DID IT!
FINALLY? WONDERFUL! UM... DID WHAT?
HERE! LOOK!
I COMPLETED THE POKÉDEX!!
250
250
YOU WHAT?!
I COULDN'T CAPTURE THE LEGENDARY POKÉMON, OF COURSE, BUT I MANAGED TO GATHER MOST OF THEIR DATA DURING THE BATTLE. AND THE REST WAS PRETTY EASY.
SO HERE YOU GO...
...COLLECTION COMPLETED!!

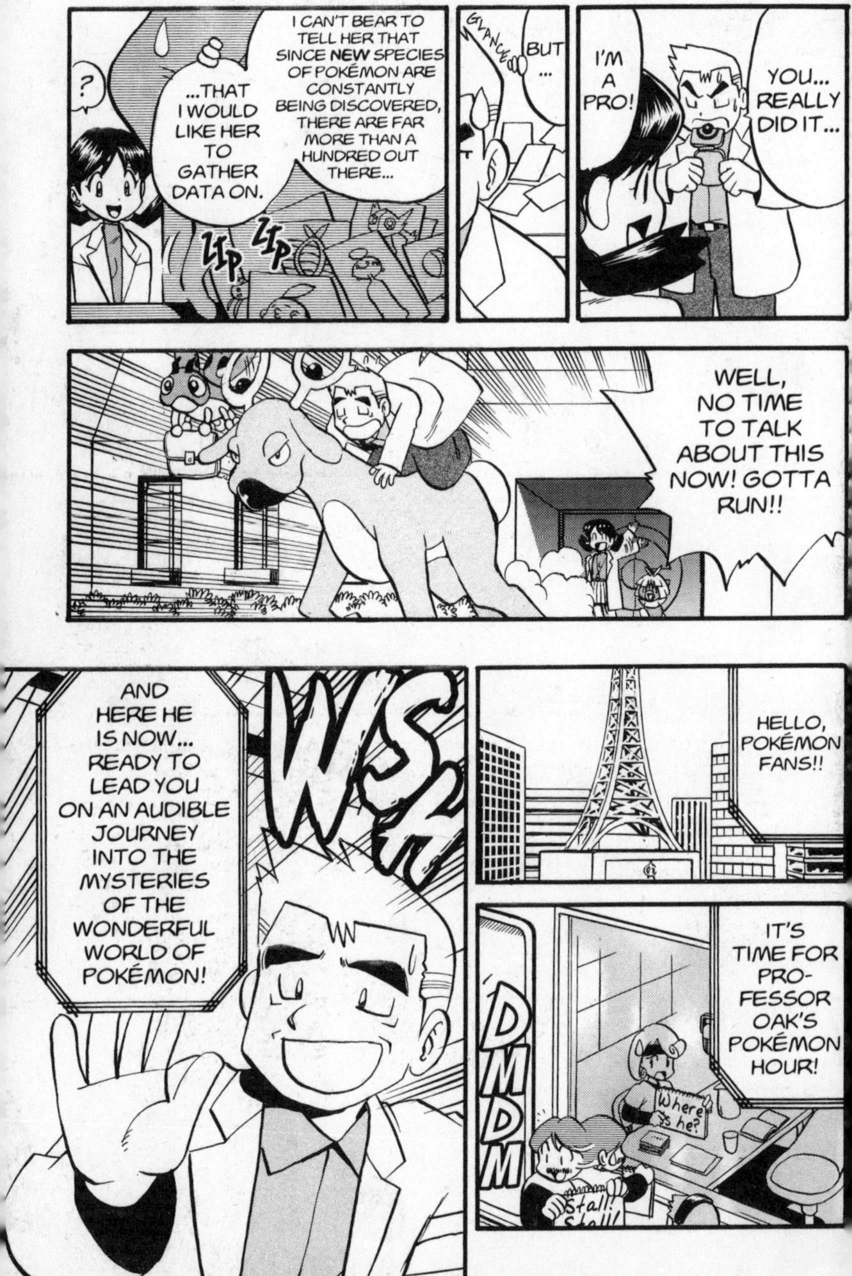
YOU... REALLY DID IT...
I'M A PRO!
GLANCE
BUT ...
I CAN'T BEAR TO TELL HER THAT SINCE **NEW** SPECIES OF POKÉMON ARE CONSTANTLY BEING DISCOVERED, THERE ARE FAR MORE THAN A HUNDRED OUT THERE...
...THAT I WOULD LIKE HER TO GATHER DATA ON.
?
ZIP
ZIP
WELL, NO TIME TO TALK ABOUT THIS NOW! GOTTA RUN!!
HELLO, POKÉMON FANS!!
IT'S TIME FOR PRO-FESSOR OAK'S POKÉMON HOUR!
DMDM
Where's he?
Stall!
WSH
AND HERE HE IS NOW... READY TO LEAD YOU ON AN AUDIBLE JOURNEY INTO THE MYSTERIES OF THE WONDERFUL WORLD OF POKÉMON!

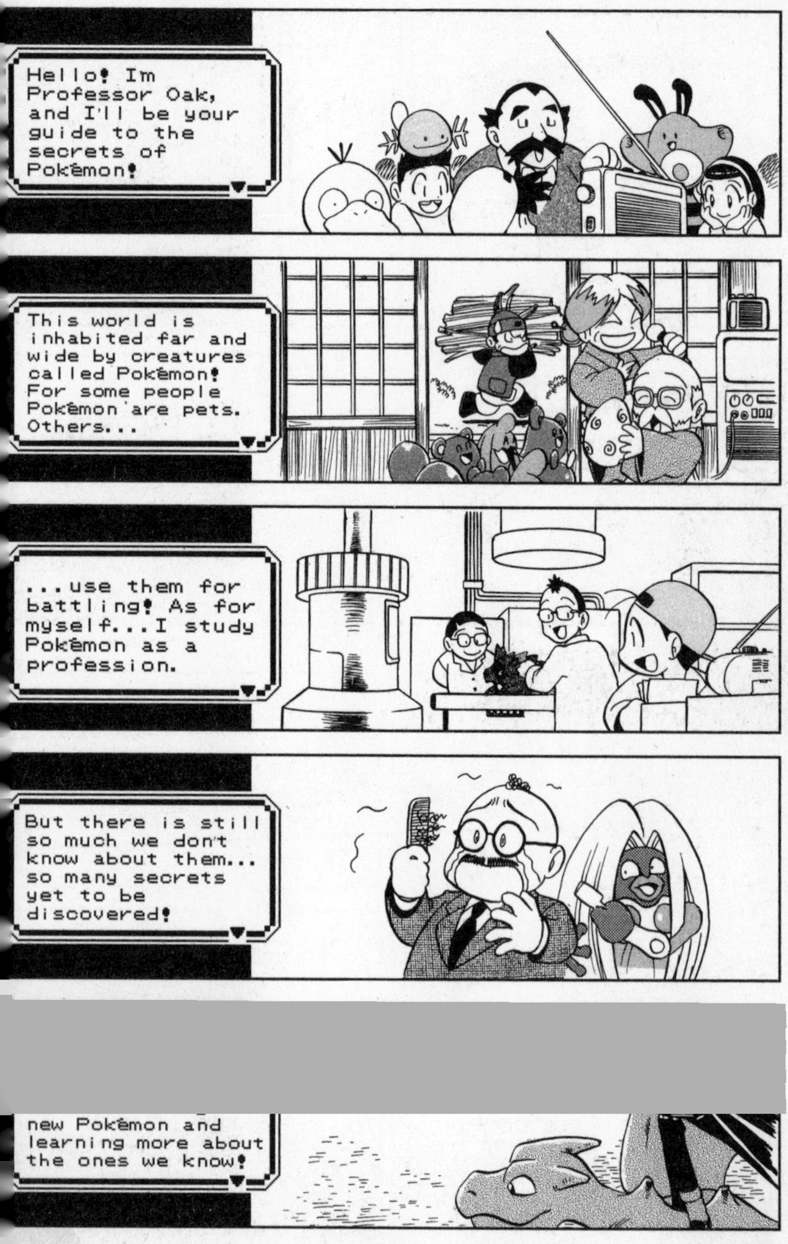
Hello! I'm Professor Oak, and I'll be your guide to the secrets of Pokémon!
This world is inhabited far and wide by creatures called Pokémon! For some people Pokémon are pets. Others...
...use them for battling! As for myself...I study Pokémon as a profession.
But there is still so much we don't know about them... so many secrets yet to be discovered!
new Pokémon and learning more about the ones we know!

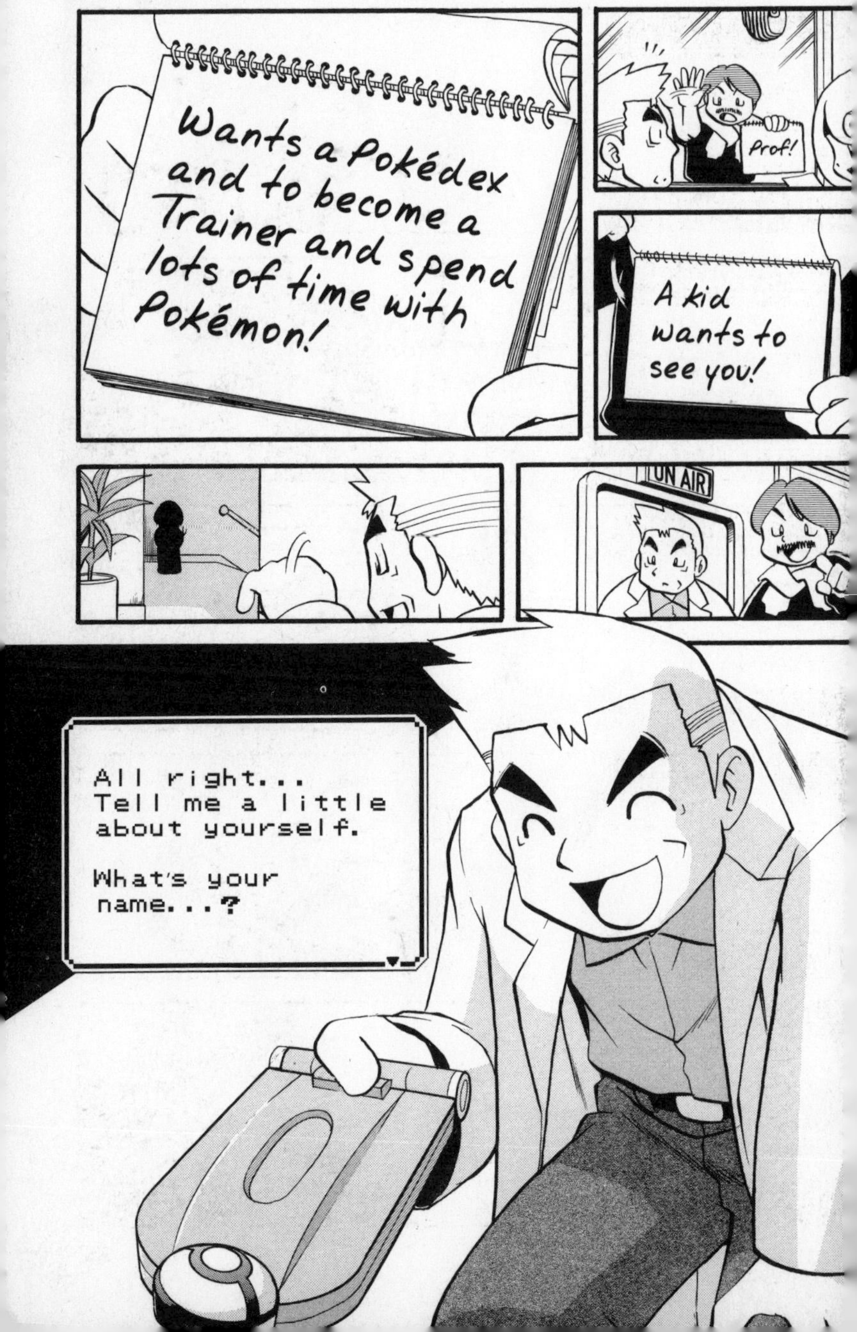
Prof!
A kid wants to see you!
Wants a Pokédex and to become a Trainer and spend lots of time with Pokémon!
ON AIR
All right... Tell me a little about yourself.
What's your name...?

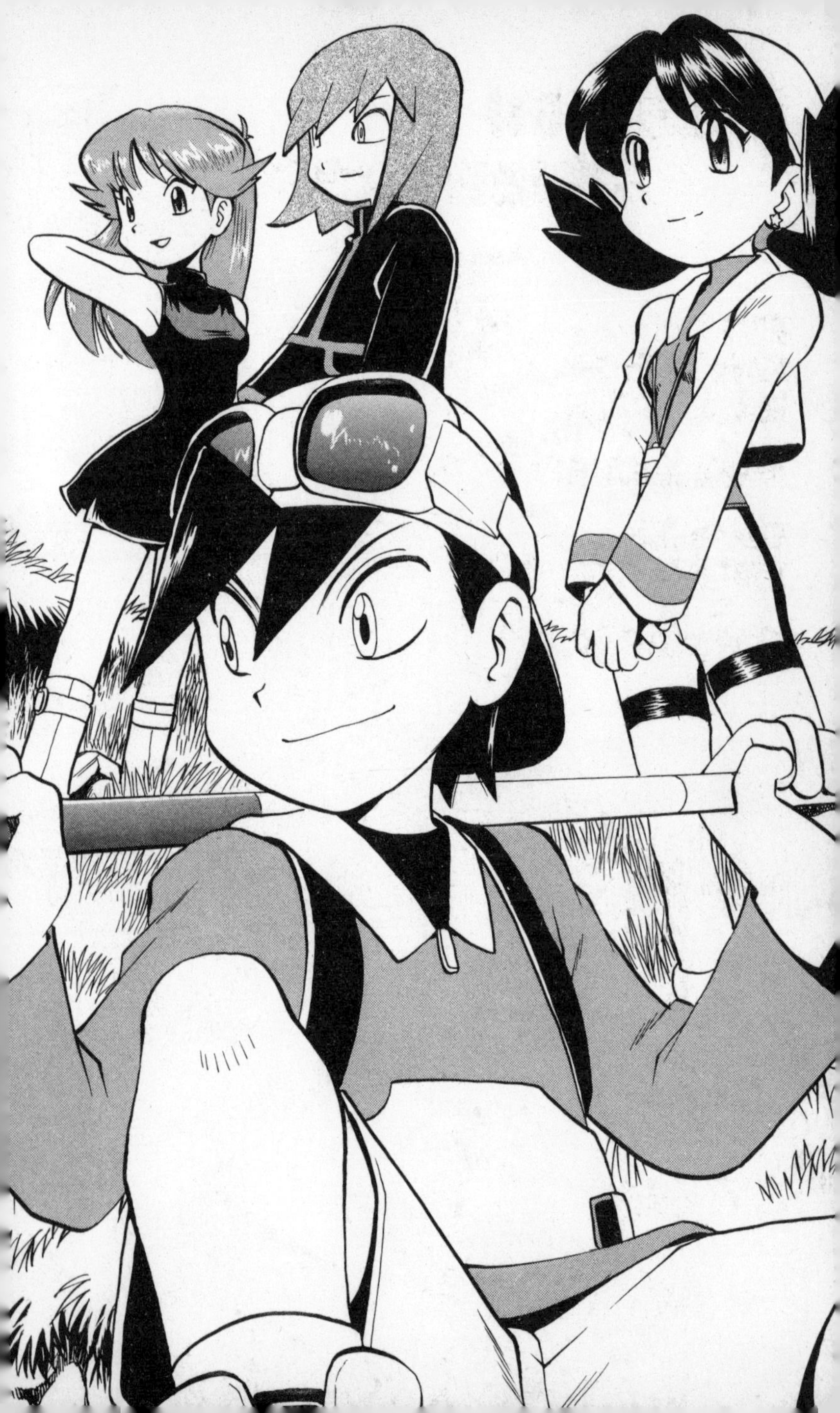

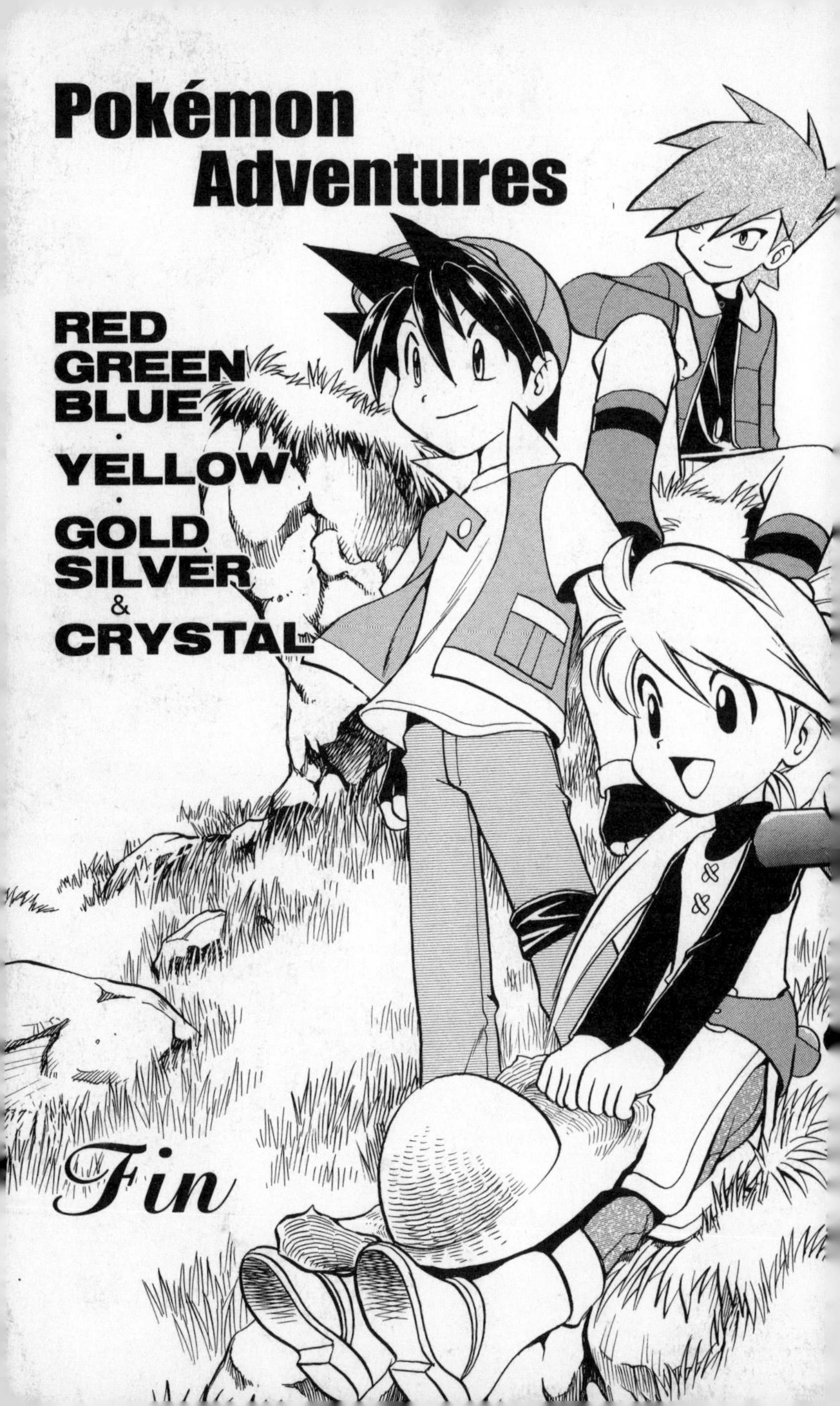
Pokémon Adventures
RED
GREEN
BLUE
·
YELLOW
·
GOLD
SILVER
&
CRYSTAL
Fin

# TRAINER DATA

## GREEN

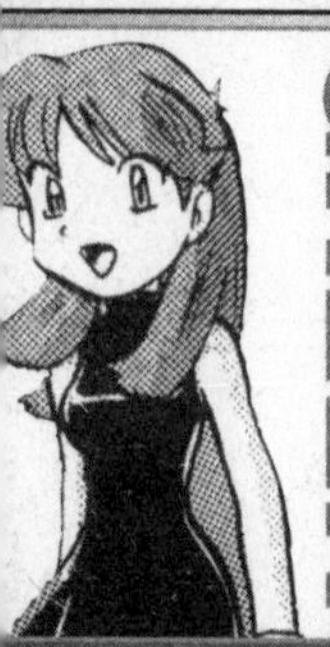

| Nickname | Pokémon | Level |
|---|---|---|
| BLASTOISE | BLASTOISE ♂ | Lv70 |
| JIGGLY | JIGGLYPUFF ♀ | Lv57 |
| DITTO | DITTO | Lv40 |
| CLEFABLE | CLEFABLE ♂ | Lv60 |
| NIDO | NIDORINA ♀ | Lv59 |
| SNUBBULL | SNUBBULL ♂ | Lv22 |

### OTHER MEMBERS

| | |
|---|---|
| ABRA ♀ | Lv 15 |

## BLUE

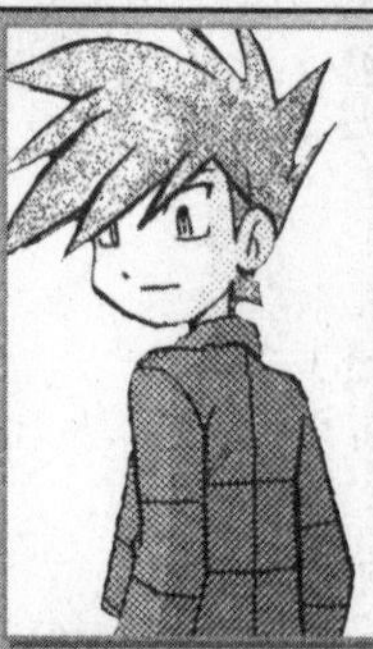

| Nickname | Pokémon | Level |
|---|---|---|
| CHARIZARD | CHARIZARD ♂ | Lv81 |
| SCIZOR | SCIZOR ♂ | Lv80 |
| PORYGON2 | PORYGON2 | Lv61 |
| GOLDUCK | GOLDUCK ♂ | Lv79 |
| RHYDON | RHYDON ♂ | Lv71 |
| PIDGEOT | PIDGEOT ♂ | Lv76 |

### OTHER MEMBERS

| | |
|---|---|
| NINETALES ♂ | Lv 68 |
| MACHAMP ♂ | Lv 70 |
| EXEGGUTOR ♂ | Lv 67 |
| ALAKAZAM ♂ | Lv 64 |
| ARCANINE ♂ | Lv 71 |

## RED

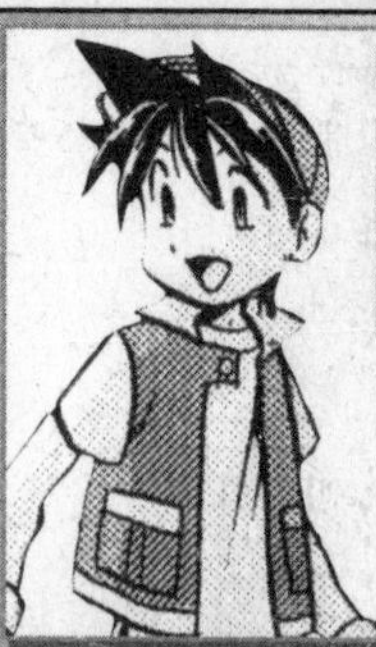

| Nickname | Pokémon | Level |
|---|---|---|
| SAUR | VENUSAUR ♂ | Lv72 |
| POLI | POLIWRATH ♂ | Lv70 |
| PIKA | PIKACHU ♂ | Lv85 |
| GYARA | GYARADOS ♂ | Lv74 |
| LAX | SNORLAX ♂ | Lv86 |
| AERO | AERODACTYL ♂ | Lv76 |

### OTHER MEMBERS

| | |
|---|---|
| ESPEON ♂ | Lv 65 |
| DIGLETT ♂ | Lv 23 |
| SANDSHREW ♂ | Lv 21 |
| NIDORINO ♂ | Lv 42 |

# TRAINER DATA

## CRYSTAL

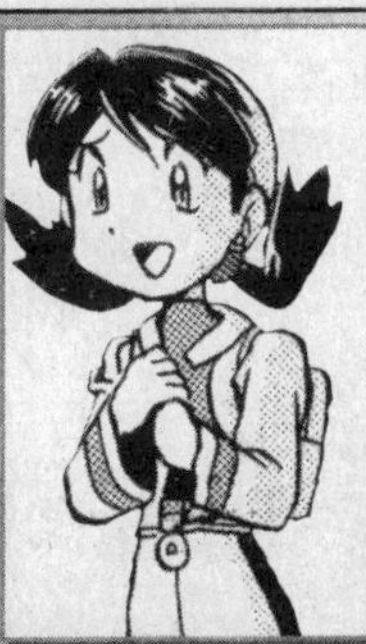

| | Nickname | Pokémon | Level |
|---|---|---|---|
| 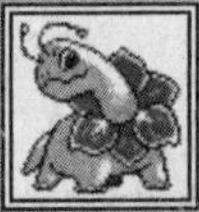 | MEGAREE | MEGANIUM ♂ | Lv40 |
| 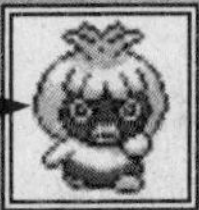 | CHUMEE | SMOOCHUM ♀ | Lv29 |
| 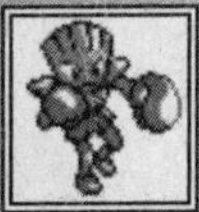 | MONLEE | HITMONCHAN ♂ | Lv54 |
| 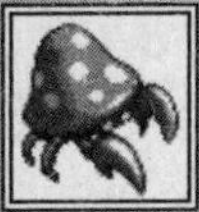 | PARASEE | PARASECT ♀ | Lv47 |
| 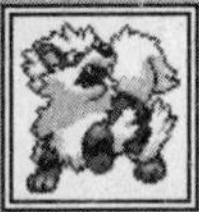 | ARCHY | ARCANINE ♂ | Lv53 |
| 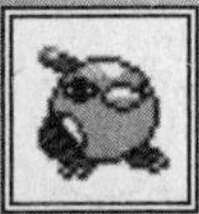 | NATEE | NATU ♀ | Lv43 |

### OTHER MEMBERS

 CUBONE ♂ Lv 47

## SILVER

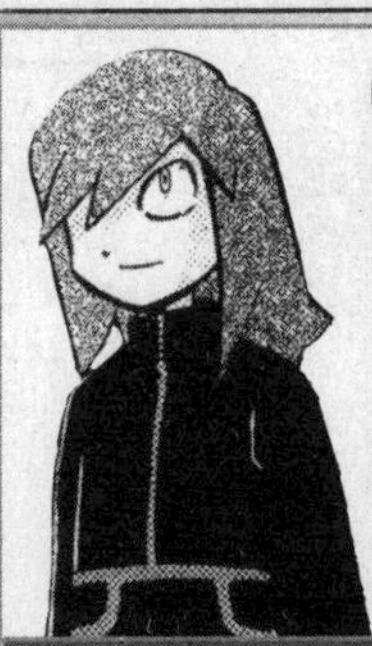

| | Nickname | Pokémon | Level |
|---|---|---|---|
| 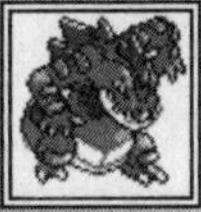 | FERALIGATR | FERALIGATR ♂ | Lv45 |
| 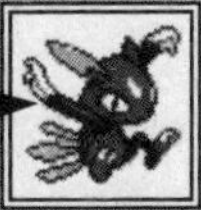 | SNEASEL | SNEASEL ♂ | Lv46 |
| 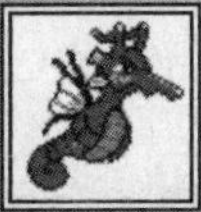 | KINGDRA | KINGDRA ♀ | Lv44 |
| 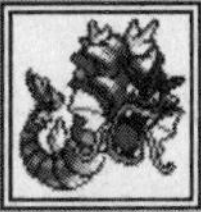 | GYARADOS | GYARADOS ♂ | Lv40 |
| 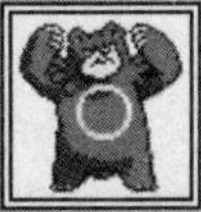 | URSARING | URSARING ♂ | Lv44 |
| 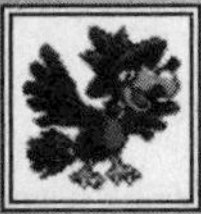 | MURKROW | MURKROW ♂ | Lv43 |

### OTHER MEMBERS

## YELLOW

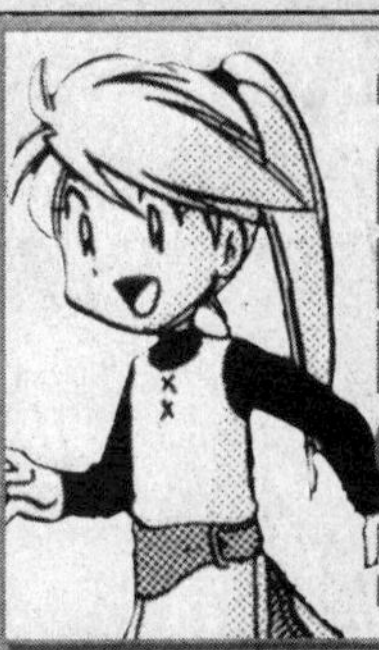

| | Nickname | Pokémon | Level |
|---|---|---|---|
| 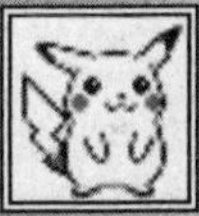 | CHUCHU | PIKACHU ♀ | Lv31 |
| 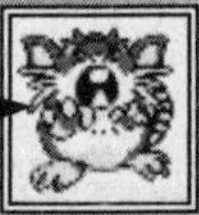 | RATTY | RATICATE ♂ | Lv25 |
| 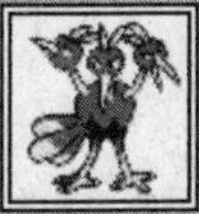 | DODY | DODRIO ♂ | Lv33 |
| 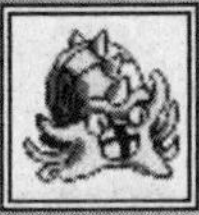 | OMNY | OMANYTE ♂ | Lv42 |
| 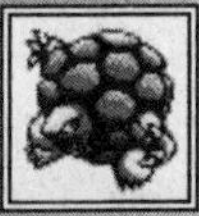 | GRAVVY | GOLEM ♂ | Lv39 |
| 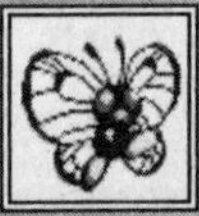 | KITTY | BUTTERFREE ♂ | Lv20 |

### OTHER MEMBERS

# TRAINER DATA

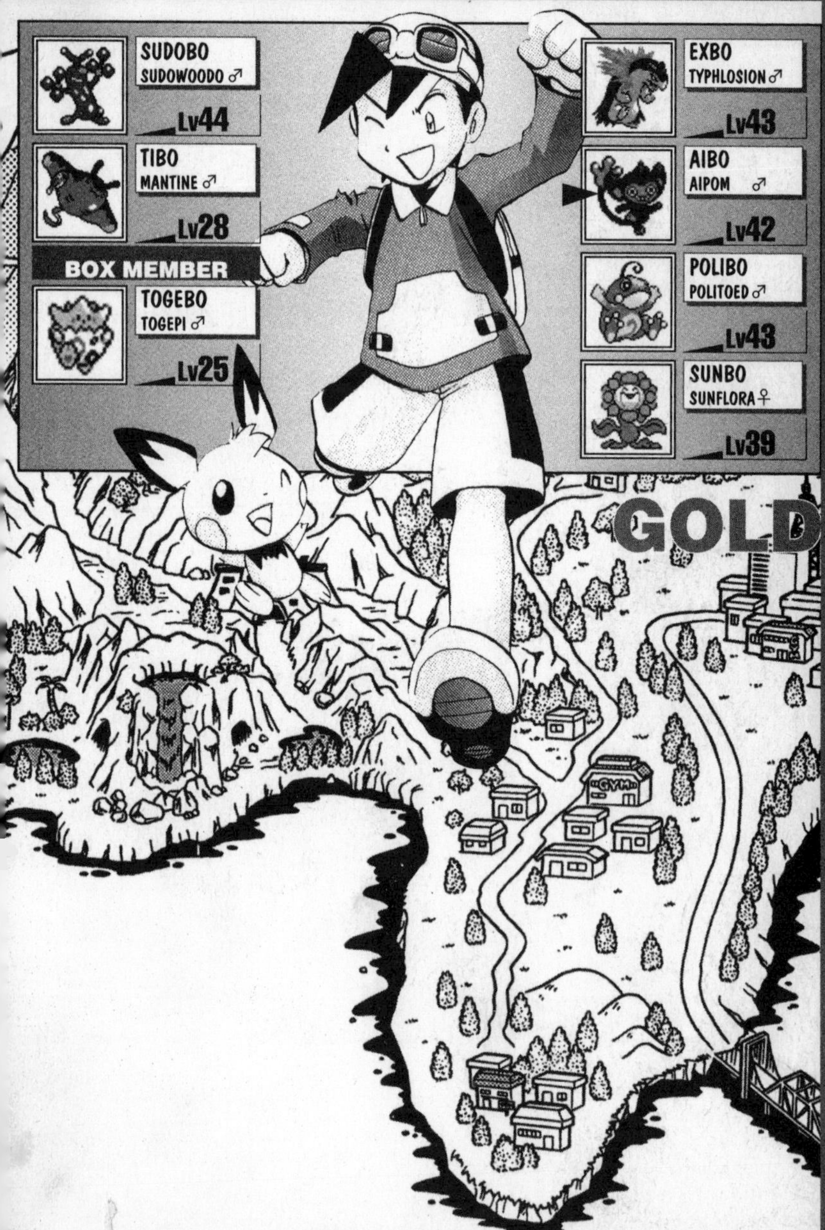
SUDOBO
SUDOWOODO ♂
Lv44
TIBO
MANTINE ♂
Lv28
BOX MEMBER
TOGEBO
TOGEPI ♂
Lv25
EXBO
TYPHLOSION ♂
Lv43
AIBO
AIPOM ♂
Lv42
POLIBO
POLITOED ♂
Lv43
SUNBO
SUNFLORA ♀
Lv39
GOLD
GYM

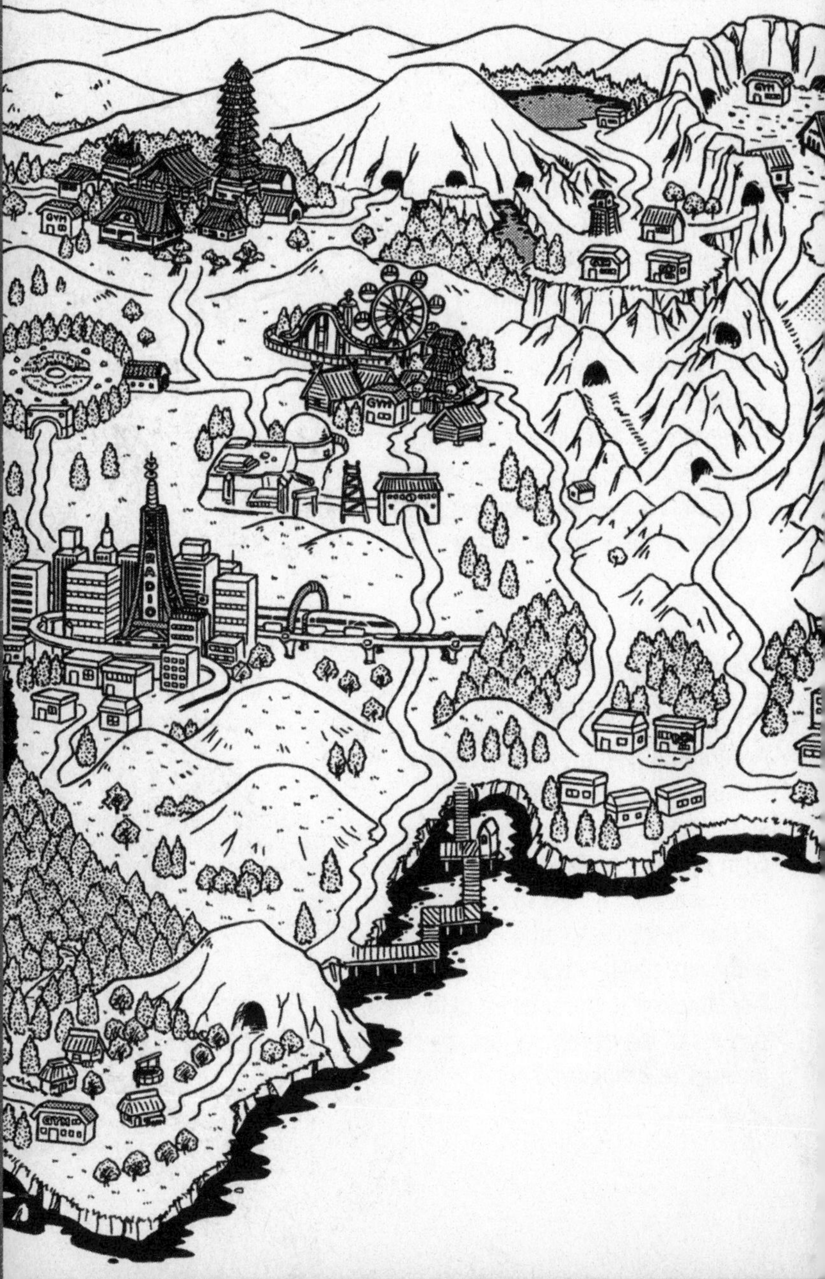
GYM
GYM
GYM
RADIO
GYM

## Message from
Hidenori Kusaka

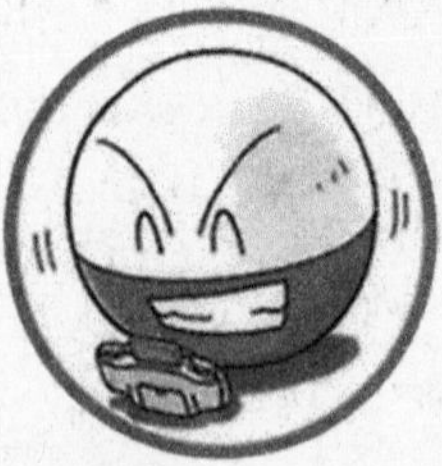

Thanks to all your support, this manga has finally reached volume 14. If we just count the Gold, Silver and Crystal episodes, we have seven volumes. Oh! Come to think of it... the Red, Blue and Green episodes plus the Yellow episodes total seven volumes also! Hmm! So...Part 3 of *Pokémon Adventures* is actually longer than Parts 1 and 2 combined! Well, anyway, this volume is the finale of this story arc! I hope you enjoy this special action-packed volume of *Pokémon Adventures*!!

## Message from
Satoshi Yamamoto

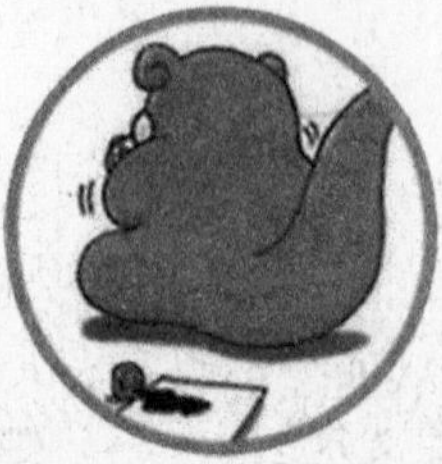

*Pokémon Adventures*...an ensemble action-adventure in which the seven main Pokémon Trainers, Gym Leaders, and supporting cast members each have a story... Finally all their stories will come together and every mystery will be resolved! Pay attention to the smallest details in the corners of the panels... Share the characters' thoughts and feelings... I'll make you cry along with them!!

# More Adventures!!

Pokémon Trainers Pearl and Diamond are starstruck! Their lifelong dream is to floor an audience with their Pokémon comedy act. So how do they wind up as bodyguards to a pampered little rich girl on a quest to reach the peak of Mt. Coronet...?!

Come along and join in the thrills and laughs as *Pokémon Adventures* continues with stories inspired by the video games *Pokémon Diamond, Pearl,* and *Platinum Version*!

**VOLS. 1 AND 2 ON SALE NOW!**

**VOL. 3 AVAILABLE OCTOBER 2011!**

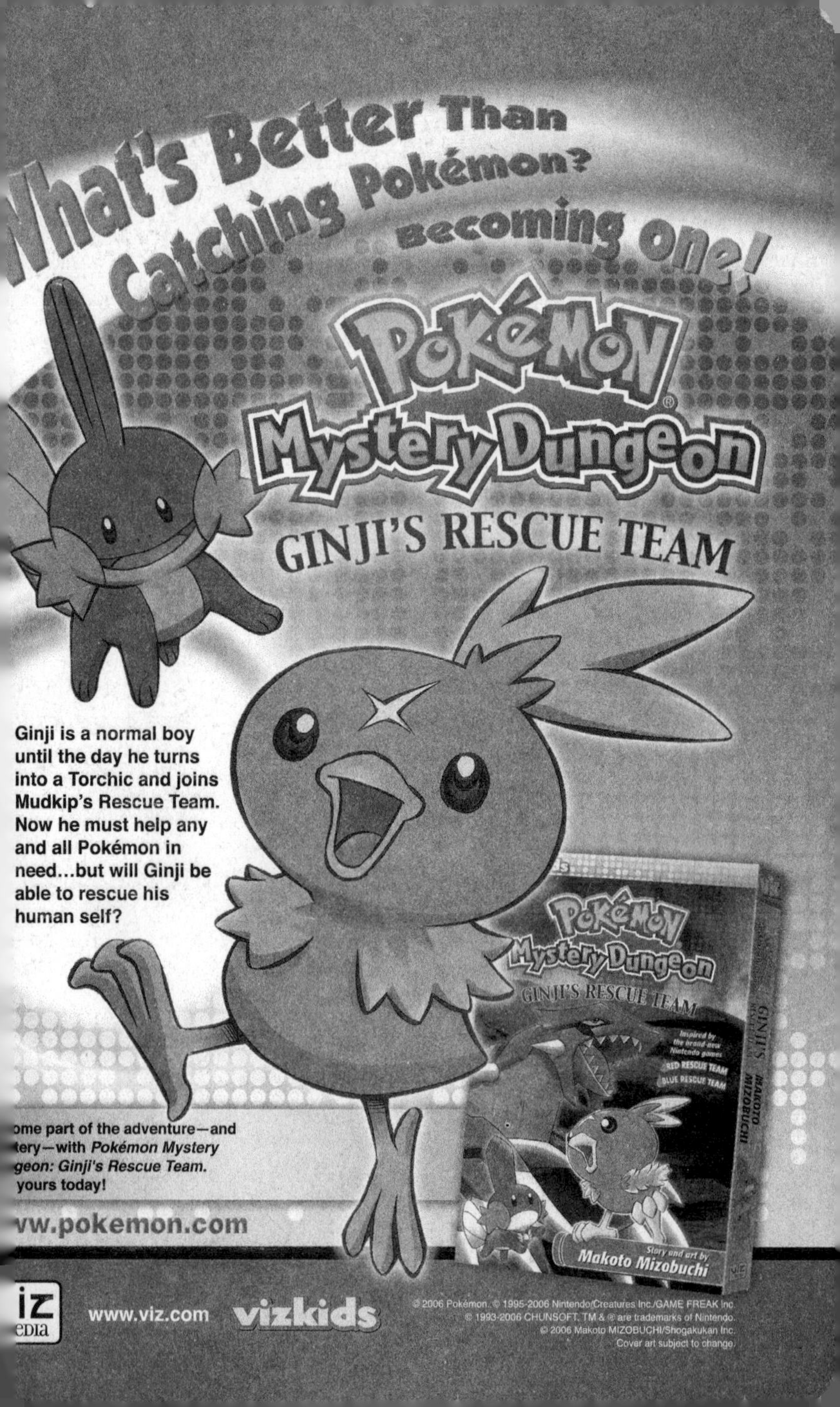

What's Better Than Catching Pokémon?
Becoming one!
Pokémon Mystery Dungeon
GINJI'S RESCUE TEAM
Ginji is a normal boy until the day he turns into a Torchic and joins Mudkip's Rescue Team. Now he must help any and all Pokémon in need...but will Ginji be able to rescue his human self?
ome part of the adventure—and tery—with *Pokémon Mystery geon: Ginji's Rescue Team.* yours today!
vw.pokemon.com
Pokémon Mystery Dungeon
GINJI'S RESCUE TEAM
Inspired by the brand-new Nintendo games
RED RESCUE TEAM
BLUE RESCUE TEAM
Story and art by
Makoto Mizobuchi
GINJI'S
MAKOTO MIZOBUCHI
iz
EDIA
www.viz.com
vizkids
© 2006 Pokémon. © 1995-2006 Nintendo/Creatures Inc./GAME FREAK Inc.
© 1993-2006 CHUNSOFT. TM & ® are trademarks of Nintendo.
© 2006 Makoto MIZOBUCHI/Shogakukan Inc.
Cover art subject to change.

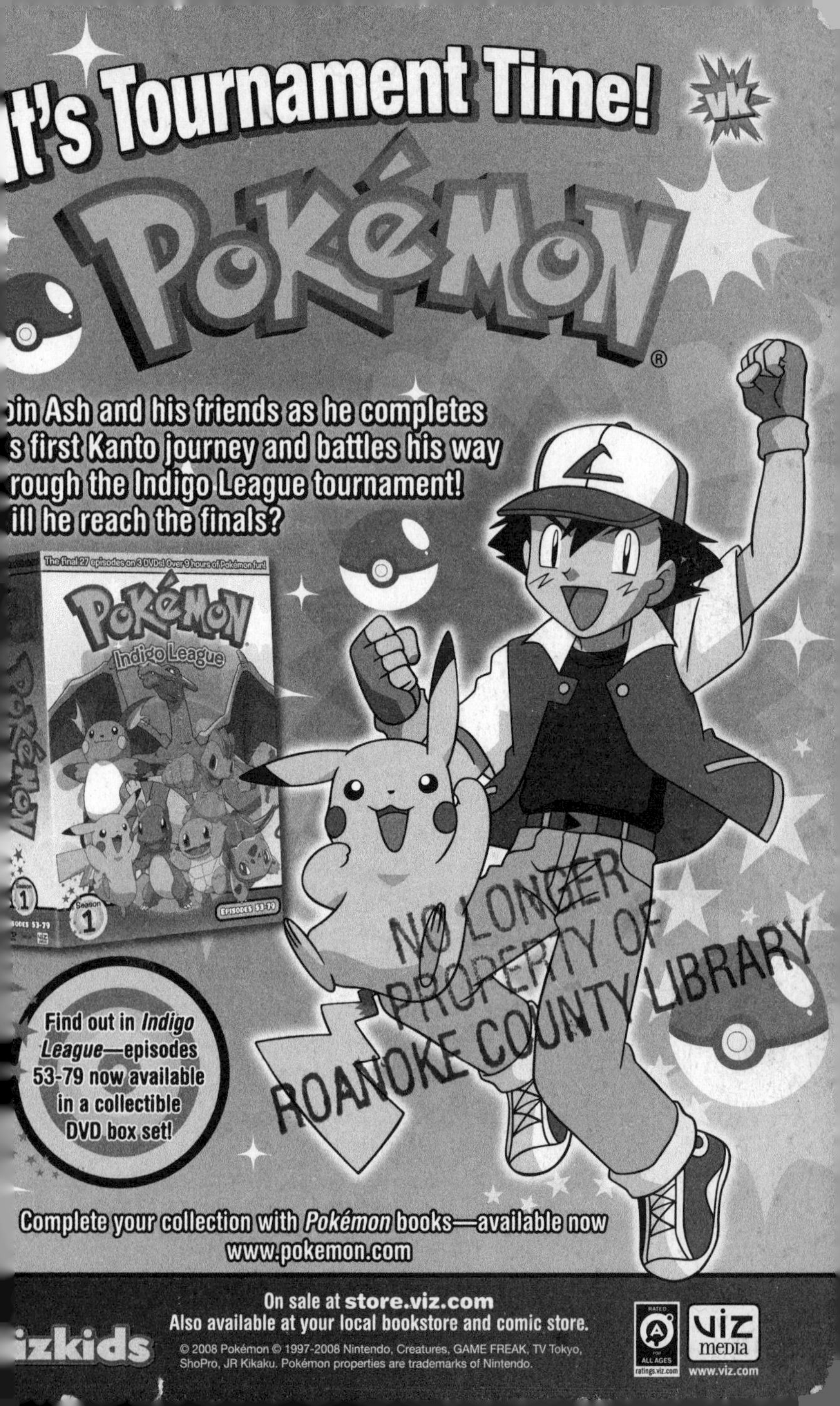

t's Tournament Time!
vk
POKéMON®
oin Ash and his friends as he completes
s first Kanto journey and battles his way
rough the Indigo League tournament!
ill he reach the finals?
The final 27 episodes on 3 DVDs! Over 9 hours of Pokémon fun!
POKéMON
Indigo League
Season 1
EPISODES 53-79
Find out in *Indigo League*—episodes 53-79 now available in a collectible DVD box set!
NO LONGER PROPERTY OF ROANOKE COUNTY LIBRARY
Complete your collection with *Pokémon* books—available now
www.pokemon.com
On sale at **store.viz.com**
Also available at your local bookstore and comic store.
izkids
© 2008 Pokémon © 1997-2008 Nintendo, Creatures, GAME FREAK, TV Tokyo, ShoPro, JR Kikaku. Pokémon properties are trademarks of Nintendo.
RATED A ALL AGES
ratings.viz.com
VIZ media
www.viz.com